A QUANTUM MYTHOLOGY

Gavin G. Smith

Copyright © Gavin G. Smith 2015
All rights reserved

First published in Great Britain in 2015
by Gollancz
An imprint of the Orion Publishing Group
Carmelite House, 50 Victoria Embankment,
London EC4Y 0DZ
An Hachette UK Company

This edition published in 2016 by Gollancz

1 3 5 7 9 10 8 6 4 2

A CIP catalogue record for this book
is available from the British Library

ISBN 978 0 575 12704 3

Typeset by Deltatype Ltd, Birkenhead, Merseyside

Printed in Great Britain by Clays Ltd, St Ives plc

The Orion Publishing Group's policy is to use papers
that are natural, renewable and recyclable products and
made from wood grown in sustainable forests. The logging
and manufacturing processes are expected to conform to
the environmental regulations of the country of origin.

www.gavingsmith.com
www.gollancz.co.uk
www.orionbooks.co.uk

To Nicola and Simon Bates, and my nieces Nell & Amelie,
who can read this when they are in their thirties.

1
Birmingham, 1791

Sir Ronald Sharpely may well have been impatient, but the Clockworker was not to be hurried.

'The innovation, Sir Ronald, is not in the pepperbox style of the weapon ...' With delicate tools inherited from his watchmaker father, the Clockworker continued finessing intricate adjustments to the complicated powder pan of the seven-barrelled flintlock pistol. 'It's not even in the rifling inside the barrel, which will make it more accurate,' he continued. His Swiss accent was very slight. He turned to look at Sharpely, a well-built man in the prime of his life with the complexion of someone who enjoyed outdoor activities. Sharpely did not like the way the brass-and-leather lens arrangement strapped to the Clockworker's head made one of the man's strangely coloured, lifeless eyes look so large.

'Damn it, man, I was told it would be ready!' Sir Ronald snapped, looking down at the pale, emaciated figure dressed in dark clothes that made him look like one of last century's Puritans. The Clockworker wasn't bald so much as someone who did not quite suit hair. Sir Ronald was pleased when the Clockworker turned back to work on the pistol's mechanism.

'You were told it would be ready today. And it will,' the artificer said absently as he worked with the tools he had rescued from his father's burning workshop. A religious man, his father. Realising that all sin came from the flesh, he had attempted to replace his children's flesh with his own devices. To the Clockworker this had been sound reasoning, inasmuch as any religious reasoning was.

'The rifling will make it much slower to reload than a smoothbore weapon, but after seven shots, if you haven't killed what you were aiming at—'

'When will it—'

'The innovation on this pistol is the mechanism for the pan. All you need to do is turn the barrels as you would normally and my

1

mechanism will refresh the pan with powder. This will of course rapidly increase the speed of your firing.' Sir Ronald watched impatiently as the Clockworker demonstrated the weapon. 'Will you be staying in Bromichan tonight?' He used the old name for the city, which was only just starting to go out of fashion.

'No, we are staying with friends in Aston,' Sir Ronald said in exasperation.

'We? So your family are with you?'

Sir Ronald stopped staring at the finely wrought seven-barrelled pistol that was being constructed for him and instead looked at the Clockworker's eyes. His face burned red with anger at being addressed so familiarly by a tradesman, even one so singularly skilled as the Clockworker. He didn't see the Clockworker cut himself with one of his tools. He didn't see the Clockworker smear blood on the butt of the pistol. He didn't see the blood absorbed into the wood of the gun as if it had never existed, and he didn't see the Clockworker's wound heal itself of its own accord.

'Damn your impudence! What business—?'

The Clockworker made one more tiny adjustment and there was an audible click from the clockwork pan mechanism.

'And we're done.' The Clockworker held up the completed pistol. The engraved silvered barrels were longer than a normal pepperbox, for greater accuracy. It was a heavy pistol but finely balanced, with a lead weight in the rounded base of the mahogany butt.

Sir Ronald took the expertly crafted weapon from the Clockworker and stared at it with awe.

'That, sir, is a fine piece of work,' Sir Ronald said. The Clockworker merely nodded. 'Excuse my rudeness. I am not a patient man.' Sir Ronald tested the weapon's action, pulling the hammer back and then lowering it without letting the flint fall and spark. The Clockworker grimaced as he turned the barrels by hand, forcing the ticking clockwork mechanism. 'My wife and Elsa, the eldest, wish to frequent the various dressmakers and seamstresses the town has to offer, whereas Alexander, my youngest—'

'Wishes to see the toy manufactories the city is so famous for?' the Clockworker finished for him.

'Just so,' Sir Ronald said, transfixed by the pistol.

'Well, I believe our business here is concluded. I make children's toys also – in fact, I prefer to do so. I am a faint-hearted man, I'm afraid, and the thought of guns ... Well, let us say I prefer to create entertainments that make children happy. I have a small workshop on Snow Hill. I would love for young Alexander to see my creations.'

'What? Oh, yes, we will look for you. If you will excuse me, sir, I must bid you good day.'

The Clockworker watched Sir Ronald walk out of the workshop. No, he wasn't a religious man, but he knew he had demons in his blood, demons that would do as he bid them.

Before it became a reality of soot-stained brick and stone buildings, the city was a cloud of black smoke pouring from thousands of chimneys on the horizon. Houses, forges, mills, manufactories, workshops and churches, all tightly packed together.

The canal boat he was travelling on brought the coal from the Black Country that powered the city's industry. The Hellaquin had never been fond of cities, and already the stink of the smoke, of the people and animals all pressed together, and of the filth in the street they created was beginning to feel oppressive. Birmingham looked like a slice of hell to the Hellaquin as the narrowboat slid through the water towards the foundry wharf in the west of the city.

The boatmen secured the narrowboat and saw to the horse that pulled the craft as the foundry-men and -women came with barrows to unload the coal. The Hellaquin picked up his belongings: a wooden case just over two feet long and a waxed-leather-wrapped stave some six feet long. The boatmen tried to ignore the two short swords the man with the hulking upper body wore at his waist under his leather coat. They just returned his nod as he climbed off the narrowboat and headed east. Behind him was the orange glow of molten metal being poured from crucibles in the foundry, accompanied by a constant thunderous clanging.

On New Street he waded through mud and excrement, both human and animal. The street was packed with people. He hated the way the wood-beamed houses crowded in over his head, almost touching, blocking out the smoke-stained sky. He had been in battles where the press of people wasn't so extreme. He was appalled to see horses, and even wagons, trying to make their way down the street. The six-foot stave he carried wasn't making him any friends, either.

There were too many of them, and with the stench, and the smoke, he was finding it harder and harder to breathe. A fat, bald, florid man in a leather apron was screaming in his face now. It may as well have been in a foreign language. The Hellaquin felt his forehead connect with the man's nose. His forehead came away wet and sticky. The man fell into the filth and ordure.

A horse bumped into him and he staggered back. He almost lost his grip on the stave. He felt the panic rising in him. He was at Poitiers again. Then the panic was gone. He felt the change. The calmness he felt in battle. He had killed horses at Poitiers, when English arrows glanced off curved French plate mail.

The Hellaquin turned away and pushed through the mass towards the edge of the street. He made it to a narrow alleyway, where a crown in the hand of a hard-faced urchin secured him a loyal back-street guide.

Where New Street had been oppressive and closed in, the Froggary may as well have been underground. It was a tangled multilevel warren of ramshackle buildings connected by narrow corridors in which people lived, and it was impossible to tell where one building ended and another began. The Hellaquin followed the urchin through rooms inhabited by entire extended families, sometimes more than one.

Other than crossing two streets, they had pretty much been moving from one building to another, occasionally looking down on crowded courtyards or walking over makeshift bridges. Then the urchin led him out onto the High Street. The Hellaquin didn't like the press of people out here, either, but his guide forced a path for him through a mixture of pedestrian agility and aggression.

They made their way south over the refuse of the different markets that ran down from New Street towards the corn market at the Bull Ring, in the shadow of St Martin's Church. The Hellaquin heard the barking of the dogs and the bellowing of a wounded bull long before he saw the small green outside the church.

The 'Bull Ring' was a heavy iron ring embedded in the ground. A badly savaged, blood-covered bull was weakly trying to fend off several dogs bred specifically for the purpose of baiting. A number of dead and dying badly gored dogs lay around the green – presumably the bull had put up quite a fight. The practice had been banned in the city some eighteen years past, but too many people insisted that the meat tasted better if the beast was baited first. Those people were prepared to pay extra for it.

The Hellaquin turned away from the death throes of the beast at the teeth of the flat-faced dogs. He could remember when this entire area had been a deer park. In fact, it hadn't been far from here, in a root-lined earthen cavern, where he'd drunk from the Red Chalice.

Just off the green a crowd had gathered by a large clanking, hissing mechanism with two black iron arms that pumped up and down, steam rising from it constantly. The whole machine must have been

4

four, five yards tall, the Hellaquin estimated. He stopped and stared at it. The urchin backpedalled to stand by him.

'What is it?' the Hellaquin asked, his tone equal parts awe and dread.

'It's one of Mr Watt's steam engines,' his grubby guide answered. Then his tone became more guarded. 'They say it's going to replace people soon – working, I mean. Then everyone will be like us. The world'll be a rookery.'

It was a machine, a device. The Hellaquin knew about those. He had been a man once, but now he was something else. He stared as long as he could manage.

The Hellaquin dismissed the boy and headed south-east into Digbeth, where three- and four-storey stone houses became two- and three-storey wood houses. With fewer crowds than the market centre, the Digbeth Road had dried to cracks and dust in the late-July sun. Horses and carts plied the route under the watchful eyes of soldiers called in to quell the recent riots. They leaned against the walls of houses, sweating in their red coats, bayonets affixed to their muskets. With his big build, his upper body so large he looked almost deformed and his thick leather coat in the hot July sun, the Hellaquin attracted their attention and they watched him go by.

It had been many years since he last felt warmth or cold like others did. So long since he last sweated.

He could remember a time when the Old Crown had been a guild-house and a school. Now it was a hostelry and tavern. The Hellaquin was a tall man, and he had to stoop to avoid banging his head on the ceiling beams inside the wooden-framed two-storey thatched building. Nobody paid any attention to him, not even when his sub-stantial bulk jostled them as he made his way through the press of customers towards the bar. The exception was the Knight. He noticed the Hellaquin. He was sitting at a table in the corner eating a large roast beef dinner that would have fed a family. Like the Hellaquin, he needed a lot of food to sate the devils within.

Their vocations meant they were natural enemies. Even allow-ing for that, the Hellaquin had never liked the Knight. He wore the clothes of a gentleman who preferred the outdoor life. The exception to his rural finery was the cavalryman's trousers with leather inner legs. The trousers were tucked into knee-length riding boots.

He wore no wig, and his fine blond hair was tied back into a ponytail with a black ribbon. Both his hair and face had been powdered. Blue eyes glanced at the Hellaquin's shabby clothes and shoulder-length, unkempt, dark hair with the easy disdain of the aristocrat. The Knight beckoned for the Hellaquin to join him as if he were calling a servant.

'When it was a guildhouse, at least the wine was better,' the Knight said by way of greeting. His French accent had become a lot less noticeable during the nearly five hundred years the Hellaquin had known the other 'man'. 'Get my friend whatever he wants and a lot of it,' he said to a passing servingwoman. The Hellaquin asked for stew, bread and ale as he put his case down and slid it under the table. He leaned the stave against the wall. 'Still carrying that thing, I see?' said the Knight.

The Hellaquin observed a brace of pistols on the table, and a belt with scabbards for a cavalry sabre and the Knight's strange Far-Eastern knife hanging over the chair next to him. The Knight noticed the Hellaquin glancing at the ornate, long-barrelled flintlock pistols.

'Nock of London. Perhaps you should consider joining this new age? I looked for you in America.'

'I was further north, Hudson Bay.'

'And the recent unpleasantness in France?' It was asked casually enough, but the Hellaquin knew it was a test.

'I don't think our masters liked my sympathies.'

The Knight stopped eating and looked up at the other man.

'Why am I here?' the Hellaquin asked in an attempt to forestall the inevitable argument.

The Knight put his fork and knife down and wiped his mouth on a linen napkin. 'Very well. I fear I have lost my appetite.' He stood and the Hellaquin followed him out of the main room of the tavern.

The Hellaquin stared at the body of the boy and tried not to shake with rage. The Knight leaned against the wall of the tavern's back room, watching the Hellaquin's response.

The boy couldn't have been much older than five or six. His blood-spattered clothing was expensive, and he looked like he had been well fed and healthy when he was alive. The back of his head had been caved in, which was clearly the wound that had killed him. By far the stranger wound, however, was the ruin of his left eye, into which a tiny, ornate brass scorpion had crawled and then curled up, clamping itself to his skull and eye socket. The Hellaquin had to turn away from the body and found himself looking at an amused expression on the Knight's face.

'What happened?' the Hellaquin asked.

'The nanny found him just after he had murdered his infant

brother. Then he turned on the nanny. It was his mother who beat his head in after she saw what he had done to her other child.'

The Hellaquin crossed himself. 'And that ... that ... thing in his eye?'

'We don't know where it came from. All we know is that young Michael here had been touring the toy manufactories of Snow Hill with his father.'

'Somebody gave it to him?'

'Would be my guess, unless he took it.'

'The Brass City?'

'Why? Say what you like about them, they always act with purpose.' He gestured towards the child.

The Knight was right. There was no purpose to this, outside of madness. The Hellaquin knew there had been questions over the Knight's views on the Brass City in the past, but when it came down to it, the other man had always acted decisively against them.

'So we go to Snow Hill?'

'Tomorrow. Now one of us has to cut that thing out of the poor boy's skull.'

The Hellaquin awoke fully alert. Even though the murmuring from the next room was faint, he could still make out every word. He even understood the *glossolalia of both voices – the human one and the strange, dry, old, less-than-human one*. He knew the Knight would be lying on the bare boards of the floor, his arms outstretched in the shape of a cross before the ancient severed head. The severed head was known as Baphomet, the Baptiser. The Knight was communing with it. The Hellaquin got out of bed and started to dress himself quickly.

A short while later, there was a gentle tap at the door and the Hellaquin opened it. The Knight saw that the other man was already dressed and simply nodded.

The Hellaquin was sure the powerful black horse was almost as unnatural as he and the Knight were. He had no wish to ride behind the other man but Baphomet had told the Knight that something was happening at that very moment, and they needed to move fast.

The city was under curfew, and as they galloped through the streets they were challenged by a number of the redcoats. Few, however, were prepared to fire on someone of the Knight's obvious station in life, regardless of how disreputable his companion looked.

Only one had dared fire his musket. The Hellaquin felt the projectile hit his back like the blow from a mace, but his leather coat had hardened with the impact and the ball had not gone through. The bruise healed so quickly it practically never existed.

Tendrils of wood and lead had grown from the pistol, passing through his hand and his arm, consuming – or transforming – his flesh as they wove in and out of it. The bones in his arm had broken to accommodate the pepperbox pistol and he felt other, smaller strands growing inside his body, his head. Then the demon in the gun started speaking to him. It told him what to do. Showed him.

He had killed his own family first. Killed both their children in front of their screaming mother as, sobbing, he shouted at her about all the times he had betrayed her with other women, most of whom he had paid. The devil had laughed as he wept. When his friend came running to investigate the gunfire, he shot to wound. Then he left a bloody trail behind him as he dragged his friend through the house so the other man could watch his family die in front of his eyes, succumbing to the wound in his stomach as he did so. Then, slowly and with purpose, he descended the stairs and entered the town house's servants' quarters. He shot a footman but only injured him. The rest had fled screaming into the night.

He went to sit in his old friend's study. He wanted to put the pistol-limb to his head and pull the trigger, but the demon in the gun did not want him to die just yet. It had told him so. The demon liked the way the man made it feel.

There is no hell, the demon told him. *No place for me but here.*

So Sir Ronald Sharpely wept and reloaded the weapon and wondered when the crowd gathering outside would come for him. Or would it be the city watch, or even the redcoats themselves? The devil in the gun – in him, now – revelled in his thoughts, though it knew the best, the sweetest, had already come and gone.

The first time he saw heat, like a desert serpent, was when the Hellaquin realised how truly damned he was. How far from God. So much further than all the killing, the stealing, the drinking and the whoring could ever have taken him.

It was a narrow four-storey stone town house in a row of similar buildings on Duke Street in the desirable suburb of Aston. It looked new and expensive, and his own cottage in Cheshire could have fitted many times within the vast swathe of lawn at the back of the house. He was standing in the shadows of the trees at the bottom of the garden, observing the crowd that had gathered on the recently cobbled street in front of the house.

8

The Hellaquin unwrapped the waxed leather from around the yew stave and flexed the wood to warm it up before stringing it. Even with his considerable strength, that was a challenge. He selected a number of arrows from the case, each one handmade from ash, each one hardened by the dripping of his blood onto the wood, each one just over two feet long. The arrowheads were armour-piercing bodkins made from something called adamantine, which the Knight had told him, long ago, just meant very, very hard. He had chosen these arrows over the ones that contained his own blood in the arrowheads' cores.

All the while he watched the house he could see the cooling heat of the bodies in the upper floors, and the vibrant oranges, reds and yellows of the murderer on the ground floor. The Hellaquin nocked the first arrow, waiting for the murderer to provide him with a shot.

Sir Ronald screamed with hopeless, impotent frustration when he heard the town house's front door thrown open, and then he was on his feet and staggering into the hall. He had but a moment to take in the well-dressed, blue-eyed, blond-haired man striding across the hall towards him, a pistol in each hand, before the figure disappeared in the smoke from his own guns.

Sir Ronald staggered back as a pistol ball caught him in the chest, but the demon moved him like a puppet now. He raised his pistol arm and fired into the smoke, rotated the barrel as the pan mechanism ticked, fired again, rotated, fired again.

The blond man strode out of the smoke, a sabre in one hand, a knife in the other. Bone poked through skin torn and bloodied by a nasty-looking head wound, but still the man came. Sir Ronald fired, the barrel turned, he fired again, and again. The man staggered as shot after shot hit him, the front of his coat darkening as blood soaked into it, but he kept coming. Sir Ronald moved to one side to get a better shot as the hall filled with yet more smoke.

The Hellaquin watched Sir Ronald's heat-ghost as his arm breathed fire at the Knight's fainter ghost. Sir Ronald moved to the left. It was the move the Hellaquin needed. He exhaled, visualised the shot, lifted the bow and drew back the string. The poundage on the weapon was such that no mortal man could have drawn it. With hundreds of years of experience and the benefits of the 'gifts' he had been given by the Red Chalice, it took him but a moment to sight, and to judge the slight breeze in the hot night. He loosed and heard the window break almost immediately.

Shot after shot and the blond man finally stopped staggering forwards and collapsed onto the marble floor of the town house's hallway. The devil was already devising plans for the body, but first Sir Ronald would have to reload.

Sir Ronald didn't hear the window break. The adamantine-tipped arrow flew through the sitting room, then through an internal wall, and finally through Sir Ronald's head before embedding itself deep in the outer wall, quivering. Sir Ronald collapsed forward onto the floor, leaving the demon to slowly fade away, trapped in cooling dead flesh.

The Hellaquin stalked through the sitting room and into the hall. He saw the man, his arm fused with what looked like a multi-barrelled pistol, lying face down on the marble in a pool of red. The Knight was lying in a similar pool on his back. The Hellaquin nearly put an arrow in the Knight when he sat up.

'I almost had him,' the Knight muttered. The Hellaquin nodded with a sceptical expression on his face. Clouds of grey and black powder-smoke hung in the air. Through the windows at the front of the house, the Hellaquin could see the milling crowd.

The archer kicked the grotesque man onto his back and knelt down next to him.

'Is he healing?' the Knight asked as he got up unsteadily and bent to retrieve his pistols, his sabre and his knife.

The Hellaquin looked at the hole in the man's head made by the arrow he'd fired.

'Is there a maker's mark on the pistol?' asked the Knight.

The Hellaquin picked up the deformed limb and checked the visible metal of the barrel, grimacing as he saw up close the fusion of wood, metal and flesh. The Knight was standing in the pool of his own blood as he sheathed his various weapons, the pool shrinking as he reabsorbed it. The healing would leave the Knight very hungry.

'There's no mark. What do we do with him?' the Hellaquin asked, glancing out at the crowd again.

'Damnation! We can't take him with us – we'll have to burn the house down and hope for the best.' As he spoke, the Knight used his Far-Eastern knife to open a wound in his hand. He squeezed some of the blood from his wound into a small silver cup he had produced from somewhere on his person.

'What are you doing?' the Hellaquin demanded.

'Just a touch of necromancy.'

The Hellaquin crossed himself. 'I have no taste for this.'

The Knight looked up at the Hellaquin. 'We need to know where he got the gun. If you don't want to bear witness, go upstairs and set the fire.' Then he poured the blood from the cup into the dead man's mouth.

The dead body started to convulse and writhe, flesh flowed like hot wax and the screaming started as the demon in the dead man's flesh fought with the devils in the Knight's blood. The Hellaquin climbed the curved marble staircase, trying not to look down, trying not hear the twisted words wrenched from the corpse.

'Where on Steelhouse Lane?' the Knight shouted at the writhing carcass.

Upstairs, the Hellaquin found the bodies. All he could offer them was a pyre on a hot summer's night.

2
A Long Time After the Fall

Vic lay dead on the deck of the Church frigate the *St Brendan's Fire*. Scab was watching the most valuable uplifted monkey in Known Space die. She was dying because foreign nanites were trying to colonise every last bit of her body.

Even as she gasped for breath, Scab was able to appreciate how beautiful she was. He might have felt nothing, but he understood aesthetics. If there was artifice in her genetic make-up, then it was old, powerful and elegant. She did not look sculpted like most in Known Space. She looked like she had been born with perfect bone structure, dark eyes and thick brown hair. She was tall, slender to the point of gauntness. Her skin had a porcelain quality to it, or at least it had until the advertising virals started crawling across it when she fell victim to the ambient nanite pollution from which most people were protected by their nano-screens.

Scab watched her die. He understood that she was a nat, unaugmented. He'd seen them before. They were bred in protected environments for study, as pets, kinks or food – curiosities, little more. So why was this one so sought-after? The Church, the Monarchist systems, the Consortium – they all wanted her. Why was this nat so important? He felt sure she was from before the Fall, but there had to be more to it than that. How could she be the key to bridge technology? Why had she been aboard the strange S-tech craft? Why had the Church monk's hand opened the cocoon?

Absently he noticed that the red steam in the air was coming from his blood meeting the still burning-hot energy dissipation grid woven into his clothes. More smoke billowed as some of his corrupted blood dripped onto the frigate's deck. Vic had done more than his fair share of damage before Scab had driven the – very illegal – S-tech energy javelin through the other bounty killer's chest. The powerfully built, hard-tech-augmented insect's chest cavity was now a hollow fused mess.

The codes Vic had 'faced to Scab before Vic chose to attack him gave the human bounty killer complete control of the Church frigate the 'sect had stolen on Scab's orders. The ship's AI was putting up a fight against the high-end control-virus program attacking it. Their erstwhile employer had been generous with the expenses, but that arrangement was at an end now as Scab intended to double-cross his employer.

Most of the few surviving crewmembers aboard the frigate were locked down. Scab absently reprogrammed the frigate's security nano-screen, weaponising it, turning it into a self-replicating flesh-eating nano-swarm.

He looked down at the girl. The closest thing he had to a sense of humour was tempted to let her die there. Let it all have been for nothing. On the other hand, that wouldn't help him get what he wanted.

Scab watched her for a moment longer. Then he picked her up, 'facing instructions to the frigate's med bay as he carried her out of the loading area. The screams of the crew being eaten by the nano-swarm echoed along the corridor. Scab found himself really craving another cigarette.

The Monk stood on one of the catwalks that ran over the dolphins' nutrient pool in the Command-and-Control chamber of the Church capital ship, the *Lazerene*. The large chamber was illuminated by the warm orange glow coming from the pool, and the smart-metal bulkheads of the chamber projected a panoramic view of the surrounding space. Holographic telemetry and other system information ran vertically down parts of the view, though all the data would be directly 'faced to the dolphins and to the crewmembers of various races bobbing around the chamber seated on AG platforms.

It had been a star system once. Now it was going dark, consumed by squirming, maggot-like forms of nothingness momentarily lit from within by the sun's fusion as they devoured the light of the system's star. The same process had already taken the fourteen planets, a number of habitats and countless asteroids.

The Monk stared fixedly at the image of the sun. The estimated number of deaths in the system was available to her, but it was large enough to be abstract.

'We give them access to an apparently infinite universe, but then we pen them in until they teem over everything like termites,' Churchman said. 'We've overpopulated space. Who'd have thought that would happen?'

'I'm not sure I want cod philosophy right now,' the Monk said angrily, knowing her fury was misplaced. The dolphins were motionless in their fluid.

Churchman wasn't actually here. Every ship in the Church fleet had AIs modelled on downloads of Churchman's personality. Each one had been allowed to develop independently, and as a result, each ship's AI was quite different. Normally the Monk liked the *Lazerene*'s AI the best. The capital vessel was a more than capable warship, but that wasn't its only purpose. The Monk didn't like the battleships', destroyers' and frigates' AIs. They tended towards imprints of an older and more warlike, single-minded Churchman. This AI looked like Churchman when she'd first met him, though the AI wore a priest's dog collar. He appeared to be standing next to her, but that was just an image she allowed to be 'faced to her neunonics.

The Monk was watching the refugee fleet making for one of the system's bridge points. The *Lazerene*, along with the rest of the small fleet sent to the system, were waiting for them. They had already sent out the signal to remove the system from the astrogation programs connected to all bridge drives. The most potent Pythian-designed viruses actual credit could buy were erasing every last piece of information regarding the system from all of Known Space's various communications networks. Once, a long time ago, the Monk had asked why this always appeared to go unnoticed. Churchman told her it didn't – people just didn't care.

'So why do we have to kill them?' she asked again, as she did every single time.

'If the masses don't know about it, they don't care. If they knew about it—'

'They'd fight it.'

Churchman turned to look at her sadly. 'At one time, maybe. I personally think the ensuing panic would play into his hands. He has the influence to manipulate them, to turn them on each other. In terms of humanity, he started breeding them towards the selfish, vicious, uncaring creatures you see now even before the Fall.'

'We're going to close the bridge point, remove the beacons anyway—' she said, feeling guilty.

'And let them try to hide and flee, living in terror until it inevitably consumes them? That only makes it easier for us. This way it is over quickly for them.'

'We could take them—' Even now she still wanted to weep each time.

'We don't have the resources,' he said softly. Even now he still explained it as patiently as he had the first time.

14

The only sound in the C&C was the water lapping against the bulkhead as the ship adjusted to the change in mass in this sector of space.

The weapons section 'faced a question to the Monk. She didn't answer. Churchman looked to her, as did a few of the crew. A number of the individualistic, heavily customised P-sats, the personal satelites the dolphins used to facilitate easier communications with the uplifted races also appeared to be paying attention to her.

'What did Scab want?' the Monk asked, to distract herself. She couldn't quite refrain from speaking his name through gritted teeth.

'Our presence at an auction.'

The Monk nodded, clenching the muscles in her jaw. 'Will we go?' she managed.

'Yes ... in some form or another. We'll certainly be represented.'

'Will you pay?'

'I imagine that if I can, I will.'

'If?'

'I'm not sure that child knows what he wants. Though in many ways he is one of the most perfectly suited people to live in this age.'

The Monk started to reply angrily but was interrupted.

'Ma'am?' said the lizard militiawoman in charge of the weapons section. The Monk nodded for her to continue. 'For the log, ma'am.'

'Fire,' the Monk all but whispered.

The darkness was lit by lances of light, the glow of manoeuvring engines, vented energy from dissipation grids and explosions of matter from reactive armour as the hulls of the surprised and betrayed refugee ships were penetrated, burst and scattered across the cold vacuum.

Only when they were sure they had hunted down the last survivor was space cut open by the ship's bridge drives to reveal the gaseous, swirling, crimson wound of Red Space.

'It's kinder this way,' Churchman said to her quietly, in her mind's eye.

'So we've come to genocide being the kinder option?'

Churchman didn't answer.

The star had been fully consumed by the time the last bridge point closed. The faint red glow was the last ever source of light in that system.

Everything had been so warm and safe. Even where she touched vacuum, her hardened skin had been long dead. She had known so much, felt so much. Now she was diminished, the tiny, frightened, alone thing she had been before and so, so cold.

15

She opened her eyes. It had taken her a while to find the courage to do so. She was staring up at a ceiling made of cold, dark metal. The lighting in the room was subdued, the sources difficult to pinpoint. It was sparsely furnished, but the door looked to be electronically controlled and very substantial. A seam ran diagonally across it. She thought she could sense a faint vibration thrumming through the metal.

She was lying on some kind of mattress that had moulded around her. There were a number of other beds in the room, and something about them made her think of hospital gurneys, although they had no wheels. She wondered if she'd been sectioned again. Perhaps the millennia in Red Space had been a bizarre hallucination, a schizophrenic loop. She looked down but couldn't see any restraints on the bed.

Some kind of apparatus with arms was folded into the ceiling above the bed/gurney. Behind her was some sort of screen showing information that looked familiar from hospital visits and medical dramas, except that the screen appeared to be part of the wall, and there was nothing attached to her that could be feeding it information.

A black sphere-thing rose from a docking station on the wall and drifted towards her, arms uncoiling as it approached. It was speaking gibberish, though she thought she recognised a few words. She fled.

She had expected her legs to give out underneath her as soon as her feet touched the cold metal but was surprised to find she could stand. Naked, she ran at the door. The door opened for her and she bolted from the strange room and the even stranger machine.

She was in a corridor made from the same dark metal as the room. She paused at an intersection ahead and looked down each of the branching corridors. Every one looked the same as the last. Slowly, it was coming to her. She realised she had to be on some kind of spaceship.

How much time has passed? It had never felt important before. She remembered the parasites crawling through her skin, then the pain of disease, and finally the burning. Then nothing. No, not nothing – sometimes she thought she felt something trying to reach her through her shell, her cocoon, her home.

Then she'd woken. She recalled a strange and horrible man in bizarre make-up standing over her. Then she couldn't breathe, her skin burned and there was noise and light. When it all went dark again, she was sure she had died.

She wrapped her arms around herself. She was starting to shake – cold, fear, she wasn't sure which. She wondered if there were any drugs back in the hospital room she had woken in. Just something to calm her a bit. Help her deal.

She hadn't heard a sound but suddenly she was sure there was someone behind her. She thought she caught the slightest whiff of tobacco. Her shaking intensified. She closed her eyes and tried to will herself to turn around.

'Please ...' she all but sobbed.

She couldn't even hear breathing, but she was still convinced that someone was standing behind her. The smell of tobacco had faded, replaced by a weird absence of almost any scents.

Slowly she managed to control her fear, though the shaking wouldn't stop. She half-convinced herself that she'd been imagining things. Slowly she turned around.

A glimpse was enough. It was the strange and horrible man. He was small, wiry and wearing a horrible brown suit and hat. He was staring at her. She couldn't read his expression – there was no desire, no lechery; her nakedness appeared to make not the slightest difference to him. No anger or hatred in those cold, dead fish eyes, either. She screamed and ran.

She sprinted along corridor after corridor. It didn't matter where she went as long as she put distance between herself and that man. Then she found herself running out of corridor.

Doors! she thought desperately. *There are doors.* She made for the closest one, looking for controls but seeing none. She raised her hand to hammer on it as she glanced back along the corridor. The skull-faced man was nowhere to be seen. The door slid open. The room was red inside. She wasn't sure how many bodies – men, women, animal people. All of them looked as if they had died violently. Many of them were in pieces.

She staggered back, bringing her hands up to cover her mouth. Strong fingers grabbed her arms, gripping her tightly. She started to scream as the doors to the red room slid shut.

'Shhh,' the skull-faced man whispered. One of his sharply filed nails pierced her skin and false calm flooded through her. The fear was still there but it mattered less. He let her go. She lurched away from him, bumping against the wall of the corridor. The metal was so cold against her skin. She slid to the ground.

Cold arse. The inane thought rose unbidden and made her giggle.

'What's your name?' The man's voice, like everything else about him, was horrible. He had a strangely accented, low, croaky voice but unlike the floating machine, he, at least, wasn't spouting gibberish.

'Talia,' she said, staring at him. The fear under control, she was fascinated by his grotesqueness.

'Talia, I can either hurt you or drug you, or you can cooperate. Which do you prefer?'

'What are you going to do with me?' She remembered the red room. The fear was trying to rise within her again. She wanted to move away from the wall. She knew there were dead people on the other side of it.

'Sell you,' the man said eventually.

She nodded as if this was an obvious answer. Then she started to cry. The skull-faced man frowned but let her cry, watching her as if it was a test of some kind.

'Don't hurt me,' she pleaded.

'I'll try, but sometimes ...' he said. 'It's not easy, you know?'

She stared up him. The soporific effects of whatever he had spiked her with were battling the terror that wanted to overwhelm her.

'What's your name?' she said at last, more for something to say than from any real interest in the answer.

'Scab,' he said. She snorted with laughter and then clamped her hand over her mouth. 'Woodbine Scab.'

'Like the cigarette?'

Scab reached into his suit jacket and drew a cigarette case from his breast pocket. Talia noticed that his teeth were stained yellow. They were also filed to points and capped with silver. He offered her a cigarette. Trembling, she took one. He took one for himself and then lit both.

Again? He wondered why Scab had killed him this time. Then came the terror. He began to thrash in the strangely murky nutrient gel of the clone tank as he remembered Ludwig, blithely ignoring the *Basilisk*'s defences, phasing through the craft's hull and into the converted corvette-class ship's interior.

An Elite! A fucking Elite had killed him! What he couldn't understand was how he was being cloned. He'd run out of clone insurance after the last time, when Scab had cloned him and refused to tell him how he'd died in the first place. More to the point, when Elite killed they tended to infect the neunonics with viruses that not only scrambled memory uploads but could remain hidden long enough to snake their way into insurance company personality/memory backups and destroy them as well.

He wondered if he was going to be cloned just long enough to appreciate the process of turning into a mentally scrambled freak, with the possibility of being a preprogramed slave to boot.

He became calmer as narcotics flooded his system. He audited himself. He was a mostly natural insect. It was the usual cloning process. The gel protected his fragile exoskeleton from the ravages of gravity, artificial or otherwise. His neunonics felt rudimentary. Presumably he was waiting for components, assuming that whoever had paid for his cloning was going to rebuild his hard-tech-enhanced body so it could be of use.

Then it struck him. If he'd been captured, any one of the massively powerful people Scab had pissed off could be holding him. The insect-run Queen's Cartel – he'd released a virus in their Arclight habitat after killing an extremely expensive blank. The Consortium – they'd wanted the cocoon Scab had been paid by a mysterious client to find. The Church, who wanted to stop everyone getting the cocoon in case it broke their monopoly on bridge technology. Or the Monarchists could be holding him, because Scab had just tried to attack the Citadel of their Elite. But none of this made sense, however. If he'd been captured, why clone him? Why not just drop his personality/memory backup into a torture immersion? The horrible thought occurred to him that he might be the prisoner of some fetishist weirdo who pre-ferred the incredibly less efficient and more time-consuming torture of actual flesh. *Oh, excrement, I've been sold to some sicko as their insect meat puppet!* It was the only possible explanation his slightly addled and drugged mind could reach.

Through the dirty gel he could see he was in an unevenly paved stone room with an arched entrance. The tank itself was made of what looked like polished dark wood with brass fittings, though he'd had to use his rudimentary neunonics to look up both materials.

The only illumination in the room came from the tank itself, a transparent-fronted cold storage made from similar material to the clone tank, and some strange burning things in a kind of specialist rack, which were called candles, according to Vic's neunonics.

Fear overcame narcotics when the red-clad monk, a cowl covering his features, walked into the chamber. He was followed by a crystal and wood cylinder, also with brass fittings, floating on an AG motor. A thick, black, viscous liquid flowed around inside the cylinder, ap-parently with a life of its own.

His first thought was the Church. That was frightening enough, but it was the realisation that this *wasn't* the Church – that he had, in fact, been cloned by a heretical cult – that really made him exude pheromonic terror.

It was difficult to tell, but he assumed the monk was watching him. He had no idea what the cylinder of black liquid was doing, or even what it was. Then the pain started. He felt something growing through the meat of his brain. Tweaking the pain centres. His neu-nonics weren't as rudimentary as he'd initially thought. They were invasive. It was an audit. Whoever was doing it didn't just want to know something. They wanted to know everything. His mandibles locked open in a constant silent scream. It lasted a long time and stimulants pumped through his system kept him awake through it all. They wanted coherent thought, not the subconscious ramblings of an insect mind modified to be more human so he could embrace his humanophile tendencies and dream.

He was exhausted and in pain from the exertion of constant thrashing in the dense gel. He recognised the shape of Scab, sitting slouched on the ornately carved dark-wood chair now next to the tank, smoking.

'I had to know,' Scab said over the 'face connection. It would never be an apology.

'What have you done?' was all Vic could manage.

'Things have moved on. We ... I have the cocoon.'

Vic was always impressed by Scab's ability to inspire more fear just when you assumed you'd reached your tolerance threshold for the emotion.

'So give it to your employer and let's get paid,' Vic said, with a sinking feeling. Scab just shook his head. 'In that case, just wait around for any number of people to come and kill you. Can you switch me off first?'

'No.'

'Why not, Scab? Why not?'

'You're useful.'

'Do you really need me, Scab?' Vic demanded. The human didn't answer. 'Then switch me the fuck off.'

'You tried to kill me,' Scab said at last. Vic thought he heard sadness in Scab's voice but then assumed he must have imagined it. 'But it's not in you. It must have happened after.'

So that was what the audit had been looking for. Apparently, after Ludwig – a machine Elite from the Monarchist systems – had killed him, Vic'd been cloned again. Then something happened that made him try to kill Scab, and Scab had him cloned yet again.

'Maybe it was after the *fucking Elite killed me*!' Vic screamed. He was pleased he'd managed to emote human screaming across the 'face link.

'Do you want to kill me now?' Scab asked.

'Fucking obviously.'

'I wasn't looking for intent. I was looking for the will.'

This stopped Vic. He often fantasised about killing Scab. He thought he'd always managed to hide it quite well from the human, even during the frequent neural auditing required by their 'partnership' agreement, though none had been as invasive, deep or all-encompassing as the last one. Scab was right, though. Even after everything, even after this, he knew he wouldn't be capable of acting on his murderous feelings towards the human. He was too frightened of him.

'They're going to send Elite after you,' Vic said weakly. 'No amount of being a vicious little prick will help you.'

'I don't think so. They can't risk me utterly destroying her. It's the Church we need to worry about.'

'Oh, well, that's all right, then,' Vic said, nailing sarcasm.

Vic hung in the tank in silence for a while. He could see the red glow of the tip of Scab's cigarette through the murky gel.

'When will this be finished?' the insect asked.

'All I can promise you is a quick and easy death if I have any control over it.' This last was difficult for Scab. He was uncomfortable admitting the possibility of a loss of control.

'I'm not like you, Scab. I want to live.'

'It's the best I can do. It's either that or I leave you in a torture immersion with the longest time dilation I can find.'

'Audit me again, see if I can kill you now,' Vic 'faced with real venom, but they both knew it was only bravado. They both knew he would do what he was told.

3
Britain, a Long Time Ago

Back when Germelqart could still think, back when there was more to him than pain, more to him than burning in the chest, agony in the screaming muscles in his legs and arms as he tried to keep swimming, back when he was a man, he wished he had never read Herodotus. He wished he had never heard of the Cassiterides, the Tin Islands, and the moon-touched Pretani who inhabited them. Wished he had never signed on with his friend and captain Hanno to use his gifts to navigate the *Will of Dagon* in his god's name.

The beach was not getting any closer. It was a dream. Once, he lived for the sea, but that was the warm blue sea within the Pillars of Herakles, not the cold, grey seas surrounding this land of mists, monsters and madmen.

It took a while for his exhausted mind to understand what the feel of the silt through the water meant. He was crawling as much as he was swimming now. He dragged himself onto the beach and collapsed, gasping for breath, trying to draw air into burning lungs.

He could not quite manage thought yet. He saw but did not understand the black, greasy smudge of smoke in the air coming from the giant burning, man-shaped cage to the west of the island on whose beach he now lay. He could smell burned flesh and effluence. Even if he had been thinking clearly he would have struggled to understand why the giant burning man of wood and metal had started to disintegrate and fall into the water.

Once, he had known that the dark tendrils in the water were blood from the hundreds who died there, reduced to a crimson froth in the feeding frenzy of the things that were neither shark nor human. The creatures that had been waiting for them in the water.

Now he just about understood that the black ships with hulls made of skins – the Pretani called them *curraghs* – that he saw surging through the water against current and wind were bad. Crewed by demons. He did not have the strength to crawl away from the black ships. He lay on the wet sand under what passed for a sun god in this cold northern land, letting the little waves break over him.

As the burning in his chest subsided, as thought slowly returned and with it understanding of his surroundings, he noticed a figure standing among the sharp grasses of the dunes further inland. He wore a robe of some kind, but even from where the navigator lay the robe looked filthy and stained. The figure held a staff with various small items hanging from it, and there was something wrong with the man's face.

Germelqart understood that there were people running across the sand towards him. He wondered if they were coming to help him. In this cursed land he thought probably not.

Bress knelt among the smoke and flame, leaning on his now quiet sword stained with the blood of Fachtna, the warrior from the *Ubh Blaosc*, the Egg Shell. They had failed. It meant less than nothing to him.

There had been enough meat left in him to feel the pain of the Muileartach, the primal goddess who dwelt beneath the waters. Her pain had been caused by the suffering he wrought in Crom Dhubh's name to summon Llwglyd Diddymder, the Hungry Nothingness.

Crom Dhubh's touch, that ever-present, disgusting violation, had been lost among the Muileartach's screaming. Now he felt the tendrils of the 'Black Crooked One's' presence creeping through his mind as the wicker man started to disintegrate. The cage of wood and metal was returning to its constituent parts. Hiding the evidence of its violation of history.

It was a mistake to kill the warrior. The words were like rotting silk in his mind.

Only in light of your failure, Bress thought. Even in his armour, the heat of the flames was becoming too much against his immortal skin. The wicker man felt progressively more unsteady underneath and around him.

Our *failure*, Crom Dhubh reminded Bress as his flesh started to smoke and blister.

I did what I set out to do ... what you wanted me to do.

This Fachtna could have shown us the way to the Ubh Blaosc. *The slaves of the Lloigor are one of the few threats to us left.* There was no anger there, not even real reproach. Reproach or anger would have required some connection, some recognition on the part of the Dark Man that Bress was an equal, or even something remotely similar to him. If that had ever been the case it was a long time ago.

23

The whereabouts of the Ubh Blaosc *are only important in light of your failure*, Bress reiterated. He didn't add that this was because things still existed. He didn't have to. Crom Dhubh, the Dark Man, knew his thoughts. There was no reply, but Bress could still feel the other as a corrupt presence living like a parasite in the back of his mind.

What now? Bress asked. His lungs were full of smoke but he did not cough, nor did tears stream down his soot-stained face. All around him the metal and wood framework of the wicker man looked as if it was eating itself.

Nothing. It was little more than a distant hiss.

He was discarded. No longer required. He had expected to feel something – relief, maybe, even so far from what could laughingly be called home. Maybe even loss as the Dark Man's presence bled out of him. He felt nothing.

He stood up as flames reached hungrily for his flesh. The wicker man shook beneath him with every movement. He searched for feeling again as he strode to what remained of the edge of the platform. There was no sky now, only thick, greasy, black smoke.

His thoughts returned to the woman. From his perspective she was little more than a savage. But he remembered her naked form, painted blue like the night, when she had come to try and kill him. He remembered feeling her skin under his long fingers.

Skin bubbled, blistered, burned and healed, again and again. Even with his tolerance for pain it was becoming too much. He stepped into the smoke. As he fell his thoughts were still of Britha. Crom Dhubh was just a receding, mocking laughter in the back of his mind.

The one called Bress had said that Fachtna was dead. Teardrop was dead, though Tangwen had the feeling he died some time before he stopped moving and talking, consumed by the crystalline magic that lived inside his swollen head. The captain of the ship that had taken them west along the Grey Father, into the lands of the Atrebates, was dead as well. Though he kept talking even after his head had been taken, until she helped kill Ettin. And she did not know where Britha was.

All her muscles ached and her chest burned, for the current was strong here. After all the swimming and the climb to the wicker man, which even now was burning as it crumbled into the water behind her, she was surprised that somehow she was still moving towards the easternmost island.

She might have grown up in a marsh, but she was beginning to think she never wanted to see water again for as long as she lived.

Judging by the moonstruck on the island towards which she now swam, who had mocked them, as they had marched towards Bress's forces, living long might not be such a problem. She had seen the feast they left for the crabs and the other things that lived in the water.

She was peripherally aware of others swimming near her as she made for the beach. Survivors. Those who'd been strong enough to live through their imprisonment, escape from the burning wicker man into the water, survive the unnatural feeding frenzy at the claws and teeth of the children of Andraste, and then swim against strong currents to the eastern island.

So few of them left.

Her hands and feet touched silt. Now she could allow the hope she had denied herself in the water. She tried to stand, but burning muscles protested and she collapsed into the water again. She would crawl if she must – she knew she had to get out of the water.

On either side of her, people were staggering up the beach and collapsing. She saw figures sprinting towards them from the dunes further inland, kicking up sand as they ran. Clothed in rags, if wearing anything at all, many of them were painted with lime, woad, blood and excrement, or decorated with crude tattoos and self-inflicted scars. Carrying makeshift weapons, they howled, and gibbered as if they were angry at the sun for not being his brother the moon.

Tangwen, the huntress of the Pobl Neidr, the People of the Snake, a tribe of the Catuvellauni to the north and east of here whose name meant Expert Warriors, knew that the mad were closer to the gods. It was this closeness that made them moonstruck. They could not but fail to be affected by what had happened. The torture of the Mother in the sea. The eating of the sky.

On the beach she could see one of the foreign traders. He had come from across the sea, far to the south, and had been the navigator on the ship. His name was strange and she was too exhausted to remember it. He wore a filthy woollen *blaidth* which had once been white. When she knew him on the ship, he had black dye painted around his eyes, a trimmed and lacquered dark beard, and a belly that told of a life of plenty. Now he was gaunt, his dark hair long and matted, his beard similarly wild. Paler than he had once been, his leathery, weather-beaten skin was still many shades darker than that of the inhabitants of her own land.

One of the moonstruck stood over him, raising a crude club made of driftwood with bits of stone, bone and shells embedded in it. Another was running towards the navigator; there were more behind that one. From further along the beach she could hear howls of pain, fear and madness. There were explosions of water as the moonstruck sprinted into the sea to reach the survivors.

Germelqart heard the screaming. He was sure it wasn't a language. He smelled the stink of the moonstruck man before he'd even opened his eyes. All he could see was thin, muscular arms swinging the crude club plummeting towards his head.

The woman – little more than a girl, the navigator thought – collided with the moonstruck man. There was sickening crunch as the rock she swung caved in the man's head. The pair of them collapsed into the sand. The man was muttering and sobbing, his head a new shape of red blood and white bone. Despite his madness, all the fight had left him.

The navigator watched as the wiry young woman pushed herself up off the sand on arms shaking with exertion. He recognised her as the warrior from the snake tribe. She was the one who knifed Ettin, the thing that had worn Hanno's still-living head when Germelqart and Kush had dragged the creature off Britha. Germelqart was sure her name was Tangwen. The young huntress had travelled with Britha, the mad woman, the sacrificer, priestess, witch, warrior and demon.

He had watched her paint her short hair with lime to spike it, but wet it lay flat on her head. Her skin bore traces of the dyes the warriors of Ynys Prydein wore for war and ritual but the sea had washed most of them off. Her only garments were a soaking-wet tunic and a leather belt around her waist.

She drew a long, iron-bladed knife from a sheath as more of the moonstruck came sprinting across the sand towards them. She was saying something to him but he did not know enough of her language, and he was too exhausted and frightened to understand her.

A naked man skidded to a halt nearby. He danced around them, into the water, screaming imprecations as he drew patterns in his flesh with the knives he held in each hand. A large woman charged them, shrieking and wielding a skull filled with lime cement hanging from the end of wooden haft.

'Get up! Run!' Tangwen tried to scream at the navigator, but she barely had the strength to croak.

She watched the grotesque ripples in the flesh of the woman charging her. The sky was cloudless and blue above her, the sun bright and warm.

Tangwen staggered to her feet. She was surprised to see she had a knife in her hand, her axe long-gone now. The large woman swung at her. Somehow Tangwen ducked. The hand with a knife in it appeared to strike of its own accord and the blade scraped across the woman's skull, cutting skin and flesh. Blood covered the moonstruck woman's face, blinding her. This just made her laugh. The woman swung the skull-headed club and Tangwen ducked under another wild blow. The woman overextended herself, staggering past. Tangwen felt the impact run up her arms as she stabbed the knife into the back of the woman's neck with enough force to sever her spine. The woman flopped to the ground like a dying fish.

More moonstruck were sprinting towards them across the beach.

Even if I had my bow, Tangwen managed to think, *I still wouldn't have the strength to draw it.*

She wanted to give up now. Lie down. Sleep. Let the inevitable happen. She wanted death to carry her back to her Serpent Father in his crystal cave. Instead she stood over the body of the frightened navigator, bloody knife in hand. They had achieved so much. It wasn't fair to die like this. She screamed so the gods could hear her anger.

Her cries were cut off as the man who had been cutting himself landed on her back, his weight sending them both crashing to the sand and rolling into the shallow water.

He was shamed. Unmanned. This small, tough woman raised in a cold, hard land was fighting, selling her life hard, whilst he lay shaking in his own water.

She hit the ground as one of the moonstruck jumped on her back. Germelqart's hand wrapped itself around the haft of the barbaric skull-headed club the moonstruck woman had dropped. Then he was on his knees. Warm blood sprayed on his face as he brought the club down again and again onto the man's head. He was screaming. The warrior woman had rolled from under her moonstruck attacker and was watching Germelqart beat the man's head in.

He stopped, looking at the ruin he had made. The warrior woman had stood up, her knife at the ready, but she swayed as if she was ready to drop. Germelqart managed to stand, still holding the crude, horrible club. He was no warrior and never had been, but he was determined to follow the young woman's example.

A group of islanders was running towards them. He wasn't sure how many. In his exhaustion, he had forgotten how to count.

The stink. Hands grabbing at her. Tangwen was kicked, punched, bludgeoned, clawed with long, ragged nails as she slashed out with the knife and cut and cut. They didn't appear to care that her knife

27

bit into their flesh again and again as they forced her back into the red-frothed water. She saw the navigator swing the skull-headed club but they were all around her by the time he went down.

She felt herself go over as she sucked in her last, deep breath before she was under the shallow water again. She tried to fight free, but as more and more hands held her down, as more of her own blood leaked out into the stinging salt water, as the need to take another breath grew stronger and stronger, the panic came and she started to thrash around ineffectually.

Suddenly she could move again. Something bumped her under the water. A weight fell on her. She struggled free and sat up in the red-tinged shallows.

A number of the moonstruck were being forced back towards land by a tall, powerfully built, brown-skinned man with no hair. He was swinging a long-hafted axe with a double-crescent bronze head at them. A decapitated body bumped against her, pushed by the gentle movement of the waves. There was another body nearby, a huge bloody rent in its midriff.

Someone grabbed her arm. She turned to stab them and realised she'd lost her knife. The navigator let go of her, recoiling, his hands held up. He was trying to help her. He said something, nodding at the axeman. She recognised the word *Kush*. It was the brown-skinned man's name.

'We must help Kush,' Germelqart repeated helplessly. The young woman turned from him and started feeling around in the silt under the red water. He saw the haft of his weapon bobbing in the gentle waves, anchored by its lime-cement-filled skull. He grabbed it and tried to run after Kush, but had to settle for stumbling.

Tangwen squeezed sand through her fingers as they closed around the hilt of her knife. Up and down the beach she could see survivors dragging themselves from the water only to be set upon by the moonstruck. All the while the *dryw*, wearing flayed faces, stood on the dunes, watching. The *dryw* with the filthy white hooded robes, who had been sent here to tend to the mad.

'We have to help the survivors,' she muttered to herself. Then she shouted it at Germelqart's back in a language the navigator would struggle to understand. She stood up in the water and staggered after the two foreign traders.

*

28

Taking the horses onto the causeway had been a huge mistake. Ysgawyn could see that now. It was overconfidence, arrogance. He had underestimated the ability of the Atrebates' warband and their allies from the Otherworld. He was not going to make the same mistake again.

It had cost them a number of warriors and more horse when they were forced off the causeway and into the swampy ground on the westernmost island. They had also lost Gwydion, his second-in-command and the Corpse People's warleader. It was just another thing Ysgawyn was going to take out on the flesh of any Atrebates survivors.

Much of the lime had been washed off their faces, bodies and armour when they were forced to pick their way back north through the marshland to the causeway. Now they looked less like the corpses they tried so hard to emulate.

They had made it back to the mainland and were standing among a large field of tree stumps where the Lochlannach had chopped wood to fuel the burning, crumbling wicker man. The clear-cut swathe was a scar on the landscape.

They had been too busy trying to navigate through the marshland and pull their people and beasts from the sucking mire to have seen the battle, or the wicker man ignited. The wind had taken the smell of cooking meat the other way, but they still heard the screams. Even from so far away they had watched the angry red sea seethe and boil under the pulsing blue rip in the air, the gateway to Annwn. They had cheered when Arawn manifested as a mass of black maggots eating the sky. But their death god had not consumed the land. The gateway had closed. Ynys Prydein, the Isle of the Mighty, had not become Ynys Annwn, the Isle of the Dead.

He could see it in the eyes of his people. Despite the blessings of Crom Dhubh, despite having stolen the power of god-touched heroes by eating their flesh, his people were beginning to doubt their invincibility. In fact, having seen how the Atrebates warband and their allies had shepherded their comrades to Annwn, the Corpse People were beginning to doubt they were dead at all.

As Ysgawyn sat on one of the few surviving horses, hand gripping the hilt of his longsword so tightly that his knuckles had gone white, he knew that his people needed a victory. More fundamentally, they needed to hurt others and then kill them.

Somewhat worryingly he had watched his allies, the blank-faced warriors from the Otherworld, sail east against the wind. The giants had slipped beneath the waves. Whether they swam beneath the black *curraghs* or returned to their sunken homeland, he did not know.

They had all seen movement on the western isle, further inland from the causeway. They were not sure who or what it was but the movement was strange. It did not look like the movement of man or beast, and there had been a lot of it. It had started in the south but appeared to be getting closer, and it was making what was left of Ysgawyn's warband even more nervous. There was something disturbing and unnatural about all that movement.

'What are we doing?' one of his warband asked. The young Corpse People warrior was looking to the south and west, where the sun had turned to red as it sank beyond the horizon. Under the lime and bravado, he looked little more than a well-built, frightened boy. The warrior was young enough that Ysgawyn hadn't bothered to learn his name.

'We're waiting for survivors,' Ysgawyn told him and then raised his voice. 'Don't you wish to avenge your humiliation?' he demanded.

'Our disgrace,' one of the long moustaches said. Owen, he was called, well built and with scars to wear, he was one of the older members of the warband. He had been a good friend of Gwydion's.

Ysgawyn seethed with anger at the correction but knew he could do nothing about it without alienating the warband further.

'It is the time between times,' Owen added. 'The connections to the Otherworld grow in strength. The borders have been broken here this day. We should leave.' Grumbles of agreement rose from the rest of the warband.

When did you become a dryw? Ysgawyn wondered.

There was movement in the dying light. They heard a distant splash and saw ripples in the water by the shore of the western isle, about half a mile from their position.

'I think the Atrebates' bitch goddess has given birth to some awful thing to revenge herself on us,' said the young warrior who had spoken first. His fear spread like a sickness through the warband.

Ysgawyn opened his mouth to curse them for cowards, though the fear was not unknown to him, either. Then the thing surged from the water and mud of the marshy terrain close to where they stood.

Stinger-tipped tendrils of translucent flesh, like those he had seen on the strange sea creatures that sometimes washed up on the shore, flew from a maw filled with rows of predatory teeth. Its mouth was surrounded by multi-segmented, spear-like mandibles. It writhed up, eyeless and wormlike, its body covered in thick shell-like armour. It surged across the land towards them, moving with surprising speed with a rapid, rippling movement.

Some readied spears or reached for swords, bracing shields, whilst others ran. Even Otherworldly steeds reared in terror at the massive creature, which was growing as they watched.

Cries of fear turned into cries of agony as tendrils wrapped around the men, their touch burning exposed skin as they were lifted into the air and dragged towards the maw – men or beasts, it didn't matter.

Ysgawyn fought frantically to control his rearing horse as his men ran past him. One of them was yanked backwards into the air by the creature's tendrils and his horse bolted from the thing. Later he would tell himself there was nothing he could have done, that the horse was too frightened for him to stand his ground. Now, with the cries of terror and agony of his own people in his ears, all he wanted to do was flee.

Despite himself, he looked back. His men weren't dying. The thing's mouth had distended to further enormity and sprays of liquids hit men and beast alike. Their skin sloughed off as their flesh fused with that of their steeds, and they screamed, and screamed, and screamed.

As he turned away to concentrate on riding north towards the hill that overlooked the three islands, he caught a glimpse of the western isle in his peripheral vision. The isle appeared to seethe as if it had a life of its own.

4
Birmingham, 1791

There was a lot of screaming. The Hellaquin caught a glance from upstairs of the dead man's skin crawling, demons and devils moving in his flesh as the Knight's necromancy tore word after word from the corpse through its gritted teeth. The Hellaquin heard the demon spit and curse at the Knight, shouting imprecations and threats, but in the end the devils in the Knight's blood had proven stronger. It told the Knight that the cursed pepperbox pistol had come from one of the gun works on Steelhouse Lane. By then the house was ablaze and an even larger crowd had gathered. The two of them left via the back garden.

'They'll blame the Dissenters,' the Hellaquin muttered.

'Let them,' the Knight said icily.

More redcoats spotted them as the Knight's powerful horse carried them back into the city, heading for Steelhouse Lane. It was difficult to avoid the soldiers in the city at the moment. A mounted officer had even given chase, but the Knight's steed easily outdistanced him. The officer fired at them on the gallop but the pistol ball went wide.

'This is the place,' the Hellaquin said when they finally reached their destination. His eyes read the plaque in the darkness as if it were broad daylight. His ability to read had also come from the chalice. The Knight moved up next to the Hellaquin, keeping an eye out all around, a pistol in each hand. The Hellaquin knew that the Knight would have no qualms about killing common soldiers if any of the redcoats found them. The Knight glanced down at the lock and then at the Hellaquin.

'You are just as capable of picking locks as I,' the Hellaquin growled.

'Except I have no picks, and surely it's much more appropriate for one of your station than for one of mine?'

The Hellaquin bit back a reply, reaching instead into his arrow case. He pulled out his picks and went to work on the lock. It was a complex modern design, very much what you would expect from Birmingham, and it gave him some trouble.

Quentin Padget felt the steel against his skin in his sleep, but it was the strong hand holding his mouth shut that woke him. The master gunsmith found himself looking down the rifled barrel of a pistol whose workmanship he had to admire, he recognised it as one of Nock's pieces.

'My apologies,' the well-dressed pistoleer told him. There was another much larger figure behind him. Padget was surprised to see that the larger figure appeared to be holding a longbow with an arrow nocked. They must have come through the workshop and somehow not woken any of the apprentices. Padget started to panic. He tried to move his head to see if his wife Susan, lying next to him, was all right, but strong fingers held him still. 'We would not have come upon you unannounced if it was not a desperate situation, but we must know certain things and we will have our knowledge. Now, if I let you go you must be quiet and still, else my large companion will murder and rape all here, possibly myself included. Do you understand?'

Padget saw the large man with the bow turn and look at the well-dressed pistoleer, but he could not make out the hulking brute's expression in the darkness of his room above the workshop. He managed to nod and the fingers came away from his mouth. He looked over at Susan and was astonished to find that she was somehow still asleep.

'Please—' he begged.

'No extraneous information, just answer our questions and we will be on our way.' Padget had no idea what 'extraneous' meant, so he kept quiet. 'A man bought a pepperbox pistol here recently—'

'Sir Ronald Sharpely—' Padget began.

'No,' the pistoleer said gravely. 'I have not asked you anything yet.'

Padget felt his bowels turn to ice water. He saw the bowman glance at the man with the pistols again.

'Who made the pistol?' the well-dressed man asked.

'I did,' Padget said as a tear ran down his cheek. 'I'm sorry, sir, I'm a master craftsman. I always look after a client of Sir Ronald's standing. One of my finest pieces.' Padget had a horrible feeling that the pistoleer had lost someone to the pepperbox in a duel and decided that the seven-barrel pistol had provided an unfair advantage. The well-dressed man appeared to be studying him. Even in the gloom it felt as if the pistoleer was looking into him somehow.

'No,' the well dressed man finally said, thoughtfully.

Padget almost pissed himself. 'Sir, I promise—'

'Quiet,' the pistoleer said. Padget only just resisted the urge to sob. 'Someone else worked on it.'

The Hellaquin observed the poor man the Knight was terrorising. The Knight had made sure the gunsmith's wife would sleep through the ordeal by using a needle of Cathayan manufacture to drug her as she slept. He watched realisation followed by relief spread across the terrified man's face at the Knight's question.

'Yes, sir – a clockworker and toymaker, he did the pan mechanism.'

'And where may we find him?'

'He has a workshop on Snow Hill, sir.'

'And where does he come from?' the Knight asked.

The Hellaquin looked sharply in his direction. Why hadn't the Knight asked for the clockworker's name first?

'Austria, I think, maybe Switzerland, one of the Germanic countries, certainly.'

'And his name?'

'Silas Scab.'

The Knight let the name hang in the silence of the night for a while. The Hellaquin only noticed because he was looking for it and could see perfectly in the dark, but there was a moment of recognition on the Knight's face, and then it was gone.

'Where exactly on Snow Hill?' the Hellaquin asked. He felt bad because the man jumped at the sound of his voice and a wet patch started to appear on the bedclothes. The gunsmith told them.

The Knight was holding up a tiny, ornately decorated brass egg.

'There's life in this – I can see the light of it. I wonder if this is an unborn baby scorpion?' He put it down. The workshop in the 'toy'-making district of Snow Hill was immaculate. 'Toy' referred to all manner of small metal goods from buttons to buckles, but it was clear that Silas Scab was a clockworker of prodigious talent. The workshop was so full of ticking, moving gears and springs that, to the Hellaquin, it appeared to be alive in the most unnatural way.

They had let themselves in again, though the lock had broken a number of his picks and then stabbed him with a needle coated in a venom that would have felled a normal man.

'You know this man?' the Hellaquin asked the Knight.

'No,' the Knight finally answered, but from the tone of his voice the Hellaquin knew there was something the Knight wasn't telling him.

'Who's in there?' a voice asked from outside. The accent was English.

The Hellaquin and the Knight looked at each other. They had been quiet and careful. Nobody should have heard them. The Knight moved quickly to one side of the double doors that opened into the workshop, drawing one of his flintlock pistols as he went. Then he nodded to the Hellaquin.

'It's the Watch – the door was open. What business is it of yours?' the Hellaquin demanded with an authority he'd learned commanding mercenaries in France. The door was pushed open a crack by the barrel of a musket, and an old but still hale-and-hearty-looking man peered in. The Knight placed the barrel of the pistol against the man's head.

'Do please come in,' he said politely. The man looked irritated but not frightened.

'How did you know we were in here?' the Hellaquin demanded, worried that they had come upon another of their kind.

'Master Scab asked me to keep an eye on his place. He gave me one of them clocks. He said that if I ever saw the bird it meant there were someone in here. I thought he was talking nonsense meself – till the damned bird woke me up.'

The Hellaquin glanced at the Knight, who shrugged.

'And where is Mr Scab?' the Knight asked.

'I don't know,' the man said stubbornly.

'You're lying.'

'What if I am? I can't see sneak thieves or assassins meaning anything but ill to Mr Scab, who's always done right by me.'

The Hellaquin saw the expression of exasperation on the Knight's face. The Knight was always confused whenever anyone whom he perceived to be lower than him in station didn't just do exactly what he wanted when he wanted it done.

'You realise I have a pistol clapped to your head,' the Knight pointed out.

'That hadn't entirely escaped my notice, but it's not the first time I've had a gun pointed at me, and I've lived a good, long life.'

Despite the man's words, the Hellaquin could see the man was frightened.

'That is your prerogative,' the Knight said and cocked the pistol. 'I'll tear what I want to know from your steaming carcass.'

'Wait,' the Hellaquin said, not least because a shot would bring the redcoats and the actual Watch running. 'He'll do it,' he told the man.

The old man turned to look at the Knight. Even in the darkness his

35

eyes had adjusted enough to see the bored expression on the Knight's face.

'I believe you,' the man finally said.

'Is this Scab worth dying for?' the Hellaquin asked.

'I'm guessing he is polite but distant,' the Knight said. 'Pleasant enough, but you've always felt there was something not quite right about him.'

'I just thought he was one of them Quakers.'

The Knight's laughter was humourless.

'He's killed a young boy and a whole family in the last few days – that we know of,' the Hellaquin said.

The old man looked between them both, then appeared to come to a decision: 'He's gone up to Soho. Old Man Boulton saw some of his work and asked for him.'

'Who?' the Knight asked.

'Mr Matthew Boulton, the manufacturer, James Watt's partner.'

'The steam-engine man?' the Knight asked.

'Yes.'

'And where can we find Mr Boulton?'

'At this hour? Abed.'

'I will shoot you,' the Knight promised.

'Try Soho House.'

The Knight removed the pistol from the old man's head.

'Go away and tell nobody that you spoke with us.'

'Why don't you go away, because I live here and I'll call the Watch?'

The Hellaquin knew that the Knight was getting ready to kill the old man just to make his life easier.

'Leave him,' the Hellaquin said firmly. The Knight looked surprised that the Hellaquin would speak to him so, but he walked out of the workshop.

Soho House was a grand, three-storey rectangle with columns. It was faced in white-painted slate, giving it the appearance of having been constructed from large bricks of stone.

The drawing room was lined with dark wood panelling and book-shelves, and the fireplace still contained the dying embers of last night's fire. The Knight was seated in a leather-upholstered chair, glancing between the tasteful finery of the room and the hastily dressed Boulton, who stood in front of the fire.

He was a formidable-looking grey-haired man in his sixties with a hawk-like nose and dark eyes. Despite the sternness of his features, the Hellaquin thought he could see a kindliness about the man. He was dressed in a black velvet housecoat, a silk waistcoat and a ruffed shirt that somehow managed not to be too ostentatious.

'I am not in the habit of accepting visitors this late at night, regardless of how histrionic they are. What is this nonsense you told Evans?' he demanded.

'Do you know a Silas Scab?' the Hellaquin asked.

Boulton's eyes narrowed. 'What business is that of yours?'

The Hellaquin opened his mouth to reply but the Knight beat him to it.

'Just answer the damned question so we can get on with our business,' the Knight demanded. He could have been talking to a stable boy. The Hellaquin let out a sigh as Boulton turned on the Knight, his face like thunder.

'Get out of my house before I have you beaten out of it!' Boulton demanded, barely able to talk through his anger. The Hellaquin could see his point. It didn't matter what your 'station' was in society, you didn't speak to a man that way in his own house.

The Knight looked equally furious at being threatened. The Hellaquin saw the other man's hand creeping towards a blade, or maybe a pistol. The archer grabbed the Knight's arm. The Knight looked about ready to kill both of them.

'Decide what's important here,' the Hellaquin hissed, 'or walk away.' He watched the Knight control his temper with some difficulty.

'Take your hand off me,' the Knight said quietly, dangerously. The Hellaquin let go of him. 'I'll leave you to converse peasant to peasant.' The Knight stood and strode out of the room. Boulton, his face a mask of fury, watched him go. If he heard the Knight's parting comment, he said nothing.

'Quickly tell me why you are here,' Boulton said, turning on the Hellaquin when he heard the front door close.

'Silas Scab has killed nine people that we know of. He is a lunatic and we believe he will kill again.'

'Why should I believe you?' Boulton demanded. 'Where is your proof?'

'We have witnesses ... back in the city—'

'You are a bad liar, sir!'

The Hellaquin shouldn't have lied, he knew that. You didn't get to be as wealthy – and obviously powerful – as Boulton without a degree of shrewdness.

'He kills families in the most horrible ways, causes as much pain as he can. You have to believe me. He is possessed by devils.'

The Hellaquin read the expression of distaste on Boulton's face as he said this last, and he knew he'd made another mistake. Boulton might believe in god but he was a man of his age, of science and clanking steam, clockwork and machinery. There was little room in this new world for devils. But then, surprisingly, Boulton's face softened.

'That at least is true, or you believe it so. Tell me, are you suffering a religious mania?'

'I'm not that kind of man. I believe what I'm forced to because of what I've seen. If they had told you of Watt's steam engine when you were a child, would you have believed them?' The Hellaquin was all but pleading. Boulton thought on this.

'No,' he said eventually. 'That I had to see to believe as well.' Boulton was staring at the strange, burly man who had come unbidden to his house as he tried to make a decision.

The Hellaquin retrieved his bow from where he'd hidden it in the bushes by the iron railings surrounding Soho House and walked over to stand by the Knight. To the south-west the forest of chimneys, steeples and spires above soot-stained brick almost filled the landscape as they looked back at Birmingham. Even now, workers would be starting to get up and break their fast before heading to toil in foundries, mills and workshops, powered by coke from Warwickshire and Staffordshire, and fed by iron from Sweden and Russia.

But the Knight wasn't staring at the city. He was staring at the massive building that was the Manufactory, just below them on South Hill. The Hellaquin started flexing his bow.

'He's down there, isn't he?' the Knight said. The Hellaquin nodded. Boulton had wanted to look into the possibility of mass manufacturing Silas Scab's clockwork. Silas had asked to see the Manufactory and Boulton asked his foreman to show him around. That was early yesterday evening. As far as Boulton knew, Silas had looked around the Manufactory and then returned to the city.

'He knows we're coming,' the Knight said.

'How?' the Hellaquin growled.

'The blood magic. He sensed me and destroyed the "devils" I sent out into the night.' He said the last bit sarcastically.

'He's strong, then?'

The Knight just nodded. 'I kill him, you understand me?'

The Hellaquin met the other man's blue eyes and held their stare. 'What is this man to you?'

The Knight didn't answer. Instead he spun on his heel and headed down the hill towards the Manufactory.

The inside of the Manufactory was a cavernous space full of noise but empty of people. Massive machinery moved of its own accord, powered by glowing furnaces. Huge copper kettle-like boilers stood here and there in various states of assembly. The flickering gaslights threw strange shadows across the filthy stone floor and the air was unpleasantly hot and humid from the venting steam. The Hellaquin didn't sweat any more, but his clothes, particularly the heavy leather coat he wore as armour, were very quickly soaked through.

I think when they've calculated all my sins I'll be sent to a place like this, the Hellaquin thought as he stalked deeper into the Manufactory, a flesh-tearing broad-head arrow nocked on the bow. Stalking or not, he did not feel like the hunter.

There was movement above him as something crossed in front of one of the windows on the third floor. The movement looked wrong, somehow, too jerky to be natural.

Even over the noise of the machinery the explosion of the pistol shot was loud and the muzzle flash momentarily bathed the interior of the building in a hellish orange glow. The Hellaquin tracked the source of the noise. One of the Knight's pistols was still smoking.

The Hellaquin heard the chains first. He had a moment to realise the shadows around him were growing, then brought the bow up and loosed the arrow, relying on instinct rather than aiming.

The Hellaquin knew he had hit the thing falling from the ceiling beams of the Manufactory. His gift allowed him to hear through the noise of the machinery and he heard the sound of flesh torn open as the arrow passed through his attacker's body. It landed in front of the Hellaquin. Whatever it was had chains wrapped around its wrists and ankles, but was otherwise shaped like a man. It moved towards the archer in jerky fashion, as if the chains were controlling it, though the Hellaquin could see that this was not the case. The Hellaquin realised the creature was supposed to look like the kind of puppets the Italians called marionettes. The wound in its chest was certainly mortal, but it kept coming. All over the Manufactory the Hellaquin could hear chains rattling, and he was aware of other things dropping from the beams running under the ceiling.

The Hellaquin loosed another arrow as he moved away from the thing and the human marionette's head shot back as the arrow tore through it. The Hellaquin was appalled when its head jerked forwards again to look at him as the thing continued advancing. He wasn't sure if he was imagining being able to see through its head or not. It swung a mattock at him, and the Hellaquin barely managed to dodge out of the way. It made no sense, the chains were getting in the way of the walking dead man's ability to move. He could hear fighting behind him.

As he reached into the long tubular pockets inside his coat for another arrow, the Hellaquin saw the small brass scorpion wrapped around the marionette's eye socket, its legs and stinger moving deeper into skin, flesh and the eye itself. The Hellaquin backed away from it rapidly as it lurched after him, swinging the mattock. He pulled an arrow with an adamantine-headed bodkin from one of the pockets, quickly nocked it, brought the bow up, took the barest moment to aim this time and loosed. The arrow hit the still-moving metal scorpion and tore the side of the man's skull off. The marionette slumped forwards in its chains. The Hellaquin was aware of some tiny thing skittering across the floor and under one of the half-completed boilers.

'Aim for the—' he cried out as the sledgehammer hit him in the back. His leather coat hardened, as did his skin, but it wasn't enough. Agony shot up his spine. The force of the blow staggered him and he collapsed to his knees as the breath exploded from his lungs. Behind him one of the human marionettes raised the sledgehammer high above its head to cave in the Hellaquin's skull. His diaphragm, aided by his 'gift', shook off its paralysis and he sucked air into his lungs again. He put both hands on the ground and kicked up, hitting his attacker in the chest. Ribs broke and the marionette was thrown backwards on its chains. The Hellaquin dropped his bow and pushed himself to standing.

'Aim for the scorpions in their eyes!' he shouted as he ducked under another sledgehammer swing. The Hellaquin had a short sword in each hand now. He took a rapid step forward and thrust the right-hand sword through the human marionette's skull, pinioning the brass scorpion and pushing it out through the other side of the human puppet's head.

'Aim for the scorpions!' the Knight shouted. 'I'm going after—'

Whatever the Knight had intended to say was drowned out by a pistol shot, followed by another in quick succession. The Hellaquin had a moment to look up towards a catwalk at the other end of the Manufactory. He could just make out a dark figure wreathed in pistol smoke, then the figure fired the pepperbox pistol again.

Silas kept firing the pepperbox pistol as the Knight leaped past one of his marionettes and onto the stairs leading to the winch platform upon which he stood. He knew he was hitting the Knight – he saw the man stagger more than once – but still he kept coming.

He was sure he knew the man. He had seen him before, walking out of his father's burning workshop covered in blood. He screamed as he fired again. The man stumbled back against the wall. One of Silas's marionettes landed in front of the man, swinging a huge spanner at him. The man ducked and sparks flew off the brick wall. Silas had to concede that the chains might have been a mistake, regardless of how much he liked the idea of human marionettes. The blond, blue-eyed man jumped up and, with little finesse but surprising force, he severed one of the marionette's arms, then the other, and then one of its legs. His puppet's torso fell forwards, leaving limbs dangling from the chains.

Silas fired again and was rewarded with a spray of blood from the man's head. The pepperbox pistol was empty now. He laid it neatly on the workbench in front of him, in its place among his other tools.

The Knight's blond hair was matted with blood by the time he reached the top of the stairs and faced Silas on the winch platform. As Silas watched, the blood was already disappearing from the Knight's hair. That was when he realised the man was just like him. He had the will to control demons and do great works. However, he also recognised the look on the Knight's face as he approached with a red and naked blade in his hand. This man wanted – no, hungered – to take his life.

The Knight moved with frightening speed, but so could Silas. Hot broken glass and iron nails hit the blond man in the face and chest as the blunderbuss kicked back into Silas's shoulder. As the smoke cleared, Silas found himself disappointed. He expected to see the Knight's chest a crimson ruin and his head all but gone. Instead the man's chest looked fine, but where his face had been there was now a skull painted red that opened its mouth so blood could bubble out. Skin and flesh were already starting to creep around from the back of the blond man's head.

Good, Silas thought, *I can take my time with this one*. He put the blunderbuss down on the workbench, in the right place, and reached for his blades just as he remembered the other man on the ground floor. He looked up as the broad-head arrow caught him in the throat and passed through, two feet of ash pinioning him to the brick wall behind him. Silas reached for it as blood ran down the shaft. He spat blood out of his mouth, more surprised than anything else.

The Hellaquin didn't waste a moment to check the effects of his shot. He nocked another arrow, drew and loosed, then fired again at a marionette swinging towards him, his ability and 'gift' guiding the shot. The marionette slumped dead in its chains, the side of its head a ruin. He spun. Behind him, yet another marionette was running towards him, almost too close to fire on. He loosed and the human puppet hit the ground, sliding over the stone. Something leaped from the marionette's head and skittered under a boiler. Then there was no more movement. Not down on the workshop floor, anyway.

The Hellaquin glanced up to the winch platform. His 'gift' made Silas look much closer than he actually was and he could see the killer drooling blood as he inched forwards on the arrow shaft. The Hellaquin drew his penultimate arrow from inside his coat. It was a broad-head.

The broad-head caught the killer in the chest and drove him back into the wall again. The Hellaquin reached the stairs to the winch platform and started climbing them as he drew the final arrow. He'd hollowed the head of this arrow and filled it with his own blood. He'd told the devils in the blood to do one thing and one thing only: to seek out others like them and kill.

The Hellaquin stopped for a moment to look down at the Knight as the other man struggled to regrow enough of his mind to be capable of movement. The Hellaquin stepped over him. He wasn't going to shoot the killer from a distance. He was going to ram the arrow straight through his heart.

Silas continued trying to pull himself off the arrows pinning him to the wall as the big archer approached him. Every movement caused agony to reverberate through him as he inched along the shafts.

The archer was standing in front of him now, bow raised and arrow nocked, ready to plunge into Silas's heart. Silas spat his blood into the archer's face and gave the devils in his blood the order to eat.

The archer started screaming. He dropped his bow, hands flying to his face as the blood started to consume skin, flesh and eyes, overwhelming the archer's own defences.

With a scream, Silas wrenched himself off the arrows, already starting to heal. The archer staggered back, much of the skin on his face gone, revealing the musculature underneath. Silas lurched to the workbench and grabbed one of his knives. A heavy knife for butchering meat, he'd modified it to include a ring for his finger where the blade met the hilt. He had a pair of them.

Knife in hand, Silas turned on the archer. He pulled the archer's hands away from his diminishing face and slit the man's throat. That act would normally involve some sawing, but Silas's superior strength and the sharpness of the blade allowed him to do it in one deft cut.

The archer grabbed at his throat as blood bubbled out. Silas's own neck wound was already starting to heal.

The killer carefully placed his bloodied knife on the workbench, next to the virgin steel of its twin, and picked up another item. He remembered when his father taught him that people were like clockwork. You could take them apart quite easily.

Silas walked around behind the archer and stepped on the back of the man's knee, forcing him to the ground. He grabbed his long hair and used it to force the archer's head sideways onto the workbench. The man tried to fight him with one red-coloured hand. Silas released the archer's hair and grasped the handle of the bone guillotine. There was sickening crunch as Silas's strength forced the guillotine's curved blade through the archer's skull and sliced off the top of the other man's head. The archer stopped struggling. Silas moved the body into a limp kneeling position. He looked around for something in which to collect the blood seeping from the neck wound, but found nothing.

I will have his knowledge, Silas thought. *I will have his power.* Strong fingers scooped out the archer's brain matter and Silas started to consume it. He managed to swallow one mouthful before he stopped. He shuddered, spat blood and grey matter out of his mouth, and then the tip of a sabre exploded out of his chest.

'I enjoyed killing your father,' the Knight whispered in his ear. Silas cursed himself for a fool. He had got far too carried away with the kill.

Du Bois wrenched the sabre out of Silas Scab. His face still burned and ached; it would be red and raw as he regrew it. The killer spun away from him with surprising vigour for a man who had just been run through, and du Bois suspected that Silas's healing ability was even better than his and the Hellaquin's. Du Bois advanced on Silas, stepping over the Hellaquin's body. He was sure the archer was dead, his ability to heal overwhelmed by the damage inflicted by Silas.

Scab grabbed a pair of knives from the workbench, one already bloody, the other clean. Du Bois held his left arm across his body, the tanto all but concealed in his left hand. The sabre flicked out lightning-fast at Silas. Silas backed away, parrying as best as he could with the long knives. The killer relied on speed and strength, du Bois on skill and hundreds of years of experience. It was a short fight.

Silas saw his moment. He stepped inside the Knight's guard, one blade ready to deflect the sabre, the other to cut into his opponent. To start to take him apart as his father had taught him. For his father. Steel rasped on steel as he turned the sabre aside. His keen blade bit deep into the Knight's left arm, eliciting a grunt of pain. Too late, Silas saw the tanto. Folded steel sliced into the killer's skin, cutting through it even as it tried to harden to armour. The chisel-like tip of the knife forced between his ribs.

Du Bois screamed with exertion as he rammed the blade with sheer strength through rib bones, cutting downwards in a C-shape to the stomach before blood made the hilt of the blade too slick to hold and he lost his grip on it. Silas dropped both of his blades. Du Bois kicked the killer in the chest, causing more of his innards to spill out, and Silas stumbled back and slipped on his own entrails.

The Knight stood over the killer. Silas stared up at him. He did not like pain – that was for others. It was nearly intolerable, but it was seeping out of him now. He felt real hatred for the man standing over him, but found he had nothing to say.

Du Bois ran the sabre through the killer's heart and left it there. He might still have the ability to heal, but not with the blade in the wound.

He spared a moment to look down at the Hellaquin. He despised archers as a breed. Filthy creatures who spread disease by covering their arrowheads with their own excrement and killed good horse, all because they were too lazy to learn to fight properly, and too cowardly to confront their enemies face to face.

Du Bois stepped over the body and went to retrieve his pistols. He holstered one and started reloading the other. He had a special pistol ball for Silas. It was hollow and filled with the Knight's blood, designed specifically to seek out and kill whatever dwelt in the blood of other immortals. He had mainly used its like to hunt down and kill agents of the Brass City.

'Malcolm?' The voice was quiet and incredibly deep. Du Bois glanced behind him. Two people were standing there. They had passed unnoticed through the blood wards he had left in the air.

'Mr Brown,' du Bois said to the taller of the two strange figures. His skin was as near black as du Bois had ever seen, yet Mr Brown did not have African features. He was a little under six and a half feet tall, dressed in understated, dark-coloured finery. He carried an elegant silver-tipped dark-wood cane. In his other hand was the always-present and ornately carved opium pipe. As du Bois watched, Mr Brown took a long draw from the pipe. As far as du Bois could see, Mr Brown derived little pleasure from the opium and it never noticeably affected him. His appearance was so singular that du Bois always wondered why he had such a hard time remembering what Mr Brown looked like.

Next to him was the Pennangalan, one of the infamous twin canni-bal queens of the South Pacific who claimed to be heirs to something called the Khmer Empire. Du Bois looked around. He was surprised to see the Pennangalan without her sister. Perhaps rumours of her twin returning to the Pacific were true after all.

She wore a featureless mask of beaten silver that covered her entire face. Her long black hair was gathered in a ponytail, which in turn was secured in a loop that reminded du Bois of a hangman's noose. She wore a loose shirt and trousers, and soft-soled hide boots. What little skin that remained on show was either intricately tattooed, tanned or weather-beaten. A curved, sabre-like *dao* hung from a scabbard on her belt. She also carried a pair of *dha-hmyaung* daggers and a brace of ornate flintlocks, their barrels carved into the shape of serpents' maws. Du Bois had once heard tell that the sisters' blood came from the mythical Naga themselves, and that Mr Brown had given them the choice of working for the Circle or being destroyed.

The Pennangalan pushed past du Bois and walked over to where Silas lay on the wooden boards of the winch platform.

'Leave him,' du Bois told her as he rammed the ball into the barrel of his pistol. The Pennangalan ignored du Bois and dragged the sabre out of Silas's body. 'And don't touch my sword.' Du Bois' sabre clat-tered to the ground.

Life returned explosively to Silas and he dragged in a long, rasping breath. The Pennangalan used a foot to keep him down on the boards.

'This man is a sickness. There is no requirement for his continued existence,' du Bois said as he primed the pistol.

'There is no requirement that you can see,' Mr Brown said softly. 'The Circle feels otherwise. He will be put in a place where he can do no harm.'

'Why?' du Bois asked.

Mr Brown spread his arms apologetically, indicating that he either did not know or could not tell him.

'I'm afraid that's not good enough.' Du Bois felt rather than heard the Pennangalan shifting position behind him.

A rasping, wet laugh arose from Silas. 'I'm going to enjoy killing you,' he mocked. 'You want there to be a reason. There isn't. You want me to be different from you. I am. I admit that I kill for pleasure. You pretend to kill for power.' Mr Brown was gesturing for Silas to be quiet. 'You pretend to be righteous, but we know the truth, you and I, don't we?'

It was too much for du Bois. He swung around, cocking the pistol as he turned. He was aware of the flare from a muzzle flash in the ceiling beams at the other end of the Manufactory. Then he heard the sound of the shot. The etched, saboted bullet hit him in the back right where his heart was. His clothing and skin were too slow to harden and the bullet went straight through him as the Pennangalan brought her *dao* down. The pistol and his hand fell to the wooden boards of the winch platform.

Du Bois hit the wall and slid down it. He felt himself being turned over. Mr Brown was standing over him with an expression of sadness on his entirely forgettable face.

'Why are you always so wilful, Malcolm?' he asked. Behind him the Pennangalan was helping Silas off the winch platform.

Du Bois knew he would heal but it still felt like dying. Mr Brown bowed his head and closed his eyes as if he was praying, and then he turned and walked away. Du Bois cried out as he felt his knowledge of these events disappear as if they were being slowly stolen. Tears sprang from blue eyes.

Outside the Manufactory the American joined them. His long-barrelled rifle was slung across his back. The Pennangalan was helping Silas into a luxurious black coach with an interior of upholstered red leather. It was pulled by four powerful-looking black horses.

'He's right – that creature is scum,' the American said.

'I am going to hide him from the sight of all good people,' Mr Brown said. 'Even you.'

The American looked sceptical, but he climbed up onto the driver's seat as Mr Brown entered the carriage and took another deep draw on his pipe. He didn't see the look of fear on Silas's face.

5

A Long Time After the Loss

The Monk strode through the passages of the immersion monastery. The door to the monastic cell gave her a moment's trouble, but she had the *Lazerene*'s AI override the lockout codes on the contemplation immersion.

The handle of the thick, iron-reinforced door felt cold against her calloused palm as it turned, and she stepped into the cramped stone cell. It was windowless, the only furniture a crude cot on the floor against one of the walls. Brother Benedict was kneeling, his cassock stripped down to the waist. His body was covered with tattooed equations describing fifth-dimensional thought experiments. He looked like he was praying, but observing the equations on his skin change, the Monk knew that his solitary contemplation was an opportunity to use his neunonics software to work on a number of extra-dimensional physics problems.

'No,' Benedict said quietly. He had the accepted body sculpt of a physically fit base male seen all across Known Space, though part of his tonsure betrayed a receding hairline that he wasn't vain enough to hide. The Monk knew that Benedict had had the same cold, dead eyes as his father until he'd had them redesigned.

'I'm sorry, Benedict.'

'You may have me backed up here but that's twice now he's killed me. I don't enjoy the experience.'

'If it's any consolation, Scab has killed me once as well.'

'It's not.'

'The first time was your own fault. You were hunting him.'

'I designed my own psycho-surgical procedures after that. I changed my mind so I wasn't like that any more. I was doing a lot of combat drugs back then.'

'It was an unsanctioned mission.'

Benedict turned to the Monk. His blue eyes looked wrong. They were somehow too expressive for his face, as if he was trying to fake warmth that just wasn't there.

'I did my penance. It did not include being repeatedly killed by that psycho until he actually manages to get a virus past our security and permanently scrambles my backups.' The Monk didn't say anything. Benedict concentrated for a moment. 'I'm not still in the Cathedral, am I?'

'No. I'm sorry – we had your body loaded aboard the *Lazerene*.'

Benedict used his thumb and forefinger to massage the bridge of his nose.

'We've lost your father—'

'Don't call him that.' It was a growl. The Monk would never admit it to Benedict, but she could see noticeable similarities in their mannerisms, despite the son only ever having met his father twice.

'This is important or we wouldn't ask. You're our expert. You studied him when you were tracking him down.'

'And I would have removed that information from my head if Churchman had let me.' He turned back to face the wall. 'Do you know, when the Church "found" me, Churchman was going to have me destroyed? He thought I was some kind of hereditary "bad seed". He was almost right.' The Monk knew this but chose to remain quiet. 'I have no connection to that man beyond being the result of him impregnating my mother and then meat-hacking her to make sure I went full term. If you were to download all the information I have on him, you would know as much.'

'Churchman doesn't believe it.'

'I know, but his belief in an intuitive connection is bordering on the superstitious.'

'When the Consortium caught him, they recorded his personality in their Psycho Banks.' The Psycho Banks were used to record significantly aberrant personalities for profiling purposes.

Benedict came up on one knee as he looked at her again. The Monk actually tensed slightly before she remembered the pointlessness of attacking someone in this particular immersion. There was emotion on his face now. Horror.

'You don't know what you're suggesting. You're talking about putting the mind of a heretical, recreational killer inside me and letting him run free?'

'You'll be in control, and under strict supervision.'

Benedict was on his feet and pacing now. 'It's all about will for him, will and control. If he has the will to do what the other guy won't, he wins. Winning is only important in that he will have control, or, more importantly, that nobody has control over him. He has two ways to resolve problems. He will often take the most direct – and probably violent – route. He will court atrocity. He will tell himself he does this as a warning to others, but I think that's the residual sickness no amount of psychosurgery could eat out of him. If he does not take that route, then he will try to come up with the most convoluted, unexpected plan. He will look to completely wrong-foot his opponents.' There was desperation in his voice.

'I'm sorry,' the Monk told him, and meant it.

'He's not giving me any choice?' Benedict asked, incredulously. The Monk just looked at him sympathetically. 'It'll be like a possession. Whatever you ... he thinks, I'm not like him. I'm going to drown.' Benedict was pleading now.

'We'll destroy you, utterly, and then clone you.'

'He's like a virus. He destroys everything he touches. You don't want my help – you want a ritual sacrifice!'

'So how are we committing suicide today?' Vic asked as he walked into the medical area of the bizarre heretical cult's asteroid habitat. Mindful of his audience, he was speaking in the pre-Loss language their captive understood.

'I'm tired of your negative attitude,' Scab said quietly. Vic could tell that the normally emotionless human was actually irritated, but he wasn't sure it was with him.

'You've got a death wish,' Vic pointed out defensively.

'Which I'm very positive about, and proactive in my pursuit thereof.'

'I knew a lot of guys like you,' Talia said from the smart-matter couch that had been designed to fit in with the general stone decor of the church. There was a tremor in her voice. She was trying to brazen through seeing a near-seven-feet-tall cybernetic insect, but the fear – bordering on terror – in her tone was difficult to disguise.

Vic had to admit the heretical sect that was sheltering them might have resources that looked rudimentary, but they'd regrown him just fine. Presumably Scab had arranged for the hard-tech augments. A lot of them had been salvaged from his last body, but there were new components, too, and even some upgrades. That was the problem with bounty killing – you always had to be upgrading, because if you didn't, you could be sure the other guy would.

Vic studied the pale girl lying on the couch. He was fairly sure she was pretty by human standards. He even ran some image analysis to be certain. Studying her through the various visual spectrums he had access to, as well as passive scans from his antennae, she looked all wrong. She was just too natural. Even the farmed nats he'd encountered in the past tended to have some tweaked genetic component to help with longevity, or whatever purpose they'd been bred for. Scab was watching him.

'She's not what she appears,' Scab said, seeming to read his thoughts. Scab moved to stand over her couch. The girl did her best not to cower away from him.

'What's that supposed to mean?' the girl demanded. Scab ignored her and 'faced the results of the human female's medical tests to the 'sect. Vic reviewed them quickly. His mandibles clattered together as he let off a complex mix of pheromones and wished he could do that whistling thing humans did when they were impressed by something. The girl was baseline human, clearly pre-Loss. Her body, however, was crawling with living Seeder bio-nano-tech.

Vic looked down at her. She was wearing a black lace dress with some kind of leather bodice and spike-heeled boots. He didn't recognise the style, so she must have used the cult's aging assembler to make it.

'You seem nicer than him,' she said warily.

'He makes that very easy,' Vic said.

'For a big insect.'

Vic held out his lower-right hand. She shrank away from the powerful-looking three-digit mechanical appendage.

'Hi. I'm Vic,' he said as cheerfully as he could manage in the circumstances. Talia plucked up the courage to shake his hand.

'So are you going to hurt me as well?' she asked, swallowing hard.

Vic glanced at Scab. 'What have you been telling her?' he demanded.

'That I can't make any promises,' Scab said, studying Talia. 'It's strange – say anything to her and she'll look for the most negative possible outcome. She's like you, in a way.'

'I suspect you bring that out in people. I was pretty upbeat when I worked the T-Squads.'

'T-Squads?' Talia asked. Vic suspected it was as much because she was tired of people talking about her in front of her as because she actually wanted the information.

'Thunder Squads, they were an elite army—'

'They destroyed cities for their masters,' Scab interrupted.

'So you're a killer, too?'

'Most people are, we're just better at it,' Vic said, and then worried that he might have sounded a little absurd. She was just staring at him.

'When are you planning to let me go?' she asked.

'Why would we do that?' Scab asked absently.

'We did go to rather a lot of trouble to get you,' Vic told her, thinking it would make her feel better, but he saw her tear-up. 'Where would you go, anyway? Without a debit rating you'd never get very far, and there are a lot of other bad people looking for you out there.'

'Who?' she asked through the tears.

'Well, the Ch—' Vic started, but Scab held a hand up for quiet.

Talia looked between the two of them. 'Those are the people you want to sell me to?' she demanded.

Vic didn't say anything. Some of the psychosurgery that had redesigned his insectile mind to be more like the humans he admired so much had left him with a feeling that he'd eventually identified as guilt. Most of the people he traded, or killed, were involved in the same world he was. Innocents were hard to find. Maybe some of the more sheltered Consortium children, but he doubted it – he'd met them on jobs and they seemed just as grasping and spiteful as everyone else. Talia, on the other hand, appeared to be as close as he was likely to find to an innocent. He found himself wanting to protect her.

'I don't want to be sold,' she told them.

'Who does?' Scab asked.

'It happens to us all in one way or another,' Vic told her. 'Look, you're a valuable—'

'Asset?' she asked.

'You'll be well looked after wherever you end up.'

'Or you'll be vivisected,' Scab pointed out.

Vic glanced at the human. 'How does that help?' the 'sect asked.

'Help what? She's a commodity, nothing more.'

Vic could tell that his human partner was starting to get exasperated again. The insect decided not to push it.

'I want to be free,' she told them. Insect and human just stared at her.

'You can't afford it,' Vic said, surprising himself with the sadness he felt.

'Your choice is you can be awake and aware, or we can drug you until we're ready to dispose of you,' Scab told her.

Vic watched her face crumple as more liquid leaked out of the corners of her eyes.

Scab looked confused. 'She does this a lot,' he told the insect.

Vic was busy looking up the meaning of certain human emotional states. After his internal liquid hardware had done some cross-referencing, he said, 'Are you surprised, the way you speak to her?' he demanded.

Scab turned to stare at the insect. 'What's that got to do with it?'

Vic searched through the available data again. 'Cause and effect?' he suggested.

'But I don't care if she cries, beyond the irritating noise, which I can filter out when I need to.'

'You're such a fucking bastard!' Talia screamed at Scab.

Scab gave an exasperated sigh and walked out of the medical area.

'Wait!' Talia cried. 'I'm sorry. You mentioned drugs?'

'I meant sedating you,' Scab said without looking at her.

'I think some drugs might help, y'know? I'll be calmer.'

Scab glanced at her. Vic was pretty sure Scab was at the end of what little patience he had. He reached into the breast pocket of his tatty brown pinstripe suit and pulled out a beaten-up metal case.

'Do you know what to do with this?' he asked. Talia looked at him, unsure. He walked over to the medical couch and opened the small case, which contained his works.

'Surely we could just have the medical suite—' Vic started.

'Shut up,' Scab told him quietly.

Talia stared at the works. Scab was watching her reaction. Vic saw Talia swallow hard. He wasn't sure but he suspected that the stainless-steel syringe and the packet of brown powder were a bit more hard core than she'd expected.

'Well?' Scab asked.

'What if it messes up, y'know, whatever it is that's in her?' Vic asked.

'It won't,' Scab said quietly, still watching Talia.

Talia nodded nervously and picked up the works. Scab reached into his other breast pocket and took out his cigarette case. To Vic's mind, the cigarettes were Scab's other pointless retro vice. The human killer took one out and lit it.

'Could I have one, please?' Talia asked. He gave her a cigarette, and even lit it for her. She smiled up at him through her tears. Something about the smile made Vic angry. Scab left the medical area. Vic watched Talia as she gingerly examined Scab's works, then followed his partner out.

'Hey!' Vic said. He watched Scab tense and pause in the vaulted corridor before turning around slowly. Vic stopped dead as he realised he might be pushing his luck. 'You don't have to be so nasty about everything.' He suddenly felt foolish. Scab took a step towards the large insect. Vic resisted the urge to take a step back.

'Did you see me being nasty in there?' Scab asked.

Vic gave this some thought. 'No,' he finally admitted. 'What's getting to you? If she annoys you that much, why not just keep her sedated, lock her in an immersion, make her think she's back wherever she came from?'

You had to know Scab pretty well to see it – emotions made little impact on his facial expressions – but Vic didn't like the unease the question had caused his partner.

'I'm looking for something.' Scab finally answered.

'From her? She's about as sophisticated as some corp kid's pet, those things you feed to the Scorpion. I don't think she even has neunonics.' Absurdly, Vic found himself feeling guilty again.

'She doesn't have neunonics,' Scab said. 'I need some insight.'

'Into what?'

'I don't know what her S-tech does.' Scab turned and started walking away.

Vic followed the much smaller, wiry human. 'I thought it's connected to bridge tech. That's why everyone wants her. That was the whole fucking point, right? I mean, that's why we're going to spend the rest of what feels like eternity in some Church torture immersion, right?'

'But how's it connected?'

'What, are you a bridge-drive engineer now?' Vic said. 'Who gives a fuck? And frankly, if we knew anything about her, that'd just make us more of a target in the highly unlikely event that your cockamamie scheme works.'

'Don't worry about it – you'll almost certainly be dead before it comes to that.'

'That's comforting.'

'Cockamamie?' Scab asked, glancing up at the big 'sect.

'I heard it in an immersion.'

The pair of them went quiet as one of the red-clad monks walked by, accompanied by the AG-powered cylinder in its wood and brass housing. Vic's shiver was a human affectation; the disapproving spray of pheromones brought on by the sight of the animated viscous black liquid in the tank was not.

'When can we get out of here?' Vic asked. Scab ignored the question. 'I mean, do you trust these guys?' Again, the human said nothing. They reached the docking arm. Scab 'faced the entry codes to the St Brendan's Fire. 'Are we going to clear out the dead?' Vic asked, almost desperately, as he followed Scab into the dark metal corridors of the frigate.

'As and when we need the space.'

Vic couldn't shake the feeling that Scab liked the idea of captaining a ship of the dead.

'Why are we trusting them?' Vic tried again, meaning the monks.

'We're not and I don't. Certain arrangements that aren't your concern have been made. Either they'll work or they won't, same as anything else.' It was clear they were heading towards Command and Control.

'Were you like them? The monks, I mean, when you were a sect leader?' Vic asked, largely for something to say.

Scab glanced up at him but kept walking. 'Back on Cyst? No, I wanted to build a temple to myself out of bone. It was about apotheosis, or self-aggrandising, I'm not sure which. I was young.'

'It's nice to see you've grown as a person since then,' Vic said wryly. They reached C&C and the armoured door slid open. Scab's P-sat rose into the air, scanning them both as they entered. Vic noticed that it was in a heavy combat chassis. He tried not to look at the dolphin in the tank in the corner of C&C. The brass-skinned S-tech terror that was the Scorpion had wrapped itself around the tortured creature.

'Remind you of anyone?' Scab asked.

Vic looked over at the pathetic cetacean, and then back to Scab. 'The Alchemist? Only in as much as they're both dolphins. Clearly I haven't got to know our ...' Scab looked over at the 'sect. 'I mean *your* victims,' Vic corrected hastily.

'I've been thinking about him recently.'

Vic was struggling to keep up with Scab's train of thought. 'What can you do? He was sent to Suburbia, wasn't he?'

Scab didn't bother answering. He was concentrating on something else. Vic checked and found that the ship was 'facing info to Scab. Vic requested and Scab granted access to the 'face. Vic saw an animatic of a worm-like dragon battling a knight wearing a white surcoat with a red cross on it, over mail. Vic amused himself by superimposing Scab's face on the dragon in his own neunonic interpretation of the animatic. He knew that the knight was the *St Brendan's Fire*'s AI. The worm was a sophisticated Pythian virus that Scab had unleashed on the AI in an attempt to make it more pliable, and thereby gain full control of the frigate.

'Still giving you trouble?' Vic asked. Scab ignored him again. The AI had lost the fight for almost all of the frigate's systems including the bridge drive, but it had gone to ground in certain core processes, including the one Scab was most eager to use. He was after the process that would enable the ship to shift from planetary Real Space into planetary Red Space. It was the very capability the Church were desperately trying to conceal from everyone else. This was probably why the AI was being so difficult about it, Vic thought.

'What's the plan, Scab?' Vic asked. 'What are we doing here?'

'Waiting.'

'What are you going to do with her?'

Scab turned to look at Vic. 'You didn't take this well the last time.'

'But I'm guessing I have to know at some point.'

'An auction.'

'That sounds just about psychotic enough for you. How's that going to work?'

'Pythia has agreed to host. The invitations have been sent. The price for tickets alone will put me into credit – you, too, if you want.'

Vic found he didn't care because he couldn't believe it would work. Though Pythia did make sense – most of the negotiations could be handled remotely. Pythia, despite being theoretically in Consortium space, would be impartial. It was one of the few entities in Known Space that was not interested in bridge tech. It could use its impressive orbital system and bridge-point defences to keep everyone in line. If those didn't work, Pythia wielded the more serious threat of an information embargo.

'Who?' Vic asked, but Scab ignored him. The 'sect knew the answer – the great and good of the Consortium and Monarchist systems, and of course the Church.

'I've never told you this, but I've always enjoyed your rudimentary attempts at human seduction,' Scab said. Vic stared at his partner/captor. He would have been less surprised if Scab had offered to orally pleasure him. 'They are' – Scab gave his next words some serious consideration – 'amusing to me.' The human looked as if his own words had surprised him. Vic knew it was an affectation but he was still staring at Scab, his mandibles agape.

'Wh ... what?' he managed.

'I'm missing something, with the girl. You want to have sex with her. Talk to her. Give me some insight.'

'What are you looking for?'

'I don't know ... insight, something strange in her life.'

'She was melded to a Seeder vessel. How strange do you want? She was a moon-fucking giant centipede?'

'I thought you'd enjoy this,' Scab said, and even he sounded a little confused.

'Why don't you speak to her?'

'I might kill her.'

'Of course you might. Fine.' Though Vic had to admit it was one of the less unpleasant tasks Scab had given him over the years.

*

Scab had made his presence known in the back of Vic's mind. He was watching Vic's efforts with Talia through the 'sect's own senses. Vic found he couldn't even get angry at the violation any more.

'Where are we going?' Talia asked as they climbed the helical stairway cut out of the asteroid's rock.

'It's a surprise,' Vic told her. He had spent a lot of time researching how to do this in various immersions. Not the colonial or humanoporn immersions he favoured, but the more gentle romantic immersions preferred by housewives and husbands of the more decadent upper-mid-corporates who could afford such luxuries. He'd even found some pre-Loss examples but they weren't immersions. There was no interaction. You were just supposed to watch them. They hadn't been very satisfying.

'Is it some sort of observation place?' the human asked.

Not that much of a surprise, then, Vic thought.

'Am I going to see space?'

Still, she sounded excited, he thought. The drugs appeared to have taken the edge off her fear a little, and she'd been allowed to use the assembler to make some narcotics and cigarettes, though she maintained that Scab's cigarettes were better. Her eyes were glassy at the moment. Vic hoped her narcotic haze wasn't the only reason she'd agreed to come with him.

The steps brought them out in a circular stone chamber with a transparent smart-matter domed roof. Vic realised his mistake as soon as he reached the observation chamber. He remembered approaching the asteroid habitat in the *Basilisk* the first time. He hadn't liked the look of space in the system then, either. It was inky, impenetrable.

'Where are the stars?' Talia asked. There was disappointment in her voice.

Vic was still staring through the dome. It was claustrophobic, somehow, closing in on him. The databanks in his neunonics provided him with the word 'malevolent'. Perhaps he was going too far to the human-side, he thought, if he had started investing natural phenomena with meanings they couldn't possibly have.

'You can see a better night sky out on the moors,' she said, and she sounded miserable.

Vic showed her the bottle he was carrying. She glanced at it, and then at him. She looked like she was about to start crying. Again.

'It's all gone, isn't it?'

Vic's studies into human culture aside, he wasn't really equipped for this sort of thing. Instead he nodded, deciding the tears were inevitable, and just stood and watched her. He spent a moment neunonically 'facing a command to the habitat's decidedly odd systems to grow something they could both sit on from the rock. The habitat was doing so but the item of stone furniture it was creating didn't look terribly comfortable.

'All my friends, my dad, even my fucking sister – all gone!' she wailed.

'Do you want some of this?' Vic asked, feeling a little helpless.

'What is it?' Talia asked, wiping away tears and mucous and then searching through the purse she'd assembled for a cigarette.

'Oh, right, we call this alcohol, we have this now.'

Talia stopped searching for a cigarette and stared at the big 'sect. Vic didn't need the image-analysis software in his neunonics to tell him she was looking at him as if he was a moron. She eventually found a cigarette and lit it.

'Don't you have time travel, or something useful like that?' she asked as she inhaled smoke from the cigarette.

Vic couldn't stop the laughter quickly enough. She glared at him. He decided to change the subject.

'Without soft-machine augments to scrub harmful substances from the smoke, won't those cause harmful and potentially life-threatening mutations?' he asked, pointing at the cigarette. Talia continued glaring at him. He decided this wasn't going well.

'Give me the "alcohol",' she demanded, and snatched the bottle of spirits, which had apparently been made here in the habitat using methods other than the aging assembler. The top of the bottle unsealed itself. Talia stared at it in wonder for a moment and then took a swig.

'Jesus, that tastes like shit.' She coughed, gagged a little and then took another swig.

'Jesus?'

'What are we doing here, Vic?'

'I want to have sex with you,' he blurted out, then took the bottle from her and let its sour ethanol taste flood his system as he neunonically turned off various toxin filters. She was staring at him.

'This is like a horrible trip,' Talia muttered. It was clear she was talking to herself. Vic wasn't sure what 'trip' meant in this context, but he was certain that the inclusion of the word 'horrible' didn't bode well for his chances.

'I just thought you might like something a bit different,' he tried. This sometimes worked with experimental types. The hard-core insectophile human women he favoured tended to be a bit more jaded. This was unfortunate, as insects weren't renowned for their imagination.

'You know that you're a big, armoured insect, right?'

'I can be careful.'

'I'm less worried about the armour, more the insect.'

'I'm an insect?' Vic asked, trying levity. 'Who's been talking? My cock won't fall off inside you.' Then he laughed to make sure she knew it was a joke. Talia stared at him. He felt exasperated confusion in the back of his mind. Talia continued staring at him. Then she reached for the bottle, took it from him, swigged and carried on staring.

'It's a joke, see – some insects, not uplifted ones, when they procreate, their—'

'Like a fly, I get it.'

'We're not having sex, are we?'

'No,' Talia confirmed. 'Don't take it the wrong way, you're by far the nicest insect I've ever spent time with, but first contact is one thing. I'm not sure my reputation can take sleeping with the first alien I meet.'

'I'm just an uplift. You were joined with a real alien. Its tech runs in your blood. There's an argument you're more alien than I am.'

Vic saw her face crumple again and wondered if she would ever run out of tears. Talia sat down hard on the seats the habitat had extruded and took another long pull from the bottle before grimacing.

'She was so beautiful. We sailed through the Red. There were things out there, you know? Not cold like the black. And now she's gone, too.' Then she turned on Vic, her face a mask of fury. 'And your fucking friend murdered her!' Vic thought she was going to throw the bottle of cleaning fluid, but she decided against it and took another swig.

'He's not my friend,' Vic said, holding all four hands up in contrition.

'He's a cunt,' Talia grizzled.

'Believe me, I hate him more than you do.'

Talia looked up at him. 'He killed part of me, the greater part of me, the best part of me. Sleeping, her in my mind, mine in hers ... it was just the best thing that ever ... better than any drug or fuck.' She looked up at him. 'Even with an insect.'

Vic was about to ask her if she'd ever had sex with any other insects before he realised she was teasing him. He was coming to the conclusion that he didn't understand pre-Loss humans. He certainly couldn't keep up with them.

He sat down next to her and awkwardly put his two right arms around her. He'd seen this move in the pre-Loss media he'd assimilated. Though, as he understood it, it required some sort of communal room projecting two-dimensional moving images to be truly effective. He was gratified when she moved closer to him, leaning against his armoured thorax.

'You're really uncomfortable,' she told him, but she didn't move away.

'Has anything weird ever happened to you?' Vic asked, mindful of what Scab had told him to do. He felt more exasperation over the experiential 'face link Scab had downloaded into Vic's neunonics.

Talia pulled away from him and stared at him as if he was mad. 'No, this is *perfectly* fucking normal! All the girls in Bradford curl up with a giant insect and watch starless space of a Saturday night!'

'Well, I don't know, do I?' Vic said in frustration. He got the feeling she was making this more difficult than it had to be. 'I don't know what's normal for you. We have a queen, workers and warriors, and that's it. I grew up in a hive. Humans have, like, five sexes alone, and every one of them is different, and weird, and really fucking difficult!'

'Five sexes? Really?'

'Some of them are fashion genders.'

'In my day we had two, maybe three, max.'

'I'm sorry I can't relate to you.'

'Look, this sea of fucking weirdness ... I mean, there are no aliens, only uplifts ...' She gestured at him. 'And you're hitting on me. It's just ... everything's been so weird, for so long, and it's not going to get better, is it? Because you're planning to sell me.'

'I'm not,' Vic told her. 'If I could, I'd send you back to your own life, but I can't.'

'So you'll be nice to me? We can be friends, right?' She cocked her head to one side in a way that Vic found very attractive. Every bit of facial and voice-analysis software he had was telling him he was being manipulated. He didn't care.

'Yes.'

'And you'll protect me from him?'

'I can't.'

'But you're like a giant insect killing machine, aren't you?' she asked. The manipulation was gone. This was desperation.

'You don't understand ...' Vic was growing less and less sure of the benefits of his human psychosurgery as time went by. He was becoming more intimate with shame than he really wanted to be.

Ask her how the weirdness started, Scab 'faced to him.

'How did the weirdness start?' Vic asked.

'Why do you want to know?' Talia demanded suspiciously. 'You're communicating with him somehow, aren't you?'

'What? How'd you—'

'I've seen you do it before ... Oh, Christ, he heard me, he's going to fucking kill me ...' She was so terrified that Vic thought she was about to be sick. 'You fucking bastard!'

'Look, that's not what he cares about. Please, just answer me.'

'I've always known I was different, special ...'

The first thing that stood out, not her feelings. Vic didn't like the sense of impatience he was picking up from Scab's 'face.

'Something specific.'

'I was held by some sick crime boss—'

'Why?'

'Something happened. We were bloodletting. I was with a boy. Others had said my blood was odd. He drank some and ... something happened.' She shook her head violently. 'I don't ... I can't think about it ... I don't know. Please don't make me think about this.' She was pleading now. 'Something terrible happened to him ... oh, god, I can't even remember his name.'

Was he a blank? Scab demanded in Vic's head. It sounded like an odd question to the 'sect.

'Was he a blank?'

'What?'

Vic searched around for a way to explain it. 'Was he biologically entangled with you?'

'Of course – we were fucking.'

Vic tried to ignore the pang of jealousy. 'No, I mean—'

'He was so sweet, sensitive. He was an artist. What was his name?'

'An artist? What? Like, he did porn or something? So what? Everyone does that.'

She looked up at him sharply. 'You know what? You're a fucking arsehole as well!' Then she stormed out of the observation chamber, taking the bottle of cleaning fluid with her, leaving the smell of cigarette smoke in her wake.

Scab changed the shape of the smart-matter vial into a pipette and the drop of blood ran down to the tip. He had been staring at it for more than an hour now. He lifted it up to his lips and opened his mouth. He held it there. He 'faced another instruction to the vial. All the smart matter connected with the heretical sect's habitat was oddly truculent, but the pipette eventually changed back into a vial. Scab put the vial down on the bench.

He knew something. No, he *sensed* something that was just beyond his understanding, something that unsettled him.

As he looked at Talia's blood in the vial, he felt something that had been foreign to him for a long time. He knew fear.

6

Ubh Blaosc

Cold metal on her skin. Britha's brain was assaulted by memories from someone else. Some*thing* else. Contact with the Muileartach, her mother, the All-Mother. Its suffering. Crom Dhubh, so hard to look at. Her head splitting as the crystal crawled into it. Things she would never do: the taste of human flesh in her mouth. Throat after throat slit, the bodies tossed into the water. Killing the boy the Corpse People had captured.

'No!'

She was in darkness. She tried to scuttle into a corner but found herself in a rounded chamber. Judging by the feel of the metal against skin, the inside of the metal chamber had been carved with various patterns or images. She curled up in a foetal position. She was frightened, but more than that she was disgusted with herself at what she had become. She would kill in battle, a necessary sacrifice to defend herself or to protect her people; but this time she had revelled in it. There was something inside her, speaking to her – the spear, the eaten flesh, Crom Dhubh's whispers. Bress.

Teardrop was dead, Bress claimed to have killed Fachtna, she had abandoned Tangwen and the others, her people. Cliodna. She had killed Cliodna. The sobs wracked her frame as she remembered what it had felt like when the head of the spear had penetrated her lover's flesh. Looking into her dark eyes. She had done that.

Sometime later she reached up to touch her head. It was no longer swollen. She felt different as well. Her sobbing had made her ache; she was no longer aware of everything around her. She felt weary. She felt like she always had before. Before Cliodna had done something to her. Before she had eaten of one of the Lochlannachs' flesh. Before her magics had become so potent.

There was light above her.

She tried to collect her thoughts and cursed herself for her weakness. Bress had lied about Fachtna. She remembered now. There had been stones. She had walked with monsters, warped creatures born of the Muileartach's womb, poisoned by Crom Dhubh's great working. They had let her be. They had known her as sister. Then she had summoned great power from the earth. *How did I do that?* Lightning had danced for her among the stones. A star had gone out in the night sky. *How did I know that?* And she had been somewhere else. Different stones. There were people all around her, tall, well made, Goidel warriors, male and female. There had been *dryw* there, brown-robed, leaning on staffs, hoods masking their features. Fachtna was there, too – she had seen his face illuminated by the light they'd caged her in. He had looked sad. Then they had killed her.

She looked up. The light was faint, the grey light of the time-between-times, dusk or dawn. She stood up. It was only then she came to realise that she was in a massive cauldron. She wondered if they were planning to eat her, but it would be a poor meal. Then she remembered the magic of men, the metalworkers. How the rounded belly of a cauldron was supposed to be the stomach of a pregnant woman.

She reached up and felt the cauldron's lip. She was not nearly as strong as she had been, but she managed to pull herself up over the lip and all but fell onto wooden boards.

Painfully she stood up and looked around. She was in a large wooden long hall any *rhi* could be proud of, though why they had covered good earth with wood was beyond her. The walls were ornately carved and stained with bright, vibrant colours. She saw knotwork, spirals, shapes she recognised as women and men, animals, chariots and *curraghs*, and other things that she did not recognise or understand.

The cauldron was a massive bronze vessel with little external decoration. It had two handles on either side, though only a giant would have been able to lift it. She shivered at the momentary reminder of the giants that had walked and fought alongside the Lochlannach. No fire had been set beneath the cauldron. In fact, it looked as if the bottom of the cauldron had been sunk into the earth beneath the boards of the long hall.

There was no source of light in the hall. Her guess was wrong – it was neither dawn nor dusk, for bright sunlight shone through cracks and gaps in the wood. She made her way towards the hall's double doors. She felt very unsteady, and more than once her legs went from underneath her, but she made it to the doors.

Vertiginous fear overwhelmed her. Things were not as they should be.

She collapsed to the floor, desperately trying to make sense of what she could see. Then she remembered where she was. Then she remembered coming to the Otherworld.

Britha collapsed onto the warm, slightly damp, lush green grass outside the hall. She clung to the ground expecting to fall into the sky. The land was enormous, too big to take in properly, and she could see so much of it – farmed fields, thick forest, mountains, rivers, lochs, even seas and, beyond the seas, other lands. Mists and cloud obscured some of the places in the distance but it went on as far as she could see, and she imagined it went much further than that.

There was no horizon. The ground curved up, so she found herself looking down at blue sky, and so much of it. Perhaps more than her mind could cope with. Above/below her, the sky was bright blue, but from where she clung to the ground she could see patches of dark sky obscured by thundery-looking clouds in the distance. Even further away she was sure a land across one of the seas looked white in colour. It was as if she stood on the inside of a sealed giant cauldron.

There were things in the sky, hanging there, floating. Rocks, strange round plants or trees, distant spheres that looked like they might also have land on them. Closer, but still too far off to make out what they were, she perceived smaller objects that moved more erratically than the sedate floating rocks and trees. The few birds she could see looked very different from the birds she knew in her realm.

Despite all the strangeness, it was the Otherworld's sun that caught her attention. It was not that different from the sun she knew, except it looked much, much larger, and closer. She could feel its warmth. Few summers in Ardestie had been this warm. Sweat started to bead on her skin.

She had to force herself to let go of the grass, though instinct told her that if she did so she would fall into the sun. Looking around, she could see that this wasn't the case. It was normal to be upside down, apparently. She stood up unsteadily, shading her eyes with her hand.

Awe and more than a little dread overcame her. She knew herself to be in the presence of the gods now. Her people had always sought to avoid their attentions as the gods only cared for themselves, and none but the gods could understand those cares. In front of the sun stood a giant figure. Difficult to make out against the brightness, it existed only in silhouette and was nearly as tall as the sun itself. She guessed it was a warrior because it carried a spear. Black lines sprouted from all over the figure, they reminded Britha of many hollow logs joined together. The lines connected the enormous figure to the sun itself, and then down to the land in a number of different places.

The figure had wings on its back. Six of them, Britha thought, though she wasn't sure as some appeared to be extended, and others folded behind it. The extended wings cast the land below them into darkness. In the closest of the dark areas she could make out what looked like tiny pinpricks of light.

'It's called the Forge.'

Britha actually screamed and jumped. She rounded on Fachtna, who was sitting on the grass, his back against the long hall's outer wall. He was barefoot and stripped to the waist, wearing only a pair of loose-fitting trews. There was no scar tissue on his chest and stomach, but she had learned that he healed faster than mortals. His body also looked strangely hairless, though a detailed tattoo of a serpent, or a dragon, in the knotwork style of the Goidels coiled around his left arm, over his shoulder and onto his chest. Its open maw surrounded the place where his heart would be. A silver torc curved around his neck and another around his upper-right arm. His beard was short and neatly trimmed, and his hair and moustache were both long and braided.

Britha took a step back from him. 'Bress told me he killed you,' she said. And then she remembered seeing his face in the crowd when she first arrived, when the lightning consumed her.

'That's disappointing,' he said. His manner was … different, somehow.

'Are we in the land of the dead?'

Fachtna picked up something from the ground next to him and held it out to her. She glanced at it suspiciously and then realised it was a folded grey woollen robe. She was more surprised when she looked back at Fachtna and found him meeting her eyes rather than staring at her naked body. Britha took the offered robe from him and started to dress. As she did so, she glanced around the local area. The long hall appeared to be on a foothill surrounded by larger wooded hills and truly grandiose snow-capped mountains in the distance. Looking downwards, the land narrowed into a long cliff-lined bay that led to what she assumed was a sea. A road meandered down through trees towards a small settlement surrounding the bay, though the huts were rectangular rather than round like those in Ardestie and most of Ynys Prydein.

The robe's material was very soft and didn't make her as hot as the scratchy, thick robe she had worn back in Ardestie. It had a hood and the belt was of leather, not rope.

'The Cauldron brought me back to life, just as it did you,' Fachtna said. She stared at him. 'I'm sorry. With the crystals and the taint of

Crom in your blood, we had no choice. We did it in the knowledge that the Cauldron could bring you back.'

'I thought the crystals came from the Otherworld?'

Fachtna grimaced. 'They are from another realm, but it is forbidden to talk about them.'

'To anyone, or just mortals?'

Fachtna looked up at her thoughtfully but said nothing. She realised what it was about him that was bothering her. He seemed quiet, more thoughtful. He hadn't said or done anything that annoyed her yet.

'Teardrop?' Britha asked. Fachtna nodded. 'Is he here?' Britha asked, eager to see the strange, wise man with the deformed skull, but Fachtna was already shaking his head.

'He struggled with the path he had to walk. His people's equivalent of the *drui*. He wants something simpler now—'

'To be a warrior?' Britha asked, unable to keep a smile from her face.

'Perhaps, or perhaps he will just work the land, but he is with his family and content.'

'Will I see him?' Britha asked, and was disappointed by Fachtna shaking his head again.

'You would not know him, and he would not know you.'

Suddenly something struck Britha. 'Is this a lie?' she asked.

Fachtna regarded her strangely for a moment. 'No, but that is a good question—'

'Don't patronise me,' Britha said evenly. 'This may be the Otherworld but I am still the *ban draoi* of the Cirig.'

Fachtna bowed his head. 'Apologies, it was not my intention to patronise. I have no memory after leaving here to journey to your world, and nor does Teardrop.'

She let this sink in. 'But then why can I—'

'Because you died here. Your body was here.'

Britha sat down on the grass. She was quiet as she tried to think through all she had been told. Fachtna watched her, concern in his expression. Britha found herself looking at some distant thing making its way through the Otherworld's endless sky. It did not move like a bird.

'What is that?' she asked.

Fachtna followed her gaze. 'A chariot.'

It was almost enough for her. The vertiginous fear returned, but she knew she had to master it. She could not show weakness here.

'You have a *rhi* here?' she asked.

'For this particular land, I am he.'

Britha stared at him; it made sense, but somehow it made her angry, too.

'And the *dryw*?'

'They wish to speak with you.'

'Can I return to my people?' she asked, ashamed that it had taken her until now to do so. She had been overwhelmed by this place, this land of plenty. It would be so easy to succumb to its apparently easy life.

'In time.'

'Am I prisoner?'

She knew the ways of the fair folk. A day in their world could be many years in her land. She thought of those in the wicker man – her people, the Cirig, taken on the beach and at the broch. She wondered what had become of Tangwen, of Kush and the navigator.

They might have stopped Crom Dhubh's summoning of the Llwglyd Diddymder, the Hungry Nothingness, but she hadn't set out to save Ynys Prydein, only to rescue her people. She cursed herself for weakness in front of a warrior as tears sprang to her eyes. Fachtna reached out for her but she slapped his arm away.

'Why—' she started, and then choked back sobs and wiped her eyes. 'Why are you different? Has death robbed you of your manhood?'

Fachtna regarded her for a moment and then leaned back against the wood of the long hall. 'You and I didn't like each other, did we?' he asked, smiling for the first time.

I considered you stupid and boorish, and in the end you believed I was a monster, Britha thought. *Because that's what I had become.*

'I went to war,' he said. 'The *drui* put certain geasa on me. They change us. As warriors we have to behave a certain way.'

'Obnoxiously? Yes, I've met warriors before.'

'No, I mean we cannot show weakness in front of others because then we would start to doubt ourselves. I took ... certain potions and preparations.'

'You mean you drank and boasted a lot?'

Fachtna was looking a little exasperated.

'So what now?' Britha demanded.

'You are not a prisoner, but to send you back is a great magical undertaking. It will require a little time.'

'My people ... ?'

'We can only know what you tell us.'

'I don't want to return a thousand winters after they are all dead.'

Fachtna shook his head. 'We wouldn't do that to you. The *drui* will want to speak with you but I don't know when. I can arrange for food and drink, and I hope you will be my guest.' Then he started to smile again. In the smile Britha saw some of his old cockiness. 'Until then, perhaps you could entertain me with tales of the great deeds I did before I died.'

She started to tell Fachtna of great and terrible deeds. She used the bards' tongue and spared him nothing. She told him of the betrayal on the Crown of Andraste. There were tears in his eyes when she described what had become of Teardrop. He tried to mask his disgust at the killings of the kneelers, and the boy the Corpse People had taken prisoner. Half the time she didn't even realise that her cheeks were wet with her own tears.

How did this happen? Britha demanded of herself. Now more than ever, so far from home and among such strange people, now was not the time to show weakness.

She had eaten well, though she was embarrassed by memories of gluttony. The *uisge beatha* was good, but not as good as what she had grown up with, it was too smooth, too easy to drink. She was also secretly pleased that their ale was not as good as her heather ale.

She found herself sitting around a fire with the people from the village and the surrounding area, down by the cliff-lined bay. They spoke a language she recognised, and of which she knew some words. All of them were intimidatingly tall and beautiful, not unlike Fachtna. Whether Fachtna was a *rhi* or just a landed warrior, Britha wasn't exactly sure. His people showed him respect, but he had a very informal relationship with them. In this he reminded her of Cruibne MaqqCirig, though that informality could only be taken so far. Britha had watched Cruibne break the teeth and split the skull of more than one young warrior who had pushed his luck too far.

Even the common folk here had access to some kind of magics. They had all learned her language with just a moment's concentration, as she had when Cliodna's blessings and the darker blessings of Crom had mixed in her blood. They made her welcome. Fachtna made her welcome. They even showed respect to her as a *ban draoi*, though in that she detected something false.

Fachtna had put on a *blaidth*, though even in the darkness that fell as one of the giant's wings obscured the Forge, Britha did not feel much of a chill. Fachtna, at the insistence of his people, played some kind of complicated, long-necked, stringed instrument. She liked the sound of it, and was even more surprised when she liked the sound of his voice, though he was no bard. He sang songs in their language. Most of them sounded a little sad to Britha. They made her think of home.

She had no idea how she had come to be lying by the dying fire in Fachtna's arms. Trying not to think about Cliodna. Trying harder not to think of Bress.

It's because he is the only familiar thing so far from home, she thought, then: *That is not a good enough reason.*

'You said the giant is called Forge?' Britha asked, looking up at the obscured red glow of the huge sun and the figure of the spear-carrying giant fixed in front of it.

'No, the sun is called the Forge. The giant is Lug, one of the Lloigor. He came from before everything was created and he changed the Forge.'

'That does not make sense,' Britha said, nestling deeper into Fachtna's arms. 'How can he come from before everything was created?'

Fachtna shrugged. 'The *drui* tell us these things. The Lloigor came from somewhere before everything. The place they came from is not there any more.'

Britha considered this. 'I have heard stories of lands that once were, that had been taken by the ocean,' she said. Fachtna shrugged non-committally. 'You call this place *Ubh Blaosc*?' He nodded. 'What does that mean?'

'The Egg Shell.'

'If this is a shell, what is beyond it?' Britha asked. Fachtna glanced down at her. He looked impressed. Britha found herself feeling irritated again, as if she was being patronised.

'The night,' he replied.

'We are in the sky.'

'We are in a different sky.'

'Then how did I get here?'

'A bridge.'

She shook her head. It was too confusing, even assuming Fachtna was telling the truth, though if he wasn't he had suddenly become a very good liar.

Britha looked around the fire. Many of the villagers had gone home and only a few other couples lingered around the dying embers. She was intrigued that one of the couples consisted of two men. She had never been able to differentiate between her attraction for women and men, but most tribes had frowned upon men who liked men, or women who liked women.

'Our people are from your world, you know?' Fachtna said. 'The Lloigor brought us here a long time ago. First us, and then the Croatan, and their slaves from the Roanoke settlement.'

She looked up at him, his face orange in the glow of the dying fire. 'They commanded great magic then, your gods?'

Fachtna nodded. 'They were gone when we arrived here, but they had changed us.'

Britha gave this some more thought. 'How old are you?'

Fachtna laughed. 'Older than you, younger than many.'

She pushed herself up and looked at him, angry more with herself than him. 'You only ever give me half an answer. You act like you don't think I would understand.' *And you were happy lying in his arms*, she admonished herself.

'And how old are you?' he asked lightly.

'That's not the point!' she said in exasperation, and then his lips were on hers. It was just too easy to reciprocate. He had not asked her permission but it was not the rough wooing of the arrogant warrior she had first met as she'd made her way south. With his arms wrapped around her, suddenly she was aware of her hand on his leg, her other hand in his hair. She felt herself responding, wanting.

Then she remembered Teardrop teasing Fachtna about bedding many mortal women. She remembered him rutting in a ditch with Tangwen. She remembered Cliodna. She remembered Bress.

Then she remembered running Cliodna through with a spear.

Britha's disgust with herself fuelled her anger as she shoved him away. She assumed the hurt expression on his face was just an act. She stood up, unsure where she might go, where she could sleep. This angered her further and she almost kicked Fachtna, thinking that he had assumed she would share his cot with him.

It took her a moment to register the gasps of surprise from the other side of the fire. She spun around and then staggered back, almost tripping over the log they had been leaning against.

She must have just emerged from the treeline. She wore the brown robes of a *dryw* and carried a staff, a sickle hanging from her belt along with several pouches. The *dryw*'s entire head was hidden by a horse's skull. Britha knew the meaning of the horse's skull. This was the *Lain Bhan*, the White Mare. This was death, night and the desolation of winter. As she was about to flee, she felt a hand on her leg.

'It's not what you think,' Fachtna told her gently. She looked around the fire. The other couples had reacted with surprise but not fear. That didn't prevent a cold feeling from running through her when the *Lain Bhan* pointed at her, and then beckoned.

The grove was almost too idyllic for Britha. A small waterfall ran over rocks that bordered one edge of the small clearing. The waterfall fed a pool, which in turn fed a stream of clear, cold, fresh water. The oaks leaned in overhead, but the nature of the wing-shrouded night under the Forge meant that it never appeared to get completely dark. It was more of a perpetual twilight.

After leading Fachtna and a very uncomfortable Britha through the woods to the grove, the woman had taken off the horse skull. Like all the inhabitants of the Otherworld she was tall and well made, though she was older than most of the people Britha had seen so far. Still handsome, her face was heavily lined and her hair white but she looked energetic. Something in her eyes and the set of her features suggested shrewdness and a penetrating intelligence to Britha. She had introduced herself as Grainne.

Another *dryw* was waiting for them in the grove. He was even older than Grainne and his skin looked like cracked leather. His hair was long and silver, as was his trimmed and shaped goatee, and his eyes a vibrant green. He sat on the fern-covered altar stone, leaning on his hands, swinging his legs forward.

'It is a ritual of life,' Britha said sceptically, glancing over at Fachtna. He was stripped to the waist again, drinking from a small clay bowl that Grainne had given him. 'Not for sealing an alliance, and I have not said yes.'

She was more than a little uncomfortable with what they were suggesting, though she knew they would not suggest it without good cause. She was not precious regarding such things but this did not sit right.

She was also uncomfortable because although these people might not be kneelers, they had a relationship with their gods, and she did not fully understand that relationship. The Pecht, her people, had learned generations before her not to trust the gods.

'It is up to you,' Sainrith, the male *dryw* said. 'But what we are talking about is more than a simple alliance. We must be joined against Crom Dhubh and Bress.'

'I cannot speak for my people.' *If any of them still live.*

'But what would you advise them to do?'

'That you have been fair and true allies this far, but that you are powerful and too much is unknown. I would advise them to be cautious,' Britha said evenly.

Sainrith raised an eyebrow. 'That is good advice,' he admitted.

'What is done can be undone,' Grainne said as she anointed

Fachtna with oil. It was exactly the sort of thing some *dryw* said that annoyed her.

'How will you have made his cock not have been in my cunt?' Britha enquired.

The other woman considered Britha's words. 'Agreed – that was a foolish thing to say.'

'And those are ... powerful ... Could you stop anointing him, please? I haven't said yes,' Britha said irritably. Grainne put down the bowl and the brush, and turned to Britha. 'It's powerful binding magics, and whether I trust you or not, I don't know enough about the ritual.'

'Bonds can be undone, is what I think Grainne was trying to say,' Sainrith said.

'Yes, but why burden myself if I don't need to?' Britha asked.

'Because it will make us stronger against Crom,' Sainrith said.

Why is everyone so eager for me to lie with Fachtna? Britha wondered. She could sense something behind it.

'Does Tansy grow here?' she asked.

'Yes,' Grainne told her. 'And we have more efficient methods, if need be.'

'I will not bear his or anyone else's child,' she said evenly.

'We're not asking you to—' Grainne started.

'With respect, could you leave us?' Britha said.

'This is a sacred—' Grainne started, but Sainrith raised his hands and motioned for quiet. He stood up and the two of them left the grove without another word spoken. Britha watched them go before turning to face Fachtna.

'We can leave here now. I'll find you a place to stay, not with me. Don't do this because you feel obligated to. Only do this if you want to,' he said before she had a chance to say anything.

And she did want to, she knew she did. She had to force herself to look him in the eyes and not at his body.

'And if it's not right?' she asked.

'Are you beholden to anyone?'

Bress. The thought was a betrayal, not least of Cliodna's memory.

'No,' she said quietly. 'Who are you?'

He moved to her, slowly, carefully, as if he was expecting her to bolt. A hand reached up to caress the side of her face. She couldn't see a lie in his features, but she didn't trust her own judgement. She felt so much younger. She wanted him. She never had before.

She could use the working, the ritual, as an excuse.

7

Micronesia, 6 Weeks Ago

Lodup was double-checking the diving gear. It was more a nervous tick than a requirement. He had checked it before he loaded it, and then again as he packed it into crates, but salvage diving tended to encourage caution.

His right arm was a sleeve of horizontal lines, tattoos forming complicated patterns on his nut-brown skin, and *Pelipel* tattoos crept out of his shorts and down his legs. Stripped to the waist, even in his mid-thirties he had managed to keep his body in the wiry, toned shape that had come so easily to him in his youth on Mwoakilloa and Pohnpei, and later in the US Navy, though he had to work harder at it then.

Early autumn, the trade winds had just started blowing. The port's floodlights and the lights on the container cranes overhead made the Pacific night as bright as a sodium-arc day. The glare reflected off the puddles created by the evening rains. It was humid, but then it was always humid.

The noise of the footsteps sounded out of place, and Lodup glanced behind him to see an odd figure approaching. She looked like she was dressed to go to one of the punk bars or nightclubs he'd seen when he was stationed in San Diego. Her hair was a spiked black Mohican that had wilted in the humidity and the shaved sides of her head were tattooed. Her ears were pierced multiple times, and her nose and one eyebrow also had rings in them. She wore sunglasses despite the lateness of the hour, and her skin looked pale to the point of unhealthy under the harsh lighting.

She was wearing what looked like a black leather corset or bodice, Lodup wasn't sure which, a black, flared miniskirt, fishnets and motorcycle boots. The short jacket over her bodice reminded Lodup of pictures he'd seen of European soldiers in the late seventeenth and early eighteenth centuries. More interesting was the fact that the jacket appeared to be poorly concealing some kind of shoulder rig for a pistol. She had a heavy-looking kit bag slung over one shoulder, though its weight didn't seem to be giving her any problems.

'Are you Lodup Satakano?' she asked as she reached him. Her accent was thick, and he was pretty sure she was from England. She was definitely armed – he could see the butt of a pistol sticking out of a shoulder holster, and below that the hilt of a knife, its blade sheathed upside down next to the pistol in the same holster.

'That depends,' he replied cautiously. Almost unconsciously, his hand moved closer to the dive knife strapped to his ankle. She followed his eyes and opened her jacket. There was another pistol and knife hanging under her right shoulder.

'It's all right, love,' she said. 'These aren't for you. This is.'

She tossed the kitbag at his feet. Lodup looked at the bag suspiciously.

'It's full of eels,' the woman said, lighting a cigarette. Lodup was beginning to think that under the make-up she was a lot younger than he'd initially thought. Late teens, perhaps, he decided.

'I don't want anything to do with anyone as heavily armed as you.'

'I've already said I'm not going to shoot you and I'm lovely when you get to know me. You really need to look in the bag.'

'Will you go away if I do?'

'I suspect you won't want me to.'

Lodup reached for the bag and pulled it towards him. Slowly and carefully he unzipped the bag, looked inside, then zipped it up again and slid it back towards the odd woman.

The bag was full of stacks of hundred dollar bills. Full to the brim.

'That's a hundred thousand dollars,' she said. 'It's completely legal.'

'So why's it in a bag?'

'I wanted to make an impression.'

'What's it for?'

'Just to come to a job interview. Whatever happens, you keep that. You get the job, there'll be a lot more than that on the table.'

Lodup nodded towards the salvage ship behind him. 'I've already got a berth.'

The woman laughed. 'Fine, give me the money back. There's other salvage divers in the Pacific.'

'This is a salvage dive?' Lodup asked. The woman just nodded. 'Difficult to believe it's legitimate.'

The punk woman was starting to look bored. 'Do you want the money or not?'

Lodup glanced down at the kitbag again. He could do all sorts of things with that money. No more contract work, refit a small craft for salvage.

'Can I take it that I'm leaving the bag with you?' she asked. Lodup was still staring at it as the woman turned and started walking away. 'Be at the Naval Air Station at Agana tomorrow at six, or zero-six-hundred, whatever you ex-Navy types call it.' Lodup stared after her. 'My name's Grace, by the way,' she shouted over her shoulder.

A thousand miles of staring out over the blue of the Pacific interspersed with islands and atolls. From the air, the atolls looked like they were waiting to be swept away by the ocean, and the shadows of reefs and sandbanks just under the water were predatory, somehow. The clouds above formed endless, mountainous continents in the sky, rendering the Pacific a sea in a hollow Earth.

Lodup had flown from Guam back to his home on Pohnpei many times before but he still wasn't bored by the Pacific's beauty, though the ocean had tried very hard to kill him on more than one occasion.

Grace had been waiting for him aboard the Grumman C-2 Greyhound Navy transport plane they took from Naval Air Station Agana. She was friendly enough but not inclined to discuss the job interview or tell him much about herself. She stank of alcohol and looked very tired. She quickly lapsed into a deep sleep, leaving him to stare out of the cabin windows at all the blue as he played games of wild speculation.

Some three hours later, Lodup found himself looking at a mountainous canopy of green sloping down into flatter jungle-covered land, interspersed by small hamlets and a few larger towns. The plane descended into Pohnpei International Airport on Takatik Island. The huge, jungle-covered rock overlooking the single runway was a welcome sight. It meant he was home.

Grace ignored customs and led him to an old battered Land Rover parked in the cargo area of the airport. She drove him over the Deketik Causeway that crossed the harbour and into the town of Kolonia.

Grace thrashed the ancient Jeep along streets lined with low corrugated-roofed buildings and down to the water near one of the jetties where a small boat was moored. Lodup thought he recognised the man at the engine. He was local, and Lodup was pretty sure he worked for the Village Hotel.

Grace gestured down into the boat.

'This is getting pretty tiresome,' Lodup told her as he went to throw his bag into the boat, but Grace stopped him.

'I'll take your bag.'

'You're not coming?'

'I'll see you later,' she said as she shouldered his bag and headed back to the Land Rover.

The boat's pilot was called Billy. Lodup chatted with him a bit but the rest of the time he just enjoyed the journey as they made their way east around the island. From the sea it was easy to ignore the odd house here and there, or glimpses of the road that ran around the island, and see only the green of the jungle.

They sped past tiny islands with unspoiled white beaches, and the water inside the protective ring of reefs was calm, as usual. Lodup was pretty sure he knew where they were going. He wondered why foreigners wanted to bring locals to Nan Madol to impress them. He'd been there many times before.

The water surrounding the ruined city was choppy. It took a number of attempts, but Billy expertly piloted the boat through the entrance and into the network of canals that ran between the ruins. Lodup climbed out of the boat and onto the narrow grass-covered path by one of the massive cornerstones on the artificial islet of Nan Dowas. He'd been taught that this islet was the main temple area of the Saudeleur Dynasty. Founded by the sorcerous twins Olisihpa and Olosohpa, the eel-worshipping Saudeleur elite had thought them-selves gods. When their demands on the common people had become too hard to bear, Isokelekel, a hero from the isle of Kosrae to the east, had overthrown them.

Even ruined, crumbling, overgrown by the encroaching jungle from Temwen Island and subject to slow erosion by the ocean, the artificial islets – built on a reef and separated by tidal canals – still looked magnificent. Lodup walked down the narrow path next to walls made of basalt blocks mined on the mainland. The blocks were interspersed with layers of basalt 'logs'. He followed the walls around until he came to the temple complex's rubble-strewn entrance. Inside, trees and undergrowth grew through walls and stone debris.

'Do you know how they got the stones here?' a voice asked. Cultured, undoubtedly European but, either because of the excellent English or despite it, Lodup could not quite place where in Europe the accent came from. He turned to face the speaker.

'Did you ask permission to come here?' Lodup said. It was unusual that none of the locals, the custodians of the site, were in evidence. The blond-haired man wore sandals, khaki shorts, a cream short-sleeved shirt, sunglasses and a straw hat. By no means massive, he nevertheless looked well built, lean. Lodup was surprised he hadn't heard the man approach.

'I did. Shall we?' He gestured into the interior of Nan Dowas. Lodup was wary. Everything about this was odd, but it occurred to Lodup that if they wished him harm there were much less resource-intensive ways of doing it. The man turned and walked into the temple complex, running his hand over the basalt blocks as he did so.

'The logs between the blocks weigh as much as eight hundred pounds on their own, and they are the lightest of the stones here. Some of the cornerstones could weigh up to fifty tonnes—'

'I know this. I grew up here. Grace works for you?'

The man glanced back at him but continued walking past the interior walls towards a small, rectangular, cave-like structure in the centre of the overgrown complex.

'I work with her, and you didn't answer my question.'

'Hard work and native ingenuity, or is that just for the Egyptians, the Greeks and the Romans?'

'Arguably different circumstances.'

'I've found that if people really want things, they normally find a way. Who are you?'

'My name is Malcolm du Bois. You were named for the Strong Man?'

'Am I supposed to be impressed that you know Mwoakilloan legends?'

'No.' The man thought for a moment. 'It's too easy for me to come by such information. Your mother was a wise woman?'

'Most women where I come from are pretty wise,' Lodup said in exasperation. The blond man stared at him, and all Lodup could see was his reflection in the sunglasses. Du Bois turned away and started to walk around the stone structure.

'What if I told you that the basalt was impregnated with super-conductors that allowed for a levitation effect by manipulating the Earth's – admittedly weak – magnetic field, and that the crystalline matrix of the stone has been engineered to act as a huge and complex computer?'

'Then I would remind you that telling stories during the day hastens the night. I know the legends. Olisihpa and Olosohpa levitated the stones here using black magic, and with the aid of a dragon—'

'Not magic, science.'

'The elders used to tell us that if we saw the shadow of the manta over us as we dived, it meant death. The manta would wrap itself around us and drain our blood. Are you telling me that's true as well?'

'I don't know. It's certainly possible.'

'What are you, some rich madman?'

'Do you believe my story?'

'Next you're going to tell me that Lidakika the octopus created Pohnpei rather than a volcanic eruption. Or offer to take me to *Kanamwayso*, perhaps. *What is this? A test to see if the islander who grew up without electricity is an ignorant, superstitious fool?*'

'*Kanamwayso, the City of the Gods. Perhaps you're closer than you think. Wasahn mehla wasa koaros.*'

Lodup stared at him for a moment. He was starting to get angry.

'Everywhere is a place for death, so a real man should not worry and should act without fear. Do you really think I am afraid?'

'I think if you had any ideas about the origins of this place that would be considered esoteric, then you'd keep them to yourself.'

'I think this place was built with the blood, sweat and tears of thousands of people. I think it was done using winches, and rafts, and possibly other techniques since lost to us.' He patted one of the rocks. 'I think if there were any kind of computer matrix in the basalt, then one of the scientific or archaeological investigations would have found something, and I think I've heard all the conspiracy theories. So what I'd say is: show me.'

'That, Mr Satakano, is a good answer. May I buy you dinner?'

'What, you're not going to make all the rocks fly around?'

Du Bois appeared to be giving the sarcastic question some thought. 'No, that would be ridiculous. I'm not a magician.'

Lodup was losing patience with the other man. It was clear he was an eccentric – and very rich – nutcase. Though his influence with the Navy was troublesome. Lodup wasn't sure he was prepared to take money from the delusional. On the other hand, it was a lot of money.

'Do you know what "Pohnpei" means?' du Bois asked.

'You do know I grew up here, right?' Lodup demanded. Du Bois just nodded. 'It means "upon a stone altar".'

'I have a tremendous appetite but I can never eat much in the tropics. Still, I'm very fond of the Tattooed Irishman's omelettes.'

'I think we're wasting each other's time.'

'Let's assume that's the case. Then by letting me waste a little more you will have a good meal to add to the hundred thousand dollars and the trip home for your wasted time.'

Lodup reluctantly agreed.

The Village was a holiday resort in the jungle comprised of wooden huts built on stilts on the side of a hill, among the palm trees, overlooking the Pacific. The veranda, also on stilts, was attached to the

Tattooed Irishman Bar and Restaurant by a short wooden bridge at treetop height.

Du Bois had changed clothes and was now wearing an immaculate white linen suit and a panama hat. Lodup was convinced the European thought he was in a Graham Greene novel: *Our Man in Pohnpei*. They were seated on wickerwork chairs at a low table, and Grace was leaning against the railings on the bridge. There was a niggle at the back of Lodup's mind telling him something wasn't right with their surroundings.

'Well?' du Bois asked Grace.

In reply, Grace reached into her jacket and drew one of her knives. It was a fighting knife of some sort, with knuckledusters on the hilt.

'Hey!' Lodup shouted as she drew it across the palm of her hand, making a red line. Grace just grinned at him.

'Us kids today, ay? With our self-harming.' She clenched her fist. Lodup didn't see any blood drip out of it. Then it hit him what was strange. There were no insects anywhere near them. The omnipresent mosquitos were simply not present. He stared at du Bois as the other man took a sip of his gin and tonic. Then he realised he hadn't seen either of them sweat.

Lodup opened his mouth to say something but du Bois held his hand up, motioning for silence, before turning to look at Grace. Grace was concentrating.

'We're clear,' she told him, re-sheathing her knife. If her hand was bleeding, Lodup couldn't see it.

'My apologies – we have to take certain precautions,' du Bois told him.

'And those precautions involve either self-harming or sleight of hand?'

'So you're a qualified master diver, once part of Mobile Diving and Salvage Unit One based out of Pearl. Freshly qualified, you worked the USS *Monitor* project, off North Carolina. You also worked on the *Ehime Maru*, served aboard the auxiliary rescue salvage craft USS *Salvor* and spent time at the US Navy's Experimental Dive Unit in Panama City, Florida. You worked with Submarine Development Squadron Five as part of the Deep Submergence Unit. You're a qualified hydronaut with experience in pressurised atmospheric diving suits. Since leaving the service you've been working as a contract salvage operator and commercial dive instructor, mostly based out of Guam.'

Lodup took a sip of his cold beer and said nothing.

'I am also aware of some of the more covert jobs you did in the service. I can list them to prove how well connected our operation is, but I do not wish to be indiscreet. Would you like to take my word for it?'

They had the influence to swing a Navy transport.

'Sure,' Lodup said. 'Is your interviewing technique always based around making the prospective employee feel uncomfortable?'

'You already have the job, if you want it. Our problem is persuading you to accept the strangeness of the situation.'

'Who do you work for?'

'Is just one of the questions we will not answer.'

'It's a salvage job, right?'

'All I can tell you is that it is a long-term contract, six months with the option of a possible extension, and you cannot tell anyone where you're going or what you're doing – largely because you won't know. We will arrange a cover story for your friends and family.'

'Is it legal?'

Grace let out a snort of laughter. Du Bois rolled his eyes.

'I assure you, that's largely irrelevant. If it makes you feel better, we're not breaking any law that I am aware of.'

Lodup glanced between the pair of them. 'Look, I'm sorry, guys, but there's just too much unknown here. I'll give you your money back but this is too weird, and I'm going to have to say no.'

'Whatever happens, the money is yours, Mr Satakano. We understand we're asking a lot, which is why the reward we're offering must be commensurate.' Du Bois reached under his chair and produced a leather folder. Unzipping it, he removed some papers and handed them to Lodup. Lodup glanced through them. It was the specs and sales details for the SS *Lady Macbeth*, a new-build deep-sea salvage vessel. Lodup felt a prickling on his skin. They couldn't be offering him what they appeared to be offering him. *Could they?*

'We thought we'd appeal to your sense of opportunity,' du Bois said, taking a cigarette case out of the breast pocket of his suit.

'Sense of greed,' Grace muttered. There was a momentary flash of exasperation on du Bois' face as he fixed a cigarette into a holder.

'This is my payment?' Lodup tried to keep the eagerness out of his voice.

'Yes.' Du Bois lit the cigarette. 'Plus a year's capital to make a run of it.'

Lodup stared at the photograph of the ship. She was a beauty. No expense had been spared. He forced himself to put the papers down on the table.

'I'm sorry, but this is too good to be true. No job is worth this much. I've got some skills, but there's others as capable as me with more experience.'

'And they'll probably be working with us as well,' du Bois told him.

Lodup shook his head. 'I haven't heard of any jobs on that scale.'

Grace sighed.

'And if you had we wouldn't be doing our job very well, would we?' du Bois pointed out.

'You'll have to fork out for a lot more salvage ships if you're buying one for every operator.'

'We try to find specific motivation for everyone,' du Bois said. Lodup wasn't sure he liked the other man's choice of words. 'We're going to ask you to take a lot on faith. We'll drop you in the middle of the ocean for pickup. All I can tell you is that you'll be working at great depth, using proven but experimental dive technologies.'

'That's it?' Lodup asked, already shaking his head.

'The *Lady Macbeth* will be signed over to you before you start to prove we mean what we say and can deliver, but then you're on a plane to Kwajalein.'

Lodup knew Kwajalein was a missile-tracking base. He had worked there as a contractor recovering test-fired missiles from the atoll.

'This may sound like a ridiculous offer, and it is, but we're in an extreme situation here.'

Lodup's mind was racing. He was trying to work out what might be so valuable that they could afford to make such offers. *They must have found a practical way for either deep-sea oil extraction or mining. Probably a mother-lode as well.* Lodup took another swig of his beer and watched a lizard run along the veranda's railing. The ship was everything he was working towards, but without the crippling debt.

'This is too easy.'

'There is nothing easy about the job you're going to be doing,' du Bois told him.

Lodup took another nervous swig from his beer.

'I'm in.'

He used to be called Kyle Nethercott, before he ascended. He used to be from somewhere in the middle of America that nobody had heard of or cared about. He used to belong to a family that was just like everyone else's. Except for his presence in it. A lot of what he used to be he had forgotten, or more precisely he'd had it erased.

It bothered him that he could not be the demon here, but he'd had to walk among them. He'd had to pretend to be one of them in first class on the flight from Boston Logan to Heathrow.

He'd spent a long time in the strangest places on the net, places he suspected had existed a long time before anyone had even heard of computers. Hiding there. Moving through them like a worm through soft earth.

There were so many murders, so many atrocities in history. He wasn't sure why these fascinated him in particular, other than their apparent use of lost tech. Perhaps it was because the other killings had always seemed impure, somehow. The murderers had always thought they were doing something else. Delusions of transformation, or power, based in a fantasy world that they didn't have the strength of will to make manifest. Whereas he felt motivated by a purer malice. He had always gone for the hurt. Like a harvest.

The defences were rudimentary. Perhaps the wards would have been potent in the nineteenth century, but spoofing them felt like walking through cobwebs. The fact they had forgotten him was a travesty.

Broadmoor was a high-security hospital that housed the most disturbed of Britain's criminals. The murderer had been transferred here from Bethlem Royal Hospital, or Bedlam, more than a hundred and fifty years ago.

In a sealed, long-forgotten bowel of the prison hospital, Inflictor let his true face grow through his human mask. He knelt down on stone and drew a sharp claw over leathery skin, then used his dripping black blood as the medium for his matter-hack. The smart-matter stone peeled open. A hand gripped the edge of the revealed oubliette.

The man's filthy skin was covered with scar tissue and scabs in the shape of arcane symbols Inflictor was sure he'd seen in some of the games he had played. The hairless, emaciated man pulled himself out of the stone hole and lay exhausted on the floor, panting for breath.

'I heard a new world,' he whispered. 'I felt it through the earth. The ground shook and I tasted blood. I heard electric screaming.'

Inflictor nodded. He did not understand the words but he liked the sound of them. He reached into his own flesh and started to drag something through it. The man watched, transfixed. Inflictor tore the Cornucopia free. He had configured it to look like a drinking horn. If King Jeremy discovered he had taken it, he would freak out.

'This is power and everything you need to know,' Inflictor told him.

The other man looked up at the demonic face made of sharp teeth and hard leather scales. 'You can't have come for me. There's no heaven or hell unless we make them.' Inflictor shook his head. 'Do you belong to me? A homunculus grown of my blood and excrement?'

Inflictor liked these words less well. 'No. I enjoyed what you did. You should be free,' Inflictor said. He did not like the nervousness he felt on meeting the man. It was a weakness. The other man nodded as if he understood.

'I think they forgot me,' the man said. His voice was sad. 'This sounds like a magnificent age. I think I understand now. They will love me. Though they will call it something else.'

The man looked up at the boy pretending to be a demon. Whilst imprisoned, he'd had fever dreams of this new world. He would see them realised.

'Lot of trouble to go to,' Grace said as she and du Bois made their way to their huts. Either side of the path lay fairly thick undergrowth. They could see insects playing in the lights on the path, but their blood-screens kept the irritation of the insects far from them.

'It's quicker this way. Besides, the ship is irrelevant.'

Grace laughed. 'The end's been coming since I started doing this. It's just another form of manipulation.'

'Control will pick that up on their next audit.'

'I can't police my thoughts, why police my mouth?'

Du Bois opened his mouth to reply. Pain lanced through his head. He screamed and dropped to his knees, clutching his head. Blood was seeping out of his nose, ears and tear ducts.

Grace had a pistol in each hand as she scanned the jungle on either side of her. She spared du Bois a concerned glance and saw the pain writ across his face. He shook his head, trying to force himself to recover enough to speak.

'Malcolm?' she asked.

'I'm okay,' he muttered. He didn't sound okay.

'An attack?'

'No, download.'

He remembered everything now. The murders, the scorpions, the fused gun-limb, how the Hellaquin died. Mr Brown coming for the monster. He remembered the disgust Silas Scab engendered. He remembered the gunshot. He now knew it was the American who had shot him. His phone started to ring. He reached into his linen suit jacket and pulled it out. He looked at the phone's blank black screen. The phone answered itself.

'He's escaped,' the voice on the phone said.

Du Bois looked up at Grace.

8
A Long Time After the Loss

Red lighting was a universal sign that things weren't going well. So was the smell of burned flesh and the pain from her wounds. The Monk could hear the mourning song the dolphins were singing. They'd lost more than a tenth of the *Lazerene*'s crew complement, over a thousand dead.

The mistake had been to try the possession immersed. The thinking was sound. A virtual Scab had to be less dangerous than the real thing. An electronic prison made from some of the best software actual credit could buy, developed by some of the best coders in Known Space. Then slave him so he had to answer questions.

Except Scab was a talented hacker before the Elite recruited him and honed his skills. The first thing he did was hack the time-dilation parameters on the immersion. Subjectively he'd had all the time in the world. From Scab's perspective it took him more than a hundred years to find his way out of the immersion-prison construct.

The Scab personality they used had been cobbled together from black thrill-kill immersions, available to the most rabid and rich of Scab's bounty-killing fan base. They purported to be pirate copies of the files held in the Consortium Psycho Banks, where they were used to help profile recreational killers. Church techs had then attempted to use predictive programs to piece together the rest of Scab's personality. The Monk was of the opinion that they had bred a younger and more feral Scab. Parts of the *Lazerene*'s interior were still burning.

They had to destroy the *Lazerene*'s AI after the Scab personality effectively possessed it and took control of certain of the ship's systems. The *Lazerene* would have to return to the Cathedral, where all of its computer systems would be stripped out and destroyed. It would take months, and the Monk was going to miss the AI. She could still smell cooked uplift flesh.

She walked into the red light of the bridge, looking down at the dolphins crowding around their dead in the tanks below the catwalk.

The flesh on her face was still knitting together, the burned, dead skin flaking off and falling to the metal of the catwalk like black snow.

It was wearing Benedict's limbless body and hanging from a harness attached below a security satellite that had its weapons angled down at him. He was grinning at her. He was basically a nat now – she'd removed his limbs and drilled into his skull to destroy Benedict's neunonics. He'd probably end up with brain cancer as a result, but the body would be destroyed as soon as it had served its purpose.

'Motivate me,' Scab demanded from the mouth of Benedict's dangling body.

'You don't tell me what we want to know, then no more playtime for you. You want to die, say so now.'

Scab gave this some thought.

'Should we accept the invitation?' the Monk asked.

Scab started laughing until there were tears in Benedict's eyes.

'The problem with what you're asking is that any Elite is a tremendous drain on resources. Even allowing for the threat you might pose, it would significantly weaken whomever met your price,' said the man with a goldfish bowl for a head. He was wearing a nappy. When he finished talking, a dummy appeared in his sculpted crystal head.

Vic knew the man. He was a player in the Consortium, an immortal trying to win a seat on the board and become a Lord of Known Space. Vic wasn't sure he'd ever known the man's name. He'd met him investigating a series of murders on the *Semektet*, a pleasure yacht for the Consortium's upper-echelon executives.

The executive had replaced his own head with a sculpted crystal replica, filled it with liquid software, downloaded his personality into the software and then added a number of very small and doubtless incredibly exotic fish. This was probably considered the height of fashion in the Consortium core worlds. Vic had thought then, and hadn't changed his mind since, that it was deeply stupid. He'd named him Goldfish Bowl Head.

'I don't care about that,' Scab told Goldfish Bowl Head. The head might be sculpted and immobile, but Vic was pretty sure he picked up the Consortium exec's exasperation.

You can't reason with a psychopath, Vic thought. It wasn't true but he thought it sounded cool. Psychopaths could be very reasonable when they were getting exactly what they wanted. Though Scab wasn't really one of those kinds of psychopaths, either. If Scab was ever reasonable, he chose to do it when Vic wasn't around.

As for the nappies: Scab had made everyone attending the

immersion auction wear them in their virtual forms. Talia told him he was being childish. Scab replied that he was interested in just how far they were willing to debase themselves to get her. As a result, the immersion had them all wearing nappies and seated on small rocking horses in some saccharine version of an upper-middle-class nursery from a pre-Loss media. Vic had initially been worried that humiliating them like this would incur their wrath, but frankly he had no clue how they could get into any more trouble than they were already in.

Vic, Talia and Scab were all dressed normally, however. Talia had tried to reason with the attendees from the Church, several of the more powerful companies in the Consortium and the aristocratic representatives from the Monarchist systems. She'd eventually lapsed into silence when she realised that they cared about her as much as Scab did. She was now sitting against the wall, arms wrapped around her legs.

Vic was crouched, comfortably, nearby, trying not to keep looking at Talia, though she constantly caught him doing just that. Scab was leaning against the wall and smoking, which was arguably even more pointless in an immersion than it was in the real world.

'Surely the offer we have made is more than sufficient,' said one of the representatives from the Monarchist Regent's Pleasure system, the dummy in his mouth disappearing as Scab neunonically allowed him to speak. 'Overlord of an entire planet. Total control of a billion-strong sentient biomass.' The man was grotesquely fat. Scab had allowed him to retain his make-up and wig. Vic was staring at the fat man. He was still behaving with a kind of pompous arrogance; they all were, despite their humiliation. Vic assumed they must have extensive conditioning which allowed them to act like pricks regardless of the circumstances. It was fascinating, Vic thought, from an anthropological perspective.

'A seat on the board is a much more valuable commodity,' Goldfish Bowl Head said, then his dummy appeared again.

'Your own subsidiary would provide effective control over a number of planets and influence over many more. Not to mention the resources you would have at your disposal . . .' This from a feline exec, the representative of Karnak Industries, one of the most powerful companies in the Consortium. Whatever sex the exec had started off as, she was now very feminine. Vic had to admit they'd done their research well. She was just Scab's type, though the nappy and bonnet spoiled the allure somewhat. At least, the 'sect hoped it did.

'But still not nearly as prestigious as a seat on the board,' Goldfish Bowl Head said in exasperation.

The feline was unable to prevent a slight hiss escaping her lips. 'You and I both know that's a hollow offer. There's no way the board would allow free rein to someone of Mr Woodbine's persuasion—'

'And what persuasion would that be?' Scab asked.

The feline turned and held his dead stare. She was good, Vic thought.

'That of a prolific murderer.'

Scab nodded. Vic was impressed. Either the feline or those who had sent her had done their research well. Scab respected that sort of honesty.

'Would you reverse my psychosurgery? Provide me with a fleet? Legion? Ground forces?'

Suddenly nobody would look at him, not even the feline.

'I don't think you understand why you're here,' Scab told them. 'This is an auction. This isn't about you having to find increasingly more extravagant ways to try and control me. It won't work. You must see that by now.'

Vic couldn't be sure, but he was starting to think that Scab was amused despite himself.

'Did I mention that the world would come with the title of emperor?' the fat, wig-wearing blue-blood asked.

Scab shook his head and glanced over at Vic with an expression of bemusement.

'How many people get to see themselves auctioned?' Talia wondered.

'Most slaves, I would imagine,' Vic suggested

The attendees had started arguing among themselves again. This had been going on for some hours now.

'This is a farce,' Talia said. 'He's not going to get what he wants because he's a psycho, and nobody wants to give a psycho power.'

Scab turned to look at the nat pre-Loss human woman. Talia smiled at him with venomous mock-sweetness.

'That's really not true,' Vic said. 'It doesn't matter if he's a psycho. They just want to give away the smallest amount of their power they can to get what they want. But you're right, they don't want to hand him that much power.'

'Yeah, but I mean, why bother with it? Why would any of them live up to their offers?'

Because, Vic thought, *they've all paid a lot of debit just to be here.* Part of the expense had resulted from Pythia agreeing to host the auction within the planet's atmosphere. The immersion had been created within the infoscape of the nano-civilisation's hive mind, and as a result was probably the single most secure immersion in the history of the uplifted races. What remained of the vast sums paid for admission had all gone into secure, occulted Pythian black accounts. Scab was now one of very few people in Known Space who was in credit.

Despite Pythia's security assurances, and assurances that Scab would deliver Talia upon the successful conclusion of the auction, they had still come in force. Consortium battle fleets, capital ships, entire Monarchist fiefdom navies. The visiting dignitaries, their entourages and their heavily armed security forces had hired out entire habitats. Pythia's orbital defences and their – now extensively augmented – fleet of military contractors watched the visiting ships nervously.

Raised voices were silenced as dummies appeared in the mouths of all the attendees again. Many of them looked less than happy about this, though Vic had noticed that a number of them were really taking advantage of having a dummy in their mouth and seemed to be enjoying it. The odd calm that spread over the nursery immersion felt very fragile.

'I don't think they really know you,' Vic said in an attempt to console his 'partner'. Scab just shook his head. He made the dummy disappear from one of the attendees' mouths. So far this attendee had said nothing.

'And what does the Church have to offer?' Scab asked.

The Monk tried to suppress a strong urge to kill. Benedict/Scab managed to get his laughter under control and looked around the *Lazerene*'s bridge. No longer able to neunonically interface with the ship, he had to make do with the parts of the smart-matter superstructure that had turned into screens showing feeds from the damage-control parties, the med bay, and the ongoing struggle to regain control of the automated weapon systems, weaponised nano-swarms, security satellites and hacked automatons.

'Was it worth it?'

'Bye.' The Monk started drawing her knife.

'Send a sacrifice,' the Scab possession told her. 'This isn't real.'

Nobody had the ability to wear a nappy and sit on a rocking horse with a dummy in their mouth and manage to look dignified. The elderly lizard, probably a cardinal, Vic guessed, came the closest.

'I think,' the lizard started, 'that the best way to win the game is not to play it.'

Scab said nothing, just looked at him, his expression unreadable.

'Well, how fucking profound,' Vic muttered.

'No threat?' Scab asked.

'I would reason with you if I could, bargain with you, threaten you, but you are insane, Mr Woodbine. What difference would it make?' the Church representative said. Talia laughed. The old lizard looked at her. She shrank away slightly, still not used to non-humans. Vic's facial-recognition software was pretty sure he saw sympathy on the lizard's face. He wondered where the Monk was. She must have been cloned by now. 'I don't suppose we could have the backups for the crew of the *St. Brendan's Fire*, could we?'

'You don't want the ship?' Scab asked. The elderly lizard shrugged. 'Offer me something.'

'There are already more than enough people here who would pander to you, and you are not a greedy man. This is a farce.'

Vic thought he saw the ghost of a smile on Scab's face. The 'sect saw the other attendees struggling to speak through their dummies.

'So nothing, no offers, no threats for me?'

'Not for you,' the lizard said. He turned to the other attendees. 'If this auction is successful, there will be one winner and many losers. As well as a placing a full embargo on bridge- and Seeder-derived tech on the winner, we will offer technical, spiritual and military aid to the losers in ensuring the utter destruction of the winner.' He turned back to Scab. 'You may put the dummy back in now.'

Vic was pretty sure a number of the attendees were going to give themselves embolisms back in their bodies if the dummies weren't removed soon. Scab removed all the dummies simultaneously and there was chaos in the nursery as everyone started screaming and shouting, except for the elderly lizard, who began rocking backwards and forwards on his hobby horse.

Threats and counterthreats were bandied around. The offerings made to Scab became increasingly ridiculous. Finally Scab held up his hands for quiet, though Vic noted that he hadn't replaced their dummies.

'None of you is prepared to meet my price. I'm afraid we're wasting time here.' Then the screaming really began. Shrieking mouths appeared, pressing through the walls of the nursery. The noise was agonising, triggering various immersion overrides in Vic's and Scab's neunonics. Talia was simply lying on the floor, blood pouring from her eyes, ears, nose and mouth even though this was only her immersion form.

Vic couldn't believe it. Someone was actually attempting a data raid on Pythia. The nursery ceased to exist as if it had been cut into ribbons. They found themselves in a blue sky, fast-moving clouds shooting by them. The attendees started to disappear. The feline executive began to scream and then fell, disintegrating as she did so. Vic knew that some kind of Pythian killer program had traced her immersion form back to her neunonics and killed her meat. That meant Karnak was responsible.

Then the sky disappeared.

'Why?' Vic asked, opening his eyes. He was lying on the couch that had been looking after his body whilst he was immersed. 'They must have known it wasn't going to work.'

Scab opened his mouth to reply.

'The scorpion and the fox,' Talia said, taking off the trodes she'd used to immerse. They had to use the assembler to manufacture them because she lacked neunonics. 'They can't help themselves.' She was wiping the blood from her nose on the back of her wrist and examining it. Vic noticed that Scab was looking at her. There was something guarded in his expression.

'Karnak are primarily a software house, and a good one, but they're feline owned and operated. They could never understand software like a machine intelligence can,' Scab said quietly.

'Seeders' sake,' Vic muttered. The smart matter of the hull went split-screen at a neunonic command from Scab, showing feed from different parts of Pythian orbital space.

'Are we safe?' Talia asked.

'They'll be looking for us,' Scab told her. 'Pythia guaranteed they would maintain our privacy as long as they could.'

'A lot of resources out there,' Vic observed. They had leaked their presence in Pythian space to various intelligence agencies, which had also proved quite lucrative, otherwise nobody would have come to the auction.

'That's the *Bubastis*,' Scab said and increased the view of a truly massive ship, its manoeuvring engines burning whilst it was still attached to an orbital habitat only slightly larger than it was. 'It's Karnak's headquarters.'

The enormous armoured behemoth was actually dragging the habitat out of its orbit, and every weapon on the habitat was pouring fire into the *Bubastis*. Reactive armour exploded outwards, lessening the impact of kinetic harpoons and AG-driven submunitions. The side of the massive craft looked as if it was bubbling as the carbon reservoirs struggled to regrow the ship's armour. The orbital space around the capital ship was filled with light as every Pythian defence platform capable of doing so fired on the ship. The *Bubastis* became a ghostly silhouette in the bright light of the craft's energy-dissipation grid as it tried to bleed off the torrent of fire.

The *Bubastis*'s own batteries fired. AG smart munitions were launched, and small ships and defence platforms caught in the lines of energy exploded. One side of the orbital habitat was shrouded in light and destruction as it fell away from the capital ship. Explosions existed momentarily before being snuffed in the vacuum. The habitat, a luxury hotel by the looks of it, started falling slowly, almost gracefully, towards the cold, grey planet, towards dark thunderclouds of a civilisation-sized, angry nano-swarm.

The manoeuvring engines on the Pythian military contractors' ships burned as they made for an orbit that would provide them with favourable firing positions. Fingers of light reached from the *Bubastis* to blister and burst their ships as AG smart munitions burst into more submunitions; counter-submunitions blossomed to meet them in almost pointless explosive displays.

Swarms of smaller craft flew out of the *Bubastis*, many of them exploding as they left the dubious safety of their mother ship, but more made it out than were destroyed. The smaller craft attacked defence platforms and got into dogfights with military contractors.

At the same time, the other auction attendees were leaving. Any resistance on the part of the Pythian authorities to their departure was being met with violence.

More than one of the more recently employed military contractors fired on the leaving ships. Whether accidentally or because another party had bought their loyalties, it didn't matter. Pythia was wreathed in violent light.

Church, Consortium and Monarchist ships that weren't heavily involved in the battle fled to high orbit, fighting off rivals and Pythian forces where they had to. They ran aggressively active scans and diverted processing power to analysis routines as they searched for the *St. Brendan's Fire*. They offered ridiculous sums to Pythia for information as to Talia and Scab's whereabouts, but the planet's nanite populace was too angry to accept bids.

Fire spread across about a fifth of the planet's sky as the falling habitat hit the atmosphere and nano-swarm thunderheads surged up to consume the burning matter. The clouds glowed with inner fire as the tiny machines converted the habitat's matter at a molecular level, using it to make more of themselves.

'Now,' Scab whispered.

*

They spent some time analysing the local conflict around the station where the *St. Brendan's Fire* was docked in high orbit, looking for the path of least resistance and then taking it, engines burning bright. They didn't pick any fights and went out of their way to avoid existing ones. They ran.

The frigate wove between rapidly firing defence platforms and dogfighting ships from various factions, and steered clear of a garishly decorated heavy cruiser from one of the Monarchist systems. The heavy cruiser's beam batteries broadsided and tore apart two squadrons of military contractor corsairs and a patrol ship.

The *St. Brendan's Fire* got a close look at the underside of a fast-moving Consortium light cruiser glowing with the fire it had taken from pursuing mercenary frigates. Moments later, it exploded. Beams of light shot out from the *St. Brendan's Fire*, destroying the debris now tumbling towards it.

A military contractor cruiser de-cohered in front of them, taking hit after hit from one of the *Bubastis*'s massive D-cannons as the enormous capital ship hove into view over the planetary horizon, still wreathed in light. The ex-Church frigate fired all its weapons systems. Submunitions exploded, beams cut and kinetic harpoons destroyed as the craft attempted to carve a path through the disintegrating cruiser's wreckage. It came out of the other side badly damaged, carbon reservoirs flowing as the self-repair systems went to work.

On the bridge of the *Stigmata*, Cardinal Hak received the active scan-sensor data in his neunonics.

'It's the *St. Brendan's Fire*,' announced Crazy Fish, his dolphin navigator. The old lizard smiled, inasmuch as lizards smiled. It was more of a baring of his teeth, truth be told.

'I can see that, old friend.'

'Well?' the dolphin asked in a series of clicks which the creature's customised P-sat translated with negligible delay. Today, the dolphin was using the voice of some saccharine teenage musical-immersion artist. The cardinal had long ago stopped letting such things annoy him. The elderly lizard sighed.

'Set an intercept course, tell the rest of the squadron to join us. We fire only in defence.'

The cardinal knew it wouldn't matter, they would have to fight. As the Church ships peeled away from Pythia towards the bridge point, chasing the *St. Brendan's Fire*, others would realise what they were doing and follow. They would be prepared to fight to capture Scab's ship.

'Here we go,' Scab said. He watched the Church squadron head away from Pythia, fighting their way free of orbital space when they had to. More and more realised what the Church squadron was doing and followed, engaging AG-driven smart weapons and other long-range weapon systems such as particle-beam cannons in an attempt to slow the pursuing Church ships.

'How many people have you just killed?' Talia asked, staring at the battle playing across the smart-matter screens. Vic glanced at the young human woman. He wasn't quite sure what he'd heard in her voice.

Orbital space was still carnage as the *Bubastis* tried to fight off Pythia's punitive attempts to destroy it.

Pythia used the burning matter it had consumed to form a massive shape, miles across, made from quintillions of constituent parts. It wasn't exactly a hand. It had eight digits, four on either side. Then it reached.

'Holy mother of...' Talia muttered. She watched as what looked like the hand of God reached up, wreathed in atmospheric fire.

'Seeders preserve us,' Cardinal Hak said as he received the feed from Pythian orbital space. Every Pythian orbital defence platform turned its attention to the treaty-breaking nanites that had just breached Pythia's atmosphere. Untold trillions of nanites died as fire rained down from the platforms, the military contractors, the remaining Karnak Industries craft and any other nearby panicking ships. Pythia fed more matter to the 'hand', which was constantly being destroyed and regrown.

The cardinal knew that signals would be transmitted all over Known Space, and that both the Consortium and the Church would scramble fleets when they received news of Pythia breaking the agreement that it would never leave its own sparse atmosphere.

The fingers clasped around the *Bubastis*. Pythia's 'arm' was tethered to the planet below. It pulled as generation after generation of its constituent nanites were destroyed. It pulled as the *Bubastis*'s engines glowed bright, trying to resist, but it was dragged inexorably down. As the massive craft hit the atmosphere its back broke, and Pythia's sky was filled with fire again. The capital craft started to disintegrate and rain down on the planet. Angry, roiling black clouds consumed the wreckage before any of it reached the ground. Lightning played through the angry nano-swarms. One word was transmitted to every craft in the Pythian system.

'Enough.'

The skin of the *St. Brendan's Fire* bubbled. Superheated armour plate flowed like liquid as accelerated charged particles penetrated the frigate's superstructure. The *St. Brendan's Fire* launched AG smart munitions. Upon leaving their racks they almost immediately burst into submunitions, forming a screen between the frigate and incoming fire. Multiple explosions rocked the frigate. It was a one-sided fight. More fire from the *Stigmata*'s particle-beam cannon lit up the frigate. Reactive armour blew out but couldn't keep up with the multiple submunition impacts. Two of the Church battleship's escort craft closed with the fast, manoeuvrable frigate and emptied their kinetic-harpoon racks. The *St. Brendan's Fire*'s reactive armour was overwhelmed and the frigate came apart, turning into a fast-moving debris field.

Behind them the *Stigmata* was being fired upon by the ships of the other interested parties who, denied what they wanted, had turned vengeful.

'Fools,' the cardinal muttered to himself. He glanced over at the pre-Loss knight in full mail standing next to him on the bridge. The knight didn't actually exist – he was a manifestation of the ship's AI. Hak was aware of the damage the *Stigmata* was talking through his 'face connection. He had served so long with the ship that he felt each burn or impact as if it was pain in his own body. 'Well?'

'I can detect no trace of a bridge drive in the wreckage,' the *Stigmata*'s AI said quietly. Hak nodded and sent that information out as a secure 'face just as the *Stigmata* died in fire and force.

Nobody saw the heavily stealthed luxury yacht leave orbit because they weren't looking for it.

'What about the dolphin?' Talia asked in a small voice. Scab ignored her. Vic wasn't really sure what to say.

Pythia knew, but then Pythia was as close to omniscient as science could get. Scab accepted the 'face transmission and the smart matter of the hull formed a holographic projection mechanism. It was primitive, but Talia couldn't receive neunonic interface communication.

Pythia was represented as a dark-haired woman in a simple and ancient-looking black dress. The dress and her hair flowed as if she was underwater. Rags were wrapped around her head, covering her face.

'This was your plan?' the manifestation of the planet-wide machine civilisation asked.

'You must have calculated that,' Scab said.

'We knew it was a distinct possibility. We underestimated uplift greed – and stupidity.'

'Perhaps I have more faith in them.'

'Why did you do it?'

'It's in my nature.'

The woman appeared to consider this. 'We will not work with you again.'

Scab just nodded. The woman disappeared.

'You did it for the money, right?' Vic asked. Scab didn't answer.

'You weren't really auctioning me?' Talia asked. Vic found the pathetic gratitude in her voice heartbreaking. He also didn't like the way she was looking at Scab. He felt the prick of jealousy in his psychosurgically modified mind.

'Not yet,' Vic said, a little too harshly. 'He lost his deep-pocket employer and needed a way to finance the next part of this idiocy.'

Scab reached up and cupped Talia's chin. 'Don't worry. You're still a commodity.'

Angrily, she slapped his hand away – Vic was surprised Scab let her – then she spat in his face and stormed out of the luxury yacht's comfortable split-level living/Command-and-Control area.

Vic turned on Scab, his mandibles clattering together as he searched frustratingly for something to say.

'I killed tens, if not hundreds of thousands of people today. Are you really that upset about what I just said to your nat girlfriend?' Scab asked, then looked up at the 'sect.

'I just want to be away from you,' Vic said quietly, and left.

The assembler on the *Basilisk II*, as Vic had decided to call the yacht, not only offered a much broader choice than the one on the *St. Brendan's Fire* had, but the choices tended to be a lot more decadent. Vic had assembled a selection of imbibable vices and some decorative flora in an attempt to try and cheer Talia up.

He 'faced the instruction to open the door to the room she'd grown for herself. The most insulting thing was that Scab hadn't even bothered to lock the door after himself. Vic saw his partner/captor's pale back first as it moved up and down. Talia moaned underneath him. Scab must have known that Vic was there. Talia opened her eyes for a moment and saw the seven-foot-tall insect in the doorway. She gestured for him to go before closing her eyes and moaning again.

Vic 'faced the instruction to close the door to Talia's room and watched it slide shut. He stared at it for a while, holding a tray of narcotics and flowers.

9
Ancient Britain

Tangwen couldn't remember a time when her throat didn't burn, when her chest didn't ache, when her muscles weren't made of pain. She sprinted through the trees, barely registering the whipping branches tearing at her skin. She heard cries of agony and the shouted gibbering of the moonstruck as they kept pace with the survivors. They were dark, hunting forms wearing masks of flayed human skin, running through the woods, attacking any survivors they found. Tangwen skidded to a halt in the dirt. She needed to breathe. Her throat felt bloody.

How many did we leave behind, how many simply couldn't keep up with us? The thought was quickly forgotten as something thundered through the woods and collided with her. The impact dragged her across the dirt as she hit the ground hard. Tangwen wasn't sure how, but she found herself on the man's back. His face came away in her hands. No, it was only a red mask. She yanked his head towards her, and he soiled himself as she sawed at his throat.

'Come to me, girl.' The language was close enough to her own that she understood each word, but she could not divine their meaning. Her head whipped around. It was just easier to be a hunting animal now.

The speaker was an old woman, but she stood tall and strong, and carried herself with confidence.

'You're not one of them,' the old woman said quietly. She was clad in tatters, her skin black with soot. Her hair was a tangled mess that the poorest slave would be ashamed of, but even in the dark beneath the canopy of branches and leaves, Tangwen could still make out her eyes. They looked bright, alert – strong, somehow. Like all the other survivors, her form was emaciated, ill-fed, though it looked like she'd had meat on her once. She had found a branch somewhere that she was leaning on it as a staff.

Tangwen hissed like an angry snake, her head whipping from side to side as she made out the many dark shapes in the woods around the woman, keeping pace with her, visibly stalking her, moving in and out of the beams of moonlight that filtered down through the trees. Most of them were watching the woman through the eyeholes in the flayed faces they wore, but a number of them looked at Tangwen.

There were screams from deeper in the woods.

'Stay close to me,' the woman said. She was doing a very good job of masking her fear as they started to move. The moonstruck were keeping pace with them as well. One of them swung at her and she hissed angrily and slashed back with her knife, more for show than anything else.

'Why do they not attack you?' Tangwen hissed when she remembered she wasn't a wild animal, a serpent.

'Well, whatever else they may be, they were brought up well enough to know to fear women.'

Tangwen glanced over at the other woman, surprised and more than a little worried that this was the extent of her plan.

'Show no weakness,' the woman told her. Only then was Tangwen fully aware of just how frightened the other woman was.

Germelqart glanced over at Kush, who was holding his head in his hands, eyes closed tight as he tried to block out the screaming, tried not to hear it. Germelqart knew his friend had been a slave and then a gladiator before winning his freedom, before earning a living protecting other people's lives and goods. Kush was not a good man. He had looked out for himself. He had lived a life of violence, and that rarely troubled Kush's conscience, but this?

Germelqart, for his part, couldn't turn away. The circular building was little more than a wooden framework set in a cleared rectangular area. To the navigator's eyes, the structure appeared to be positioned to catch the light of the moon. Maybe it had seen other ritual uses before this day, but now it was a place to hang the living and make them suffer. It was a place of casual torture where lifeblood stained the earth black in the moonlight.

The survivors strong enough to make it to the island who hadn't immediately been killed outright by the moonstruck had been brought here. Here the *dryw* tended to them, their white robes stained red and brown. Even in this poor light, Germelqart could make out the lack of life in the *dryws'* eyes. He knew that the priests of this cold, harsh land practised blood rites, as did the priests in his land and all lands he had visited. The gods were greedy, they had to be appeased or bargained with, and for the greatest boons, the greatest sacrifices were required.

But this – this was a mockery. This could serve no purpose. This was the gluttony of the darkest gods. The giant wicker man within whom he had been imprisoned was the same. In this land they spoiled the worst of their gods.

'We have to do something,' Kush whispered. Germelqart glanced at his friend and then back the way they had come. There were around twenty survivors from the wicker man hidden in the woods. Germelqart was exhausted. He knew, despite the other man's strength, that Kush was, too.

Kush's head sagged and tears sprang from his eyes. There were so few warriors among the survivors – most had either died resisting the Lochlannach or been enslaved by their magics. It was a daemon's choice: either protect those already with them, or risk all by trying to rescue those already taken.

'We cannot leave them ...' Kush muttered.

You may not be a good man, Germelqart thought, *but you are no monster*.

'We have to,' Germelqart whispered. That was when they brought the child in. A strong child, a fierce child of a fierce people, who struggled and fought his captors but just wasn't strong enough to break free. Not after climbing down from the wicker man, not after swimming to the island, not after trying to escape the moonstruck.

The moonstruck started to rope the boy to the frame. One of the *dryw*, a shaven-headed woman with a dripping robe – the face she wore was a male's – approached the struggling figure. Germelqart turned to Kush but it was too late. The tall, dark-skinned man had already charged into the clearing.

Still breathing hard, Tangwen looked down at the *dryw* she had just killed. She spat and made the sign to avert evil. To harm or kill a *dryw* was a great crime, but her serpent father had always struck her as a very practical god, and she was sure he would forgive her. If she lived.

More survivors joined them. Tangwen killed more of the moonstruck, and others did the same. They caught up with the other survivors, those whom Kush and Germelqart were leading, whilst she protected their rear. Through the trees she saw the obscenity that the *dryw* had made of their holy place, their shrine to their god of the moon.

Tangwen watched Germelqart and Kush fighting for their lives, a boy battling desperately by their side. Something made her glance at the old woman she had been walking with. A beam of moonlight shining through the canopy of trees illuminated her face and Tangwen saw the look of fear. The woman knew the boy.

'You fight in threes. Two of you grab one of them, the third kills them as quickly as they can, then you move onto the next one. Do you understand?' Tangwen told the survivors.

'We are not warriors,' replied one man. 'I can barely move, let alone fight.'

'Then you are already dead,' she told him and moved quickly to where he stood. She remembered Britha and tried not to puke as she knifed him to death as quickly as she could. The rest of the survivors stared at their erstwhile saviour, appalled. Some whimpered, some cried, but none moved.

'Die helpless or die fighting. Decide now,' the old woman told them with no little authority. Slowly they started to get up. The woman turned to Tangwen and nodded, and Tangwen all but fled into the woods. She would do more good on her own, she told herself, and then threw up. She felt a lot worse about killing the frightened man with the survivors than she had about the *dryw*.

She swallowed bile and scuttled forwards on all fours towards the rear of the press of moonstruck closing in on Kush. She cursed as one of them turned around, having heard something, but he did not look down. She stabbed him though the back of his ankle. He fell, his cries lost among the squeals of the moonstruck and the shouted devotions of the *dryw*. One of the others turned to face her, and she rammed the dagger up into his throat from her crouching position. The moonstruck woman sank to her knees, blood bubbling from the wound and from her mouth. Another turned around at the movement but did not look down quickly enough, and his screams cut through the other noise as Tangwen rammed her blade up into his groin. Now they knew she was there. She rolled away from them, coming unsteadily to her feet before backing into the woods. A number of them followed her. As exhausted as she was, as sickened by the violence, she started to hunt them.

The survivors came out of the woods. They grabbed at the moonstruck, trying to bear them to the ground as they clubbed or stabbed at them. Frantic, panicked, but somehow holding it together enough to fight. While they distracted the moonstruck, Kush started to swing his axe. Short, fast cuts with the blade, or hitting them with the head of the axe, wounding blows, blows that forced them back, gave them room until he could make longer swings. Then he started to cut the wounded moonstruck down.

Germelqart protected Kush with his club. He landed few blows and fewer still did significant damage, but it was enough to keep them off his warrior friend.

The boy had been trained. He held himself together in the face of the moonstruck and knew enough to bide his time, to pick his attacks with the small dagger, but when he saw an opportunity, he took it.

They fought their way through the moonstruck. Kush raised his axe high to strike down another half-naked, blood-covered savage with a dripping blade.

'No!' Tangwen shouted at him. Too late, Germelqart realised what was happening and made a grab for the axe. Kush cried out from the effort but at the last moment he diverted the path of the axe. The weapon dug deep into the earth next to a shaking Tangwen. She stared at him, eyes wide with the horror of the day. She sagged. He caught her as she fell, but then realised he was falling as well, barely able to move. All around them was murder as the remaining survivors dispatched the moonstruck and their *dryw* masters. It was only then that they started to feel the pain of all the wounds they had taken. Kush slumped forwards. Sleep or unconsciousness was trying to claim him.

'No!' Tangwen said fiercely. 'We need to get off this island!' She struggled to her feet and tried to pull Kush up with her.

The older woman was called Anharad. She was the mother of a minor chieftain of the Trinovantes, whose tribal name meant the Vigorous People. Tangwen's own tribe, the Pobl Neidr, the People of the Snake, were part of the Catuvellauni. The Trinovantes were their northern neighbours on the east coast of Ynys Prydain, the Isle of the Mighty. Tangwen had scouted into their territory for more than one raid, but none of that mattered now.

The boy's name was Mabon. He was Anharad's grandson and had been abducted from the children's camp, where he had been training to be a warrior, to follow in his parents' footsteps. He had not said a word since the fight at the moonstrucks' holy place, though he had been helping some of the other survivors.

There appeared to be few of the moonstruck left, and those that had escaped were keeping their distance. If any of the corrupt *dryw* survived, Tangwen had not seen them.

Their band had swollen to about fifty people now, though many were injured, a few so seriously that they needed to be carried, and all were exhausted. Tangwen, with Kush and the formidable Anharad's help, pushed them onwards, north towards the mainland. Germelqart led the way.

They reached the shore by dawn as a faint grey light illuminated the land. Tangwen sighed as they staggered out of the trees only to be confronted by thick mud and a narrow stream.

'We have to cross,' Anharad said as she came to stand by the young woman. Tangwen didn't think she'd ever been so tired. She nodded numbly and half-staggered, half-slipped towards the thick mud. Kush was by her side, helping Germelqart through the clinging ooze. Tangwen was forced to use her hands to drag her legs out of the sucking mud. Behind her she could hear Anharad ordering the survivors to follow.

Something exploded out of the mud, showering them all with dirt as it reared up on its hind legs. Tangwen caught a glimpse of a creature that looked like a flayed man fused with a flayed horse. Limbs poked from skinless flesh at odd angles, as though rider and beast had melted into each other. At first she thought the rider carried a sword, but then she realised the blade was fused with the monster's arm. Tangwen found herself sitting in the mud, staring up at the creature. The muscles on its face contorted into a silent, agonised scream. It vomited a stream of bile. Numbly she felt it hit her. Then it started to burn her flesh. Tangwen found that she wasn't so numb she couldn't feel pain.

Kush had staggered away from the creature. He saw Tangwen rolling in the mud, her face smoking, and he could hear her cries of pain. The strange protean creature's forelegs came down on the mud. One leg was a horse's; the other looked like a skinless human leg. It stabbed forwards with its sword-limb and ran one of the survivors through as he tried to scramble across the mud to get away from the monstrosity. The creature lifted the screaming man up out of the mud on the blade.

Kush charged the creature, or tried to, but got bogged down in the mud. He swung his axe at it. The creature deflected the axe with what Kush thought at first was a shield, but then he realised it was a fused growth of bone. He swung again, but weakly. The fused-bone shield caught him in the chest and face, breaking his nose, cracking something in his chest. The force of the blow lifted him out of the sucking mud and sent him flying through the air. He lost his grip on the axe.

Germelqart had been knocked over when the creature exploded from the mud. He managed to stagger back to his feet and was frenziedly swinging his club at the creature's flanks. It moved forwards slightly and kicked out with its rear legs, catching the navigator with a glancing blow to his hip. It was still hard enough to send him spinning into the air.

The horrific crunching noise was heard over the other sounds of violence. Another survivor, a woman Kush was sure had been trained as a warrior, had hit the creature in the face of its human head with the butt of the branch she'd been using as a staff. As the flayed face caved in, the horse's head lunged forwards. There was a ripping noise as the woman's face was bitten off and she stumbled backwards when the creature reared. Its forelegs came down, trampling the warrior's broken body into the mud.

Then Tangwen was on the creature's back, its skinless horse's back, behind where the fused 'rider' grew out of the steed's flesh. Half her face and part of her chest were a ruined smoking mess. She grabbed the creature's human head and pulled it back, sawing at its throat with her dagger. Red blood bubbled out of the wound, but it was healing even as she sawed. The dagger she carried now had not been bathed in the blood of Britha and Fachtna, unlike the weapons she had taken with her to the wicker man. Kush knew she could not win this fight as he scrabbled in the mud for his axe. The creature circled in the mud, reaching back for Tangwen with its sword-limb.

Howling, Kush swung his axe hard enough to bury one of its crescent heads in the creature's torso. The creature shrieked and reared again and Tangwen held on for dear life. The movement tore the axe free. Kush stumbled back from its fury, changed his grip on the weapon and swung again. The axe bit deep, decapitating the horse. The creature tried to rear once more but instead it flopped sideways. Tangwen screamed, too slow. The falling horse had landed on her leg.

The creature was still thrashing in the mud. As Kush staggered towards it, the 'rider' swung weakly at him with its blade. Kush stood on it. The axe came down and Kush harvested another head.

Tangwen grunted as she pushed her way out from underneath the dead monstrosity. Had she not landed in soft mud, she was pretty sure it would have broken her leg. She staggered to her feet. Blood and melted flesh ran down the ruin of one side of her face, a tear down the other. It was just pain, she told herself.

Kush waded through the mud towards where Germelqart was lying in the shallow water, groaning.

Something made Tangwen look to the west.

'What is it?' Kush shouted to her.

Distantly she could make out movement in the brightening light.

'The fruits of Andraste's poisoned womb,' she said, shrugging. 'Where did you get that axe?'

Kush looked up sharply from examining a painful-looking red

mark on Germelqart's side, but he didn't answer. Blood ran freely down the axeman's face and he winced with every movement.

The axe is blessed, she realised, *soaked in the blood of gods or heroes.*

'Can he move?' Tangwen asked.

'I don't think anything is broken in him.'

'Then get him up!' Tangwen snapped. Kush looked askance at the harshness of her tone but started to help Germelqart to his feet.

'Are you okay?' Anharad asked, gasping for breath. Mabon was looking all around for danger, dagger in hand. Tangwen turned the smoking ruin of her face towards them. Anharad took an involuntary step back. Mabon could not keep the expression of disgust from his face. He would have been taught that such a deformity made Tangwen less than a whole person.

Tangwen glanced down at the monstrosity's corpse and something caught her eye. It looked like horse and rider had, at one time, been separate, and the steed had worn a saddle and bridle. Those items were also fused with the flesh. She reached down and scraped something off the edge of the saddle, which protruded through both horse's and rider's flesh.

'What is it?' Anharad asked.

'I think it was lime, once,' Tangwen told her.

'So?'

'The Corpse People paint their horses with lime.'

She touched the ruin of her face. The land was changing. She had to change, too.

'We cross now,' she told the survivors quietly. They started to move out onto the mud.

10
Birmingham, 6 Weeks Ago

Inge Street was on the edge of Birmingham's Chinatown. Bars, restaurants and a theatre huddled at the end of the street closer to the town centre, while the adult shop and cinema lay at the other end.

There weren't many people out and about on the cold, dreary, wet Wednesday afternoon as the woman made her way unsteadily towards the adult shop and cinema. She pushed open the door and walked in, ignoring all the garish pictures of human bodies reduced to product, all the costumes and toys, and made straight for the stairs leading down to the basement cinema.

'Oi,' the man behind the counter shouted. She wasn't the first woman to come into his shop but it was pretty rare that they wanted to visit the cinema. Oddly, given that the cinemagoers were there to look at women in an objectified form, the presence of an actual woman tended to put off the masturbators.

The woman didn't look quite right, he thought, as she made her unsteady way downstairs. She was in her late thirties, early forties, attractive in a slightly mutton-dressed-up-as-lamb way in her low-cut top and miniskirt. Or would have been if not for the slack expression on her overly made-up face and the drool coming out of the side of her mouth. Her long hair looked like it had been bleached once too often.

'You need to pay!' the man behind the counter shouted as he heard the door to the cinema open and close beneath him. 'Fuck's sake.' He glanced at the monitor showing a black and white image of the cinema. He tried not to look at it too often because he didn't want to watch portly middle-aged men wanking. The woman had slumped down in the front row. He sighed, lifted the countertop and headed downstairs.

'I'm sorry, love, but you either need to pay or get out,' he told her. She didn't respond. He leaned down to shake her, trying to ignore the smell of stale cum and desperation in the cinema. She didn't respond.

She did not look at all well. 'Oh, fuck,' he muttered. It wasn't the first time, he thought. An old guy had suffered a heart attack during a particularly spicy scene in *Latex Anal Queen Two*. He took out his mobile phone and started dialling. The few other punters in the cinema began to sidle out. 'Hello, ambulance, please.' He reckoned he had about four minutes to hide anything particularly dodgy in the shop upstairs.

The air/spacecraft was designed to look like an experimental stealth military version of the EADS Astrium commercial spaceplane. That was only for show. The shell of the aircraft and its internal workings were nearly pure L-tech, and artificial gravity simulated an Earthly 1G. The cabin looked like the inside of a luxurious executive jet.

Du Bois was seated in one of the comfortable chairs in the cabin, hand propping up his head as he stared down at Earth from orbit and brooded. He could just about make out one of the Circle's orbital facilities but only because he knew where to look. It was little more than a dot against the rising sun. He'd swapped his white linen suit for a pair of jeans and a smart, tailored black shirt.

'Fucking Birmingham!' Grace threw her phone down onto one of the leather chairs. She slid off the table she'd been using as a seat and joined the phone in the chair. Du Bois wasn't paying any attention to her. She watched him brood for a bit. 'I said, fucking Birmingham.'

'Silas has returned there. We go to Broadmoor first,' du Bois said, and then lapsed back into silence.

'Control do it all the time,' Grace told him, meaning the removing of sensitive data from their memories. 'None of us likes it, but we live with it because of the need for security.'

Du Bois looked over at her. 'I understand all that.' He didn't like the feeling that he was being patronised by someone many years his junior, though he knew she was only trying to make him feel better. 'What I don't understand is why he was allowed to live. Silas was a clear security risk. He ate the brains of one of our people. He clearly had access to S- or L-tech, we don't know which. If he interrogated the archer's nanites then he could know a great deal about us.'

'They must have wiped him. Or at least removed any sensitive data,' Grace said.

'We kill,' he continued as if he hadn't heard her. 'But we serve a greater purpose ...' He shook his head.

'Sounding hollow?' Grace asked. She was leaning back in the comfortable leather-upholstered chair, her boots up on the table as she took long swigs from a bottle of beer. The spaceplane was flying itself, piloted by a limited AI. Both of them had the skills to take over the flight, either remotely or physically, hardwired into their systems.

'Is that an excuse?' he asked her.

'I don't like where you're going with this,' Grace told him.

'You question and even disobey orders all the time.'

'I've always seen them as polite requests – suggestions rather than orders.' She gave this some thought. 'Those were orders? Really?'

Du Bois ignored her. Grace was a lot younger than him but older than any other naturally aging human. She was still much better at adapting to the spirits of different ages than he was.

'Is your first instinct to kill?' she asked him.

'No, but nor is it my last resort.'

'Do you enjoy it?' she asked, raising an eyebrow. He didn't want to answer that. 'I'll give you a moment to torture yourself, then I'll answer for you, make you feel better.'

'How? Moral relativism?'

'It's either that or vast amounts of drugs and alcohol.' Grace grinned at him as he looked at her ruefully.

'This doesn't bother you?'

Du Bois got up to help himself to a glass of twenty-five-year-old Glenmorangie.

'We sometimes have to do bad things,' she said. 'I don't like that, so afterwards I go on a bender, do some damage to others and myself. Y'know, generally torture myself for a bit.'

'Is that what was going on in Seattle in ninety-two?'

She nodded, taking her legs off the table and leaning forward. 'It was after what happened in the Balkans. Nobody deserves that.' She looked thoughtful for a moment and then took another swig of the beer. 'Other times, the people we take down have it coming and I'm glad we're here. Remember that fucker in Tibet?'

'Yes, somehow it's very difficult to feel bad about killing Nazis.'

'What about Spitalfields?' Grace asked. Du Bois looked over at her. He could still see the filthy, terrified but brave street urchin he'd first met back then.

'That gave me no pleasure. Hawksmoor was one of our brightest minds. I was sorry that went as far as it did. Killing him was an act of mercy.'

'He got too close,' Grace said quietly. Du Bois frowned at her. 'Whatever it is, whatever's coming, I think his genius gave him insight, somehow, perhaps even contact.'

Du Bois just stared at her. Perhaps she was right, but he didn't like to think about it.

'You don't like killing, Malcolm. You like action, and sometimes killing's a part of that. If you want to torture yourself about it, then go ahead. I think more often than not, you do the right thing. When you can.'

'Is that an excuse, though? Few can stand up to me.'

'The Brass City can. Hawksmoor's constructs could. We've found more than a few independents who gave us a run for our money.'

Outside the window was fire. They had barely felt the spaceplane start re-entry. Through the flames, du Bois could just about make out the British Isles so far below, his adopted home since the suppression of his order.

'The question isn't, *Do you enjoy killing?* I don't think you do. This guy, this Silas Scab, he enjoys inflicting suffering, and I've seen you make others suffer. You're a bastard when you want to be, but you've always got a reason. I think if you went a hundred years and didn't kill, you wouldn't miss it. He kills for fun, for sport.'

'I've certainly seen that before,' du Bois said quietly, thinking back to a hot, dusty, blood-soaked land.

'Besides, you can always go and pray for forgiveness from your god. The one you know for certain doesn't exist.' Du Bois turned to glare at the punk girl. She was grinning at him. 'Seriously, though, you know they can hear this?'

'I don't care,' du Bois snapped. 'I don't understand his continued existence. What possible reason can there be to let such a creature exist – especially one with access to the tech? Silas exists for one reason – to create atrocity. How can that serve us?'

'Self-doubt won't—'

'It's not me I'm doubting. And frankly, if the Circle doesn't like it they can send the American, or Wassermann, or the Pennangalan, though I notice she rarely leaves his side these days. And they want us to catch him—'

Grace's message came in across their occulted link. They had set it up in the sixties and were pretty sure the Circle didn't know about it. He heard her answer directly in his head.

'He doesn't have to survive.'

Du Bois didn't nod or show any outward sign that he'd received any communication.

'But do you know what pisses me off the most?' du Bois said.

'People using the acronym "LOL" in conversation?'

'Now, *that* is an example of when you can kill without a trace of guilt,' du Bois admitted. Grace laughed. 'No, relocation from Pohnpei, a tropical paradise, to fucking Birmingham.'

'Yes, that truly sucks,' Grace mused. Du Bois looked less than impressed by her use of language.

Du Bois and Grace were in the cockpit as they came in over the Channel, looking down at the maps of towns drawn by their street lights. They followed the Thames, making their way over London.

Re-entry had been easier than the subsequent landing in the rain with high crosswinds in the early hours of the morning. They taxied the aircraft to the small hanger the Circle kept at Farnborough Airport. There was no visible human security, no customs or passport control, nobody to bother them about the weapons they were carrying.

They walked across the hanger to their vehicles, which Control had arranged to be brought to the airport. Grace threw du Bois her kitbag, which he loaded, along with his own, into the back of the black, armoured Range Rover. Grace had changed into her bike leathers in the spaceplane. She straddled the Triumph Speed Triple motorcycle.

'It's cold and wet – are you sure you don't want to come with me?'

'You know I don't feel it,' she said, sorting out her helmet. 'Besides, you drive like an old person.' She put the helmet on, started the bike, gunned the engine, then spun the bike around and shot out of the hanger. Du Bois watched her go.

'I am old.' He climbed into the Range Rover.

Grace and du Bois sat on the bonnet of the Range Rover, drinking tea and smoking, watching the sunrise. Behind them were the high razor-wire-topped walls of Broadmoor Psychiatric Hospital. The institutional red-brick Victorian buildings housed some of the most dangerous patients within the British legal and health systems.

The sun was coming up over wooded, somewhat swampy-looking moorland. Beyond that was a small suburban area that his internal systems told him was called Owlsmoor, and he knew the wooded area he could see beyond the suburbs was part of the Royal Military Academy Sandhurst, the officer training school for the British Army.

'It's one of those places you never really come to, isn't it?' du Bois said, nodding at Owlsmoor. 'There's no reason to visit. It's neither one thing nor another.'

'I have a theory about suburbs,' Grace mused. They still had an hour to go until their appointment. 'I think it's where it all happens.'

Du Bois gave that some thought. 'Expand.'

'Well, so many people must live in them now. People don't just go into suspended animation when they live in boring places.'

'They're sedated by television and prescription antidepressants.'

'No, I think it all happens here, all the great crimes, kept hidden until they're too loud to contain. Quiet perversions, quiet substance abuse, quiet violence, quiet art. We just don't hear about it until something big happens. You mark my words – in one of those houses down there is a man with a needle in his arm, fucking a dog whilst composing the greatest poetry since Homer.' Grace nodded, happy with her explanation, and took another drag of her cigarette.

Du Bois was staring at her. 'I'm not sure you're all right, Grace.'

'Really? With everything you've seen, *that* shocks you? With your sister ...' Grace said, eyebrow raised. Du Bois just about managed not to flinch at the mention of his sibling. 'How is Alexia?'

'Enough,' du Bois told her. Grace knew she'd pushed him too hard. His relationship with his brother/sister was problematic at best. She held her hands up in contrition.

'Sorry,' she told him.

Du Bois said nothing, just unclipped the holster that held his Accursed Colt .45 and stored it with his tanto and the pouch of ammo in a secure compartment in the Range Rover's central console.

'We can take those in if we want,' Grace pointed out. 'We've got clearance.'

'Let's save ourselves the argument and not mess with their security protocols.'

Grace looked like she was about to argue, but instead she removed the leather jacket and slipped out of the double shoulder holster. She took off the two ammo pouches and stored everything in the larger hidden weapons compartment in the back of du Bois' jeep.

The interior of the hospital was faded in places, but it was clear that recent investment had made much of it look modern, comfortable and very security conscious. As one of the guards led them along corridors protected by multiple locked doors, it struck du Bois that the modernity was just a facade laid over something older and far more forbidding. He knew the Victorian edifice had seen so many inmates who had done unspeakable things. He knew that their 'evil' couldn't seep into the building. Except in the case of Silas Scab. The tiny, ancient nanites in his blood could have crept out, depending on how securely he had been imprisoned.

Du Bois and Grace were reviewing footage from the hospital's security cameras as they followed the guard deeper into the bowels of the building. Grace had downloaded it straight into her mind. Du Bois felt more comfortable watching it on his phone's screen. He'd never quite come to terms with merging with technology.

The CCTV footage only offered glimpses of the individual who had freed Silas. Those images were indeterminate, showing a flickering, vibrating, ghostlike vision of a screaming woman.

'Hmm,' Grace said. Du Bois noticed that she'd sent him something and opened the link in his phone. It was a clip from a recent horror film which showed exactly the same vibrating woman. Du Bois sent an intelligent program into the hospital's security systems to upgrade it sufficiently so du Bois could perform a more thorough diagnostic. It would take a while due to the limits of the hospital's computer system.

They were moving further and further into the older and less used parts of the hospital. The guard with them was giving every indication of becoming more and more uncomfortable.

'Mr Patel?' du Bois said. 'We can handle it from here. We'll buzz you when we need to get out.'

'Are you sure?' the guard began. Du Bois reassured the man and sent him on his way, whilst Grace looked bored.

'Think he was frightened of ghosts?' Grace asked as soon as the guard was out of earshot. They were underground now, in a vaulted corridor made from the same red brick as the rest of the original buildings.

'I think if Scab was locked down here, then genuinely odd things could have happened. It would be understandable if the staff didn't like it.' Du Bois reviewed the location of the oubliette and wondered, 'How did they know?'

'That Silas was here? We live in the world of mass communication, even in the world of black tech. Someone, somewhere always knows, and someone, somewhere always puts it out there.'

'You think we have a leak?'

'She would've known.'

'The traitor? She'd gone before we captured him.'

'She would've known, but frankly a reasonably intuitive L-tech program could have heard about the events in Birmingham and Switzerland and worked out the details itself. Do you not remember that craziness we found in Lubyanka Square?'

Du Bois looked unconvinced. They had come to a heavy cell door. It was the only door in the corridor and it was actually bonded to the frame around it. Du Bois sent the code. The door unsealed itself and swung open.

'And suddenly I want my gun,' he muttered.

'You're a very insecure person.'

Grace pushed the door open and stepped into the dark room. Du

Bois followed, his eyes adjusting immediately, illuminating the near total darkness as if it was daylight.

'Who's doing it?' Grace asked him. Du Bois removed the small carbon fibre punch-blade disguised as a belt buckle and passed it to her. 'You realise with my look, you're stereotyping me?'

'Rank has its privileges,' du Bois muttered as he knelt down next to the man-sized hole in the floor. He'd seen oubliettes before. They were usually secured by a metal hatch with a grate in it. This one had been sealed over by the stone floor. It must have been like being buried alive, standing upright.

'Age has its privileges,' Grace muttered as she drew the blade across the pale skin of her arm. Blood welled in the wound but it didn't bleed. Instead the nanites in her body reproduced and dispersed into the surrounding area as a nano-screen. The tiny molecule-sized machines settled on every surface, searching for information.

The stench in the oubliette was indescribable. Du Bois had to all but switch off his senses of smell and taste to put his head in the hole and look around. He saw crude symbols painted on the stone. He didn't want to think too much about what they'd been painted with. He started to run the images through a recognition program. It was a relief to take his head out of the hole.

'There was no facility for food,' du Bois mused. 'They just left him here to rot.'

'Maybe Mr Brown wanted him punished after all,' Grace suggested absently. Then more attentively: 'So some of the wards had failed. He wasn't going to get out soon but he'd ... Eugh—'

'What?' du Bois asked. Grace was wearing an expression of distinct distaste.

'So he used his nanites, probably instinctively, to create a network. He used matter from his own faeces.'

'Lovely,' du Bois said, grimacing. 'For what?'

'As far as I can tell, it was a receiver.'

'He was learning.' He pointed into the hole. 'Looks like crude rendering of occult symbols. If the program is reading it right – and it consulted one of the sleeping minds on this – then they're a mixture of pop-satanic symbolism.'

'Probably harvested from the Internet. It's how he's rationalising his abilities,' Grace suggested.

Du Bois looked unconvinced. 'He didn't seem the type,' he said.

'Then what?'

'I think he believes he's having some kind of relationship.'

'With Satan?' Grace asked, trying not to laugh.

'With something bad.'

'Like what? Some broken Lloigor information entity that thinks it's a dark god?' she asked.

'Something like that.'

'Here's what I don't understand. You want to imprison this guy, just suspend him – drop his mind into a virtual construct and punish him or keep him happy. But locking him in here on his own, with nothing to do except feed on his own body and never die – that's only going to do one thing—'

'Make him madder,' du Bois finished.

Grace nodded and then went back to concentrating. 'I've found something else.' Du Bois glanced at her. 'Tiny traces, I nearly missed them. It looks like the nanites that broke the wards and did the matter-hack to let him out self-destructed when they were finished.'

'Brass City?' du Bois asked.

'This feel like their kind of madness?'

Du Bois had to concede that it did not. 'L-tech? S-tech?'

Grace was shaking her head. 'I can't tell. The Egg Shell?' She said the last hopefully.

'If they exist, I don't think this would be their sort of thing, either. I suspect we're dealing with an independent, or rogue tech. Perhaps a possessor.'

'Brilliant.'

Du Bois stood and brushed himself off. He had decided that before he got into the car he was going to use his nano-screen to hunt down every scent molecule native to this hole and destroy it.

'Birmingham?' du Bois asked.

'Yaay!' Grace cheered sarcastically.

Du Bois received the results of his interrogation of the CCTV system. He sent a smart worm to destroy his upgrades and erase any trace of their presence in the hospital's systems. He shared the results with Grace as the door closed behind them, and he sent the command codes to seal it again.

'So the CCTV caught the footage of whoever let Silas out. Someone's gone into the system, removed their image and replaced it with—' Grace said.

'These cheap theatrics.' Du Bois interrupted, lighting a cigarette as he walked, desperate to smell and taste something other than the oubliette. 'Do you think the images on the CCTV looked a little immature?'

*

It took them around two and half hours to reach Inge Street in Birmingham. Grace could have got there much quicker but she decided to keep pace with du Bois. They managed to arrive just before the rush hour, when the city's streets all but ground to a halt.

They pulled up by the police cordon around the sex shop. A crowd of angry detectives and forensic investigators were awaiting their arrival. The police had been ordered by the Home Office to keep clear of the scene until du Bois and Grace had shown up.

Du Bois got out of the Range Rover and looked at the police officers glaring at him. He sighed inwardly. Grace took off her crash helmet.

'Surely it's your turn to deal with them?' du Bois said.

'Not me,' Grace said as she climbed off the Speed Triple. 'I'm a biker chick' – she frowned as she started playing with her hair – 'with a very floppy Mohican, so they're not going to listen to me. Besides, you know I'd just end up knocking one of them out.'

'I remain convinced that you only punch them so I'm forced to deal with them.'

A particularly angry-looking, florid, paunchy police officer in uniform was making his way towards du Bois.

'You have such a suspicious mind,' Grace said, and stepped out of the policeman's way.

One screaming argument with a chief superintendent later, Du Bois found himself staring at a vibrator that he thought would be quite uncomfortable for all but the most accommodating of orifices.

'I've got one of those!' Grace said brightly. 'I mean a smaller one.' She looked very pleased when du Bois actually blushed. 'So the vic is—'

'Vic?' du Bois enquired.

'Victim. Okay, I've been watching some police shows.'

'Were they American?'

'You've already got one of those dildos lodged in your arse, haven't you?' an exasperated Grace asked as she looked around at the collection of adult DVDs, sex toys and underwear. 'I've lived too long – this all looks really boring to me.' She grinned at du Bois. 'Still, must make a pleasant change from the hair shirt and self-flagellation.'

'I haven't done that in—' du Bois began before he realised she was making fun of him. He ignored her, concentrating on the task at hand; downloading the information on the victim from the buffer he kept on his phone into his head. Her name was Linda Galforg and she was forty-three years old. She had moved to Birmingham from Somerset to attend art college twenty-five years ago. She dropped out of college but stayed in the city. Unmarried, no children, reported missing by her housemate late last night. She had walked to an appointment less than a quarter of a mile from her home in Kings Norton. She left the appointment but never came home.

'Quick work,' du Bois muttered. Silas had been free for less than twenty-four hours. Du Bois sent search routines out all over the country to see if he could trace Silas's whereabouts from the moment he left Broadmoor to the time the body walked into the cinema. There was always the slight chance that the two things were unconnected, but he thought it unlikely.

The body had flagged in their system because its temperature put the time of death several hours before Linda Galforg had walked into the adult shop.

'A psychic?' du Bois said.

Grace shrugged. 'Let's go and look at the body.' She sounded a little subdued.

With the lights on, the small, cramped cinema was an unpleasantly seedy affair. Worn seating, threadbare carpets, and everything appeared to be encrusted with dried stains.

Grace crossed her arms. 'I am not inflicting this place on my nanites,' she said with a degree of finality.

Du Bois sighed, drew his tanto and cut across his palm. Grace was looking at the body of the dead woman. Linda Galforg, who'd had a life, experiences, connections and relationships, had been reduced to a limp, lifeless doll, a plaything for a damaged mind. Du Bois could see Grace reliving events more than a hundred years in the past, and knew there was nothing he could do help her. He leaned against the wall and lit a cigarette, sending instructions to the forensically programmed nano-screen to ignore the ash.

'It's him,' du Bois said after what felt like an interminable wait for results. Then he shook his head. 'Her brain is missing.'

Grace stared at him. 'That's a little B-movie, isn't it?' she asked, disgusted.

'He mended the skull after he opened it. The nanites formed a small CPU – enough to control her nervous system, to animate her.'

'Anything else?' Grace asked.

'There's a lot of semen residue in this room.'

Grace stared at him, her sense of humour gone. Du Bois frowned as he started receiving new information from the forensic nano-screen. Linda Galforg stood up. Grace was already reaching for her pistols and backing away from the reanimated corpse. Du Bois held his hand up, motioning for Grace to hold position. He stepped out of the way as the woman lurched towards him. When she reached the blank white screen, she fumbled in the pocket of her skirt for a lipstick, which she used to write the words 'I lied' clumsily on the screen. Then she turned to look at du Bois.

'Shit,' he swore under his breath. 'Come on,' he said to Grace. The corpse opened its mouth and let out a rasping scream. Then ignited. The nanite-fuelled conflagration fed on the flesh it burned. Du Bois and Grace beat a hasty retreat as the cinema caught fire and headed back into the street.

'What triggered it?' Grace whispered before they were overwhelmed by questions as smoke started pouring out of the sex shop.

'My investigation, the nano-screen. He was waiting for me.'

'I really want this guy,' Grace said.

Du Bois could hear the repressed fury in her voice.

11
A Long Time After the Loss

Elodie Negrinotti strode along the walkway miles above the surface of Ubaste. The planet had started off as a Rakshasa park world, named for one of the felines' semi-mythic ancestral heroes, a warrior queen. When the Consortium arrived in the system, it had briefly become a conflict resolution world, but there was a push to preserve its natural resources. During its exploited phase, Ubaste was wealthy enough to spend just under a century as a Consortium core world. Its glory days were now long gone, but a central position along a number of Red Space trade routes meant that the planet had not fallen as far as New Coventry – or worse, Cyst.

Like most former core worlds, Ubaste was a planet-sized city built over a resource-gutted planet. They ran out of ground space quickly, so they built up. Many of the starscrapers pierced the atmosphere, and each of the massive buildings contained a population equivalent to that of a pre-Loss city. The lower levels never saw light from the system's sun. Many of the buildings had acquired shanty towns of platform settlements molecularly bonded to the vertical arcologies.

From up high the planet looked like a labyrinthine collection of deep canyons. Few people ever left their home arcology, and when the inhabitants of Ubaste did travel, it was largely via the skyways, skyline and, more rarely, skywalks between the buildings. Very few of them could afford personal G-carriers.

At this height, on an open skywalk, Elodie needed an oxygen mask to augment her internal systems. Her nano-screen was also pushed to its limit resisting the high levels of nano-pollution, which were far worse in the open than inside the filter-protected arcologies. She had heard stories of naturally occurring nano-swarms formed of ancient nano-advertising viruses. There had even been unconfirmed reports of nano-storms.

Elodie was tall, slender and long-legged. Like a lot of other felines, she moved in a way that accentuated her assets, though it looked less forced with her than many. She was comfortable with her body and carried herself with an easy confidence. Elodie had modified her appearance to look more human. Her skin was a dark brown, her short, downy fur the same colour as her skin, and her whiskers were mostly gone. But while her facial features favoured the human augment, her eyes were the pure vertical slits of a cat and her pointed ears also showed her true heritage. Her long black hair hung down almost to her knees in a complex braid tipped with a silver-coloured metal ornament that came to vicious-looking point.

The feline showed little in the way of hard-tech augments, which suggested extensive soft-machine augmentation. She wore a 'sect-made segmented armoured bodice resembling part of a chitinous exoskeleton and thigh-length high-heeled boots.

It was Elodie's P-Sat, a simple but elegant black sphere floating just over her left shoulder, that detected the other pedestrian coming towards her across the windy skywalk. Her nano-screen was too busy trying to cope with the nanite pollution. The fact that anyone else was out here at all warned her that something was going on. She sent the P-sat to loop under the walkway and set the device to running active scans, but to no avail – either the interference from the nano-pollution was too great or her devices were being jammed by someone with a great deal of skill and a surprising degree of subtlety. Elodie stopped and had a good look around. She couldn't see anyone else, but the massive steel-coloured buildings surrounding her limited her vision.

The figure approaching her looked like a human, a hairless monkey. One of their baseline genders, a pure female despite the completely hairless head. She wore loose-fitting black clothing and walked like a seasoned fighter, someone who'd learned through practice, training and experience rather than via hardwired off-the-shelf skills. Elodie had learned the difference the hard way many years ago. Above her, the pale light of the sun was trying to make its way through the star-scraper spires and the nano-haze, with limited success. Everything about the bald woman screamed Church monk.

Elodie glanced behind her, but she knew that if the other woman was there for her – and it seemed unlikely that this was a bizarre coincidence – then they'd have her retreat covered. She felt the first spots of gritty rain touch her skin as the beleaguered weather-control system attempted to use what was left of the planet's water system as a heat sink. She looked up and decided to let the other woman come to her. She put her hands on her hips. Her P-sat was 'facing imagery and sensor data direct to her neunonics.

Fuck you, Scab, Elodie thought.

'Elodie Negrinotti?' the woman asked.

'No,' Elodie suggested.

'I think you are.'

'Then why did you ask? I know what you want, and I haven't seen him in more than ten standards.' Then she saw what she was looking for – a slight atmospheric disturbance just behind the woman. Something was definitely jamming her P-sat's active scans, and they were smart enough to use the ambient nano-pollution to help them do so. They were good and they were packing high-end cloaks. 'I've had every bounty killer and wannabe in the surrounding systems 'face me or visit me, demanding to know where he is. I don't know, I don't care and I don't owe him anything. Now I'm going to get on with my day, okay?'

Elodie started to move past the Monk. The Monk moved slightly to stand in the feline's way.

'Look,' Elodie said, trying to hold onto her waning patience, 'you have resources and appear to know what you're doing, so you must know I'm more trouble than I'm worth, and all you'd get is exactly what I've just told you.'

'How many of them did you kill?'

'Everyone that didn't take the hint. You know what I do for a living, right?' Elodie said, simultaneously trying to keep her temper and look for more of the atmospheric disturbances.

'You're a kick-murder and intrusion specialist. You work physical as well as information intrusion. In short, you're a thief and a murderer.'

'I only murder when the thieving isn't going well.' *Like now.*

'You're also one of the few bounties who got away from Scab. Or, more accurately, that he allowed to get away.'

Elodie was pretty sure she heard disgust in the Monk's voice. *Is this where the hostility is coming from? She thinks I whored myself.*

'If you think I fucked him and he let me go, then you know as little about me as you do about him. I can't help you, you judgmental bitch.'

The Monk bristled in a way that didn't strike Elodie as terribly professional. There was something about her that was getting under the human's skin. Perhaps she was just another human racist, envious of the effortless sexual attractiveness of the female feline.

'We don't believe that's the case. I don't think he has been in contact with you because he has no use for you at the moment. But other than his partner, Vic Matto, you're probably the person with

119

the greatest insight into him. We think this insight could aid us in finding him.'

'What's he done?' Elodie asked, genuinely interested now.

'That doesn't matter. We'll pay you the going rate for your services.'

Elodie was nodding, trying to look interested. 'I'm expensive.'

'I bet.'

'Well, let's agree on a price so I can at least pretend I have a choice in this.'

'How much—'

Elodie scorpion-kicked the Monk. The Monk staggered back as her nose spread over her face, blood squirting from the nostrils. Elodie took a step and executed a reverse turning kick. It made contact with something, apparently in empty air, just behind the Monk. The soft-tech-augmented kick impacted hard enough to crack the cloaked militia soldier's composite combat armour and the soldier staggered into the Monk. The soldier's form was revealed as their armour struggled to project an image of the surroundings fast enough to react to the sudden movement and maintain the cloak.

Elodie's braid darted forwards over her head. The pointed ornament on the end of the braid was now a potent viral-delivering stinger. Cross-eyed and frantic, the Monk clapped her hands together, capturing the braid, the dripping point inches from her face. Elodie cartwheeled backwards, tearing the braid out of the Monk's grip. Elodie's foot caught the Monk in the chin, hard. The Monk's reinforced bones stopped the blow from powdering her jaw, but the force of the kick sent her staggering back into two of the cloaked militia.

Elodie kicked another militiaman coming up behind her as she completed the cartwheel, her boot catching him in the head with enough force to crack his helmet. Back on her feet, Elodie ran at the skywalk's railing. One foot on the railing and then she was over and diving gracefully into Ubaste's sky, miles above the surface. Her P-sat zipped after her.

The Monk was angry. It wasn't that Elodie was necessarily faster or better than her. It was a sucker kick, but a good one. The Monk hadn't seen it coming, hadn't read the movement in Elodie's body.

'All units move in,' the Monk 'faced to all her personnel. The twenty or so militia on the bridge with her became fully visible. They would be moving too fast for the cloaks on their combat armour to be effective once they stepped off the skywalk and into the air. The weak AG drives on the P-sats clipped to their armour slowed and guided their fall, sending them after Elodie. The Monk threw herself off the skywalk into free-fall, her augmented vision just about able to make out the plummeting feline. Four G-carriers banked around a nearby building and sped after their prey. There was no way she could escape now. It was just a question of how long the feline wanted to draw this out.

Elodie had dropped several miles, travelling at terminal velocity in the .8 G. She was heading for the side of one of the other arcologies. She held out one hand and her speeding P-sat extruded a handgrip. *One day this isn't going to work*, she thought as molecular hooks on the handle bonded to her palm. Her neunonics sent signals to her soft-machine-augmented physiology and the correct muscle groups and joints were reinforced. It was still going to hurt. She 'faced the order to the P-sat to brake. The P-sat tried to reverse her momentum and pull her arm out of its socket. As she hit the side of the starscraper, hard, she bent her knees, augmented physiology managing to absorb most of the impact, but it was still jarring. Sharp, predatory teeth clattered painfully together.

Aided by the P-sat, she was running horizontally around the building. Scan data told her that the Monk had hit the arcology starscraper behind her and was giving chase with the aid of her own P-sat. Presumably that had been cloaked as well. The militia were landing behind the Monk.

More worrying were the G-carriers. One of them dropped down level with her, its coaxial strobe gun tracking her movement. She killed the P-sat's AG drive and pushed off the building back into free-fall. The G-carrier dropped into a dive after her. There was another behind that and two more spiralling down, trying to lock on to her position from further out.

It was a long dive. Elodie took them out of the weak sunlight and into Ubaste's dark levels where the lights on the arcology starscraper windows resembled a strangely regular star field. She gave herself much longer to decelerate this time. It still hurt her arm. Nanites flooded to the area, trying to repair damage to strained muscles and stressed joints. She still hit the side of the enormous building hard. She slid down the outer wall, her armour protecting her, using the P-sat to slow her descent. She landed on the roof of one of the parasitical shanty-town buildings bonded to the side of the arcology starscraper. She heard shouting from within the structure.

The Monk hit the side of the starscraper level with the shanty-town rooftops and started running horizontally along the building towards Elodie with the aid of her P-sat. Elodie beckoned the other woman towards her. Two of the G-carriers dropped down to cover her but they'd had all the time in the world to burn her out of the sky and they hadn't done it. They could try killing her and pick her up when she cloned, but her clone insurance was black and they couldn't guarantee they'd find her before she was back on the street.

The armoured militia started landing on the roof.

Time to teach some lessons. She axe-kicked the closest militiaman in the head, cracking his helmet. Her P-sat started firing its laser, momentarily lighting up the energy-dissipation matrices on their combat armour. The Monk's P-sat opened fire on Elodie's. The feline couldn't risk losing it. Elodie's P-sat stopped firing and plummeted out of sight. She was already spinning to face the next militia soldier. The sting on her braid shot through the cracked helmet of the militia soldier she'd kicked, found warm flesh and injected its viral venom. He started to fall, already dead, until his P-sat caught him, dangling him in mid-air.

Elodie went low and swept the legs out from underneath another militiaman with a tail. She assumed he was a lizard. As he fell off the side of the building, she 'faced a hack to his P-sat. Church security resisted the hack for a moment, but this was what she did for a living. His P-sat unclipped itself from his armour. He started screaming as he dropped. Elodie continued spinning.

The Monk was charging Elodie as she leaped at the next militiawoman. The Monk was in the air, a flying kick aimed at Elodie's back when Elodie landed on the militiawoman. Her right hand shot forwards, hardened claws penetrating the helmet's reflective visor and the militiawoman's flesh. The momentum of the blow carried both of them off the roof and into the side of one of the hovering G-carriers. The militiawoman's P-sat sprang its clip. Elodie knew she wasn't going to be able to pull that trick too many more times – the Church's electronic warfare specialists would be on to her now. Both of them dropped. The Monk flying-kicked the side of the G-carrier and dropped after them.

Elodie pushed the dead militiawoman away from her. Her envenomed claws had done their work. She controlled her free-fall and reached out. She felt her P-sat's handle and grasped it. The P-sat was under relentless electronic attack now. Elodie knew how to protect her own gear, but they would get through eventually. Still, three of them were dead. Two more had scrambled uploads and would have to use older backups when they were cloned.

One of the G-carriers dropped in front of her and she used the AG to change course again. Her arm was almost pulled out of its socket and she hit the top of the G-carrier a lot harder than she wanted. The

G-carrier stopped. The four roof-mounted strobe guns turned towards her, but she ignored them. When one of the roof hatches opened, she started to run. The militiaman was climbing out of the hatch when she punted him in the head, cracking the visor on his helmet and breaking even his reinforced neck. As he started to slip back into the G-carrier, Elodie let go of the P-sat and caught him. She pulled him out of the hatch. A different hack to a different part of the militia-man's kit activated the four thermal grenades on his webbing. The Monk landed on the G-carrier behind her just as Elodie dropped the militiaman back into the vehicle, cartwheeled to one side and then somersaulted off the side. Above her the G-carrier lurched and then started to drop, smoke pouring from the open hatch. The Monk had thrown herself off the vehicle and was diving after Elodie.

As the P-sat struggled to stop her momentum, Elodie felt something rip in her arm and screamed. She hit the roof of a shanty-town structure messy and hard and staggered to her feet. She didn't like how easy the Monk made her landing look. G-carriers swooped in level with her. The militia started dropping in, keeping their distance, landing on other structures nearby, covering her with their advanced combat rifles.

The downpour intensified. She flinched as rain turned to steam in the red laser light as one of the strobe guns on the closest G-carrier took out her P-sat.

'Finished?' the Monk asked.

'I think I'll force you to kill me. See if you can find me, and then we'll play chase again, on my terms.'

'You understand who we are, right?' the Monk asked, obviously struggling to control her temper. 'The amount we'll pay for you? Whoever your black-market clone insurance is with will offer you up gladly. Cost us money, but frankly save us the hassle.'

'Fine. You still have to come and get me.'

'Oh, for Christ's sake.' The Monk shook her head. 'Realise it's over.'

'Was it worth it?' Elodie asked.

'They'll be cloned! We could stop that happening to you!'

'Why are you so angry?' Elodie wondered out loud. 'You know him, don't you?' The Monk didn't answer but it was written all over her face. She knew Scab and hated him.

'I could try and explain this to you,' the Monk replied, 'the im-portance of finding him, but you wouldn't understand. You see, it involves being able to look beyond your own gratification, your own selfishness, and I just don't think any of you people would get it.' She sounded genuinely exasperated. Elodie thought about her words and dismissed them. They were just people trying to grab what they could. Scab had clearly got in the way of something the Church wanted.

'You know he'll kill you, don't you? I mean *properly* kill you.'

'What for? Messing with his girl?' the Monk mocked. Elodie was surprised, and a little concerned, that the Monk wasn't using the conversation as an opportunity to close with her. 'Is it love?' she asked sarcastically.

Elodie's laugh was humourless. 'Never.' *Not with Scab.* 'Ready?'

The Monk just shook her head. The burst from the ACR hit Elodie in the knee. The armour-piercing tips of the caseless rounds tore through her armoured boots and her armoured skin. The rounds exploded when the smart bullets sensed flesh around them and the bottom part of Elodie's left leg spun off. She cried out and collapsed onto the roof as pain shot through her. Her internal augments flooded her system with analgesics, shutting off the pain reaction in her brain.

Controlling herself, Elodie stared at the Monk, shaking with a rage born of helplessness. The Monk kept her distance, but knelt down so she was level with Elodie.

'What is it with you people? Does sociopathy so heavily outweigh common sense? You're coming with me. I'll take you apart piece by piece if I have to. You won't be the only fucking self-inflicted quadriplegic helping us with our fucking enquiries, believe me.'

'One day we're going to revisit this.'

'I don't care who's harder. It can be you. Can we just get going, or do you need to lose more limbs fir—' There was a rush of air, Elodie's mask was torn off her face and it became hard to breathe. Everything was bathed in red. Incredible heat bubbled and blistered the skin of the feline's neck and the Monk disappeared, replaced by a cloud of red steam.

Something tried to suck Elodie off the roof. She dug her claws in, panels of the composite roofing material tearing off and tumbling past her. She watched as a lizard-made power disc cut the face off the nearest militiaman to her. Over the roaring from the powerful sucking wind she heard the sound of firearms and superheated air exploding so rapidly it became a constant noise, one bang running into the next.

Ordnance hit the militia around her, destroying sections of their armour and exploding the flesh beneath it, leaving behind messy red cavities. Others were lit up, dressed in the neon of heavy laser fire, the energy-dissipation grids on their armour rapidly overwhelmed, the flesh beneath superheated and cooked inside the fused armour.

Parts of the arcology were scorched or burst open as militia and the structures they'd been standing on ceased to exist in bursts of red light. An explosion bounced Elodie into the side of the arcology and she dropped back onto the roof of the shanty-town structure. Her neunonics were telling her all the ways she was hurt now. The sucking wind started dragging her across the roof again and her claws made deep rents in the composite material. She watched militia torn off the roof and then shot or lasered in the air.

Everything had happened so quickly, it was only now that she turned to look behind her. She was bathed in the blood-coloured light of Red Space and her mind struggled to deal with the concept of the rent in space inside Ubaste's atmosphere. A ship was coming through the rent. She didn't recognise the configuration – it looked custom, expensive. Its smart-matter hull was flexing and changing the ship's configuration, presumably for atmospheric operations. A yacht, she guessed, but a heavily armed one. Its laser batteries raked the side of the arcology, seeking out and utterly destroying the fleeing militia. One of the G-carriers was already superheated wreckage tumbling into the darkness. The other two had dived, all eight of their top and bottom strobe guns rotating at full speed, pouring laser fire onto the ship but barely making its energy-dissipation grid glow.

A ramp was open at the front of the ship. There were two figures on it. One of them was just short of seven feet tall and had four arms. His lower limbs were firing a strobe gun. His upper limbs were firing an ACR. The other figure was shorter, only two arms. He was clipping an empty automatic shotgun to the back of his servo-assisted combat armour with one hand whilst smoothly drawing a double-barrelled laser rifle with an underslung disc gun over the other shoulder. He started firing short, rapid double bursts, killing the remaining militia as efficiently as he could. The ship was moving ever closer to her.

Elodie heard panicked screams from within as the shanty town structure started to fall away from the starscraper. The nose of the ship dipped as it surged forwards, the open hatch closing on her like an open mouth, tearing up the roof as it approached. She tried to fall into it and felt power-assisted hard-tech hands grab her armoured bodice, crushing it as they gripped and yanked her inside the craft. She fell against someone as the ramp closed and the craft reared up, rose and banked hard. There was a disconcerting moment before the ship's G-field kicked in and she was able to tell which way was down.

She looked up at the big four-limbed 'sect holding her. 'Hey, Vic.'
'Hi, Elodie.'
'You guys have really fucked up this time, haven't you?'

'You have no idea, darling. I'm going to put you down. Hold on to my P-sat, okay?'

Elodie nodded. The big 'sect lowered her to the deck and his P-sat – handgrip already extruded – zipped around to hover by her head. She reached for it and took a quick glance around. She was in a well-equipped loading bay.

'What happened to the *Basilisk*?'

'Scab sacrificed it to the Church.'

'Yeah, they really want to speak to him.'

On the other side of the airlock/loading bay, Scab was already taking off his combat armour's helmet.

'You making their life difficult?' Vic asked, following her gaze to Scab.

'Well, they didn't ask nice. I really don't like that bald bitch, and she seems really angry with Scab. What'd he do, fuck her?' she asked absently, still looking at Scab, who was ignoring her as he unclipped his armour.

'No,' Vic said. 'Yes.' He thought for a moment. 'Not really. It was complicated. They weren't themselves.'

'Vic,' Scab said. 'Shut up.'

Elodie turned back to Vic, put her arm around his head and pulled him down to her level to kiss the armoured chitin.

'Thanks,' she said.

'Sorry we bought trouble your way,' the 'sect replied.

Elodie started to hop towards Scab with the P-sat's help. Her internal drug supply meant she was feeling no pain now and her knee had healed into a stump.

'I don't like your new girlfriend,' Elodie told him. Scab ignored her. He was almost naked now. 'How'd we get away? Are we in Red Space?' Scab still didn't say anything.

'Yeah,' Vic said from behind her.

'I thought you couldn't do that,' she said.

'Church secret, and the *Basilisk II* here is rocking one of their stolen bridge drives.'

Elodie glared at Scab, fear and anger warring within her. Engines weren't transferable. Any messing with bridge tech usually junked it, and then you got a visit from the Church. Anyone capable of successfully swapping engines had to have Church knowledge. That was heresy. And the Church hunted down and exterminated heretics, destroying their ships and anyone even remotely connected to them. At best. There hadn't been a heresy capable of manipulating bridge tech in over a thousand standard years.

'Is that why my life is being disturbed? Is that why I'm half a leg short?'

'Not even close,' Vic said.

'Vic,' Scab began, just the trace of a warning in his dead voice.

'Fuck, and you, Scab,' Vic said quietly.

Elodie stared at Vic. Nobody spoke to Scab like that. Certainly the Vic she knew wouldn't have dared. Scab, naked now, straightened up to look at his 'sect partner.

'What?' Vic demanded over Elodie's head. 'Threats getting a little redundant now?'

'Which means I have to start acting on them.'

'Fine. I'll go and plug myself into a torture immersion.'

Scab opened his mouth but Elodie got in first.

'Hey,' she said. 'Why am I here? That wasn't a rescue – you don't do that.'

'I need you,' Scab said simply.

'Of course you do,' she said angrily. 'Getting in somewhere, or getting something out?'

'Getting someone out.'

'Where?'

'Suburbia.'

Vic started muttering angrily behind her.

'It can't be done,' Elodie said.

'You had contingencies in case you ever got caught.'

'No, I had ideas.'

'I'll take ideas.'

'You're like a meat-grinder, aren't you?' Elodie demanded. 'Unrelenting.'

Scab crossed the deck to her. She grabbed his face. Envenomed nails pierced armoured skin and smoking, poisoned blood scored a line in his make-up.

'I will kill you,' she told him, and meant it.

She heard mandibles clatter together behind her and detected a release of pheromones. It was what passed for a 'sect chuckling. Scab just shook his head.

'That's not the way I'll be going out.' He 'faced a command to the ship and the airlock/loading bay opened into the plush interior of the yacht. Elodie saw a terrified-looking, attractive, young human woman dressed in black, gauzy clothing. She was staring at Elodie. Scab picked the feline up and carried her past the other human.

'Who the fuck is she?' the woman demanded.

'Fuck you, monkey girl,' Elodie told her. She was doubtless another one of Scab's victims.

'Fuck! Fuck! Fuck!'

The *Templar*'s AI, dressed in full knightly regalia, watched the recently cloned human rage. There was little in the clone lab to destroy but soft-machine-augmented muscles were denting panels. The phrase was bandied about, but few people ever saw a genuinely murderous rage.

They'd had to reconstruct the last moments of her memory from footage of the confrontation with Elodie on Ubaste. She'd died too quickly, and there had been too little of her left to upload.

With a sigh, the AI overrode the Monk's internal systems and flooded them with enough sedative to calm her down. He was only able to do this because she was so recently cloned that the medical systems still had access to her neunonics. Even so, it took a while for her to calm down. A couch grew out of the smart matter for her to slump into.

'I need you composed.'

'Fucking twice,' she spat. 'The same way both times.'

'Which suggests that he doesn't want to take you down personally.'

'Don't fucking placate me,' she snapped. The image of the AI stared at her. AI copy or not, he wouldn't tolerate being spoken to like that. 'Sorry,' she said, calming herself with difficulty. 'It didn't stop him in the Living Cities.'

'I think that was a test. He hides shrewdness behind psychosis, but he's more calculating than he appears.'

'Benedict/Scab was right. He took the drive out of the *St. Brendan's Fire* so he could bridge into atmosphere.'

'So where did he acquire the expertise to do that?' the AI asked.

'The Church,' the Monk said. 'A breakaway heretical sect? But we wiped out any with that knowledge millennia ago.'

'And yet ...'

'I thought you were supposed to be an angrier, more warlike and less irritating version of him.' The *Templar* was the fastest light cruiser in the Church fleet. As a warship its AI was based on a younger, more aggressive version of Churchman.

'Somebody has knowledge they shouldn't possess. And Benedict/Scab also predicted he'd go for Miss Negrinotti—'

'No,' the Monk said. 'He guessed.'

'Nevertheless, he guessed right. Which means he requires her skills for something.'

'He got lucky, but it suggests he wants to steal something. Steal what? He already has the most valuable thing in Known Space.'

'Or he wants to break in somewhere. But why bother?' the *Templar*'s AI asked. 'Pythia was a test run. He needs to find a way to profit from what he has without being destroyed, that will be difficult.'

'So one of the Citadels? The Cathedral?'

'As with Miss Negrinotti, the answer has to lie with what he knows. His past.'

The Monk sighed. 'He's on board, then?' she asked.

'Transferred from the poor *Lazerene* as she limped back towards the Cathedral. Still limbless, no neunonics, and I'm holding him in a secure airlock.'

'Therapeutically, I need to kill him.'

The AI knew she didn't mean it. She wasn't that sort of person. But she had meant it before the sedative, when she'd been caught in a rage.

The door opened. In the constant light pollution, the diminutive figure with the tall hat sitting in the wicker bath chair cast a long shadow. The chair rolled forwards. Security had deprived him of his faceless automaton attendants. In front of him was a marble desk so large it looked like a piece of pre-Loss architecture. The tall man behind the desk was difficult to make out even with augmented eyes. The harsh glare from the large window, which looked out onto the core world's crowded high orbit, turned everything into a silhouette.

The lizard 'faced an instruction to the bath chair and it stopped just in front of the desk. The door closed behind him like a tomb being sealed. He wasn't sure – information on the man behind the desk had proved elusive – but the lizard had the feeling he was on the board.

'I like your reputation,' the human started. His voice was so deep that the lizard found himself becoming aroused by the vibrations. With a thought he rearranged biochemical stimuli so he didn't embarrass himself. 'Unlike many bounty killers, you are not simply a gunman. You know how investigate, how to track.'

'I come from a clan of hunters.'

The tall human's nod was slow, almost ponderous. 'Can you find him?'

'With the resources you're offering me? I believe so.'

Mr Hat suddenly found himself in credit.

12
Ubh Blaosc

Hollow animal skulls looked upon her. The horse of winter held her down on the warm, moss-covered stone altar. She knew it had been a trick. The ritual sex, the joining with Fachtna, it was in preparation. They wanted her with child. That would make the sacrifice all the more powerful. One life, some of it spent, and a new life, full of potential.

She tried to struggle but the frail-looking hand was surprisingly strong. Words were spoken from behind bone in a language she almost understood and she froze, unable to move. Then she really started to panic. There was another robed figure wearing an animal skull standing over her. Britha was sure this one was a woman under the bone. She moved a wand of ash over Britha's naked body, chanting some kind of invocation as she did so. Britha tried to shout at her but found she had no voice.

The horse of winter was smearing some kind of ointment onto her skin. It was disappearing as it touched her, almost as if it was being sucked through into her body.

The female animal skull held up the wand. Britha was sure she saw some kind of glow from within the bone mask. The horse of winter was looking at the female animal skull, who nodded. Britha heard herself scream as blackness engulfed her.

Her own cries woke her as she sat bolt upright on the cot, touching her stomach. Nausea overwhelmed her. She scrambled out from between the furs and grabbed for a bronze bowl close to the smouldering fire pit. She just managed to get hold of it before she started to throw up. There were muttered complaints from some of the others trying to sleep in Fachtna's hall.

Britha sat down, feeling miserable, her buttocks on the warm stone floor, the bowl of vomit cradled in her lap, and looked back into the cot she now shared with Fachtna. He hadn't woken. He slept soundly. Peaceful. Beautiful. It had been so easy. He was not the Fachtna she had known back in her own world. This one was gentle, softly spoken, strong but not boorish, capable but not arrogant. After she had gone with him to the grove, after they had lain together on the stone altar, it had been so easy to keep doing that and time had passed. He was well made, and not unskilled as a lover.

Though no rites had been performed, she lived as a royal lady. She wanted for nothing. She did not work her magics any more. She was not required for childbirth, nor sickness, nor animal husbandry.

She was not herself and she knew it. There was so little strength left in her. People didn't respect or fear her, and they didn't seek out her wisdom. She didn't inflict her will on them, not even when she knew herself to be right.

She remembered the spear speaking to her, the demon in wood and iron urging her towards blood, to make wounds in others. She remembered the sickening feeling, the violation, of Crom Dhubh whispering to her inside her head. The agony of the crystal in her mind. The connection to the Muileartach. That had not been her, either. There had been so many conflicts inside her. Voices foreign to her flesh. When had she last been herself? Had she been herself with Cliodna? Had the selkie done something to her? If she could not recall when she had last been herself, what difference did it make? Let Fachtna provide for her. Make the hard decisions. Shoulder the burdens. Though in this land of plenty, her lover's responsibilities appeared light indeed. The people were healthy and strong, as were the animals, and the crops abundant.

Except she remembered what Fachtna told her when she first arrived: 'I went to war. The drui *put certain geasa on me. They change us. As warriors we have to behave a certain way.*' Perhaps it had been a long time since she was last herself, but she didn't recall being the soft and compliant creature she had become. All the knowledge she had learned about the fair folk told her that you should not eat of their food, or drink of their drink. She had done both. Had they glamoured her? Geased her? Changed the way she thought?

Yes, this was comfortable, easy. Yes, it had been a hard time before she was reborn in the cauldron, but she did not like the way that her oaths, her duties to the Cirig, her people, felt so distant. As if that life had happened to another person. As if the memory was wrapped in heavy fog.

Nausea surged through her again. She drooled and spat vomit into the bowl.

Fachtna was awake when she finally climbed back into the pallet they shared. He didn't say anything to her, just wrapped his long, powerful arms around her and held her. Strong, calloused fingers

131

found just the right points on her back to rub and press to ease her discomfort. He kissed her hair.

And Fachtna was nearly perfect. Accepting him was easiest of all. Except he wasn't Cliodna. Except he wasn't Bress.

Maybe this is happiness, she thought, *and I just can't accept it*. She felt Fachtna touch her stomach. *Of course I would end up with child*, Britha thought, *the* dryw *lie for the good of their people*. She knew this because she had done it all the time. *Back when I was a ban draoi*. Distantly she wondered when she had stopped being one.

The chariot was sleek and fast. Its armoured skin looked like handsomely carved wood inlaid with semi-precious and precious metals. Not too ostentatious, just enough to let you know that the warrior who rode in it was someone of rank and means.

Teardrop shaded his eyes from the sun to watch it land. There was nothing difficult about the manoeuvre but it was obvious that the charioteer knew what he was doing. Part of the larger rear section – the weapon's cupola – split open and Fachtna stepped out onto the plain. He walked to the arrowhead-shaped forward compartment and spoke a few words to Adarc, his charioteer. He was dressed in thin woollen trews and a light shirt, his skin already darkening. The Forge burned fierce, hot and close above them. They were beyond the shade of Lug here. Teardrop was more bemused than insulted that his friend still wore a sword and dagger at his hip. No torc, though, he noted. His position notwithstanding, the metal got hot in this climate.

Fachtna walked through the haze and dust towards the Croatan. He smiled and held out his hand. They grasped forearm to forearm, and Teardrop pulled the grinning Gael to him as they hugged. Stepping back, Fachtna looked down at Teardrop's lean, hard body. The other man was stripped to the waist, wearing only buckskin leggings and calf-length moccasins. His long, dark hair was tied back in a simple braid.

'You're looking good,' Fachtna said. There was little or no fat on Teardrop's lean frame. 'The warrior's path must agree with you.' For a moment, a shadow appeared to cross Teardrop's face.

'It's a simpler path to walk. It must be if one as foolish as you can excel at it.'

Fachtna laughed, shaking his head. 'Sword, spear – I will meet you with whatever weapon you wish.'

'Wit?'

'And already I see where this conversation is going.'

Teardrop laughed as well then and turned, leading Fachtna towards what appeared to be a large crater in the plain. There were a number of Croatan warriors around the crater, and more further afield on the fast ponies they bred specifically for their warriors. Fachtna knew there would be many more he could not see, and that the Croatans' medicine people would have also spun many protective wards around the site.

'And how is your mortal girl?' Teardrop asked. The humour had gone.

'Don't call her that,' Fachtna said quietly. 'You should visit. She remembers you.'

Teardrop was already shaking his head. 'She does not remember me. Never me. Laughs told me what that Teardrop was like—'

'He was in pain. He was going to die.'

'This' – Teardrop pointed at the crater – 'this is a better way.'

'We didn't know where and when to find Bress,' Fachtna said. Teardrop nodded, looking grim. 'He lives yet.'

'That can't be our problem any more. We've given enough.'

'We didn't give anything.'

Teardrop stopped walking and looked at Fachtna. 'What?'

'What we're doing, it's wrong,' the Gael said.

'Providing for her in a place of plenty. Where she can always be healthy, never has to worry about her next meal, about being attacked. I'm not sure we're quite the monsters you want us to be. If she so chooses, she can stay here, live for ever.'

'We're manipulating her. *I'm* manipulating her.'

Teardrop narrowed his eyes, studying the Gael for a moment. 'We need what she has. These bridges, these trods use too much power. Each use shortens the life of the Forge. If we want to leave, to be able to travel, to see what is beyond this shell—'

'To take the war to the Naga?' Fachtna asked.

This time Teardrop looked irritated. 'To defend ourselves – or are you going to tell me you would not do that?'

'I'm no coward.'

'You fall in love with every mortal you meet, you always have—'

'Three women! Three!'

'You like them because their lives are fleeting, and to you that makes them more vibrant, more alive. Much more so than our staid existence, but we are fighting a war—'

'Very slowly.'

'And she is only one person. We are not going to harm her, but we must harvest the gifts she was given by the—'

'Muileartach.'

'The Seeder.'

'She is carrying our child, and what we are is built on a lie.'

Teardrop put his arm around Fachtna's shoulders. 'You are a romantic. Marry this woman. Have children. Stepping in baby shit will soon drive thoughts of romance from you,' the Croatan told him. Fachtna stopped dead. Teardrop sighed. 'You really like this one?' Fachtna said nothing. 'Then learn to live with the lie. Anything else will lead to misery.'

Fachtna turned and walked away. Teardrop watched him go. It was all a lie. They changed so much, in their bodies, in their heads. Who knew what was real, and what was put there by the *drui*, by the medicine societies?

Teardrop glanced up at the Forge. He could see the pipes trailing down from the sun in the distance, carrying the raw materials they needed to survive, to create, to build, all harvested from the sun. He muttered something that was half a prayer, half a working, to the gods who made this place, whose magic had brought them here. Then he followed Fachtna to the edge of the enormous crater.

The Gael was looking down at the hemispherical scar in the earth. The rock looked raw, and ill-used where it had been removed. Fachtna knew that none of the quarried rock would go to waste, but it still looked ugly to him, a wound.

He concentrated and the distant lowest point of the crater came into focus. He could see the simple circle of standing stones and just about make out the pictograms on the rock. Painted members of one of the Croatan's medicine societies danced among them, chanting, instructing the stones to their purpose. In the centre of the stones was a large, egg-shaped dolmen.

'What did they make it from in the end?' Fachtna asked.

'Quartz,' Teardrop told him. Fachtna nodded. The hard rock would have been made harder still.

'And this will work?' Fachtna asked. Teardrop shrugged. 'A lot of resources wasted if it doesn't.' Fachtna glanced up at the Forge again.

'The auguries were favourable.'

Fachtna rolled his eyes. The medicine people climbed into a large chariot. It lifted off silently and circled lazily around the stones before it started to rise. Teardrop turned away and let out a loud warbling cry. It was answered across the plain as the Croatan warriors warned each other to be ready.

The ground beneath them shook.

*

134

The water was freezing, but Britha had finally warmed up after swimming hard. The crystal-blue water in the cliff-lined fjord was little like the grey northern sea of her home. She'd still had to force Cliodna from her mind.

She reached the rocks just outside Fachtna's village. The dress was where she had left it. It was a warm day, though, so she lay out on the rock, basking in the sun, her hand unconsciously touching her stomach. She was growing more used to the idea of motherhood.

Suddenly it became darker. Britha sat up and looked at the Forge, expecting to see clouds, or even one of Lug's wings stretching across its surface for some reason, despite the hour. Instead her breath caught in her throat as she watched the Forge flicker.

She felt pain in her hand. Something hot and warm. She looked down and saw blood where her nails had pierced the skin of her palm. She stared at the blood. Let it drip down onto the rock and into the water.

The ground stopped shaking as light shone through the pictographic symbols on the stones in the circle. Suddenly there was a pool of black water among the stones. It was gone so quickly that Fachtna knew he had only seen it because of the Lloigor magics the *drui* granted the warrior caste. Then a nearly perfect pillar of water shot miles into the sky as if forced through a hole at tremendous pressure.

'Something's just occurred to me,' Teardrop said.

'We're standing too close, aren't we?' Fachtna said as the column became spray miles above them and started to collapse. Teardrop had already turned and was running for all he was worth. Fachtna followed.

The medicine society had carefully calculated the amount of water that would be displaced and the size of crater needed to contain it. Teardrop and Fachtna, however, had failed to respect the violence of the water's re-entry into the crater.

They had one last moment to gasp at air before the wave hit them both as it spread out across the plain. The force of the water tore them off their feet and then slammed them to the ground, through trees and against any rocks that had somehow remained anchored to the earth.

Fachtna's entire body felt like a very tender and painful bruise. He cried out when he felt bones grind as they knitted together. He gasped for breath and ended up with a mouthful of funny-tasting water. Instinctively he tried to thrash around but more pain shot through his

135

body. Finally he worked out that all he had to do was push his head up. He broke the surface of the water and was able to breathe again. He felt the Forge's heat on his skin.

He was floating on water so clear he could see all the way to the bottom of the crater. Air began to bubble up through the rock walls but Fachtna could still make out the circle of standing stones. The quartz egg had gone.

He felt the disturbance in the air above him. The chariot was hovering just over the water. The rear section split open and a battered-looking Teardrop leaned out, reaching for him.

'You used to be a *drui* and you couldn't work that out beforehand?' Fachtna managed through the pain.

Britha had used the voice of authority, one of the twelve voices she had learned in the groves. Her position as Fachtna's pregnant lover may have had no real standing in the Otherworld, but even the warriors had obeyed her and left the hall. She was waiting for him, alone, when he returned, his clothes torn, his hair a mess, but otherwise he looked well. Though the expression on his face told her he was troubled.

'The Forge?' she asked.

'What of it?' he asked.

She narrowed her eyes. 'Something happened to it today?' she asked. Fachtna nodded. 'You have nothing to say to me?'

'Do you tell me all your secrets?' he demanded. It was the harshest tone he'd ever used with her.

'It's something to do with how you get from the Otherworld back to my world, isn't it?' she demanded.

Fachtna opened his mouth to speak and Britha read the falsehood on his lips before he spoke it. She crossed the stone floor to him quickly.

'Don't,' she said, pointing at him. 'I was ... I *am* a *ban draoi*. Do I need a robe and a hollowed-out horse's head before you'll respect me enough not to lie to me?'

'Yes. We opened a trod.'

'To my home?'

'Not exactly. You could not have gone through – it would have killed you.'

'Your magics never fail, do they?'

'Not so badly that it matters.'

'And they are a gift from your gods?' she asked. Fachtna nodded. 'Do your gods still walk among you?'

'If they do, then they have not revealed themselves to us. There were only plants and animals when we arrived here.'

'You're no different from us, are you?'

Fachtna went and sat down on some furs close to the fire pit and helped himself to a clay mug of heather ale.

'The magics of the Lloigor change us. We can do many things that you cannot. You've seen them.'

'But it is different from the magic of Cliodna – that is the magic of blood and quim, the magic of life,' she said. He nodded. 'Cliodna changed me.' He nodded again. 'And there were no magics before that, were there?' Fachtna said nothing. He wouldn't meet her eyes, either, but the answer was written all over his face. 'It all comes from the gods, doesn't it?'

'It not that simple – the way of healing, the way of birth, the knowledge of man, woman, animal, the laws, the stories—'

'You made the sun dim!' she screamed at him. He looked up at her, alarmed and more than a little frightened, as his instinctual fear and respect for the *drui* took over. She was shaking with anger.

'It was a powerful working.' It was all he could think to say.

'What am I to you?' she demanded. 'A slave? A plaything to be glamoured? A pet? A broodmare?'

Fachtna took a deep breath. He ran his hands through his long, sandy-blond hair, shaking with emotion.

'I love you,' he told her.

She could see the plain truth of it, but she could also see he was holding something back as well.

'Are you sure? I am not what I was,' she said quietly. 'Did you do something?' She was whispering now. It was the voice of fear. Her magics might have been nothing more than words and stories, but this worked. He couldn't look her in the eyes.

'I didn't ...' he started, and then swallowed.

'So who did? Grainne and Sainrith?' she asked. Fachtna nodded. 'Who rules here?' she demanded.

'I do!' Fachtna was on his feet now. Britha was nose to nose with him.

'Are you sure?' He looked away, which was all the answer she needed. 'It doesn't matter how many blessings your gods give, a weak man is a weak man.' The words hit home like a stabbed dirk. 'How is it fair that Talorcan, Cruibne, Feroth, even Nechtan never had any of the power you possess, yet each of them was worth twenty of you, and they are all dead?' she flung at him.

'I don't know what you talk of—'

'I am talking of you being nothing! An empty vessel for the magics of long-forgotten gods! You say you love me. How would you know? You dance to your *dryw*'s tune, hollow man.' She was savaging him now for the sake of it. There was no reason for it other than to cause pain.

'And you never manipulated anyone for the good of your tribe?' he shouted back with such fury that she took a step away, but then regained her ground quickly.

'Manipulated? Perhaps! But not controlled. The women of the Cirig were their own people!' she spat. 'And the men at least had cock and balls, three things you'll be missing if you ever try and touch me again! And the only way you will ever see this child is if you draw your whispering sword and cut it out of me now!' With that, she stormed out of the hall.

Fachtna's head dropped. He was surprised how fast the tears came. Anger, sadness, self-pity and more than a little confusion. She was right. He had no way of knowing which thoughts in his head were his own. He recalled what Teardrop had said to him just before he climbed back into the chariot for the ride home.

'Perhaps they will let you have children in the future, but the first one, the one she carries now, that child is for them.'

Britha had no idea where she was going other than away from Fachtna. Of course they were waiting for her. The *Lain Bhan* and her black horse-skulled consort were standing at the edge of the trees that came up to the hall. She stared at them.

'Take off the skulls,' she demanded through angry tears. The *Lain Bhan*, the white mare who is death, raised her gnarled staff and dropped it back onto the earth. Britha collapsed to the ground.

She awoke once. She was in the grove again. Lying on the altar stone. They leaned over her, the animal skulls long and grotesque. She tried to fight but she was too weak. She fought against sleep as it tried to claim her but she lost the battle even as she felt fingers gently probing her stomach.

'What have you done?' There was genuine horror in Grainne's voice.

Britha tried to move but she only succeeded in making her head loll to one side. Then strong arms were picking her up, lifting her. She recognised the feel of boiled leather against her skin. She felt absurdly pleased when she managed to work out that someone wearing armour was carrying her.

Then she saw the *Lain Bhan*. No, that wasn't right – she had no head. No, she wasn't wearing her skull. *Her name is Grainne,* Britha thought. Through her befuddlement she remembered that she hated Grainne. She tried to spit at her but only drooled on herself. She was naked, she realised. Grainne was staring at them in horror. Britha's head fell forward and she saw the red body on the floor. Sainrith, she remembered. Then realisation of what had happened cut through her fugue.

'Put me down,' she demanded.

'I can't,' Fachtna said.

Grainne was shouting at them in her own language, but Britha knew a curse when she heard one. Fachtna was damned. He had killed a *dryw*. It was just about the worst crime she could think of. Then she touched her stomach. There was nothing. Her skin was smooth and unmarked under her fingers but she knew it was gone. She started to thrash around in his arms. She was looking for it. Expecting to see its tiny bloodied form hanging sacrificially from one of the branches in the grove.

'They've given our child to your gods!' she screamed.

'Stop! Britha, please! She's alive, but you have to stop fighting!'
She?

Then a branch clawed at Fachtna's face, drawing a red rent in his perfect skin. He let go of her with one arm and she all but collapsed to the ground. He was holding her up and trying to drag her along with his left arm. She heard his sword sing. Saw its shimmering ghostly blade as he cleaved the branch. All the trees were coming to life now. The altar stone was sinking, being reclaimed by the earth.

'I can carry you, or I can fight,' he told her.

'I can walk,' she said. Fachtna put her down and she collapsed the rest of the way to the ground. He reached for her. 'No!' She forced herself to her feet. She was in awe of the power she could see as trees moved towards them. Branches reached for her. The sword was a blur. She stared at Grainne, who stood her ground, cursing them. Britha realised that she wanted this power. She wanted to kill Grainne, and she wanted her daughter back.

'Run!' Fachtna shouted.

Still unsteady on her feet, Britha ran into the woods. She tore through branches that grabbed at her, leaped or ducked any that were too large to break through.

She was aware of Fachtna running with her, the sword moving, flowing like liquid light. He fought and stumbled as the now-living trees and undergrowth reached for him.

Britha was trying to push her way past the branches that were wrapping themselves around her bloodied body. It was only a matter of time now. She could hear Fachtna's cries, his beautiful face a mask of dark blood as the trees clawed at him.

The woods were turned to silhouette as a bright light all but blinded her. She felt a force push against her. Heard the sword sing close enough to her that she was sure she had lost hair. She was being dragged. More of her skin was opened as she was pulled free of the grasping trees and pushed into something hard. She felt herself rising. She looked out through an opening and saw the grasping trees dropping past them. Then they were over the woods, broken branches falling from the craft as the wood's canopy reached for them.

She looked down at her blood-covered body. She saw the thick, still-living branch that stuck out of her skin just below her ribs. She could feel it trying to pull its way up into her chest cavity.

'No, no, no, no!' Fachtna yanked off his gauntlet and the leather vambraces on his right arm. He had a dirk in his left hand. It took him some effort to push the blade through into the flesh of his wrist with an ugly sawing motion. Then she saw the dark blood flow from the wound. She tried to fight him off as he held his bloodied wrist to her mouth, but she was too weak. It was her final thought as darkness claimed her. This place was too soft. It had made her weak.

'Don't do this to me,' Teardrop muttered to himself as he looked up into the night sky. Lug's wings shielded them from the Forge's light at this hour.

'He's coming here, isn't he?' Raven's Laughter, asked. Teardrop turned to look at his beautiful wife. He held a tomahawk casually in one hand, a knife in the other. He could see Rain, his eldest, standing in the doorway of his home.

'Inside, now!' he told Rain. 'Look to your brother and sisters!' He thought she was going to argue, but she relented and went inside. Teardrop turned back. He could make out other warriors on ponyback moving rapidly across the network of causeways that covered the marshy river lands he called home. He knew there would be chariots and maybe even a war-*curragh* making their way here, but he also knew instinctively that the craft he saw in the sky racing towards them was Fachtna's chariot.

They waited a few more moments, and then the chariot was above them. Adarc brought the craft in to land. The weapons cupola split open and a bloody Fachtna stepped out. Within the darkened interior,

Raven and Teardrop could see the bloodied form of the woman lying on the floor of the craft.

Fachtna was armoured and held his shimmering sword in his hand.

Raven bristled. 'You come to my home with an unsheathed sword! What nonsense is this? Sheathe it immediately and bring the mortal into the house,' Raven's Laughter admonished Fachtna. Even through the dried blood that covered Fachtna's face, Teardrop could see the guilt written all over it.

'I'm sorry,' he told her, and then turned to Teardrop. 'Give it to me.'

'Your *drui* have driven you to madness,' Teardrop told him evenly.

'Give him what?' Raven said suspiciously.

Teardrop closed his eyes for a moment. He suddenly felt very tired. He had always known that someday he would pay for his moment of madness, now hundreds of years in the past.

'I will go through you if I have to,' Fachtna told him.

'Fachtna!' Raven shouted at him, angry now, and then moved closer to her husband.

Fachtna approached them. Teardrop brought his spear up.

'I may be new enough to the straight path of the warrior that you could defeat me, but not both of us, and my children are in that home.'

Fachtna looked around, desperate. He was now one of the worst criminals in the history of the *Ubh Blaosc*. He could see the riders. He knew there were more chariots on their way. He would probably be executed for this, never to be reborn.

'If you use it, you shorten the life of the Forge, and we don't know by how much. You risk all of us for one,' Teardrop told his friend.

'What are you talking about?' Raven demanded, now very suspicious.

Fachtna looked at Raven, and then back to Teardrop. He lowered his sword. He left the question unasked. *What would you do?*

Teardrop glanced at his wife, and then back into his home.

'Stay here. I don't want the children to see their Uncle Fachtna like this.' *I'm going to be standing next to him when he's executed*, Teardrop thought. He turned and started heading towards the house, but Raven was in his way.

'I asked you a question,' she told him.

'Please,' was all he said, and then he pushed past her.

Raven turned on the stricken Fachtna. 'What trouble have you brought to my house?' she demanded.

'I'm so sorry.'

She could tell he meant it. She could tell he knew it wasn't enough. She stared at him angrily until Teardrop came back out of the house carrying something wrapped in a beaded medicine bag. He held it out to Fachtna. Fachtna reached for it, but Teardrop didn't relinquish it.

'You go as well,' he told the Gael.

'I have to—'

'You go as well, or my wife and I kill you here and now.'

Fachtna stared at his friend but then finally nodded.

'What is tha—' Raven started. Her eyes widened as Fachtna took a small bronze rod shaped like a cross out of the bag.

'Is that one of the control rods?' she demanded.

Teardrop swallowed hard, and then nodded. 'We found it in the sourlands during the first war with the Naga.'

'Why didn't you give it to one of the medicine societies?' she demanded.

He had no good answer for her. 'Because I coveted it.'

'You can't—' Raven started, but Fachtna was already climbing into the chariot's weapon cupola as the chariot rose up from the ground. Teardrop moved closer to his wife and tried to hold her, but she jerked away from him.

'Please,' he begged. 'Shout at me all you want later. I'm so sorry, but please just hold me now.'

She glared at him but then wrapped her arms around him. She could feel the sobs wracking his body, and she cursed the bonds that men formed in war.

His blood had stabilised her well enough that she could stare at him with accusing eyes.

'You killed a *dryw*,' she said quietly. He looked away from her and tried very hard not to think about it. He'd been concentrating on getting the still-living branch out of her flesh on the way to Teardrop's. Making sure her now slightly more than mortal, fragile form survived. He felt the chariot bank.

'We're here,' Adarc called from the head of the chariot. A warrior was always close to his charioteer, but he could hear the distance in Adarc's voice as well. Not least because the charioteer knew he would be judged for aiding Fachtna.

He had a moment to take in the scene as they circled the crater full of crystal-clear water. Every inch of the chariot's skin fed imagery and data directly to Fachtna's mind. They'd picked their course well, flown low and dark when they could, but angry warriors were closing on them now. In the distance, the hard terminator between the night and the day was creeping towards them as the wings of Lug moved.

Lightning shot from the ground. The chariot was cut in two. And they were falling. The cupola hit the water so hard it might as well have been rock. The matter of the chariot softened to try and cushion the blow, but it was too little, too late. The cold, clear water was filling the cupola as it sank. It was the water that kept him awake. Many of his bones were broken and he could see bones sticking out of Britha's flesh, blood bubbling from her mouth. Somehow her chest was still moving as she tried to breathe. Fachtna reached for her.

13
Close to the Oceanic Pole of Inaccessibility, 6 Weeks Ago

Lodup hated the feeling of falling that sometimes accompanied drifting off to sleep.

He had arrived at the Ronald Reagan Ballistic Missile Defence Test Site on the Kwajalein Atoll earlier in the day. He had gone to sleep in his room at the Kwaj Lodge after working out and trying to catch up with the advances in atmospheric diving suit, or ADS, technology.

Lodup opened his eyes. He had a moment, only a moment, to register an HV-22 Osprey tilt-rotor aircraft hovering in the night sky above him with its rear loading ramp down. Then he hit the ocean, hard, and immediately went under. Panic overwhelmed him and he started to flail wildly. He forced himself to calm down, and then realised he was being dragged deeper. Something heavy was tugging at his leg. He looked down and saw a lanyard with a heavy kitbag attached to it.

He tried to ignore the odd feelings in his chest. For a fleeting moment he wondered if he was having a heart attack but there was no pain, just a sensation of movement inside him. He felt water flood his ears. He assumed his eardrums had burst, though he didn't think he was deep enough. Lodup started to flail again as he felt liquid rushing into his sinuses. This didn't fit with what he knew about drowning, what he had experienced of it during training exercises and on two separate occasions when things had gone disastrously wrong.

Lodup reached down to release the tether around his ankle but found that the lanyard was securely locked. Then he realised he was also heavily weighted. When he tried to remove the weights, he found them locked in place as well. That was when panic really took over. That was when he truly knew he was dead. He was too frightened even to wonder why they had gone to such extravagant lengths to kill him.

He made no conscious decision to get it over with or to try and breathe water. He held his breath for as long as he could with the air he'd managed to inhale before he hit the water. Then he opened his mouth and tried to do the impossible. He tried to breathe seawater.

It was a curious feeling. It was less like drowning, more like being sick in reverse, if the vomit was cold water. Coldness spread throughout his chest but then was replaced, almost immediately, with a very peculiar warm, liquid feeling, not unlike pissing yourself, but again the sensation was inside his chest. It grew darker and darker as he dropped. It took him a number of minutes to realise he was somehow breathing water. It was a lot more strenuous than breathing air.

As he managed to control his panic, he realised he wasn't suffering any of the ill-effects of pressure, either. He was in total darkness now. The tugging sensation on his leg and the feeling of falling told him he was still being dragged down, but there were no visual clues to his predicament.

He felt around and found that he was wearing some kind of dive suit. The material was unfamiliar; it was a little less bulky than a semi-dry suit and completely form-fitting. A hood covered his head and face and appeared to have some sort of built-in mask.

Then he realised he could see something – a counter with luminous numbers. Those numbers were increasing and he knew he was looking at a depth reading. He had just passed five hundred metres. He should be dead.

Lodup found himself desperately wishing for a dive light. A beam of light shot out from the centre of his head, another from his right wrist. It didn't make that much difference – he was surrounded by black water, and all the light illuminated was particulate matter. He reckoned he was mid-ocean somewhere, judging by the utter lack of visible sea life. He was surprised by how perfect his vision was, as if the lenses of the built-in mask were compensating for the visual distortion caused by the liquid medium.

He noticed a dive knife strapped to his right ankle. He reached for it, thinking he could at least cut away the heavy pack that was dragging him down and try to control his descent. He drew the knife, then realised that it had an oddly crystalline-looking blade.

Lodup noticed his descent was slowing. He concentrated on controlling it some more and finally stopped as he managed, somehow, to attain neutral buoyancy. If the number in his vision was correct, he was at a depth of a little less than a thousand metres. He hung there in the darkness. He could feel the water pressing in all around him, but he was the warmest he could remember being on any deep dive not in an ADS. In fact, other than the effort it took to breathe, he felt pretty good. Except for the terror.

He wasn't sure why he hadn't tried to ascend. He also wasn't sure if it was his imagination, but was beginning to suspect there was a faint light coming from far below.

He did know that he had been hanging there motionless for exactly seventeen minutes and forty-three seconds before the beam of light cut through the water and his vision darkened, compensating for the sudden brightness. Lodup moved himself around carefully in the water, the waterproof kitbag hanging from his ankle hampering his ability to manoeuvre. Though he was impressed that the bag appeared to be able to withstand the depth.

Beyond the light he could make out a mechanical shape moving towards him. It looked like some kind of submersible. Lodup reckoned it was fitted for salvage, with a large flatbed area on top of it for storing tools and carrying salvage material. Its multidirectional impellers would give it manoeuvrability and power. There were lights and cameras all over the vehicle, and the observation bubble at the front of the submersible was large enough to provide a good all-round view. He noticed that the powerful-looking waldos on the front of the vehicle had grips that looked more like hands with fully opposable thumbs, which could be capable of quite delicate work. In fact, Lodup was somewhat surprised to see it this deep. An observation bubble that size, at this depth, had to be on the very edge of its material tolerances.

The pilot was wearing beige overalls with no logo on them. He looked Asian – Japanese, Lodup guessed – in his early- to mid-twenties. His head was shorn and he had a curiously slack, emotionless expression on his face. He worked the joystick controls with some expertise, using the impellers to make tiny adjustments to hold the submersible completely steady.

The pilot looked up at Lodup but didn't appear to register his presence. Then a shiver ran through the man and he was smiling at Lodup, and pointing down under the submersible. With some difficulty because of the kitbag, Lodup made his way towards the submersible. He located a series of rungs that led beneath the vehicle to a hatch embedded in its hull. This was insanity, Lodup decided. Surely the submersible pilot didn't mean for him to enter the craft. They couldn't be running it at ambient pressure, not at a thousand metres, which would put it at a hundred atmospheres or a hundred times the pressure at the surface. Lodup actually pulled himself back into the pilot's line of sight again to double-check, but the pilot just smiled and repeated the gesture.

Suit yourself, Lodup thought. *I can breathe water, apparently*. Lodup moved back and reached up to unscrew the hatch. He pushed it open and then climbed up into warmth, dryness and air – or a breathable gas, at least. The submersible didn't crumple. The interior was surprisingly spacious. Due to material tolerances when working under pressure, space was normally at a premium in such vehicles. He also observed that the controls looked surprisingly simple, though he noticed a pair of odd-looking gloves lying on the transparent material of the observation dome.

He opened his mouth to ask something and gurgled liquid into the hood/mask covering his face and head.

The pilot turned to look at him. 'You'll need to purge, my man. I'd prefer it if you do it outside before you close the hatch. You'll need to take the hood off first, though. Grasp it at the base of your neck and pull.'

Lodup did what the man suggested and the hood slipped easily over his head to hang down the front of the suit. He noticed that the suit was dripping very little water. He leaned forwards and thought about throwing up. Water surged from his mouth. It was unpleasant but not as bad as vomiting. There appeared to be a lot of water and it was coming in a constant stream. He also noticed two streams of water gushing from his chest. He felt movement inside him. He wondered if that was his lungs reinflating.

'Now, when you see them you're going to freak,' the pilot said, 'so we might as well get this out of the way now. You have what look like grilles implanted in your chest. They're mechanical gills. You'll need to get used to them.'

'What? The fuck?' Lodup exploded.

'A reasonable question. My name's Hideo, by the way. Could you secure the hatch?'

Lodup did as he was bid and felt the submersible start to descend.

'You're going deeper?' Lodup demanded.

'Oh yeah,' Hideo said. He was facing away from Lodup, but the Mwoakilloan was pretty sure the other man was grinning. He also realised that their voices sounded normal, regardless of the gas they were breathing.

'Dude, I know it's harsh, but trust me, we all got dropped in the first time round. They tried explaining beforehand but people never believed it, you know what I mean? They defeated themselves with their minds, panic attacks, wouldn't put their heads underwater, that sort of thing.'

'Nitrogen?'

'Scrubbed from your system.'

'By what?'

'The same thing that's modifying your body to allow you to deal with other pressure issues, which reinforced your joints, and which rebuilt you for submarine operations. You know what nanites are?' Hideo asked, glancing around. Lodup stared at the man. The pilot's English was slightly accented, but otherwise flawless.

'You injected me with nanites?'

'Wooah! I'm just a working stiff like you.'

Lodup was appalled. 'Bullshit! Nano-technology is nothing like advanced enough to do that.'

'Fine, *you* explain it.'

'So you, what, drugged me on Kwaj, modified me and threw me out of an Osprey in the middle of ... where the fuck are we?'

'Forty-seven by nine degrees south, and a hundred and twenty-six by forty-three degrees west, and again I didn't do shit to you other than come and pick you up.'

The coordinates sounded familiar to Lodup. 'Point Nemo?'

'We're not far from there.'

'Look, you can't just—'

Hideo looked back at Lodup, a sympathetic expression on his face. 'This is so far above classified it's just not true. They take liberties, but that's why you're getting paid what you're getting paid.'

Lodup lapsed into silence. He was aware of the pressure adjusting as they descended but felt no real effect from it. He didn't even have to equalise. He was now certain there was a cold blue glow coming from beneath them. Ahead of him, some of the water looked darker than the rest, and he could just about make out what looked like a mountain, but its jagged outline stretched in either direction as far as he could see.

'Is that a ridge line?' he asked. Hideo nodded and started playing the searchlight around in the water. Lodup glimpsed what looked like high-tech spiked balls hanging motionless in the water. More distantly he could see a small, sleek sled-like vehicle.

'Smart mines, and that's a patrol AUV,' Hideo told him, meaning an autonomous underwater vehicle, but now Lodup was staring down at the bright lights below him.

The first thing he noticed was the black lake. His mind tried to cope with the absurdity of finding a lake at the bottom of the ocean, particularly as it appeared to have a beach.

'Is that a cold seep?' he asked. Again Hideo nodded. Lodup knew this phenomenon consisted of salty brine much thicker than the surrounding water, while the 'beach' was made up of hundreds of thousands of mussels existing in a methane-eating bacteria-based food chain. A forest of swaying tubeworms also bordered the lake. The tubeworms survived by harvesting sulphides from the seabed itself

'We stay away from the lake,' Hideo said, genuine fear in his voice, but Lodup was too overcome by awe to notice.

Water bubbled above towering chimneys at the base of the ridge-line – black smokers venting hydrogen-sulphide-saturated water, hot as molten lead, into below-freezing water maintained in a liquid state by the immense pressure. The same pressure kept the water liquid around the mouths of the bubbling chimneys at temperatures as high as four hundred degrees centigrade. The forest of chimneys vented black smoke in the form of iron sulphite which dissolved into the water, and when the minerals in the boiling water hit the freezing water, the smokers were created. Their existence at the base of the ridge made sense. The ridge itself would have been formed by solidi-fied molten volcanic rock. Lodup knew that there were probably Pompeii worms, crabs and shrimps around the vents, all filled with bacteria that turned the sulphides in the water into simple sugars which allowed them to exist in a food chain separated from the Sun by – Lodup checked his depth – what must be over four thousand metres.

The mass of chimneys gave the whole scene a curiously industrial look, but it was whatever lay between the chimneys at the base of the ridge and the eerie black lake that stunned Lodup. That disquieted him. That hurt to look at. That made him feel nauseous. That filled him with equal parts awe and dread.

It took him a while to realise what he was looking at. The geometry was all wrong.

'What is it?' Lodup asked, stumbling over the words.

'One of the changes they make to you before you can work here involves neurosurgery that enables you to perceive this safely, so that it doesn't cause neurological and psychological damage.' Hideo paused. 'So they say.'

The whole area was illuminated by cold artificial light. Lodup was having trouble coping with the idea of a place that required brain surgery before you could see it without going mad. Parts of it looked as if they'd been carved from massive pieces of rock that appeared to share characteristics with both soapstone and basalt. The forms were disturbingly organic.

It had to be one of the tricks the ocean occasionally played on people – naturally occurring rock formations that looked like intelligent design. It was the sort of thing that convinced people they'd found Atlantis when in fact they'd just stumbled across an interesting geological curiosity.

The odd-looking rock formed megaliths, off-kilter pyramids and ziggurat shapes, and there was something sepulchral, something tomblike about them. They formed labyrinthine streets and blind culs-de-sac of disquieting proportions which, if they were the result of intelligent design, had not been built for human physiology – not just in scale, but also in perceptual terms. The whole place appeared to be one massive nausea-inducing optical illusion.

Lodup found there were tears on his cheeks without really knowing why he was crying. Blood was trickling out of his nose, and he was shaking.

In the centre of the city was a circle of enormous stones, each easily the size of four-storey town house. They looked more like gravestones than standing stones. Like most of the 'buildings', they were covered with strange symbols, pictographs that he didn't want to look at too closely, which appeared to squirm in his peripheral vision. The pictographs confirmed the conclusion he'd been trying to resist. This was a city. The submersible's searchlight was playing over urban streets. The black-smoker chimneys turned the scene into a twisted mockery of an industrial cityscape.

By far the most disquieting sight were the things he had taken initially to be statuary. The strange biological shapes consisted of sacs, tentacles and odd appendages that looked like nothing he had ever seen, but somehow he knew they represented organs of some sort. Other shapes looked like a cross between massive seed-pods and some kind of bottom-feeding sea creature. They were fused to the moulded rock. Pain shot through Lodup's head. Somehow he knew they weren't statuary. Somehow he knew these things had once been alive. Somehow he knew that he was looking at a city of dead things, a corpse city, and it was teeming with activity.

Lodup almost lost it all over again when he heard the whale song. The creature passed the submersible at a leisurely pace, glancing at the vehicle. It looked like an orca, only fatter; its eyes were camera lenses and parts of its body were reinforced with a machine exoskeleton. The almost-orca was covered with plating that wouldn't have been out of place on an armoured vehicle, but the strangest thing about it was the arm-like waldos.

'That's Marvin. He took out an experimental Chinese deep-diving sub recently. They're not just good for security. They're living magnetometers. They have—'

'Crystals of iron oxide in their heads,' Lodup said, his voice filled with a kind of horrified wonder.

'They augment the crystals, make them more sensitive. The dolphins were better at surveying, they helped us find and excavate most of the city ... but there was trouble.'

'You've got dolphins down here?'

'Not any more.'

The orca dived towards the horrible city. Lodup saw other submersibles, many of them larger than the one he was in at the moment. There were smaller figures in the water, too – modified divers like him, he assumed – and large metal humanoid forms which he guessed were atmospheric diving suits, though they looked more like the robot battlesuits he'd seen in Japanese animations when he'd worked with their Navy. Stranger still were creatures that looked like *Architeuthis* – giant squid – only much, much larger, armoured like the almost-orca and sporting reinforced exoskeletons, with various mechanical devices attached to their multiple limbs. They appeared to be working as cranes. He watched one of them take some kind of cutting torch to a massive block of stone fused with one of the petrified seed-pods, light from the torch cutting through dark, now boiling water.

A number of roughly rectangular metal constructs were tethered to the seabed but floating some fifty metres above it. Their shape reminded Lodup of an inverted dry dock, though they were open to the water. Several were hives of activity. Inside one, Lodup thought he saw something that looked like the shaped stones he'd glimpsed in the city, but he couldn't quite make out the exact form of the stone, or what was being done to it.

'The squid aren't so much controlled by telepresence as influenced by it,' Hideo told him.

'What are those?' Lodup pointed at some large spherical tanks from which pipes ran into more of the petrified organic-looking forms.

Hideo laughed, but there was little humour in his voice. 'All the sedative in the world.'

Lodup stared at him. He did not want to accept the implications of Hideo's explanation. He felt dread mounting.

'I don't think I want this job,' he said quietly. He had not felt this frightened since he was a child.

'I get that,' Hideo said softly. 'This is important, man, give it some time.'

Hideo was manoeuvring the submersible towards some sort of large habitat which obviously wasn't part of the horrible sunken city. The habitat consisted of a series of black domes made of small, bubble-like hemispheres. At first Lodup thought the habitat was moving in some kind of deep current, but on closer inspection, he decided the movement looked more like breathing. It was situated on open ground within the city atop constantly adjusting heavy-duty struts.

As Hideo brought the submersible in low, Lodup tried to cope with the fact that he was now in an underwater vehicle moving through the streets of some alien city. Hideo played the lights over strange stone architecture and Lodup glimpsed more of the disquieting pictographic symbols. He also noticed some smaller things fused with the stone – humanoid figures with a piscean quality to them, locked in silent screams of agony, and several snake-headed figures. Towering over a smaller block of stone, one of the armoured hi-tech squid was moving between tomblike buildings.

Ahead he could see light flooding out of the domed habitat. An ADS strode across the street in front of them as a submersible left the domes. Black-clad faceless-looking divers were clinging to the side of the other vehicle.

One of the armoured orcas swam down to the habitat and suckled on a nipple-like protrusion coming from what looked like an inflatable bladder.

'Gas?' Lodup asked.

'Food. It's chum, effectively, with growth hormones, a high fat content and other supplements to augment bone. They have what amounts to an artificial lung, like us, although they do occasionally replenish their emergency internal gas supplies, but they do that in the moon pool.'

'That place has ambient pressure? What the fuck's it made out of?'

Hideo leaned forwards and knocked on the submersible's observation bubble. 'Condensed adamantanes.'

'What?'

'Synthetic diamond, actually a diamondoid.'

'The expense—'

'Not if you can manipulate matter on a molecular level. You see those pipes?' Hideo indicated pipes running out of the rear of the habitat; some were sunk into the seabed, while others ran through the city. 'They pull in raw matter, anything from silt to rock, and break it down. The matter is then manipulated into diamondoids, helium to breathe and whatever else we need.'

'The power—'

'Stable geothermal energy, with two backup cold-fusion generators.'

'So we're breathing ... ?'

'Mostly helium but more oxygen than you might think. Your body's been—'

'Adapted to deal with it.'

Hideo nodded. 'You put a normal human down here, if the pain in their joints didn't kill them, then oxygen toxicity would.'

'And some modification to the larynx so we don't sound like cartoon characters?' Lodup asked. Hideo nodded again. 'But this level of technology, the difference you could make ...'

Hideo took the submarine under the habitat and brought it up into a huge brightly lit moon pool. The horrific city gone, Lodup found himself looking around in wonder as his vision darkened to adjust for the brightness.

The area reminded him of American football stadiums he'd visited in Florida and California when he was stationed there. It was a massive domed chamber containing a number of jetties where the submersibles docked and there were cradles for the ADSs, some of which were open and being worked on. Banks of tools and other equipment were scattered about the vast space.

He saw orcas poking their heads out of the water for their cybernetic systems to be adjusted. He started for a moment when an armoured mechanical tentacle reached into the habitat until people started to hook a large crate to it.

There were small cranes on the jetties and more heavy-duty versions running on a network of rails overhead. One of them had lifted a large submersible out of the water for repairs.

Lodup was craning his neck, looking all around.

'We can get out now,' Hideo said, grinning. 'Welcome to *Kanamwayso*.'

'You're kidding?'

Hideo got up and started undoing the top hatch. He pushed it open and Lodup felt the air currents change in the submersible.

'They had to call it something. Mu and Lemuria sounded a bit geeky, I reckon.' Hideo pulled himself out of the sub. Lodup hesitated for a moment and then followed, dragging his kitbag out after him.

Outside the submersible it was cold and damp but that didn't bother him. He climbed down and Hideo helped him onto the jetty. It was then that he started noticing the armed guards and gun emplacements resembling smaller versions of the Phalanx Close-In Weapons System rotary cannon used for missile defence on US Navy ships.

'You expecting trouble?' Lodup asked.

'It's mostly precautionary, but sometimes things happen,' Hideo said evasively.

'What things?'

Hideo pointed up towards a large window shaped like an eye. Lodup saw a woman standing in the window, arms behind her back, looking down on the moon pool.

'That's Command and Control. I'm supposed to take you up there.'

'That the boss?'

'That's Siska – she's the overseer. We don't see much of the boss man. C'mon, I'll show you the way.'

Lodup hoisted the kitbag onto his shoulder. He wasn't even surprised that it was dry now. He found himself scratching at his face, which felt itchy for some reason.

As Lodup turned to walk along the jetty, he found a very strange figure in front of him. The figure was wearing an expertly tailored and expensive-looking business suit and had the head of a black-scaled lizard.

'Kasalehlia Lodup Satakano, my name is Siraja Odap-odap. I am the artificial intelligence that runs the systems in Kanamwayso, and I am at your service. This image of me is appearing only in your internal systems. The skin irritation you are feeling is the habitat's protective nano-screen interfacing with you for the first time. This is for your protection, and the irritation will pass quickly. I will leave you in peace, but should you require anything, please do not hesitate to call on me.'

'Er ...' Lodup started. The dragon-headed man bowed and disappeared.

'Did you just meet Siraja?' Hideo asked as he began to walk along the jetty. Lodup nodded, then followed Hideo. 'Siraja's cool, he'll look after you.'

'Isn't Siraja Odap-odap an Indonesian god?' Hideo shrugged. 'How long have you been down here?' With technology that could revolutionise mankind, he didn't add.

'Let's put it this way – I used to hunt you lot in submarines.'

Lodup stared at Hideo. 'You're not the oldest person down here, are you?' The other man just shook his head. 'But your English, your accent—'

'I've watched a lot of TV. I avoid war films, though.'

Lodup almost walked into a tall, well-built woman. Her hair was tied back in a ponytail, and the one-piece dive suit covering her muscular frame was the same as his. She was loading what looked like cutting gear into a toolbox attached to the flatbed of a submersible very similar to Hideo's.

'Sal?' Lodup asked. The woman looked at him blankly. Lodup frowned. 'Sal, it's Lodup.' He'd first met the woman when she joined

Mobile Diving and Salvage Unit 2 based out of Little Creek, Virginia Beach, on loan from the Royal Australian Navy Salvage Team. Both of them had been involved with the project to recover the Civil War Ironclad warship USS *Monitor*, and he'd worked with her a number of times since they'd left the service. 'How long have you been down here? I thought you were in the Gulf of Mexico?'

She continued to stare at him blankly for a few more moments, and then appeared to shake herself out of it.

'Lodup!' She gave him a hug. 'How you doing, man? I wondered when they were going to recruit you. Bit of a culture shock, huh?'

'Culture shock? I don't believe all this shit.'

'You'll get used to it ... Actually, you won't, but—'

'Who else is down here?'

'Anyone who's anyone is down here.'

'You all getting paid—'

'A lot, man, and I mean a *lot*.' She whistled, nodding. It made sense, Lodup thought; if they could manipulate matter, they could effectively create anything they needed – including money and resources to recruit whoever they wanted. 'Look, we'll catch up later – I need to get going.'

Lodup nodded.

'C'mon, dude,' Hideo said.

A thick blast door separated the moon pool from the rest of the habitat. On the other side of the door, Lodup was surprised to find that the corridors were carpeted and heated by warm air blowing through them. This was disconcerting at first – the warm wind felt a little like being breathed on, and they hadn't quite managed to eliminate humidity. The carpet was particularly springy underfoot.

'It's a grass analogue, would you believe?' Hideo told him. 'I'm not sure how it works, but it helps scrub for carbon dioxide build-up and takes some of the pressure off the habitat's lungs.'

Hideo took him up a flight of stairs and along a corridor to another blast door.

'I'll leave you to it, man, okay?'

'Em, yeah,' Lodup said, still trying to assimilate everything he'd seen. 'Thanks, man.'

Hideo patted him on the shoulder, then turned and headed back the way they had come. The blast door slid open and Lodup stepped into C&C. It wasn't quite what he was expecting. Instead of banks of machinery and screens, he found a large, open-plan, split-level room decorated in subdued dark colours. On either side of the door was a pair of huge ornate brass cannon, their barrels carved into the fanciful shapes of Chinese dragons. A long elliptical hardwood table stood just in front of the oval window overlooking the moon pool. A number of people were seated around the table, reclining on comfortable leather couches. Most of them had their eyes closed.

The woman he'd seen earlier was standing on a raised level between the table and the window. She wore dark combat trousers and a simple T-shirt. Lodup guessed she was Cambodian, though she was surprisingly tall, and her spare frame suggested a lot of wiry muscle. Her skin was dark and weather-beaten; a scar ran down the left side of her face. Her long, black hair was tied back in a simple braid. What surprised Lodup the most were the holstered pistols, on each hip. Her belt had pouches for extra ammo and a pair of sheathed, curved knives.

Standing in the shadows provided by the subdued lighting was a squat, powerfully built man with a flat-top haircut. His eyes were bright blue, but Lodup didn't like the look of them, too cold. His arms were crossed over a T-shirt that was just a little too tight for his muscular torso. A complicated-looking sub-machine gun with an underslung grenade-launcher hung across his chest. There was a sidearm at his hip and his utility belt held a selection of less lethal weaponry in various pouches attached to it. Lodup recognised the type. He'd worked with Special Forces operatives in the past.

'My name is Siska, and I'm the overseer at this facility. This is Yaroslav, my head of security.'

'Are you expecting trouble?' Lodup asked.

Siska studied him for a moment. 'As you might imagine, there's a great deal we can't tell you. That said, I will be as honest as I can be with what I'm allowed to divulge. There are external threats. There are other organisations with comparable technology who are interested in *Kanamwayso*. There are also certain environmental challenges, but the single biggest problem we face is that we are dealing with a population of over five hundred powerfully augmented humans and a significant number of augmented fauna. This place changes people. It affects them in ways we cannot predict.'

'Are you saying this place will drive me mad?' Lodup asked, thinking back to the disquiet, the fear, he had felt during the descent when he first saw the alien city.

'I'm saying it will affect you, but it's nothing that can't be reversed when you return to the surface to receive your payment.'

Lodup looked over at Yaroslav. 'What are you? Ex-Naval Spetsnaz?' Lodup asked. Yaroslav said nothing. Lodup shook his head at the hard-man act.

'And he fought in the Great Patriotic War,' Siska said.

Lodup looked up at her sharply. 'What is this place? That city out there?'

'Does it look human to you?'

'No, it looks ... I don't know ... older.'

'It is. Imagine a species, very advanced, whose technology and biology are indistinguishable.'

'How long have you known about this? Had access to this knowledge?'

'We call ourselves the Circle, and we have been in existence for more than two thousand years.'

Lodup just stared at her. He felt like sitting down on the grass/carpet and taking some time to process what he'd just been told. The fact that he'd seen the city on the way in made this information somewhat easier to believe.

'But with this technology, think of everything you could ...' he managed after a few moments.

'We have been responsible for many technological advances throughout history, but we can't control human social evolution. Himmler had an inkling regarding the existence of this technology. He had units searching for it. Could you imagine what would have happened if he had got his hands on any of it?'

'So what makes your Circle the guardians of this technology? Why do they get to make the decisions for the rest of us?' Lodup demanded, but he could feel his anger diminishing. He felt rather than saw Yaroslav shift slightly.

Siska laughed. 'Happenstance, or, if you prefer, sheer dumb luck,' the scarred woman told him. Lodup couldn't think of anything to say to that. 'We are not perfect, we have made a lot of mistakes, but we try.'

'You try what? To harvest the technology here for ... yourselves?'

'For the future of mankind. Some of the greatest minds in human history have been, or are, members of the Circle. We have weapons because those who would use this technology malevolently also have weapons.'

'Why should I believe you?'

Siska stared at him for another moment, and Lodup could not make up his mind whether she was losing patience with him or not. Despite himself, he glanced over at the brooding presence of Yaroslav, but the Russian remained impassive.

'You have no reason to believe what I say. That can only be gained by you working with us, seeing what we do, and either coming to trust us – or not. You are here, however, because we are paying you, and paying you very well, to do a job. If you feel this is all too much, we can return you to the surface. The augments will be removed. You will not receive your payment. We will modify your memory ...' Lodup started to object but Siska held up her hand. 'I'm sorry, but otherwise you would represent too big a security risk. More to the point, it would make you and those close to you targets. You would, however, still have the hundred thousand dollars you've already been paid.' Lodup opened his mouth to speak again, but she shook her head. 'Mr Satakano, I'm sure you have a great many questions, but I am afraid a lot of the answers will have to be found on the job. I appreciate that this is a great deal to take in, but I must press you for an answer.'

'If I say no, it would be a lot easier to just have him put two in the back of my head,' Lodup said, nodding at Yaroslav.

'There are a great many things we could have done to make this easier for us, but that is not how we operate. Yaroslav is an exceptional soldier and a very capable guardian of this facility. He is not, despite his skill set, an assassin.'

'Who is in command of the facility?'

'As far as you are concerned, I am. If for some unlikely reason that proves insufficient, we will deal with the situation as required.'

Now Lodup could hear irritation in her voice. He took a good look around C&C. The lack of visible equipment and screens still didn't feel right.

Answering his unspoken question, she said, 'Our internal nano-tech translate all the information supplied by the systems and the feeds from various cameras and sensors and relays it directly to our minds.' This time there was no irritation in her voice. 'However, we can also do this.'

All over the walls and along the length of the elliptical table, images from various parts of the operation appeared – footage from the moon pool, from within the habitat and throughout the city, footage from submersibles, AUVs, ROVs and ADSs, and feeds from the alien corpse city. In one picture he thought he saw the wreck of a World War Two-era submarine. In the centre of C&C, an image was being created in light, and he found himself standing in a hologramatic representation of the base and the city, surrounded by all the divers, fauna, submersibles and other vehicles.

'Programmable smart matter. Effectively, it can be whatever we want it to be,' Siska said, gesturing at the images on the wall.

'How does comms work?' Lodup asked, his discomfort with the

situation momentarily overwhelmed by technological awe.

'We hardwire what we can – it's the most reliable way. In addition we use ultrasound over short range – one hundred metres or less, and over greater distances we burst-send packets of low-frequency infrasound.'

Lodup knew that under normal circumstances the equipment required to achieve this would be quite large, but assumed they must have found a way to miniaturise it.

'We also use ultrasonic pulse emitters as point-defence weapons, and to deal with hostile flora.' Yaroslav's voice was a deep rumble and his Russian accent very strong. 'Mr Satakano, this environment is more difficult to survive in, long term, than space. We have had to become something other than human to do so. On top of that there are many other dangers intrinsic to the nature of our operation. This is, however, the single greatest challenge for any diver on the planet. Forgive me for using a crude American idiom, but you need to man-the-fuck-up.'

Siska said nothing, her hands still behind her back as she watched Lodup impassively. Lodup glanced at Yaroslav. The Russian was holding the same position he'd been in since Lodup entered the room, but his eyes looked more alive, somehow. Slowly, Lodup started to smile.

'I think you're right. Maybe you and I should have a drink sometime?'

'Perhaps when you rotate out,' Yaroslav replied. 'I make it a policy not to get too friendly with people I may have to kill.'

Lodup didn't think this was bravado on the Russian's part, just a simple statement of fact.

'Your first shift starts in twelve hours,' Siska said. 'You will want to get some food and then some sleep.' It was obvious that the meeting was over, so Lodup picked up his kitbag as the screens disappeared, leaving bare walls and the table. The hologram erased itself line by line. He nodded at Siska, the door slid open behind him, and he walked out.

'Well?' Siska asked once the door had slid closed again.

'He is a diver. This is the Grail for him.'

'Is that a joke?'

Yaroslav's slow laughter sounded like the rumble of distant thunder. 'He complicates things, but then we always knew he would,' the Russian said.

'This was the most expedient solution.'

'I'm less worried about him than I am about the city's reaction to him. He is more like us than the other workers, only far less prepared and not nearly as well augmented.'

Siska gave this some thought. 'We can't predict the city's reaction,' she said eventually. 'Keep an eye on him.' Yaroslav nodded. 'That means you as well, Siraja.'

The dragon-headed image of the AI appeared in Siska's and Yaroslav's vision.

'Of course,' the AI said, bowing to Siska.

14

A long Time After the Loss

The Monk opened the airlock door, then crossed to the other side of the corridor and sat down, leaning against the opposite bulkhead. When she saw the smug expression on Benedict/Scab's face, she actually had to instruct her systems to release a reasonably strong sedative to calm her.

The harness he was hanging from was an old-fashioned sling molecularly bonded to the ceiling. They had decided against providing him with an AG motor of any description. He was limbless. Her previous self had spayed his neunonics and internal liquid software, but even though he looked helpless in his sling, he still gave the impression of being in total control of the situation. *Who knows*, the Monk thought bitterly, *maybe he is.*

'There's something different about you,' Benedict/Scab started.

'Fuck off,' the Monk muttered.

'Is that a whole new body? Did I kill you again?'

'No, you didn't, the one with limbs—'

'And one of your bridge drives, and the secret to bridge technology—'

'. . . did,' the Monk finished.

'Outside of Vic, the closest person I have to someone remotely useful is Elodie. If I went to get her, that means I want her skills. She is an excellent kick-murder specialist—'

'She's not that good.'

'She got you.'

'A fucking spaceship shot me!'

'But as far as violence goes, there's nothing she can do that Vic and I couldn't cover.'

'Are you referring to him as "I" just to annoy me?'

'Yes. I'll stop if you give me my limbs back.'

'You'd best keep doing it, then. She's an intrusion specialist.'

'Physical, electronic and personal.'

The Monk sat up straighter. 'How could we have missed that?'

'Simple – it's not something she advertises, she never does it for clients, only for herself, and she's very careful to dispose of any evidence.'

She kept the secret the old-fashioned way, the Monk thought. *She didn't tell anyone. And here's me thinking privacy was dead.*

'She's another class-A psycho, then?'

'Who isn't?'

'How do you know this?'

'I can only assume that the Psycho Bank who sold you my possessing personality was very good.'

'Okay, how did proper Scab work it out?'

'Motivate me.'

'I could use you as a kick bag?'

'I'll try not to sport an erection whilst you do it.'

'You're different from him. More talkative, and you've modified your personality to be more ... irritating,' the Monk said. Benedict/Scab said nothing, just looked at her, his expression unreadable. 'You don't do anything without a reason. You're talking more because it's the only means of communication you have left. Still desperately jockeying for position. How sad.'

He started to laugh. There was no humour in it whatsoever. The Monk was surprised that, even after all this, it chilled her.

'What astonishing insight. I talk more when my limbs have been cut off. Yes, if I still had my limbs, our communication would be of a *much* more physical nature. Speaking of which, the "real" me has been inside you, hasn't he?'

The Monk knew she'd given herself away before she even started to lie. 'Not in any way that matters,' she said. She barely had memories of the time she'd spent disguised as Zabilla Haq, biophysicist and player on Game, with Scab masquerading as her paramour Dracup.

'Oh, I think it *does* matter. Are you more angry that he killed you, or that he fucked you? Do you hate Elodie because you're jealous?'

The Monk stared at him. For a moment his words felt like a heated blade shoved into her guts, and then she started laughing.

'Is that the best you've got? Yes, the idea of him touching me repels me, but it may as well have happened to another person, and frankly I think it bothered him a lot more than it bothered me. In fact, let's put that to the test.'

She rolled onto her feet and quickly crossed the distance between them. She knelt down next to the sling and leaned in close to him.

'See, there's more than just you helping us. We've got some of the best minds, AI and otherwise, working on this. Scab's profile is exhaustive. The attention to detail is incredible, and the one thing it says again and again is that control is *very* important to Scab. So I think control would be important to a fifth-rate third-generation carbon copy like yourself.'

She pulled back and looked at him. His features were expressionless but there was something in his eyes. She leaned forward and kissed him, and felt his whole torso flinch in response.

'Now, without your neunonics, do you think you can control your physiological responses sufficiently not to get hard if I go down on you? I might struggle to get wet enough, but as soon as you're hard, I am going to slide you inside me and rock you back and forth in your little sex swing here.' She pushed the harness and let him swing for a while. He couldn't contain himself any longer. He was shaking with fury, though the Monk suspected he was a little aroused as well. 'Or you can stop fucking around, tell me what I want to know and I'll go and assemble a packet of fags for you.' Benedict/Scab frowned. The Monk cursed herself. 'Cigarettes.'

He nodded as he struggled to control his – ultimately impotent – rage. 'That,' he said. 'That's how you'll get him.'

'What, threaten to rape his limbless body?'

'No,' he said, his tone serious. 'What you just did – make him realise he's not in control.'

She nodded. *What's wrong with you?* she wondered, appalled at what she'd just done.

'And I'm going to find a way to kill you,' he told her with real feeling.

The Monk sighed, but there was something about the way he said it this time.

'So what's it to be? Information or a hand-job?' she asked as she sat back down, this time against the airlock's bulkhead.

'I told you, after Elodie, I don't know. Beyond wanting to get into a facility, a system or someone's head, none of this makes sense to me. He must know something I don't.'

'Why?'

'Because I don't understand his play. What's he got to gain from it?'

'He has one of the most valuable things in Known Space,' the Monk said bitterly.

'Not if he can't use that value. He's dead once he's sold her, and unless I'm missing something, his best chance to sell her was an immersion auction. Anything else is too risky.'

'But you called that – it was about financing.'

'Yes, but financing for what? The next auction carries the same risk.'

'He could go to a buyer on the quiet.'

'Then he gets less, and what he was already offered wasn't enough.'

'So what does he want?'

Benedict/Scab hesitated. The Monk raised an eyebrow. The possessing download had been extensively conditioned to cooperate with them, but still the core personality resisted somehow.

'He cares about control, freedom. Being a god, because that can provide those things. Or dying.'

Which is nothing we don't already know, the Monk thought.

'There's something I can't see,' said Benedict/Scab. 'I'm formed of information from the Legion obtained when they first captured him on Cyst; information declassified by the Consortium from his time as an Elite; black-personality immersions; and a composite put together by an intelligent Pythian profiling program based on the available information about him. He resisted being recorded after he left the Elite. He doesn't use clones, so he didn't have a backup personality.'

'So you're missing a lot post-Elite?' the Monk asked.

'I'm missing a lot post-Legion, though I don't think he knows much about his time as an Elite.'

'Do you believe the information we need is from that time? You might think it's a convenient excuse to be uncooperative, but it does limit your usefulness somewhat.'

Benedict/Scab narrowed his eyes. 'You understand what I just said, don't you?'

'He doesn't have friends, he has few contacts, he eschews publicity as much as any high-profile bounty killer can, and he doesn't keep company with other bounty crews.'

'It has to be a job,' Benedict/Scab said.

The Monk found it odd. In some ways the possessing personality appeared to be enjoying this, almost as if it relished the challenge, a trait largely dead outside of Church personnel.

'So, which job?'

'I would need to review.'

Then she saw it. She laughed. 'We're not giving you your neunonics back.'

'Then it's going to take a very long time.'

She 'faced instructions to have a screen painted on the airlock hull and for a holographic projector delivered, but he was right – it was going to take a long time.

'Let me ask you something,' Benedict/Scab said. 'Why can't your beacons find his bridge drive signature?'

Because he's managed to modify it as well as put it in a new ship, and because he has help, the Monk didn't tell Benedict/Scab, *and we thought all the heretic sects capable of doing such things had been destroyed a long time ago.* They were also sure that Pythia had arranged for the sale of a ship capable of changing the shape of its smart-matter superstructure sufficiently to disguise itself. Scab had used some of the proceeds from the fake auction to pay for a data lock. That hadn't expired yet, and when it did it would cost the Church and all the other interested parties a fortune to buy Scab's ship info.

'That should tell you something in itself. Now give me my smokes.'

Elodie was better than her competitors for the same reason that he and Scab were, Vic thought. The 'sect was watching her practise – hand-to-hand combat, quick cripple and kill kick-murder moves. They had all the right soft- and hard-tech augments. They were carrying all the right gear. They had a lot of experience, but the reason they were better, the slight edge they had, was because they practised. They kept their skills sharp, regardless of whether they were hardwired in or hard learned.

Elodie cycled through the various improvised patterns. She used moves from many different fighting forms, particularly lizard and feline as they were considered the two uplift species with the best martial arts. She had woven them into a form that suited her, though Vic knew she was always looking for more, always adapting, always improvising, so her moves couldn't be predicted. She had a number of chaos fact algorithms programmed into her neunonics, which helped her mix it up a bit, fight counter-intuitively and put her opponents off balance.

If anything she was a better fighter than Scab, but Scab would always win. Viciousness went a long way towards victory.

She was putting her leg through its paces, helping to integrate the recently grown new flesh with the rest of her body.

'What do you want, Vic?' Elodie asked without missing a beat of her pattern. 'You looking for an advantage?'

'I don't want to fight you. I like you,' the 'sect said. 'Y'know, as a person.'

'Really?' A series of quick kicks rising higher and higher until the final one had her practically doing vertical splits. 'Good. Tell me what's going on.'

Vic didn't answer. Elodie practised in silence for a while. Her breathing wasn't laboured; her feet barely made a sound on the replica wood of the deck.

'Church trouble? Who's the whiny hairless monkey?' she asked. Vic still didn't say anything. 'If I hand her over to the Church, does my life get easier?'

Elodie executed a spinning kick in the air, landed into a leg sweep and then delivered a series of fast kicks from the ground.

'You rely on kicks too much,' Vic said. 'They're too slow, particularly the ones in the air. And he can hear you. Not just Church trouble. Board-level Consortium, Monarchist nobility and Elite involvement.'

She was good, but Vic caught the moment of hesitation when he mentioned the Elite.

'Leg muscles are stronger than arm muscles, so kicks are my best hope against anyone with serious augments.' She came to a halt and looked at the 'sect. The smart matter in her chamber started to reformat the room back to luxurious living quarters. 'Like you. And fuck him.' She concentrated for a moment and then smiled. 'So I'm in.'

Vic saw the security warning from the *Basilisk II*'s systems that Scab had allowed him access to. He also saw Scab's response – a hydra of seek-and-destroy programs, some subtle, most not, Pythian-designed programs which he used to counter-attack rather than defend. Some of the heads of the counter-attack program would cripple her; others would burn out her mind, subject her to meat-hack slavery or kill her, painfully. He wasn't holding back.

'A test.' Elodie smiled. 'Tell me, if it comes down to him and me, whose side are you going to be on?'

Vic felt a tickle of excitement. Together they just might stand a chance against him. But just as quickly as the optimism came, it was gone again.

'You'll do what he wants in the end as well. Don't fool yourself.'

'You want to fuck me, Vic?'

Vic gave the blunt question some thought. She was moments away from being crippled, enslaved or dead thanks to the heavily converted yacht's systems.

'Yes—'

'But only to get back at him.'

'Yes.'

'I'm not enough of a hairless monkey for you to find fuckable?'

'Close, though.'

'Brave. I'm not Scab's woman, but I think he believes he's sprayed me.'

'I can certainly smell him on you.'

'It wouldn't make any difference to him anyway.'

'As I said, I like you.'

'You think you like anyone who's not him,' she told him. Vic wasn't convinced she was wrong. 'What happened to you?'

'I don't care any more.'

'That's what I mean.'

The conflict between Scab and Elodie in the yacht's systems went beyond what Vic's clearance allowed him to see. He opened his mandibles to speak but Elodie held up her hand. He waited, only slightly resentful. Finally she blinked, obviously dealing with some pain, and spat out blood, which the now plushly carpeted floor absorbed. The tailored enzymes in her saliva would have destroyed any DNA and then self-destructed before it even touched the carpet. That wouldn't stop Scab making the yacht's systems analyse it.

'So what have we got here?' she muttered to herself. 'There you go.' She gave Vic open access to the yacht's systems, presumably just to annoy Scab. Moments later, a worm ate that access and he found himself limited again. 'Petty. So we've got a high-performance yacht with frankly illegal stealth systems, and it's armed to the teeth. Hmm. A little above you guys' pay grade. A spayed AI – typical control freak Scab. Medical systems. Want to tell me who she is now?' Vic still didn't answer. She concentrated for a moment longer, then she was looking at Vic. 'She's pre-Loss, and she's carrying pure-strain S-tech.' Vic still didn't say anything. There was nothing to say. 'I already don't like her. I don't like the venomous looks she gives me, as if she thinks she matters. I don't like the sobbing, or the whining. Felines have sensitive hearing, you know? I don't like her smell, and frankly her clothes are fucking stupid. What sex is she, anyway? Girly girl?'

'Base human female. There were only two, possibly three genders originally.'

'If I kill her, do my problems go away?'

'In that Scab will kill you, permanently, then I suppose so,' Vic told her. Elodie nodded as she considered this. 'She's under my protection.'

Elodie snorted with laughter. 'Oh, Vic,' she said, grinning. 'Is it love?' Then her face hardened. 'Don't be so fucking stupid. If she's here, she's a commodity.'

'You think you're not?' Vic asked.

Elodie strode across the room to him and reached up to hold his face in her hand. Vic felt claws hard enough to do some damage tap against his armoured chitin.

'I may have to dance for a while but that's all. You can't make him jealous. The only thing he cares about is if something inconveniences him, and then he'll just destroy it.'

Vic removed Elodie's hand from his face. 'Stay away from her.'

'No,' Elodie told him. 'You keep her out of my way.'

Vic turned to go. He was wondering how he, someone who'd helped destroy cities on CR worlds as part of a Thunder Squad, who was half of the most feared bounty killer duo in Known Space, had somehow managed to end up even further down the pecking order on a ship with only four people on it.

'I like you, Vic. It's probably the contrast,' Elodie said as he left, the room sealing behind him.

Vic found her curled up in one of the corridors on the plush, wine-red carpeted floor. Half the wall was similarly carpeted, and above that the smart matter had taken the form of dark wood panels. It was odd, the 'sect thought as he looked at the sobbing pre-Loss nat human. She was visibly miserable but had decided to be out in the corridor rather than inside her chamber, which at least gave the illusion of providing solitude even though she was monitored at all times.

Vic watched her cry for a while. Her sobs were wracking her body in a way that looked positively painful, and as a humanophile, he was slightly envious of them. He wandered off again, the carpet deadening the sound of his heavy armoured frame. He 'faced some instructions to the yacht's assembler – it had kept his preferences from previous attempts. This time, instead of having the assembler attempt to re-create a real flower, he had the *Basilisk II* construct one from surgical steel.

He returned a few minutes later with the tray of assorted drugs. Talia was still curled up on the carpet, sobbing.

'I'm not sure what the human protocol for this is,' Vic said. Few of the human genders were this emotional and vulnerable these days, not even in immersions, although some of the historical ones suggested an early human predisposition towards hysteria. 'I have chocolate, red wine and morphine,' he said cheerfully.

She looked up at him with a tear-stained face, her make-up running. Scab didn't understand the make-up. He was getting better and better at judging human aesthetics, and the make-up just obscured her actual attractiveness.

'Do you want to get fucked-up?' he asked hopefully. He was learning that direct sexual enquiries were not always the way forward. They only worked for monsters like Scab, apparently.

*

'So it's just, like, every guy I choose is a bigger wanker than the previous one.'

Vic accessed the pre-Loss lexicon he'd been building to look up 'wanker'. If his information on human mores was correct, then he was pretty sure that most humans, and indeed most uplifts bar the 'sects, were 'wankers' unless they belonged to some of the more extreme ascetic orders within the Church. He hoped it wasn't a member of the Church she was looking for.

Her chamber within the yacht was odd. It was very dark, for a start, and cluttered with many things she had fabricated in the assembler that looked unnecessary to Vic, but then he remembered that she didn't have access to all the entertainment. She'd had the smart-matter hull create a circular porthole that reminded him of a spider's web, and Red Space bathed the room in its deceptively warm glow. Her bed was very soft and extremely large for her small frame, which gave Vic hope. It also held a number of strangely inanimate stuffed toys, which he thought she was too old for, and all of which looked slightly grotesque. He'd been quite surprised to see actual paper books. In many ways she was lucky that the yacht's entertainment libraries were equipped with old-fashioned audio and visual entertainments. He was less sure about the odd keening noise the room was playing. Talia had assured him it was music, though apparently it had no accompanying soundscape, either emotive, psychological or even visual.

'It's like I find the single biggest bastard I can in any given situation and latch on to him.' This Vic could understand. She was smoking a cigarette made of tetrahydrocannabinol. She had offered him some, but his various filters would have made it pointless even if he inhaled like humans. Instead he had been trying to use his internal drug stores to synthesise a similar effect. He'd only succeeded in making himself lethargic and slightly paranoid – or rather, had caused a slight increase in his healthy baseline paranoia.

'I think I do that, too,' Vic told her. She nodded, though Vic suspected this had more to do with social conventions than her actually listening to him. Talia took another swig of red wine from the bottle. 'Is that why you fucked Scab?' Vic asked, more to try and coax out of her the next thing he was supposed to feel sympathetic about than anything else. He panicked when her face started to crumple again. He decided at this point he wasn't going to say anything else until he had cross-referenced it with the human social-interaction library stored in his neunonics.

She started crying again. He tried patting her shoulder. It was one of the appropriate responses, apparently. She almost managed not to flinch away from his armoured chitinous touch this time.

'Well, why did you?' he asked, forgetting to cross-reference. He'd been a little hurt. He did feel sympathy for her. She was thousands of years away from anything she even remotely knew. The last thing she'd had any kind of relationship with was a living alien spaceship they'd murdered, she was going to be sold to the highest bidder, and if she was lucky, it wouldn't result in vivisection. 'Look, I'm sorry, I'm not really very good at this. Normally I just find a human female who wants to experiment, try not to crush her whilst we copulate, use a cocktail of drugs to fake an orgasm and then listen to her tell me it was just a phase she was going through.'

Talia was staring at him. Then she burst out laughing, much to Vic's relief.

'Oh my god, this is so weird! I'm in space, talking to a giant insect. This is like ... I don't know ... William Burroughs or something.' She reached out to touch him. Vic's tactile sensors appeared to enjoy it. 'Look, seriously, you don't want to be involved with me—'

'Do you mean get sexed-up?'

'I'm a fucking mess, I really am,' she carried on as if she hadn't heard him. 'I mean, the thing with Scab. It's classic me, and we're just too different.' She glanced up at the big insect. Vic thought her eyes looked particularly big, for some reason.

'But why Scab? I'm not trying to make you weep like an infant again. I'm much nicer than him, but I've also killed rather a lot of people as well.'

Talia stared at him for a while. 'Well, he's human. We don't really think of insects as things we have sex with where I come from.'

'Things?'

'I'm sorry, people. And look at it from my perspective – I'm alone out here and everything's strange. He appears to be the most dangerous person ever. I thought if I could get him to like me even a little—'

'He doesn't really like people,' Vic told her. 'So you weren't really attracted to him?' She didn't answer. Instead she looked away from him and drew her legs up to hug them more tightly.

'Oh,' Vic said. She had told him about her boyfriends. The one who beat her, who her mean sister had killed. The one who had stolen her stuff and thrown her out. Another who wouldn't share his drugs with her. The last one had apparently pimped her out. Then she was kidnapped for her blood. Vic assumed it was for the strange application of pure-strain S-tech she contained within her. Then Scab. It made sense, he thought.

'It sounds like the best one you were intimate with was the Seeder ship.'

This time the tears in her eyes were different. They weren't coming from big body-wracking sobs. She turned away and lay down.

'You know I can't remember it. I keep reaching for it. It feels so close but I can never get to it. I think I was at peace. I think it was beautiful. Imagine if you felt the universe, and it wasn't all cold? Imagine if it sang, and you could hear it?' She didn't say anything else for a long time. 'And then you guys murdered her, didn't you?' she said angrily.

Oh, fuck, Vic thought, and struggled to find a correlation in the library of human interaction to murdering the alien spaceship that the girl he fancied was bonded to. 'Sorry,' he hazarded.

She rolled back over and sat upright. Analysis subroutines in his neunonics told him she was struggling to control rage. She exhaled smoke at him.

'Sorry? *Sorry!* It's all just predator and prey to you guys, isn't it?'

'Yes,' Vic answered honestly.

'And now pussycat super-bitch is on board, the ultimate psycho has a new fucktoy, so screw you, Talia, you're still going up on the block for auction.'

Vic reached over to touch her again. This time she flinched from him. This time she couldn't hide the expression of disgust quickly enough.

'I don't want to hurt you,' he told her. He was starting to think he'd pushed the whole human thing too far. It just wasn't worth feeling like this.

Then she looked up at him and her expression completely changed again. He was pretty sure it was contrite. She reached out to touch his upper arm.

'No, I'm sorry. Look, you have to understand this sort of thing doesn't happen. I have a boring life. I'm from a boring family, in a boring town. To me this is like living a nightmare. Everyone I know is dead – my dad, my friends, my fucking sister, all gone. There's not even some future Earth to go back to, and nobody seems to really know why. I'm doing the best I can, but can you help me?'

She sounded desperate. She was pleading. He reached down to place the hand of one of his lower arms on her shoulder. This time she didn't flinch.

'Yes,' he told her.

'Protect me from him. Please. Don't let him sell me.'

There was pain but with no actual apparent physiological cause. He ran a diagnostic of all his physical and mechanical systems but found nothing amiss.

'I can't do that, Talia. I don't think anyone can.'

She threw herself down on the bed and rolled away from him. 'Please go,' she said coldly.

Vic stood up and left the room. He knew Scab could have heard every word if he'd been monitoring them. He almost expected to find him out in the corridor, leaning on the wall, smoking. Holding something hard, sharp and pain-inducing in his hand. Wanting to make it wet. But the corridor was empty.

Mr Hat sat in his temple. He was in his bath chair. The bath chair was on a jagged, irregular spike of glass rising from a blasted, blackened landscape into a starless, dark-purple sky.

Images of violence and atrocity cascaded down the glass of the temple to play across Mr Hat's scaled features. They were visual representations of the history of his current prey, Woodbine Scab, uploaded as raw immersive audio and visual data. The display was completely unnecessary, of course, but it was a ritual he enjoyed at the start of a hunt. He felt it mimicked ancient lizard hunting rites that had involved the consumption of the image of the prey they intended to hunt.

As he assimilated the information on Scab, intelligent investigation programs began sifting through it using criteria he had selected. Far above him, black-immersion simulations of Scab howled in their cages as interrogation, torture and psychosurgical subroutines went to work on them. Mr Hat suspected only the psychosurgical programs would be of use against the shade of Woodbine Scab.

As the software sifted through the raw data, he relaxed in his bath chair and leaned back. The featureless dataforms of his automatons were naked and writhing all over each other, creating a living carpet on the floor of the temple as they debased themselves before him.

A while later he found something of interest. He dropped out of the illegal deification immersion and back into the black metal and brass of his ship's Command and Control. He started 'facing instructions to the ship. He spared a moment to glance at the eyeless human blank seated in the tailored couch at the base of his command column. The blank's S-tech-augmented, biologically entangled twin remained with his employer. Their means of instantaneous communication for the moment when Mr Hat found Scab.

15

Ancient Britain

Everything sickened with life. It was the opposite of what they thought they wanted. It was a corruption of the order of the gods. Things moved that shouldn't move. Creature merged and fused with creature in a perversion and a mockery of the hated gods of birth and life. It was as if the principles of the male magic of iron and the forge had fused with the principles of the female magic of birth and life. Even as they made it back to the Plain of the Dead, Ysgawyn knew that his dreams of ruling part of Annwn, the land of the dead, had been shattered. He had prayed and sacrificed for a quiet, chill place, a kingdom of fear where his will was paramount. That dream was over, because even here on the plain, in the borderlands between the two worlds of the living and the dead, the sickness of fecund, unrestrained life still threatened.

They had ridden hard, fleeing the monstrosities emerging from the sea between the three islands. Riding west back to their mound homes. Even the horses blessed by Crom Dhubh, those he had turned into white, Otherworldly steeds with red eyes, were pressed to their limits. Their flanks were soaked with salt sweat, panting for breath when they risked slowing their gallop.

Some of the weaker ones had succumbed to the sickness of life, and their skins had started to slough off as they sank into their mounts, fusing with them. Others developed screaming mouths in their flesh or vestigial limbs. Where possible, the other members of the tribe killed them and left them where they fell. No burial, no ritual, no words said.

'We need to rest,' Gwynn said. He was one of the seven remaining warriors from the original warband. Ysgawyn was beyond speech. He simply nodded and slipped down from his horse. His knees came close to buckling, but he managed to stagger back to his feet.

'What's that?' asked Brys, the only remaining greybeard. He had been a close friend of Gwydion's, before their old warmaster was killed during the battle on the causeway. Ysgawyn closed his eyes. He did not want to look. This was home, that was enough. He could bear no more. The sacrificers could wall them in their tombs, inscribe wards sacred to Arawn on the stone and leave him there, for all he cared.

'People,' Gwynn said, and even as tired as the young warrior was, Ysgawyn could hear the surprise in his voice.

His head nodded forward tiredly as he forced himself to look at the plain. The full moon cast long shadows of the figures lurching towards them, emaciated to the point of skeletal.

'Unless they have something very compelling to say, kill them,' Ysgawyn managed, slurring only slightly. He heard the satisfying noise of iron sliding from leather. He drew his own sword, though he barely felt strong enough to hold it. He forced himself to walk to where his men stood. He counted about thirty of the emaciated shadows staggering across the plain towards them.

'Ysgawyn,' Brys said quietly. The *rhi* turned to look at the greybeard. The big, once powerfully built man looked gaunt and haggard. Worse, he looked afraid. 'I think one of them just came out of a mound.'

Ysgawyn turned back to the figures lurching towards them, suspicion mounting with fear.

'If they have trespassed, they must fall. Gwynn – a casting spear.'

Gwynn was the youngest among them and still had the strength to throw one of the light casting spears. It caught the closest figure in the ribs. The sound that echoed across the plain was wrong. It did not sound like a spearhead sinking into flesh. All eyes turned to Ysgawyn. Ysgawyn closed his eyes and took a deep breath. He opened his eyes and slowly, tiredly, took his limed, leather-covered oak shield from his saddle before walking out onto the plain ahead of his watching men. He made his way towards the closest one with a vigour and an air of courage he did not feel.

'Do you trespass in these borderlands because you wish to travel to Annwn?' he managed to demand. 'Know that you will do so as our slaves.'

There was no answer. For the first time, the quiet of the plain bothered Ysgawyn. He moved closer to the figure. There was movement, some kind of slithering around the man's legs, and pale metal glinted in the moonlight. The skeletal form was wearing arm and neck torcs and its eyes were black holes. Its desiccated skin was limed in the style of the Corpse People. It reached out a bony hand for Ysgawyn. The *rhi* of the Corpse People was appalled to see something move around the arm and push under the cracking skin, fattening up the limb before returning the arm to more normal proportions. Ysgawyn realised there was also movement in the thing's rib cage. It looked like hanging, bloody, soil-covered fruit, more rudimentary than the internal organs he had seen before in the split-open battle wounded and the dead. As the figure moved, it had to pull at its leg to separate it from the earth, yanking dirt up with each step. The dirt flowed like liquid as it climbed the thing's leg.

Ysgawyn swallowed hard. Dead skin fell from the thing's face like snow, but not before he recognised the figure reaching for him. He did not soil himself because he had eaten so little, but he did piss himself as his long-dead father reached out for him. He swung wildly with his sword. He heard dry bones crack. It did not feel like he had hit flesh.

'Run! Run!' he screamed.

Tangwen was younger, but not much younger. She was still a hunter for her tribe, but her face didn't hurt all the time, or make her want to weep when she caught its reflection in the water. She was sitting in the crystal cave on the ground, looking up at Father on his wooden chair.

They kept Father secret, and his magics hid him from insane gods. She was, however, only slightly aware of how unnatural many other tribes would find his serpentine appearance.

Here, on the floor, was a good place. This was where he told stories of long ago and places far away. He said that the land was vast, and round like an apple, and filled with many wondrous people, creatures and things. They knew he made these stories up to amuse the children. What he spoke of simply wasn't possible, even with the mightiest of magics, but she had always liked the stories anyway.

She was not, however, here for stories.

'Daughter, I am so sorry, what I do this night is wrong. I swore I would never invade the mind of one of your people, but this is too important.'

'There is nothing I would hide from you,' she said. Too late she thought of her weakness, her hesitation at the wicker man. She thought about the boy that Britha had killed. The one they rescued from the Corpse People. She turned away from Father. She felt the familiar, gentle touch of cold, dry, scaled, clawed hands against the skin of her face. Then they faded. She looked up and saw him shimmer. The cave started to disappear, but then it returned.

'It's all right, child. I do not judge. I sing the mindsong to the blood we share as you sleep, but the magics are weak. We do not have long.'

'We are coming back. I have people with me. More than died fighting the Lochlannach, but some will return to their own tribes—'

'No, you must not return here,' Father told her. She could hear the hiss

in his words now. She heard it rarely, and it had always frightened her. It meant he was agitated, and she was used to him being the calm centre of her tribe's life.

I have to return, she thought. Being told not to come home made her want to weep so much. She missed the marshes and the swamps, her close family and her larger family. She had done enough. She wanted to go home.

'The family are leaving, going west across the sea to Gaul. The Muileartach's womb has burst and spilled out poisoned life fathered by the Dark Man. We cannot stand against this. We must run. Ynys Prydain is lost.'

'We can fight this—' Tangwen began, though war with the monstrous things she had witnessed was the last thing she wanted. She just wanted to rest.

'We do not have the magics,' Father said sadly.

'But we fought the Lochlannach, and we beat them!'

'Your friends – Britha, Fachtna, Teardrop – they could fight this poisoned tide, but they are too few—'

'And they are gone,' she said sadly.

'Their weapons?'

'Gone. But you have their magics, we have drunk of your blood, soaked our arrowheads and speartips in it.'

'They had the blood of the Muileartach, and the magics of the Ubh Blaosc, though I do not know that name. I am weak by comparison. Some of your blood on your weapons might help, but it would need to be replenished so often that it would never be enough.'

'I heal quickly!'

'Because of that same blood. You would heal more slowly if you were to do this.'

'Do I need a ritual? The help of the drywр?' she asked, thinking back to the ritual Teardrop had performed on the Crown of Andraste when she thought Britha and Fachtna were dead.

'No, daughter. No ritual. The magic is in the blood. Just think on what you want it to do before you cut yourself.'

'There must be other magics powerful enough.'

She saw him hesitate. She could tell he was trying to hide something from her. For all that people said of serpents, Father had always been a bad liar.

'Please,' she said.

'Only the Lochlannach have magics powerful enough.'

She felt her heart sink. 'Kush's axe?'

'He is but one man,' he finally said. 'There is no hope for this land. Take your people north and then make for the coast. Go to Gaul and meet your family there.'

She realised what was wrong with what he had said.

'And you will travel with them?' she demanded, feeling the tears come, knowing the answer.

'I cannot leave this place—'

'I will come back for you—'

'No! I forbid it!' Suddenly Father looked over his shoulder. A moment of fear, which he forced down, and turned back to look at her. Bending in close, cradling her head in his arms.

Over his serpentine form she could see something indistinct, a shimmering dark shape she couldn't quite make out, and which made her sick to look at it.

'Tangwen! Tangwen! They are close now.' The voice came from so far away.

'You have to go now,' Father told her. She wanted to look at him one last time but she couldn't take her eyes off the dark shape in the crystal cave. She felt something dirty and corrupt squirm in the back of her mind, like the thoughts she knew she shouldn't have, but which came unbidden anyway.

'Enough!' Half-hiss, half-shout. She shrank away. She had never seen Father angry before. He stood and turned on the thing behind him.

Tangwen found herself reaching for her spear, looking up at Anharad.

'I have broken the mindsong. She is nothing to you,' Father said.

'Her blood is weak,' Crom Dhubh said, from where he stood in the crystal cave that existed in the mindsong. The Dark Man had pushed his way into it.

'You failed,' Father told him.

'Tell me, do you know me? Did we walk the same streets?'

'You can have me if you leave my children be,' Father said, visibly afraid.

'I don't want you. I probably won't even be that amused when our poisoned children find you and drag you from your hole so that you can hear the sleeping gods.'

Father stared at him, the fear slowly draining away. 'You are a petty, spiteful creature.'

Crom Dhubh considered this. 'I just don't lie to myself. The first lesson we all learn is pain.' Suddenly the Dark Man looked directly up at him. 'Did you feel that?'

And he had. Something had moved deep in the earth. Part of the network of ancient gates had been activated. A bridge from another place.

Tangwen had made the spear by securely tying the knife she'd taken from the Isle of Madness to a stout branch she'd found. Still tired, she carried it as she followed Anharad. They had rested for the night on a rise looking down over a densely wooded valley. After escaping from the Isle of Madness, they had travelled for days. Tangwen had no idea where they were, but somehow the thirty or so survivors from the wicker man were looking to her for leadership. She didn't want the responsibility. She didn't want their hopes pinned on her.

They had passed a number of settlements, most of them abandoned fortified farms, sometimes villages of roundhouses where the richness of the land could support them. They had only seen one fort, built on a low hill not much higher than the surrounding countryside. All the settlements had been abandoned and some of them raided, presumably by the Corpse People.

Tangwen had not felt any guilt whatsoever about looting these places for food and clothing. There was little in the way of weapons left behind.

They were in the territory of the Atrebates at the moment. She assumed they had sent scouts south when the Corpse People raided. The scouts would have returned with news of the plague of monstrous things that had crawled from the sea. What was bothering Tangwen was that the Atrebates, and indeed many of the inhabitants of Ynys Prydain, were not a cowardly or timid people. She was surprised they had run. But she was also relieved. She believed Father – there was no fighting the madness at her back.

The thirty or so survivors with them were either strong, clever or simply very lucky. She could not think about how many had died because it made her sick. Other than her and Kush, there were no other real warriors. The boy, Mabon, was learning to be a warrior when he was taken, and Anharad, his grandmother, had been schooled in the use of sword and shield when she was younger. Many of the others had been spear-carriers at one time or another, landsmen and -women pressed into service to support their tribes' warriors during times of conflict. They were from many different tribes, though mostly coastal ones like her own Catuvellauni; the Cantiaci; the Trinovantes, old enemies of her people; the fearsome Iceni who lived directly to the north of her people's lands; the Corielatavi; the Parisi; the Brigantes. Then stranger people from further north of whom she had only ever heard stories. The Goddodin and others who spoke a language so different from her own that she barely understood them, though they looked and sounded a little like Britha. Most of them were young, because it was the young who had been strong enough to survive. There were only a few children other than Mabon. Two of them, a boy and a girl, were with their mother, a fierce Corielatavi woman who, even now, kept her children strictly disciplined. Tangwen was of the opinion that was why they were still alive. The other child was a silent, terrified-looking northern girl. She was on her own and spoke little. Tangwen and Anharad were taking turns keeping an eye on her.

Tangwen tried to ignore how tired she felt, the weariness and the ache in her bones, the pain from the ruined side of her face. She followed Anharad to the edge of the rise and looked down on the woods in the bowl-shaped valley. The tree canopy was thick and just starting to turn from green to brown as the days became shorter, colder and wetter. As Tangwen watched, she saw it – it looked like the canopy was moving. As if it had come to life.

'It's moving faster,' Anharad said. Tangwen glanced over at the older woman. The Trinovantes noblewoman looked haggard and tired, but despite her age – she had seen close to fifty winters – she'd managed to keep pace with the rest.

'Get them up,' Tangwen said.

She knew what was happening down below in the valley because she'd seen it close up. The abominations from Andraste's poisoned womb were creating more of themselves. They corrupted animals, made trees move and brought rocks to horrible life. The Parisi with them – a timid, nervous but powerful man called Twrch who had some training as a *dryw* because he had been learning how to work metal – had suggested that somehow the things spread seeds that made life. Anything not brought to life was consumed by the monstrous horde. All they left behind them was a plain of muddy grey waste.

'What of Essyllt?' Anharad asked.

Tangwen tried not to sigh out loud. The young woman, one of the Brigantes from far to the north, had complained of pain in her leg and then collapsed screaming, except the screaming hadn't been coming from her mouth. When they unwrapped the rags around her leg, they found a hideous growth. The flesh of her thigh had reshaped itself into a mouth, and in that mouth were other growths that Tangwen did not understand. It was the mouth that screamed, and that was all it did. They gagged the mouth as best they could, and two of her own tribe had made a litter on which to carry her. They had done so uncomplaining, but Tangwen could see the resentment building in them.

Others had developed strange growths – patches of fur or bark, extra toes, fingers and even tails emerging from strange places. Tangwen wasn't sure if it was a sickness caused by the seeds Twrch had talked about or some other form of magic. Not that it mattered, as she had no way of countering it. Unless they started turning on the group, those affected stayed with them. Though some had asked for them to be cast out.

Tangwen made her way over to Essyllt's litter as Anharad set about getting the others up and ready to move. Mabon fell in next to her. The boy still hadn't said anything, not even to his grandmother, but he acted as if he was someone of rank in his bearing alone.

The young Brigante woman was lying on her litter, moaning in pain. The mouth on her leg still had a rag stuffed in it, and there was something obscene about the way it was trying to chew its way through the fabric. Tangwen glanced up at the two men tasked with dragging and carrying the litter. They had done so valiantly, Tangwen had to concede, but they were close to exhaustion. Neither of them would meet Tangwen's eyes.

'What?' Tangwen demanded. Neither man answered immediately. She had been told their names many times, but she couldn't remember them now.

'She is close to death,' one of them said.

'You're a *dryw*, are you? You know this?' Tangwen asked. He did not answer. 'You mean you don't want to carry her any more?'

'I don't think we can,' the other said. The shame was written all over his face.

That at least is honest, Tangwen thought. 'Fine, kill her,' Tangwen told them. She could feel Mabon looking at her. She glanced down at the boy but couldn't decipher the expression on his face. She looked back up at the two Brigantes, but neither of them had moved. 'Or do you want to leave her here for what follows?'

'We were hoping that—' began the one who had spoken first.

'That I would do it? If she asked me to, then perhaps.'

'Then *you* carry her!' the same man hissed. Others were starting to look over at the three of them.

'No,' Tangwen said simply. She could not be bothered to explain that her skills were of more use to them elsewhere. The man sat down hard on a rotted log, his head in his hands. 'We will not always be trudging through this wood, fleeing Andraste's brood. One day we will be safe, warm, rested, our bellies full. We will be seated with friends and family. How do you want to remember this day then? I can't force you to carry her.'

The man on the log stared up at her with unbridled hatred. Tangwen walked away. She did not look back but she heard them picking up the litter. She would speak with Twrch and some of the stronger ones, get them to help. The thing was, the two men were probably right. Essyllt would most likely die, but Tangwen could not face losing any more people.

*

Kush had told her that one of the reasons why the *Will of Dagon* had been such a successful trading vessel was because Germelqart appeared to be able to see perfectly in the darkness, and therefore navigate at night. This meant that the ship could move further and faster than their competition.

Tangwen moved quietly to where the navigator was standing in the woods, looking north. She would rather have been in those woods on her own, scouting ahead or hunting for food for them all, but she needed to be at the head of the column of survivors, leading them. Kush, whose skin colour alone made many of the survivors nervous, was at the back of the column, chivvying them on, making sure none fell behind.

Kush's command of the language appeared to be improving daily. He was a quick learner. She was pretty sure Germelqart's speech was improving as well, but the navigator kept very quiet.

'Can you see something?' Tangwen asked quietly.

'I thought ... movement ... but far away,' Germelqart said haltingly.

'Andraste's brood?' Tangwen whispered.

The Carthaginian shook his head. 'Not like that.'

Tangwen could hear the others coming up behind her. She had no choice but to go on, for dealing with anything that lay ahead was better than what lay behind. She was too tired to think beyond the task of trudging onwards. The ground was rising in front of them and they had glimpsed a line of hills through the trees ahead.

As they continued, Tangwen became more and more convinced that they were being watched. Keeping pace with her, Germelqart was also anxious, darting his gaze one way and then another very suddenly.

'More than one,' he said quietly.

Tangwen felt as if she was being hunted, and was frustrated that Germelqart was seeing what she could not. Suddenly he pointed forward. At first Tangwen thought it was one of the strange fusions of creatures that Andraste had made, for it looked like a person with the tufted head of a lynx. It took her a moment to realise that the lynx head was made from thin, light wood, leather and furs. It was not unlike the snakeheads her people wore when they went to war. She was sure the figure was a woman. She wore a short cloak made of lynx fur, which had helped hide her in the woods, and beneath that soft, supple leather with moulded pieces of stiffer leather sewn to it to protect various parts of her body. She held a bow and a short sword and a dagger hung at her hip. Germelqart started looking elsewhere the moment she appeared.

'She's showing herself to us,' Tangwen said. That meant there were others she could not see, ready to act if the survivors proved hostile. She knew that whoever they were, they invoked the spirit of the lynx to hunt, as she did the snake when she wore the snakehead. This would make them difficult to spot within the woods.

The others had seen the newcomer now and stopped. She heard a few gasps and the sound of makeshift weapons being readied. She held up her hand. The lynx-headed woman took her time looking them over.

'Counting,' Germelqart said quietly. Tangwen nodded. The scout was taking a good look at them. Finally the strange figure made an exaggerated step to one side and pointed north.

'Which is the direction we were going anyway,' Tangwen muttered. She gestured for the others to follow. Glancing behind her, she saw that Kush had moved up the line, his axe at the ready. She motioned to him that everything was okay and then moved closer to the lynx-headed woman. Now she could feel them, the others in the woods. She saw a branch move in her peripheral vision. *It's movement that gives you away*, she thought. They would have arrows nocked but not drawn, watching her.

'Can you understand me?' Tangwen asked. The lynx-headed scout nodded, once. 'Cythrawl,' she said, using the word for the worst evil her people knew. 'Follows us.' The lynx-head nodded. 'Your people cannot fight it.' There was no movement from the scout. 'Will you have to learn this with your death?' There was no immediate answer, but finally the woman pointed north again. Tangwen turned to watch the survivors pass. When Kush was level with her she joined him, and after one last glance at the scout she headed north with the rest.

'Do you know who she is?' Kush asked. Tangwen just shook her head.

It was close to nightfall when they found them. At the base of the hills they'd seen in the distance, they found a trench that ran in either direction as far as the eye could see. In the trench were warriors and horses, more of each than Tangwen had ever seen in one place before. The ones closest to Tangwen wore armour made of metal chains like the type the traders from Gaul were always trying to sell her people, but the heavy armour would only be a hindrance in the marsh. A number of them wore thick cloaks of bear fur and the skulls of bears as headdresses. They carried heavy, long iron swords and large leather-covered shields stained black. The hafts of both their long and casting spears were also stained black.

A few of them glanced up but paid little or no attention to the ragged band of survivors. Scanning along the ditch, it was clear there were warriors from a number of tribes here, and it looked as though there were more out of sight. Tangwen estimated there could be as many as two hundred warriors.

She had seen ravens and other scavengers feasting on bodies scattered among the trees. This was the inevitable result of warriors from many different tribes jockeying for status and position.

'They're going to try and fight,' Kush said quietly.

'They have no idea what is coming,' Tangwen all but whispered.

Carrion eaters took flight as the stones glowed from within. There was a bright, pulsing, blue and white light, then water swamped the stones, the force of it tearing off the corpses hanging from them and carrying them away. The light stopped and with it the flow of water, though what was left spread out, soaking the surrounding dry earth.

Fachtna had caught a glimpse of one of the glowing stones rushing towards him as the freezing water carried him along. Then everything went black. He awoke to pain and nausea and managed to stagger to his feet. He found Britha, whose wounds made her look more dead than alive. He had told his blood what to do when he forced it into her mouth. He vomited his blood onto her wounds and then into her mouth, praying to Lug, whom he knew he had wounded deeply through his actions. He needed her to have held on to just a vestige of life. Then he blacked out again.

'How do we get back? How do we get back?' It was a shriek.

'We can't,' he said as he struggled to consciousness.

'Liar! Child thief! Murderer of *dryw*!' Each accusation was punctuated by a kick. Fachtna managed to open his eyes. He had never seen her so angry. He had never been so pleased to see her. She was naked and covered in blood but her wounds looked healed, though her body had feasted on itself to do so. She was gaunt and would need to eat soon. He was less than pleased when he saw her hold up his sword. The blade was dull, though, and there was no song. 'The laws are the same in the *Ubh Blaosc* as they are anywhere else. The price for killing a *dryw* is death!'

'No!' he managed, but the sword plunged down. His armour hardened under the blow, but even though it was not alive, the sword point was sharp enough, and she put enough force behind it to pierce the armour. He felt it go through, the blade driven deep into the sodden earth beneath him. It started to grow dark again. He reached for

Britha as she turned from him and walked away. He had seen the tears in her eyes.

'Did you feel that?'

Bress was alone on the *curragh* as it made its way up the river. Many of the slave warriors were close at hand, but he was always on his own. Looking down at the river, he could make out the dark shape of one of the 'giants' swimming close to the surface as they headed further inland. The people from the settlements along the banks of the river had fled. The Lochlannach had raided this area when they were taking people for the wicker man. The people here knew to fear the black *curraghs*.

Even though he was alone, he felt Crom Dhubh all over him like a treacherous, diseased lover. Bress closed his eyes and nodded.

'I want to know,' the Dark Man whispered.

16
Birmingham, 5 Weeks Ago

Grace leaned back on the chair while Du Bois sat on the edge of the bed, concentrating. They had been reviewing the data internally.

'He can't have gone from spending more than two centuries in a hole to being able to hide from the most technologically advanced organisation on the planet,' she said through a yawn. They had been looking for him for the better part of a week now. All the CCTV cameras in the city were linked to a recognition program and they'd run down thousands of possible matches in facial features and stature. The city and the surrounding area was under geosynchronous surveillance from one of the satellites in the Circle's ancient network. They had seeded the local rat population with nanite cameras but found nothing. Given that most of this work could have been done from anywhere in the country, du Bois was reasonably sure they were being kept in Birmingham as a punishment of some kind.

'We may be technologically advanced but our operation's small and our resources stretched tight – particularly at the moment. And he had help.'

'You believe the rumours, then?' Grace asked, scratching absently at her legs through her fishnets. They were in his comfortably appointed room at the Malmaison in the Mailbox, close to the centre of Birmingham. They were in du Bois' room because you could see the floor.

'Which ones – about the Pacific situation, or that the Brass City is planning something?' Grace shrugged. 'I think the situation in the Pacific is getting worse, and the Brass City is always planning something. That doesn't help us.'

They had found CCTV footage of Silas Scab at Crowthorne railway station, and then again at Reading. After much enhancement, the grainy images appeared to show him carrying some kind of goblet. After Reading, they'd lost him.

'Do you think he's still being helped?'

It wasn't the first time they'd discussed this. 'Of some kind. It doesn't have to be direct.'

'The cup?' she asked. Du Bois shrugged. 'He must have gone somewhere else,' Grace suggested, not for the first time. She lit a cigarette. Du Bois glanced at her irritably.

'But there's nothing anywhere else in the world, as far as we can tell, that fits his MO. And if you're going to do that, could you at least open the window?' Du Bois enjoyed smoking as well, but he tended not to do it in the room he was staying in. Grace ignored him. 'Control must have a reason for keeping us here.'

'You're such a good boy, aren't you?' Grace earned herself another glare. '"I lied",' she mused, referring to the words the dead woman had written on the cinema screen.

'Well, she did,' du Bois said simply. It had transpired that Linda Galforg was not such a nice person after all. She advertised herself as a psychic but wasn't a true believer, apparently. In fact, according to those who had known her best she was something of a con woman who prayed on the desperate, the gullible and the bereaved.

'So does he care that she lied?' Grace asked. 'Is he punishing liars? Because he will be very busy.'

'They didn't really have psychological profiling the first time around.'

'But you caught him quickly.'

'Because he didn't know to expect us,' du Bois said. 'He thought he was unique, a god.'

'But you killed his father.'

'He probably rationalised it as a freak occurrence.'

'Did he give you the feeling that he would care about lying?'

Du Bois lay back on his bed. 'He appeared to be most interested in causing pain.'

'Which suggests that if he was bothered by her lying, it was because it got in the way of something he wanted.'

'To do what he does, he has to be able to objectify his victims.' Du Bois was relying for this insight on the criminal psychology books and papers he had downloaded and assimilated into his neural systems.

'And he's the worst kind of criminal, because with access to S- or L-tech he can make his fantasies come true.' Grace had assimilated the same information. 'In which case he'll only care about the lying inasmuch as it affects him.'

'Which suggests he was expecting Galforg to be a real psychic,' du Bois said, somewhat sceptically.

'Bit naive, isn't it? So much for the Age of Enlightenment.'

'I grew up believing in dragons,' du Bois pointed out.

'You may have been right.' Grace was grinning. 'So we think this was a practice kill, and he's actually looking for a real psychic?'

Du Bois sighed and closed his eyes. The smell of Grace's cigarette was both irritating him and making him want one as well. They'd been down this route before. They'd cut themselves and left veritable networks of nanite bugs in the vicinity of just about every 'psychic' they could find in Birmingham. So far nothing.

'Do you know what really bothers me?' du Bois asked.

'The abandonment of feudalism?'

'I mean other than the emancipation of women.'

'I will cut you.'

'He killed one of us—'

'The archer?'

Du Bois nodded. 'He also ate part of his brain. Now, I think he did that because he was insane. Because he wanted to symbolically steal the archer's knowledge. But what if he actually did? What if the tech subconsciously obeyed his desires? He could know a lot about us.'

'Two-hundred-year-old information,' said Grace, and then thought about it for a moment. 'He wouldn't know about me,' she said brightly.

'No, but he'd know about certain key things that just don't change. That's why I still don't get—'

'Why Mr Brown took him prisoner,' Grace finished for him.

'And why he was so lightly protected. The guy is a walking security risk.'

'So something else is at work here?'

'There's certainly something we're not seeing, and Control won't tell us.'

Grace just shrugged. 'Well, in the absence of anything worth doing, I'm going to head out, get outrageously drunk and start fights.'

'You know it's not fair fighting them, don't you?'

'Does it offend your chivalric code?' Grace mocked. 'Besides, it's fairer when I'm drunk.' She stood up and wandered towards the door before turning back to du Bois, who was looking up at her. 'Perhaps some sport sex with multiple partners as well!' She grinned, taking pleasure in du Bois' obvious discomfort before heading for the door. 'You stay here, have fun. You can put on your best hair shirt, maybe flagellate yourself for a bit,' she shouted over her shoulder as she left the room.

It was a private facility not far from the centre of the city. He could not believe how much things had changed. Everything was overwhelming, but how the world treated the mad had come a long way. Admittedly the wealthy had always been able to provide better facilities and care for members of their families who fell ill. Even if that meant locking them up somewhere else in the house where they couldn't embarrass anyone.

The goblet the demon had given him spoke to him. Told him everything he needed to know. Perhaps he shouldn't have trusted it, but his own demons had assured him it was under control. Without it he was sure he would have been discovered curled up sobbing in a ditch somewhere, overwhelmed by the world he found himself in.

A prick of his finger, a drop of blood touched to the electronic lock, and he was in. The 'phone', which had been born of the goblet, sent electronic information to the cameras in the hospital, making them record false images. A slash from one of the knives he had forged from the goblet released the demons in his blood and the staff fell asleep. He would keep the inmates – sorry, the *patients* – in the secure mental hospital awake, though. He would let them see him. He was pretty sure people would think he was like them. He wasn't. He had just enough insight to see it for what it was. A joke.

Through the thick metal security doors the hospital was clean and white. Nurses, orderlies and security staff were asleep on the floor, where they had fallen. He stepped over them carefully. The goblet had shown him how to make the demons in his blood surround him and remove traces of his presence that were somehow visible to modern forensic science, which to Silas's mind bordered on necromancy. But he was invisible now, a ghost and a near-god walking among them.

He could hear the disquiet of the patients. Whether his presence played into their own illnesses – it was, after all, a secure unit for privileged schizophrenics – or some preternatural sense, they were certainly reacting to him. A few screamed or shouted, mainly the ones in restraints. Many muttered to themselves, or talked in glossolalia that Silas was half-convinced he understood. Others hurt themselves or ran at the doors to their rooms. Most just cowered as far away from him as they could manage. He made sure he looked in every window he passed.

Finally he came to the room he wanted. Their security was as nothing to him. The blood seeped into the lock and the door opened.

He was little more than a boy. His head had been shaved for his own safety. He had a number of self-inflicted wounds and was strapped to his bed with padded leather restraints. *That will make things easier*, Silas thought.

'No ... please,' the boy begged.

Silas stepped into the room and opened the leather doctor's bag he was carrying. He pulled the glass slides out of the bag. The last time had been humiliating, and he was determined that wouldn't happen again. Next came the stainless-steel clamps. The boy wasn't even begging now. The forceps, the long knife, scalpels. Everything he'd fabricated himself and stylised slightly.

'P-please, it hurts so much – can you make it stop?'

Silas regarded the boy thoughtfully. 'Will you lie to me?' More than two hundred years might have passed, but Silas still retained the trace of his Swiss accent.

The boy stared up at him through a fog of pain. He appeared to understand what was happening to him.

'Then I won't lie to you. This will hurt. What will come after will hurt more. It doesn't matter.'

Silas walked over to the bed and the boy started to scream.

Du Bois picked Grace up from Broad Street. She left a drunken thug lying in his own blood on the street as she climbed into the Range Rover, her body converting the alcohol into something useful.

They assimilated what information was available before they arrived at the resentful cordon of police surrounding the private residential mental health facility. The victim's name was Alan Songhurst, a nineteen year old from a reasonably wealthy middle-class family in Warwickshire.

'What does "non-traditional schizophrenia" mean?' du Bois mused.

Grace looked at him as if he was a moron. 'Maybe there's a clue in the words used?' she suggested. Du Bois sighed and concentrated some more. A police officer waved them through the cordon and into the car park of the wood-panelled building. Flashing blue lights illuminated the entire area. Despite the attempt to make the facility look homely and pleasant, there was still no mistaking its institutional purpose.

'The disorder presented unconventionally,' du Bois mused, mostly to himself.

'You think that's significant?' Grace asked, sober now, as they both climbed out of the Range Rover. She was also reviewing Songhurst's medical files, downloaded from the facility's secure systems directly into her head.

As they pushed the door open and walked into the private facility, Grace reached under her leather jacket and drew one of her fighting knives from its upside-down sheath.

'My turn to self-harm, then?' She ran the sharp blade down her palm and released her blood-screen into the facility's interior.

'Nothing,' Grace said. 'Just junked fragments of DNA and carbon – everything's been broken down by a blood-screen programmed to remove evidence.' They were walking along the corridor towards Songhurst's room.

'Same with the security,' du Bois said grimly. 'Something went in there and spoofed it, but I can find no trace. The blood tests on the sleeping personnel will come back with nothing as well.' He had called the chief superintendent, whose name he was determined not to remember, to order the forensics team to start taking blood samples from the staff.

'So clearly he understands the modern world and how to circumvent it,' Grace pointed out.

'Though I suspect his approach to it will be coloured by his eighteenth-century upbringing—'

'And the fact that he's a screaming nut job?'

'Well, yes, but if we can find out how that manifests within in him, it will provide some insight.'

'I don't want to understand him, I just want to find him. What about the inmates?' Grace asked.

'I imagine we'll get some quite prosaic descriptions and interesting insights, but I suspect it won't bring us any closer to finding out where he is. I'll task the police to sit in on interviews with the staff psychologists.'

They arrived at Songhurst's door. Du Bois reached for the handle but paused.

'You ready?'

Grace pushed past him into the room.

Songhurst lay on the bed, still in the padded restraints. The top part of his head was missing, his skull a hollowed-out red bowl. Silas had laid a towel down on the desk in the room. The towel was red. The top part of Songhurst's skull had been placed on it. Grace stared at it whilst du Bois examined the hollowed-out head.

'Clamp marks, regular wounds – this was surgical. And the brain again.'

'Look at his eyes,' Grace said quietly. 'He was terrified, in agony. He didn't sedate him. He paralysed him, kept the nerve endings active. That poor bastard felt the whole thing. But there's more to this than just causing pain.'

Du Bois straightened. He didn't like the way Grace was looking at the corpse.

'Are you all right?'

Slowly, Grace turned to look at him. 'You ask me that again, Malcolm, and you and I are going to fall out.' Du Bois held his hand up in surrender. 'Now, I wonder – did Songhurst lie?' She started to concentrate. 'Non-traditional schizophrenia. The patient claims that the auditory hallucinations he hears are the thoughts of other people around him,' she recited from one of the medical reports she'd downloaded.

'You think he was psychic?' du Bois asked, somewhat sceptically. He reached down and dipped a finger into the residual blood around the bowl of Songhurst's hollowed-out skull. Grace grimaced as he brought the finger to his mouth and tasted it. She took her phone out of her pocket, downloaded a number into it from her mind and dialled it with a thought. Du Bois appeared to be concentrating on the taste of the dead boy's blood.

'Doctor Agarwal? My name is Grace Soggin, I'm involved with the Songhurst investigation.' She paused as she listened to the response. 'I'm sure the chief superintendent will vouch for me. I have a bit of an odd question for you. In your case files you say that the presentation of the auditory hallucinations was non-traditional – that Alan thought he could hear others' thoughts ...' Another pause while Grace listened. 'I appreciate that, Doctor, and you're absolutely correct, I'm not a mental-health professional, but did Alan ever correctly guess what you were thinking?' There was a longer pause this time, and at one point she rolled her eyes. 'Okay, Doctor, thank you.'

'Thought he was faking the auditory hallucinations, and instead had a talent for cold reading?' Du Bois asked.

Grace nodded. 'He was starting to come around to the idea that Alan was delusional, paranoid, but not schizophrenic,' Grace told him. 'Enjoy your taste?'

'If there's S-tech or anything else in his blood, it's so diluted I can't find it. You're thinking he was a real psychic?'

'According to the doctor, he was frequently frighteningly accurate in guessing what people were thinking. Do you know what the Ganzfeld experiment is?'

Du Bois sighed. 'Hold on.' He concentrated for a moment, wishing he could use the comfort blanket of his phone to read/assimilate the information. 'An experiment utilizing what is, effectively, sensory deprivation to test for extrasensory perception. It's the closest thing to empirical evidence of psychic phenomenon.' He sounded unconvinced.

Grace looked at the body. 'We got everything we need here?' she asked.

'We can wait for the police forensic team to identify the tools he used.'

'Then let's get out of here,' she said as she left the room, slamming the door behind her.

Du Bois caught up with her in the corridor. 'It's different this time,' he said quietly.

She turned on him angrily. 'Is it? I see some psycho hurting people again, and I tell you there's something driving this, something we can't see. Hawksmoor didn't just go mad – something he found in the architecture, in the geometry, drove him that way.'

Du Bois regarded her for a moment, worried. She had been a normal person when Hawksmoor started his Geometry of Violence experiments. She was caught up in the middle of it. A street-fighting hard girl, she'd been looking to protect her 'family' – the other gang members, beggars, thieves, prostitutes. She must have gone back and researched what happened. He wondered how she'd obtained clearance. Her dwelling on it made him uncomfortable, but on the other hand, he could understand why she'd want to know what had happened to her, and to those around her.

'And you think something's driving him?'

'What's he want a psychic's brain for?'

'If he *was* psychic. Or maybe Silas just thinks he was. Like—'

'I do?'

'That isn't what I meant.'

'Here's the thing, though,' Grace said. 'Nobody, anywhere, has suggested that Songhurst was psychic. Galforg advertised in the newspaper, she had a website. Everybody just thought Songhurst was some mad kid.'

'He's widening his search parameters,' du Bois said.

Grace nodded. 'And the closest thing to a connection we have is the psychic link, whether it's real or not.'

That, at least, du Bois had to agree with.

They walked across the car park towards the Range Rover, bathed in the flashing blue lights, ignoring the unhappy looks of the local constabulary. Du Bois stopped.

'What?' Grace asked.

Du Bois started heading back to the building. Grace followed, reluctantly.

'He's learned to circumvent our tech,' he said.

'So?'

'We're too hung up on it. Too used to everything being easy and convenient. We forgot to do something.'

'What?'

'Look.'

It was mid-morning. They had been searching for more than ten hours when they found it. It was just the two of them, moving out from the mental health facility in an ever-widening spiral. They'd used the police to form a cordon to try and minimise local residents fouling up any evidence.

The River Rea passed close to the back of the facility and they had been searching the banks. Grace's spike-heeled boots were hopelessly fouled, and not even augmented reactions had stopped her from toppling over more than once. She couldn't shake the feeling that du Bois was enjoying her discomfort more than a little, particularly when he offered to help her up.

'Over here,' du Bois said quietly, kneeling down in the undergrowth close to the river's muddy bank. Grace struggled through the mire towards him.

'You know there's not much opportunity to learn to hunt growing up in Spitalfields, Mr Lord-of-the-Manor, sir,' Grace muttered. Du Bois just smiled. Grace crouched and du Bois pointed out the bootprint. 'What makes you think it's him?'

'Right length of stride, anachronistic boots and they lead to the hospital.'

Grace glared at him. 'You mean you backtracked them here?' she asked. He nodded. 'So why have I been skating around in this fucking mud, risking falling into the fucking river?' she demanded.

'Mostly for my amusement,' he told her. Grace opened her mouth with an angry retort. Du Bois cut her off. 'That's not the point. The point is that the tracks lead from – and to – the river.'

'He's moving around using the river?'

'Well, he did this time. Birmingham has more miles of waterway than Venice. Pretty much the whole city is close to water, one way or another.'

'If he was in the water he'd be soaked – we'd have seen his tracks in the hospital.'

'What would happen if we fell in?'

Grace knew that the intelligent clothing they wore would either repel or expel the water, wicking it away from the skin.

'Where the fuck's he getting this tech from?' she muttered, but she knew the answer. From the same person who had helped him escape. 'So we seed the fish?'

'In that water? We're better sticking with the rats, and you're going to need a proper pair of walking shoes because we'll have to keep looking the hard way.'

'You're enjoying this, aren't you?'

Du Bois just smiled at her.

He rose out of the clammy, oily water and pulled himself easily onto the muddy bank. The water practically fell off him and he was dry by the time he stood up. It was unpleasant and undignified travelling this way. He had reduced himself to the level of some river-dwelling bogeyman in a child's fairy tale, but it served his purpose for the time being.

The leather doctor's bag hung across his back on a strap. He took it off and grasped the handle. As soon as he did so, he knew that the glass slides in the bag's sealed interior were secure.

He turned to walk towards his hideout and noticed the semicircle of dead rats surrounding a small tree growing out from the base of a graffiti-covered red-brick wall.

'Hello, my darling boy.' The woman who climbed down from the lower branches of the small tree was clad in layers of frayed and ragged cloth. Her hair was matted and filthy and she smelled horrible. She was leaning on a thick, staff-like stick.

'You weren't there a moment ago,' Silas said. He didn't like this at all. His left hand was already reaching inside his coat for one of his knives.

'Oh, darling boy, believe me, I have always been here.' She nodded towards the mud on the riverbank. 'And you want to be careful about the tracks you leave.'

Silas glanced down and saw his boot-prints, irritated that what she had said was correct.

'What do you want? How did you find me?' Silas demanded.

'You've got a little cup, haven't you – a horn, a trinket? It's a toy, nothing more. I know what you really want.'

'And what is that, hag?' Silas demanded. Her filth offended him. He wasn't sure that he wanted to soil his knife on her.

She smiled at his words. 'You think that's an insult but I know where hags come from, and they'll steal your breath and strip the flesh from your bones with their teeth. You're the child of cannibals, little one, and I know what you tasted on the Hellaquin's mind.'

Suddenly Silas was more interested, and even more disturbed. His eyes narrowed suspiciously. 'And why would you tell me anything?'

'Because them that's got it have lost their way. Because a bad man wants it for no good.'

'Some would say I'm a bad man.'

'You're just a warning. Besides, you're blood.'

A Long Time After the Loss

17

A Long Time After the Loss

The Monk stared at the image projected onto the airlock wall.

'Why?'

'It's him, or Negrinotti. The rest fit his pattern of going for the most difficult jobs, the biggest pay-offs. Those two are the only ones with anything significantly different about them. It's either that or he'll try for a Citadel.'

'Could he have the resources for it?'

Benedict/Scab's cold, dead eyes met hers. His head and torso were still hanging from the support sling. He didn't dignify the question with an answer.

'What about a cloner?'

'For what? If you saw Vic with him then he's already got access to cloning facilities.'

'Would you clone the girl?'

'Yes, if I thought it would benefit me, and if I could. In fact, what I don't understand is why he *didn't* clone her and sell you all copies.'

'We would have checked, of course, but that does suggest he can't clone her.'

'Which takes us back to ...' Scab nodded at the image on the wall.

'It doesn't matter – the Consortium would never let us near him.'

'If only you had access to an intrusion specialist like—'

'Negrinotti, yes, but even so. There's a reason that place is a prison.' The Monk shivered slightly.

Talia had almost crept into the yacht's large, open-plan lounge area. It was bathed in the blood-coloured light of Red Space shining through the transparent hull. Scab was sitting in the centre of the lounge, slumped in an armchair, naked, sunglasses on, a smouldering cigarette between two fingers.

'What are you doing?' she asked, leaning against the wall. He didn't answer. She suspected he might be on a heroin nod, or just ignoring her, again, but then the crimson glow of Red Space lessened as the hull became opaque and started to show what she assumed passed for news footage in this age. It displayed something that looked like a kind of slowly spinning, polygonal beehive made of what appeared to be plastic, inside a huge cavern that she guessed was a hollowed-out asteroid. Parts of it were burning, other parts had been destroyed. Heavily armed aircraft hovered around it. There were no captions to explain what was happening.

Another image showed a number of figures in armour that resembled a high-tech version of what she thought knights used to wear. They were led by a human with two heads. One of the heads was that of an ugly, completely bald human. The other looked like an idealised machine version of the human head. The armoured figures were carrying a still-living torso and escorting a heavily restrained multi-limbed figure. The torso looked a little like Vic if Vic had been larger, more heavily armoured, more insectile, spikier and had his limbs removed. The other figure was female, Talia thought, but she had no idea where she got that idea. It was smaller and had eight limbs, like a spider rather than an insect. Both the 'sect and the arachnid didn't so much look badly hurt as badly damaged, and both of them were more machine than biological.

'Where's that?' Talia asked, more for something to say than actual interest.

'The Solitude Hive,' Scab said.

Talia was little the wiser, though she guessed by the use of the word 'hive', and by the way it looked, that it was a place where the insect people lived.

'You have spider people as well?' she asked, looking at the restrained eight-armed female. There was a long silence.

'It's an arachnid augment, she's a princess 'sect. A worker-caste 'sect who's had a gender change.'

Talia nodded, as if any of it made sense to her.

'Have you seen Vic?' she asked. The silence stretched out. 'So what's happening?' she eventually asked when she realised he wasn't going to answer her previous question. The ash fell off Scab's cigarette and was absorbed by the carpet as he brought it to his mouth and took a long drag.

'The two-headed guy is called Crabber. He's a media whore who leads a bounty crew. The other 'sect is General Nix. He's warrior caste, a war criminal. The princess 'sect is known as the Widow. She was Nix's second-in-command, an immersion-warfare specialist. Crabber's crew have just taken him down.'

She could tell that her questions were irritating him but something Scab had said struck her as strange.

'In this day and age, how do you become a war criminal?' she asked before she realised she didn't want to hear the answer. Scab told her anyway.

The *Amuser* had come in with the Consortium naval squadron from one of the larger military contractor companies. There were two heavy cruisers, four light cruisers, a screen of eight destroyers and numerous smaller craft from corsairs down to fighters. Needless to say, Mr Hat had to ask permission to join them in Red Space. His employer's influence must have been remarkable indeed as the naval squadron had allowed him to accompany them, although they kept multiple weapon locks on him at all times.

Mr Hat had wondered if this was all because of Scab. Had they come to the same conclusion? If so, what did they expect to accomplish with a naval squadron? It wasn't how Scab worked.

He was further impressed by his employer's influence when Suburbia agreed to his request to see one of the prisoners. He had been of the belief that mostly they didn't do that kind of thing. There were too many secrets locked in too many heads in Suburbia.

Nolly Berger finished his breakfast and kissed his wife. She smiled at him, but she was distracted as she was getting the children ready. As he did every morning, Nolly wondered what they had done to end up here.

He went out of his front door, just like he always did, then walked down the drive to the ground car and climbed in. It was a bright, sunny day. It was always a bright, sunny day. All along his street of identical detached houses, his neighbours were doing exactly the same thing, though each was slightly staggered so they could make use of the transport network as efficiently as possible.

'Where to today?' the habitat's AI asked, accompanied by the sound of canned laughter.

'Work, please, Al,' Nolly said cheerfully. Inside he was screaming, and he wanted to tear out his own tongue. There was more canned laughter. It was funny because it was where he always went, and the AI, who they all called Al, which was also funny, knew that.

The car slid out onto the road and drove itself towards work, along with the rest of the all-but-identical cars driven by the other inmates. He knew that on each of the three non-window segments of the cylinder habitat, a similar scene would be playing out in every residential street.

In many ways, that was the worst thing about the cylinder habitat – the three window sections, which let in sunlight or showed space. They revealed the darkness outside. Occasionally they would see a pulsing red slash in space as the prisoner transports bridged into the system. He was sure that Nolly wasn't his real name, just as he was sure he hadn't always been human. He glanced up through the windscreen and felt the familiar vertiginous sensation as he looked at the other two inhabited sections. Boring streets, set out in boring grids, each the same as the next. They had malls but no town centres. There were light-industrial and business parks where they all worked within neatly landscaped grounds.

The only break he ever got was when one member of the family was chosen to flip out and torture to death the rest of the family. Then they would be cloned and have to go back into the program still aware of the violence, feeling resentment towards whomever had done it. Last time it was little Suzy. He still remembered her sitting on top of him, playing with the kitchen knife. He would hate her if he didn't fear her so much.

Suburbia was based on pre-Loss punishment media – twisted parodies of a perceived idyllic existence. There was no law-enforcement presence because none was needed, and if an inmate did manage to break their programming, there were incredibly efficient S-sats to deal with them. They were all good, law-abiding citizens until their houses were sealed and one family member was programmed to hunt the others. After their murders they were downloaded into newly cloned bodies the following morning, so they could wash the blood off the walls and pretend that everything was okay. More than that, he worried about when it would be his turn to brutalise his family. He didn't think he'd been a violent criminal.

There was no attempt at rehabilitation. It wasn't even incarceration. It was designed to do one thing, and one thing only: torture inmates who had pissed off the great and the good of Consortium space.

Nolly arrived at work praying for death. His mouth hurt so much from the fixed grin. He shared inanities with the unconvincing automaton-torso receptionist, which incurred more canned laughter that made him want to weep.

Seated at his desk, he pointlessly moved data around and talked to people just as inane as him on antiquated audio-communication devices. He accomplished nothing; he produced nothing. Initially he wondered if the work was modular, and all of them incarcerated on Suburbia were somehow parts of a greater whole – number-crunching some giant computation, perhaps. Now he was sure they were just going through the motions, doing busywork designed to remind them of the ultimate pointlessness of their existence. They were incapable of suicide.

'Nolly, old buddy.' Geoff's plump and affable head appeared over the office partitioning. Nolly was sure he could see the look of desperation on his boss's face under the painfully fixed smile. He wondered who Geoff had been before and what he had done to piss the Consortium off this badly. 'Hey, how about that local sporting fixture?' Geoff asked. There was more canned laughter. It was funny because, unlike all the other 'men' in the office, Geoff didn't really like sport. He was a little effeminate, because that was funny, too, but when the time came he still had a wife and two kids to murder, just like the rest of them.

'Uh, which one, Geoff?' Nolly asked. Nolly eyed the stapler and wondered if he could get it to his eye before the control protocols took over, but he knew the answer. He didn't think this was a normal thought that normal people had. Geoff's painful-looking smile grew wider and more painful-looking. There was more canned laughter. Nolly suspected that parts of this nightmare were viewed in some kind of media format within Consortium space.

'There's somebody here to see you, in the back office,' Geoff told him. Even through the rictus smile, Nolly could see the jealousy. He could practically hear Geoff's thoughts. He was thinking that he'd worked hard to get promoted, to find himself the butt of everyone's jokes. Why couldn't he go to the back office? Why couldn't he be destroyed, or released?

'Okay, Geoff.' Nolly stood up and headed towards the nondescript door that led to the back office. Beads of sweat appeared all over his face. *Is this it?* he prayed. His hand gripped the handle and turned it.

The door opened into a long corridor with another door at the end of it. He had a strange feeling that the walls had just finished shifting in his peripheral vision. He stepped forwards and closed the door after him. The corridor smelled of some kind of cleaning product. He started walking. Excitement and hope building in him, he began to increase his pace. Pain lanced through his skull and the corridor tipped. He tried to grab the wall but failed and found himself on the floor. He could taste vomit in the back of his throat, the pain was so extreme. The pain didn't go, just subsided enough that he was functional again. He tried to stand up, but he wasn't supposed to have legs. He turned to one side and threw up the nutritional breakfast that had been lovingly prepared by the prisoner locked inside his 'wife'. He managed not to throw up on himself. He started pulling himself along the floor, avoiding the vomit, towards the other door.

He could remember who he was, what he was and what he'd done. He reached for the door handle.

Nolly half-crawled, half-flopped into the room, looking up at the odd figure sitting on the other side of the table in the utterly nondescript room. It was a diminutive lizard in a very tall hat, body tucked under itchy-looking blankets in a strange wheeled chair made from a material Nolly didn't recognise.

Nolly managed to pull himself up into a chair on the near side of the table as the small lizard watched. Nolly could imagine few things more alien and uncomfortable than sitting in the hard plastic moulded chair.

'Would you prefer I call you Mr Berger, or the Alchemist?' the lizard asked. Nolly reached for him but the small lizard recoiled, hissing in distaste, forked tongue flicking out between his teeth.

'Please,' Nolly begged with an unfamiliar larynx. 'You have to get me out of here.' His tears dripped down onto the pitted surface of the plastic table.

'If you help me with my inquiries, that is a distinct possibility. What can you tell me about Woodbine Scab?'

Nolly stared at the lizard. Slowly, pleading desperation was replaced by a look of anger bordering on fury.

'That fucking vicious, vile cunt!' Nolly spat. 'He did this to me. He caught me! It's his fault I got sent here! We weren't doing much harm. It was the people's own choice.'

'I am, of course, familiar with your crimes—'

'Crimes! Crimes? I wasn't doing anything different from what everyone else was doing. Know why the debt relief on my bounty was so high?'

'Because you used to be part of the Church?'

'Because I used to be part of the Church!' Nolly slammed unfamiliar hands down on the table and almost slid off the chair. He recovered himself and pointed at the lizard. 'I'm in this ... fucking *hell* to deny me to the Church, and all because the Consortium can't break Church conditioning!'

'Indeed.'

'See, I probably knows what they want to knows, but they can't get it.' He tapped the side of his head and slid off the chair, the lizard's eyes following him as he did so. He continued watching as Nolly pulled himself back up into the chair. 'I shouldn't be in this body, it's not right,' he muttered.

'Why would Mr Scab wish to break you out?'

Nolly stared at the lizard. 'It'll be for some cuntish reason,' Nolly eventually answered.

'Could you be more specific?'

'I don't know. He wouldn't.' Then a look of horror crossed his face. 'Maybe the Church has hired him.'

'That sounds unlikely. He wants you for his own purposes.'

'Then I don't know. You're one of them, ain't you? A bounty killer.'

'I am a hunter. If you want to get out of here, Mr Berger, then you need to cooperate. You were a bridge drive engineer, is that correct?'

Nolly looked exasperated. To Mr Hat, the expression was exaggerated, as if he was trying it out for the first time.

'Yes, but even if they hadn't mindfucked me in here, I couldn't get at what I know, and neither can he, because the Church mindfucked me first. The conditioning can't be broken.'

Mr Hat knew that the Alchemist was one of the few bridge techs ever to escape from the Church, which had to be significant. He wondered if Miss Negrinotti actually thought she had found a way to break Church conditioning.

'You were apprehended for selling psychotropic drugs, is that correct?'

'No, for cooking them, and I mean – who gets done for drugs? I didn't even realise I was breaking any laws until they came through the skylight.'

Mr Hat had to concede he had a point. He could not recall ever hearing of a bounty on a drug chemist before. It seemed highly unlikely that Scab was interested in the Alchemist's ability to make drugs. Scab was insane and as much of a junkie as everyone else in Known Space, but there was a definite method to his madness, even if it was nothing more than a psychopath's requirement to get what he wanted regardless of the cost. It was only problematic when the psychopath in question was ex-Elite. What an Elite thought an acceptable cost was scaled far above what a normal criminal would consider as such.

'Please,' Nolly begged. 'Can I go now?'

'Of course,' Mr Hat said, and then realised his mistake as he saw pathetic hope spread unconvincingly across the Alchemist's now-human face. 'I mean back to your job.'

'Then kill me! Please!' Nolly started to beg. The room began to

202

distend. It looked like the lizard in the strange wheeled chair was moving further and further away from him.

'Why would I do that?' Mr Hat asked, genuinely confused.

'Are you okay, Nolly, old fella'?' Geoff asked. Nolly looked up at his boss and friend to the sound of canned laughter as his identity and memories melted away. He could see the smugness behind Geoff's smiling facade. Nolly wanted to tear at Geoff's face, he wanted to weep and scream. Instead he smiled until it hurt.

'Yes, I'm fine, thank you, Geoff. Will you be watching the local sporting fixture tonight?' he asked in a gently mocking manner to the sound of yet more canned laughter.

As the AI drove Nolly back to his fake, loving family, he saw something very odd. Two building custodians were trying to clean writing off the side of the mall. Someone had scrawled the words THE EMPIRE NEVER ENDED on the wall. Nolly was mortified.

'Who on earth would do such a thing?' he muttered disapprovingly.

18
Ancient Britain

The water had washed much of the blood off her but left her freezing. The wounds that should have killed her were just fading scar-tissue reminders now. As she walked the cold left her. She stopped staggering and her stride became more purposeful. She felt the familiar, gluttonous hunger threaten to overwhelm her, but she felt something else, too – she felt the old power in her blood. She wasn't as strong as she had been, perhaps, but then she didn't have demons screaming in her head, either, and Crom Dhubh wasn't whispering to her any more. She felt strong, fast and aware again. She had stolen Fachtna's strength.

She heard them first: the sound of hoofbeats across the plain she had found herself on. She glanced behind her, knowing instinctively they had come from the south-west. They didn't have to get much closer for her to recognise their ill-used steeds as the white-coated and red-eyed horses of the Otherworld. It took her longer to recognise the five riders as equally ill-used-looking Corpse People, their lime long since washed off by their trials. She placed her hands on her hips and waited for them to approach.

'You!' Ysgawyn spat at her. Britha understood the language like she understood her own.

The five riders circled her. Their mounts' coats were covered in foamy sweat, their red eyes rolling, and more than one of them snapped at her with their wolf-like teeth. They used the horses to knock her around a bit. She understood it for what it was: intimidation, an attempt to establish dominance. She held her ground as best she could. She noticed Ysgawyn looking back the way he had come.

'You should consider yourself lucky,' he said, eyeing her naked body, 'that we don't have the time to take turns with you.' He drew his sword. Notched, bloodstained and patchy with rust, the blade had obviously not seen much care recently. 'We will just have to kill you instead.'

'A choice all women would take rather than receive the ministrations of your cock, I suspect.'

He swung at her. Britha bent so the blade whistled over her, then straightened and grabbed his arm as he tried to pull it back for another blow. She yanked the arm hard, easily pulling Ysgawyn from his saddle and throwing him to the ground. The other Corpse People began to draw their swords. All of them appeared to have lost their spears.

'I am a *dryw*!' she all but shrieked at them in the voice of anger. She watched them shrink back and wondered how much of it was just nonsense, if what Fachtna had told her was true – that she'd had no magic. She did now, though, with his blood in her body. She pointed at Ysgawyn. 'This one has already been punished for threatening a *dryw*. Who wishes to join him? Who would have woman, man and beast turn their backs on him?'

The other riders looked less sure, though they still had naked blades in their hands. Ysgawyn struggled to his feet, his fatigue self-evident. Every movement was a significant effort for him, but that effort was fuelled by his hatred. He swung the heavy blade at her two-handed. It was an easy matter for Britha to step to one side and he lurched forwards, off balance. Britha struck both his arms and he dropped his sword. She punched him to the ground and then reached down to pick up his sword.

'You do not look after this as a warrior should,' she said, examining the rusted, pitted blade.

Ysgawyn looked up at her. His animating anger was fading, but the burning hatred remained.

'What are you frightened of?' Britha asked. Ysgawyn just glared at her.

'Andraste's children,' one of the other warriors said.

'Is that why your numbers are so few?'

'They are too numerous,' the young warrior continued, 'and even with weapons washed in the blood of heroes they are very difficult to kill.'

'Not like running down unarmed landsmen and -women as they flee, then?' Britha enquired.

'Kill me, sacrifice me to your northern gods, just get on with it,' Ysgawyn said, his voice so tired that Britha suspected he'd welcome death. She wasn't feeling particularly merciful, however.

Britha ran the sword down her palm. The five men watched her nervously as a red line of blood appeared. Ysgawyn's horse reared away from her. She wasn't sure how she knew to do this, but she smeared the blood on the horse's neck and then darted out of the way before it could bite her. The blood disappeared as if it had been sucked through the animal's skin. In her mind she saw the horse calming, accepting her, and she thought of herself riding the horse. Finally she turned to Ysgawyn.

'Take your armour off,' she told him. She didn't want his armour so much as the clothes underneath. 'Do you have anything to eat?'

Britha gorged herself on what little food the five Corpse People riders carried with them but she still felt hungry. They watched her miserably. She was considering what they had told her. She had a mind to kill their horses, hamstring the warriors and then wait for their returned-to-life ancestors to find them. She found herself curious as to what would happen. These were the thoughts of a *dryw*, she decided. To seek knowledge, and power, and the Corpse People had put themselves well beyond any decent consideration with their own behaviour.

'So what will you do now?' Britha asked instead. Ysgawyn shrugged and looked to the south-west. He had been doing this since they found her. Britha followed his gaze. The sun was setting, just a faint glow on the horizon now. Britha squinted. She wasn't sure, but she thought there might be movement to the south-west.

'We're going to find Bress,' Ysgawyn said softly.

His name was like a dagger. She was overcome with absurd guilt as she thought back to lying with Fachtna. She pushed the feeling down. It was ridiculous. She owed Bress nothing but death. She wished she had taken Fachtna's sword with her. Unless more had survived than she had seen, it looked as though Bress was responsible for all but wiping out her people.

'Did any survive the wicker man?' she asked quietly.

'Horse, armour, sword, spear and brand,' said Ysgawyn. 'Our enemies fell before us like wheat to a sickle. We weren't terrified victims kept in our own filth. If this is what has become of us, what chance did the people in the wicker man have? They are either dead or afflicted with the sickness Andraste spreads. To think otherwise is to lie to yourself.'

Britha took this in. She became aware she was touching her stomach. Thinking of her child, one moment part of her, the next gone, but she had felt it nonetheless. She moved her hand away. Ysgawyn was watching her carefully. It was becoming clear to her that he had been made the *rhi* of his tribe as a result of his mind and probably his tongue, but not as a result of his sword arm.

'Very well,' Britha said quietly.

'Very well what?' Ysgawyn demanded, but tiredly.

'I will come with you.' If Fachtna had lacked the magics to take her back then perhaps it was a secret she could steal from Bress's corpse. One thing she had decided: she was sick of the Otherworld's presence in these lands.

'I had thought you finished with me,' Bress said.

'I had, but I want to know what came through,' Crom whispered in his ear like a lover. He was standing behind, always just out of sight, little more than a presence.

'Why should I serve you again?' Bress almost flinched as he felt a hand brush against him.

'What do you want?' The whisper sounded sweet, or it would have if Bress hadn't known of the corruption it promised.

'You know what I want.'

'You could do that yourself.'

'There would always be echoes.'

'Do you want to go home? I will murder a sun for you. Lay it out on an altar and sacrifice it for your return.'

Bress could turn around, he supposed. He knew, even in this darkness, that he would be able to make out Crom Dhubh's form, little more than a crooked shadow, a dark ghost so malformed it would hurt to look at him.

'It's not my home, I ... we ... changed it.'

The laughter was low and sickly. Bress knew that Crom Dhubh was weak now. What had happened inside the Muileartach had lessened him.

'The Muileartach sleeps again. Her energy is spent. It will be years before she wakes again, millennia, but during that time, the sickness that infuses the human mind will leak into her, poisoning her, driving her mad.'

'Why don't you tell the others? Whisper it to their poisoned minds?'

'They are too far beyond madness to hear me.'

'And I find myself asking again – what do you want from me?'

'What do I want? I am a servant, just like you—'

'Of an idiot god stinging itself—'

'Rail against it all you want, but we serve the same master. You were born for this.'

'I don't think I was born—'

'If it's someone from the Ubh Blaosc, if we can get to them before they are destroyed—'

'We can find out where the Ubh Blaosc is. Why?'

'Because they oppose us.'

207

'For the Naga?' Bress asked, spat and then wondered if he had spent too long in this land.

'They are tools, nothing more. This wouldn't have mattered if we had succeeded.'

'Nothing would have mattered. I have a condition.'

'The bargain is an illusion.'

'Leave the woman be.'

'Do you think she's alive?'

'Yes,' he said simply. She had struck him as someone who wouldn't stop fighting.

'But she wants—'

'I said, leave her be.'

'You are a fool, but I agree.'

He felt the task he had been charged with settle into him like a weight. Initially it did not seem as bad as his previous task, but if he succeeded he could be responsible for so many more deaths. He wasn't necessarily opposed to that. He just couldn't see the point.

'I tire of slavery,' Bress said quietly.

'That is a pretence, a lie we all tell ourselves. If we didn't like it we would do something about it.'

Bress awoke in his cot. He sat up and saw his moulded 'leather' armour hanging from the framework of the skin tent. He pushed the fur blanket aside and stood. He had to find one or two people in this whole, empty land. He would have to ride to the stones and try tracking them from there. That said, if they had access to the stones, there was a good chance that whoever they were would be coming for him. The age of gods was over, and there weren't many with the blood of 'heroes' in this part of the world.

Still, he thought, at least he had something for his army of blood slaves to do. Though first he'd have to find some horses.

She made Ysgawyn ride behind Gwynn, the youngest of the Corpse People, and she took his horse after mastering it with her blood magic. They found a well-trodden road, one that looked like it had been used much for trade, judging by the grooves wagon tracks had dug in the hard-packed dirt. There was nobody on the road today. The road climbed up onto a ridge line looking down on woodland, farmland and patches of swampy lowland.

Behind them was the plain. Britha could just about make out the large circle of stones. She assumed it was where she had appeared. Beyond that the land looked wrong, dead, stunted, twisted and strange. She could see shapes moving across the plain. They looked larger than anything not living in the sea had any right to be, and their movement was all wrong.

The land before the creatures appeared to be normal but behind them was sourland. They were changing it, turning it from good, rich earth that could be sown and harvested by people into material for some other purpose. She saw smaller shapes as well, scattered over the plain, but always heading inexorably north.

The road on the ridge was taking them east. The beleaguered Corpse People did not know where Bress and the Lochlannach had gone, but they had last been seen sailing east away from the Isle of Madness. Ysgawyn's plan was to head north and east, try to distance themselves from the Muileartach's spawn. Where Bress went there would be stories for them to follow.

They travelled for weeks, finding only abandoned settlements and villages. Britha shamefully joined with the Corpse People in scavenging for supplies.

They came across a hill fort guarded by spear-carriers. All their warriors had ridden east to fight the army of giant serpents coming from the south. Britha and her companions were refused hospitality because someone from within recognised the Corpse People who had raided the Atrebates for many years. Ysgawyn cursed them, and told them there was no fighting what was coming, and that they were all dead anyway.

As they followed the road further north and east, they started to see more people using it. Nearly all of them were warriors who had either missed the chance to do battle with the Lochlannach or, shamed by running and hiding, were heading south. The warriors came from disparate tribes and there appeared to be an uneasy truce among them.

Britha and the others were cursed for cowards when it became apparent they were heading away from the spawn, which resulted in a series of challenges being fought along the road. Ysgawyn made sure they picked their victims very shrewdly, and each new victory meant that the dead warrior's horse, armour and weapons were forfeit to the Corpse People. They took what they could use and traded the rest.

Ysgawyn made one miscalculation and another of the Corpse People died. Now only four remained: Brys and Gwynn – both of whom Britha was starting to like despite herself, Ysgawyn and Madawg. Madawg looked too frail to be a warrior, particularly after the ravages of the Corpse People's flight. He was nearly silent, and his odd, narrow face had a complexion so sallow he looked ill. His dark hair was thin and receding. Despite his appearance, however, he was a cunning, vicious and very fast fighter. He'd won the challenge he fought because the other warrior had woefully underestimated him.

They turned off the trade route and started travelling north after they met a bard heading south for the mighty battle. He had heard rumours of sightings of the black *curraghs* on a river further north. The river was said to have a fearsome spirit living in it that made it burst its banks and drown the surrounding land with remarkable frequency. The river was called the *Tros Hynt*.

Britha had a spear now and a dagger traded from Ysgawyn after he'd won a challenge. It was the dagger, not the spear, which she took into the woods on the darkest night, when the moon's light was little more than a sliver in the heavens. It was the dagger that she worked her will and her blood magic on. It was the dagger that she whispered her purpose to. It would be easier to get the dagger closer to Bress.

He had known of them as soon as the first of his slave army became aware of them. They rode in with the points of their longspears pointed down. He recognised their horses first – Crom Dhubh had transformed them – but it took a moment for him to place the people without their corpse paint. They were members of some ridiculous warrior cult Crom Dhubh had controlled. At Crom's behest they had hunted down those who still possessed some residual power in their blood and bones, leftover blessings given to their ancestors by the remnants of ancient civilisations. The warrior cult who thought themselves already dead, who consumed their prey to steal their power. They were nothing more than parasites as far as Bress was concerned. They were only still alive because *she* was with them.

He wore a simple *blaidh* and trews. No armour, not even his boots. His sword remained in his hide tent, only a dagger hanging from the belt at his waist. It didn't matter. They were no threat to him.

They had come as far west as they could on the *Tros Hynt*, but beyond this point the river was simply not navigable. The hide-hulled *curraghs* were much smaller now that the ships did not have to carry so many prisoners. They held themselves steady in the water against the forceful current. He had left the giants submerged further upriver, but he could call them with a thought. His slaves pitched his hide tent on the driest patch of ground they could find in a small clearing close to the riverbank.

After raiding the surrounding area extensively for good horseflesh which he subsequently transformed with the Red Chalice, he had been ranging out for some time now but found little. He used the Red Chalice to control and interrogate those they did find but learned nothing. Then he drew the metal out of them again – he would create no more slaves. Whoever had arrived was keeping very quiet. He was aware of the mortal warriors heading south to die or be warped by the children of the Muileartach, but he gave them little thought.

'I am Ysgawyn, son of—'

'Be quiet,' Bress said softly, but his voice carried. They had ridden in through the silent ranks of his Lochlannach. He could smell their fear.

'Careful,' the one called Ysgawyn hissed, but Bress was only looking at Britha. He could not read her expression, but he could sense the power born of the *Ubh Blaosc* in her blood. She had changed. This was not her first form. He did not like the pain he felt in his chest at the thought that she was little more than an *Ubh Blaosc* changeling sent to kill him.

'We had an alliance,' Ysgawyn insisted. 'I demand you honour it!'

Bress turned reluctantly from Britha to look at the angry man. 'You demand what?'

'Your aid, access to your magics as per the terms of our alliance sworn in blood—'

'Stop,' Bress said. Ysgawyn did so. 'There was no alliance.'

Bress didn't look the man in the eye as Ysgawyn replied, 'We served the same master and he has betrayed us. Where there should be death, there is more life than ever before.'

'Are you a child? You slavishly worshipped my master and he used you for his own ends. Go and ask him for aid and magics. I suspect they will not be forthcoming as you appear to have little to offer in return. I owe you nothing.' Bress started moving towards Britha and Ysgawyn opened his mouth to protest again. This time Bress merely looked at him and Ysgawyn knew to be quiet. 'Was this not what you expected? Having made enemies of all others, did you hope for succour from me? Because you have travelled here with her, I will grant you a great boon. If you leave now I will neither kill nor enslave you, but if you say one more word to me ...' Bress let his voice trail off almost sadly. There were tears of frustration and rage on Ysgawyn's face, but he turned and walked back to his horse. The Lochlannach watched him all the while.

'And what of me?' Britha asked quietly. Bress moved quickly to her. He lifted his hand to her face, long, powerful fingers almost touching her skin. She did not shrink from him. Her expression was guarded, but he could see water gathering in the corners of her eyes.

'You can stay and do what you want. All I ask is that you don't leave.'

She stared at him, saying nothing. The silence was broken by the sound of the remaining Corpse People galloping out of the camp, Ysgawyn hurling insults as he rode away.

'Have you come to kill me?' he asked, lowering his hand, clenching it into a fist before forcing it back to his side. She nodded, and a tear ran down her cheek.

'I'm sorry,' he whispered. The trees, the clearing, the riverbank were filled with the silent Lochlannach, but they were, to all intents and purposes, alone.

Her hand moved to the hilt of her dagger. Bress glanced down at it but did not move.

'It's you, isn't it?' he asked quietly. She nodded as more tears ran down her cheek. He looked back into her eyes. 'What did they do to you?'

She started to collapse. Bress gathered her into his arms, knowing how much she must hate this weakness. She started to beat him with her fists as she sobbed into his chest. He carried her to the ground with him and held her.

Fachtna came to. He concentrated, working out exactly how hurt he was. Then he registered the pain from his leg. He opened his eyes and looked down past the sword protruding from his chest. He screamed. Some half-formed thing, a corpse-like mockery of life with beating, pulsing rudimentary organs hanging down from rotted bones was chewing on his leg, harvesting flesh – and presumably the magics contained within – for itself.

Fachtna kicked out but only succeeded in bucking the creature up and down on his leg. Every movement caused the sword wound to widen, and blood coursed from the gash as pain shot through him. Fachtna brought to mind the calming exercises he'd learned in warrior camp and managed to control himself. He reached for the sword sticking out of him and closed his fingers around its hilt. He wanted to cry out as teeth tore into this flesh. He did cry out as he ripped the sword from his body, and his cries echoed across the plain. He felt darkness closing all around him as he started to drift away. He was bolted back into consciousness as a large chunk of his leg was torn away by the living-corpse-thing's teeth. This time his scream was joined by his sword's song. He only just had the presence of mind to use the correct magics to activate it.

He pushed the sword through the undead thing's head, being as careful as he could not to cut off his own foot. It did not want to die even after he all but bisected it, and he started grabbing at it and flinging its constituent parts away.

The wards drawn by the *drui* on his bones and flesh told him he was being attacked. It was not dissimilar to Naga magics. If anything, this attack was more potent. He recognised this as the magics of the Muileartach.

He saw other shapes moving across the plain through the broad circle of standing stones. The stones were little more than markers for the great power in the earth many miles beneath the plain.

His wounds were starting to heal, but the process was being complicated by whatever the Muileartach's spawn had filled the air with. Her magics weren't trying to kill him, rather they were trying to change him, and they were ancient, and powerful, but the wards of the *drui* were trying to keep him safe.

Another of the living-corpse creatures reached for him. The shimmering blade of his sword flicked out and cut it in two as Fachtna staggered away. He knew there were too many to fight, unless his wards could protect him long enough to heal. He glanced down at the blood still pulsing through the wound in his chest. Even his armour was struggling to repair itself. In fact, it looked as if it was trying to grow screaming mouths.

It was a desperate act and he was no *drui*, but there was magic in his blood, too. As the closest of the things reached for him he shut his eyes and concentrated. He felt fingers brush against his armour. He felt them as he would on his skin. He stopped trying to fight the Muileartach's magics. Instead, as he bled into the air, he simply tried to influence it, make it his and ultimately control it. He felt himself fuse with his armour, his flesh changing, becoming stronger, his feet growing into the earth, branching out for more material to fuel his transformation. Finally he opened his eyes. The living-corpse creatures were standing all around him. Staring at him. He smiled.

19

Close to the Oceanic Pole of Inaccessibility, 6 Weeks Ago

There was no real way to handle it other than by going through the motions. What Lodup had seen and heard in the last twenty-four hours should have been more than enough to shut him down. He had worked underwater, at frightening depths, for his entire adult life. He had always known that the oceans, unexplored as they were and arguably as inimical to human life as space, had many more secrets to give up. It had never occurred to him that these secrets would be of this nature. It was so far beyond the realm of his experience and understanding that he couldn't process it. He felt numb.

While he found that he wasn't shutting down with the sheer enormity of it, he couldn't embrace the wonder of it, either. He was left feeling as if the weight of all that black water between the habitat and the surface had a palpable presence and was pressing against the fragile breathing, diamond hull of the habitat, looking for a way in. He was left with a profound sense of unease by the twisted, dead, sense-defying city that he felt lurking in the water outside.

His berth was comfortable enough. It wasn't very big, consisting of a wet room with bathroom facilities, a desalinated shower and a sink, plus a desk, bunk and under-bunk storage. He was looking for some kind of TV and started to wonder if there was a communal area when Siraja had, rather disconcertingly, appeared as an image on the wall. Apparently the entire wall could become a screen, if need be. The dragon-headed AI explained that Lodup only needed to ask for whatever media he wanted and it would appear. He explained that it all came from the habitat's library as communication with the mainland was highly limited.

Lodup thanked him and asked how much privacy he had. Siraja told him he was monitored for his safety, but that this monitoring was low key and the AI understood the need for privacy. Lodup was coming to terms with the fact that he would probably struggle to masturbate in these conditions. He tried out the media system, requesting the most obscure music and films he could think of. The habitat had them all. There was also a detachable tablet he could use to read books, magazines and graphic novels.

Lodup unpacked and got himself fully squared away, a habit from his days in the Navy. Then he decided to go for a walk to meet the neighbours.

The dorm block Lodup was staying in was four storeys of tightly packed cubicles like his own overlooking an open central plaza that contained hanging plants, palm trees and other bits of decorative landscaping. Overhead UV strip lighting embedded in the breathing-diamond skin of the habitat provided the light required by the plants. Balconies connected the cubicles and a number of bridges crossed over the central area. Several similar dorm blocks adjoined the one in which Lodup was berthed.

It was quiet. There was little conversation and the cubicles appeared to be very well soundproofed. What little noise there was came from media being played inside cubicles with the doors open. Every so often one of the security guards patrolled the catwalks and balconies. They looked very heavily armed to Lodup and carried the same odd-looking SMGs as Yaroslav, as well as side arms, collapsible batons, restraints and a number of non-lethal weapons. The only difference from Yaroslav was that their SMGs lacked the underslung grenade-launcher mounted on a Picatinny rail. Instead they had another underslung weapon that Lodup suspected was some kind of short-barrelled shotgun.

Lodup had always been used to his own company, but even so, the quiet was getting to him and making him wish for a poker game, or a few beers and some pool with his fellow divers. He felt like he was staying in an unfriendly hotel in a completely alien culture.

Returning to his cubicle, he started to watch a film, but it only made him miss the surface. He switched to a nature documentary but couldn't stick with that, either. He looked for technical specs to read for the equipment he was going to be using but discovered that he already knew them, which further increased his discomfort. Finally he settled for some music and some reading. By the time he felt it was late enough to sleep, he was pretty sure he would be too restless to do so, though he drifted off easily enough. He did not, however, dream well.

Breakfast came from a microwave-sized compartment that appeared in the cabin's wall. It tasted like it should, but also as if there was something missing from it. He showered and then put on the dive suit, which he now knew was a thermal sheath designed to both conserve and provide heat, and to augment the artificial gills that had been implanted in his chest. Live bacteria held in tiny rib-like bladders within the sheath added to what little oxygen there was in the aphotic water at this depth as it flowed through the membranous smart material of the suit.

As he'd found out yesterday, the suit could be pulled up over his head, providing a one-way transparent hood. The material was thinner around the gloves to allow for delicate work and the heating properties increased. Fins could be grown from the feet, the size depending on space and speed requirements, and for long distances the fins could merge to form a self-rippling monofin. He strapped the diamond-bladed utility knife to his calf.

When he was ready, he sat on his bunk and asked Siraja what he should do next. He was told that Hideo was coming to get him, and that he would be working with him and Andreas, an ADS operator.

When Hideo appeared at his door, Lodup felt almost pathetically happy to see a face he recognised.

'You ready for this, bro?' Hideo asked.

'Sure,' Lodup told him.

Hideo looked at him sceptically. 'No, no you're not, but you'll cope, man, we all do.'

They walked along the balcony, passing others leaving their cabins dressed in either thermal sheaths or overalls. It was still very quiet.

'This place ever liven up?' Lodup asked.

'It's the job, man, it gets to you,' Hideo replied.

'People normally talk when they're nervous.'

'I'm right there with you, man.'

They made their way over a bridge and along several catwalks under the tent-like diamond ceiling. Lodup looked down into another landscaped central plaza where a group of personnel of visibly different ethnicities had gathered around a small statue of some kind. The murmuring coming from them didn't sound like anything Lodup could identify as a language. He glanced over at Hideo, who shrugged.

'Freedom of religion, man.'

The small statue appeared to be made of a material similar to the city outside.

'Andreas is a good guy, but he's German, so he's a little intense,' Hideo started. It sounded like he was talking for the sake of talking. Lodup kept glancing back at the ad hoc ceremony.

They arrived at the door to one of the cabins and Hideo reached out to touch it. The submersible pilot seemed surprised that the door just slid open. Every surface inside the cabin was a screen showing a documentary about germ cultures. The blood coating the walls obscured the images. A well-built man with a crew cut and a chiselled jawline was lying on the floor of the cabin. He was red also, his body covered with multiple gashes. His diamond-bladed knife was still gripped tightly in his hand.

Hideo and Lodup stared into the room.

'Yaroslav is on his way.' Lodup jumped as Siraja appeared next to him.

'Why didn't you know about this already?' Lodup asked as the door to the red cabin slid shut.

'I respect privacy,' Siraja said, his voice low and reverent.

Lodup felt Hideo take him by the arm and pull him away. He noticed one of the security detail making his way towards Andreas's berth.

'What—' Lodup managed.

'It happens,' Hideo told him. 'Sometimes people crack before their rotation is up. I liked Andreas, but he was wound too tight.'

Lodup looked around at the blank faces of the men and women he was passing on the balcony. None of them looked like they'd been wound at all. What he couldn't quite work out was why, after all the strangeness and now this, he still wanted to stay.

Charles Deane was too tall for a diver, Lodup thought. With his sideburns and his gangly body, he looked more like Abraham Lincoln than the dive supervisor of a secret underwater habitat. He was stripped to the waist, the top part of his thermal sheath tied around his midriff. His upper torso was covered with fading blue tattoos of ships, fish, mermaids and kanji script. They looked very old to Lodup.

They were standing on one of the jetties in the moon pool, next to Hideo's submersible. An ADS was perched on the jetty next to the submersible, its armoured back split open, and Lodup couldn't resist taking a look inside. He wasn't sure what he'd been expecting, but it certainly wasn't the soft, dark, faintly biological-looking contoured padded interior.

Sal had joined them and was sitting on a pack of crates nearby. The ex-Australian Navy diver looked less than happy, but she had greeted Lodup warmly enough. Sal was going to be piloting the ADS, having been transferred to their dive detail due to Andreas's suicide.

'Okay, nobody's happy about what transpired this morning,' Deane said. 'Not a good start for the new lad, but we've still got things that need doing.' Deane's accent was odd. Lodup was pretty sure it had started out British – London, he suspected – but it had become mixed up with all sorts of other accents along the way. Lodup wasn't quite sure what to think about the claims of longevity he'd heard with regard to the crew. He supposed the level of technology they were displaying made just about anything possible. Deane certainly looked as if he belonged in another age.

'So we're going to keep Mr Satakano's first shift very simple. Eastern quadrant.' Lodup caught a brief change in Hideo's expression. The submersible driver didn't look happy, but it was gone almost as quickly as it had appeared. 'I want a survey. Use a towfish, and Big Henry's coming to help. You find anything, you set up to dredge. There should be a structure there according to the model, but it's been buried by silt over the years.'

'Seed-pod, Chief?' Hideo asked. Lodup glanced at the submersible pilot but said nothing.

'Nothing that grandiose, lad. I think we found all we're going to find of them, start of the last century.' Deane's accent made such a mangled mush of the words that Lodup had to play them back to understand them. 'The bioengineers are looking for a harvest.'

'If the tech's active,' Hideo persisted, 'the building could have a large network. That means—'

'Anything active, I think we would have felt it before now.'

'Tell that to Hidepole's crew,' Sal muttered.

'Different time, different protocols in place. We'll send AUVs in first to check it out, mind,' Deane told the Australian. Sal nodded. 'Okay. Lodup, you're support diver – most of the work's going to be done by Sal and Hideo, you'll ride in the submersible unless you're needed.'

'Chief,' Lodup said, 'if it's all the same to you I'd like to get wet, see what it's all about. Familiarise myself with the gear, and the conditions.'

Deane looked at him for a while, as if he was trying to make his mind up about something. 'Okay, lad. The gear's mostly instinctive, and I believe Siraja downloaded the safety protocols for you – most of them're what you've been used to. You listen to Sal and Hideo and do what they tell you, okay?'

Lodup nodded. He didn't like being called 'lad', and in fact he felt that Deane had a somewhat patronising attitude towards all three of them, but the dive supervisor appeared to be practical, competent and have a degree of common sense.

'Off you go, then,' the Brit told them.

It was almost like driving as Hideo took the sub through the sunken streets of the strange city. The submersible's lights cut through the grotesque shadows thrown by the backlit statuary.

Lodup was holding on to the railing surrounding the submersible's flatbed. He'd felt the cold, rushing sensation through his chest again as the folds of skin protecting the mechanical gills opened. His respiratory system collapsed and his red blood cells became more efficient. Sinuses and other cavities filled with a saline solution, and his metabolism changed to become a thermo-conformer rather than a regulator. Oddly, he felt neither the cold nor the pressure, although he was aware of both. He felt like the living dead. A drowned man still moving.

Sal kept pace with the submersible, just behind and above them in the powerful-looking *ADS* exoskeleton. She piloted with a finesse Lodup had rarely seen in *ADS* jockeys. He had watched her climb into the exoskeleton, and how it sealed itself, and he couldn't shake the feeling that she was being consumed.

Further behind, shining their own lights through the crystal-clear water, were two *AUV*s. They looked like a cross between a stubby torpedo and a technological cuttlefish.

It was clear that going through the streets was a mixture of Hideo showing off his piloting skills and a tour for Lodup's benefit, as it would have been quicker simply to pass over the strange city. Seeing the metropolis close up was as disturbing, if not more so, as seeing it from far away. It wasn't just the giant statues – every structure appeared to contain bas-reliefs of odd-looking people and other animalistic forms. There were creatures with serpentine heads, and occasionally vaguely insectile, multi-limbed, armoured creatures with angular, slab-like heads. Worse still, the strange architecture of the city played tricks with perception, causing optical illusions. He kept thinking there was movement in his peripheral vision.

'This isn't right,' Lodup subvocalized, the words turned into a short-range ultrasound transmission. 'These aren't statues, are they?'

He heard Sal's reply in his head. 'The boffins think it was some kind of petrification effect. Probably caused by nano-technology.'

'These things existed on this planet?' Lodup still couldn't quite believe it, despite what he was seeing. Nobody replied. 'This petrifaction effect – either they were attacked, or they did it to themselves, presumably?' Again, nobody replied. 'Can it be reversed?'

Hideo answered this time. 'To a certain extent, that's what we're doing.' He sounded subdued. 'Reverse-engineering, anyway.'

Lodup tried to imagine what it would be like if the city came to life again. He figured most of its inhabitants would drown, assuming they could withstand the pressure, but he still didn't like the thoughts he was having.

Hideo deftly swung the submersible around a corner. The impellers tilted to point downwards and the vehicle rose over an obstruction ahead of them that stretched across the street. Lodup couldn't quite work out what it was at first as the submersible's lights played across it. It looked like an elongated tin can that someone had stomped on. Slowly he worked out that it was a submarine. A Japanese U-boat from World War II, he guessed. He wondered if that was why Hideo hadn't been overjoyed about working this part of the city.

They were on what, in a normal city, would be considered a long, narrow boulevard. Lodup could just about make out where the boulevard ended as the seabed rose up into the ridge. As they moved closer, he saw where some of the sepulchral structures had been covered with silt, rock and other benthic debris. Off to his right, the sea was boiling around the forest of chimney-like smokers. Wonder and disquiet warred within him.

Lodup became aware of movement in the water above him and glanced up to see one of the orcas lazily swimming overhead. Up close it looked like an unholy amalgamation of killer whale and armoured attack helicopter.

'I'm going to deploy the towfish – can you come in?' Hideo asked.

Lodup pulled himself under the submersible to the hatch and unscrewed it as Hideo held the submersible steady so as not to flood it. The thermal sheath was already drying as Lodup pulled himself into the warm interior. He felt movement within his head and torso as he slowly transformed back into something more human rather than a technologically adapted man-shaped fish.

'You okay?' Lodup asked Hideo. The submersible pilot nodded curtly.

Through the vehicle's observation bubble he watched the orca – Big Henry, Lodup assumed – glide easily down the boulevard and then out over the seabed. A holographic representation of the area appeared, floating in the air within the cabin. Lodup wasn't entirely sure if it was actually holography or, like Siraja, an image that had just been uploaded into his perception. Whatever its origin, the map was incomplete. As Big Henry swam down the boulevard, the information gathered by the augmented iron oxide crystals in his head were transmitted to the submersible and back to C&C in infrasound packets, to form a more complete map.

'Big Henry will do the broad strokes then we'll use the towfish to fill in the details,' Hideo told him. Lodup had watched the towfish being lowered onto the flatbed by one of the moon pool's overhead cranes before they left. It looked like a truly ancient piece of kit – some kind of brass antique from the history of diving, well before the invention of sonar, let alone magnetometers.

'So what's with the towfish?' he asked Hideo.

'We've got *AUV*s and teleprescence ROVs that use a kind of bio-mechanical water-jet propulsion which doesn't get in the way of the instruments, but they're all busy today.'

Sal had set the *ADS* down on one of the nearby buildings. She was using the exoskeleton's arms for support and occasionally kicking the suit's legs. It made for a strangely incongruous image.

They watched as Big Henry made another couple of passes down the boulevard and out over the seabed.

'Hideo?' Lodup asked. 'Sometimes people go nuts, right?' Hideo didn't say anything. 'What about the orcas?' Hideo's lack of answer told him everything he needed to know. 'What happened with the dolphins?'

'Thanks, Big Henry,' Hideo said, ignoring Lodup. Lodup heard answering whale song, and the armoured creature swam up and disappeared over the roofs of the city. The holographic map was no-ticeably more complete but was still missing information. It definitely looked like there was another building under the mound of silt. 'So, we're going to take a number of passes. We'll be using a mixture of acoustic swept-frequency pulses, a sensitive bottom and sub-bottom magnetometer and high-res multispectrum images from the cameras.' He paused for a moment. 'Sal, you stay put whilst we do this.'

'Understood,' Sal answered.

Lodup could hear the winch unspooling the towfish's cable through the submersible's hull.

'Parts of it can't be mapped,' Hideo said quietly. All traces of the effusive cheerfulness he'd greeted Lodup with had disappeared. 'It changes.'

'Hideo, are you alright, man?'

Again, Hideo didn't answer. With the cable unwound, the submers-ible began its first pass. Lodup heard the first chirps as more detail was added to the three-dimensional map. He found the architecture revealed by the multispectrum scans disquieting, unnatural and all the more sinister, somehow, for currently being buried.

The silt dredge was a dense-looking cube on the submersible's flatbed. Lodup had left the craft and watched as the cube grew several concer-tinaed tubes. Lodup and Sal grabbed two of the tubes, whilst a larger one snaked of its own volition through the city and then out onto the seabed. Lodup and Sal wrangled the tubes they were holding roughly into place, but then the tubes came to life, reminding Lodup of the Hydra in old movies about Greek mythology. Sal explained that Hideo had taken the results from the towfish and Big Henry's passes and fed them into the silt pump, then programmed it to remove the silt from designated areas. They were largely there to troubleshoot. She shared the data stream from the silt pump with Lodup. It was more than a little disconcerting how the telemetry appeared to cascade down his vision.

'This is Hideo in flatbed four-two to Deane. Requesting permission to task a nano-screen for mapping in the upper-east quadrant?' Hideo shared the infrasound packet burst with Lodup and Sal.

'Flatbed four-two, this is Siska in C&C, permission denied.'

'Thanks for thinking about it, at least,' Hideo muttered over the local short-range ultrasound link.

'Not getting jittery on me are you, Hideo?' Sal asked over the ultra-sound link. Hideo didn't answer. Sal turned the exoskeleton's head turn to look at Lodup. He gave her a very exaggerated shrug.

They watched the tubes writhe around in the silt like angry snakes, sucking up the granular material and pumping it across the city to the seabed, where it was deposited in billowing clouds. They were slowly revealing a building made of the ubiquitous black, faintly organic stone. It was roughly rectangular, but again the angles were just off-kilter enough to cause confusion. It reminded Lodup of a warped version of the Egyptian tombs he'd seen on history and archaeological documentaries. If he understood what he'd been told properly, then the technology of this civilisation was fused into the very matter they used to build the city.

Lodup couldn't shake the feeling that he was being watched. He repeatedly glanced behind him. He told himself it was just the strangeness of the horrible architecture surrounding him. He was still struggling to believe that the larger 'statues' had once been somehow alive. He glanced behind him again.

'You okay, dude?' Sal asked. 'You look spooked.'

'Just getting used to the place, I guess.'

'Go up about ten metres, check to the west down among the buildings.'

Lodup headed over the building and found himself looking across the strange cityscape. He could just about make out the stone circle in the centre of the city. From this angle, alien statues made the tomb-like buildings they sat atop look like thrones.

He glanced to the west, the direction they had come from. The buildings that way looked lower. At first he saw nothing, then eventually glimpsed a large shadow moving low and slow among the buildings. He'd seen that sort of movement before. It was a marine predator hunting. At first he thought it was a shark, but the depth made that unlikely.

'Is that one of the orcas?' Lodup asked across the ultrasound link.

'It's Marvin, I think,' Sal answered. 'I'd ask for verification but they don't like being disturbed.'

'What's he hunting?' Lodup asked. He was a little surprised, as he thought the orcas fed on chum from the nipples on the underside of the habitat. He really didn't want to think too much about what would be down here that was big enough for an orca to hunt. His reply was a burst of ultrasonically delivered laughter, which prompted him to ask, 'Is he hunting me?'

'More sort of stalking. Seeing what you're made of. The pod's almost tribal and all male, so there's a lot of macho bullshit. They do this to all the newcomers. You're probably fine as long as you don't bolt,' Sal told him.

Great. A submarine-destroying cyborg killer whale is hazing me, Lodup thought as he watched the submersible bank and move sideways around the structure that was appearing through the cloud of silt.

'Do you want to try and matter-hack the entrance?' Sal asked. Lodup assumed she was talking to Hideo as he had no idea what she meant.

'Fuck it. If they won't task a screen for mapping, they won't for a matter-hack, or a swarm for eating our way in,' Hideo answered. Lodup could see what looked like some kind of cutting torch among the waldos and other tools on the front of the submersible. 'Lodup, you stay well out of our way, understood?'

Yeah, I'll just stay out here being stalked by the armoured killer whale, Lodup thought and glanced behind him again. This time he caught a glimpse of Marvin. He was of the opinion he was supposed to. It didn't matter how much of a game Sal told him it was, it was still difficult to suppress fear when a predator like that was playing with you.

Sal moved closer to the building. Lodup's augmented vision enabled him to watch the cutting torch unfold itself from a wrist mount on the ADS. There was a sudden strobing white and blue light as both fusion torches bit into the petrified material of the tomblike structure. Around the arc of the torches the superheated water bubbled and boiled, almost simultaneously going from steam back to water again.

'Lodup,' Sal said over the ultrasound link, 'there's a toolkit on the flatbed. You might want to grab the U-pulse.'

'Why?' Lodup asked as he joined his feet together, the thermal sheath's fins bonding to form a rippling monofin. It made his swim to the submersible look somewhat mermaid-like, but it was quick. He found the toolkit and opened it up, removing something that resembled a stubby sonar pistol. He knew that the U-pulse emitted a weaponised burst of ultrasound at a frequency that *could damage or even kill most unshielded biological creatures. At the very least it should discourage them.*

'We're kicking up a lot of shit and making heat and noise. It's bound to attract something.'

'Anything down here that can hurt us?' Lodup asked, starting to get worried. Most deep-sea life was too fragile to be any real threat to humans. Most of the dangerous stuff remained in shallower depths where all the food was. Other than psychotic work colleagues, cultists, rebellious dolphins and orca practical jokers, he thought, but kept that to himself.

'Well, some of them have fed off the city,' Sal said.

'Them? What them? What're you talking about?' Lodup said, trying to fight off a sense of panic as he looked at the horrible statues. He found himself glancing all around, and suddenly Marvin didn't feel like such a threat.

'It changes them,' Sal added in a way that really didn't put Lodup's mind at ease.

Gradually, Marvin's stalking became less frightening as the armoured orca weaved through the nearby streets of the submerged city. Lodup had his back to the light of the two fusion torches and bubbling plumes of water. Standing guard with him were the two autonomous underwater vehicles. Occasionally he heard one or other of them 'chirp' as they sent out a sonar pulse.

'Here they come,' Sal said over the ultrasound link.

'Huh?' Lodup said. 'Where—' Then he saw the shared telemetry from the AUVs. Ghost images of wriggling worm-like fish. They looked like hagfish – deep-sea carrion-eaters with no jaw, rather two rasping rows of teeth that they used to scavenge sunken carcasses for meat. Except these were much larger and looked like they were covered in some kind of segmented armoured shell. 'Guys?'

He was aware of the two AUVs rapidly firing directed pulses of ultrasound, and saw some of the mutated hagfish start spiralling towards the seabed, which in this case was the basalt streets of the strange city. Others veered off suddenly but then turned back, coming at the source of heat and light from another angle.

'You'll want to start firing at some point,' Sal suggested over the ultrasound comms. Lodup was staring at the vast shoal heading towards them. They looked like they were wriggling rather than swimming through the water.

Lodup raised the U-pulse and his vision filled with target solutions. With a thought, he sorted them in terms of urgency. He squeezed the trigger. The closest eel-like hagfish all but exploded from the blast of ultrasound. He shifted, fired, then again, and again. Suddenly the normally crystal-clear water was full of sinking hagfish remains. Those closest to him exploded and some dropped, either dead or stunned but still intact. Others ran from the pain of the ultrasound burst transmitted through a liquid medium. The AUVs shifted slightly, making sure their fields of fire overlapped and that they had all possible approaches covered.

It was like a sick video game, Lodup thought as he killed the mutated hagfish en masse. He felt pressure on his left leg rather than actual pain. Glancing down, he saw one of the monstrous, alien-looking things clamped to his leg as it tried to rasp its way through the thermal sheath. On some level he knew that the thermal sheath was hardening against the hagfish's attack. On another level, Lodup had a terrifying thing the size of an adult alligator attached to his leg and trying to eat him. He dropped the U-pulse and grabbed at the hilt of the diamond-bladed dive knife strapped to his right calf, somehow managing to draw it.

'No!' Sal shouted across comms, but it was too late. Lodup stabbed the blade through the top of the creature's body, close to its mouth. The blade cracked the armour, passed straight through its primitive body and bisected its mutation-reinforced vertebrate, then out of the other side, through Lodup's thermal sheath and into his leg. Lodup tried to scream in the liquid environment of his own larynx, and failed.

He had a moment to register that the black ink he was seeing in the water was actually his own blood, and then the water was full of hagfish. He felt their teeth against the thermal sheath and tried to cry out as they found the rip in it, and the wound beneath.

The burst of ultrasound was agonising. He felt his eardrums burst, and things tearing inside his body. The hagfish were now just so much chum sinking in the water. He saw the armoured maw of the orca swimming straight at him. It opened wide, displaying metal teeth. Then darkness.

Light, heat, panic overwhelmed him. He reached down for his leg even as he managed to work out where he was. Hideo was standing over him inside the submersible.

'Dude, you all right?' The submersible driver was smiling again. At least Lodup's brush with death had cheered him up.

'I hate this place,' Lodup said quietly. He was running his hand down the left leg of his thermal sheath. He couldn't even find a cut in the material.

'The suit's repaired itself, so has your leg, and your ruptured internal organs. Marvin pretty much saved your life. They're not that dangerous unless they can swarm you. They're parasites.'

'They live off the city?' Lodup asked incredulously. 'Anything else I need to know.'

Hideo tapped his head. 'Anything that's not classified is in there. You just need to find a way to assimilate it.'

'With all this tech, your only means of dealing with those things is zapping them with ultrasound?' he demanded.

Hideo looked uncomfortable. 'No, there's lots of other ways,' the submersible pilot said. 'But sometimes, particularly in and around the buildings, there isn't.'

'So this was training rather than a set-up?'

'Sorry, dude, not my idea.'

'Can you tell Siska to go and fuck herself?'

'Not verbally. I could maybe glare at her while she's not looking if you want, but this was more likely Yaroslav.'

'Okay, so now that I've failed my training and the killer whales think I'm a pussy, can I go home?'

'Do you want to?'

This stopped Lodup dead. He thought about it for a long time.

'No,' he finally admitted.

'You've got a choice, man. The building's open, the AUVs have been inside and mapped it. The interior's too small for the ADS.'

Normally after any kind of accident, a dive would be called off. This clearly wasn't that sort of environment.

'Any more fucking surprises?'

'If there are, they'll be a surprise to me as well,' Hideo said, grinning.

'Comforting,' Lodup muttered.

Lodup dropped out of the bottom of the submersible into water illuminated by the flatbed and the ADS's running lights. Light projected from his mask and right wrist as the feet of the thermal sheath grew into fins, and he carefully made his way across to the dark, rectangular-shaped hole they'd cut in the low, tomblike building.

'You all right, love?' Sal asked.

'Yes, Sal, thanks.'

He gripped the side of the doorway and was surprised by the tactile feedback through the thermal sheath's glove. The rock felt smooth, like a pebble in a riverbed, and despite the recent heat of the fusion torch it was cold again. The interior was illuminated by the AUVs. Sal dropped down behind him, using the ADS's propulsion system to keep the exoskeleton off the seabed to avoid kicking up more silt.

Lodup dived down a little and then gently finned into the building. Normally he'd use a line for any form of entry into a restricted environment, but the structure had been mapped, it was open plan, there was nowhere to get trapped.

The interior was basically an oddly angled, almost rectangular chamber. Low panels of differing heights protruded from the walls, floor and ceilings. Something about them suggested they were incomplete, as if they'd been frozen in place at the moment the city was petrified.

The AUVs were hovering in opposite corners of the long, low chamber, illuminating the interior with their running lights.

Lodup realised this was some kind of rite of passage. He played his wrist light over the walls as he slowly finned around the chamber. He jumped in mid-water and almost cried out when he saw them. Two figures. Largely humanoid, though their hairless heads looked slightly too large, and there was something wrong with their eyes. They had terrified expressions on their faces. They were both female, one of them a child. They were fused with the wall, as if they had been running through it and hadn't quite made it.

Lodup swallowed hard. He cast the light around but there were no more of them.

'Now what?' he subvocalized nervously.

'Now we've done our piece, they'll send in the bioengineers to see if it can be mined for anything useful,' Sal said.

Lodup made a thorough sweep of the place and then tried not to move too quickly as he finned back towards the exit. He didn't look at the two figures fused with the wall. He couldn't shake the feeling that they were watching him.

Lodup tried to scream, again, but it didn't happen, again. He thrashed backwards in the water, trying to get away from them as he grabbed at the U-pulse where it had adhered to his thermal sheath. They were simply hanging there, moving just enough to keep them level in the water. They were squid, just under a metre long and about half that across. A web of skin, like a shroud, stretched between their tentacles, and the shroud was lined with sharp-looking metal spikes. The creatures were covered with segmented metal armour and their eyes were lenses.

'It's okay, they're ours,' Hideo said across the short-range comms.

'Why are they hanging around out here?' Lodup asked, trying to control his anger. *And this is just my first day at work*, he thought.

Back in C&C, Siska shook her head as she listened and watched the feed from flatbed 4-2. Behind her she could hear laughter from the other C&C personnel. She glanced back – even Yaroslav had a smirk on his normally emotionless face.

The engineered *Ampyroteuthis infernalis*, or 'vampire squid of hell', weren't even guard-fauna, really, just a side project the bioengineers had thought was 'cool', and which she had okayed.

'You have to be a bit careful with them in the moon pool. They can launch themselves out of the water up to about five metres.' Hideo used the short-range ultrasound to tell Lodup, and the long-range infrasound to tell C&C. There was renewed laughter in C&C. Siska turned around to face the room.

'Okay, that's enough fun with the new guy. I want everyone back to work,' she said firmly, though even she was struggling to suppress a smirk.

20
A Long Time After the Loss

Everything felt strangely soft and warm to General Nix. He should have felt hard chitin, sinew and the armour and machinery required to survive in higher-G combat environments. Not only was his mind no longer connected to a powerful neunonic and liquid-software computer, but his thought processes were odd. They were fragmented, chaotic, unfocused. There was no residual connection to Queen or Hive. He opened his eyes to a bizarre mono-image which looked too narrow in scope, as if his eyes only faced forwards.

He felt rage rise in him. He normally killed out of cold necessity, but now he wanted to kill in a cold fury, just for the sake of it. He also wanted to pick up the kids from soccer practice while the pot roast was cooking, and make sure Frank was able to relax in front of the TV without the kids bothering him too much.

The General was confused. He held up a hand. Where there had been a power-assisted hard-tech claw, there was now a perfectly manicured human-looking hand. Despite all the housework he liked to keep his hands and nails nice— No! General Nix looked down. He was astonished to find two bizarre mounds of flesh protruding from his chest. He was wearing some kind of pink garment that was open at the back, and his legs were encased in a deeply uncomfortable skintight covering. He was undeniably a hairless monkey. He was pretty sure he was a baseline female but couldn't be absolutely certain as they all looked the same to him.

He glanced around the bizarre house. It was large and spacious, the furniture old enough not to be made of smart matter. Outside there was even more space, covered in green stuff. The word 'garden' rose unbidden in General Nix's head. From where he was sitting in the 'lounge' he could see one of the massive sun windows on the cylindrical habitat. Above the vast window was another strip of land covered with neatly laid out streets. Slowly Nix started to work out where he was. He tried to emit angry pheromone secretions but some kind of biological override prevented him from pissing and shitting himself. His face contorted as he tried, but failed, to scream.

Mr Hat was seated in his bath chair directly in front of General Nix, watching the human woman's face contort in the real-time immersion rendering of the war criminal's suburban hell.

'Surely if he does that in front of anyone, his partner, his children, he'll give the game away?' the diminutive lizard said.

'You'd be surprised what an unaugmented human mind is capable of rationalising away, actually,' the warden said. He was a nondescript, handsome male-plus, a corporate rather than a combat model. His fixed, ingratiating grin and predatory eyes were already starting to annoy Mr Hat. He was practically bleeding testosterone from his pores. The warden, who had introduced himself as Isaiah, obviously resented the bounty killer's presence. He wasn't terribly happy about the presence of the naval contractor's squadron of ships, either.

'He's fighting the programme here. It's designed to allow that to a degree, particularly when there's nobody present, like other family members, to see. It causes quite a lot of pain, whereas when they voluntarily go along with the programming they receive a serotonin reward.'

'So they effectively end up conditioning themselves?' Mr Hat asked. He was watching one of the most notorious war criminals in Consortium space doing mundane housework of the type that probably hadn't been necessary since the hairless monkeys had very carelessly lost their home planet.

'Pretty much. They're criminals, people unable to embrace the free market and succeed, which makes them weak-minded. Addicting them to their own serotonin is simple enough.'

The human face General Nix was wearing looked as if it desperately wanted to scream.

'So if you were locked in there, with your thirst for success and competitiveness, you wouldn't succumb to the serotonin, then?' Mr Hat asked. He could feel the warden glaring at him. The immersion disappeared as Isaiah closed it down.

'Whatever they do, they cannot break the fourth wall,' Isaiah told Mr Hat, ignoring the lizard's question.

'But they are aware of their core personalities, who they really are?'

'Initially, but that fades – there's too much bleed from the program personality. It needs to be strong enough to stop them taking over, after all. AI is working on a way to extend their self-awareness whilst keeping them trapped, perhaps indefinitely.'

'AI is the habitat's artificial intelligence?'

'Yes, and, if you ask me, something of a sick fuck,' Isaiah added smugly.

'You feel they deserve this?' Mr Hat enquired. He glanced up at Isaiah, who looked genuinely perturbed by the question. The immersion was replaced with the nearly featureless control room. It was little more than a series of couches on which the warden and his staff lay as they neunonically interfaced with the habitat's systems. The control room was at one end of the cylinder, and transparent smart matter provided a vertiginous view of the six segments. Three windows and three strips of land stretched away from the control room as the entire cylinder slowly rotated.

'Every single form of control has been tried at one time or another,' the warden said. 'Only one has won out over all others and proven to be the way forward for the uplifted races. If you don't believe me, then perhaps you should move to the anarchy of the Monarchist systems.'

'FIFO, ay?' Mr Hat asked, smiling slightly. Isaiah frowned. FIFO was the unofficial motto of the Consortium: Fit In or Fuck Off. 'Tell me, have you ever been to the Monarchist systems?' He could feel the answering glare without turning around to look at Isaiah.

'This facility is as secure as a Citadel. I am a little confused by your presence here, let alone a naval squadron.'

No it is not as secure as a Citadel, you silly little man, Mr Hat thought. Though having reviewed the habitat's security, he could not see an obvious way in.

'Why the murders?' Mr Hat asked.

'So that even when they go along with the programming, they still live in fear.'

'These are hard people. Violence does not scare them.'

'Hello, Mr Hat,' a very jolly voice said. 'Loss of control scares them, their helplessness in the face of pain and violence. The tension and anticipation of it makes them suffer, as does the memory of it, and not knowing when it will happen again, and who will initiate it. Though some of the sicker minds may enjoy it.'

'Hello, AI,' Mr Hat said to the AI. He was forced to agree with Isaiah – the AI didn't sound entirely healthy. 'Where is the Widow?'

'That is the beauty of it,' Isaiah said.

'We tell partners, friends or other bonded groups that they will be close,' the AI added. 'That they will interact in day-to-day life, but as a result of never being able to break the fourth wall they will never know who the other is.'

The AI sounded absurdly pleased with this. It sounded petty to Mr Hat.

'Do you use experiential ware? Like in the Game?' Mr Hat asked. The pause before the answer came told him everything.

'No, soft tech. The split-level mind-imprisonment systems we use are too sophisticated to be compatible with something like experiential ware.' It was Al who answered. As jolly as it was, it sounded rehearsed to Mr Hat.

You mean you don't have the processing power to listen in to more than a million minds and their prisoners at one time, Mr Hat thought. Experiential ware allowed for thought-policing. It was the ultimate in surveillance.

'Suburbia's status as the longest-running situation comedy soap opera in Known Space means that it is a total surveillance environment, a panopticon,' Isaiah told him. Mr Hat nodded as he looked out over the hexagonal cylinder habitat. 'Now, Mr Hat, I don't mean to be rude but we allowed you to interview Prisoner Berger. We have been very cooperative, but you can see for yourself that we are perfectly secure. Woodbine Scab will not come here. Not unless he's an inmate.'

Even if I caught him, I do not see him coming here, Mr Hat thought. He couldn't see the programming taking, somehow.

'I don't recall you being given any choice about allowing my interview of the prisoner. Just like you've not been given any choice about my presence here. There is something you should bear in mind about your "perfectly secure" habitat, however. Mr Scab infiltrated the Game, and he now has one of the best intrusion specialists in Known Space helping him.' Isaiah opened his mouth to retort but Mr Hat had tired of the corporate mouthpiece's narrow-minded ignorance. 'Just make sure you keep me 'faced in to all surveillance feeds around Mr Berger.'

With that, Mr Hat's bath chair started trundling towards the door. Two of his eyeless automatons, a male and a female, appeared out of the corners of the room. The male moved behind the bath chair and started pushing it, unnecessarily. As Mr Hat left the control room, he couldn't shake the feeling that he was missing something.

The garden had been torn up a little. Plant pots had been knocked over, saplings uprooted, a garden gnome smashed.

A small hand picked up the vial lying on the disturbed lawn.

'What just happened?' Isaiah asked. There was a blinking red symbol in his mind.

'Slight change in pressure, very localised,' Al answered, a razor-thin edge to his jollity.

'Should we inform Mr Hat?'

'I see no real reason to,' the AI said. 'After all, security at this facility is our responsibility, not his.'

'Can we dispatch a stealthed S-sat to the area, to be on the safe side?'

'Sure, why not?' Al said.

Nix discovered that his name was Hilda Swanson now. This angered him further. Then the pain started. He was crying out, clutching at his head and careening around the house to the sound of canned laughter. He felt as if the inside of his head was being eaten. He was losing himself, remembering less and less of his former life, slowly ceasing to exist.

'What's going on with Prisoner Swanson?' Isaiah asked. He was receiving the direct feed from inside the house as Nix staggered around the lounge, screaming.

'The core personality must have downloaded corrupt – we'll need to pull him and run a diagnostic,' Al said, sounding less jolly than normal.

'That hasn't happened in a while,' Isaiah said. 'It's going to look bad on the weekly report.' Then they lost the feed. 'What the fuck?' That hadn't happened before. 'Al?'

'We're losing more feeds. Looks localised. Something's eating the nano-cams.'

Al 'faced the macro-cam feeds to Isaiah. They showed footage of the area shot by powerful cameras mounted on rails running along the window supports. They could provide very detailed shots but did not have the total coverage the nano-cams provided, and all they could pick up through the walls of the houses were heat signatures. They focused on the garden that had been disturbed.

'More vandalism?' Isaiah asked. Another feed kicked in showing the wreckage of the garden from a different angle as the stealthed S-sat hovered over it.

'No, look at the pattern of destruction,' Al's disembodied voice said. 'That's caused by depressurisation.'

'The S-sat's picking up traces of Cherenkov radiation,' Isaiah said, frowning. Al turned part of the smart matter of the control room into a screen, his circular, yellow cartoon happy face no longer smiling. Its mouth was now a big downward curve. 'Al, has someone just established a bridge point within the habitat?'

'We may not have the mass of a planet but that should still be impossible,' the frowning cartoon face on the wall said.

'Does it fit the data?' Isaiah demanded.

There was a moment's pause. Then: 'Yes.'

'Review the footage leading up to it.'

'There isn't any.'

'It went down after the pressure change?'

'Someone has released a very powerful privacy swarm in the area,' the AI told him.

Isaiah checked the macro- and S-sat feeds. 'The area looks okay. Can we counter it?' he asked.

'Eventually.'

'Eventually! We're supposed to be the highest security prison in Consortium space! I want stealthed S-sats patrolling the area constantly until that privacy swarm is fucking eaten and we know what's going on. It's the Church, it fucking has to be.'

'If it is, then they are after Prisoner Berger. Do you want to bring him in?' the AI asked.

'No, I want to catch whoever's doing this. Besides, why bother? They'd want him dead and we have his personality in our Psycho Bank – they've got nothing to gain.'

'Do you want me to notify Mr Hat?'

The vial transformed into a syringe. The child put it against his skull. There was a crunch and he grimaced at the pain. He wasn't used to it. The needle grew through the bone and squirted its contents into the soft matter beneath it.

Nix died in the mind of Hilda Swanson and Vic was reborn. He looked down at his strange new body.

'Oh,' he said, crestfallen. He was wondering what the fuck Scab had done to him this time. He glanced down at his human female form again and then went looking for a reflective surface. His appreciation of the human form allowed him to recognise the baseline female body. His favourite of the human sexes, he even preferred it to the girly-girl, which was just a bit too much for him. His self-taught understanding of human aesthetics told him he was in good shape and attractive enough, if a little ordinary-looking. He was certainly no Talia, but he liked his auburn hair and brown eyes. He started feeling the body. 'Oh,' he said again, this time a little more salaciously. He glanced at the fridge, and then at the open bedroom door.

He was probably here to do something really stupid for Scab. Some secret mission. In terms of his humanophilia, it did occur to him that this could be a case of 'be careful what you wish for'. *On the other hand*, he thought, *how many times do you get a chance to investigate such things first hand?*

Sated, Vic had finally fallen asleep after deciding that being a human female was the best thing ever, though he was struggling with the distinct lack of limbs. When he eventually awoke, he had no idea how long he'd slept for as his new body didn't appear to have any neunonics. He got up and dressed himself, looking for the most practical clothing he could find. Not much of it was terribly practical. In the end he settled for a pair of slacks, some tennis shoes and a blouse that tied across the stomach. It was then he heard a noise. Instinct took over and he glanced around for a weapon.

Vic crept into the kitchen, bedside lamp at the ready. There was a young human male, perhaps twelve or so years old, sitting at the breakfast bar. He was balancing a large and sharp-looking kitchen knife on its point and spinning it.

'Who the fuck are you, and why the fuck are you in this house, which may actually be mine?'

The boy glanced up at him. Without the human-expression recognition-ware in his neunonics Vic couldn't be entirely sure, but he thought the kid was looking at him as if he was an utter moron. He noticed a vial full of quicksilver-like liquid lying on the surface of the breakfast bar close to the knife.

'It's Elodie, Vic, you can put the lamp down.'

A bizarre set of expressions crossed Vic's now-human face as he tried to mimic human confusion. Elodie just watched him.

'Er ...' Vic started.

'Why don't you have a beverage of some kind and I'll explain it to you?'

Vic went to the fridge and spent some time trying to open it. He pulled out a bottle of beer and waited for the smart cap to open. It didn't.

'Any idea how to open this?' Vic asked.

The kid rolled his eyes. 'Get me one, too,' Elodie told him. Vic took another beer from the fridge and handed them both to Elodie. She opened both bottles by knocking the lids off against the edge of the breakfast bar.

'So ...?' Vic asked.

'We're on Suburbia,' Elodie told him.

'Are we prisoners? Did they get Scab?' Vic was unable to keep the hopeful tone out of his last question.

'No. We snuck in as fragmented personalities hidden in the minds of two criminals who we shopped to a bounty crew—'

'Who?'

'Crabber— Does it matter?'

'Is this Living City tech?'

'What?' Elodie was getting exasperated. 'Yes.'

'Why didn't we just bridge in?'

'Because we'd have been torn apart by the internal security in a moment. Scab opened a pinpoint bridge and dropped some neunonics' – Elodie tapped the vial – 'and the most potent privacy swarm we could afford.'

'Is that for me?' Vic asked, pointing at the vial. Elodie nodded. Vic picked it up and held the vial to his head. The smart-matter vial transformed into a syringe, the needle grew through his skull with a crack and a rivulet of blood ran down Vic's human face. 'Ouch. That really fucking hurts.'

'Hold still and stop being such a pussy.'

Vic was aware of, rather than actually feeling, the neunonics growing through the soft matter of his brain. Telemetry started to appear in his vision as his mind expanded and all sorts of information became available. Skills were hardwired into the grey matter that he hoped the meat of the body would be able to live up to.

'Why am I here?' Vic asked. 'You're the intrusion expert.'

'Muscle.'

'You want me to do violence in this body?' he asked incredulously. It was so soft and brittle he was worried it would explode if he threw one solid punch.

'I've found the Alchemist,' Elodie told him, ignoring the question.

Elodie and Vic were lying under a tree looking across at a house. Vic was watching it carefully. Finally he saw it – a disturbance in the air that suggested a cloak. He nodded to Elodie and both of them backed away. It was only a matter of time before the cloaked S-sat would pick them up with passive scans, even at that range. They made their way back to Vic's house.

'How many, do you think?' Vic asked.

'I made three earlier,' Elodie told him.

'In these bodies, no weapons to speak of, we wouldn't stand a chance.' Elodie nodded in agreement. 'So what's the extraction plan?'

'Basically, we didn't know where the Alchemist was prior to getting in here, so we needed to locate him and then take him to an agreed-upon point at a certain time.'

'How did you find him?'

'I looked.'

'So how are we going to get him out? The S-sats will just cut us down.'

'What would Scab do?' Elodie asked.

Vic considered this. 'Something violent and grandiose.'

'No, he'd think laterally,' Elodie growled.

Vic was at a loss as to why she was irritated with him. 'Okay, he'd do something violent and grandiose laterally.'

Vic arrived back at the house to find the odd curved plastic machine in a cradle was vibrating and making a ringing noise.

'What is it?' Vic asked.

'Some sort of rudimentary communications device,' Elodie hazarded a guess. 'Pick it up.' Vic did as Elodie suggested. There was a tinny noise coming from the device. 'Hold it to your ear.'

Vic did so, though he was very much of the opinion that his antennas were vastly superior sensory organs. He listened to the voice on the end of the phone.

'What would you like me to do about that?' he eventually asked. He listened to the reply. 'I see, and how would I do that?' He listened again. 'Okay, I'll get right on it.' He put the plastic device back down on its cradle. Elodie had an enquiring expression on her face. 'It appears I have two human larvae, they are stranded at an institution called a "school" and I am required to retrieve them.'

Elodie nodded.

Conflict resolution worlds were easier, Vic thought, though they inspired similar genocidal thoughts. There was no assembler, and he had been expected to provide the larvae with nutrition that he somehow created himself. After muddling through that, he was expected to do the same for a male human mate. The male human appeared to think he was 'acting strangely', and kept pausing as if he was expecting to hear something after every time he said this.

The meal preparation, which was decreed by all to be a horrible failure, resulted in water leaking from Vic's eyes out of pure frustration. Vic's human mate fed the larvae something called ice cream, which appeared to cheer them up. Vic was then subjected to several hours of mind-numbing tedium that passed itself off as entertainment, in the form of odd two-dimensional media that were played on a large device attached to a dumb-matter wall. When Vic mentioned immersions, everyone looked at him oddly.

The worst came after the larvae retired to their rooms. Vic discovered that being a human female was great fun with a cucumber, but less fun with a human male. He then had to wait until his 'mate' was sound asleep before he could risk sneaking out.

Vic was still a bit shaky when he met up with Elodie.

'What's wrong with you?' she asked.

'I don't want to talk about it,' Vic snapped.

'Look, I've been pretending to be a human kitten for days now, don't get me started.'

Elodie led them through the streets until she found what she was looking for – one of the automated ground cars on a driveway rather than its garage.

'This car clearly belongs to some kind of radical free-thinker,' Elodie muttered.

'You can get us out of here, right? That's why Scab recruited you, wasn't it? Because you had a plan to get out of here if you were ever caught, right?'

Elodie looked up at Vic. She'd heard panic, but she was pretty sure Vic had got the accompanying facial expression wrong.

'Why? Missing your nat girlfriend?'

'She's not my—' Vic started.

'Keep your fucking voice down!' Elodie snapped.

Vic lapsed into silence. He wondered if explaining that practising with a cucumber had made him more responsive to her needs would impress Talia. He suspected he lacked the perspective to know for sure. He was coming to the conclusion that he just didn't get human females, even if he was one at the moment.

'And to answer your question – no,' Elodie told him.

'What?'

Elodie turned on him. 'Do I have to cut your fucking tongue out?' she hissed.

Vic looked down at the diminutive human larva standing in front of him, glaring at him angrily. He burst out laughing.

'Oh, fuck you, Vic.' Elodie turned and stalked away from him. She moved quickly up the driveway and knelt by one of the ground car's doors. She hawked and spat on the lock mechanism.

'Then seriously, what are we doing here? I can't stay here – it's like one of Scab's torture immersions but without the fucking irony.'

Elodie was concentrating on the nanites in the spittle she was using as the medium for the hack to unlock the vehicle, then spoof it into not contacting the AI to tell it that the vehicle was active.

'We're testing a theory,' a somewhat distracted Elodie told Vic.

'A theory? A fucking theory! Do you know what he put in me?' Vic hissed. Elodie glared at Vic. 'What theory?'

The ground car's door clicked open but the systems remained dark. Elodie climbed in and scooted to the passenger seat to make room for Vic.

'Okay, so none of the inmates have neunonics. All the internal security, the control program, is soft-machine bioware. I mean, unless a house has been secured for murder, people leave their doors unlocked.'

'So?'

'All the security is on the outside. Who'd break in, particularly as it's a total surveillance system?'

Vic was staring at her. 'This is a fucking guess?' he demanded, appalled.

'Pretty much,' Elodie said as she produced a hammer, a screwdriver and a number of tea-towels from her coat.

'And what do you do if you're fucking wrong?'

'Well, I don't know about you, but I'm going to attack the S-sats and hope they kill me, and eventually Scab will decide to download a backup personality into my body. I certainly can't do another day of school without fucking murdering someone.' She paused. 'Possibly everyone.'

'So a privacy swarm to buy some time, and then what?'

Elodie took the hammer and the screwdriver and, using the tea-towels in an attempt to mask the sound, she started trying to drive the chisel point through the hard plastic case of the ground car's central column.

'I'm not saying there won't be a lot of internal security,' she said as she hammered the screwdriver through the plastic. 'I think they'll have amazing security. What I'm hoping is that they're overconfident enough that a good intrusion expert and some top-end Pythian programs will be enough to bypass it.'

'To do what?'

'To create a diversion.'

'And we're in the car because there's no 'face tech, but the cars are linked to the AI.'

Elodie nodded. 'Give me a hand with this,' she said. Vic reached down, and the two of them pulled open the crack in the plastic that Elodie had made with the screwdriver. 'It was either here, or try and use one of the comms or media devices in the houses, but I reckoned there was more chance of someone finding us there.'

The central plastic column contained material that looked more like tech to Vic. A number of wires ran from a cylinder containing a blue gel. Elodie removed the kitchen knife she had taken from Vic's house.

'Hey! I could have used that earlier, when I was preparing dinner,' Vic said. Elodie gave him a disparaging look. 'Sorry.'

Elodie hawked up another mouthful of phlegm and then used the knife to pierce the cylinder before spitting on it. The spit visibly branched out inside the blue gel, reminding Vic of arteries. The spittle also sealed the hole made by the knife. Elodie closed her eyes and started to concentrate. Vic watched her. His skin was starting to itch. It had turned red and blotchy in places, and he suspected this was the result of Elodie's privacy nano-swarm, and whatever counter-swarm their jailers had released.

'Well?' Vic asked.

'Vic, I need you to shut up.'

Vic lapsed into a sulky silence and tried not to scratch his fragile skin. The porch light of the house they were sitting outside came on. A man in a dressing gown, wearing glasses and looking just like every other male inmate on Suburbia, was walking down the drive towards them. He opened the car door. Vic looked up at him and tried to smile, but ended up sort of grimacing.

'Hi there, can I help you?'

'This is your problem,' Elodie muttered, her eyes closed, still concentrating.

'Do you want to have human sex?' Vic blurted.

Elodie actually opened her eyes and turned to stare at Vic.

He shrugged. 'I panicked,' he told her. The man was confused, since he had expected canned laughter.

'Well, gee, I'd love to but I'm—' He stopped, his expression suddenly fixed and blank. The whole cast of his features became more calculating and malevolent. 'This isn't going to last, is it?' he said.

'Er, what?' Vic asked.

The man grabbed him by the hair – Vic was surprised by just how much that hurt – and dragged him out of the car.

'I think I'll take you up on your offer.' He threw Vic to the ground. Vic turned it awkwardly into a roll and came up on his feet. His body still felt very awkward, too fleshy and with not enough limbs.

'It was just a distraction!' Vic shouted desperately. 'I didn't really want to do it.'

The man advanced on Vic. Vic hooked a kick into the back of the man's leg, sending him staggering down onto one knee. Vic threw a punch with his left lower arm. Too late, he remembered that he didn't have lower arms. The man got back to his feet. Vic kneed him in the groin, the chest and the face in quick succession. As the man staggered back, Vic hit him with a right-fisted haymaker, then back-fisted the man with the same hand. There was the solid, flat sound of meat hitting meat at velocity. The pain that shot through Vic's hand surprised him. The skills may have been hardwired into this body, but that didn't mean the body, though healthy, was conditioned for combat.

Something glittering and made of steel flew through the night air towards him. Vic caught the kitchen knife Elodie had thrown by its handle. As the man turned back towards Vic, he rammed the blade through his neck so hard that the point of the knife came out of the back. The man dropped to his knees drooling a lot of blood from his mouth, the neck wound bubbling. Then he slumped to the ground.

'Cucumbers are better, motherfucker,' Vic told the corpse.

Elodie was standing in the passenger doorway of the ground car. Despite the violence, and the dead person, the night appeared quiet and still.

'Well?' Vic asked. 'What did you do?'

It started with the sound of grass breaking – the universal sign of impending chaos. Then the screams began.

'I just woke everyone up.'

Isaiah's vision was red. It was filled with warning symbols from the habitat's systems. Through the transparent wall of the control room he could see the first explosions blossom as fires sprang up in all three sections. *The Church wouldn't do it this way*, Isaiah managed to think through the drug-suppressed panic.

'Inform Mr Hat,' Isaiah told Al.

21
Ancient Britain

There were more than two hundred horse-mounted warriors in the broad, shallow trench. Tangwen had walked up and down counting them. She was sure some were from the Regni, others were definitely from the Atrebates, but many were from tribes she did not know. There were no spear-carrying landsmen or -women with them, only the warrior nobility. Most were men, though the scouts who wore the lynx headdresses appeared to be mainly female.

'Not like this,' Tangwen muttered to herself.

The warriors had mostly ignored her. She was a small, wiry female with a scarred face, of no interest to them. Some were nervously preparing for battle, others talking a bit too loudly, using bravado to mask their fear. Many who had seen war before were just waiting grimly for it to start. The whole area carried the stink of horse, leather and sweat.

The horses, seasoned though they might be, were obviously nervous. They knew something unnatural was coming. Many of the warriors had dismounted to calm their horses, and would mount again at the last moment. They intended to charge into the forest and face the monsters. It was madness, but Tangwen knew the warrior mindset. She would no more be able to dissuade them from their actions than teach them to fly. Many would need to die before the rest understood what was happening.

Tangwen heard cries from where she had left the rest of the survivors. She turned and ran down the line, still ignored by most of the warriors present. Then she heard angry shouting, the unmistakable sound of metal hitting flesh, hard, and then more cries.

Ahead of her through the trees she could see a number of the bear-skull-wearing warriors surrounding Kush, who was crouched low, his red-dripping axe at the ready. She watched as one moved towards him. Kush swung the axe. Even as she ran, Tangwen saw the bear-skull-wearing warrior's shield break, and the warrior was taken off his feet by the force of Kush's blow. As she closed on them, she saw another of the warriors lying on the ground, his chest a red mess of split bones.

'So you're one of the demons,' she heard a warrior say. He started turning as he heard Tangwen's approach. Tangwen caught him just below the chin with the butt of her spear, forcing the leather armour around his neck into his throat. He went down choking. Another of the warriors turned and swung at her. She rolled under the blade and up on her feet, back-to-back with Kush.

'What do you think you're doing?' she demanded furiously.

Nearby, Essyllt was lying on the ground, close to her litter. One of the two Brigante who'd been helping to carry the litter was lying senseless next to her, a livid red mark showing where he'd been hit in the head. The other litter-bearer had a bloodied mouth, but was trying to help Essyllt back to her pallet.

'Who are you to speak to us like that, woman?' one of the warriors demanded. His nose exploded and spread itself across his face as the butt of Tangwen's spear crushed it. He staggered back. He looked ready to use the heavy iron blade he was holding easily in his right hand.

'I'll have courtesy, or you'll have the sharp end of my spear,' she told him.

The man glared at her and then smiled through his thick, white-streaked, bushy beard. He was a large man, about equal parts fat and muscle. A half-closed dead-eye, two fingers remaining on his left hand and a patchwork of scar tissue on his face told of a long life as a warrior. His boiled-leather armour was also well scarred, and had been stained black at some point in its past. He started to laugh, a low, rumbling sound.

'I like you, but I want to kill the demon,' he told her.

'So did your friend, and look where that got him.' She nodded to the corpse on the ground. 'And this is no demon. Don't make excuses for your people's weakness.'

'They wanted to burn Essyllt and some of the others,' Kush managed.

'Why?' she demanded of the thick-set bearded man. The man she'd hit in the throat appeared to be recovering and more warriors were surrounding them. Back in the trees she could see the other survivors advancing. Some of them had makeshift weapons and looked just about desperate enough to use them. Germelqart had his club. She saw Mabon, knife in hand, moving and ready to attack one of the armoured warriors. It would be a massacre.

243

'They have the sickness,' the bearded man said.

'So?' replied Tangwen.

'We burn them, it doesn't spread.'

'They have travelled with us, and none of us has caught it. It comes from the spawn of Andraste, abominations of the goddess, not the afflicted themselves.'

'Are you a *dryw*, to know this?'

'Are *you*?' Tangwen demanded angrily.

The warrior opened his mouth to answer.

'Nerthach acts under my orders.' The voice was quiet enough, but carried. Tangwen risked a quick glance in the direction from which it came. The speaker wore the black robe of a *dryw*, one of the sacrificers. The robe was open – he wore armour underneath it – and although he leaned on a gnarled staff, a sheathed sword hung from his belt. The hood of his robe hid most of his facial features, but a long beard with a braided moustache hung down from it. He was built similarly to the warrior with the dead-eye but looked to be less fat and more muscle. Tangwen was pretty sure she knew who he was.

'You're Bladud, aren't you?' she asked warily. She left out the rest of the name he was known by.

'I am Bladud, called Witch King, and I was trained as a *dryw*. I ordered the sick burned.'

'You intend to fight their sickness with iron when they come, yet you would burn the afflicted now? That makes no sense,' Tangwen said. Her spear was still ready, as was Kush's axe. She knew Bladud by reputation. All knew his name. Formerly a *dryw*, he had broken the ban on *dryw* taking part in battles. For his actions he had been censored on a number of occasions, and once even subject to the great disgrace that was a satire. When the last king of the Brigante died, Bladud claimed there was nobody other than himself fit to lead, and his people agreed. He was cast out of the *dryw* and told he was forever hidden from the sight of the gods. He had a fearsome reputation for conducting warfare with the aid of his magics.

'You will all catch the sickness when they get close enough to you. Will you burn yourself on a pyre?' Tangwen asked him.

Bladud pushed his hood down. He was quite old, by Tangwen's reckoning, perhaps even as much as forty summers. His head was shorn of hair and a spiderweb of scar tissue covered the skin of his scalp.

'If need be.'

'Your weapons cannot harm them.'

'How do we know she isn't one of them?' the man called Nerthach asked. 'She walks and fights alongside a demon.'

'He's no demon,' Bladud said, and turned to Kush. 'Numibian?'

Kush narrowed his eyes suspiciously. 'How did you know that?'

'I travelled when I was younger and learned the secrets of many different places. Will you put up your weapons so we can talk?'

'Or we can just kill them,' Nerthach suggested.

'Then how will we learn anything?' Bladud asked. 'We will still be able to kill them later, if we wish.'

'The reason only one of your people lies dead is because Tangwen was merciful to them,' Kush said in his deep baritone.

A rasping noise came from the one she had hit in the throat. Tangwen realised he was trying to speak.

'That ... I can attest to,' the warrior finally managed. There was laughter from the other warriors, including Nerthach. Bladud smiled.

'Our people are not to be harmed,' Kush said.

'The diseased ones are dead already,' Bladud said. 'It is a kindness.'

'Mine to give, not yours,' Tangwen said evenly.

Bladud regarded her carefully. She was aware of the bear-skulled warriors shifting slightly, ready to attack if the Witch King willed it.

'They stay forward of the line,' Bladud said.

'We will pass when we wish it,' Kush said. 'You can clear as big a gap in your line for a group of tired, weary and sick people as your courage dictates.'

Tangwen glanced at him. The speed with which he was picking up the language was astonishing. Bladud turned another thoughtful look on the Numibian.

'No agreement, but let's talk first. We can always kill each other later.'

'I have your word that nobody will be harmed whilst we talk?' Tangwen asked.

'Who are you?' Bladud asked, sounding a little irritated now.

'Tangwen of the Pobl Neidr.'

Bladud narrowed his eyes, the slightest smile curving the corner of his mouth. 'How many summers have you seen?'

'What does that matter? I am a warrior of my people.'

'Answer me.' Bladud did not sound angry, but his tone made it clear that he wouldn't brook much more insolence.

'I have seen nineteen summers,' she said begrudgingly.

'Then you are too young to remember. I have met your father. Do you understand me?'

Tangwen just stared at him. 'I find that hard to believe.'

'Nevertheless, it's true, and I mislike being called a liar. Would you have me describe him?' Bladud asked. Tangwen shook her head.

Bladud turned to his men. 'Sheathe your swords now,' he told his warriors.

'The demon?' Nerthach asked.

'If you are afraid of him, then keep your sword in your hand,' Bladud told him. Nerthach thought about it for a moment, laughed at himself and sheathed his sword. Then he walked straight to Kush, his hand extended. Kush glanced at Tangwen, who relaxed. Kush lowered his axe and grasped Nerthach's proffered arm

'I am Kush,' the dark-skinned man said, 'and nothing is easy in this land.'

Nerthach started to laugh and slapped Kush on the shoulder, much to the other's man's irritation. 'That at least is true. It is a sorry thing to kill the sick, but it must be done. When it comes time, then you and I will fight, agreed?'

Kush frowned, looking down at the thick-set, bearded man. 'I would wish it otherwise. I think your people will be poorer for your loss, but so be it.'

'I like you, demon,' Nerthach told Kush.

'Well, this is … pleasant,' Bladud said. 'In the meantime, Kush, Tangwen and their charges are under my protection. They are not to be harmed.' Nerthach opened his mouth to ask a question. 'Not even the sick.' Nerthach nodded. Bladud turned to Tangwen. He reached out to touch her burned face. Tangwen wanted to flinch away from him but didn't.

'This still hurts.' It wasn't a question. 'I have a salve which will help. I think there is much we need to speak of, but what I need to know first is how far behind you are they?'

'No more than half a day,' Tangwen told him.

'Give them food and water, but keep away from them,' Bladud told Nerthach, nodding towards the survivors. He then gestured for Tangwen and Kush to follow him. Germelqart hesitated for a moment and then joined them as well.

The camp was further up the slope, set back amongst the trees, and was busy with all the various retinues that accompanied travelling warriors. Food was being prepared, weapons honed and maintained, horses shod. Bladud exchanged words with most he passed as he led Kush, Germelqart and Tangwen to a shelter made from branches and the surrounding undergrowth. Inside was a cluttered mess, many of the things Tangwen recognised as the tools and accoutrements of the *dryw*. Bladud rummaged around until he found a small clay pot sealed with wax.

'It would be better if I did this, but if you would prefer to do it yourself ...'

Tangwen regarded him for a moment. She was not sure what to make of him. The one thing she did know was that he was powerful, and powerful people tended to be ruthless because they had to be. His outcast status should have made him a pariah, but that was clearly not the case if he commanded two hundred warriors from different tribes.

'Where were you when the black *curraghs* came?' she blurted out angrily.

Bladud went very still. 'I was in the west on Ynys Dywyll with my warriors. I was petitioning for the ban on me to be removed.' There was something in his voice – shame, she thought. 'If I had ...' he started. 'There is no excuse. I failed my people.' He would not meet her eyes. Instead he broke the wax seal on the pot and started to smear some of the salve within across the acid scar on Tangwen's face. For the first time since she received the wound the burning lessened, became tolerable. She felt like weeping with relief, but knew that this was not the time to show weakness. When he had finished dressing the wound, Bladud left the shelter. He returned with bread and horns filled with ale. Kush, Tangwen and even Germelqart all but snatched them out of his hands.

'There will be meat to follow. I have sent the same to your people,' he told them. They thanked him through mouths full of bread and ale. Bowls of stew did indeed follow, which they attacked with equal gusto.

'Tell me what happened, as much as you are willing,' Bladud said after furnishing them with a second horn of ale.

Kush remained mostly quiet and Germelqart was entirely silent while Tangwen told Bladud the story. She kept certain details to herself, but recounted broadly what had happened. Britha, Fachtna and Teardrop coming to her village. Tangwen guiding them to the Crown of Andraste. The wicker man, Andraste's awakening, the Isle of Madness, Andraste's spawn and what they were doing to the land.

'They change everything they touch, warp it, twist it. They are horrors of the Otherworld, born of a goddess, perverted by the Dark Man, and weapons cannot harm them.'

Bladud was regarding her thoughtfully. He had asked few questions throughout her story, content simply to listen.

'Your warriors will all die,' Kush told him quietly.

'And yet you fought one and lived,' Bladud said.

'A small one, and it killed two of our number almost before we could move against it,' Tangwen told him.

247

'But if no weapons can harm it?' Bladud said. Tangwen and Kush said nothing, but Kush couldn't help glancing towards where his axe lay. Bladud followed his glance. Kush turned back to find the Witch King looking at him, one eyebrow raised.

'Your axe has been blessed with the blood of the gods,' Bladud said. It was not a question. Kush did not reply. 'Tell me, Kush, have you ever heard of the Brass City?'

The Numibian did everything he could to try and mask his reaction, but Tangwen could tell he knew the name. Germelqart was fixedly staring down, avoiding looking at either Bladud or Kush.

'Even in this land you would do well not to speak those words again,' Kush said. Tangwen did not think he meant it as a threat. She thought he was frightened.

'The blood of the gods flows in some of our veins,' Bladud said. 'It is weakened, yes, but it drives us to do great things.'

'In this you will die,' Kush assured him.

'My Father ...' Tangwen began. This time Bladud looked to her with interest. 'He sang the mindsong to me in my sleep. He said that even the blood magics would not be enough to fight them.'

Kush was staring at her, his expression unreadable.

Bladud's expression became grim. 'In my youth I searched out every wonder I could—'

'I think you searched too far,' Kush muttered.

'Perhaps, but if any would know, it would be Tangwen's father. What did he counsel on this matter?'

'To flee to Gaul, or further,' Tangwen said. 'That Ynys Prydain is lost.'

'Bitter news indeed,' he said, looking down. 'But I have to see this, judge for myself. I have to know what we are facing.'

'Nothing will be served by all these warriors dying here,' Tangwen said.

'Agreed. Did your father offer no hope at all?' Bladud asked. Tangwen opened her mouth to say no, but hesitated. 'Tell me,' he said quietly.

'There are magics strong enough to fight the spawn.'

'Where?'

'The Lochlannach. The raiders in the black *curraghs*.'

Bladud thought on her words. 'We have no choice. We must have their power,' the Witch King said.

'You do not know what you are saying,' Kush said harshly. 'Those they do not kill become nothing more than steeds to be ridden by demons.'

Bladud reached down and tore a handful of earth from the ground. 'Then what?' he asked the Numibian quietly. He held the handful of dirt out to him. 'Let them defile and murder our Mother? Then what are we?'

'If it was a matter of simple death I would say go with your gods, but you will accomplish the opposite of what you intend,' Kush told the Witch King.

'Such is the folly of most people.'

Kush shook his head but smiled.

'Can our people pass?' Tangwen asked.

'Will you let me speak with them first?' Bladud asked.

The three pyres illuminated the dark wood with a hot, flickering, orange light. Bladud stood in front of the central pyre, its light throwing him into shadow. It was Essyllt's pyre.

Tangwen had watched him as he spoke to Essyllt, and to the other two survivors showing signs of the sickness. He spoke to them in low tones, frank and earnest. The voice of persuasion. Tangwen had watched tears roll down their cheeks, but it was to their and Bladud's credit that they had not broken down. The same could not be said for the two Brigante who had carried Essyllt's litter. Tangwen had finally learned their names: Duach and Sel. Both had been landsmen and were, in fact, subjects of the Witch King. Duach stood watching the pyre, sobbing openly and loudly. Sel was on his knees, head buried in his hands, also weeping. Bladud had talked the sick into allowing themselves to be sacrificed. He had lit the flames himself and given them to Nodens, who was the sun and the moon. In return he asked for wisdom and protection from sickness. This drew cries of anger from the warriors gathered around the pyres. They wanted the sacrifices to be given to the Red God, blood-stained Cocidius.

Tangwen watched Nerthach help Sel to his feet. 'This is not right. You must be as strong as they were,' he told his fellow Brigante, not unkindly.

Tangwen felt a hand on her shoulder. 'It was their decision,' Kush told her quietly. She nodded. She hadn't even realised she was crying. Anharad, Twrch and the silent Mabon had come to stand with them, watching the flames. All the survivors had been treated well and given food. Bladud had even gone so far as to find armour, a hatchet, and bow and arrows for Tangwen. They were gifts of great generosity, worthy of a great king. He had offered her a knife, but she decided to keep the one she carried with her on the Isle of Madness. She had worked hard to scour the rust from the blade and hone the edge on whetstone. Nerthach had even managed to find a suit of boiled leather armour that fitted Kush's, tall, deceptively thin frame. The bear-skull-wearing warrior appeared to like the Numibian, though Tangwen suspected Nerthach was just hoping to keep Kush alive long enough so the pair of them could fight.

Bladud held up his hands and called for quiet. 'We go north,' he said simply. There were cries of outrage from the assembled warriors. Bladud lowered his hands and let them get it out of their system.

'Why?' demanded a large warrior with an impressive moustache but no beard.

'Because they will be on us this night. Tell me what happens when this many horse fight in woods in the dark.'

'It's never been done before,' the warrior answered. Tangwen rolled her eyes.

'Pretend you're not a lackwit,' Nerthach suggested. The moustachioed warrior bristled.

'This is taking too long,' Kush muttered. Tangwen had been thinking the same thing. The spawn of Andraste were not that far behind them.

'There would be chaos. We would be about our enemy's business,' Bladud told the assembled warriors.

'So we run like cowards!' another warrior demanded.

'Mind your tongue,' Nerthach told him.

'Do all Pretani warriors think with their cocks?' Kush asked Tangwen.

'Only the male ones,' she muttered.

'Know that if you fight, you fight against the wisdom of the gods, and against my advice,' Bladud told them.

'You brought us here!' Another warrior, this one a heavy-set woman covered with scars and missing lumps of hair and scalp.

'Things are not as I believed,' Bladud replied. 'We will have our war, but it will not be this night. Stay if you will, but if you wish victory then we head north. Those of you who do decide to stay, I have a use for you, but know that every last one of you will die – or worse.'

Tangwen recognised the voice. She had heard *dryw* use it before. It was the voice of absolute truth. When something was so important that all had to believe it without question.

There was muttering among the warriors. Tangwen was trying to look beyond the pyres, cursing the flames for ruining her night-sight, expecting the forest to come to life at any moment. She tensed when she saw movement and felt Kush do the same. She was reaching for her knife and hatchet when the figures walked through the flames.

All of them wore lightweight leather armour that provided a degree of protection, but more importantly allowed them to move quickly and freely. All of them carried light, short weapons – hand axes, short swords, daggers, cudgels – and each of them had a bow. All of them wore wicker masks and the furs of the lynx, like the scout they had seen earlier in the day. And all of them were female.

One of them, the first to appear between the flames, went to speak to Bladud. He leaned down and they conversed in whispers. It was clear that the presence of the lynx-headed scouts made a lot of the warriors nervous.

'Who are they?' Kush whispered. Tangwen shook her head. She had never heard of them before.

'We have little time,' Bladud said, straightening up. 'Those of you who are truly prepared to die, step forward. The rest of you, go now!'

Tangwen watched as a number of the older warriors stepped forwards. Nobody tried to talk them out of it, but there were tears in the eyes of some of their comrades as they said their goodbyes, grasped arms and hugged. The older warriors gathered around Bladud. Tangwen moved to join them, but Kush grabbed her.

'What are you doing?'

'Take Germelqart and the others, follow this warband north. I will not be far behind you.'

'This is madness!' Kush hissed.

Tangwen turned to look up at the tall, dark-skinned warrior. 'I will not sell my life freely, but please, I am a hunter. They will not even see me, and I will catch up with you soon. I promise.'

Kush looked decidedly unconvinced and opened his mouth as if he was about to argue further, but Tangwen reached up and squeezed his arm.

'All on this island are mad,' he said, before turning away and stalking back up the hill.

Tangwen moved over to Bladud. He had just finished explaining his plan to the greybeard warriors. Most had grim expressions on their faces. One or two were smiling.

'Why does this one carry my old bow?' demanded the tall, powerfully built woman with the lynx mask. Braided long brown hair ran down from beneath her mask. In the flames her eyes looked quite dark.

'Ah,' Bladud said. 'I was going to speak to you about that. This is Tangwen of the Pobl Neidr – she escaped from the wicker man. She has need of the bow, and I will compensate you for it.'

'Pobl Neidr? Catuvellauni weaklings. That's why they were in the wicker man.'

Tangwen didn't think she was going to get on with the other woman.

'Tangwen, may I introduce Sadhbh of the Iceni.'

'You will be hiding while these others die, then?' Tangwen asked. She knew of the Iceni. They were a warlike tribe from the lands to the north of the Trinovantes, who in turn bordered Tangwen's people's lands. Tangwen suspected that had the Iceni been less warlike, the Trinovantes would have troubled her people more. As it was they spent a lot of time and resources defending their northern borders from the aggressive Iceni.

The other woman bristled. 'We will be watching—' she snapped.

'And reporting back to me,' Bladud said. 'I have more than enough swinging cocks and prideful warriors. Do not let these warriors' sacrifices mean nothing. We need information.'

'I'm going as well,' Tangwen told them. Sadhbh opened her mouth but Tangwen got there first: 'Keep your people out of my way.'

Bladud started to say something, but Nerthach was at his side.

'It is time to go,' the big warrior told his *rhi* and began to all but drag him back up the hill.

Tangwen turned back, but the other woman had gone. Behind her the warriors were mounting nervous steeds and coaxing them up out of the trench. Tangwen cursed her own foolishness. Then she walked between the flames of the pyres.

She walked into the woods, all but blind because of the fire. She knew that if any of Andraste's spawn were nearby, her lack of night-sight would get her killed. She found a place to hide, then lay down and waited for her vision to return.

The woods were very busy tonight. She could hear the sounds of the warriors – the chink of metal, the creak of leather and wood. The warriors were advancing in a staggered line, experienced enough to control their nervous mounts. She watched one ride by close to where she hid. His polished and honed iron blade was caught in a beam of moonlight that had pierced the thinning autumn canopy of leaves. The sword blade looked as if it was glowing for a moment, and Tangwen thought of Fachtna.

When she was happy she could see as clearly as she would be able to, when she was happy she had been still long enough for the woods to get used to her, she started to move. She whispered a prayer to her father, and another to the night. She tried to move as she thought the other creatures of the forest would. It was only then that she realised what had been irking her, what felt odd about the forest: there were no noises other than the sounds of the horses. The warriors riding through the woods would disturb the local animals, but there should be noises further afield. Bats, owls, wolves and even bears were all night-hunters, but she heard nothing of them. *The Lord of the Woods has warned them,* she thought, and then wondered why she hadn't heeded the same warning.

If the Iceni scouts were out there with her, she couldn't hear them, which meant they were good. She started trailing the warriors who were ahead of her now, moving as if she was hunting them.

She heard noises the like of which she had never heard before. There was movement and lots of it; it sounded unnatural, too large for any normal creatures. She heard the warriors' voices, they spoke as though they were trying to suppress their fear, a few shouted with false bravado. She continued moving forwards, flitting from shadow to shadow, an arrow nocked on the bowstring, for all the good it would do her.

Ahead of her it looked as if the entire forest was moving of its own accord. She glanced down and found the ground alive with crawling, fast-moving life. She could not make out what the creatures were, but they looked wrong. Larger, more twisted shapes, little more than shadows, moved through the beams of moonlight that broke through the forest canopy.

She could see several of the warriors on horseback advancing in a broken line, shields in one hand, longspears in the other. She moved closer still, though the fast-moving carpet of crawling, warped life made her nervous.

She heard screaming, forced herself to turn slowly so sudden movement didn't give her position away. She saw one of the horses rearing. Its rider had dropped his spear and was desperately trying to control the animal. Living things surged up the horse's legs from the moving forest floor. She watched as the flesh and then the bones of horse and rider were stripped and consumed. The rider's cries only lasted a moment.

Emerging from the trees, which even now were beginning to change, warp and move of their own accord, were mockeries of life. She saw strange and horrible creatures that were patchwork fusions of other life, swollen to enormous size.

She heard battle cries, turned back to see a warrior charge something that looked like a tree with a mouth, four legs which ended in cloven hooves and flailing branch-like tendrils. A tendril flicked out and a man's head tumbled through the night air. The horse ran by the thing, but more branch-like tendrils dropped down from newly moving trees and tore the creature off the ground. Chunks of horseflesh rained down on the seething, moving earth. Tangwen flinched at the sound of bones splintering, as blood sprayed the tree-thing's bark-like skin.

The night air was full of the sounds of tearing flesh and human screams. She looked down and saw lines of tiny creatures, part insect, part lizard and snake, even part bird, moving across the ground. The closest was almost upon her. They had too many mouths, legs, pincers, stings, fingers. It was enough for her. She ran.

Tangwen hit something solid and living. She tumbled to the ground on top of it, losing her bow as she fell. She managed to suppress a cry as the thing beneath her fought violently. She yanked her dagger free. Wide, white eyes stared up at her. The face was dark, woaded to aid with concealment. Tangwen stayed her hand, though it took her a moment to realise she had almost stabbed Bladud. She climbed off him, grabbing her bow.

'I had to see,' he whispered. Tangwen held a finger to his mouth and gestured towards the hills. She didn't help him up. Instead she sheathed her dagger and nocked an arrow to her bowstring.

Bladud was getting to his feet. The staff was gone, as was the armour. He wore his dark robes, and his sword still hung from his hip. As the last of the screams was cut off suddenly, he started running back towards the hills. Tangwen followed him, continually glancing behind her. Suddenly she grabbed him and dragged him to the ground by the root structure of a tree.

'Be still,' she whispered.

Something landed with a thump nearby. Tangwen was all but lying on Bladud. She could see over the root and remained still – she knew it was movement that gave you away. She heard a shuffling noise. Slowly it crept into sight. What looked like a single, massive, powerful leg was in fact two legs fused together. A single withered arm ending in long claws grew from its muscular torso. A mouth too big for its head was filled with rows of strange, sharp-looking, half-circle-shaped teeth. It had an oversized nose, a huge single eye, and instead of hair it sported a mane of black feathers.

Tangwen swallowed hard and tried not to wet herself. Bladud had gone still beneath her. The thing was sniffing the air. Tangwen stared at the abomination, afraid that it would hear her heart hammering in her chest. She felt Bladud shift beneath her, his hand reaching for his sword. The creature stopped shuffling and stood stock still. Tangwen willed Bladud to stop moving but he didn't. Suddenly the creature's head jerked towards them.

Tangwen knelt on Bladud, drawing the bow and loosing before

Bladud had a chance to move and spoil her aim. She had aimed for the eye, and at such close range she was good enough to hit her mark. But the creature had crouched at the last moment and the arrow hit the top of its head, skidding across the hard bone of its skull. The creature leaped high into the air on mutated leg muscles. Tangwen dropped the bow and moved off Bladud, drawing her dagger and hatchet.

Arrows filled the air. The creature practically landed on Bladud as he tried to get up and draw his sword. He started to cry out but managed to stifle it.

Tangwen sensed rather than heard movement behind her. She spun around and almost swung her hatchet at the lynx-headed form of Sadhbh. The other woman was lifting a short sword to parry when Tangwen stopped herself.

'Fools,' the other woman spat. She still clutched her bow in her other hand.

Bladud disentangled himself from the corpse and stood up. 'So they *can* die,' he muttered, looking down at the thing. 'This was a man once.'

'We need to go now,' Sadhbh hissed.

'No,' Tangwen said to Bladud. 'Look.' The arrows were melting as they were pulled into the wounds, which were already beginning to seal. Then the one-legged thing started to move. Even Sadhbh was staring at it in horror. She grabbed Bladud and all but pulled him away.

'I had to see,' Tangwen heard Bladud mutter as Sadhbh led him back towards the hills.

They ran into a furious Nerthach, who soundly berated his *rhi* for giving him the slip. They climbed the hill and crossed down into a broad, flat valley of woods and farmland.

Eventually Tangwen caught up with the other survivors, who were trailing behind the warband. As the sky started to turn red in the distance, Tangwen found herself walking beside Germelqart.

'What does *Brenin Uchel* mean?' Germelqart asked.

'High King,' Tangwen said. 'Why?'

'I think this Bladud seeks to rule over all the tribes,' the navigator told her.

22
Birmingham, 4 Weeks Ago

Du Bois was meandering along the side of the Grand Union Canal, checking all around him. His blood-screen was doing pretty much the same thing but on the molecular scale. Grace and du Bois had spent the better part of a week scouring the canals of Birmingham and further afield, looking for Silas. The city might have had more miles of canals than Venice, but Grace had decided that they lacked some of the Italian city's romantic appeal. Other than a few dead rats they had found nothing. Grace quickly grew bored of checking the canals, but something kept dragging du Bois back to them.

They continued seeding the city's rats, but still nothing had come of it. Grace suggested that their quarry might have only used the canals on that particular occasion, or even that he was taking the time to come in from much further afield. They dropped some extensively genetically engineered koi into the canals, but they discovered as much as the nano-seeded rats had.

At first du Bois found the canals a depressing place. Many of the factories that backed onto them were derelict, overrun by weeds and covered in graffiti. The canals looked like a graveyard for the city's past industrial glories. Then he started noticing the redevelopment. He began to recognise common images in the graffiti – codes of some sort. He found secret gardens of plastic statues, modern-day groves of some unknown postmodern religion analogy. They were the history of the city on display, a kind of living archaeology telling its story better than any dry museum exhibit, for those who cared to look. The canals weren't really a place. They were woven between places. They were the back doors, a strange borderland. Perhaps that was why he kept returning to them looking for Silas.

Du Bois found himself thinking about one particular piece of graffiti a lot. It wasn't actually on the canal side, but on a garage attached to one of the nearby buildings. The image was of a hand, but the fingers had eyes, and the nails were mouths with teeth. Du Bois wondered what the artist knew about his world, even if it was only subconsciously.

Du Bois recognised the sound of the motorbike before he saw it. Ahead of him a narrow road bridge crossed over the canal, and just behind that was a much higher, dark brick rail bridge. Grace brought the Triumph Speed Triple to a halt and looked down along the canal towards du Bois. Du Bois gave her a wave, but he could tell by her body language that she was less than happy.

'What's up?' he asked when he'd climbed the steps up to the roadway.

Grace's riding was one of the few things that still managed to frighten him. She pulled into the taxi lane in front of the ugly brutalist concrete building that housed Birmingham New Street, the city's main train station, and braked hard. Du Bois climbed off, trying not to let his irritation show. He handed her the helmet, walked to the edge of the raised taxi lane and looked down on the platforms. A train had been cordoned off and a tent erected over the platform next to it. Grace came over to stand next to him, removing her helmet. Her Mohican was a flattened mess on her head.

Du Bois noticed a group of people of various ages surrounded by a loose cordon of police. He pointed at them as he and Grace walked past, making for the escalator that would carry them down to the platforms beneath the main concourse.

'Witnesses, would you believe?' Grace told him.

Du Bois gaped at her incredulously. 'We're not going to have interview them, are we?'

'I think they'll all tell the same story – for reasons they can't explain, they all stood up and exited the carriage as one, leaving a man they can't describe and the victim in the carriage alone.'

'He did this publicly?'

Grace nodded. 'I've got the police taking blood samples from them. I suspect we'll find they were slaved and their memories modified.'

'This could be good,' du Bois said. Grace gave him a questioning look. 'Does this not strike you as overconfidence?'

'No, I think this is *actual* confidence.'

They reached the platforms. Like the exterior of the building, they were mainly ugly concrete architecture, and the whole area was dimly lit by flickering electric lights. Pillars supporting the main concourse were interspersed along the platforms. Despite the sun shining outside the station, the covered platforms had all the charm of an ugly underground car park.

Du Bois and Grace walked past the forensic team, who were taking off their protective crime scene suits. The forensic team glared at them angrily as, without any protective clothing, it looked like du Bois and Grace weren't even trying to preserve evidence.

'They want to make a case,' Grace said quietly. Both of them knew that wasn't going to happen.

'Did they leave the body *in situ*?' du Bois asked. Grace didn't say anything. Instead she pushed through the well-lit tent the forensic team had set up, which somehow looked more cheerful than the actual platforms themselves, and into the railway carriage murder scene. Du Bois followed her and saw the body for himself.

The victim was an attractive young man, if a little gaunt. He had long dark hair, and du Bois suspected he had taken himself very seriously when he was alive. In fact, du Bois mused, he looked exactly like the sort of person Grace would spend time with, and then complain bitterly about it after the fact.

'He was pretty,' Grace said. Du Bois tried not to let a smile creep across his face. He glanced at her. She didn't appear to be letting this one get to her quite as much as the last. She was capable of killing ruthlessly when she had to, but their pursuit of Silas was creating too many reminders of what Hawksmoor had done.

Du Bois leaned down and looked at the thin line of red bisecting the man's head. Almost absently, he reached for the tanto at his hip. The folded steel cut into his skin and he released the blood-screen into the air, programming it to look for evidence with a thought.

'He took the brain again but it's neater,' du Bois muttered to himself. Grace was concentrating, collating, searching and then downloading relevant CCTV footage.

Du Bois reached into the man's coat, looking for – and finding – a wallet, which he extracted carefully. Rigor mortis was still hours away, and he didn't want move the body too much in case the top of the man's bisected head fell off.

'Robert Jaggard,' du Bois said. He sent the instruction to his Circle-modified phone to find and download everything it could find on Jaggard. He pulled the phone out of his jacket and took a picture of Jaggard for the image-recognition routines he was running.

'You know you can do that in your head, right?' Grace asked.

'I don't like doing that.'

'It slows you down.'

'When it matters I'll do it in my head.' It was a conversation that they'd had many times before.

Du Bois' blood-screen was coming back with nothing. Another

blood-screen, presumably Silas's, had already sanitised the area.

'Look at this.' Grace sent him CCTV footage. His phone buffered it. 'Just run it in your damn head,' Grace said irritably. Du Bois opened the connection in his mind and the images uploaded instantly. As he did this he took a vial from his pocket. With a thought, he changed the vial's shape and pushed the needle end into Jaggard's cold flesh. It took blood and tissue samples from the body. Du Bois knew he was going to find that Silas had paralysed the man's body but left him aware. The nerve endings would be intact so that his victim could experience what was happening to him. Absently du Bois wondered why this atrocity felt so commonplace. Why didn't it bother him so much any more?

As the samples confirmed his suspicions he ran the CCTV footage, spooling through it quickly. There had been no footage of him getting on or off the train at any of the stations.

As the train reached Birmingham, rolling on raised tracks past the rooftops of houses, over factories, shops, motorways and canals, all the passengers had stood up and started filing out of the carriage. Jaggard, who'd been reading, had looked up, frowning, and then glanced out of the window, presumably to see if they were arriving at a station. Eventually he returned to his book.

Du Bois' internal systems were cleaning up the resolution of the image. As he reviewed it, the grainy footage was becoming clearer. He watched the long, thin, black-clad arm reach in through an open window and unlock the carriage door. Somehow it reminded him of the expressionist films that had come out of Germany between the two wars.

Silas opened the door and climbed into the carriage. There was something predatory and insectile about his movements, as if he had unfolded himself into the train. His face was a shimmering blur. Du Bois had no idea how the killer had achieved that particular effect, but even with the masking of his face du Bois recognised the tall, thin frame and unmistakable movement of Silas Scab.

In the film running in his mind, Jaggard still hadn't looked up, despite the open door. Du Bois enlarged the image of Jaggard's face and then used an intelligent program to add resolution, effectively filling in the blanks left by the initially grainy footage. Jaggard's face was a grimace. It was clear he'd already been paralysed and was struggling against it. All his facial muscles were contorted as he tried to look up at the figure walking down the carriage towards him.

Silas was crouched over Jaggard now, his frame partially obscuring du Bois' view of his victim. Silas took his time. With unerring accuracy he drew a line in the skin with a scalpel, cleaned up the blood, then drew another line in the tissue with a heavier blade, paring the flesh down to the bone. Then he drew the bone saw from his bag.

'It will feed some part of his fantasy,' Grace suggested.

Du Bois watched as Silas quickly but skilfully sawed off the top of Jaggard's head. Blood and tears poured down the young man's face.

'It's not a fantasy,' du Bois said quietly.

Silas removed the brain.

'It's always fantasy to these sick bastards.'

'Yes,' du Bois conceded. 'They try to make their fantasy real, but Silas may actually have the ability to do so.'

Silas turned to the camera and walked towards it until his shimmering, vibrating non-face filled the screen. Then the screen went blank. Du Bois turned to Grace.

'He doesn't want us to see what he's doing with the brains,' Grace said.

Du Bois nodded. 'And the CCTV footage was meant for us?' he asked. Grace nodded in agreement. 'Which leaves us where?'

Grace shrugged. 'Well, I'm for looking under bridges to see if he's living there like a troll,' she suggested. 'No sign of him on the New Street cameras. Frankly I'm surprised he didn't stuff his cock between his legs and do a little dance for us.'

'What?'

'Never mind.'

'So he got off the train—' du Bois started before one of his search routines turned something up. He sent the footage to Grace. It was from a CCTV run by a private security company on top of one of their clients' workshops in the Digbeth area, just south-east of the station. It showed a tall, thin, darkly clothed figure leaping from the raised railway line that ran above the area's decaying industrial rooftops. The figure dropped quickly out of view.

'I don't think he meant for us to find that,' Grace said.

Du Bois accessed the information his search routines had turned up about Jaggard, half-expecting to find another history of schizophrenia.

'He was an artist,' he said superfluously. Grace had access to the same information. Du Bois was running through reviews of the victim's most recent exhibition, which used words like 'disturbing' and 'unease'.

'That's a bit of a coincidence,' Grace said. Jaggard's ongoing exhibition was being held in a gallery in Digbeth.

*

Du Bois walked. He met Grace in the Old Crown pub for lunch. He had long since stopped being surprised by how places changed over periods of hundreds of years. He had never quite liked the feeling of violated nostalgia he felt revisiting them, but he still always went and looked. He was less than impressed with the quality of the wine and the food, however. That didn't appear to bother Grace. She ate, as she always did, as if she didn't know where her next meal was coming from.

Digbeth was a run-down and crumbling area. It was the city's industrial past paved over with ugly concrete from the 1960s, '70s and '80s. Weed-encrusted brick bridges carried the trains above the area's rooftops towards New Street and the city's other stations. The graffiti that covered many of the buildings looked like an alien language, or modern cave paintings with their own complex codified meanings.

To get to the gallery, du Bois and Grace walked through a brightly coloured redeveloped factory that had been turned into a series of trendy shops, cafes and bars. Something about it reminded du Bois of a cavalry fort he'd once visited in Apache territory, if the cavalry soldiers had enjoyed lattes and impractical-looking footwear. A large statue of a Green Man, half-human, half-tree, caught his eye. Something about its pagan countenance took him back to the earthen cave and the last night he had been truly mortal, truly human. He stopped to look at it. Grace had to backpedal and drag him away from it.

'What's wrong with you?' she demanded. It was a good question.

They found the gallery close to where Heath Mill Lane crossed the Grand Union Canal, where trendy galleries competed with garages for space. The gallery was a one-storey building, the same red brick as everything else, opposite a wall made of compacted cars. The gallery looked a little like a community centre or village hall on the outside. Inside it was a wide-open space painted white. The white contrasted with the dark colours of the canvasses Jaggard had created.

Grace and du Bois stared at one of the pictures. Predominantly black, at first sight it looked like a nebulous starscape, but it lacked the grandeur that such images often displayed. Instead the artist had managed to imbue the picture with a sense of anima, as if the space itself was alive with an unseen malevolence. The oil painting gave such a sense of depth, of existing in three dimensions, that it almost looked like an optical illusion, as if the picture moved with a life of its own when it was in the periphery of their vision. Jaggard had instilled a sense of hunger into his starscape. The critics had been right – the images were unsettling. Even more unsettling was a feeling du Bois couldn't shake that the artist had instinctively understood something about the world that he and Grace inhabited, about the true nature of reality.

The other canvasses were all variations on the same theme. Jaggard's genius wasn't in what he painted, it was in what he implied. That and the sense that he was painting from life, painting things he had somehow seen.

Grace glanced up at du Bois. She looked unsure, almost frightened, and it wasn't an expression he was used to seeing on her face. Not for a long time.

Stredder shouldn't have felt anything. The L-tech device had altered itself to fit in with his reconfigured flesh. He knew that the feeling of having a foreign body inside his stomach was largely psychosomatic, regardless of the actual truth of the matter. Carrying the oldest piece of L-tech the Circle owned, particularly one with so much history to it, always felt different from the other courier jobs he did.

He shifted uncomfortably in his spacious seat and looked around the first-class cabin of the 747. He didn't like any of this at all. Normally it travelled on one of the stealthed orbital transports. These came with their own set of risks but were considered worth it given the value of what he was now carrying inside himself. After all, it provided all of the Circle's operatives with the templates for their augmentations. He had drunk from it himself on one of the Circle's orbital stations after the Siege of Paris.

The chalice had been used in the Pacific, he presumed in connection with the city, and was on its way to London having come through Tokyo. The use of an unsecured civilian aircraft was very irregular, but there had been a sudden increase in recruitment. Stredder was worried that this increase was due to the end becoming a lot more nigh.

He had his blood-screen spread throughout the entire aircraft like a spiderweb. The best hope for safety lay in secrecy. He remained convinced that if the Brass City knew what he was carrying, they would almost certainly try to take it. The healthy paranoia that was part and parcel of being a good courier had him wondering if that was the point. Was Mr Brown using him as bait, for some reason?

The Brass City was not the only threat, either. The situation in Birmingham had caught his attention. He had worked with du Bois a number of times, and with Soggin on fewer occasions. She was undisciplined, in his opinion, but capable, and du Bois was more than competent, though given to questioning Control too much. That this madman, Silas Scab, had managed to so effectively escape the pair of them worried him very much indeed. Less than two days had passed since Silas had last killed.

The stewardess offered him another drink; he accepted. His augmented body would break the alcohol down into sugar, and then efficiently convert that into actual useful energy before he could feel any effect from the alcohol. That didn't stop the stewardess from looking at him like he was an alcoholic.

Once again he glanced around at his fellow passengers. As he looked from one to the other, the information he had on them cascaded down through his vision. They were upper-echelon executives, playboys and -girls, children of the rich, one mid-range celebrity. If any of them worked for the Brass City or one of the independents, their cover was immaculate.

Something snagged his spiderweb. He allowed himself a moment. He closed his eyes before standing up.

'Sir, you must remain seated,' the stewardess told him firmly. They were on their final approach into Heathrow. 'Sir!'

Stredder ignored the woman and moved down the narrow corridor between the seats into the business-class section. His enhanced hearing blocked out the stewardess trailing him, and he could hear another similarly one-sided conversation going on in the economy-class section of the passenger jet.

He felt the stewardess grab him and swung around to face her. She took a step back from the violence of his action. He wanted to tell her something but couldn't think of anything to say. Instead he grabbed the chairs on either side of the isle. The soles of his shoes melted and he began sinking into the floor as his fingers dug into the seats, pushing into their matter as if it was putty. His vision was full of the 747's technical schematics. There was only so much matter he could steal before the airframe became unstable and fell apart in the sky.

'Sir, return to your seat now!' The voice was all male authority. Stredder wrenched himself free of the now putty-like consistency of the seats and the floor. Already the molecule-sized alien machines that lived in his body were converting the matter sucked in through the pores on his skin and turning it into muscle mass. It was reinforcing his skeleton, toughening his skin. It was being broken down and converted into energy.

Stredder turned around and took a step forwards as if he was trapped in sucking mud. As he suspected, the authority in the man's voice was bolstered by the automatic pistol in his hand. Stredder watched the man's confidence turn to fear as he grew in front of him. He pushed now-clawed hands into another row of seats so the transformation could continue. He heard the screams start. Screams had accompanied him throughout his life.

The air marshal fired. A frangible bullet exploded into harmless powder against Stredder's armoured chest, which was now covered with short bristly fur that may have looked canine but had more in common with sharkskin. Just touching it would draw blood. His clothes had sunk into his body now, their matter adding to his bulk.

'You are all going to die,' he growled before his elongated maw, full of canines, robbed him of the ability to speak. The air marshal fired again, and again. The low-impact bullets were useless against Stredder's armoured half-human, half-wolf form. He had only meant to warn them, but now the passengers were climbing over each other to get away from him. He wanted to reach out and turn the air marshal into a red mess as chemically and neurally programmed rage coursed through his body. He could smell the little man's fear.

He felt the pain for a moment. He saw the point of the blade appear through his chest. Then the nerve endings were locked down. The information that was pain was transformed into fury.

'I even coated the blade with silver,' the voice said from behind him. It didn't matter. Stredder was beyond understanding anything as complex as language.

Stredder tore himself free of the now mud-like matter of the aircraft. He had absorbed several of the seats and left progressively larger and more animalistic footprints in the cabin floor. The blade was pulled out of the wound as he swung around. His system was already trying to heal the wound, but the blade had impregnated it with nanites that were already attacking his own systems.

The figure in front of him was tall and slender, dressed in dark clothes, pale, and his narrow head with its painfully sharp-looking features and dead eyes was utterly devoid of hair. He had a long, silver-bladed knife in each hand and was looking up at Stredder quizzically. His lack of fear gave the courier pause for a moment. Then he raised his foot and kicked the tall, thin man very hard.

Silas flew backwards, battering himself against the corner of the partition between business and economy class. He landed on the ground by the steward's compartment. He had a momentary glimpse of a terrified-looking steward and stewardess as he tried to pick himself up. He wondered if they knew who the monster was in this fight. Then the courier was on him, tearing at him so viciously he was lifted off his feet and carried back into the economy section. Claws tore into his flesh and injected tiny venomous demons into his system. His own demon-infected blood whispered to him, telling him that the invaders were eating him from within. Chunks of his flesh were torn off by the raging technological hybrid. He laughed, spat blood and stabbed the courier time and time again. Teeth dug into his shoulder and he was flung across the central aisle of the 747's economy-class cabin. He hit his back on the top of one of the chairs. Terrified passengers tried to scramble away from him and the air filled with the smell of faeces. His own spilled blood tried to find its way back into his body. The courier's demonic venom was trying to prevent this, making his blood smoke. His wounds opened and closed like mouths. His skin crawled and muscles contorted as his body became a battleground for the tiny demons. He heard screams, but one of the first tricks he had ever taught the demons in his blood was to turn the sound of screams into music.

Silas tumbled off the chair backs and hit the floor. The courier was standing over him now, bloodied claws raised. Silas knew it was over. He was not sure that this death would be good enough. Suddenly it was much colder. A raging wind blew. Everything tipped sharply and he was falling, bouncing painfully off things. So was the hybrid. Tears appeared in the fabric of the aircraft.

They stopped falling. They had landed on something, a wall with moving pictures on it. Silas wasn't sure how it had happened but he was on top of the courier. He found himself laughing as he stabbed and slashed down into the hybrid as it thrashed beneath him. Silas made the creature red. He could see the night sky now.

The courier was being eaten from within. The demonic venom on Silas's blades had won their battle inside the technological hybrid's flesh. Silas pushed his blade into the creature's body, burying it so deep that his hand was inside the courier. With a thought, he cast his spell through the blade. Controlling the courier's flesh, demanding it reveal its secrets. Around him the aircraft bucked and lurched, the airframe flexing dangerously. The courier was flopping weakly beneath him now. Silas pushed sharpened nails and then his long, powerful fingers into the creature's flesh, and curled them around a metal stem. He tore the Red Chalice out of the courier's flesh and the dying thing beneath him howled in agony. He lifted the hot metal to his lips. He had a moment to feel the pain of the molten metal pouring down his throat, then the plane tore itself in two.

*

She stood on top of an aircraft engine in a large trench where part of suburban Isleworth used to be, leaning on her staff. She was surprised how quiet it was, although she could hear the sound of sirens in the distance. There was the crackle of flames, of course, a sound that was welcoming more often than not. It was a comfort to her. Even in this age when she found herself standing around with other unwanted people, sharing borderline poisonous cheap alcohol.

She leaped the twenty feet down into the trench with ease and started making her way through the wreckage, ignoring the burning pools of aviation fuel. She walked across what used to be a railway line and found herself gazing at something that didn't look very human. It was little more than half a blackened face fused with the equally blackened fuselage of the 747. It was still moving.

'You risked death. Why?' the bag lady asked.

An eye turned to look at her. 'I am dead,' it managed in a voice full of pain.

'I don't think so, my dark little boy.'

'I don't like what I am.'

'Change, then.'

The laughter was a truly horrible sound. 'Let me die,' the fused mess that was all that remained of Silas managed. The bag lady said nothing. 'Are you real?'

'No. You're insane, you know this. What if I told you that none of this mattered? What if I told you it was coming anyway? What if I asked you to stop now?'

'I ... I ... just want to see god.' There were tears now. The bag lady turned away, a look of profound sadness on her face as, without thinking, she walked into a large pool of burning aviation fuel.

'Aren't you going to take the chalice?' His voice was stronger now. She heard the sound of metal straining. She stopped and looked over her shoulder.

'I don't need it. It didn't work. I just don't want them to have it,' she said as the flames licked all around her. She started walking again, slowly sinking into the burning earth. 'Though I'm not sure I can tell the difference any more.'

23

A Long Time After the Loss

'Are ... you ... sure?' Mr Hat left a long pause between each of the words. He wanted to emphasise the seriousness of the situation.

'Who else could it be?' Isaiah asked.

Mr Hat was sitting on the throne-topped control column in the *Amuser*'s Command and Control centre. The transparent part of the smart hull, which he had configured into a window, was magnifying and displaying separate incidents of violent chaos all the way along the prison habitat, on all three strips of land. Some of the inmates had even managed to start a fire on one of the windows. There was more feed arriving from the cameras in Suburbia itself. The lizard found himself wondering if it was still being shown as a reality soapcom throughout Consortium space. He imagined so. They always found some way to capitalise.

'Mr Isaiah, I am about to tell some very powerful people that Scab is either here, or on his way here, on your say-so and some very circumstantial evidence. If there has been an incursion from Red Space, does it not seem a lot more likely that the Church is involved?'

The image of Isaiah being projected into Mr Hat's visual cortex by his neunonics froze. 'But you said Berger was the bait ...' Isaiah managed.

Mr Hat moved the *Amuser* with a thought, sending it to the docking arm closest to where Berger lived. He requested feed from local nano-cams but found that the whole area was still overrun by a privacy nano-swarm. He switched to macro-cam feed, but all he saw was chaos.

'I understand the need for catharsis, but imagine what they could achieve if they were to organise,' he mused to one of his human-looking eyeless servant automatons. 'Wake all my children.' The automaton nodded. Mr Hat turned his attention back to Isaiah. 'The Church also wants Scab. Has it not occurred to you that *they* might want to use inmate Berger as bait, too?'

'We can't fight the Church as well!' Isaiah said, appalled.

'Fight them, Mr Isaiah? We will need to erase the very fact they have this capability, lest we wish to be assassinated.' Over the 'face link he actually saw the other man blanch. He felt the thud and reverberating clang of the *Amuser* docking. All the while he was analysing the macrocam footage, looking for something out of place. 'I want G-carriers or hoppers ready to transport my servants to Mr Berger's residence.'

'What? You can't go in there!'

'Why not? The inmates have no augments to speak of and rudimentary weapons. The only thing I have to worry about is being rushed by what would have to be, frankly, a suicidal horde. Otherwise all I will be doing is committing mass murder on any who bother me. Now, do you want to task the G-carriers, or would you prefer I waste time communicating with the board and have them tell you to do it once it is too late?'

There was a moment's silence. Mr Hat could see the sweat coating Isaiah's face. The human made him feel faintly disgusted.

'There will be G-carriers waiting for you,' Isaiah told him.

'Thank you, Mr Isaiah. The question is, what are *you* going to do?'

'What?' He sounded surprised that Mr Hat had even asked the question.

The *Amuser*'s control column sank into the ground and one of the automatons carried Mr Hat to his bath chair, taking the time to tuck him in with the tartan blanket.

'Shall we thaw our guest?' the automaton's collective mind asked as one of them started rapidly wheeling the bath chair towards the airlock. Mr Hat considered the question. If it was a false alarm, did he want to be seen to be wasting this person's time?

'Yes, but tell him it is a Red Space incursion, and that I believe the Church is trying to secure Mr Berger as bait for Mr Woodbine.'

He felt the acquiescence of his loyal flock. One would stay behind to secure the *Amuser* and to take the blank from storage, and then contact their employer. He had almost forgotten about Mr Isaiah stammering his way through his delusions of adequacy.

'Mr Isaiah, my advice would be to find the largest areas of unrest and use the automated weapon systems to make examples of them—'

'But the damage—'

'You need control before you can count the cost. If you turn over control of the facility to me ...' Mr Hat had reached the airlock door. It slid open. Now all the automatons were following him. They made their way down the docking arm.

'Thank you for your advice, Mr Hat, but I think we can handle it from here.' Isaiah's 'face link had gone down and now he was hearing Al's voice, and seeing his yellow cartoon smiling face.

'Understood,' Mr Hat said. He assumed Isaiah's career with the Consortium was over. They had reached the maglev platform at the end of the docking arm where a carriage awaited them. He was wheeled aboard and the carriage moved smoothly away from the platform the moment all of his automatons were on board. 'Mr Al, please be aware that we will be handling the Berger situation, and that I have board clearance that says I can.'

There was a worryingly long pause that made Mr Hat wonder if the AI had become corrupt and was now making decisions based on ego.

'Understood.'

The maglev came to a halt. Mr Hat clambered out of the bath chair. Two of the block-shaped armoured G-carriers were waiting for them. They were armed with rotary strobe guns at each of their eight corners, with missile batteries locked away inside armoured housings. Mr Hat climbed into the rear G-carrier. Half the automatons went with him, and the others climbed into the front carrier.

Mr Hat started receiving the feed from the vehicles as they rose towards heavily armoured doors that were in the process of opening. Suburbia lay beyond the doors. He could see clouds of smoke rising from the three land sections to pool in the centre of the hexagonal cylinder.

Mr Hat's neunonic search routines finally found what they were looking for in the macro-cam footage, something that stood out. A ground car that was still moving, albeit erratically, when Al was directly controlling all the others.

Vic watched the columns of smoke rising into the sky. He wasn't sure it was the way to go, but he could understand the outpouring of rage from prisoners whose experience had not been unlike his. The problem was that not all the prisoners were there as a result of committing violent crimes, or any crimes at all, in fact. Suburbia was where the Consortium punished people who had irritated someone powerful. This meant that some prisoners were considerably less able to cope with violent situations than others. It was rapidly turning into a two-tier system: the victims and their victimisers. Which was the same as anywhere else really, he supposed, just the line was a little better defined here.

Elodie had her eyes closed, concentrating as she tried to steer the ground car via neunonic interface. The fact that they had a working ground car was drawing some attention.

Vic flinched as a spanner hit the passenger-side window of the car, cracking the safety glass. He saw a bloodstained woman with a knife in each hand standing on the edge of her perfect lawn. She watched them go by. He caught a glimpse of man running between houses, hopping from back garden to back garden, pursued by a horde of children who had daubed themselves with blood, like some kind of lizard tribal markings. He watched a man sitting atop another on the pavement, beating him into a pulped mess of blood, exposed bone and flesh.

Many of the prisoners, even with their personalities reasserted, were just milling around, not really sure what to do. A lot of them were drinking. Great pyres of belongings burned on lawns, driveways and pavements and in the roads. Elodie had to skirt around more than one bonfire while people hammered on the ground car. They saw rapes, murders and more than one large group of people who looked organised and were being led.

In the distance they could hear gunfire. Occasionally, lines of red light connected the laser batteries on the window segments with the land segments of the cylinder habitat. Tracer-tipped cannon fire from track-mounted rail guns on the window sections looked like a rain of violent light and explosions bloomed across all three land segments. Vic watched an S-sat fly by, skimming the roofs and treetops of the street they were travelling along, weapons firing.

'They're holding back,' Vic muttered to himself. The car lurched as it drove over something lying in the road.

'This is entertainment,' Elodie said, her eyes still closed. On a nearby lawn, four children held a woman down while a fifth cut her face off. Three of the other children already wore dead-skin masks. The one without a mask watched them drive by. Vic found himself wondering how many people were still sitting in their houses, either out of fear or years of conditioning, and hoping this would end. He giggled a little bit when he thought of adding the canned laughter track to what was currently happening.

'Scab would like it here,' he said when he'd suppressed the nearly hysterical urge to keep giggling. He was finding human mood swings almost impossible to control without drugs. 'It would remind him of home.' Then he clapped his hand to his mouth to prevent more giggling.

Elodie opened her eyes and turned to glare at him. 'Look, it's hard enough to control this thing without—'

Vic felt the impact. His teeth banged together as everything slowed down. The concussion wave battered through the liquid in his body and squeezed all the air out of his lungs. The world started to spin and he found himself looking down at the cratered road from an aerial position. Much of the road appeared to be in the air as well, and reaching for the car. Then the second impact came as the car landed on its roof.

'Too soon,' Mr Hat muttered as he saw the mass driver miss the ground car. The G-carriers coming in from high above were still several moments out. He thought about 'facing a protest to the AI, but other than having it on record for a board review, he couldn't really see what good it would do. 'Now just let them run.'

Vic opened his eyes. He was desperately gasping for breath. He started to thrash around, hanging upside down in his seat. Finally his lungs inflated before panic utterly overwhelmed him. He looked to his right. Elodie was hanging in her seat restraints, apparently unconscious. Vic took a moment to check she was breathing. She looked banged-up but otherwise okay.

It took several kicks to get the door open before Vic could crawl out and stagger to his feet. The air was still full of dust from the impact of whatever had hit them. Everything hurt, and he couldn't cut off nerve sensations or flood his system with sweet, sweet painkillers.

Vic lurched around the car and spent some time trying to yank the driver's door open. By the time he finally managed to scrape it open, Elodie was conscious enough to climb out of her seat.

'Ow,' was all she said.

They started tottering through the dust. They were less than a block away from where the Alchemist had lived/been imprisoned. All they had to do was figure out a way to get past the S-sats.

The S-sat's weren't going to be a problem.

'How'd they do this so quickly?' Elodie wondered. They were hiding in the still-smoking wreckage of a house.

'Seriously, these people have almost as limited a way of expressing themselves as Scab does,' Vic muttered.

The street the Alchemist lived on was called Eden Street. A faceless corpse hung from every tree and lamp post that lined it. The street was filled with over a thousand people, all of them wearing dead-skin masks. They were standing surprisingly still, not even talking to each other. Vic, still struggling to control his emotions without drugs, found the whole scene very creepy. They were approaching the night cycle now and the entire street was illuminated by the hellish red glow from a number of bonfires.

The Alchemist's house was a collapsed ruin. It was littered with dead bodies, and among the pile of bodies was the wreckage of four S-sat's. When Vic noticed that, he turned to stare at Elodie. She ignored him and continued scanning the crowd.

'There,' she said and pointed. Vic turned to look and saw their target tied to the bonnet of a ground car. He was naked, and it looked like someone had written all over his body in blood.

'Charging S-sats until you overwhelm them. That's fanatical bullshit, that is,' Vic muttered.

'Quiet,' Elodie said. She was still looking all around, trying to figure out a way to get to the Alchemist. 'The real question is, how did they know to grab the Alchemist?' Vic looked both uncomfortable and preoccupied. 'Did the Consortium imprison an entire gang, some heretic street cult? Why? And why imprison them so close together?' Elodie contemplated that a bit longer. 'I'm beginning to think the system here had already been hacked. I think the personality downloads were corrupted somehow.' Then she turned around and glared at Vic. 'What are you doing?' she demanded.

'I've actually wet myself,' Vic announced.

Elodie glanced down despite herself. 'You need to get a grip,' she told him.

'Look,' he hissed, 'it has occurred to me that, frankly, without all the hardware and a vast quantity of fucking drugs, I'm just not that brave!'

'I think you had too much brain surgery,' Elodie hissed back. 'Took all that nice smoothness and turned it into folds, and then filled it with human bullshit! Now fucking control yourself, because if you shit yourself I will just fucking leave you!'

Someone cleared their throat behind them. Vic felt his heart sink. Elodie turned around to see seven of them, wearing the dead-skin masks, standing on the ruined lawn.

'You know what you were saying about me shitting myself ...?'

Through his fear, Vic calculated that at least one of the Dead-Skin Masks was deceased, another was crippled and the third would be unconscious for quite some time. After the first fight he had decided that committing acts of blunt-force trauma with a body that was both soft and brittle wasn't a great idea. So instead he'd decided on viciousness as a tactic.

The other four got them, however, and as they'd fought and struggled, more of the Dead-Skin Masks had joined them. They had taken quite a beating, and Vic was pretty sure something inside him was broken. Elodie's body didn't look like it was in good shape either. They had been dragged across the road and into Eden Street, and brought before another of the Dead-Skin Masks. He looked the same as all the others: a nondescript, suburban, generically bland adult male wearing someone else's face. The only real difference was the six-foot-long stick he was holding. Bloodied bones and other grisly trophies hung from it.

'Do you have any drugs?' Vic asked the man. 'It's just I'm really struggling with everything that's happening.' He heard running and glanced to one side. He saw five children wearing dead-skin masks joining the throng.

'I am—' the man with the stick began.

'I don't care,' Elodie said. 'What do you want, and what will it take for you to let us go?'

'Elodie!' Vic hissed at her. Elodie glared at him. Vic groaned inwardly, having realised he'd just given her name away.

'Well, either one of you cuts the face off the other and gives themselves to the Hungry Nothingness that waits just outside, or—'

'Okay, let's do that!' Vic said, a little too eagerly. Elodie started struggling, mostly so she could do something violent to Vic.

'Or we saw off both your faces and gang-rape you to death.'

Elodie stopped struggling. She had one of the Dead-Skin Masks on either side of her, both gripping her arms tightly. She kicked the man with the grisly stick very hard between the legs. There was a wet popping noise and he started screaming. It was very high-pitched. Elodie was already swinging up and the high-pitched scream was cut off suddenly as she kicked him in the face hard enough to powder bone. He collapsed to the ground.

'This is a child's body!' she shouted at the crumpled figure on the floor. A number of the Dead-Skin Masks scrambled for the grisly stick, which was grabbed by an inmate with the body of young girl. The scramble stopped and the other Dead-Skin Masks stepped deferentially aside.

'This changes nothing,' the girl said. 'Make your choice.'

'All praise the Hungry Somethingness!' Vic shouted with mock enthusiasm.

'I am going to kill you,' Elodie told him.

'Excuse me,' a cultured voice asked, slightly stressing the sibilant. Vic saw people looking at someone behind him and eventually he was dragged around. He was surprised to see a diminutive lizard in a very tall cylindrical hat. He was wearing a black smock and holding an EM needler in each of his scaly, clawed hands. Vic was even more surprised when he recognised the lizard. His name was Mr Hat, and he was a bounty killer. The lizard hadn't been too far below Scab and Vic in the ratings, before all their ex-colleagues had started hunting them. For a moment Vic was sure the lizard was there for them, and his bowels would have turned to ice had he not already evacuated them.

'Look,' Elodie whispered. Vic followed her gaze as she nodded towards the roof of a nearby house. Mr Hat glanced that way, too. It took Vic a moment to realise what he was looking at. A tall figure dressed in a pre-Loss-era suit, with tails, a waistcoat, a bow tie and a hat, similar in style and shape – though not size – to the lizard's, was crouched, unmoving, on the roof. The figure was pale and looked human except for the lack of eyes. At first Vic thought it was an ornately dressed and peculiarly active blank but then he realised it was one of Mr Hat's famed eyeless automatons.

Movement in the periphery of his vision caught Vic's eye, and he glanced up to see another automaton, this one female in design. The automaton was wearing a long, black lace dress that looked like a more chaste and reserved version of the sort of thing Talia wore sometimes. She/it leaped from the roof of a house and into a tree that had a faceless body hanging from it. The leaves shook, but she hadn't made a sound when she landed.

'I'm terribly sorry to bother you,' Mr Hat continued, 'but I am afraid I will be needing Mr Berger to come with me.' He pointed to where the Alchemist was bound to the car. Berger was conscious now. He was sobbing and making begging noises, but little of it appeared to be in any kind of rational language.

'You are the one!' the little girl with the grisly stick said. 'You can arrange for our release.'

Even on the reptilian face, the confusion was obvious. 'I cannot, I am afraid. I am just here to take him. Would you excuse me, please?'

The little girl stared at him. Even with most of her face concealed by a dead-skin mask, Vic was pretty sure she was about to have a tantrum.

Mr Hat watched the words form in the girl's mouth. She was about to order the inmates to attack him. He sighed inwardly, pretending to himself that he didn't want violence, but had that been the case, he wouldn't have left his comfortable bath chair behind. His automaton worshippers were perched in trees, or on the roofs of the surrounding houses, like a silent murder of crows.

The girl opened her mouth to shout the order and her head went spinning into the air. For Mr Hat, everything slowed down. It took an age for the other people in the dead-skin masks to react. The three thermal blades on the smart monofilament rotated around his hat at speed. Normally he couldn't use this weapon because most of his opponents wore armour, but here he could walk among all this soft flesh, the white-hot blades spinning like a rotor. The smart monofilament changed length and height, guiding the weapons to where they could cause the most damage. People went down as if they were being reaped. There was a nearly constant circle of red spray around him. He moved forwards, making for Mr Berger.

Mr Hat lowered his tail and fired the clustered-disc grenade from the launcher attached to it. The canister flew out and then transformed into secondary munitions. The tiny razor-sharp, spinning discs cleared a cone-shaped hole in the people who had closed in behind the lizard.

Mr Hat had synched the needlers with the revolutions of the three spinning blades. He target-locked one of the inmates and 'faced the order to fire. The needles would only fire when they could travel through the spinning blades cleanly. Each needle load had a different neurotoxin – again, they weren't weapons he got to use very often, but the non-augmented environment was allowing him to have some fun. Some of his targets' hearts stopped, others had their respiratory systems paralysed, a few tried to flee in abject terror and died from shock, several hit the ground in the throes of a terrible, final orgasm that would eventually overwhelm their nervous systems and kill them, and a couple were caught in the throes of powerful hallucinations.

Still they kept coming, charging him. Few of them made it anywhere near him, and those who did were mostly limbless when they got there. They were, however, slowing him down, particularly when he had to start walking across a carpet of slippery corpses. He used his clawed feet to dig into the human bodies for more purchase.

Vic found himself lying on the ground, painted red from head to foot. Elodie was standing over him, a knife in each hand. She was also covered in red. Vic looked up at her, panicking.

'When I said I'd cut off your face, I didn't—'

'Get up!' Elodie demanded, not even trying to hide the contempt in her voice. She did, however, hand him one of the red knives. 'Down!' she shouted and landed on top of him, forcing him to the ground. The multiple bangs of superheated air came so rapidly that they merged into a long ripping sound. The night became red as two G-carriers rose over the houses firting their forward rotary lasers, reducing hundreds of people to a humid red mist. The G-carriers stopped firing but remained hanging in the night air above the houses.

'C'mon!' Elodie said and rolled into a crouch.

'I don't wanna!' Vic protested.

Elodie turned on him, the young boy's face a mask of fury. 'I will stab you in the fucking stomach and then tell them who you are!'

Vic thought about killing her right there and then, but she was too frightening for him to act against her. He started to get up.

The slaved G-carriers had momentarily cleared a path for him. Mr Hat's augmented vision pierced the red mist as he quickened his pace. He couldn't risk firing the strobe guns too close to Mr Berger. As quickly as the rotary lasers killed hundreds of people, still more filled the gap, charging into the spinning blades and deadly needles.

Now, he thought. His automaton worshippers launched themselves from the roofs and out of the trees. They landed in a line and charged the dead-skin mask-wearing inmates. It looked like a wave breaking. Soft, unaugmented human flesh met the armoured superstructure of the eyeless, anachronistically dressed automatons, and broken human bodies went flying through the air.

Mr Hat brought the spinning blades in closer to his hat and followed behind the automatons, pausing only momentarily to dispatch an inmate they had missed. More came from behind. He turned and began firing as the blades started spinning again. He was almost at the car.

It looked as if houses, trees, ground cars and road had suddenly thrown themselves into the air in a long line. The heavy electromagnetically driven shells fired from the window-frame-mounted cannon batteries all but disintegrated any inmates they hit and churned up the earth where they impacted. The air was filled with fragmented of bodies and larger chunks of spinning debris.

'No!' Mr Hat screamed in rage and frustration. 'What the fuck are you doing?' he demanded over the 'face link.

'We—' a frightened-sounding Isaiah began.

'Not you, the other moron!' he demanded. A chunk of concrete hit his hat and sent him flying. Only a chemically and neunonically controlled nervous system allowed him the presence of mind to continue 'facing.

'We detected a large-scale disturbance,' Al told him. 'We were dealing with it.'

'Cease the barrage immediately. That large-scale disturbance is me committing mass murder, you fucking idiot!' He'd stopped the blades spinning as he fell and the monofilament had sucked them back into the mechanism of the hat. Crouched in a ball on the ground, he was suddenly underneath a pile of automatons. He was receiving information about how many of them had been destroyed in the cannon barrage. Another was destroyed when a large chunk of masonry landed on the pile of automatons shielding him. They kept him safe, but several at the top of the pile were badly damaged.

'You're in the privacy nano-swarm,' Al explained.

'That's what the macro-cams are for! Do you think I'm fucking lying to you? Stop fucking firing! Or I will find an immersion to keep you in that will allow you to be constantly anally raped to death!'

The hypersonic bang of the cannon fire stopped, followed by the sound of debris falling to the ground. Slowly the automatons started disentangling themselves and standing up. Finally Mr Hat pushed himself back onto his feet and brushed himself down. The air was full of dust, which was causing his lung filters problems and obscuring his vision. Even through the dust he was able to see that the suburban street had been turned into a series of craters. He walked quickly through the red-smeared rubble towards the ground car. A cordon of his automatons killed any of the surviving Dead-Skin Masks who tried to charge him through the dust. The ground car was mostly intact. Berger was gone.

'Nooooo!' he shrieked. 'Find him! Bring him and anyone with him to me!'

The automatons spread out. When they left the blast area, they leaped upwards and started moving from rooftop to rooftop, tree to tree.

'Well, try and fucking run!' Vic said, all but dragging the Alchemist with him after Elodie.

'I'm a fucking dolphin. We're not built to run!' Berger/the Alchemist complained.

'I'm an insect. I'm coping with the lack of limbs!'

'It's not the same. It would be like asking you to echolocate!'

'No, it'd be like asking me to swim! Which I can!'

'Shut the fuck up! Both of you!' Elodie hissed. She was crouched down and looking all around. All three of them were covered from head to foot in blood and dust after running through gardens at the back of the houses.

'Where's the rendezvous?' Vic demanded.

'Here,' Elodie said, pointing at the garden they'd paused in. They'd managed to flee about two miles away from Eden Street.

'Where are they, then?'

'You get that we can't communicate with them, right?'

Vic's human eyes widened. 'So when are they coming?'

'Another two hours?'

'Two hours!'

Elodie stood up and strode over to Vic. 'You have not contributed. In fact, you have been nothing but a whiny pain in the arse since we started!' she hissed, waving a bloody kitchen knife at him for emphasis. 'Now either cope, or I end you right here, right now!'

'All right, calm down,' Vic said, a little taken aback.

'Inside, now!' She pushed them into the closest house.

It was a spacious open-plan bungalow. They entered through the kitchen door. From the lounge, five faces turned to look their way. The two adults had been tied to chairs placed back to back and looked like they had been pretty extensively tortured. The three children had just stopped dancing around the adults. The children were carrying a mixture of household utensils, tools and caustic cleaning products.

Elodie stepped forwards. 'Get out of here, take the adults with you, torture them to death somewhere else,' she told them. The kids stared at her. She stared back, the knife in her hand dripping blood. To Vic it felt as if the stand-off went on for a very long time. Then the kids bolted, leaping through the already broken lounge window. Elodie sighed. They'd left the adults. The adults immediately started begging.

'Put him in the fridge and get the kettle on,' Elodie told Vic. 'I'll deal with them.' Elodie started walking towards the two tied-up adults, knife at the ready. They started to beg and plead for their lives.

'Breathe,' Elodie told Vic as he hyperventilated into a brown paper bag. She took another sip of the coffee. It was quite good, she decided.

Vic jumped as something landed on the roof. He opened his mouth but suddenly Elodie's hand was over it. There was a scrabbling noise, and then the sound of breaking glass as a figure dressed in a blood-smeared suit complete with tails and tall hat dropped through a skylight and landed in a crouch. The tall, thin, eyeless figure stood up straight.

'Just keep hyperventilating into the bag,' Elodie said. Vic nodded and got on with his panic attack. Elodie took another sip of coffee as the automaton slowly turned around, looking without eyes. Then it stalked off to search the rest of the house. Vic opened his mouth to ask a question – between wheezing for breath – but Elodie held up her hand for silence.

The automaton stalked back into the lounge. Vic could feel his human heart trying to batter itself through his ribs. Elodie just looked back, her expression blank and uninterested. It stood there staring at them, without eyes, for what felt like a very long time. Then it turned, ignoring the two bodies still tied to chairs in the centre of the lounge, and leaped upwards through the broken skylight.

Vic tried to speak but was still hyperventilating.

'Bag,' Elodie ordered, and waited.

'What the fuck?' Vic finally managed.

'Even with active scans, they're basically looking for movement or heat. A forensic search screen will suffer information overload in this environment.'

'Which is why you put him in the fridge?' Vic asked. Elodie nodded. The Alchemist/Berger had protested a lot, but Elodie had managed to convince him that he should be quiet and still.

'Nobody thinks to actually look these days. We just rely on technology.' She paused for a moment. 'Almost time.'

The 'face feeds from the bridge-point beacons were a few seconds old, but they showed the pulsing blue rip of the opening, and through it the crimson wound of Red Space. Al brought the footage to Isaiah's attention. It wasn't a ship that came through.

'Oh,' Isaiah said. Then he started to get really frightened.

Mr Hat stood at the crossroads. The two slaved G-carriers circled overhead, their strobe guns lighting up the night whenever anyone got too close to the diminutive lizard. He was using various neunonic search routines to sort through all the data his automaton worshippers were 'facing to him.

He stopped on the image of the hyperventilating woman and the child. He cross-referenced their images. He replayed footage from earlier in the night in his mind. When he first arrived to speak to the Dead-Skin Masks, they were there. Prisoners of the strangely organised flayed-face cultists.

'Them!' he snapped. With a thought, all his automatons started leaping from rooftop to rooftop towards the house where they had last been seen.

'We've detected a change in pressure. It's much larger,' Al said. Isaiah didn't answer. 'Well?' the AI demanded.

'Enact Cauterise Protocol.' Isaiah couldn't keep the tremor from his voice.

*

A panel of glass the size of several football pitches blew out of one of the window segments. Huge daggers of glass were sucked out into space and destroyed by the point-defence systems of the naval contractor frigate. The frigate was buffeted by the escaping atmosphere as it made its way through the hole in the window segment.

He was so occulted that Suburbia's defences didn't even register his existence. He switched physical states as he sank through the glass and found himself dropping into the habitat's atmosphere towards one of the scarred land segments.

The wind sucked everything towards, and then through, the pulsing blue rip and into Red Space. Vic and the Alchemist were holding on to the house for all they were worth. Over the rush of escaping atmosphere and the lack of available oxygen, Elodie couldn't even hear them screaming at her that they weren't going.

She felt a hand touch her and pluck her off the breakfast bar she was clinging to. Elodie turned and her small human heart actually skipped a beat. She was looking at a surprisingly small and slight figure clothed in black liquid glass. She had a moment to feel fear, then a strange narcotic calmness flooded through her. She saw the beatific face of the small human body she was in grow out of the liquid glass the strange figure wore, and then she died.

Mr Hat looked up at the sound of breaking glass, which echoed the length of the prison. He saw the frigate slowly making its way into the cylinder. A sucking wind whipped at his smock, but it wasn't coming from the hole in the window. The size of the hole and the volume of air in the cylinder meant that it would be a long time before they'd feel the loss of atmosphere. The sucking wind was coming from somewhere closer.

He had a moment to reflect just how badly Al and Isaiah had mismanaged this entire situation as he saw thick beams of dangerous light reach out from the blunt, armoured head of the frigate, and heard the hypersonic rip of multiple kinetic harpoons and AG-powered intelligent munitions being launched.

Vic was clinging to the breakfast bar for dear life. The Alchemist/Berger was right next to him. He saw some of the anachronistically dressed eyeless automatons appear at the doorway. Others were climbing in through broken windows, with difficulty in the sucking, roaring wind. He wasn't sure what made him look at Elodie, but he did so just in time to see the Elite let go of her body. It was sucked out of the kitchen, bouncing off the window frame and into the back garden, where it was pulled through the rip into Red Space. Vic let go of the breakfast bar and grabbed the Alchemist/Berger, tearing him free. They hit the window frame hard. He was still conscious. The Elite was reaching towards him. Everything was red. He couldn't breathe. There was no Suburbia. An arm encased in black liquid glass was spinning nearby.

The Elite looked at the missing arm with interest. He enjoyed the sensation for a moment, and then, with a thought, he started regrowing it. The black liquid glass of his armour wrapped itself around the flesh as it regenerated.

He changed physical state again as he found himself living within the fire and force from the frigate's various weapon impacts. He appreciated this at a subatomic particle level for a moment, and then flew through it. He hacked the frigate's control systems, sending the ship plummeting towards the inner surface of the habitat. He weaponised the frigate's internal security nano-screen into a flesh-eating swarm to finish off any survivors and burned the ship's AI in electronic fire. He did the same to the C&C staff of Suburbia, and its AI. It wasn't really their fault, particularly not the crew of the frigate, but you couldn't attack one of the Elite without a response. He was aware of the habitat shaking as the frigate finished its slow, strangely graceful fall through its atmosphere.

His vision was full of blood and his joints were in agony.

'Drugs!' Vic begged from the floor of the *Basilisk II*'s cargo bay. He'd felt strong hands pull him through the airlock. He glanced over and saw Elodie kneeling next to the gasping body of the Alchemist/Berger, injecting him with nanites. 'Please, help me,' Vic pleaded. Then he realised Elodie was in her real feline body. It was agony, but he rolled over and saw Talia, a horrified expression on her face, and a bored-looking Scab smoking a cigarette. Words could not express how much he hated that man. The other Vic, the insect Vic, the Vic that wasn't just a possessing program modelled on his personality, was pointing his triple-barrelled shotgun pistol at him.

'But you don't know what I've been through!' the possessing program in the human body said.

'Sorry, buddy,' the real Vic said. Possessing-Program-Vic's image was filled with muzzle flash.

*

Vic looked down sympathetically at the red smear on the cargo bay floor. Talia had cried out and turned away, shaking and looking sick. Vic wondered what she'd expected to see.

'He'll be fine,' Elodie said nodding at the prone figure of the Alchemist/Berger. She stood up. 'My copy had better be fucking dead as well,' she told Scab

'He is,' the Alchemist managed, sitting up. 'An Elite got him ... her ... whatever.' Elodie and Vic glared at Scab.

'What's an Elite?' Talia asked.

'You can't be surprised,' Scab said to Elodie and Vic.

The Alchemist stared at the headless human body, then looked up at Vic. 'I don't suppose you could shoot me as well?'

Out in the red, black liquid flowed over the stump of the severed arm. It turned itself into a rough lozenge shape and started making its slow way home.

He felt the point of the metal on his skin. He could sense the power in the dagger. If she chose to push the blade home he would die. He opened his eyes. She was looking down on him, straddling him under the furs that covered his cot. There were tears running down her cheeks.

'You killed them all,' she said. There might have been tears on her face, but her words were clear and strong.

'Yes,' Bress said, simply.

'I hate you,' she told him, meaning it. Britha had no reason to love him and he would not make excuses for his actions. There were none. He concentrated on ensuring that total control of the Lochlannach went to her when he died.

Bress felt the point push against his skin, which was already hardening to deflect the iron blade infused with her blood. He could tell she wanted to do it. Bress almost wished she would. They'd had their night. Few explanations, little talking. He had taken her by the hand as they walked through the Lochlannach, who remained as still as stone. They spent the night finding out all they could about how to bring pleasure to each other. Uncaring, unrestrained, wild. Bress would have liked to put it down to pure carnal desire, but he knew there was something here, a far more deeply seated feeling that he was loath to admit to himself. He could practically hear Crom Dhubh's laughter, a creeping violation in the back of his mind. He could sense the ghost of the crooked man's amusement.

He didn't understand it. This woman should have been nothing to him, another victim, nothing more. He ought to have killed her the first time they met. Or enslaved her, or given her to Ettin. She was a mud-dwelling savage, a primitive, a mortal, no more capable of understanding what was happening to her and all those around her than his horse was. So why did he care?

'What you did to those children,' she spat. Ettin had enslaved them and shaped their flesh. He found it entertaining to take children and turn them into hunting animals, but that didn't matter. Bress had controlled Ettin. He hadn't said no. It was his responsibility, as if he had done it himself. He looked up at her and said nothing. There were so many reasons he should die now. He had committed crimes that would not come to fruition for millennia, and he would commit more unless he was stopped.

'Do it,' he whispered to her, his throat suddenly dry. Even with Fachtna's blood in her – and that thought burned in him like hatred – he was pretty sure he could take the knife from her any time he wanted.

'There is no honour, no glory, in this,' she said. She was looking for something in his eyes. Bress was saddened. He could hear her faltering.

'There is no honour or glory in anything I do. None here can stand against me. What I don't destroy, I enslave.'

'We stood against you.' She was fierce again. He felt the dagger's point break through his hardened skin.

'You altered the form of this land's destruction. You were merely a setback to my master's plans. All you have done is drawn the matter out. There will be more suffering now.' *Could he goad her into killing him?* he wondered. *Would his words be enough?* He saw her face harden and felt the iron point dig deeper into his flesh.

'And will that change if I kill you?' she demanded.

'I am redundant now. Do what you will.'

For a moment he thought she would do it. There was pressure on the dagger, but then she dropped it and stood up, more tears rolling down her cheeks. She grabbed her robe as she fled the hide tent. Bress watched her go. He could still feel the memory of her touch all over his skin.

He tried to ignore the feeling of nausea as he turned to look at Crom Dhubh's shadowy, indeterminate form in the tent's shadows.

'I'll do what you want if you will leave her be.'

Do kings bargain with slaves?

'It is my experience that everyone does what they must.'

You can have her after I know where the Ubh Blaosc *is. Until then she belongs to me.*

'You're going to send *them*, aren't you? They see us only as food and a place to lay their eggs.'

That is what you are, nothing more. To them, anyway. You want an end to all things. This is the cost.

'She is strong, she might not come to you.'

She does not look strong.

He found Britha in the copse of trees close to the riverbank. One of the giants was standing in the river. The water frothed around him, the fast-flowing river coming up to the strange, gnarled figure's waist. Bress knew the only time Britha had seen them up close before was when she had been fighting them: on the beach in the north, her home, and then again in the south, again on a beach. Britha, however, was ignoring the giant in favour of staring at one of the Lochlannach.

Ettin picked the slaves who would become the Lochlannach. They were predominantly male, all strong and healthy and, where possible, fast. Few of them had been warriors, since most of the warriors had died in the fighting. Many had been spear-carriers, particularly in the north, but that didn't matter. The ability to fight was given to them by the howling metal demons they drank down when they supped from the Red Chalice.

Britha's eyes were red but her face was dry. Bress did not think she was used to experiencing this kind of vulnerability.

'I know this man,' she said. 'I forget his name but he is a landsman, one of the Ce from north of the Cirig lands.' She started moving among the Lochlannach, studying them as she went. 'This one's name is Mealchionn, he is one of us, a fisherman. This one was a Cait warrior in the service of Calgacus of the Bitter Tongue. And she is one of the Fib from across the Tatha.'

Bress followed her as she walked from person to person. She studied every face, pointing out the ones she knew before finally turning to him.

'The demons lived in my flesh, and screamed, and snarled in my head, and I came back. So can they.'

'Your lover blessed you with the blood of the Muileartach. They have received no such blessing,'

'This is for the Muileartach.' Britha spat on the ground. 'And all gods.' Then she looked him straight in the eyes. Brown eyes staring into pale, colourless, almost dead eyes. 'It is a cage, a wicker man the size of your own body. The demons imprison you. Inside you can see everything they make you do. Is that how the magic of the Otherworld works? Does it have to be so cruel?'

'No,' Bress admitted quietly.

'You are a cruel man, Bress. I have met men and women who enjoy their cruelty, but you do not. I think you would be cruel for an end, but I don't see the purpose here.'

'It was done for the sake of it ...' He looked as if he was about to say more, but didn't.

'Ettin?'

'I'll not make excuses.'

'To feed Crom?'

'He might see it that way.'

'But they are still in there?' He nodded. She moved closer, looking up at him but not touching him, her eyes narrowing. 'Let them go.'

'They would not be as they were. They have been made to do things. They saw things. They were tormented by what was in their blood.'

'Just my people, then, the Pecht, that's all I care about. It is my job to protect them still. Let them go and I will stay here with you. There is nothing for me in the north any more.'

Crom Dhubh was a strangely silent black smudge on the periphery of Bress's vision. 'As much as you would spit on the gods, you will come to serve him.'

'Then you will kill me,' she said evenly, her eyes never leaving his. He felt something catch in his throat. It took him a moment to realise that the sensation in his eye was a tear. He was starting to resent these strange emotions. They did not feel as if they should belong to him. He glanced to where he was sure Crom Dhubh was standing, in the periphery of his vision, but there was nothing. He sensed he was being manipulated but couldn't be sure by whom. He struggled with the idea that it was Britha. She might be one of the learned among her people, but they were an unsophisticated race. He thought he could hear Crom Dhubh's mocking laughter, but it was just his mind playing tricks on him.

'My people,' she said again.

Bress nodded.

Is this enough? she asked herself. This was all that was left of her people. She had failed to protect them. Perhaps she should have been sacrificed in punishment for her failure, blood and bone given to a land bereft of people. She should seek vengeance on Bress, but he appeared to be a slave. On Crom Dhubh, but he was a spent force, a ghost. She did not know what mattered now, other than the life that had been taken from her.

They marched the Lochlannach far from the copse of woods on the banks of the *Tros Hynt*. She rode with Bress, feeling less like a *dryw* and more like nobility. They found a natural bowl in the land amongst rolling hills. Bress made the Lochlannach march down into the bowl, while he remained on the rim, looking down.

'Their weapons?' Britha asked.

'I will excise the demons from them as well, otherwise the demons will still control them, and it would start all over again. They may keep them, though few will remember how to use them well. They must know, however, that to bear them against myself or the other Lochlannach will result in their deaths.'

'They may welcome that,' Britha said grimly as she looked down on the dozen men and one woman she had recognised among the ranks of the Lochlannach.

'I can kill those who wish to die,' Bress said, not looking at her, his voice devoid of emotion. Britha reached over and gripped his arm fiercely.

'This has nothing to do with you now. You release them and go on your way,' she told him fiercely.

He thought for a moment and then nodded. 'It is done.' Bress wheeled his horse around and began to ride slowly away from Britha and her mount. The Otherworldly horses were such that they did not even flinch when the screaming started.

Some screamed, most cried, a few remained silent, staring. One killed himself immediately and two attempted to follow Bress to attack him, but were still respectful enough of Britha's position to obey her when she said no.

Only one, the woman, attacked her. Under normal circumstances it would have been enough for her to be cast out. The first thing the woman had been made to do, after Ettin had forced her to drink from the Red Chalice, was to murder her four children, for sport. Britha disarmed her easily. After all, she was as one of the Fair Folk now. Then she held the woman as she shrieked and tore at Britha's flesh.

Bitter words were exchanged. Most headed north, a few didn't. The woman, whose name was Derith, demanded that Britha kill her. The triple death, the hardest death, the greatest of the sacrifices. They found an oak, and in the dying grey light of dusk Britha felt the rock's impact on the woman's head run up her arm before she strangled her with her rope belt. Finally Britha pushed her dirk home between Derith's shoulder blades.

Only one, the warrior from the Cait, asked to be enslaved again, to continue to serve Bress. Britha wasn't able to hide her disgust, for some of it was aimed at herself. She wondered how different she really was from the Cait warrior.

Nails had drawn red lines on his skin that healed moments later. They were both covered in sweat and gasping for breath. She tried to drive unwanted thoughts from her head, but even as she threw herself down on the cot next to Bress, still feeling the residual warmth of the pleasure, she knew the thoughts would be waiting for her when she closed her eyes.

She turned away from Bress. She wanted to hide these thoughts from him, but she knew it would be difficult lying naked next to him. She heard him shift to prop himself up on an elbow. She could feel his eyes on her.

'What did they do to you?' he asked, so quietly that she barely heard him. She squeezed her eyes shut and tried to will herself not to cry. It didn't stop the tears. At the back of her mind she was impressed that somehow he knew enough not to touch her, or try to comfort her. She said nothing for a while. Finally she rolled over to look at him. She had not wiped away the tears. They were hers. She should not be ashamed of them. There was so much more she could be ashamed of.

'They stole a child from me.'

Bress said nothing. He looked away from her. 'Who was the father?' he asked quietly.

'The Muileartach.' She had no idea why she said that. She had opened her mouth to say Fachtna. Bress jerked his head around to look at her. He felt for Crom Dhubh's presence but could not sense it. He looked for the shadow, but did not see it.

'Is it me you want, or power?' he asked. There was no judgement in his question.

Britha knew that she could reach over to touch him, to manipulate him, lie to him. Tell him what he wanted to hear.

'I want my child back. They took her from me before she was even born. They took her from me because some of what the Muileartach was ... is ... it's inside me. If power is required to get her back, then I will take it where I can.'

Bress looked away from her again. 'And you like it, don't you?'

She thought back to killing the warped bear at the siege of Andraste's Crown. She thought back to her salmon leap when they fought the Lochlannach on the beach.

'Yes,' she finally said. 'And I wield it well. Now tell me, do you think that is why I am here with you?'

Bress considered the question. 'In part—'

Britha started to climb out of the cot. Bress grabbed her arm. She turned on him.

'Mind yourself, warrior! Just because I have chosen to lie with you does not mean you can take liberties with me!' she spat.

'I think part of the reason you want me is because I have power.'

Britha froze. It was true that she had lain with Cruibne for reasons of ritual, but despite the fact that he was ugly, covered in scars, more than a little fat and stank of too much meat and heather ale, she had enjoyed the experience. Was this the reason why? Even Cliodna had power. Bress was beautiful, but so was Fachtna, arguably more so, and less strange, but it was Bress she truly wanted. Fachtna had been easy, a convenience. She sagged.

'It doesn't matter. Do you want me?' Bress asked.

'Yes,' she admitted weakly.

'I'll give you what you want. Only lie with me if you want.'

'I said yes.'

'You sound as if you wish it otherwise.'

She turned on him, angry again. 'Do you want to remind me of all the reasons I should hate you?' she demanded.

'I will remind you of that every time you look at me. There is no point pretending that I have not done what I have done.'

'I want you to suffer and die,' she said, in a small voice that Bress did not think sounded like her. 'And I want you as my lover.'

Bress nodded. 'Fachtna's here, isn't he?'

This time it was Britha who looked away. 'Fachtna's dead. I put a sword through him, his own. He killed a *dryw*, he had to die.' Britha knew that Bress had probably killed or enslaved or sacrificed many *dryw*, as they would have attempted to negotiate with him when the black *curraghs* raided. She hoped he would not tell her this now.

'Then we should go to his body. He has something we want. If he has it, then we can try to get your child.'

She nodded.

'But if you want power, you will have to come with me to Oeth first.'

'The Place of Bones?' she asked suspiciously.

'If you want power, that is where it will be found.'

As they rode away from the camp, the *curraghs* were sinking into the fast-moving water of the *Tros Hynt*. She had stopped questioning the magics of the Otherworld.

About twenty of the Lochlannach joined them on horseback. Bress left the rest of the Lochlannach at the camp.

They headed north and east. The powerful horses covered the ground far swifter than the ponies Britha was used to. She was a skilled horsewoman, but she mostly found herself merely holding on.

Every village and settlement they passed had been destroyed and carrion-eaters fed on the corpses of the livestock. After they rode by the first, Britha glanced over at Bress. He didn't appear to have noticed the village, though it was clear the Lochlannach had been there before.

The terrain became progressively higher as they made their way through long river valleys. The landscape was dominated by tall, rounded hills, many with rocky escarpments. Woodland and scattered farmland eventually gave way to heather-covered moorland. They spotted burial mounds and a stone circle as they travelled, proof that this land had been inhabited for a long time, and interfered with by the gods. It was at the stone circle she saw the only bodies, but they were long dead. They had been left for the ravens to slowly take to the Underworld, morsel by morsel.

After a night's rest, wrapped in Bress's cloak and in his arms, they continued onwards. The light had just started to fade when they entered the long valley. At the west end Britha could make out a roughly dome-shaped hill surrounded by a number of smaller mounds. Even from this distance she could see the hill fort. Some of it was built on platforms suspended out over the sheer drop of the cliff. It was only when they got closer, however, that she saw the bodies hanging from the ramparts, and the reddish brown smears on the rock. She glanced over at Bress. Again he said nothing.

'You kill everything,' she said quietly, though she knew Bress would hear her.

Just before they reached the rounded hill at the end of the valley they turned south, where the horses carried them up a steep slope towards a large, gaping, dark hole in the cliffside. Britha began to feel distinctly uncomfortable. Like most people she feared caves. Leaving aside the fact that bears, wolf packs and the most desperate and degenerate of people – those who had been cast out from their tribes – often lived in them, they were also gateways to the Underworld.

She tried to mask her fear as she spurred her mount on and followed Bress and the rest of the Lochlannach into the dark cave-mouth.

They were already dismounting when Britha finally rode into the cave. She climbed off her own horse, watching Bress as she did so. He remained silent, and then stalked into the darkness. As Britha watched him go, her eyes adjusted to the darkness, though colour was sucked from her vision. He turned around to look at her and she took an involuntary step back. His eyes glowed. The fear felt like a fast-rising tide inside her. She was standing still but wanted to bolt. The other Lochlannach were following Bress, and she would lose him soon if she did not do the same. She forced her feet to move. She forced herself to remember who and what she was. That dealing with the Underworld was as much her responsibility as dealing with the Otherworld. *No*, she reminded herself, *protecting your people from the Underworld and the Otherworld was your responsibility.*

She was no longer in mortal lands. They had waded through water under what looked like a naturally made gate, and her vision was caught in the half-light of permanent dusk. She knew this must be the Underworld. She was travelling into the land of the dead. Even though she could see Bress and the other Lochlannach ahead, she felt very alone.

They climbed down through small waterfalls and rocks into one cavern, and then down again into another that was half-flooded. They moved through it slowly, half-wading, half-swimming, despite the weapons they carried and the armour they wore.

The deeper they went, the further from the light they travelled, the more her fear grew, but she forced herself to keep going. She could feel her heart in her chest, pounding like a blacksmith beating metal into shape.

Finally they found themselves standing over a chasm where she looked down into darkness. She wanted to tell Bress that she couldn't go on, but remained quiet.

The Lochlannach leaned their spears and shields against the rock alongside other spears and shields already laid there, all of them identical. Britha added her spear to the collection.

One by one, the Lochlannach started climbing down the chasm wall. Frightened though she was, Britha had the presence of mind to watch where they moved and noticed that they all went exactly the same way. Finally only Bress was left with her. He lay down and all but slithered over the edge into the chasm.

Would you be frightened if you were doing this climb back under the sky? she admonished herself. *But I'm not. I am in the land of the dead.* She pulled off her boots. It took her a long time to force herself over the edge, even though she could recall perfectly from her observations where the hand- and footholds were. By the time she began the descent, Bress and the Lochlannach had long since been swallowed by the blackness below her. She descended alone into the darkness.

*

Clinging on with fingers and toes, Britha looked down and saw water just below her. She pushed out from the rock face and glanced all around, but all she could see was water. She had climbed down into a massive cavern, the roof of which was covered with sharp, pointed rocks that looked like teeth. The whole place made her think of the mouth of some gigantic beast. The water was utterly still; she could not even hear it lapping against the rock.

Britha lowered herself into the freezing water. For a brief moment she wondered how the Lochlannach had not drowned in their mail. Then all her thoughts were on the coldness of the water. From the first moment, she knew she was not feeling it as she should, for it was nowhere near as debilitating as it should have been.

Where she entered the underground loch, it was deep enough that her feet did not touch the rock of the cavern floor. Treading water, she looked for some clue as to where the others had gone. It took her a while, peering through the murky darkness, but finally she thought she saw something. She started to swim towards what looked like an island, little more than a mound that broke the surface of the water.

Either that or I am lost in the Underworld, she thought.

It was an obscenity. The broch that rose from the muddy island looked as if it had sprouted from the rock, but it had in fact been grown from bones. She had swum through the rotted, boneless remains of hundreds of people in the water surrounding the island.

Everywhere she looked in the Underworld's strange half-light she was sure she saw things moving in the shadows, as if there were many Crom Dhubhs, but when she focused there was nothing.

The Lochlannach stood around the broch, gazing up at it. Smaller figures moved between them, playing with odd, strangely regular rootlike growths which ran from the tower into the water. It was with a dawning horror that she recognised the hunched over, twisted shapes. They were like the malformed children Ettin had used as hunting dogs, except these were blind and had webs between their fingers and toes.

There was a glow coming from the other side of the small island. Britha was close to hysteria now. She wasn't sure why she went to look, but she did, forcing herself to take one step after another. There were no boneless bodies floating in the water on this side of the island. She could not work out where the light was coming from, but in the still, clear water she saw a circle of stones, like the cairns in the north and the many others she had passed on her travels. She was about to turn away when she caught sight of something else. At the edge of the light she could make out what might be a structure of some kind, in the water, but she could see too little of it to be sure.

Her skin crawled, and she jumped as she felt something cold and clammy touch her hand. She looked down at the small childlike creature. Its mouth was smeared with a dark fluid and it was still chewing something. It pulled her gently towards the broch of bone that reached up to the toothed roof of the cavern like a skeletal finger. He/she/it gestured for Britha to go inside.

Britha wasn't sure how or why she was still moving. She felt bone against her bare feet and looked down at the geometric arrangements of bones on the floor. A helical staircase rose against the inner wall and she started to climb.

At the top of the broch, she looked out over the dark underground loch. On one side she could see the floating collection of split and boned corpses, and on the other the glow of the stones. The cavern walls were lost in the darkness.

There was a hearthstone in the centre of the roof, firewood stacked on top of it. As she moved closer the firewood burst into flames, illuminating the cavern with a red glow.

Bress was on the other side of the fire. Britha looked down at the bones on which she stood, then again at the floating corpses and the things that fed on them.

'You all need to die, don't you?' she said quietly, feeling the ache in her chest as she did so.

'Reach into the flames,' he told her.

Britha stared at him as she shrugged off her wet robe. Then, with only a moment's hesitation, she thrust her arm into the flame. Her cries echoed out across the cavern.

Somehow her fingers clasped around cold metal and she yanked the chalice of red gold from the fire. Agony coursed through her body. She forced the chalice to her mouth but could not scream this time as the molten metal filled her mouth. She did not so much drink it as feel tendrils of the burning, liquid red gold claw and crawl their way down her throat. She collapsed to the bone floor. Her body convulsed violently, her throat and then her stomach glowing from within, and then the light began to branch throughout her body.

'This pleases me,' Crom Dhubh whispered to Bress. Bress squeezed his eyes shut as the tears rolled down his cheeks.

'I think you should leave this place whilst you can,' Fachtna said. The dead that followed him, those that still moved, stood in the open area of the hill fort, swaying gently in an unfelt wind. The fort offered a commanding view over the surrounding, transformed terrain. Its gates hung off their posts. The dead, those that no longer moved, lay around them, fused with the earth itself, strange flowers growing from their wounds and through their skulls. 'Please, before it's too late.' He wanted to help them, but he was torn. It was all so beautiful.

25

Close to the Oceanic Pole of Inaccessibility, 5 Weeks Ago

I've only been here a week, Lodup thought. Given the extraordinary nature of his environment, he felt that there should be more to the job than the constant sense of unease, which frequently spilled over into outright fear. He had dreams he couldn't remember, that he didn't want to remember. He had been told that without neurosurgery, his mind simply wouldn't have coped with the geometry of the architecture alone, never mind anything else. He didn't like that he was 'okay' with the fact that someone had operated on his brain and radically changed his body so he could work down here. His acceptance of this place wasn't natural, but he didn't leave, and it wasn't just the neurosurgery that kept him there. At some level he was aware of how incredible what they were doing was. Though even that excitement was dulled by the strong antidepressants and anti-anxiety medication that were turning everything into a kind of fugue state.

He wasn't the only one behaving strangely. There were people working on *Kanamwayso* that he'd known for years – mostly acquaintances, a few he considered actual friends. They were quiet and unresponsive when he spoke to them and got out of the conversation as quickly as possible. He would have been offended if he hadn't felt so numb himself.

Hideo swung between periods of almost invasive, enthusiastic companionship, and periods of withdrawn despondency. After a few days, Lodup had found his way into Sal's bed. It was more for comfort than anything else. It hadn't taken him long to see through her up-for-it, can-do attitude. Underneath, this place was eating away at her just like everyone else.

There'd been two more suicides and a murder since he arrived. One of the divers had taken his knife to his lover. Siraja alerted Yaroslav's security team immediately and one of them killed the murderer. Lodup had known the killer, though not well. His name was Antonio something-or-other, a diver in the Italian Navy. They'd worked a job together in the Mediterranean. Lodup's memory of him was as a competent diver who was good enough company, particularly as they'd spent long periods of time together in decompression chambers.

The small cult groups continued to fascinate Lodup. They used salvaged pieces of the city's 'statuary' as altars and spoke in tongues. Lodup was beginning to wonder if the cultists might actually be the most well-balanced people down here. He wondered if their faith was what was required to stay without killing yourself or someone else. At the back of his mind he couldn't help but wonder if they genuinely knew something, had some insight that was lost to the rest of them. Maybe they've just made peace with the city, Lodup thought, not for the first time.

Only the immortals, as Lodup found himself thinking of them, appeared immune to the effects of the alien city. The only constants were Deane, Siska, Yaroslav and Siraja.

Eight hours of cold a day didn't help, either, and the feeling of water being flushed through his chest, the false sensation of drowning and vomiting at the same time, only added to the feeling of numbness. It half-helped to convince his mind that it was already dead. That he was just going through the motions.

The fusion torch made the water bubble around what Lodup was still trying to think of as a statue. It was fused to one of the tomblike buildings. It had a biomechanical look to it, reminding Lodup of a cross between some kind of bottom-feeding fish, perhaps even a ray, and some enormous seed-pod. He'd seen another statue similar to this one in a different part of the city, and the tethered wet workshops contained more that looked just like it.

They were working in the shadow of one of the reengineered 'Archies', or giant squid, which stood over the statue like an enormous crane, its segmented, armoured tentacles reaching down and curling under the 'seed-pod'. Powerful lights running along the underside of the Archie illuminated the area with a cold, steel-blue light.

Sal was working the ADS and Hideo was in the flatbed submersible, both of them cutting into the 'masonry'. Lodup was standing on top of the flatbed making sure the gel dispenser's hose spooled properly, telemetry playing down his vision. He had been feeling a little odd since the cutting began: on edge, phantom sensations shooting through his body. Hideo stopped cutting, expertly controlling the impellers to rapidly manoeuvre the submersible through the crystal-clear water. He started the fusion torch again, the water bubbling around the cutting flame. Lodup cried out in shock, making no noise at all as his body was flooded with water and other liquids. He felt the suggestion of agony but none of the pain. Then his vision whited out.

He regained consciousness lying on the seabed, a cloud of particulate matter rising around him.

'Are you all right, sir?' Siraja asked. Lodup heard the words in his mind. The AI was somehow managing to convey concern despite his draconic features. Lodup knew that the AI wasn't really standing in the cloud of silt wearing a business suit, but was instead transmitting the image direct to Lodup's visual-perception centres.

Lodup opened his mouth to speak and then remembered to subvocalize. 'Yes, I'm fine. I lost my balance for a moment, is all,' he told the AI. He could see Sal in the ADS falling through the water towards him. Hideo was still using the fusion torch to cut into the basalt-like material above them.

'We detected some anomalies with you, some kind of ghost signals,' Siraja said.

'You all right, hon?' Sal asked over the shortwave comms.

'Fine, not really sure what happened,' Lodup said.

'Perhaps you should report to sick-bay,' Siraja suggested.

'Maybe after the shift,' Lodup told him.

'How are your dreams, Mr Satakano?'

Lodup stared at Siraja. 'I don't remember my dreams.'

The image of the dragon-headed AI nodded. 'Let me know if I can be of any further assistance.'

'I will.'

Siraja bowed slightly and disappeared.

'Lodup, if you've finished, I want to get the gel in place,' Hideo said over the ultrasound comms. This was proving to be one of the Japanese submersible pilot's more despondent days. Lodup pushed himself off the seabed in a cloud of silt and finned towards the hovering vehicle. The glowing area where the masonry had been cut was cooling quickly in the sub-zero water kept liquid by the immense pressure.

They hadn't attempted to cut the entire thing from the tomblike structure. Instead Sal and Hideo had incised a gash around the statue. Sal and Lodup then wrangled the hose connected to a large tank bolted to the submersible's flatbed and pushed it into the still-hot gash. They moved around the statue using the hose to extrude an unbroken line of dark gel into the cut. Lodup didn't understand it fully, but something to do with the petrification process rendered the surface of the structure resistant to the gel. They cut into it first to weaken it and, apparently, to bypass some sort of innate defence mechanism that resulted from the molecular bonding.

'Clear,' Hideo said over the comms. Sal and Lodup moved back from the statue. 'Sending the command now.' With a thought from Hideo, the nanites in the gel started to eat their way through the base of the statue.

'You going back in?' Sal asked over a closed link. They had some time before the gel finished its job.

'Not the mood he's in,' Lodup said.

'At least he's not filling the comms with bullshit waffle,' Sal said.

'What do you think they are?' Lodup asked, changing the subject. There was no reply from Sal for several moments.

'I don't know, and we don't ask.'

Lodup lapsed into silence, hanging neutrally buoyant in the water, waiting for the nanites in the gel to do their work.

They were joined by a number of security AUVs and one of the killer whales – Lodup was pretty sure it was Marvin. In the last week he'd seen the armoured orca on several occasions. Sal – and Hideo when he was in a more cheerful mood – had teased him about the whale stalking him. Lodup wasn't sure what was so funny about being stalked by a deep-diving armoured predator.

They removed the piscean/seed-pod structure using a combination of the Archie's armoured tentacles, its winch/crane systems and smart-matter airlifts, which were basically self-inflating, buoyancy-regulating underwater balloons.

Lodup was finning along next to the Archie with its cargo cradled beneath it. Marvin wasn't far behind. Sal and Hideo were on the other side of the giant squid. They were moving the piscean/seed-pod to one of the tethered wet sheds. Lodup had seen what happened to the statues earlier in the week. They cut into the basalt-like material and implanted what looked like eggs made of a material that resembled mercury. The eggs were then attached to hoses sunk in the seabed. Lodup assumed this would collect raw material for whatever it was they were doing.

Even allowing for his modified metabolism and the efficiency of the monofin, Lodup was reaching the end of his shift and starting to feel very tired. He moved closer to the seed-pod. Most of its surface was smooth and organic-looking, free from any sort of marine growth, but he found a slight protrusion and reached out to grab on to it and allow himself to be pulled along by the Archie, which was half-propelling itself, and half-using its free tentacles to stride across the seabed. He touched the basalt skin of the statue.

*

Glancing up as he made his way through the crowds, he saw one of the wedge-headed guardian servitors crouched atop the corner of a changing building, looking down at the bustling street. The air was filled with the smell of spices and the stink of so many peoples in close quarters that even the strong breeze blowing in from the azure ocean could not freshen the air.

He jostled one of the snake-headed people in ornate brocade robes that looked too heavy for the warmth of the day. The bad-tempered creature turned and hissed at him. He took a step back but it was on its way in a moment. Most of the other people in the street were humans of one kind or another, though many of them were pale, their skin starting to scale, their eyes becoming black pools. The favoured were taller, stronger, wore little but loincloths, and there was no hair anywhere on their bodies.

A pulsing blue light came from the centre of the city. He felt the power in the air, the strange taste in his mouth, the hairs on his arms standing up. Somehow he knew there would be one less star in the sky tonight. A shadow fell across him and he looked up. With a thrill he saw a massive tentacle, its tip transforming into much smaller tendrils and growing eyes. It reached through the wall of one of the changing buildings.

He heard a voice say something in a language he didn't quite understand, but which was tantalisingly familiar.

The light looked very bright. It washed out everything else for a while, but then his eyes polarised and things started to come into focus. Personal medical telemetry cascaded down his vision. He was breathing air – or what passed for it in Kanamwayso – and he was as warm as he ever got these days. His stress markers were elevated and he'd been given a sedative – which he could wipe from his system any time he wanted – but other than that he was fine.

Despite the lack of any apparent medical machinery other than the bed he was lying on, there was no mistaking that he was in some kind of sick-bay.

Siraja was kind enough to walk into his perception as if he had entered the room through the door. 'Hello, Mr Satakano,' the dragon-headed AI said.

'What happened?' Lodup asked.

'We were hoping you could tell us,' the AI said. 'You appeared to black out, and then we registered some interesting brain activity. Tell me, Mr Satakano, did you dream?'

Lodup considered the question. 'I sort of remember dreaming, but

I never remember my dreams,' he told the AI. He wasn't sure why he lied. He remembered the dream vividly. He was outside, in the city, but it was above the water under a bright blue, nearly cloudless sky. The architecture was still strange, difficult to look at, but much less ominous. He'd found the sense of wonder he'd been missing.

'I see,' Siraja said. It was very difficult to gauge the AI's draconic expression, though it probably had enough physiological and neural information to realise Lodup was lying. 'Mr Deane has taken you off the dive rota for a couple of days so that we can monitor you and make sure you're okay—'

'I'm not staying in sick-bay.'

'Understood.'

'There's nothing to do here – I may as well dive.' His day was divided into eight hours of getting wet, eight hours of troubled and not very restful sleep, and then eight hours of leisure time. After he had washed, eaten and performed the few chores that were not done for him, those hours were the most difficult. Those hours left him time to think, to wonder, to try and deal with the environment and the strange behaviour of his co-workers, and Siraja wanted to increase them.

'Until we're sure that you are fine and that you don't pose a risk to yourself, your fellow divers and the project, I'm afraid you will not be diving,' he said, not unkindly.

'What is the project, exactly?' Lodup asked.

'You are paid very well precisely so we don't have to answer questions like that,' Siraja said apologetically.

Lodup got up and looked around for something to wear. He found a pair of his shorts and one of his T-shirts. He started dressing.

'Let me get some sleep and I'll be good to go,' he muttered.

'That's Mr Deane's decision.'

'Yes, but it will be based on the data you provide for him.' Lodup stopped dressing and looked over at at Siraja. 'How do they do it? Siska, Yaroslav, Deane and whoever actually runs this place? Keep calm, I mean. Not lose it like the others. Because I think they've been down here a while.' Siraja didn't answer. 'Okay then, tell me this. The dreams, blacking out – am I on my way to losing it? To going thatch? Is this how it starts?'

The dragon-headed AI's reptilian eyes were unreadable. 'Sometimes.'

Lodup looked at Siraja for a moment. Then he nodded and finished dressing.

*

He tried reading, watching films, watching documentaries, watching mind-numbing sitcoms, listening to music, but he couldn't concentrate on anything. He had run over the dream again and again in his head. As far as he could tell, he didn't want to kill himself or anyone else. He was, however, left with the distinct feeling that there was something out there, in the city, something that wasn't alive, exactly, but which could still at least think.

The knock on the door made him jump. Lodup opened it with a thought. Hideo's features were slack, his eyes lifeless and focused elsewhere.

'Hideo?' Lodup asked.

Hideo stepped into Lodup's room. 'I need someone to talk to.'

'Er, come in,' Lodup told the submersible jockey. He was already dreading what was about to happen. He was pretty sure it would be incredibly awkward.

Hideo stepped into the room but stayed standing. 'Could we speak in private?' He was looking down, not making eye contact with Lodup. The door slid shut behind him.

'You okay, man?' Lodup was starting to get concerned now. He saw that Siraja was trying to open a comms link. He accepted it.

'Is everything okay?' the AI's voice asked.

'I'm not sure,' Lodup answered, subvocalizing. 'Hideo doesn't look right.'

'Who are you talking to?' Hideo asked.

'Siraja,' Lodup told him. 'He's worried about you.'

Hideo sat down on the end of Lodup's bed. Lodup moved his feet out of the way. As Hideo sat down, he moved a plastic bag he'd been carrying behind his back and put it in his lap.

'What's in the bag?' Lodup asked.

'I've been here for more than seventy years now, you know that? I can't go back, how would I explain it? I'm over a hundred years old.'

'What's in the bag?' Lodup asked again, nervously this time. He glanced down and saw that Hideo's dive knife was strapped to his calf.

'Lodup,' Siraja said, uncharacteristically using his first name, 'we have security personnel on the way to your location. Nod if you understand.'

'And the thing is,' Hideo said, 'more than anyone else – more than Sal, certainly – you and I are alike.'

Lodup nodded as if he was agreeing, though it was really for Siraja's benefit.

'Just keep him talking and as calm as possible,' the AI told him.

'We're like the immortals. We're real.'

'What do you mean?' Lodup asked, his curiosity overwhelming the fear that he had a crazy person sitting on the end of his bed.

Hideo stared at Lodup, who resisted the urge to curl up, to get as far away from the other man as possible. There was genuine hate and anger on Hideo's face. All of it appeared to be directed at Lodup.

'Why did they pick you?' he asked quietly. 'Do you think if I saw your face off and wear it, they'll believe that I'm you?' Lodup swallowed and stared at Hideo. The cheerful submersible pilot who had brought him down here a week ago, explained how everything worked, shown him the ropes, was gone. This was a different person. The only similarity was the skin the man wore. 'Do you want to see what's in the bag?'

'Erm, I don't think so,' Lodup said. He was bigger, he was pretty sure he was fitter and he had a black belt in Kajukenbo. All he needed to do was send the instruction for the door to open and make it past Hideo. Lodup was also no coward, and had worked in a number of dangerous situations. On two occasions he had been fired upon: once by suspected terrorists in the Philippines, and once by Indonesian pirates. On neither occasion had he frozen up as he had now.

'We are almost with you,' Siraja assured him.

'You're talking to him, aren't you?' Hideo asked. He opened the bag and started taking things out of it.

'Lodup,' Siraja said, 'when I tell you to, you need to curl up in the corner of the bed and make yourself as small a target as possible.'

Hideo placed a gun on the bed. A pistol – it looked like a Luger of the sort Lodup had seen in World War Two films, but wrong somehow. It was so close. He could have reached out and picked it up, but the distance between him and the gun appeared to stretch, distend, until the gun looked very far away. Next Hideo put some kind of electronic device down on the bed. It took a moment for Lodup to realise it was a heavily modified version of one of the entertainment tablets. That was followed by something hairy, and red, and wet. Lodup swallowed. He'd worked out what it was but didn't want to admit it. All moisture disappeared from his mouth.

'Wh-what did you do to her?' he managed.

Hideo's brief laugh was utterly devoid of humour. 'Isn't it self-evident? That's Sal's scalp. You took something from me, so I took something from you. That's fair, isn't it?'

'What did I take from you, Hideo?' Lodup had found a kernel of anger. He tried to nurse it, hoped it would be enough to get him through this. Hideo was playing with the tablet, tapping a series of commands on its touch screen.

'We are coming in now,' Siraja told him.

Lodup curled up in a ball on his bed as the room went dark. His night vision kicked in, and he could see Hideo sitting on the end of his bed. His eyes glowed, as did the tablet's screen. He was pointing the gun at Lodup.

'The routine was developed in the fifties. Yaroslav was making it more and more difficult for people to go thatch, total surveillance and all that. I think it was created by one of the dolphins, but a lot of folks think they had outside help. I've sealed the door, by the way. Oh, they'll get through, but this will give us some privacy.'

Lodup jumped as something hit the outside of the door. It took him several attempts to speak.

'I thought we were friends?'

Hideo was on his feet. 'No!' he screamed, his face apoplectic with rage. 'I thought we were friends!' He was brandishing the gun at Lodup, who was holding his hands up in front of him. 'But it's you!' He started poking himself in the head with the index finger of his left hand. 'You they talk to.'

'I don't know what you mean!' Lodup shouted.

Hideo appeared to calm down a little. 'You should have seen Sal at the end, Lodup. I gave her wings. Beautiful red wings, like a butterfly.' He cocked his head as if he was examining Lodup anew. The pistol was pointed at the Lodup's face. Hideo lowered it so it was pointing at his chest and pulled the trigger. The gun went click. Hideo stared at the gun in fury. Lodup all but evacuated his bowels. He was also staring at the gun. Then he looked up at Hideo, and Hideo looked down at him.

Lodup acted before he could think. He threw himself off the bed, tackling the smaller man around the waist, picking him up and slamming him into the wall. Hideo brought the pistol down repeatedly and painfully on Lodup's neck and the back of his head. Somehow Lodup managed to straighten up. He dropped Hideo over his shoulder, onto his head. The submersible pilot lost his grip on the pistol and reached for the dive knife. Lodup turned around, feeling nauseous from the head hits. He saw Hideo on the floor and started trying to kick and stamp, every Kajukenbo lesson forgotten in his desperation.

Hideo cried out as a number of the kicks and stamps contacted, but he managed to tear the dive knife from its sheath. Lodup jumped onto his bed to try and get away from the sharp, impossibly hard blade as Hideo slashed at him again and again. Lodup kept trying to back away but ran out of room. The blade was so sharp that he didn't even know he'd been cut. It was only when he felt something hot and wet that he glanced down and realised he and the bed were red.

Hideo's lack of expertise as a knife fighter meant that none of the slashes were fatal, but Lodup was still losing a lot of blood. Thinking he was dead and panicking, Lodup threw himself at Hideo again and managed to grab the wrist of the hand with the blade in it. The two of them crashed to the ground. Lodup was stronger, heavier and desperate. Hideo was insane. They thrashed around on the floor. Hideo's face was a mask of hatred and he was desperate to hurt Lodup. Lodup found himself underneath the other man, looking up at the diamond tip of the blade slowly being forced towards him. He didn't even notice the glow in the periphery of his night vision, coming from the door.

The thermite cutting charge blew a large hole in the sealed door. The rectangle of hardened composite material hit the ground, its glowing edges dulling from white to orange. Yaroslav was through first.

Suddenly Hideo disappeared as Yaroslav yanked the pilot into the air and threw him into a corner. As Hideo hit the wall, the room was illuminated by the flickering light of muzzle flare from the weapon of the woman who followed Yaroslav in.

Yaroslav picked Lodup up easily and pushed him into another corner, shielding him with his wide, squat body. There were another two short bursts from the other operative's SMG. Even suppressed, the noise of the gunfire was loud in the confined space. The first two three-round bursts in the chest had killed Hideo. The third all but decapitated him, spreading his head over the wall. The woman advanced, smoking SMG at the ready, to examine the body.

'Clear,' she said.

Yaroslav grabbed Lodup and half-dragged, half-carried him out of the room onto the catwalk outside. He saw more security personnel. Yaroslav deposited him on a gurney and the medical team started to look him over. Yaroslav turned and went straight back into the room.

'He's going into shock,' one of the medics said. Lodup was aware of a smashing noise from within his room and the lights came back on. He was injected with something. His clothes were being cut off. They sprayed the narrow wounds with a substance that looked like shaving cream. He glanced around at the other habitat staff out on the catwalks, all of them watching the show. Their faces were devoid of expression.

Yaroslav came out of the room holding Hideo's pistol. He ejected the round in the chamber, removed the magazine and made the weapon safe.

'Type ninety-four Nambu, standard-issue sidearm of the Japanese

Imperial Forces during World War Two,' he said, showing it to the security operative who'd done the shooting.

'Unreliable peace of shit,' the woman said. Lodup couldn't place her accent. Maybe Israeli. She looked down at him. 'Still, you're lucky to be alive.'

He was relieved when the sedative brought unconsciousness.

Consciousness returning wasn't entirely welcome. The sedative had resulted in dreamless sleep but he didn't feel rested. He was back in sick-bay with Siraja standing over him like a concerned relative.

'How are you feeling?' Siraja asked.

'You're monitoring my medical status, you probably know better than me,' Lodup said as he pushed the covers down and checked his body. He found a number of dressings across his stomach, chest and thighs, and there were more on his arms, covering defensive wounds. He pulled one of the dressings back. The wound was now ugly red scar tissue.

Lodup climbed off the bed. He was only wearing his boxer shorts. He couldn't face going back to the bloodstained room, though maybe it had been cleaned already. They were, after all, very efficient down here.

'Perhaps you should rest before—' Siraja started.

Lodup turned on the dragon-headed AI. 'How long before I go crazy?' he demanded. He knew that to anyone watching it would look as if he was shouting at nothing, but he didn't care.

'That doesn't happen to everyone,' Siraja said quietly.

'Did he kill Sal?' Lodup asked. Siraja simply nodded. Lodup closed his eyes, his fists clenching. They had been lovers but not in love. It had never felt close or intimate, more convenient, but he had liked her. She certainly hadn't deserved that. He opened his eyes again, glared at Siraja and then walked past the image of the AI.

Siraja appeared in the corridor next to Lodup.

'Where are you going?' Siraja enquired.

Lodup didn't answer. The grass-like carpet felt warm under his bare feet. None of the people who passed him in the corridor gave him a second glance, despite the fact that he wasn't wearing anything other than his boxer shorts. He reached the stairwell and went up the stairs two at a time. Siraja was waiting for him at the top.

'If you return to sick-bay, I could answer all your questions.'

Lodup made a point of walking through the dragon-headed AI's image.

Siraja was waiting at the door to C&C.

'Going to stop me?' Lodup asked.

Siraja opened his mouth to answer as the door opened. Lodup walked past the AI but wasn't surprised to find the image of Siraja waiting for him inside. Siska was standing, hands behind her back, in front of the large window overlooking the moon pool. The window was polarising, dimming the harsh white light coming from beyond it.

Lodup glanced to his left and wasn't surprised to see Yaroslav there, too.

'Thank you,' Lodup said. The Russian just nodded.

'Enact privacy protocol,' Siska said. Lodup was pretty sure the order was given out loud for his benefit. 'They cannot hear you now,' Siska said to Lodup, referring to the C&C staff lying on their couches.

'Well, I'll just have to take your word for it, won't I?' Lodup said acidly.

'Do you want Siraja present?' Siska asked.

'Does it make any difference what I want?'

'Not really.'

'Then he can stay, but I'd rather he kept quiet.'

The look of hurt on Siraja's draconic features was practically comical.

'Who's in charge?' Lodup demanded.

'As far as you're concerned, I am,' Siska said.

'And as far as you're concerned?'

Siska's expression hadn't really changed but Lodup felt as if the temperature had dropped in the room. Actually, he wouldn't put it past them to try such a theatrical move.

'We are making a special effort with you, Mr Satakano, but that only extends so far. I don't like you coming in here and barking at me.'

Lodup stared at her incredulously. 'I just got fucking slashed!' he shouted at her. Her face hardened, but she didn't say anything. Lodup glanced over at Yaroslav, but the Russian hadn't moved. 'Look, you're going to modify my memory anyway, aren't you? So what difference does it make if you tell me?'

'What do you wish to know?' Siska asked coldly. Today her long braided ponytail had been arranged into a loop. It looked like a hangman's knot to Lodup.

'Why are you making a special effort with me? Why am I different? Why was Hideo, why Sal? What's wrong with the people here?'

'They're clones,' Siska said evenly.

It took a moment for what she'd said to sink in. Lodup's first instinct was to accuse her of bullshit, but it made sense. With the level of technology they had, why wouldn't they be able to clone?

'We need people with certain skill sets. If they started disappearing all over the world, people would notice. Cloning made them easier to modify—'

'And easier to control?' Lodup suggested. Yaroslav actually laughed. It explained why people he'd known for years had barely acknowledged him. 'Am I a clone?'

'No,' Siska said. 'Neither was Hideo, which was why we thought he would be good company for you.'

Lodup laughed bitterly. 'And Sal?'

'She was a clone.'

'What was she supposed to be, a sex toy?'

Siska sighed. 'We fully reinitiated her personality and left you to it.'

Then something occurred to Lodup. 'So Hideo was a survivor from a Japanese U-boat, right?'

'Yes. He'd seen too much, his rescue was arguably an oversight, we could have wiped his memories. But he elected to stay, and he was very good at his job.'

'Which explains why he wasn't a clone, and I'm guessing you're not, either,' he said to Siska. He pointed a thumb at Yaroslav. 'He's not. Deane?' Siska said nothing. 'So why aren't I a clone?'

'You were,' Siska told him. 'There was an accident.'

'You went thatch,' Yaroslav said.

Lodup turned to stare angrily at the Russian. 'You mean this place has driven me insane before?' he demanded.

'You killed five people, and nearly killed one of my team,' Yaroslav told him, his strong Russian accent devoid of emotion. 'I put you down myself.'

Lodup could not imagine killing anyone, let alone with the brutality he'd seen evident in Hideo and the others who had gone thatch during his short time here.

'So you thought you'd get the real me down here? Why not just clone me again?' he asked, mostly to avoid thinking about his alternative self as a murderer.

'You're one of the best salvage operators in the business. We required your skills. It takes time to bring a clone to maturity,' Siska told him.

'So you're in a hurry?'

Neither Yaroslav nor Siska said anything.

'What are you doing here?'

'We told you, we're harvesting—' Siska told him.

'Alien technology. What are these things? And don't just skate over the subject this time. Like I said, you'll wipe my memory anyway, so there's no reason not to tell me.'

'Very well,' Siska replied. 'They are the source of all life on this planet.'

Lodup stared at her and then laughed. 'So Darwin was wrong – there is an intelligent creator after all?' he finally managed. He could accept the city, the technology, though he wondered how much of that was due to the modifications they'd made to his brain. This was stretching credulity just a little too far.

'No, Darwin was right about most of it. Some of it was engineered to happen. Certain organisms, like humans, were given a hand, but the rest of it evolved naturally, slowly responding to the stimulus of the environment after its initial creation. We're not talking about a god, though their biotechnology was such that it's easy to make that mistake. What we're talking about is bioengineering on a massive scale.'

'Bullshit,' Lodup told her.

'Why would I lie?' Siska asked. 'You asked for the truth. Do you know what panspermia is?' Lodup shook his head. 'It's the theory that life is distributed through the universe via spores. What you did today was surgery – you cut an extremophile seed-pod from that building.'

'Where did they come from?' Lodup asked, still trying desperately to grasp what he'd just been told.

'We don't know, but we suspect they were also bioengineered.' There was a degree of cruel relish in her voice.

'By what?' Lodup asked, appalled.

'We don't know. Maybe god. Tell me, now that you know, do you feel any better?'

Lodup shook his head. 'Everything we know—'

'Is a smoke-screen based on partial truths propagated by the Circle.'

'This is monstrous.'

'We operated on your brain so you would be capable of dealing with what you see and experience here. We purposefully engineer people so they can cope, and even then it doesn't always work. What do you think the knowledge of this place would do to humanity?' Siska demanded angrily. She was leaning on the hardwood of the elliptical table.

Lodup thought about it. If the knowledge didn't drive humanity itself mad, there would certainly be attempts to try and take control of the Kanamwayso.

'What happened here?' Lodup asked, for something to say, for a moment's respite.

'We don't know,' Siska said, guardedly.

'They were attacked,' Yaroslav said.

'By what?' Lodup asked. He did not wish to think too much about what could attack such creatures and win.

'We don't know that for sure,' Siska said irritably, glaring at Yaroslav. 'All we know is that there was some kind of disaster.'

'And it killed them?' Lodup asked. Neither Yaroslav nor Siska said anything. 'They're dead, aren't they?'

Siska looked down and refused to meet Lodup's demanding glare. 'We cannot find any evidence to suggest that they are anything other than dead.'

'But?' Lodup said. Siska shook her head angrily. 'Fucking but!'

'Some here believe they are in contact with the sleeping minds of the Seeders.' It was Siraja who spoke. 'And I know you are thinking of your dreams, Mr Satakano, but working in the city takes its psychological toll. They are probably nothing more than dreams.'

'Probably?' Lodup repeated. Nobody said anything. 'That's what the cults are about, isn't it?' Silence. 'So if they're seed-pods, what are you doing to them in the sheds? What are those egg-shaped things? Nano-tech?'

Siska opened her mouth to answer.

'I'm afraid that will have to be enough,' Siraja said quietly.

'Shut the fuck up, lizard,' Lodup snapped, and then to Siska: 'Answer my question.'

Siska looked up at him. 'And I think that's about as much insubordination as I will tolerate today. I have indulged you because of the incident—'

'Incident? Incident! You mean—' Lodup started angrily.

'That's enough.' Siska's quiet tone was enough to silence Lodup. 'Do you wish to leave?'

'No,' Lodup said after some thought, though the answer surprised him. 'But I wonder if that's because you've tampered with my brain. One final question – the cult activity, the dreams, people going thatch. It's getting worse, isn't it?'

Nobody answered. Lodup just nodded, then turned on his heel and walked out of C&C.

Siska waited until the door closed.

'Well?' she asked.

'I agree with your assessment,' Siraja said. 'I don't believe he is any greater a risk than he was before. There's nothing he can do with what he knows. The Brass City already know a great deal more than what we have just told Mr Satakano.'

'Besides, it will all be irrelevant soon,' Yaroslav said.

26
A Long Time After the Loss

The Alchemist looked up at the psychopath, the insect, the feline woman and the human natural. He wanted to make distressed clicking noises and swim in ever-decreasing circles, but he didn't have the physiology for it. The tears that sprang from his eyes were simply an autonomic response.

'I don't suppose you have a cetacean body and a large pool on board, do you?' he asked through the tears. Scab shook his head.

'We could probably configure some kind of pool—' Vic started, but Scab cut him off with a look.

'What do you want a dolphin's body for?' the female human nat asked. A device on a choker around her throat was translating her voice. Vic had fabricated it for her. She also had an ear crystal that translated what she heard into common. The Alchemist looked at her like she was an idiot.

'He is one,' Vic said quietly.

'I was just thinking how much he resembled a large fish-like mammal,' the nat muttered. Her own words in pre-Loss were getting mixed up with the louder transmissions from the translator. 'Is he part of the plan to sell me into slavery?' She was wearing what looked like multiple layers of lace. She was unarmed and moved so sluggishly compared to Scab, Vic and the feline woman that she was obviously unaugmented.

'He's a Church bridge tech, isn't he?' the feline asked.

'What do you fucking want from me?' the dolphin-downloaded-into-human-form demanded. He had decided to remain lying on the cold metal floor of the ship's cargo bay, close to the airlock. He had always considered himself a coward, but he was hoping for an opportunity to be ejected out of the airlock, even if it was into the strange vacuum of Red Space.

'Hi, I'm Talia,' the human woman said pettishly. 'You'll probably be vivisecting me later, but it's so nice to meet another kidnap victim.'

She stepped forward, bent down and offered the Alchemist her hand. He looked at it as if it was covered in excrement. 'No, that's not right at all. What you do is take the hand, shake it and introduce yourself.'

'I don't want to touch you,' he said, though he remembered the human greeting convention from his time on Suburbia.

Talia withdrew the hand and straightened up. 'Everybody's so fucking rude and kidnappy,' she groused. 'Can you manage a name?'

'He's the Alchemist,' Vic said, trying to be helpful.

'Really? He doesn't have a proper name like John, or Steve, or Scab?' she asked sarcastically.

'Look, my name's a series of clicks and ... Why am I here?'

'Did you like where you were?' the feline woman asked. As far as he could make out, her expression was one of curiosity, though not necessarily with regard to the question she had just asked.

'Have you any idea what you fucking did to me?' he demanded, turning on Scab.

'I got paid for apprehending you.'

'You fucking shot me!'

'I thought you were a talking insect,' Scab told him, as if that explained everything.

Talia looked up at Vic. The 'sect had one of his upper hands pressed against his forehead in a very human gesture.

'It's kind of difficult to explain,' Vic said.

A pause.

'She is the key to bridge tech,' Scab finally said.

'Yaaay me!' Talia mock-cheered.

The Alchemist stared at Scab, then at Talia, and then back at Scab. Scab lit a cigarette and leaned against the bulkhead of the cargo bay.

'You don't look all that surprised,' the feline said.

'Do have you any idea what that place was like? The constant repetitive inanity of it all? Being locked in this ungainly body, forced to look on as, day after day, I helped condition myself into an utterly pointless existence? They take everything from you. Your cell is one hundred and eighty pounds of sweating, stinking flesh and desperation. They teach you that you are nothing, meaningless, that your will is irrelevant.'

Scab sighed audibly. 'So?' he asked.

'I'd like to go back.'

'Do you think that's likely?' Scab asked.

'They took everything. Just how do you propose to get me to co-operate? I'm ready to die. I've lived in the torture immersion—'

'You'll do as you're told. Everybody does,' Scab said quietly. Talia glared at him and Vic looked down. The feline's expression was unreadable. Scab shrugged himself off the bulkhead and headed towards the ramp leading out of the cargo bay. Talia looked at him hopefully but he ignored her. She missed the contemptuous glance the feline gave her. Scab's P-sat appeared out of the gloom and fell in behind him.

'Make life easy on yourself,' the feline said.

'I think I'm going to call him Steve. Steve the dolphin,' Talia said mock-cheerfully.

'Fuck you,' the Alchemist muttered.

'This is Elodie Negrinotti,' Vic told the dolphin. 'I'm afraid you'll be getting to know each other very intimately.'

'Actually, *I'll* be getting to know *him* very intimately,' the feline said.

The Alchemist, Steve, didn't like the way she said it one bit.

Vic and a somewhat peevish Talia helped the newly christened 'Steve' settle in. They assembled clothes and food. They instructed the quantum dots – which acted like programmable atoms – at the heart of the smart matter from which the converted yacht had been grown to create a room for Scab's latest prisoner. They gave him a smart sedative designed to fool human physiology into actually falling asleep, rather than just a state of sedation. When he finally awoke, Vic administered the dolphin a cocktail of drugs at 'Steve's' request, and with Scab's permission. Those enabled him to keep emotions like fear, anger and an overwhelming hatred of Scab down to a manageable level.

Summoned by Scab, they assembled in the *Basilisk II*'s lounge. The spacious yacht was reconfiguring the room into a large open-plan, split-level area with lots of low, comfortable, immaculately white sofas. Vic still had problems getting them to conform to his insectile physiology, despite 'facing custom specs to the ship's neutered AI. He'd been told this was because the programmers of assembly templates for luxury goods never envisaged selling them to the utilitarian 'sects. Vic, however, suspected that Scab played with the furniture's programming just to mess with him.

'I see where this is going. She's got something to do with bridge tech, I used to be a bridge technician for the Church, but it's just not that simple,' Steve told them when they were all assembled. He was seated at a table that had grown out of the floor. It was rather grandiose, bathed in a blue glow from the large arched window formed from parts of the smart-metal hull turned transparent. The window looked out onto Red Space, but a filter in the smart matter turned the red light blue. Steve was tucking into a mock-lobster the assembler had managed to create. He was using smart utensils, as he had to relearn how to use his bipedal form now that his core personality was dominant in the human body. He took a sip from a large glass of champagne the yacht had also assembled. 'For a start, they're just going to—'

'Hunt us down?' Vic suggested as he tried to make himself comfortable on the constantly reconfiguring sofa. 'Kill us? Drop us into time-contracted torture immersions for all eternity? Wow, it hadn't occurred to any of us that having access to the most valuable secret in Known Space would cause us any inconvenience whatsoever.'

'It won't just be the—'

'Church?' Vic finished. 'Really? You think the Consortium and the Monarchist systems might be interested, too, put all sorts of resources onto us, like, oh, I don't know, the fucking Elite that chased you out of Suburbia? Not to mention a massive price on our heads.'

Steve chuckled at this last.

'He goes on about this a lot,' Scab said. Everyone turned to look at the human, unsure if he was joking or not. He had an expression of mild consternation on his made-up, normally emotionless face. He was half-slouched, half-lying in his shirtsleeves on one of the sofas and basking in the blue glow. Oddly, though, he was still wearing his hat.

'Shame,' Steve said. For someone with the psychological profile of an abject coward, he appeared to have little trouble standing up to Scab.

'Just out of interest, does anyone have any idea what this big secret is?' Talia demanded. She was curled up on the sofa with her now nearly omnipresent large glass of red wine and a burning inhalable narcotic.

'You do,' Scab said quietly. 'There's a reason you were hooked up to the Seeder ship.'

Steve turned to look at Talia, appalled.

'And so does he,' Elodie said, nodding at the dolphin in human form.

'But I can't help you!' Steve looked like he was close to tears again. It didn't appear to be stopping him digging into his lobster, however. Vic didn't like watching him eat it. The crustacean was just a little too close to insect for his taste. 'Do you think after you guys turned me over to the Consortium they didn't try and break my conditioning? Do you know what kind of resources they threw at me?' He stood up and screamed at Scab: 'Have you any idea how they fucking tortured me until, out of pure fucking frustration, they threw me in that horrible place instead of just killing me?'

Vic motioned with all four hands for Steve to calm himself.

'I've never really understood why people think I'd have any interest in what I've done to them,' Scab said.

Elodie sighed, lay down on the back of one of the sofas and then slithered onto the seat, stretching in a very feline manner. 'It's not all to do with you,' she told Scab. 'This is for him, its catharsis. Probably the same reason you kill people, blow up buildings, spay AIs, that sort of thing.'

'Oh,' Scab said after some consideration. 'You would have more insight into that than me.' Elodie's laughter sounded humourless. Scab glanced over at Talia and pointed at Steve. The gesture looked odd to Vic. 'He knows your secret.'

'Once, when I worked at the Cathedral. It would have been eaten out of me when I escaped,' Steve said through a mouthful of crustacean. His anger had apparently given away to hunger.

'Perhaps, perhaps not,' Scab said.

'It's not quite that simple,' Elodie said. 'After all, you worked out the connection between bridge technology and our pre-Loss friend here.'

Steve looked over at at Talia. She raised her glass to him. He opened his mouth to say something, but instead clasped his head and started to scream, then collapsed onto the carpet. He dragged the lobster down with him. The carpet immediately began reabsorbing the matter of his meal, breaking it down into its constituent carbon molecules. His face convulsed and then locked in a fixed expression. The tone of his voice changed, but he was still screaming.

Talia looked shocked and then jumped up to help him.

'Wait!' It was Scab.

Despite herself, Talia stopped. 'What for?' she demanded.

'I want to see this.'

Talia shook her head and moved over to kneel by Steve.

'There's nothing you can do,' Elodie said, inspecting her nails. She sounded extremely bored. 'It's Church conditioning. He was about to say something he shouldn't.' Steve had stopped screaming now. His facial muscles still appeared to be paralysed, but he was making a wheezing, rattling noise. 'It's actually a multiple-redundancy system. Steve's right – an aggressive neunonic process eats most of a bridge tech's knowledge as soon as they leave the Cathedral, or a Church ship, but the process isn't total, so they add the conditioning. Any thought of divulging information on bridge technology, they cease talking and are overcome with agony. Attempt to remove the information neurologically and the subject is mindwiped and killed.'

'See, I told you,' a very hoarse Steve managed as he gripped the edge of the table and pulled himself onto his knees. 'Please stop touching me,' he told Talia, who was still trying to help him.

'Why is everyone in the future an arsehole?' she muttered as she returned to the sofa.

'So he's of no use?' Vic asked. 'I'm *so* glad we went to all the effort to get him out.'

'If it's any consolation, I don't think you were a great deal of help in my escape,' Steve croaked as he pulled himself back into his chair. 'Can I have some more drugs, please?'

Vic glanced over at Scab, who nodded. Vic 'faced instructions to the ship, and a moment later, he reached down as the primitive hypodermic of narcotics grew through the sofa's upholstery. He walked over and injected its contents into Steve. A few moments after that, the dolphin's pained expression dissolved.

'It wasn't for nothing,' Scab said as he lit a cigarette. Vic wondered if the cigarette was a Pavlovian response to the drugs he'd just administered to Steve. 'I have one of the best intrusion specialists in Known Space working for me—'

'No!' a now blissfully drugged Steve shouted, slurring slightly. Scab frowned at the interruption. 'You don't have the best intrusion specialist in Known Space. The Consortium does, because they have all the credit, all the resources and even *they* couldn't break it. You're wasting your time.'

'No—' Scab started.

'Yes! I was there, I fucking lived through it, thanks to you, you—' Steve stopped just short of whatever he was about to say. Scab had his own way of conditioning people, Vic thought, though the look of genuine irritation on his partner's face boded ill for Steve. 'It's not going to be something else just because you will it so.'

'It was only one company within the Consortium. One board member,' Scab said.

Elodie was paying more attention now, her expression deeply sceptical.

'It doesn't matter. We're going to try, and you're going to cooperate,' Scab said. Steve opened his mouth to argue. 'Besides, that's not all I want you for.'

'Put me in a pool and I can normally do one and half somersaults before I hit the water,' Steve suggested.

'I need you to make me some Key,' Scab told Steve. This got Elodie and Vic's full attention.

'What's Key?' Talia asked.

'A hallucinogen so potent it's actually illegal,' Vic said. 'Very difficult and expensive to produce. It's what he went down for.' Vic nodded at Steve.

'No, I was heavily protected. The people who could afford it wanted me there. I went down because I'm an ex-Church bridge tech,' Steve said bitterly. 'But sure, Scab, why not. I'll do six impossible things before breakfast.' Elodie and Vic looked puzzled, Scab was oblivious, but Talia was pleased that she finally understood a reference. 'And where are we supposed to get the dragons from?' he demanded sarcastically.

'It's not a hallucinogen. I'll find the dragons,' Scab said.

Steve just stared at him. 'Oh, well, if that's the case, it's simply a matter of me agreeing to help you, then.' Steve pretended to give the subject some thought. 'So, having given it some thought, go and fuck yourself.'

Talia stifled a laugh.

'I'd raise an eyebrow if I had one,' Vic commented.

Scab was watching Steve impassively. Then he looked down. 'I don't understand this,' he began quietly. 'I have explained what we're going to be doing. Why do we have to talk about it?' Scab looked up at Steve with his dead eyes. Only Vic knew him well enough to be aware that violence was now even closer than it usually was with his 'partner', and it was normally pretty close.

Despite his bravado, Steve blanched. Then he appeared to bolster himself. 'You don't get it,' Steve said. 'You can't do anything to me any more.'

Scab was on his feet and heading towards Steve.

'Wait!' Elodie shouted. Scab ignored her. 'If you kill him, then we've just been wasting our time.' Scab stopped. Long-term gratification warred with short-term pleasure. He looked calm, but Vic knew his partner was furious. If there was one thing Scab hated, it was being defied. 'Just give me a moment, please,' Elodie said turning to Steve. 'What do you want?'

Scab turned around to look at Elodie, his expression unreadable. She ignored him.

'Fine,' Steve said. 'I want access to whatever this ship can produce in terms of food and drugs. I want neunonics and augments to a specification that I will provide. I'll need this for the work. I'll require some equipment, much of it specialised enough that the ship won't be able to assemble it. I want a cetacean body – again, I'll provide the specs – which of course means I'll need a pool and a P-sat with manipulators.'

'Yes, yes,' Scab said, 'but I'll decide the specs and install a meat-hack backdoor, and yes, you can have the body but you're not getting the pool so it will be pretty useless, and yes, but I'll have override,' Scab told him.

'Then no deal,' Steve replied and crossed his arms petulantly.

'The ship can't sustain a pool,' Scab told him.

'It can, actually,' Vic said helpfully. 'It's in the original template. It'll need a bit of reconfiguration, and we'll have to find an external source to feed the carbon reservoirs whilst it's being reconfigured, but it's completely doable.' It was only when he'd finished that it occurred to Vic that Scab would have known all that. Scab was staring at him.

'I think a pool's a great idea,' Talia announced, and took another long draw on her smouldering inhalable narcotic.

'You're a prisoner,' Scab said, a slight tone of irritation creeping into his voice.

'Fine, then I'm not going to cooperate, either,' Talia said and crossed her arms.

'I can't see a lack of cooperation being problematic during vivi-section,' Elodie said. Talia glared at the other woman. 'Why not the pool?' she asked Scab.

'Because there's no need for me to do it,' Scab said. 'And I don't like the smell.'

'The environmental systems will scrub it—' Vic started.

'It doesn't matter how good they are, you can always smell it on a ship of this size.'

'What about an immersion?' Elodie asked.

'I want a pool!' Talia demanded. Vic caught the look Elodie gave her. He suspected the feline was trying hard not to slap the pre-Loss human.

'I know the difference,' Steve answered.

'You know what immersion means, right?' Vic asked.

'I know the difference.'

'From an expeditious perspective, it's easier to give him what he wants,' Elodie told Scab. 'His cooperation will make what I have to do easier.' Steve laughed at that.

'I thought cats didn't like water,' Talia said waspishly. Elodie ig-nored her.

'I don't care about his cooperation or making your job easier. Those factors are both irrelevant as long as I get what I want,' Scab told the feline.

Talia laughed. 'You sound like a child,' the pre-Loss human told him. Scab glanced over at her, now openly irritated, and Vic started to fear for her. He reached out and put a hand on her shoulder. She looked up at him and he just shook his head, hoping she'd take the hint.

'Okay, let me put it this way.' Elodie sounded like she was reaching the limits of her patience as well. 'You are more likely to get what you want if you use your godlike power over all of us and allow this magnanimous concession.'

Scab gave this some thought. 'Agreed, but I never want to have another conversation like this again. They're ... difficult.'

'One more thing,' Steve said.

Scab's tumbler pistol was suddenly in his hand. With someone other than Scab, Vic would have taken the gesture to be somewhat melodramatic. From Scab, Vic was pretty sure it was just a coping mechanism to get him through the next few difficult moments.

'That looks like release to me,' Steve said, nodding at the anachronistic revolver. Scab looked confused until he glanced down. He appeared to be genuinely surprised to find that he was holding the tumbler pistol. 'I want a suicide solution.'

Elodie sighed.

'Obviously. Not.' Scab took his time enunciating the words carefully.

'You're not going to like any of the things I'll be doing to you. You're going to want to die a lot,' Elodie told him.

'It's not for you. It's for when the Church finds you, or an Elite comes knocking on the hull. This is non-negotiable.'

'This isn't a negotiation!' Scab suddenly shouted. Elodie looked up sharply. Talia let out a little scream. Vic emitted terror-signifying pheromones. He had never heard Scab shout before. Scab stalked out of the lounge. Vic was pretty sure it was so he wouldn't kill everyone in it.

Steve turned to Elodie. 'We'll come up with some compromise,' she told the dolphin.

'Yes, Scab appears to be all about the compromise,' Steve replied caustically. 'The prisoners wearing other people's faces?'

'Nothing to do with us,' Elodie told him.

'An imprisoned street sect?' Vic asked.

'That many? In the same place? Bit of a coincidence. I think it was a meat-hack. I think their core personalities were corrupted when they reasserted. Any idea who would do that?' Steve asked a series of blank expressions. 'Do you know what the Hungry Nothingness is?' The expressions remained blank.

'The ship,' Talia started. 'It was afraid of something. It was alone because its family had caught madness like a disease.'

'What does that mean?' Elodie demanded. Talia lapsed into sulky silence.

'Talia?' Vic coaxed gently.

'I don't know! All right? It ... I ... we didn't think like I do now, okay?'

Vic just nodded. Elodie glanced over at Vic; the feline looked worried. He suspected it had more to do with Scab than the meat-hack on Suburbia.

Nobody saw Scab for two days. They couldn't even detect his whereabouts on the ship. They had no idea where they were going as he'd locked everyone out of the navigation systems. All they knew was that they were in Red Space somewhere, though they appeared to be quite a distance from the Church beacons. This was making everyone nervous. Vic theorised that Scab was taking time to calm himself down. He suspected that Scab had sunk into the *Basilisk II*'s superstructure, feeding himself drugs and living in horrible immersions.

Then Scab returned, apparently back to his old self. He did not provide an explanation for his disappearance – not that any of them had expected one.

The lounge disappeared, to be replaced by some deckchairs and sunloungers around a large, deep and very empty swimming pool. They hadn't dropped back into Real Space to mine matter to fill it yet. Scab's early reconfiguration felt a little like petty spite.

Talia was sitting on the carpeted corridor outside Scab's room, cross-legged on a blanket she'd had assembled. She was smoking a mentholated cigarette. It didn't matter how many times she'd tried to explain the concept of a mentholated cigarette to the ship, they still didn't taste right. She'd been there for some time. The white carpet should have shown the evidence of this in stubbed-out cigarettes, but the carpet kept on eating them. Finally Scab walked by.

'Hey,' she said, looking up at him, her eyes wide, only a little water in them. 'Can we talk?'

'About what?' he asked, genuinely confused. Talia wasn't sure what to say next. He turned to leave, but she grabbed his trouser leg. Suddenly he was standing several steps away, relaxing into a more normal pose, and she no longer had hold of anything. Talia had barely seen him move.

'I mean, we slept together,' she told him, her voice sounding small. He shook his head, looking for relevance. 'That means nothing?'

'It's something I've done, I suppose. Why are you crying?'

'I'm not,' she snapped, wiping away tears. Scab turned to leave. 'Wait!' Scab stopped and turned back. 'Look, I want to do something.'

'So?'

'I mean other than just be a prisoner.'

'You are a prisoner.'

'The things in your head.'

'Neunonics.'

'Yes. I want them. I want to be improved, to have ... augments.'

Scab looked at her for a moment, as if he was studying her anew. 'No.'

'Why not?'

'Don't speak to me like that,' he said. She looked defiant for a moment, but her resolve soon crumbled and she looked down. 'It could affect whatever's inside you. I can't take the risk. If you want to know things, learn skills, then you'll have to do it the hard way.'

'Like you did?' she spat. There was a certain assumption on her part that he was little more than a technological horror.

'Yes,' he said simply.

'I want to be like you and El—' Talia started. Scab's hand shot out and grabbed her around the neck. Squeezing the air out of her, he picked her up and dangled her above the carpeted floor. Stared into her panicked eyes as she clawed at him and fought for breath. He watched her with dead eyes. She felt herself starting to lose consciousness. Then he let go and she collapsed into a sobbing, gasping heap on the floor. Scab walked into his room.

'Well, that was beyond pathetic,' a voice said from further down the corridor. Talia's head jerked up at the sound of the voice to see Elodie move out of the shadows. Talia wasn't sure how she did it but Elodie always appeared to be advancing out of shadow. 'Looking for short cuts?'

'Y ... you ... *you* use them,' Talia managed between the sobs and gasping for breath.

'To keep up with the competition. But neunonics and augments will only get you so far. My skills are hard earned, and you're too soft to learn them.'

'Would you—'

'No,' Elodie said, laughing.

'Why not?'

'I don't even like you.'

'Why not?'

Elodie knelt down by Talia and reached out to wipe one of the human girl's tears away. Then she tasted it.

'You annoy me because you're weak. Tell me, why are you crying? You've been choked and beaten by lovers before, right? Are you angry because you didn't get what you want, or because your violent bastard of an ex-lover isn't interested in you any more?' Talia glared at the feline woman. 'Do you know why he fucked you?' she asked, rhetorically. 'Because he collects experiences in a desperate attempt to feel something.'

'What do you do for him, then?' Talia demanded angrily.

'Why would I tell you that?' she asked. Talia spat in her face. Elodie glared at her, genuinely surprised that Talia had the gall to do something like that. Her fingernails grew into claws. 'Do you know how easy it would be for me to kill you right now?' she asked, her tone dangerous.

'You can't!' Talia cried triumphantly. 'Your fucking psycho boyfriend wouldn't let you!'

Elodie glared at her, stood up and headed towards Scab's room, wiping the spit off her face. She paused by the door and looked back over her shoulder.

'Fuck the insect. It'll be good for your self-esteem,' Elodie told her. Talia honestly wasn't sure if she was being cruel or not.

Vic was coming to the conclusion that a tear-stained invitation to a human woman's room to watch her drink too much red wine must be an intrinsic part of some long-winded human mating ritual.

Talia complained that he was too hard – which set her giggling – and angular for hugs. She covered him with something called a duvet and lay wrapped in that, cradled by his four arms, complaining bitterly about both Scab, which Vic could understand, and Elodie, who Vic rather liked.

'It's okay to spit and hiss at her, right?' Talia asked.

Vic pondered this. 'She's a feline. I imagine she'd be better at it than you.'

A more-than-a-little-drunk Talia gave this some thought and finally nodded in agreement. 'There's nothing for me here,' she said. 'With the ship it was different. We shared something, but here everything I ever knew is gone. All my friends ...' She appeared to be hunting for the right words. 'Everything and everyone here is really mean. Even the dolphin, and I thought they were supposed to be cute.'

'You've got me,' Vic said, hopefully. He was trying to stop his mandibles clattering together so he didn't sound threatening in any way.

Talia looked up at him but he couldn't decipher her expression.

'We're not friends,' Talia said.

Vic had researched this feeling after her last rejection of him. It was sung about in pre-Loss songs a lot. Apparently it was the result of the neurosurgery to make him more human, and it was called having your heart broken.

'This is just Stockholm Syndrome,' she told him. Vic had no idea what Stockholm was. 'These immersion things – can you customise them?'

'Yes,' Vic managed, feeling miserable. She hadn't noticed.

'Can you, I don't know, take my memories and make one like it used to be for me, only better?'

Vic nodded. 'But your mind will know,' he told her. 'It always knows.'

There were tears on her face now. She sat up. 'I don't want to be a slave. I don't want to be vivisected. When the time comes, will you kill me?' she asked earnestly through the tears.

Vic looked at her for a very long time. 'No,' he said eventually, holding her stare. 'I can't do that.'

'Fucking coward!' she spat and turned away from him. 'Get out.'

'Talia!'

'Now! Or are you determined to drive home the fact that I'm utterly powerless?'

Vic got up and headed for the door. He wanted to tell her that they were in a total surveillance environment. A panopticon. Whatever he said, Scab would find out. Vic would kill Talia if that was what it would take to prove himself to her, but he hid that decision deep down where Scab couldn't find it with anything other than the most thorough mental audit. But he set certain parameters on what would need to happen before this decision – his resolve to kill Talia for her own sake – would come to the fore.

27
Ancient Britain

Fachtna stood transfixed, bathed in the red glow, looking at the flames. He was different now. Things didn't make sense and hadn't for quite some time, but what he was seeing now didn't make sense even in terms of the transformed land, the land that had changed to suit the fevered nightmares inflicted on the Muileartach. This land that seethed and churned with new life. This land that he now served. There shouldn't be any people left. There should only be the goddess's children.

There were just enough roundhouses to form a small village. They had built a deep defensive ditch around them, then fed it with wood, peat, oil and other fuel. Then they set light to it, surrounding the village with a ring of fire. Behind the ring they had made a rough palisade wall of earth, stone and wood. It might have been enough to keep out some of the Muileartach's smaller children, but the village should have fallen quickly. Instead one of her giant idiot children, something part-worm, part-slug and part-insect, lay across the burning ditch, patches of its flesh bubbling and bursting from the heat of the flames. Its head had destroyed part of the palisade.

The land around was so fecund with plant life – much of it animated – and blister-like growths in the earth itself gestating more monstrosities that it was difficult to tell what the land was like before the spawn came. Judging by the people manning the ramparts, he suspected it had been rich land and their granaries had been full. To protect themselves from the seeds in the air they would have needed their own wards, and powerful ones, for not even those of the *Ubh Blaosc*, gifted to his people by the Lloigor, long since gone, had been enough to fully protect him. Though he could still feel the war being fought within his body between the Lloigor magic and that of Muileartach.

Around him, the idiot living dead that followed him – though he was not sure if they obeyed him – swayed in the warm wind and the smoke from the fire. Fachtna felt some of his now-living armour grow deeper into his flesh. He had become used to the pain.

'I am Fachtna, the Gael!' he shouted. *I am Fachtna the outcast, Fachtna the* drui-*killer*, he thought bitterly. 'Why did you not flee when you could?' *And why do I care?* he wondered.

'This is our home!' one of the defenders answered. He was a fleshy man with no beard or moustache. He wore good armour, perhaps a little too small for him, though he had the air of a landsman rather than a warrior. He held a longspear and had a sword at his hip, but all of it looked somehow uncomfortable on him.

Fachtna studied him carefully, trying to decide if he carried the blood of the gods in his veins, but he was too far away to tell and the fire was already kicking up too many sparks to be sure even if he moved closer.

'You cannot hold here!' Fachtna told them. 'The whole land is changing – you will be consumed, or changed!'

'Like you?' The man demanded. Fachtna noticed that more of the defenders were becoming interested in this exchange. Most were like the man he was speaking to, wealthy farmers wearing quality armour and carrying warriors' weapons they did not know how to use.

'I do not serve her in any way. I understand, and I would do you no harm, but you cannot stay here!'

'You would do us no harm, but you would force us off our land!' one of the other villagers shouted, a woman. She was not just fleshy, she was fat. Other than chiefs and the odd very successful merchant, there were few fat people in a land as harsh as this, not even in the richer farmlands of the south. He could see no children manning the palisades. This was also unusual – in times of warfare or raiding, the older children in a village would fight alongside their parents. The flames crackled and there was a popping noise. Fachtna wasn't sure if it was a log snapping or a blister bursting on the worm-creature's flesh, spewing more seeds into the air.

'Look around you. Does this still look like your land? Tell me how you can farm this.' The only sound was wood crackling in the flames. Even that was unsustainable. They would quickly run out of wood – they had to.

'I am a warrior of great renown.' *Or I was before I betrayed my people and committed the worst crime possible.* 'To relate my many deeds to you would take more time than we have left.' Fachtna knew that in the past he had been geased to enjoy the boasting part of a warrior introducing himself, but now he merely felt foolish. 'Yet I think I would struggle to kill a creature such as this.' He nodded towards the massive worm-creature.

'Perhaps we are greater warriors than you,' one of the other defenders shouted, a younger man than the first, he too was well fed. There was laughter from the defenders.

Fachtna looked down, considering the man's words. 'Perhaps you are. I have certainly been bested before.' He looked up at the man. 'But I do not think so. I think you made an agreement with something, a bargain, a sacrifice. I think you've grown fat on your betrayal, and I think you exist here on borrowed power.'

All of them were glaring at him now. He felt his living armour flex inside his flesh, responding to something unseen. It was sufficiently painful to make him grimace. The bargain had been struck far enough in the past that there was no guilt on the faces made red in the firelight. They had probably justified it to themselves a long time ago. Perhaps there had been a famine.

'And while I have introduced myself to you, I still do not know who I speak with.'

'We owe you nothing. You are a low thing that walks with the dead—'

'Enough.' Fachtna said it quietly, but he made sure his voice carried. 'Why do you fools stay here?'

The fleshy man opened his mouth to retort angrily, then his face contorted and writhed unnaturally. Fachtna watched as his eyes went black.

'We've been waiting for you.' The man's voice was different now. The words appeared to crawl up his contorted skin and out of his mouth, each one an effort. Fachtna knew that he now spoke with Crom Dhubh.

'What do you want? You've lost. Look around you. Life has won out.' Fachtna found it difficult not to smile. The people in the fort were moving differently now. Through the flame and smoke they shifted from side to side like predatory animals looking for an opening to strike. They had paid the price for their bargain. They had opened themselves to Crom, and now he would take what he was owed. Fachtna understood why they were fat now: for the same reason that he gorged himself before and after a fight. Crom would feed on them for power when he changed their bodies.

'This isn't about life or death. I am parent to these creatures as much as the Muileartach. The traitor to her kind is the Mother. Life is suffering, life is pain.'

Fachtna started laughing. 'I should have known when I saw the wicker man. Is that it – the actions of a spiteful child writ large because you stumbled on power?'

'You do not stumble on power like mine.'

Fachtna jerked his head around at the sound of the woman's voice.

'You seek it out.' The other man uttered Crom's words.

'You foster it in you.' Another of the villagers. They were starting to burn with an inner light.

'Where you find it, you take it,' a different villager intoned.

'Why were you waiting for me?' Fachtna asked.

The villager who had spoken first stepped onto the rampart. It looked as if there was fire under his skin, in his blood. His fat belly was deflating even as his legs swelled with new muscle. The man started to scream, and it sounded like his real voice now. Crom Dhubh had released control of the man's speech but not his body. Fachtna would have felt sorry for him, but he was pretty sure there were no children in the village for a reason. He felt a sort of detached calmness descend over him as he stepped back and drew his sword. It shimmered until it became a white blur, a ghost in the night.

Fachtna glanced over at the reborn dead. They had regrown flesh, sucking the dirt from the earth and using it to make mockeries of life. They looked like hastily formed effigies of the men and women they had once been. Fachtna had no idea what they would do.

The gate spokesman was no longer fat as he leaped high into the air on new muscles. His body was changing shape even as his leap carried him over the burning ditch, his longspear pointed down at Fachtna. The other defenders were doing the same. They were in obvious agony as Crom Dhubh's magic transformed them into more capable warriors.

Fachtna had all the time he needed. At the last moment he moved out of the way of the spear point. The villager who had done most of the speaking tried to shift the spear as he fell. Fachtna swung his sword two-handed and the blade cut through the man's midriff before his feet touched the ground, bisecting him. Some of his flesh turned into glowing ashes, consumed by the magics of his transformation.

More of the villagers had leaped through the fire towards him. Fachtna spun and swung his blade through another. The reborn dead fell upon them, tearing the villagers apart even as they burned with an inner fire.

Fachtna wasn't fighting. It felt more like a murderous dance. He found himself laughing as he spun and slashed. The air was full of sparks illuminating the alien landscape.

Too late, he looked up. Blackened flesh glowing from within, black eyes steaming, the figure dropped out of the sky. The spear pierced Fachtna's flesh at the shoulder, running through his chest and out of his lower torso, pinioning him to the ground. Fachtna cried out.

He was still human enough to feel the pain of iron and wood forced through his body.

The figure landed in front of him, stinking of burning fat. Fachtna felt hot fingers on the armour that had become his skin as the villager started to search him. With difficulty, Fachtna reached down and grabbed the haft of the spear that was pinning him to the ground. His fingers curled around the wood. He could feel the demon in it, put there with blood magic. His own blood flowed out of the wound and around the shaft of the spear, weakening and corroding the wood. He snapped the haft and staggered back, collapsing to his knees.

He felt hot fingers find the control rod Teardrop had given him. It was pushed through the back of his belt.

Fachtna reversed his grip on the haft of the broken spear, turned and rammed it up into the villager's head, through the bottom of his jaw and into his brain in an explosion of sparks and papery ashes.

The cool ground came up to meet him as blackness filled his vision and he began to lose consciousness. His body, which now encompassed the living armour that had fused with him, responded to his last thought: to protect the control rod. It sank into his flesh, succumbing to the Muileartach's power, reconfiguring itself into something resembling a cross with multiple crossbars. The brass-like metal became malleable and started to wrap itself around the back of Fachtna's ribs and his spine.

The last thing he saw was the confused reborn dead moving between faintly human-looking piles of glowing ashes, disappointed at the lack of carrion to harvest for new flesh.

'This is no way to behave,' Bladud said.

Tangwen was forced to agree with him, but little was surprising to her these days. They had continued moving north, chased by the inexorable advance of Andraste's spawn.

Bladud spoke to the people of any settlement they came to, asked them to gather all the food and livestock they could manage and join them. If they chose not to heed the warnings of what was coming, the Witch King burned their homes and took their food and livestock. This encouraged most of them to join the other survivors.

The bodies hanging from the trees had been flayed. Their heads were gone, and there was something else wrong with them that Tangwen could not quite put her finger on.

'Their blood has been taken,' Kush said in his deep, mellifluous voice. Germelqart was nodding in agreement. 'Is this a thing your people do?'

'No, we cut their heads off and drink ale from their hollowed-out skulls like normal people,' Bladud said, and then looked somewhat irritated when Kush could not keep a smile from his face.

'They have taken the heads,' the tall black man pointed out. There were more than twenty decapitated bodies, a mixture of landsfolk and the warriors who were riding escort for them. They had been at the head of the massive ragged column when they stopped for the night. Someone had taken them from where they camped, either dead or alive, and carried them into the woods.

They had come to what appeared to be an uninhabited area of woods and shallow river valleys. To the north lay a wooded plateau. There was little evidence of settlements or farmlands, but it looked as though someone had claimed these lands as their own.

'We will hunt them,' Sadhbh said. Tangwen glanced over at the warrior, and the smile on the Iceni's face only made Tangwen dislike her more. She wished she did not feel so indebted to the other woman for the bow. She also had to admit that Sadhbh was probably her equal, if not better, as a scout and hunter.

'I would seek them as allies,' the normally quiet Germelqart said. Kush raised an eyebrow and then nodded. This had been done right under the noses of the rest of Bladud's forces.

'I don't think they are interested in being our allies,' Nerthach said, scratching his beard.

'They came in the night like cowards,' Bladud spat. 'They dared not face us.'

'If this is their land, they have seen a massive army invade it. If they are fewer in number than us, they are forced to fight like this,' Tangwen said, with no little exasperation in her voice.

'Spoken like the child of a cowardly people,' Sadhbh said. Tangwen bristled but did not rise to the insult.

'Spoken like a shrewd and clever foe,' Kush said. 'And I have witnessed Tangwen's bravery proven time and time again. All I've seen you do is sneak off into the woods.'

'And return with game that you are happy enough to eat,' Bladud said. 'But Kush has the right of it – there's enough fighting among ourselves.'

'Who claims these lands?' Tangwen asked. It was too far inland for her to know much about the local peoples.

Bladud shrugged. 'That's difficult to say. It borders the lands of the Cornovii, the Corielatavi and the Dobunni.'

'We have a choice. Go through, or go around,' Tangwen said. She could feel Sadhbh glaring at her. Tangwen continued to ignore her.

'If we go through then we'll have to fight these people. Our own people.'

'If they will attack us in force,' Nerthach said.

'They won't,' Tangwen said. 'They'll pick at us until we are few enough for them to deal with. And if we go around—'

'The children of Andraste will catch and consume us,' Kush said.

'Then let us hunt them,' the angry Iceni repeated.

'On their territory? For them to have killed this many, and to have done so quietly, there must be at least fifty competent warriors, probably a lot more,' Tangwen said. 'I do not think you would be doing the hunting.'

'Coward!' Sadhbh spat.

'Indeed,' Tangwen mused. This time she felt Kush bristle on the other side of her. She reached over to touch his arm before he said anything.

'We have no choice but to march on,' Bladud said. 'We will bring the people closer together, and there will be no sleep for the warriors until we make it into Cornovii territory.'

'That is a long way from here,' Nerthach said gravely.

'Do you still counsel allying with these people?' Tangwen asked Kush.

'I would rather have them with us than not, but Nerthach is right – I do not think they will ally with us.'

'Aye, but will you walk into the woods with a known coward,' Tangwen asked, grinning.

Kush smiled back and glanced over at Sadhbh. 'Depends on the coward.'

'There must be someone with us who knows of these people,' Tangwen said, turning to Bladud. 'We will walk among the people and see who we can find.' Then, after a moment's thought: 'Are you a great king, Bladud?'

Bladud narrowed his eyes suspiciously. Nerthach was laughing.

'Why?' Bladud asked.

'You must prove your greatness with generosity.'

It was an impressive gift indeed: a skull that Bladud had personally taken from a warrior who had caused the Witch King several scars. The skull had been lined with beaten silver to hold Bladud's beer, after it had been picked clean of flesh and preserved with cedar wood oil. Kush had muttered something about 'civilisation' when he saw the skull. It wasn't a word Tangwen knew. Kush and Germelqart tried explaining it to her. It sounded quite frightening to her, and something to be fought against.

Her idea had felt like a good one when she was standing around with the other warriors. Now, out among the trees, she was less sure. It might have been a bright and sunny day, but the canopy provided by the dense forest was thick, and they walked through the woods in cool, green shadow interspersed with beams of sunlight shining down through the leaves. It was quiet in the woods. Birdsong and the cries of animals sounded distant. She found enough traces of tracks to confirm there were people nearby, but unseen.

They had walked among the refugees, asking about these lands. The only person they found who knew anything was a young man, little more than a boy, from the eastern Dobunni.

It had taken a while for the boy to work out where he was in conjunction with the stories he knew. When he did, he became terrified. He said that no people lived in the woods or even entered them. That it was a place of fierce forest spirits who would feast on the skin of those who trespassed there. He spat and made the sign against evil before he would utter their name. He called the spirits the *gwyllion*, meaning 'night wanderers'. Tangwen had silently scoffed at the stories. Now, under the trees in the midst of the quiet woods, she was less sure.

First the Lynx Women, and now this. Tangwen was growing sick and tired of being treated like prey.

'I have to leave you,' she suddenly said.

'What?' Kush demanded.

Tangwen handed him the skull. 'I'm sorry,' she told him. 'You have to believe that I will be watching over you.' She was looking all around them. She had spent so long watching over others that she had forgotten how to be on her own, how to hunt.

'What do you expect me to do?'

'Walk into the woods,' she said, not paying him much attention.

'Like leaving out meat for lions?'

She looked at him. 'I promise you that if you die, I will die, too.'

'But we will be claimed by different gods, and go to different places, and I will not be able castigate you for your foolishness,' he told her, only half-joking.

Tangwen continued to hold his gaze, conscious that he had not yet given his permission.

'Go, you don't have to die with me.' Kush smiled at her.

Tangwen nodded, then turned and headed off into the woods. She could hear the sound of running water. That was what she had been looking for.

Kush could not make up his mind about what he thought of all the trees he had seen since he arrived in this land of mad men, women and monsters. It was so different from his arid home, but there was an undeniable beauty to it. What the canopy of green leaves did to the light made him feel as if he had moved into a different realm: the realm of the gods.

The walking was aimless but not unpleasant. His faultless sense of direction told him he had walked directly away from the survivors and held that course for the better part of a day. Kush decided this was far enough. He stopped and leaned against a tree, an ancient lichen-encrusted oak. He grabbed the sack he had slung across his back with a piece of rope and opened it, pulling out some bread, cheese and a small wax-sealed earthen jug of wine. He had been saving the wine. Kush knew that protecting the survivors was the right thing to do, and for the most part he liked the people of this ridiculous land, even if they thought him a demon, but it felt like a long time since he had been on his own. He needed that now – even if it meant that his head would be taken, his blood drunk and his skin flayed off.

Kush was thinking of Hanno. When Hanno first bought him, and again when he freed him, Kush was given a cup of blood to drink. He was told this was part of a rite to seal the deal made between him and Hanno. He never learned whose blood it was. He had drunk it on both occasions, and everything had changed. He became stronger and faster, he learned to pick up languages more quickly, he could see further and, like Germelqart, he could see at night. He had heard stories of heroes who had drunk the blood of the gods, whispered tales of Sumer and the milk of the goddess Innana. It was this power that enabled Hanno to trade further than any other Carthaginian trader dared. The gods, particularly Dagon, had blessed him.

The blood he drank had also made Kush's hearing far superior to those who had not been similarly blessed.

He had been aware of them for some time now, and he resented them disturbing his thoughts and his dinner. He put down the bread and the jug and placed his hands on the haft of his bronze axe. The axe had been pulled from the ruins of Troy. It, too, had been blessed by the gods.

'I am as happy to give gifts and to share bread and wine as I am to die at your hands standing on a pile of your dead,' he said in the difficult tongue of the Pretani.

There was no answer. He was concerned that, his excellent eyesight notwithstanding, he had barely seen a leaf move, let alone glimpsed one of these *gwyllion*, if that's who they were. Even with his exceptional hearing, he had no idea how many they were.

'I am Kush the Numibian. I am no demon. Reveal yourself so we can talk or fight. To do less shows fear,' he said, climbing to his feet, his axe already held loosely in one hand.

There was a crash followed by the sound of flesh hitting flesh, hard, and branches splitting. A strangely coloured, misshapen creature rolled out of the undergrowth. *No*, Kush realised, *not one creature, but two fighting*. He moved towards them, shifting his axe in his grip but still unwilling to strike first. They were difficult to make out. One was a grey colour and had horns like a ram. He suspected that the Muileartach's children had caught up with them until the horns fell off. The other was mottled brown, with patterns on his skin that reminded him of the scales on a serpent.

They separated and the serpent-like one rolled into a crouch, an iron-bladed dagger at the ready, hissing. It took Kush a moment to realise it was Tangwen. She was wearing only a loincloth and a strip of hide to hold her small breasts in place. She had painted herself with mud and then used some kind of dye to add the black, mottled patterns to help camouflage herself. It wasn't just the mud that made it difficult to recognise her. Her tongue was out as she hissed, and she looked less like the scarred young woman he knew and more like an angry serpent.

The other figure was coated with grey ash, much of which had been scraped off during the fight. He was naked except for a narrow hide belt and a quiver across his back. His body was lithe and lean, filled out with wiry muscle, and various complex spiral symbols had been painted over the ash with a flaking, dry, brown substance that Kush was fairly certain was blood.

The *gwyll*, if such he was, held a club of stone in one hand and a knife in the other. Kush had learned in the arena to look for fear on which he could capitalise. There was no fear in the *gwyll*'s eyes, but he did not look happy to be facing Tangwen. Tangwen's knife darted out again and again, like a snake striking. The blade opened slashes in the *gwyll*'s skin as she wove from side to side, seeking an opening to finish him. To Kush it looked as if Tangwen was lost to the snake. The man scrambled backwards, leaping a fallen log. He was trying to avoid the dagger's blade and waiting for an opening to strike.

'Tangwen,' Kush said. She ignored him, trying to press her attack home. 'Tangwen,' he said again, with more urgency in his voice.

The *gwyll* was still backing away from her. He swung his club at the hunter, but her weaving from side to side had confused him and she was not where the weapon fell. 'Tangwen!'

This time she hesitated. The *gwyllion* were all around them: naked ash-covered warriors painted with symbols of blood, rams' horns on their heads. They carried various weapons – bows with arrows nocked, spears, clubs, hand axes, daggers and even a few swords. Their weapons were made from wood, stone, flint and bone. Only a few were of bronze, and fewer still were made of iron. Kush could see why they might be mistaken for forest spirits, but all he could smell was other humans.

'Remember why we are here,' Kush told the scarred woman. She looked at him uncomprehendingly, then, slowly, understanding returned to her contorted features and she relaxed. She took a deep breath and looked around warily. The warrior she had slashed was watching her, similarly wary, but there was no fear, hatred or anger in his expression.

'We would treat with you,' Kush said. 'We bring gifts.'

A shadow fell across him and Kush looked up. Standing on an earthen rise in the woods, the sun behind it, was a figure. Kush shielded his eyes with his hand, but even then the form was only a silhouette. The robed figure looked old and quite frail, and was carrying a staff or spear. A mantle of antlers rose from its head.

28
Birmingham, 3 Weeks Ago

Nanette Hollis was her own biggest critic. To her mind it was one of her strengths. She felt it was the main reason why she'd been accepted on the course she wanted at the Birmingham Conservatoire. It was this perfectionism, this drive, that she knew would in time lead to a job with a prestigious orchestra, and finally to becoming virtuoso violinist.

Despite being her biggest critic, she knew that the music she was playing at the moment was truly beautiful, so beautiful it was making her cry. The music was beautiful despite – indeed, perhaps even enhanced by – the disturbing discordant undertones in the complex counter-melody. She knew there was a story in the music. It was about someone in extraordinary pain who could also see, and was tormented by, the presence of extraordinary beauty.

And it had just come to her. She just started to play it, completely improvised yet fully formed. She had worked extraordinarily hard on all her previous compositions, but this one arrived straight out of the air, as they had when she was a child. She'd always thought that her father's fear of her improvised tunes was jealousy. Now she wasn't so sure. The tears in her eyes were partly a response to the beauty of the music and partly fear. She might have been playing the music, but she couldn't shake the feeling that it had been created somewhere else. She kept reaching for it in her mind, but it was beyond her understanding. She thought of Paganini, and the accusations of being possessed by the devil levelled at him during his life.

She wasn't sure how long she'd been playing in the empty practice room, but there was blood on the strings now. Somehow she would have to try and remember the strange, haunting double tune, one melodic, the other discordant. She knew she would never play it as well as she had this night. She was weeping. And then it was gone. She just stopped playing.

She stared through the practice room window over the Queensway, where traffic was still heavy and slow-moving despite the lateness of the hour. She could see the side of the neoclassical town hall.

Nanette felt empty, bereft, hollow inside, as if something had left her. She reached over and used the mouse to stop the recording software. Then she wiped the tears off her face with the arm of her woolly jumper.

'I've been watching you for a while. I heard you when I slept.'

Nanette jumped, let out a small scream, felt her heart skip a beat at the unexpected voice. She swung around. He was tall, thin, hairless, dressed like an undertaker or a Mennonite traditionalist. He was holding a hat in his hand, gaze downcast, not on her. He looked the picture of humility. She assumed he must be some Internet stalker, someone who'd heard the music she posted online.

'What are you doing in—' Nanette started.

'Please don't spoil this with banality,' he said. His voice was rich and deep, with just the hint of a central European accent. 'I think this was your finest moment. I am ... It was just so fortuitous that I was here to witness this.' Then she noticed the tears on his face.

'Look, arsehole—' She started reaching for her phone. He shook his head sadly and then strode towards her, reaching for her. She opened her mouth to scream.

'What has this got to do with us?' du Bois asked as he walked across Centenary Square towards Baskerville House, a renovated modern facade superimposed on pre-World War Two mock-imperial splendour. A council building originally, it was now expensive city-centre office space.

Grace didn't answer. He glanced down. She was wearing headphones. He glared at her until she took them off.

'What?' she asked innocently.

'Is it my turn to point out that you can do that in your head?' he asked. 'Not to mention you can multitask – and I mean *really* multitask – so you could be listening to whatever noise you call music and still be courteous enough to answer my question.' Du Bois looked genuinely irritated. Grace was losing the fight against the smirk she was trying to suppress.

'Do you think there's any way you could sound more like someone's dad?' she asked. This only succeeded in irritating him further.

'You know I don't like it when—'

'Sorry, Dad,' she said, grinning.

'Grace!'

'Malcolm!' Even this she managed to make sound like a daughter mocking a parent by using their name. Grace decided she was pushing him a bit too hard. 'Anyway, it's not "noise" – it's your stuff.'

He glanced down at her again as they approached the police cordon. He was aware that Grace had sent a file to his phone.

'It's the violinist from the Conservatory,' she said, pointing in the Conservatoire's rough direction with her thumb.

'The missing girl?' Malcolm asked. Grace nodded. 'You think it was Silas?'

'I don't know, but there's something about the music she posted. A lot of it's just the boring stuff that you like—'

'That would be actual music,' du Bois told her.

'But some of her own stuff ...' Grace started. Du Bois glanced down at her. She looked a little disquieted.

'Yes?' he asked, but she was saved from replying by their arrival at the cordon.

They showed their IDs and made their way past the line of suspicious, resentful police, then pushed through the revolving door and into Baskerville House.

The reception area was a marble mixture of modern and neoclassical that made du Bois wince. The decor was further spoiled by the presence of a number of West Midland Police armed-response officers crouching behind cover, aiming MP5s and G36s into the interior of Baskerville House. They were surprised to see du Bois. They were even more surprised to see Grace.

'You didn't answer my question,' du Bois said.

Baskerville House had a large open space at its centre, surrounded by five floors of glass-fronted open-plan offices. There was a bloody smear against the glass on the fourth floor overlooking the open area. Du Bois could just about make out the body slumped against the window.

'I don't know, is the answer,' Grace told him. They were making their way back towards the fire escape on the fifth floor having observed the floor below. They hadn't caught a glimpse of the gunman yet. With all the glass walls around, the gunman was obviously keeping his head down to avoid police marksmen.

'Is this intuition?' du Bois asked, surprise in his voice. He glanced over at Grace. She looked less than happy. 'Grace?'

'Have you got anything better to go on?' she snapped. 'This Renaissance arsehole is running rings around both of us.'

Du Bois stopped and they both crouched next to a desk partition.

'More early modern,' du Bois said. 'Are we killing this guy because he's hurt people? Because he's sick? We've had this conversation before. We can't solve all the world's ills.'

'We could if we tried,' Grace said, very quietly.

'What?' du Bois demanded, though his augmented hearing meant he'd heard her perfectly well.

'We're in the middle of a hostage situation! You want to have this conversation right here?'

Du Bois just stared at her.

'Dennis Letchford, thirty-one, quiet guy, keeps himself to himself. One day he walks into work complaining of something in his head and blows away one of his co-workers.'

'Which sounds like mental illness to me,' du Bois said.

'So I ran a check on the guy, his online history. He goes to the darkest parts of the net—'

'S-tech?'

'No, torture porn, grim stuff, sick art. He's even posted photo-manipulated images of co-workers and other people he knows. He was flagged by West Midlands Police's intelligence unit, but they never did anything because there was no child porn involved.'

'So he's a sick bastard—'

'So it's fucking intuition, okay!' Grace spat, exasperated.

'Grace, every time we get involved we risk exposure,' du Bois started.

'But it's all right to exercise your problems with authority?'

'*My* problems with authority? You're a punk!'

'You don't even know what that means!'

They were glaring at each other now.

'Fine,' du Bois relented. 'What's your plan?'

'You go in there and talk to him while I sneak up on him,' Grace said.

'That's it! *That's* your fucking plan?'

'And no is the answer to your next question.'

'What?'

'We're not killing this guy. We need to take him alive.'

Du Bois shook his head. Grace was glaring up at him fiercely.

'You know we're going to get someone killed, right?' he asked.

Du Bois pushed the fourth-floor fire escape door open as Grace crawled into the open-plan office and made straight for the cover of one of the desks. Du Bois walked in slowly, hands held high, thinking that he wouldn't be surprised if this action alone got him shot. He was wondering how many police marksmen had him in their sights at that moment.

'Who the fuck are you?' Letchford's scream sounded like it would have been at home on some of the music Grace listened to.

'My name is Malcolm du Bois. I'm with the police. I just want to talk to you.'

He couldn't see the man yet but thought he glimpsed movement deeper in the office. He glanced down at the desk Grace had crawled under, but she'd already moved on.

'I'm moving forward. Please don't shoot.'

Malcolm continued walking into the office, feeling very exposed. He now had a clear view of the body lying against the glass wall overlooking the central lobby. The man was missing most of his face. He could hear sobbing from a number of different people. The police had put the hostage count at an unlucky thirteen. There was a smell of faeces in the air.

As du Bois moved closer to the frenetic, nervous movement he'd glimpsed, he heard a dripping noise. He rounded one of the office partitions and saw another body lying over a desk, wrists and ankles cable-tied to it. A kitchen knife was embedded in the desk next to the body. The person had been gutted, the midriff little more than a red cavity.

Looking around, du Bois counted about a dozen people crouched on the floor, also cable-tied to the desk legs.

'Are you armed?' Letchford appeared from behind one of the partitions, keeping low. He was wearing a smart dark-coloured business suit and black leather gloves. The suit was soaked with blood. He had shaved his head, clumsily – chunks of his scalp were missing – and shaved off his eyebrows, then painted his entire head pitch black. For an absurd moment he reminded du Bois of Mr Brown, though he was much shorter and had a considerable paunch. Even through the black face paint, du Bois could see that Letchford was sweating heavily. He looked jittery, nervous. And he was holding a double-barrelled twelve-gauge shotgun.

'I am,' du Bois said. He held his leather coat open and let Letchford see his holstered Accursed Colt .45 automatic and sheathed tanto. 'Would you like me to put them somewhere out of reach?'

Letchford started pacing backwards and forwards, twitching, before turning to du Bois.

'Yes!' he screamed.

'Okay, where do you want me to put them?'

Letchford gestured with his shotgun towards a nearby desk. Du Bois unclipped the holster and the sheath from his belt and placed them on the table. Letchford gestured for him to move away from the weapons. Du Bois backed off, hands in the air. Letchford strolled towards the table and glanced at the knife and the pistol. The shotgun was pointing vaguely in du Bois' direction. Du Bois considered closing the distance and taking the shotgun from Letchford, but success wasn't a certainty. He decided to wait for Grace's play.

'Cool,' Letchford said, looking at the pistol and the Japanese fighting knife. Then he looked at du Bois. 'But you're a dumb fuck!'

Du Bois wasn't entirely sure he disagreed. 'It's Dennis, isn't it?' he asked.

'Don't ... use ... my ... fucking *name*! Teachers, fathers, employers – all want to use my fucking name!' The prisoners flinched away from him as he paced back and forth and ranted, his lips coated with spittle. Du Bois noticed an open sports bag on one of the desks.

'Okay, so what are we doing here? Why have you taken these people hostage?'

Letchford stopped pacing and looked confused. 'What are you talking about?' he demanded.

Du Bois raised an eyebrow, then pointed at the man's co-workers cable-tied to the desks.

Letchford leaned towards him. 'What makes you think they're hostages?' he asked quietly.

'I'll admit that was an assumption,' du Bois said.

Letchford pointed a shaking finger at the gutted body lying on the desk. 'Does that look like a hostage? These' – he gestured at the hostages, who cringed away from him, some sobbing even more loudly – 'are sacrifices.'

Well, shit, du Bois thought. He resisted the urge to look around for Grace. 'Who to?' he asked, more out of curiosity than anything else.

Letchford stared at him. 'Well, me, of course,' he said, as if it ought to be obvious.

'Oh, of course,' du Bois said. 'I'm going to lower my hands and sit down, okay?' Du Bois didn't wait for an answer. He pulled out a chair and sat, then reached into the breast pocket of his leather coat.

'What are you doing?' Letchford screamed, moving forwards and brandishing the shotgun at du Bois.

'Relax.' Du Bois drew out his cigarette case and showed it to Letchford. 'You don't mind if I smoke, do you?'

'I hate smoking!' Letchford's scream was somewhere beyond histrionic.

'Stop fucking antagonising him!' one of the sacrifices hissed. Du Bois lit a cigarette, then made calming motions towards Letchford and the sacrifice.

'I'll be honest, Dennis—'

'Don't call me Dennis!' Letchford screamed, drool dripping off his chin.

'I'm not very good at this. You're obviously a lunatic with social skills that would make the average politician pity you, but what I'd really like to know is – what set this off?'

Letchford's eyes went wide. For a moment it looked as if they were bugging out of his skull. Then he calmed down, but it was a twitching sort of calmness.

'There was a tall man. He came to me,' Letchford said. Then he raised the shotgun to his shoulder and aimed it straight at du Bois. *This might really hurt*, du Bois thought. 'He knew what was in my head. He said he'd heard it while he was sleeping. Then he put something in my head. He stole my warm red thoughts. This,' he said, glancing around at the office and the sobbing potential sacrifices, 'this is nothing compared to what I could have been before he took the dreams.' Du Bois nodded as if he understood. 'You're just like him, aren't you?'

Du Bois went very still. 'What did he look like?'

'You should—' Letchford spun around and fired one of the barrels of the shotgun through an office partition. A cry of pain rose from behind it. Letchford swung the shotgun back, aiming at one of the potential sacrifices, the one who had admonished du Bois. A red hole appeared in Letchford's face, then another, and finally a third. Letchford slumped to the ground. Du Bois was still sitting down, his cigarette smoke mixing with the bluer cordite haze drifting from the shrouded snub-nosed .38's suppressor. Du Bois stood up and walked over to Letchford, keeping him covered. The .38 had slid smoothly out of his coat sleeve on the custom-built hopper. Its twin was still nestled safely up his left-hand sleeve.

He checked Letchford. The man was dead.

'Why didn't you do that in the first place?' the man who'd admonished him for antagonising Letchford spat.

'For someone who's just been rescued, you complain a lot,' du Bois said without looking at the man. He walked over to the partition. Grace was a bloody mess on the other side. The shotgun blast had caught her in the torso.

'Did you have to shoot him?' she asked. Her internal systems had dulled the pain, and du Bois could see the wounds already closing, flesh knitting together. She would need to eat soon, he knew.

'Sorry, force of habit,' he said. 'What happened?'

It wasn't actual pain that caused the pained expression on Grace's face. 'I really don't know,' she said.

Du Bois wasn't happy. Grace was too good to make mistakes like this.

'He went for one of the hostages,' du Bois pointed out. 'He didn't try to take me out.'

'Suicide?' she asked.

'Or he wanted to create suffering.'

Grace grimaced and forced herself to her feet. 'This skirt's ruined!' she complained.

'Why aren't all your clothes laced with armouring nanites?' du Bois muttered as he wandered over to the open sports bag and looked inside. The intended hostages/sacrifices shrank away from him as he passed. The bag contained more knives and cable ties, handcuffs, a Taser, various chemicals, gloves, make-up and spare shells for the shotgun.

'This is a murder kit,' du Bois said, glancing back at Letchford. He flicked open the cylinder on his .38, emptied the spent rounds and reloaded three more Glaser bullets.

'He's a spree killer,' Grace said. 'Unless it's a bag full of guns, a murder kit's a serial-killer thing.'

'Or he's just a psycho. We've done our good deed for the day – let's go.'

'You could let us go, too?' one of the hostages suggested hopefully.

'As soon as we release you the police will be up here,' Grace said.

'You're not going to take us hostage as well, are you?' the same woman asked.

'So?' du Bois asked, ignoring the hostage.

'Something's not right here,' Grace said. Du Bois looked at the gutted sacrifice victim cable-tied to the desk and then back at Grace with a raised eyebrow.

'Close your eyes, everyone,' Grace said to the hostages as she drew one of her knuckle-duster-hilted fighting knives from the sheath under her arm. A few of the hostages let out little cries. Grace knelt down next to Letchford's body.

'What're you—' du Bois started. He heard the sound of bone cracking. 'Really? In front of all the—' There were more cries from the hostages, then more cracking sounds followed by a wet slurping noise. 'That's disgusting.' One hostage threw up, then another. Grace threw something at du Bois. Despite his better judgement, he caught it. It was covered with blood and lumps of bone and grey matter. It was still moving. Tendrils were being sucked into wriggling legs. The stinger tried to puncture his flesh, but du Bois' skin hardened. He found himself looking down at a tiny bronze scorpion.

'Are you changing?' du Bois asked. Most of the blood had disappeared, the matter reclaimed through the skin, but her clothes were a torn mess.

'Why? Am I showing too much flesh for your puritan tendencies?' Grace asked through a mouthful of cheeseburger.

Du Bois looked over at her in the passenger seat of the Range Rover as they made their way down Alcester Road towards Kings Heath. He was more than a little irritated. He hated people eating in his car. Even with a blood-screen hunting down scent molecules, it always took for ever to get rid of the smell of processed meat. On the other hand, Grace needed to eat to replenish energy and rebuild the matter she'd expended when she was shot.

'Sorry,' Grace said. 'I'm being a bitch.'

'You are,' du Bois agreed. 'And can you get your feet down off the leather?' Grace removed her motorcycle boots from the Range Rover's dashboard. 'What's wrong?' There seemed more to her current attitude than her normal attempts to wind him up.

'He shouldn't have got the drop on me like that.'

'Agreed. Now tell me what's really wrong.'

Grace didn't answer for a moment. Instead she took another bite of hamburger. Then: 'You know ...' she said, her voice sounding small.

Dead family, dead friends. Made to feel helpless, Du Bois thought.

'I hate these guys,' Grace said. 'It's almost like the madness is an excuse. They think their fantasies are more important than other people's lives.'

'He was different, though,' du Bois said as Alcester Road became Kings Heath High Street. Du Bois pulled off the High Street and onto a road lined with narrow terraced houses and cars parked bumper to bumper. He looked for a place to park. They would have to do this expeditiously. He'd made some phone calls as they left Baskerville House, but chances were that the police would be less than pleased about the mutilation of Letchford's body.

Du Bois found a parking space and squeezed the Range Rover in. He had to shunt the car in front forwards but was sure the Range Rover's armoured body could handle it.

'You really are a Range Rover driver, aren't you?' Grace said.

Du Bois ignored her. Instead he opened the armoured compartment in the central console and pulled his phone out. The bronze scorpion was attached to one end of it, inert now, like a pinned insect. Du Bois tapped commands onto the touchscreen. It was isolated from external communications while it analysed the bronze scorpion, which was clearly an S- or L-tech derivative.

'Well, the good news is we killed it,' du Bois said as he speed-read the result of the invasive analysis.

'Was he just another zombie?' Grace asked, then answered her own question. 'No, that doesn't work. His Internet history shows he was a sick fuck long before Silas appeared on the scene.'

'It's a transmitter,' du Bois said. 'Basically it's a sophisticated electroencephalograph that can transmit Alpha and Theta waves.'

Grace was staring at him. 'Causing dreams?' she asked.

'No, more like stimulating the imagination.'

'This is Silas, right?' Grace asked. 'Silas did this?' Du Bois stared at the tiny brass scorpion and nodded. 'Letchford wasn't supposed to be a victim, right?' Du Bois nodded again. 'Can we trace the transmissions?'

'Not now we've killed it,' du Bois said. 'We should speak to Control, but frankly I'm not even sure what we'd look for.'

Du Bois pulled the inert bronze scorpion off the end of his phone and dropped it back into the armoured compartment, which he closed and locked with a thought. The pair of them climbed out of the Range Rover.

'Well, you'd think his landlady would have noticed,' Grace said, looking around at Letchford's room.

The room was oppressive, he felt like it was closing in on him. The dark curtains didn't help. Neither did the wallpaper of imagery: cutouts from magazines, printouts from the Internet. Most of the images were pornographic and/or violent. Here and there were pictures of people du Bois reckoned Letchford must have known. He was pretty sure he recognised a few of the hostages, their images mixed in with the rest, often manipulated or modified to form part of the collage of violence.

Letchford's bed was in the centre of the room, a wardrobe and a chest of drawers the only other furniture. There was a laptop on the bed.

'I think he lived through that,' du Bois said, pointing at the computer.

'I'm almost too frightened to search this place,' Grace said.

Du Bois was concentrating. The laptop actually had quite sophisticated security, but it was no match for the tech they used. Letchford kept his computer sanitised. He'd wiped his browsing history and then run custom programs to try and wipe out further traces, but du Bois was able to find indications of what Letchford had been looking at. It had been hundreds of years since such material last shocked him, but he wasn't so desensitised that it didn't still disgust him. What he'd never understand was how someone could wallow in it.

Meanwhile Grace had found a locked metal box in the bottom of the chest of drawers. She drew one of her knives and cut the tip of a finger open. She pulled the motorcycle key out of her pocket and smeared some of her blood on it before closing the wound with a thought, then pushed the tip of the key against the box's lock. The key changed shape and oozed into the lock. She opened it with a twist.

'Flash drives,' she told du Bois. She chose one at random, steeled herself and then plugged it into the bottom of her phone. She began skimming through the contents in her mind's eye. 'I need to bleach my brain,' she said grimly.

'What?' du Bois asked. 'And just tell me – don't transfer the file to me.'

'Some images and films. Precious ones, I guess. Looks like he believed they were real-life torture or snuff, not simulated. I don't want to think too much about that. Needless to say he's got excellent security by normal standards. And then just lots of text.' Grace concentrated a bit longer as she speed-read some of it, disgust crawling across her face.

'What you'd expect?' du Bois asked.

'Yes,' Grace said, although she sounded slightly unsure. Du Bois gave her a questioning look. 'Well, how do I put this? He's actually quite good.' That wasn't what du Bois expected her to say. 'Don't get me wrong, it's power-fantasy bullshit that screams inadequacy and he's a sick fuck, but if he'd been eighteenth-century minor nobility he might have had a writing career.'

'He had a prodigious imagination?' du Bois asked.

'Dear old Dennis had a pot of boiling snakes where most people keep their reason. This guy was a serial-killer-in-waiting. I don't know how he was functional day-to-day.'

'And Silas wanted his thoughts,' du Bois said. He could hear sirens in the distance.

'His imagination. The odd thing is that serial killers and spree murderers have different pathologies. Whatever happened knocked him off course.'

The sirens were getting louder.

'Well, from what he was saying, I guess he met Silas,' du Bois said. Grace didn't answer. She'd hacked Letchford's records a while back and sent the police to the wrong address. Presumably they'd managed to speak to someone who knew where he actually lived. 'I think we should leave, give our Home Office influence some time to smooth ruffled police feathers over corpse mutilations.'

If Grace felt repentant, she didn't show it.

'Silas strike you as the kind of guy who'd run out of ideas?' Grace asked as they climbed the steps towards the Malmaison's reception.

'He really didn't,' du Bois replied.

'C'mon, we've had a hard day. I got shot and everything. Let's have a drink.' Du Bois couldn't think of a good reason not to agree so they made their way to the hotel's bar. It was comfortable, illuminated with subdued lighting, mood music playing softly in the background and stocked with overpriced drinks. Grace got carded and had to show fake ID to prove she was over eighteen.

'Hello, Malcolm.' The voice was feminine and sensuous.

He'd just taken the first sip of his Glenmorangie. The whisky turned sour in his mouth. He turned around to look at his brother.

Alex was now a female-identifying hermaphrodite. She went by the name Alexia and looked like a stunning, dark-haired, statuesque woman. She was wearing a pair of black jeans, a suit jacket and a fitted T-shirt advertising some kind of heavy-metal band. Du Bois was vaguely aware that his brother/sister had been involved with the music scene, in one way or another, since the late sixties.

'Whatever it is, I don't have time for it. I'm working,' du Bois told her, his face set in an angry expression.

'Nice way to greet your sister,' Alexia said. She tried to take his rejection lightly, but du Bois could tell she was hurt.

Grace looked up at du Bois. 'You monster,' Grace admonished. 'I invited her here. She can help us.' Then she went and hugged Alexia.

'Seventy-seven? Was that when Malcolm had to stop you assassinating the Queen?' Alexia asked. They were sitting at a table next to the window looking out over the busy Suffolk Street Queensway. It was a grey day outside, raining, but the bar felt warm and cosy.

Alexia and Grace had been talking so quickly as they attempted to catch up that Malcolm had struggled to follow their conversation. Though if he was being honest, he was sulking a little bit. He did not like the easy way his strange and unnatural brother had always got along with everyone else but still managed to be nothing but trouble and pain for him.

'The Queen?' Grace said. 'The whole lot of them. I was convinced there were hidden messages in "God Save the Queen", and that the whole family were baby-eating Naga infiltrators.'

'What on earth made you think that?' Alexia asked.

'Well, I'd reprogrammed my filters so I could better enjoy the jubilee and then went and got ergot poisoning from some dodgy amphetamines.'

Alexia sat back in her chair, a look of comical confusion on her face. 'How the hell did you manage that?'

'The dirty hippy I bought them from had smuggled them in some of his organic bread dough,' Grace said. Alexia laughed, her hand shooting to her mouth. 'I was roaming Buckingham Palace wearing a tutu, fishnets, a Sex Pistols T-Shirt and a tiara and carrying a Thompson sub-machine gun when Malcolm caught up with me.'

Du Bois watched as Alexia took another sip from her champagne cocktail and then glanced over at him. He was less than happy, and doing his best to ignore the conversation.

'I would imagine that "dad" was less than pleased,' Alexia said, a wry smile curving her lips. Grace giggled in a way that further irritated du Bois.

'Well, it's good that we've caught up,' du Bois said, sitting forwards, 'but we really are working, and it's reasonably serious.'

'I told you I asked her here to help,' Grace said.

'With what?' du Bois demanded, finally losing his patience.

'I listened to the music,' Alexia said.

It took du Bois a moment to realise what she was talking about. 'Nanette Hollis. The missing girl? You really think she's connected?' he asked Grace.

'I was right about Letchford, and I was right because I'm involved, immersed in it.'

'And what if you're just seeing connections where none exist?' du Bois asked.

'I don't think she is,' Alexia said.

Du Bois sighed in frustration. 'By all means, I think the world's only immortal playboy should share his ever-so-sensitive, artful insight with us,' he spat.

Alexia stared at him. Then she stood up and walked out of the bar.

'Your body is full of nanites derived from alien technology probably thousands of years in advance of current human capabilities. How is it that you're still not evolved enough to know that sometimes people are born with the wrong bodies?' Grace demanded, before standing up. Du Bois opened his mouth to retort. Grace swung on him, pointing her finger at his face. 'We can be whatever we want to be. You don't get to choose for her, or anyone else. If I can talk her into coming back inside, you're going to be nice to her, or I'm going to pistol-whip you, understand me?' Du Bois just glared at his partner. Grace glared back. 'Actually, I won't,' Grace said maliciously. 'I'm going to sleep with her again.' Then she turned and strode away from the appalled du Bois.

Grace found Alexia outside the hotel, huddled under a denim jacket in the rain, smoking. Grace could see the tears in her eyes, the tears she'd managed to hide from du Bois.

'I'm sorry,' Grace said awkwardly.

'What are you sorry about? You're not the one being a stubborn dickhead. I'm not sure he ever got over the "monk" part of being a so-called "warrior monk",' Alexia muttered.

'Yeah, I take the piss about that,' Grace said, grinning.

Alexia didn't smile back. 'They put so much shit into his … our heads.' Alexia looked lost in thought. 'I suppose that still happens. Just different shit from different sources.'

'The Empire never ended?' Grace asked.

Alexia looked down at the shorter woman. 'I'm not still the mess he thinks I am. He's just so …'

'Prejudiced?'

'I don't even know it's that. He risked so much for me. We both would have been burned at the stake, and he believed, he really believed, but his loyalty to me outweighed his fear of God. Can you imagine that?'

'I can't really imagine fearing god,' Grace said. 'He doesn't hate you. He's not disgusted by you. I just don't think he understands you, and I suspect that makes him afraid—'

'Which makes him act like a dickhead.' Alexia flicked away the forgotten cigarette. 'There are lots of things he doesn't understand. Some of those he follows blindly.'

'Are you coming back in?'

Alexia thought for a moment and then nodded.

'Be nice. Remember what I said,' Grace told du Bois as she slid back into the booth. He looked less than pleased but nodded. He was sipping his second double Glenmorangie. Alexia sat down opposite him.

'Well?' he asked sharply. 'Ow!' Grace was glaring at him, having just kicked him under the table.

'She knows something,' Alexia said.

'The missing girl? Nanette Hollis?' du Bois asked.

Alexia nodded. 'There's something about her recent music, particularly compared to the rest of her compositions. It ... I don't know, it implies that she's aware of, or in contact with, something else.'

'Something supernatural?' du Bois asked sceptically.

'Says the man who still prays,' Grace muttered, earning herself an angry glare.

'There's an underlying theme to it,' Alexa said, 'a discordant counterpoint melody that's strange to the point of being alien. There's an insight there, one I couldn't match even knowing what I know about our world. If she turns up I'll be asking to sample some of her stuff, perhaps even get her in to do session work on our next album.'

'I'm not hearing anything that would suggest there's more to this than Miss Hollis writing odd music.'

'Have you listened to it?' Grace asked.

'No,' du Bois admitted.

'What about Jaggard's work?' Grace asked.

'The artist? What about it?'

'Are you telling me you didn't find it at all disconcerting?'

'That just means it's disconcerting,' du Bois said. Grace sighed and slumped back in her seat. 'Look, I can see where this has come from but frankly we're clutching at straws—'

'Because we've got fucking nothing,' Grace pointed out in exasperation. 'Except a possible connection between the victims. At the very least he appears to think the same thing I do – he kills the first one because she claims to be a psychic but he discovers she's lying. Then—'

'What? He starts killing the real deal?'

'I'm not sure why you're so quick to discount it, knowing what you do,' Alexia said.

'Other than what he put in Letchford, there's no tech in any of the victims,' du Bois pointed out.

'No tech that we found,' Grace said. 'He's taken the brains.'

'There still would have been some trace,' du Bois insisted stubbornly.

Alexia sighed. 'What if it's an ancient piece of S-tech spliced into an ancestor thousands of generations ago?' Alexia asked. 'Something that's been diluted down until it's just a sensitivity. Do you understand all the tech?'

'None of that matters. What matters is whether Silas believes it,' Grace pointed out.

'What about Letchford?' du Bois asked.

'Silas didn't kill him, you did,' Grace observed. She took a sip from her beer and then belched loud enough to make du Bois cringe. Alexia giggled as the other people in the bar turned and glared at the punk girl.

'But we know Silas did something to Letchford,' du Bois said.

'Then it must have been for a different reason,' Grace replied.

'Which leaves us where?' du Bois asked.

'There can't be that many possible victims for him to choose from,' Grace said.

Du Bois received a text message from Control. He read it as Grace did the same in her head. He ordered his body to break down the alcohol in his system and slid out of the booth. 'We have to go,' he told Alexia. Grace was following him, an apologetic expression on her face.

'Wait!' Alexia said. The pair of them stopped. Alexia stood up and hugged Grace. The smaller woman hugged her back fiercely. 'Come down and see me in London once this is over.' Grace nodded. Alexia turned to du Bois. 'Do we really have to shake hands?' she asked. Du Bois looked at her for a moment, obviously uncomfortable. Then he hugged her. 'Be safe,' Alexia whispered. 'I worry about you.'

'Please get out of the city,' he whispered to her. She nodded.

The gala pool – which had once been the first-class pool – of the Edwardian Moseley Road Swimming Baths had been closed and drained for renovation.

'This takes me back,' Grace muttered as they walked into the building. 'Not that I would have been allowed in this bit,' she said, taking in the arched ceiling supported by white-painted iron beams. Spectator seating, balconettes and scaffolding installed for the renovation work surrounded the empty pool.

Nanette Hollis was lying in the middle of the drained pool, her eyes glassy and unseeing as she stared up at the ceiling. Her legs were together and her arms outstretched. Du Bois didn't need to use the forensic application of his blood-screen to know that her brain was missing.

Grace turned away from the body in a cold fury.

29
A Long Time After the Loss

It was the contempt that did it, his utter and total contempt for nearly everything and everyone. Mish Tullar had always known he was inadequate. It didn't matter how much time he spent in counselling immersions; his parents had made that clear to him when they gave him to the Church. They hadn't even bothered to sell him. They must have known they wouldn't get much. Perhaps if he could afford neurosurgery he might feel better about himself, but most of his money went on items of worship.

Realising he was a piece of shit, Mish started looking for someone – or something – better than himself to cling to. What he'd found hadn't been terribly inspiring. They were people every bit as weak and unpleasant as he was, just too lacking in self-awareness to realise it. Even his so-called 'betters' appeared petty, venal and despotic in his eyes.

Then Mish saw 'him' dealing with an unregistered media stalker and had gained an idea of the kind of contempt in which Woodbine Scab held everyone who wasn't Woodbine Scab.

Here was someone who saw people for what they were. Knew what he was, and was obviously better than the others Mish had latched on to because of the power he wielded. That was when Mish Tullar started drinking his own urine to debase himself.

The Church had some old-fashioned ideas. Among its own people it did not practise the panopticon of total surveillance, but even so he decided it would be best to keep his worship (the immersion counsellors called it 'obsession', but he knew it was something purer and much less tawdry than simple obsession) to himself, particularly as some of the black immersions he owned, recorded from Scab's point of view during a number of his bounty kills, were very illegal.

He scoured the media, even saved up for Pythian search programs, to try and get hold of every piece of footage he could about Scab. He put himself on the very edge of his debt threshold purchasing immersions made about his hero. Many of the immersions had resulted in the 'accidental' deaths of those involved in their production, particularly those who played Scab. His pride and joy, however, was what purported to be a corrupted partial copy of Scab's personality from a Psycho Bank. It had been recorded whilst Scab was fighting in the Art Wars with the Penal Legions. He'd only had the guts to upload it once. It nearly overwhelmed him and partially corrupted his neunonics before he managed to shut it down. As a coder and a system tech, he was able to isolate and repair the damage, but it had been touch and go for a while. He suffered residual spasms and twitches for several months after.

When Mish heard he would be serving aboard the *Templar* with Woodbine Scab's surviving son he had become very excited. He was more than a little disappointed when Benedict rebuffed his offers of oral pleasure to honour his father. Clearly the apple had dropped very far from the tree and Benedict was just another arsehole. That aside, what happened was still wrong.

They downloaded an uncorrupted copy of Scab's personality into his own son. They then removed Benedict's neunonics, and his limbs, before sealing him in an airlock. Mish had done nothing with his worthless life. He decided that now was his time to do something. He needed to prove himself, beyond just drinking his own urine.

He hacked one of the ship's assemblers to make himself some weapons. He modelled them on those Scab used, but wasn't sure if he'd got the template quite right. He spent some time stealing or requisitioning a few other bits and pieces. The neunonics he paid for himself. They were top-of-the-line, and he added several quasi-legal combat routines as well. The cost of the neunonics put him well over his debt threshold, but it didn't really matter.

As he walked through the corridors of the *Templar* he found himself shaking. He released some chemicals into his bloodstream and ran calming routines through his neunonics as he went over his plan again and again. He even ran through the simulations he'd created. He paused and waited for the drugs to take effect. Then he took a few steadying breaths and turned the corner. The moment he did so, the two Church militia turned to face him, bringing their ACRs up to bear. Mish immediately raised his hands but kept walking towards them. He had an intelligent program overriding autonomic responses, forcing him to keep walking into the barrels of the two guns.

'Whoa! Easy, I'm just here to run a systems check on the door mechanism, it's been glitching!' Again this was a pre-programmed response.

351

'We've got no record of that. Turn around and go the other way or we will fire.' It was impossible to tell which one of them was talking. Both had their visors down, the outer surfaces playing animatics of important events in Church history.

'Could you just check? I don't want to have to go all the way—'

The rifles fired a short burst at Mish's central mass, but he had seen their fingers tighten – or rather his newly programmed neunonic combat skills had. He spun out of the way, drawing both of his tumbler pistols. He moved forwards in a crouching position, firing the large revolvers. The targeting software in his neunonics guided his muscles to aim the pistols. Twelve bullets were in the air. He'd been hit, but drugs and intercepted nerve signals deadened the pain and kept him moving.

The two Church militia shifted aim, but they'd not been expecting this level of violence. They had expected a clerical error, and that someone would get bawled out when the system tech had to be cloned, but their orders were to take absolutely no risks with the quadriplegic prisoner in the airlock.

The Monk's eyes flicked open. She was instantly alert as the alarm was transmitted direct to her neunonics. She rolled off her futon and onto her feet. She grabbed weapons and something else on her way out of the room.

The two Church militia fired again, this time wildly as rounds from Mish's tumbler pistols started impacting on their armour. A number of the bullets hit the carapaces. Not even the spinning armour-penetrating qualities of the tumbler pistol rounds could penetrate full combat armour, but Mish had aimed for the visors. Three rounds hit one visor; two hit the other. The rounds drilled into them, spiderwebbing them with cracks.

Mish dropped the tumbler pistols and drew the two spawn blades. Bullets thudded into him and he staggered back against the metal wall of the corridor. He came off the wall again and thrust the diamond-hard point of one blade forward into the visor of the first guard. The visor shattered like glass and the woman dropped her ACR. She reached up for the blade, grabbing Mish's wrist. When the point of the spawn blade detected skin, the carbon reservoir inside the weapon's hilt fed the assembler in the blade, making it grow. It pushed through hardening skin, took hold of armoured bone and started to push its way into the woman's skull. She let go of Mish to grab the blade's hilt and tried to pull it out.

Both guards' P-sats popped out of their clips on the back of their combat armour. They would be the easiest things to deal with. Mish had been one of the techs who integrated their systems with the *Templar*'s C&C. The emergency shutdown codes dropped them to the floor like so much dead weight.

Mish was already spinning around, the other spawn blade still in his fist. The second guard, a lizard, re-aimed his ACR and fired a three-round burst. Mish felt burning on the side of his face for just a moment before the information was deadened. The blade's diamond tip pierced the lizard's visor and penetrated his eye, hooked on to bone and began pulling itself into his brain.

Mish staggered away from the flailing guards. The woman slumped against the bulkhead next to the airlock and slid to the ground. The lizard fought for a while longer, wasting his time trying to pull the blade out as the weapon split into roots and branched out through his head. Had he been strong enough, he would have pulled out part of his skull and a sizeable chunk of the meat of his brain along with the blade.

Mish 'faced the hack command he'd been working on ever since he first found out what they'd done. An anxious moment passed, and then the airlock door opened. He looked on the face of his god. *How many people can say they've done that?* he wondered. His body didn't appear to be working correctly, but he managed to force it into action. Scab stared at him with Benedict's eyes.

'Well?' Benedict/Scab asked.

'I'm sorry,' Mish said. He stepped forward and began attaching assemblers with portable carbon reservoirs and graft attachments to each of Benedict/Scab's stumps. As well as rebuilding his limbs, they had been hacked to inject into Benedict/Scab's body whatever soft-machine augments Mish had been able to get hold of. Next he took out a smart syringe and pressed it against his deity's temple. The needle guided itself through the prisoner's skull and into his brain before ejecting its payload. The nanites crawled through his mind, creating a neunonic network.

'There may be time for me to orally pleasure you,' Mish said.

'I think that's highly unlikely. Besides, I believe you're dead.'

Mish looked down at himself. He was mostly red. His neunonics were telling him that it was mostly technology and chemicals keeping him alive. They weren't going to do that for much longer.

'Oh,' he said. 'I'm sorry.' He opened his jacket to reveal more fastloaders for the tumbler pistols secured in various loops. 'These are for you.' Benedict/Scab nodded. Mish fell forward. He felt a thrill of excitement as his face touched his god's torso on the way down. *Finally I've done something with my life!* His last thought was that he wished his parents could see him now.

The *Templar*'s AI manifested as Churchman dressed in the bloodied and battle-scarred armour of a pre-Loss knight. The knight was keeping pace with the Monk as she attached a piece of L-tech to her belt and neunonically ran a diagnostic on the fast-cycling double-barrelled laser carbine and its underslung grenade-launcher. Holsters had grown out of her gi, and she had an advanced combat pistol holstered at each hip, along with pouches for spare magazines and batteries.

'This goes badly, space everything,' the Monk said. 'And I want to know who that little shit is.'

'I have spoken to Bishop Hollis and he concurs. Do you want it done now?'

The Monk considered this. *It would be the safest option*, she thought.

And you couldn't have undone the restraints first? Benedict/Scab thought. He felt the familiar, uncomfortable itching sensation within his head – he knew it was largely psychosomatic – and then the neunonics started feeding his mind information. His limbs and augmentations were coming online. They were nothing like as sophisticated as he was used to. He went through them quickly, integrating everything for the best performance.

It wouldn't be enough. The Monk on her own was a match for him in this body, with these shoddy neunonics, never mind the ship's automated security systems and the complement of Church militia. But Mish had provided him with systems access, which included various backdoors he'd installed over the years. That access, along with his own ability in electronic warfare, might just give him the edge he needed. If only his limbs would grow faster.

As his limbs regrew, he was quickly forming a dragon program in his neunonics to keep the *Templar*'s AI busy, just as he'd done on the *Lazerene*. He unleashed it and then hacked his restraints. They clicked open and he fell on his face. His limbs weren't quite ready, apparently. He cursed himself for his stupidity and continued looking around the ship's systems. He found something that was heavily protected. He looked for his dead 'saviour's' backdoor, located it, occulted his presence and went in to have a look.

Face down on the deck of the airlock, Benedict/Scab started to smile. His arms and legs were raw but he was sure he could stand now. He looked down at his saviour.

'Loser,' he muttered. He just needed to slow down security.

The AI cried out and disappeared. That made sense. If Benedict/Scab were to have a chance of escaping, he'd need to tie up the AI. She came to a crossroads in the corridor and continued straight on. Two squads of militia fell in behind her.

Two heavily armed S-sats appeared in the corridor ahead. Instantly she realised they were going the wrong way. With a thought she triggered the L-tech device she'd brought from her room. The protective coherent-energy field surrounded her, obscuring her image behind a shimmering yellowish aurora. The S-sats began firing. The energy field absorbed the lasers and deadened the kinetic energy of the projectiles, but the AG-powered smart munitions hit with sufficient force to make her stagger.

She noticed that the S-sats weren't targeting any of the militia, though those closest to her were catching stray beams and bolts, and were being knocked around by the multiple explosions. The barrage forced her to her knees, and her internal medical systems were constantly healing bruises, but that was the worst of it. She knew the S-sats would soon run out of smart munitions, and it would take their built-in assemblers a while to regrow the sophisticated weapons. Then all of the militia personnel's P-sats popped their clasps, shot into the air and targeted the Monk with their on-board lasers. She became a prism.

He was through the defences and into the database the *Templar* had been trying to keep secure and hidden. Benedict/Scab could certainly see why. He went looking for the meat-hack that had allowed him to possess the body of his own son. He found it, and then there was another back door. It was almost as if his saviour had some insight into what he was going to do when he got free.

He checked on the progress of the various security teams on their way to him. Unusually, he did not want to kill any of them unless he had to if his plan was to work. For that reason he'd left the various nano-screens inert rather than weaponising them into nano-swarms, and would avoid doing so unless he had no other choice.

He was less than pleased to see the Monk using an L-tech energy field. He'd gathered up the two tumbler pistols, the spawn blades and the ACRs, though he'd had to hack the ACR's control systems before he could use them. He'd also taken his saviour's trousers and top so he could use the material to grow holsters and pouches for the various weapons and ammunition. Ideally he'd have liked to put on one of the combat armour suits the two guards had been wearing, but he didn't have time. His saviour had added some armour properties to his clothes, but clearly not enough.

He heard the sound of gunfire. That would be the militia squads destroying their own P-sats. He checked the security footage. He saw the Monk extruding blades from her protective energy field as she destroyed the two S-sats that had attacked her. The only good news about the energy field was that while it could stop bullets, beams and anything else from getting in, it also stopped them from getting out. If she wanted to kill him, she was going to have to do it up close and personal.

'This might even work,' he muttered. One thing was for sure – they weren't going to be so quick to re-create him in the stinking meat of his son's body again. He sent the command.

The last of the P-sats was taken out with sustained fire from the ACRs and thudded to the corridor floor like so much junk. The Monk continued heading towards the airlock.

Almost as one, the militia started screaming. She couldn't hear it, but she could see their contorted features through the energy field. She assumed Scab had managed to weaponise the various protective nano-screens, but as she couldn't 'face with the *Templar* she had no way to be sure. There was nothing she could do to help them. The priority was to deal with Benedict/Scab as expeditiously and violently as possible.

She marched around the corner into the corridor Scab was in. He was waiting for her, ACR at the ready. He started firing immediately, one short, controlled burst after another fired so quickly that it was almost a constant stream of fire. The solid-state magazine was eaten away as it provided the ingredients for each bullet. The Monk saw the impacts of the electromagnetically driven armour-piercing explosive rounds as sparks of light from inside the safety of the shield. She kept walking.

Scab started firing the underslung grenade-launcher. The thirty-millimetre high-explosive armour-piercing grenades knocked her back. Impact after impact sent her tumbling down the corridor. Then the explosions relented.

The Monk climbed to her feet. Benedict/Scab was discarding the first ACR and aiming the second. This time he didn't start with the rifle, just fired the underslung grenade-launcher again and again. Inside the energy field, all the Monk could see was fire as she was battered off the corridor's walls, floor and ceiling.

Finally the barrage relented. The Monk stood up slowly, her entire body one large, painful bruise. Sparks played all over the energy shield as Benedict/Scab fired burst after burst from the ACR. She started walking through the bullets towards him. He was backing away from her as he fired. She picked up the pace and started to run. She wanted to kill him more than she had ever wanted to kill anyone before. Scab tossed the second ACR and fast-drew the two tumbler pistols, firing them rapidly as he backed away from her. The slower, spinning bullets hit the energy field and were held there for a moment, rotating in the pale yellow aura before dropping to the ground. The pistols ran dry. Scab holstered them and drew the two spawn blades. That was when the Monk realised there was something wrong. Just as she was level with the airlock.

Benedict/Scab was a little surprised it had worked. The external airlock door was already open. All he'd had to do was open the internal one. This was not as easy as it sounded, as one of the key things about spaceships was the requirement that the inside never met the outside, due to the detrimental effect such a meeting would have on biological functions. This made the airlock systems among the most heavily protected on any ship. Getting the *Templar*'s systems to open the external airlock door had been easy enough. Getting it to open the internal door at the same time should have been almost impossible. Except his dead saviour, who apparently had extensive systems access, had already hacked the internal door. All Benedict/Scab needed to do was modify the original hack.

Benedict/Scab expelled all the air from his lungs and closed his eyes,

Too late, the Monk realised what was happening. She caught the red glow in her periphery. There was absolutely nothing she could grab on to as she was sucked out of the corridor. She reached for the lip of the airlock but the energy field surrounding her would not allow any purchase. She just bounced off the edge of the airlock and headed out into Red Space with the other three bodies.

Benedict/Scab was sucked off his feet. He left it as long as he could before 'facing the command to shut the airlock. He hit the floor of the corridor hard. He was next to the airlock. Had it been open another moment he would have joined the Monk in Red Space. The corridor was otherwise empty. He breathed in a lungful of thin air, gratefully. Then he allowed himself to enjoy the cries echoing through the *Templar*'s dark corridors.

When they purchased a copy of his personality, they had been forced to buy an entire Psycho Bank. A secure database containing the personalities of some of the most dangerous, criminally deranged and psychologically compromised individuals in whatever sector of Known Space the Bank had come from. This included, but was not limited to, recreational killers, spree murderers and career assassins. Psycho Banks were set up so that the personalities could be interrogated by governing AIs to provide insight into other cases.

Benedict/Scab found the meat-hack program that allowed him to possess Benedict's body, and then used that to download the personalities from the Psycho Bank into the neunonics of the *Templar*'s entire crew. As the screams began to die out, he knew the possession process was almost complete. It was easier than it should have been because of his system access, and the fact that the 'face connections between ship and crew were so closely linked.

The energy field would keep her safe from the worst effects of space, and she would live as long as her internal oxygen supply held out. It was depressing watching the *Templar* receding as she spun away from it through the gases of Red Space, though she was still travelling at the same velocity as the ship. She ran through her options. None of them was good.

That little fucker's done it again. She sent the destruction command to the energy field. She couldn't risk Scab salvaging such potent L-tech. The re-engineered copy of an ancient code turned the piece of alien tech into expensive junk. The field came down, but she had already engaged her own suicide solution.

'Listen to me,' Scab said. His voice echoed through the ship as he took control of an antiquated PA system. 'This is Woodbine Scab. Not the spayed weakling bounty killer, not the Legion slave, not the pathetic wannabe who bared his arse to the Consortium for Elitehood. This is the Woodbine Scab who carved out the Kingdom of Bone on Cyst. Do you understand?' He paused to let that sink in. 'The ship you are on is a Church light cruiser, one of the most powerful warships ever made, and I am in control of it. Now, some of you are bad people, nasty folk who will want to be Daddy on this ship. Well, you can step up or hide and bide your time – the end result will be the same. But if you follow me, I promise you every sick little thing your dark, twisted, shrunken hearts could desire. We have atrocities to commit! Who's with me?'

He would have to make examples, he knew, but despite his

contempt for nearly everyone else in Known Space, the answering cheers were strangely gratifying.

Every surface in the empty swimming pool area that had once been the *Basilisk II*'s lounge had been turned into a screen. Scab was standing among the various media feeds, bathed in the red flames from the various fires on the habitat the *Templar* had raided. He was trembling with rage.

'It's very simple,' Benedict/Scab said. 'If the *Templar* appears, you will give us exactly what we want, or you and everyone you know will suffer until you're all ultimately destroyed. There will be no coming back, I promise.' Benedict/Scab had made the promise to Known Space against a backdrop of snuff/torture immersions and mutilated bodies bonded to the habitat's smart-matter windows. In the wake of the attack there had been mass outcry against the Church for letting Benedict/Scab get hold of such a sophisticated warship. The Church had in turn promised to dispatch a significant part of its fleet to find and destroy the *Templar*.

Vic was keeping well back from Scab. He wanted to leave the pool area but was too frightened to move.

'We can either go after him, or we can continue on the path we've already started on,' Elodie told him.

Scab looked over at her. The feline actually took a step back.

'This.' It came out as a slow hiss. 'Has to be answered.'

In the Cathedral, the Monk opened her eyes. He first thought was fury at Scab successfully murdering her again.

30
Ancient Britain

Britha wasn't sure why she'd done it. Shaved off half her hair. She was sitting on one of the wooden platforms sticking out from the fort on the Mother Hill, looking down the valley. She'd been sitting there for so long that her presence had stopped bothering the crows and the ravens picking over the bones of the dead.

She felt dirty. *As well I should,* she admonished herself. After she'd sheared off the hair, she had collected it to burn so nobody else could use it to gain power over her.

Her woad tattoo of a Z-shaped broken spear with a serpent entwined around it wasn't blue any more. The molten, living red gold she had chosen to drink had pushed through the surface of her skin. It had taken the form of her tattoo and crept over her body, forming disconcerting patterns.

She could hear the whispering constantly – from her dirk, from her spear, from her flesh – but she was pretty sure she was under her own control because of how disgusted she felt with herself. Her robes were black now, like those of the feared sacrificers who performed the tasks the other *dryw* balked at. She had worn masks as a *dryw*. The shy maiden when it was time for the sex rituals, the stern mother of the tribe, the fearsome hag when war threatened. This was another mask she would have to wear.

Her people were gone, so there was nobody to serve now. This had to become about her child. She couldn't fail the child like she had the people of Ardestie.

Below, on one of the smaller hills to which the Mother Hill had given birth, the Lochlannach were preparing their mounts.

'Are you ready?' Bress asked softly from behind her. Britha glanced back at him. He looked beautiful, Otherworldly. His leather armour had been moulded to fit his body. His sword was sheathed at his waist, its blade too long to have been forged from mortal metal. His fur-lined cloak fluttered in the wind, its hood up to cover his long silvery blond hair. She wondered if this was how she would look to mortals now. Had the demons in her blood cast a glamour on her human form to make her look prettier? To add to their sense of awe when they met her?

'Am I ready to hunt someone I fought beside, someone I lay beside?' Britha asked.

'If he brought you both here, then he knows the way back to the *Ubh Blaosc*, to your child. He must also have a rod – to your eyes it would look to be made of copper or bronze.'

If Fachtna had this rod on him she had not seen it, but she had been badly injured.

'And that is what we go to take from him?' Britha asked quietly. 'He fought beside me, at the wicker man.'

'I know. I killed him,' Bress said.

Britha didn't look back again. 'We fought against your evil,' she added. Bress did not reply. 'It was the right thing to do, but I did evil to accomplish it.' The silence stretched out. 'Do you come from a place like the *Ubh Blaosc*?'

'No,' Bress said.

'Where do you come from?'

'Cythrawl,' he told her. It was an old word for hell. This time she turned to look back at him, searching for a lie, searching for warrior bravado. She found neither. That was the thing about Bress: his heart might be black as pitch, he might be capable of the most awful things, but she didn't think he lied much.

'I'm sorry,' she said, meaning it, and feeling lost. 'I want you, and I will do what I must to get my baby back. I will wear the mask for you, not for your master—'

'I ...' Bress started.

'Quiet,' she told him. It was one of her old voices, one she had learned among ancient oak trees, their bark coated with long-dried blood. Cythrawl or not, Bress respected her enough to remain quiet. 'I will be your terror, for you. I will be like you, but that' – she pointed down to where she knew the entry to the cave was – 'is a thing which should not be.'

'I helped murder your future,' he said, and there was something pathetic in his voice that she had not heard before.

They rode south through the cliff-edged hills, past farms, settlements and small villages, all burned out. Their people had been harvested for their bones to build the obscene tower far beneath the hills. Britha, like Bress and the rest of the Lochlannach, rode in silence. It was a cold, wet morning when they started out and mist shrouded the land. She realised she had become one of the things people feared in the mist. She was one of the things that made people spit to avert evil.

Bress's eyes were closed as he concentrated. Britha had the disconcerting feeling that he was looking through the eyes of one of the Lochlannach he had sent ahead to scout. The sky remained cloudy, but the worst of the mist was gone now. The day had been interspersed with heavy showers, though none of them had lasted long, and somehow her robe still wasn't soaked through. They had been riding, more slowly now, along a track next to a river in a narrow cliff-lined valley. They stopped on the track and Bress had ordered them into the woods, though the trees were providing little in the way of cover for their large white horses and more than a dozen fully armoured warriors.

'Well?' Britha asked.

'Many warriors, easily in the hundreds, and they are escorting a column of landsfolk in their thousands.'

'They will be fleeing the Muileartach's children,' Britha said.

'And they will come upon us soon.'

'You don't mean to fight them?' Britha asked incredulously. 'Not even your Lochlannach could fight that many.' Then she thought about it and knew that wasn't true. Bress's expression hadn't changed. 'You can't – the slaughter would be appalling.'

'They are in my way and they are no friends of ours.'

'Because you raided their villages, killed their families, enslaved the rest and tried to sacrifice them!'

'All true, but none of it matters.'

'We could go around the valley rather than through it.'

'That would put many days on the journey. Each day we waste means that we will have to ride further into the changed land of the Muileartach's spawn, and they will be able to hurt us. We will ride through them, and keep riding. We will kill as few as possible.'

'All to make sure you kill as many people of this island as you possibly can!' Britha spat.

'I've just said—'

'This isn't ruthlessness, this is the red pleasure in taking lives, in hurting others, in spreading pain. You're no different from that ... that sick thing back in the cave!'

For a moment, Britha thought she had pushed him too far, and she saw his face harden.

'I take no pleasure in it. I just don't care,' he told her.

'There has to be another way,' she said evenly.

'Those are nothing but words. *Find* me another way.'

They had been keeping pace with her in the woods for some time now. They were good. At first Britha thought that an animal, perhaps a lynx, was stalking her, as she had caught sight of something with fur moving in the trees. Quickly she realised it was scouts moving ahead of the huge column of warriors and landsfolk they were approaching.

She rode down the muddy track, her spear pointed down to show that she came with peaceful intent. That and her robes, which marked her as *dryw*, should be enough to keep her safe. *Initially, at least,* she thought.

She did not recognise the tribe of the warriors who met her on the track. They all favoured long, intricately braided moustaches but eschewed beards. They carried longspears and shields, with sword and daggers at their hips, as Britha would expect. Casting spears had been driven into the earth close to where the warriors stood. A number of them had skulls they had taken hanging from their belts. A few wore mail, but most had armour made of plates of boiled leather. They looked tired, and travel-worn, but they were alert. Most of them were scarred in some way, and many were missing fingers. Britha knew that these were real warriors, not pretenders. She also knew they were on edge.

Beyond them she could see the refugee camp, which spread up the hillside on both sides of the track and out of the valley. It was odd that they were not moving if they sought to escape the children of Muileartach.

'Are you come from them?' one of the warriors demanded. He was a big man, his face a scarred and mangled mess, which suggested that either he was not a particularly good warrior, or he had been around for a long time. Judging by the skulls hanging from his belt, Britha suspected the latter.

'Who?' Britha asked.

'The spirits from the forest,' another warrior answered, this one younger.

'I come from a place where warriors are not too afraid to introduce themselves before they question strangers. I am Britha, *ban draoi* to the Cirig, a people who come from far to the North.'

'What do you want—' the younger man started, but the scarred warrior cuffed him around the back of the head.

'I am Borth, whom they call the Tall, Borth of a Hundred Battles, the Head-Harvester, the Child of the Red Man,' the scarred man said.

'And you have my apologies for my rudeness. You may claim what you want of me, and I will of course submit to any judgement you make.'

'That will not be necessary,' Britha replied. 'It is easy to forget your manners when times are hard, and enemies are at your front and back.'

'Aye, true enough,' Borth said, nodding. 'Will you eat and sup with us? As you see, we have many under our care, but what we have is yours.' It was a formal offer of hospitality.

'Now I must be rude, I am afraid,' Britha told him. She saw a frown appear on the warrior's scarred visage. 'I feel that to accept your offer of hospitality, well made though it is, would be to do you a disservice and mislead you.'

Borth remained silent for a moment as he thought on her words. Then he turned to the younger warrior he'd cuffed and nodded towards the camp. The young man loped off in that direction.

'Speak plainly,' Borth said, turning back to Britha.

'I come on behalf of the Lochlannach and their warleader Bress,' she told them.

Borth was shaking his head. 'You speak as though I should know who this is.'

'The raiders in the black *curraghs*.'

That got their attention. There was the sound of sharp iron sliding out of leather. Others readied their longspears or picked up casting spears. Borth held his hand up to stop them from attacking.

'Those are sour words indeed, as they are no friends to any here.' His tone was cold now. 'They harvested great suffering among our people.'

'Let me kill her,' one of the other warriors said, a short, squat, powerfully built woman almost as badly scarred as Borth.

Britha faced her. 'I am still a *dryw*, and you will respect that unless you would see your line cursed,' Britha told her in the voice that brooked no argument.

'What line?' the woman spat, taking a step towards Britha. 'Those you didn't kill you took away in your *curraghs* to sacrifice to your god who is a sickness, so I hear it.'

'Enough, Eithne,' Borth said quietly. He appeared to command enough respect among his warriors that the woman lapsed into an uneasy brooding silence and settled for just glaring at Britha. 'You have come with your spear down, so we will listen,' Borth told her. 'What would you have of us?'

'Yes, what would you have of us?' another voice asked. Five figures were making their way down the trail. The one who had spoken wore a dark robe not unlike hers, except the shape suggested that it covered armour, which was very unusual for a *dryw*, and he looked to be well built beneath it. A hood covered his features, a sword hung from his hip – also unusual for a *dryw* – and he carried a staff.

With him was a large warrior with an equally large belly, clad in mail with a black cloak, thick beard and long, black hair shot through with white. One of his eyes was milky and clearly blind.

There was a wiry-looking boy of about ten or twelve. Something in the boy's movement and his guarded expression reminded Britha of a wild animal.

A woman who looked old enough to have seen forty summers accompanied the boy. Her emaciated frame and the rags barely covering it told of her recent trials, but she still carried herself with strength and dignity.

The fifth person with the group was Germelqart.

She felt a warmth spreading through her at the sight of the Carthaginian navigator who, along with Kush and Tangwen, had saved her from Ettin. Then she saw his expression: guarded suspicion, bordering on fear.

She was also aware of quiet, careful movement in the woods at her back but resisted the urge to turn and look. She assumed it was the scouts who had kept pace with her, preparing to act in case she tried something.

'Why do you hide your face?' Britha demanded of the black-robed, armoured man as the five figures stopped by Borth. The other warriors had made way for them. The man reached up and pushed his hood down. He had a long beard and moustache, both intricately braided, and his head was shorn of hair.

'To keep the rain from my head. I am Bladud, who some call the Witch King. This is Nerthach, my strong right arm. This is Anharad of the Trinovantes and her grandson Mabon.' The boy was now glaring at Britha with hatred. 'And—'

'And Germelqart, the Carthaginian,' Britha finished for the Witch King. 'I am glad to see you well.'

The navigator inclined his head slightly but remained quiet. She felt like he was studying her.

'She is with the raiders,' Borth told them.

Britha noticed that Mabon was still moving towards her. She was worried he would do something stupid and force her to hurt or kill him. The woman was also glaring at her with undisguised hatred. She looked familiar to Britha but she couldn't place her.

'Indeed,' Bladud said. There was no hint of hostility in his voice, though she noticed Nerthach's hand was resting on the pommel of his sheathed sword. 'And what would they have of us?'

'I beg your forgiveness, but I must ask Germelqart something.' She turned to face the navigator. 'What of Kush and Tangwen?' She could see the conflict written all over the quiet man's face.

'I do not think I should answer that,' he said eventually.

Britha had half-expected this response, but she was still surprised by how much it hurt. On the other hand, she now knew they were still alive.

'Why not?' she asked, but she knew the answer.

'Because you have fallen.'

She had not expected him to put it that way. 'I ...' she started, but found she had nothing to say.

The woman, Anharad, spat on the ground and made the sign to ward off evil.

'Fallen or no,' Germelqart said to Anharad, 'you owe this woman your life, as do we all.'

Nerthach grunted his disdain and spat as well. Britha felt her fingers tighten around the shaft of her spear.

'She will be dealt with fairly,' Bladud said.

'I mistrust a warrior who dresses as a *dryw* and styles himself a king,' Britha said. Nerthach bristled and stepped forwards. Bladud put a hand on his shoulder.

'Understandable, for you do not know me, but I am afraid you'll just have to accept it,' he said, affably enough.

'I have come from Bress, warleader of the Lochlannach. He and his warband wish to pass this way and do you no harm. Will you let us by?'

There was a lot of angry muttering from the people gathered there. Mabon actually hissed at her. Bladud just looked thoughtful.

'Why are you asking?' Bladud asked. 'He has never cared about the niceties before.'

'Our business is not with you. It is with our mutual enemies that follow behind you, and I would not see bloodshed here.'

'She cannot be trusted. She is a traitor to her people,' Anharad said. Britha turned to glare at her, a look that would cow most people. The other woman held it, and gave it back.

'*You* do not wish bloodshed, or *he* does not wish bloodshed?' Bladud asked.

'You cannot be considering this?' Anharad demanded, forcefully enough to make Nerthach turn a questioning eye on her.

'I do not wish bloodshed,' Britha said. 'He truly does not care.'

'Then let him come here,' said Borth the Tall, 'and we will meet him with sword and spear. His people fared well enough against landsfolk and a few warriors taken unawares. Let us see how he does against an Iceni shield wall.' There were nods and muttered agreements from the other warriors present, including Nerthach.

'Bring him here,' Bladud said. The others stared at him, and then a clamour of angry shouting broke out. The so-called Witch King let it wash over him. He never took his eyes off her. Britha knew she was being studied. What worried her more was that she was struggling to read his intent. Finally Bladud looked over at Nerthach and nodded.

'Quiet!' the black-bearded warrior roared.

'Will he be attacked if I bring him to you?' Britha asked.

'Is he frightened?' Bladud enquired. Some of the warriors laughed.

Britha sighed. 'I ask you this for your own safety, but I think you will not believe me.'

The warriors present were still laughing and said exactly what she expected them to. She kept her eyes on Bladud. He gave little away.

Then Bladud spoke. 'He does not have hospitality because I will not suffer those he has wronged so grievously to have to share meat and drink with him. Whilst we treat, however, he is under my protection. If any attack him, then I will defend him to my death.'

'As will I, and all warriors sworn to Bladud,' Nerthach said begrudgingly. Borth the Tall and the other warriors that Britha guessed were Iceni looked less than pleased about this.

'And how do I know—' Britha asked. Bladud held his hand up. It was a simple gesture, but she fell silent despite herself.

'You are about to insult me. Please don't, because then I will be forced to act, and nobody will get what they want. Rest assured that I was learning the laws and the lore in the groves whilst your father's father was a young man.'

Britha stared at him for a while. 'Very well,' she said, and turned her horse around. She kicked the beast into a gallop along the muddy trail. She glanced back, again despite herself. The others were talking amongst themselves, but Germelqart stood apart from them, watching her ride away. Britha wondered if Tangwen was watching her from the woods, an arrow nocked, her bow ready.

'What is this? You would betray all these people?' Anharad demanded.

'If only the Trinovantes warriors were as fearsome as their women ...' Nerthach suggested. Anharad turned on him, but Bladud called for calm.

'Please, peace,' Bladud said. 'When we fight among ourselves we do our enemies' bidding. Can you please trust me? If I do not do right by you then you can choose another leader.'

'Not if we have all been put in another wicker man and set on fire!' Anharad snapped. Bladud had come to value the Trinovantes woman's council. She came from warrior stock and had a good head on her shoulders. A practical and no-nonsense woman, she had obviously helped run the village her husband ruled. Bladud had never seen her so angry.

'Anharad is right,' Borth the Tall said. 'We need to prepare to fight them.'

'We should,' Bladud said, 'but I would speak to them first.'

'Why?' Anharad demanded. 'They are of the Otherworld, the fair folk. Why would you give them the opportunity to glamour you?'

Because, Bladud thought, *Tangwen was told by her father that only the Otherworldly raiders have the power to defeat the Muileartach, and I must find a way to steal that power from them.*

31

Close to the Oceanic Pole of Inaccessibility, 3 Weeks Ago

He shouldn't feel pain when he dreamed, not like this. He shouldn't have to keep waking up with blood pouring out of his eyes, nose and ears, a concerned-looking Siraja standing over him.

He didn't think he had the senses necessary to interpret it all. Instinctively, he saw, heard, felt, smelled and tasted in many different angles and from all perspectives. Even with his augmentations it was far too much information.

He heard birds on the wing over still-forming continents; felt the warmth of the sun as he moved through/with the living stone of the city; tasted the salt spray of the ocean; smelled the smoke, incense, sweat and funk of human, guardian, sea people and serpent alike. He could hear his sisters speaking to him throughout his – no, her – entire form. And he saw the ceremony.

The boy was exotic-looking, his homeland very difficult to pin down. He was impossibly tall and androgynously beautiful. He had been ceremonially shaved.

Most of the denizens of the city had come to see the ascension. They crowded the steps of the surrounding ziggurats and the basalt rooftops of the sepulchral buildings. Guardians clung, partially melded to the edge of the buildings. Serpents stood under complex silk parasols held up by multiple eunuchs. Those from the sea kept themselves wet in the cool, clear pools, little more than their black eyes showing above the water, and all found themselves sometimes in the shadow of waving tentacles and the massive, palpating bulks of the first as they drew themselves from their cooling melds with the living stone of the city.

The priest was a shortish man with an average build and a bit of a paunch. His features were those of someone from far to the east, and his skin was swarthy, leathery and weather-beaten, suggesting time spent at sea. He had a small, neatly trimmed and lacquered beard, black with just a few grey hairs, and he wore kohl around his dark eyes. His robe was of simple white linen.

The ceremony was taking place on one of the split-level ziggurats, around a pool on a platform about halfway up the stepped structure. The tall boy and the much shorter priest stood on one of the steps overlooking the green water, which was choked with strange plant life. Sinuous ripples in the water and the occasional glimpses of a blunt, reptilian maw were the only clues to the pool's inhabitants.

There was little or no fear in the boy's face. Even when one of the guardian servitors leaped from a nearby roof to land on the ziggurat's steps and partially sank into the stone, the boy showed little reaction. His mind had already been opened by the consumption of various narcotic compounds.

The small, bearded, pot-bellied man stepped into the pool and then reached up for the boy. The boy turned around and leaned back, letting himself fall. The priest caught him and lowered him down into the water. The sinuous movement in the water increased as something eel-like moved just below the surface. Electricity played across the water and strange flowers bloomed, though only beneath the surface.

The priest stepped out of the pool with as much dignity as his haste could afford him. He did not see the boy open his eyes as dragon-headed serpentine forms entwined themselves around him. He did not see the boy open his eyes, and the gulfs behind them, but Lidakika did. Then she felt the tear, and then everything was pulsing blue light.

'Lodup!'

Lidakika, that was his name, her name. He wasn't sure if this had been imparted to him in the dream, or whether it was just the way he had come to try and understand her, to try and fit her in his head. He had grown up hearing stories of the octopus that guided the god Sapkini and the crew of his canoe to the reef from which Pohnpei would spring.

'Lodup!'

He always struggled to wake from these dreams. It was as if they clung to him, reluctant to relinquish him to the waking world.

'Lodup, get up now!'

The clone-zombie – as he had started thinking of them – trying to wake him up sounded a lot more excitable than they usually did. Lodup opened his eyes to pulsing blue light flooding the submersible through its diamondoid observation bubble. He was crying tears of blood. Blood was also coming out of his mouth and ears. Again.

'What's happening . . . ?' Lodup started, then something hit the submersible hard. Everything slowed down as his augmented reactions stepped up his response time. Something gave in the submersible. Lodup had time to think: *That's not supposed to happen.* The water that breached the submersible was under so much pressure that it punched straight through the clone-zombie's hardening overalls and his toughened skin and cut a red rent through his flesh. The water that came out through the other side of his body was red.

This is going to hurt, Lodup thought. Then he hit the submersible's internal bulkhead. There was another impact as the vessel hit something hard that stopped them dead, and then it was tumbling slowly through the water. Lodup tried to find something to hold on to. His foot dropped through the jet of water. He yanked it out, but it was too late. The pain was only momentary. He barely had time to scream before the signals from his nerve endings in that area were cut off. He somehow had the presence of mind to pull his legs up and curl into a foetal position as he held on to the handle for the hatch.

Outside he could see the city slowly spinning. It took him a moment to realise that the submersible was turning end-over-end. He could hear someone talking in urgent tones in his ear but didn't want to focus on the voice. The blue pulsing light was fading. There was a final impact and an explosion of silt and other particulate matter as the submersible hit the seabed. He could understand the words he was hearing now.

'All divers recall, I repeat, recall.' It was Siska. This had to be serious. Lodup looked down numbly at his blood swirling in the crystal-clear water that was rapidly filling the submersible. He stared at the ruin of his foot. In his mind he was receiving information about the bruises, contusions and at least two fractures that had resulted due to whatever had hit the submersible, which was now lying on its side. The clone-zombie was dead. Lodup hadn't even bothered to learn the name of the person he was a copy of.

Lodup forced himself to stop looking at the stump of his foot. Already nanites were fixing his other injuries, making flesh from his fat stores. Skin grew over the stump. He took a moment to artificially correct his breathing and chemically alter his anxiety and fear, and then looked around.

They had been surveying some of the rooms within one of the tomblike structures, looking for tech they might have missed on earlier visits. They were heading back towards the habitat. Deane was supporting them in an ADS. The dive supervisor had been working with him a lot more recently, since the blackouts and the dreams started. Since Hideo had gone thatch and murdered Sal. He was pretty sure Siska wanted one of the 'immortals' keeping an eye on him at all times.

He pulled himself up and moved forwards, careful to avoid the jet of water still rapidly filling the submersible. They'd hit one of the ziggurats and tumbled down the steps to the seabed. Lodup was pretty sure it was the one from his dream – it had the same split-level look to it. Above him he could make out the sled-like AUVs moving quickly through the water to converge on something. Lodup saw tubular ripples as the AUVs fired torpedo after torpedo at an unseen target. An orange light glowed behind him. Water boiled, then one of the AUVs came apart. The submersible rocked as the water-amplified shock wave hit it. Lodup saw the spiked balls of the smart mines dropping through the water, then lost sight of them. There was light, and distorted noise, followed by the concussive force of successive rapid shock waves battering the submersible. He was thrown about in the water now half-filling the vessel and only just avoided losing another piece of his body to the jet of water. His severed foot bounced off his head.

There was more bright orange light above him, and part of the ziggurat exploded. He was appalled at the force that would be required to do that. He saw lumps of the alien-technology-infused masonry raining down on the submersible and held on to the hatch handle for dear life as the craft took another battering. The water started rising even more rapidly. He could hear the creaks of the stressed matter of the hull as the crack weakened the vessel's structural integrity.

'Deane?' Lodup subvocalized as he evacuated air from his body and started to fill hollow cavities with saline, sucking water through the intakes in the technological gills implanted in his chest.

'I've got you, Lodup,' Deane said. Even though he knew the dive supervisor was subvocalizing, the other man sounded particularly quiet, subdued, frightened.

'Okay, the sub's taking on water. I'm going to need to let it fill completely to equalise the pressure and hope it doesn't collapse before I can get out.'

'Understood. You're covered in debris at the moment—'

'Don't try moving it until the submersible's full of water, copy?'

'Understood. How's John?'

'Who?' Lodup asked before he realised Deane must be talking about the submersible pilot. 'He's dead.' *Or as dead as anyone gets around here*, he added silently. 'What's going on?'

'I don't know,' Deane said quietly. 'We're being attacked.'

By who? The light and the explosions appeared to be getting further away, but they were moving towards the habitat. There was no more information coming from C&C other than the repeating diver recall, though it was Siraja's voice now, not Siska's. He lay there, occasionally feeling a slight tremor from distant shock waves. At last, the submersible was completely flooded.

'Now,' he subvocalized to Deane. He felt the vessel shaking as the dive supervisor used the ADS's exoskeleton to remove the rubble. Finally the submersible was shifted to make it easier for him to use the hatch. He didn't like the sound of stressed metal echoing through the water. He started to turn the lock. At first it wouldn't shift, so Lodup internally shifted matter and energy to his arm muscles. He felt himself becoming thinner. Slowly the lock started turning. He managed to move it all the way around, but when he pushed the hatch wouldn't open.

'Deane, I can't get the hatch open,' Lodup said. He knew that even with the power of the ADS he wouldn't be able to breach the observation bubble. That would take something insidious and truly powerful, like water under pressure.

'It looks warped from this side,' Deane said. Lodup heard a scraping sound on the hull and the submersible moved as the ADS shifted its position outside. 'Okay, get away from the hatch. I have to do some cutting, and it's going to get hot in there.'

Lodup moved all the way forward and stared out of the observation bubble. Part of it was buried in the debris, and it looked like someone had taken a bite out of the ziggurat. The water above him was empty, but behind him, he could see nearly constant flashes of light.

The condensed adamantine hull next to the hatch was glowing white, the water around it bubbling as the heat of the ADS's fusion torch boiled it. When Deane finished cutting, Lodup craned his neck to look through the submersible's observation bubble. He saw Deane's ADS holding up the submersible with one hand while the other pulled on the hatch. The creaks from the stressed hull were louder now. The water amplified the noise, making it sound much worse than it was. The submersible shook as the hatch was finally wrenched open and Lodup made his way through, careful to avoid the parts of the hull still glowing red.

When Lodup was clear, the ADS dropped the submersible, which caused an explosion of silt and a slide of debris. Lodup found Siraja standing in the silt cloud.

'Where have you been?' Lodup subvocalized as he looked around. About half a mile from his position there was a lot of light refracting through the water. He saw bubbles of fire encasing explosions rising above the roofs of the once-living buildings. A line of orange, flame-like light that reminded Lodup of lava reached up from an unseen street in the city and pierced the armoured body of one of the orcas. The body ruptured, glowing armour plate and chunks of cooked meat drifting towards the sea floor, boiling the water around them.

'I was busy,' Siraja said tersely. Three Archies were silhouetted above the lights, half-striding, half-propelling themselves towards the area of disturbance. 'You need to move quickly and return to the habitat. I have plotted you a safe but circuitous route.'

Suddenly a three-dimensional map of the city's confusing layout appeared in Lodup's mind. Siraja's suggested route was highlighted in red.

'Won't whoever is attacking us be going there, too?' Lodup asked.

'Yes,' Deane said over the ultrasound link, 'but it's also heavily defended. It's either that or we stay out here and get picked off on our own.'

'Who's attack—' Lodup started to ask Siraja, but the dragon-headed AI had already disappeared. It occurred to him that the AI became considerably less polite during stressful situations.

They watched as torpedo after torpedo disappeared between the ziggurats and tomblike buildings of the city. The structures between them and the fight-zone were thrown into sharp relief by the light of the bubbles of explosions and the shock waves buffeted them. The thick lava-like beams of force reached out again, drawing scorch marks and glowing lines of cooked meat through one of the massive Archies. Lodup was appalled when he saw the massive creature topple. The lights of the city were dimmed as tonnes of silt were thrown up into the water.

Now smaller lines of the same lava-like force were boiling water as they destroyed incoming torpedoes, smart mines and AUVs. Lodup and Deane watched as several of the security-pod orcas dived down into the city, firing various munitions at the unseen attacker. The thicker line of force was almost constant, like a searchlight, as it sought out, ruptured and destroyed one orca after another until they broke off their attack.

'Have you got security feed from the habitat?' Lodup asked.

'Nothing,' Deane said.

'What do you think? The habitat's a tin can.'

'They said to go back,' Deane replied, though the dive supervisor still hadn't moved. 'Siraja's right, it's heavily defended.' The 'immortal' sounded like he was trying to convince himself.

Lodup just pointed at the demonstration of fire and force happening in the streets of the sunken city.

'Let's head back,' Deane said. Some of his authority appeared to be returning.

Or his obedience, Lodup thought.

Lodup finned over to the ADS and grabbed one of the diver handholds on its armoured form. Deane expertly manoeuvred the impellers to send them floating over the seabed. He kept low, under the height of the buildings, skimming through the streets.

The light from the explosions and the strange beam weapons made a show of disconcerting, grotesque, flickering shadows. Lodup looked towards the fight, trying to catch glimpses of it between the buildings, along twisting streets, in the junctions and crossroads. He saw orcas swimming down low between the buildings, firing electromagnetically propelled harpoons and torpedoes of various sizes before seeking cover. The strange beam cut relentlessly through the buildings as if they didn't exist. He watched as one of the heavily armed submersibles used by the security force was ruptured by several of the thinner beams. The superstructure buckled and the submersible was crushed as four hundred atmospheres of pressure did the rest.

Lodup caught a glimpse of the thing that was attacking them down an avenue lined with strange, petrified, tree-like growths as they moved parallel with it. It had a blocky body, not organic but not mechanical-looking either. He couldn't make out much in the way of detail. Then it started to glow with an inner light and spiral patterns inscribed on its body lit up from within. Its head, which looked hollow, vomited the lava-like light. As it fired the beam, Lodup noticed that its legs tapered off into glowing rootlike structures which pierced the seabed.

Tethers attached smaller, floating constructs to the walking thing. They were broadly triangular in shape and reminded Lodup of flowers for some reason. They emitted the thinner beams of the lava-like force. Lodup guessed they were something like tethered ROVs. As he watched, another one grew from the walking thing's body and propelled itself away through the water as far as the connecting tether would allow.

The walking thing fell into darkness as one of the Archies loomed over it, probably the last of the three giant creatures that remained, Lodup thought. An armoured tentacle wrapped around the construct. The roots on the thing's legs flexed, grew and anchored it more deeply into the seabed as it started to glow from within. Then it was gone from sight, but he could still see the burning light stabbed up, again and again, cooking, cutting and blistering wherever the beam hit.

Over the infrasound link, Lodup was aware of Deane sending packets of information warning the base that they were incoming. As they got closer to the habitat, they could see batteries of torpedo launchers firing, while others regrew new payloads from the surrounding matter.

*

They surfaced into the bright light and semi-organised chaos of the moon pool.

The ADS dumped Lodup unceremoniously onto the pontoon jetty. Deane didn't wait for one of the roof-mounted cranes to hoist the ADS out of the water. Instead, he grabbed the metal framework of the jetty, which buckled slightly as the ADS pulled itself awkwardly out of the water, its back already splitting open. As soon as it stopped moving, Deane's hands appeared out of the dark, organic-looking matter that filled the ADS and he pulled himself from the exoskeleton.

'C'mon!' Despite his tall, wiry frame, Deane had no problems hoisting Lodup over his shoulder. The healing abilities of his augmented body could only do so much, and his foot was still just a stump.

Lodup tried calling Siraja to find out what was going on and request access to the external camera feeds, but the AI wasn't answering. He assumed Siraja was securing the habitat's electronic systems from intrusion, which probably necessitated cutting off all comms access.

Divers were surfacing constantly and clambering out of the moon pool alongside submersibles being hastily secured as their crews clambered out. ADSs were climbing or being lifted out of the water.

'C'mon, move! *Now!*' Yaroslav's voice filled the moon pool chamber. He was changing the magazine in his weapon – a modified .45 calibre Vector sub-machine gun, standard issue for all members of the security teams. The guns were equipped with suppressors to deaden the noise from the weapons in a confined area, and Lodup noticed that most of the visible security personnel had removed the suppressors and were changing the magazines on their weapons. The majority of the SMGs had M26 Modular Accessory Shotgun Systems mounted on Picatinny rails under the barrels. They were also replacing the magazines on the shotguns. Yaroslav had an M320 40 millimetre grenade-launcher mounted beneath his SMG.

'Each of you will empty the magazines from your primary and secondary weapons in an orderly and accurate manner, before falling back and switching to your sidearms!' Yaroslav shouted, addressing his security personnel, who were staying out of the way as divers, submersible pilots and ADS jocks evacuated the moon pool chamber.

Yaroslav was changing the magazine on his sidearm, a .45 calibre Heckler & Koch USP, as Deane carried Lodup past him.

Above them, the multi-barrelled rotary weapons were moving back and forth under their inverted, tower-like ammunition drums.

They were among the last out of the moon pool chamber. Deane stood by the door, his earlier hesitation, his earlier fear forgotten as he made sure all his personnel were clear of the chamber.

The security detail formed up along the edge of the pool. They didn't bother with cover. They knew there was no point. More security personnel lined the synthetic-grass-carpeted corridors beyond the moon pool chamber, leaving a narrow throughway should any retreating comrades need to pass.

'Right, not much more we can do here – let's go and hide,' Deane suggested over the nearly constant thudding of repeated shock waves breaking against the diamondoid superstructure of the habitat.

'C-and-C?' Lodup said.

The habitat shifted slightly underneath them from a particularly heavy impact. Then everything went quiet.

'I'll drop you off and then you're on your own,' Deane told him.

Lodup had to hop into C&C. Deane left him propped up against the blast door, and he had to bang a few times before it finally opened just wide enough to admit him, then closed immediately behind him.

Inside the dimly lit control area there was little sign of panic or chaos, with the exception of the images playing across the wall. The staff remained lying on their couches, presumably linked into the habitat's systems. A blast door now covered the window that normally looked out over the moon pool. Siraja was standing motionless in front of the blast shield. It was difficult to tell with his draconic features, but Lodup was pretty sure he was concentrating intently.

'I indulge you because you actually have real meat between your ears,' Siska told him as she reloaded her twin .45 calibre Sig Sauer P220 automatic pistols. She chambered rounds and re-holstered them at her hips, safeties off. 'However, if you want to stay here, you need to keep out of the way and remain fucking silent.'

Lodup didn't answer. He was looking at the feeds from various cameras being played across the wall: Yaroslav and the security detail in the pool below; the slow-motion rain of debris on the city; the wreckage and remains of the three Archies and the gutted corpses of several orcas; the damage done to the alien architecture; the destroyed submersibles, torpedo batteries and AUVs. Then finally he saw it, walking inexorably across the seabed, leaving a trail of silt in its wake. There was little left out there still attacking it.

Lodup got a clearer look at the thing this time as it strode past one of the cameras. It was about fifteen feet tall and looked like it was made of granite. A series of small torpedoes detonated around it, staggering and buffeting it, but the rootlike stone structures growing from its legs anchored it firmly to the seabed. As it glowed with internal light, Lodup saw in more detail the spiral and knotwork patterns inscribed on it. They reminded him of the tattoos on some of his former Navy shipmates. It vomited the lava-like light from its hollow head and one of the few remaining AUVs was destroyed.

It started walking up the ramp into the moon pool. On the local feed, Lodup watched the rotary weapons start firing hydrodynamic rounds into the water, the barrage audible even through the blast shield covering the window. The water frothed, but it continued walking up the ramp. There were so many impacts on the creature that Lodup couldn't make out whether or not the weapons were doing any damage. Surely something in the centre of a firestorm that intense would be totally destroyed. He was appalled when the onslaught didn't even slow the thing down. Then its head rose from the water.

The security detail started firing their Vector SMGs and M26 shotguns. Lodup knew that the nanite-tipped ordnance they were now loaded with would eat through or otherwise break down any matter they came into contact with. As they fired measured, accurate bursts with the SMGs, Lodup wondered how many of the bullets collided in mid-air because the fire was so heavily concentrated. They didn't slow the thing down, either.

Lodup glanced over at Siska. She looked concerned, which worried him. In the three weeks he'd been working here, he'd never seen her look anything other than in complete control.

Some of the cameras whited out. Lodup felt heat rise from the floor as C&C lurched and glanced at the moon pool feed as it came back online. The thing's hollow head was still glowing white and there was a massive rent in the wall of the chamber where its beam had cut straight through it. Parts of the diamondoid structure were burning in a way he knew they shouldn't. Little more than a few smoking chunks of flesh remained of the security detail. The few who had been on the edge of the staggered line were still alive, but horribly burned and screaming.

Yaroslav was somehow still up, his left side and most of his back blackened and blistered with still-bubbling flesh. His face was a mask of agony as he tried to pull a member of the security detail back towards the moon pool's exit, firing his Vector one-handed as he did so.

'We have to do it now,' Siraja said, an urgency in his voice that Lodup had never heard before.

The ROV analogues tethered to the creature, which Lodup had thought looked a little like flowers, rose from the water, their thinner beams reaching out to burn the air and turn the rotary weapons into slag.

'Request permission,' Siska said. Lodup had no idea who she was talking to. He suspected it was a sign of her nervousness that she had even spoken the words out loud. 'No, sir, I cannot see another way. It's either this or we lose the whole facility.'

The granite-skinned thing was stepping out of the water now. Small-arms fire sparked off its granite body from the corridor, which it ignored. It knelt down, its massive hands growing, mimicking the rootlike structure of its legs, and reached into the floor of the habitat.

Siraja opened his draconic maw to say something but it turned into an agonised electronic scream, then his image was burning, and then it was gone.

'Sending the signal,' Siska said, staring at the space where Siraja's image had been.

Agony shot through Lodup. He cried out and then vomited blood as it squirted out of his nose and ran out of his ears and eyes. The world went away and there was only the white light of agony filling his vision. He wasn't aware of collapsing. As the pain faded, he was nearly overwhelmed by a primal, instinctive fear. He knew something utterly inimical to his very existence was out there. Moving.

Through the blood in his eyes and the white-light pain, he was barely able to make out one of the feeds. It showed the black lake, the cold seep consisting of salty brine much thicker than the surrounding water, with its beach of mussels. Something was climbing out of the black lake. It looked like a living oil slick. It filled Lodup with terror that sprang from something hardwired and ancient within him, a racial memory.

He became aware of Siska nearby. She was crying tears of blood as more leaked from her ears and nose. She spat red on the carpet as she looked down at him.

The thing stretched from the black lake, moving across the seabed rapidly, forming pseudopods and tendrils of a black, viscous material that appeared plastic and liquid at the same time. Sluggish initially, its pace increased as it seeped through the streets of the sunken city towards the light, energy and life of the habitat. Whatever it was, it absorbed the glow of the city's floodlights, only noticeable by its movement.

'We're sealing the moon pool. Anyone not through the blast door is dead,' Siska said quietly, her voice amplified throughout the habitat.

Lodup glanced at the moon pool feed. There was nobody left alive there. The stone thing was still growing roots into the habitat's superstructure.

'What is it?' Lodup managed, meaning the thing from the black lake.

'Programmable biomass,' Siska answered.

'You didn't make that thing.'

'No, it's much, much older than us.'

The lights went out in the moon pool. Lodup looked at one of the feeds and saw inky black tendrils and pseudopods wrap around the stone thing. The living-oil-slick-thing pulled part of its mass up and out of the water. The stone thing's head turned a hundred and eighty degrees and started to glow. Where the oily pseudopods touched it, the granite-skinned creature started to dissolve. Lodup watched its roots withering. The stone thing was torn off the habitat and pulled into the water, engulfed by the black oil, which started to seep away from the habitat, but slowly, as if reluctantly.

Lodup glanced up at Siska. She had a look of great concentration on her face.

Lodup was not, and had never been, a fearful man. He was not a great risk-taker or an adrenalin junkie, which were factors that made him such a good diver. He could think on his feet and hold it together in difficult situations. After it was over, he sat against the wall of the C&C and wept. A shadow fell across him. He looked up at Siska.

'You wanted to see,' she said, but not unkindly.

'What...?' he started.

She knelt down next to him. 'You're a curious fellow, aren't you?' she said, smiling slightly. 'And no.'

'It won't make any difference—' he started. Then he realised that things would never be the same knowing he shared a planet with the 'programmable biomass'. The worst thing was that he still didn't want to leave.

'We're never going to tell you everything. I don't know everything. We have enemies. The more you know, the more of a risk you are.'

'What enemies? Who did that?' he asked, desperation in his voice. Siska shook her head. 'Why don't I want to go home?'

'That's not our conditioning any more,' she said. 'You're not a clone, you're real meat, and you don't have quite the level of protection that lifers like myself, Yaroslav and Deane have. Siraja thinks something in the city is reaching out to you. Trying to communicate.'

'I want to leave.'

'That's the thing, Lodup – you really don't.'

And he knew she was right.

Half of Yaroslav's face was a flaking, blackened mess. He had lost body mass and was eating energy bar after energy bar as his flesh healed itself and shed large scabs of skin like burned dandruff. He was running through the footage as he healed.

It started at the stone circle with the ground shaking. Then a light began to fill the stones from within, rising up from the seabed and into the stones, until the pictograms carved into them burned brightly with the internal glow. The water was boiling all around them. Then a sphere of pulsing blue light appeared in the centre of the stones and became a sucking vortex. Water poured through it into apparent nothingness. Then it was gone, leaving in its place a large, egg-shaped granite boulder. Initially it looked as if the granite egg was hatching, but it was growing limbs, then a hollow head, transforming into the thing that had attacked the base.

'He does not think it was the Brass City,' Siska said quietly to Yaroslav.

'It was a data raid,' Yaroslav said in his thick accent as he took another bite of energy bar.

'It was a data attack, and it wasn't their style. Besides, how would they hack the stones? The Brass City are subtler, more thorough. He thinks it was the Egg Shell.'

Yaroslav stared at her. 'Because it was L-tech?' he asked. 'The Brass City use L-tech. They specialise in infoscapes—'

'It was a fetch. Geothermal-powered or not, its weapon was the sun. It was a thing of Lug's.'

'How long?' Yaroslav asked.

'Thousands of years.'

Yaroslav just nodded.

32
A Long Time after the Loss

The *Basilisk II* might have been an elegant yacht designed for speed and augmented for stealth and combat, but as it sank into the meteorite to harvest matter for raw materials, she looked like a parasitical insect.

The window tint had been removed and the pool room was bathed in the unsettling crimson glow of Red Space. Talia was wearing plastic polarised glasses as she stared out through the ornate circular window, watching the pool fill with water. She had a smouldering inhalable narcotic in one hand and a bottle of red wine in the other.

'You consume everything,' she said quietly, her voice full of sad awe. Vic hoped she wasn't going to start crying again. He'd been waiting for a quiet time to review some footage taken from the mind of his possessed copy, the one who had been imprisoned on Suburbia. He interrogated the neunonics in the human form before he let the ship absorb and claim the body's matter as raw material. He absently wondered if the carbon that had been harvested would eventually end up in one of his meals.

He wasn't sure why he hadn't told Scab about what he'd done. He guessed it was a false sense of independence.

He recognised the featureless automatons in the strange pre-Loss clothes. They belonged to a bounty killer called Mr Hat, a diminutive lizard with an enormous hat who had inadvertently saved them when he attacked the Dead-Skin Masks. According to the bounty killer ratings, Mr Hat was as good as – if not better than – Scab and Vic had been before they became fugitives. He had an impressive record, but was dogged by persistent rumours that his automatons were programmed with highly illegal deification routines. Vic had a feeling he'd met the lizard bounty killer before, but that was one of the periods Scab had edited out of his memory during his frequent neural audits. It may even have been the first time Scab killed him.

Vic felt strangely calm. He had known that someone they had

angered would send people after them. This was confirmation. That was all.

'Are you going to tell him?' Elodie asked. Even with the augmented aural abilities of his skin, Vic had struggled to hear the feline enter the pool area, though he picked up her disturbance of the air particles via the passive motion detectors in his antennae. Talia, on the other hand, jumped when she heard Elodie's voice. She turned and glared at the feline and then stormed out.

Vic did pick up the quiet hiss as Talia walked past Elodie. After all, it had to be loud enough for the human nat to hear, too.

'You should be nicer to her,' Vic said. Elodie just shrugged. 'And tell him what?'

'About the automatons and their boss?'

Vic swivelled his head around just over two hundred degrees in a way that most non-'sects found disconcerting and stared at Elodie.

'I've got enough problems with Scab mind-fucking me.' Vic tapped his head. 'I can live without you hacking my neunonics as well. Besides, there's some insect-on-sentient-mammal porn in here that I think you'd find very distasteful.'

Elodie raised an eyebrow. 'You never know,' she said salaciously. Vic put it down to standard feline flirting. 'I've not hacked your neunonics, and if I had I certainly wouldn't admit it over something so trivial. I did the same thing you did – interrogated the neunonics on your hairless-monkey copy before the body was destroyed. I wanted to know what happened to my copy. You're a coward without neurosurgery, augmentations and drugs, by the way.'

Vic attempted a human shrug. He came to the conclusion that shrugging looked odd when you had as many limbs as he did.

'I assumed you'd do the same,' Elodie said, 'and you had that slack-mandibled look you always have when you're concentrating. It was a deductive guess, nothing more. So will you tell him?' she asked again.

'Well, now you've brought it up he already knows.'

'Only if he cares to.'

'He cares.' Both of them looked around at the sound of Scab's voice. He was naked, again, growing out of the smart matter next to the now full swimming pool as if the ship was extruding him. He had taken to living within the ship's smart matter. Vic suspected it was so the situation with his possessed son and his crew of serial-killer pirates wouldn't cause him to lose his temper and kill everyone else on the *Basilisk II*. Nobody else, not even Elodie, appeared to realise how close they were to dying every time a new story came in, or one of them made a comment. Scab's pale skin glowed red with the light from space outside. He wore two polarised lenses over his eyes.

'Why?' Vic asked. 'We knew we were going to have bounties on us.'

'Did we?' Scab replied. 'Nobody wants anybody else to get their hands on Talia. Even among the Consortium and the Monarchists, there's internal competition for her.'

'So?' Vic asked. He didn't really see how that mattered.

'So Mr Hat must be working for someone in particular, one of the factions,' Elodie said. 'Though I agree with Vic – what difference does that make?'

'I think he was my erstwhile employer's second choice,' Scab replied. 'If the theft of the cocoon hadn't been so out-and-out criminal, I think my employer would have preferred to use Mr Hat.'

'Because he's not such a psycho?' Vic asked.

Elodie raised an eyebrow, the ghost of a smile on her mouth.

'He programs automatons to worship him,' Scab said. There was no trace of irritation. He was merely imparting information.

'I stand by my initial statement,' Vic said. Elodie actually laughed this time. Scab frowned.

'So what?' Elodie said. 'He's employed by someone who's probably a little bit more pissed off at you than the rest of Known Space is. We get caught, we get fucked, whoever catches us.'

'I want to know how he is communicating with my erstwhile employer,' Scab said.

'He was on the other end of the blank at Arclight,' Vic pointed out.

'You think he may have a blank?' Elodie asked.

'The blank belonged to the Queen's Cartel,' Vic told them.

'The stakes have been raised,' Scab said simply. 'And he has access to blanks.'

'Again, so what?' Elodie asked. 'Are you going to tell us who he is?'

'No,' Scab told her.

Vic was regarding his partner carefully. 'You want a blank, don't you?' the 'sect asked. Scab looked over at him.

'What for?' Elodie asked. 'Blanks are twinned. You'll only be able to talk to your old employer.'

Scab ignored her. He concentrated on his cigarette.

'The person who hired you to steal the cocoon is on the Consortium board, isn't he?' Vic asked. Scab still said nothing.

'Wow! What a great pool!' The Alchemist – who Talia was insisting everyone should call Steve – said as he walked into the pool area. He was wearing some stained boxer shorts and an equally filthy, wide-open bathrobe. 'Full of water and everything! Are there any dream dragons in it? No. Weird. Imagine that. Just a shame I'm not currently in the body of a waterborne mammal, isn't it?'

Vic's olfactory sensors could pick up the stench from the other side of the pool room. Steve had gone on hygiene strike until he either got a dolphin body or his lack of hygiene annoyed Scab and the human killed him, whichever happened first. Elodie's nose wrinkled in disgust. As a feline she was suffering the worst from it.

'Why aren't the ship's nano-screens eliminating the scent molecules?' she demanded.

'I asked them not to,' Steve told her. 'Gee, I hope I can swim.' He jumped into the pool. A small slick of grime spread out from his body but it was quickly sanitised by the ship's nanites.

Elodie opened her mouth to say something but then received the neuronic warning from the ship at the same time as Vic and Scab. Elodie looked less than impressed. Vic and Scab started running. Scab sent instructions to the ship with a thought.

Scab had already overridden the door lock on Talia's room and it was wide open when he reached it. Vic was right behind him. Talia was struggling with the smart-matter bed, which had morphed to restrain the human nat. Beside her was a rapidly diminishing red-wine stain and the carpet was already absorbing a broken bottle. The bedsheets and carpet were absorbing blood from a ragged red gash on her wrist. Pills from a half-empty bottle were also scattered around the bed.

Scab stood next to the bed and looked at her. He took a drag on his cigarette.

'Talia!' Vic said, stopping just behind Scab. 'What did you do?'

Scab glanced at his partner.

'Let go of me!' Talia shouted at the bed.

Then the realisation of what she'd been trying to do hit Vic. 'Were you trying to kill yourself?' the 'sect demanded. He turned as he heard laughter. Elodie was walking down the carpeted hallway towards them.

'I don't think so,' the feline said. Scab was shaking his head. 'If she was, it was a pretty half-hearted attempt, don't you think?'

Vic returned his attention to Talia. He suspected he was never going to be able to understand humans.

She stopped struggling and looked up at him pathetically. 'I don't want to be here,' she told them.

'It's been ten minutes since her last little psychodrama,' Elodie said, coming to stand by Vic. 'She just wanted some attention. With

'Why didn't you come and talk to me?' Vic asked Talia.

'Because you don't care. You won't kill me,' she said plaintively.

I will, he thought, *I promise.*

Elodie glanced at the insect.

'Well, she's got my attention,' Scab said quietly and took another drag on his cigarette. 'We can't risk her actually managing to damage herself.' He turned to Vic. 'Sort out her wrist, purge her and then drop her into an immersion. I don't care which one. You can visit her there.'

Vic nodded.

'Bastards!' Talia shouted at them.

Elodie and Scab turned and walked out of the room, leaving Vic standing over the bed.

It had cost a fortune in terraforming to tint the atmosphere to make Lotus Eater's sun appear green in the sky, but then it was a privately owned planet. The owner, one of the Lords of the Monarchist systems, clearly liked it. Most of the planet was bespoke – designer flora and fauna, all of it set up to be appealingly 'alien' to once-human minds. Unlike most planets, it was almost empty. It had a tiny population.

The estate was suspended hundreds of feet above a garishly coloured savannah with oddly shaped plant life. Bizarre and exotic flying, stalking and grazing fauna populated the plain. Sculpted mountains rose in the distance.

The estate itself was made up of a series of steps surrounding a slowly revolving segmented house, each flight rotating counter to the direction of the ones above and below. Each step level had a garden, and each garden had a theme.

A crimson wound bordered with pulsing blue light appeared in the sky above the grasslands. With it came a sucking wind that tore plant-life, birds, flying lizards and six-legged, vacuum-mouthed herbivores off the plain and through the wound. The *Basilisk II* emerged from Red Space, its ordnance already firing. The forward airlock hung open like a mouth.

'Shiiiit!' Vic howled as a herbivore the size of a G-carrier narrowly missed him, bouncing off one of the airlock's support struts. The strut bent under the impact, but the smart matter immediately began repairing the damage.

There was a hypersonic ripping sound as the *Basilisk II* fired its current payload of kinetic harpoons at the orbital weapons platforms that would doubtless be targeting them by now. AG-driven smart munitions followed. The ship then began to regrow new munitions from its carbon reservoirs, running the base matter through military-grade assemblers programmed with complex weapon templates.

The wound in the air snapped shut behind them. The *Basilisk II*'s closer-range weapons – EM-driven assault cannon blisters, rotary laser batteries – were already firing, acting as point-defence weaponry. A storm of light and force fluctuated back and forth between the estate and the *Basilisk II* as it circled. In addition to destroying incoming munitions, the *Basilisk*'s short-range weapons systems were also targeting the estate's heavy weaponry and destroying the hardpoints. It looked as if the rotating anti-gravity estate had exploded.

Vic, Scab and the nearly invisible Elodie launched their armoured combat-exoskeleton forms from the airlock ramp and the airlock closed behind them. P-sats in heavy-combat chassis carried them into the firefight, sensors feeding a dazzling display of trajectories into their neunonics as tactical programs tried to find the safest route.

The sky lit up above them as the orbital defence network recovered from the surprise of a heavily armed ship appearing out of nowhere. Beams of energy destroyed kinetic harpoons and AG smart munitions, despite the latter's evasive manoeuvres and countermeasures.

The estate was beginning to recover as well. Vic and Scab felt the first weaponised nano-swarm, viral and electronic attacks. They were the best the money that allowed you to own and redesign a planet could buy. Not so long ago they would have overwhelmed Vic and Scab's countermeasures. That was before the fake auction and Scab going into credit, even if it was black credit. Their defences held. Nobody had noticed Elodie yet.

The *Basilisk II*'s energy-dissipation grid was constantly lit up, the ship's armour smoking, running in places as the carbon reservoirs struggled to regrow it. Kinetic harpoons rained down, hammering the vessel repeatedly towards the plain. Some missed the yacht and hit the plain, causing small tectonic events and large fauna stampedes.

Lasers and assault cannon rounds cleared the way for Scab, Vic and Elodie's flight. Any weapons systems that targeted them, the *Basilisk II* destroyed. Even so, Vic and Scab were glowing neon figures as their combat exoskeletons attempted to deal with the incoming laser-fire, and they were battered around in the air by explosions and projectile hits. Every time the ship destroyed one weapon system, another took over. Elodie still remained unnoticed.

Scab was flying the *Basilisk II*. He had multitasked, essentially forking his mind to control flight and defensive and offensive weapons, with a little help from the yacht's personality-spayed AI.

They landed on the third of six rotating levels. The garden had once consisted of artfully arranged stones, sand, lacquered wood and water features. It was now glass, ash, molten slag and steam. Security shutters had slid down, turning the AG estate into a floating fortress. It was also moving at speed towards rapid-reaction forces despatched from other estates owned by Lotus Eater's ruling family.

Vic aimed the strobe gun at nearby automated anti-personnel weapons that were targeting Scab and himself, pouring on fire from the rapidly cycling laser. One of the automated weapon systems glowed neon and exploded. Vic covered Scab as his human partner/captor advanced, double-barrelled laser rifle at the ready. Vic had no idea where Elodie was. The *Basilisk II* was a smoking mess. Most of the ship's armoured skin was bubbling as it was battered around in the air, hit again and again from orbit.

Scab threw programmed thermal seeds at the armoured shutters protecting the estate. The seeds glowed red, orange and finally white as they cut a large circle through the armour. Vic strode forwards, still firing the six-barrelled strobe gun, and kicked the armoured shutter in the centre of the circle cut by the thermal seeds. His power-assisted hard-tech leg knocked it in, and the white-hot edge of the armour plate set fire to the carpet inside. Vic felt something move past him. He assumed it was Elodie. He threw his strobe gun in through the hole, the weapon's spipod unfolding in mid-air. The six-barrelled rotary laser landed on the spipod's four legs and scuttled into the AG mansion. Vic immediately started receiving sensor feed from the ambulatory weapon which he shared with Scab. They had to move quickly now. The information coming from the *Basilisk II* suggested that the ship couldn't take much more of the kind of punishment it was currently receiving.

Vic unclipped his advanced combat rifle from the back of his exoskeleton with his upper limbs and sent information to his lizard power disc. The strobe gun was already firing. Vic stepped through the hole in the armoured shutter into the mansion, taking out targets provided by the strobe gun's sensor feed. As he advanced into the open-plan room, his P-sat separated from his exoskeleton and rose up towards the ceiling beams.

Vic stepped to one side, still advancing and firing. He was receiving a lot of return fire and the room was starting to fill with smoke as the strobe gun wandered around, destroying carefully selected targets. Scab followed Vic in, taking out target after target with his double-barrelled laser rifle. A member of the security team died with each double beam.

Vic grabbed the power disc from its housing on the back of his exoskeleton with his right-lower limb and threw it. The moment he released the disc, he drew both of his double-barrelled laser pistols with his lower limbs. The security team were competent and had responded quickly and proficiently to an attack that shouldn't have been possible. Vic and Scab started receiving accurate return fire the moment they came through the armoured shutter. The security team's main problem, however, was their smart attire – while their armoured clothes had energy-dissipation grids woven into them, but their faces were bare.

The disc flew across their exposed skin, opening flesh, removing eyes. The majority were still combat effective, but at the very least the power disc surprised them. As soon as the disc scythed their skin open, either Vic or Scab hit them with headshots. They fell back, faces either red, steaming, superheated messes from Scab's lasers, or full of holes from the electromagnetically propelled, caseless, armour-piercing explosive rounds fired from Vic's ACR.

Everything went quiet inside. Outside, the *Basilisk II* was still taking a battering. The strobe gun leaped up onto a counter, rotating three-hundred-and-sixty degrees, seeking more targets.

'I've got him,' Elodie said over the 'face link and revealed her position to their sensors. Vic and Scab instantly let their various weapons systems know she wasn't a target. She was standing, holding on to a very fat human with a lot of dark-coloured hair and a large bushy beard. He was wearing a stained toga of the type popular in certain parts of the Monarchist systems. He was blubbering, almost hysterically, and had soiled himself. This confused Vic, because the human should have been able to neuronically and chemically control his response. Despite Elodie's lightweight, stealth-adapted combat exoskeleton, Vic could still make out the feline's distaste in her body language. The bearded human looked familiar to Vic. At first he couldn't work out why, then realised that he reminded him, some-how, of the Living City's spokesperson they had met with on Pangea. Perhaps all the Monarchist humans looked the same, he mused. Then Vic saw the tendrils of animated wire running from under Elodie's retracted claws and into his head.

The light and the thunder from outside stopped as Elodie used the man's hacked neuronics to spoof the orbital defence network and the estate itself into ceasing fire.

'How long do we have?' Vic asked.

'We've got G-carriers and hoppers plus several ships from the security fleet all inbound,' Elodie said. 'The ships are coming from high orbit so they'll take a while, but they'll be in range in less than a hundred and twenty seconds.'

'Is the estate ours?' Scab asked.

Elodie nodded.

Missiles and other autonomous munitions were speeding across the plain and through the sky towards the *Basilisk II* as Vic, Scab and Elodie were carried by their P-sats back towards the partially melted-looking ship. The fore airlock opened and swallowed them even as the sky lit up overhead with incoming ordnance.

The *Basilisk II* banked sharply, its internal gravity keeping the passengers upright. The sky above them lit up again, this time with green fire as frigates from the naval contractor fleet pierced the tinted atmosphere. Light and energy reached out for the *Basilisk II* as it flew low over the savannah, scattering herds of fauna in its thunderous wake. Then the red, sucking tear appeared in the air over the grasslands and the *Basilisk II* disappeared.

Vic's and Scab's combat exoskeletons were still smoking as they cooled. Vic carried the two recently assembled tanks using all four of his limbs. Scab and Elodie followed the armoured 'sect through the ship and into the pool room.

Steve was curled up on the floor, sobbing.

'It's okay, it's over,' Elodie told the dolphin imprisoned in human form.

Vic walked over to the pool and 'faced instructions to the two tanks. Their bottoms split open and the contents fell into the pool. They uncoiled, writhing through the water in a display of angry hissing and flickering electricity. With a thought, Scab dimmed the lights and let their electrical displays illuminate the room. Steve was staring at them, awe all over his face.

'A breeding pair?' he asked. Scab nodded.

Vic watched the two serpents with their flat reptilian maws and bright reflective rainbow scales coil angrily through the water. He sort-of understood the fascination with the beauty of the creatures, though it wasn't really something he'd taught himself to appreciate yet. They made him nervous, however. He'd undergone Key hallucinations in the past. It was a trip to a place he had no intention of returning to.

'What you can't assemble you'll find in the cargo hold,' Scab said.

Steve nodded dumbly, still staring at the two dream dragons as they sinuously explored their new home. Vic glanced over at Scab.

His human partner had opened the faceplate on his armour to watch the dragons, his pale features bathed in their electric light. Vic wasn't sure what the expression on his partner's face was, but he knew it made him uncomfortable. After a few moments, Vic, still smoking gently, turned and walked out of the pool room.

Talia was curled into a foetal position, sitting on the bare wooden boards of the floor with her back against the wall, hands over her ears, screaming. Yellow-powder disc guns blew holes in the walls, while thrown and crossbow-fired discs thudded into the wood all around her. She knew that outside the hut, war-painted humanoid lizards mounted on flesh-eating dinosaurs and armed with spears and blades, both curved and circular, were galloping around the flimsy wooden house. She hoped they were simply going to kill her, although she had a suspicion they would eat her alive.

Vic appeared, standing over her. 'Are you enjoying yourself?' he asked as a serrated disc blade impacted into the wall next to him. Talia stared up at him, eyes wide with fear. It took her a moment to realise what he'd said. Then she threw herself at him, clawing at his armoured body.

'Can you make it stop?' she cried. Vic looked down at her, utterly mystified, then froze the immersion. She collapsed sobbing into his arms. He didn't think he'd ever felt more like his namesake and hero than he did right then as he scooped her up, carried her into the colonial homestead's bedroom and laid her down on the bed.

'Did you not like the immersion?' he asked.

She stared at him, chest heaving as she gasped for breath. 'What are you talking about?' she managed. 'I just appeared here. Then these lizards starting attacking me.'

'Yes, it's my favourite. Vic Matto and *All's Quiet on the New Croydon Front.*'

'You're Vic Matto,' Talia managed as she tried to persuade her confused brain to work through all the terror.

'No, I took my name from him. He was an immersion star till he died of a drug overdose so massive it scrambled his personality when they tried to clone him. A shame, really, as he was in his prime when he died. A lot of people think Monarchist assassins killed him. A pre-emptive taste-strike during the build-up to the Art Wars.'

Talia was still breathing heavily and staring at him wild-eyed. 'We're in a fucking *film*?' she spat.

'A film of what?' Vic asked, confused.

'This is a movie, a story?'

'It's an immersion, yes.'

'Why?'

Vic was mystified. 'What do you mean? It's an adventure. You had entertainment, right?'

Talia stared at him. 'Subjectively, what do you think just happened to me?' she asked.

Vic thought about that for a moment. 'Subjectively, you were dropped into a homestead during the humans' diaspora period.'

'And?' she demanded.

'You were attacked by a lizard hunter tribe,' Vic said as he started to see what she was getting at.

'And it didn't occur to you that might be just a little fucking *frightening* if you're not a seven-foot-tall, armoured insect violence junkie?' she screamed at him, spittle flecking her chin.

'So, not your thing, then?'

'We watch stories, read them, sometimes listen to them. We never want to be in them because they're too fucking *dangerous*!' she shouted.

'Sorry,' Vic ventured.

'I thought you were punishing me.'

'What? No!'

Vic sat down on the bed, which creaked under the weight of his virtual hard-tech form.

'You do this for fun?' she asked. 'How much violence is too much for you guys?'

Vic gave the question some thought. He remembered watching starscrapers collapsing and thinking the sight beautiful. He remembered watching an Elite destroy a habitat and being frightened by the raw power being displayed.

'I've never really thought about it like that,' he mused. 'I don't know for me. I don't think there's enough for Scab.'

'So I'm not really here?' Talia asked.

Vic shook his head. 'No, you're wrapped in the ship, asleep. So you won't hurt yourself.'

Talia looked somewhat sheepish. 'Can you take me somewhere else?' she asked.

'Scab has oversight, but he's got some new pets to keep him occupied so we can try. Where do you want to go?'

Talia leaned against the bedstead and looked out of the window. 'Do you have something of Earth, from—'

'Before you guys lost it?'

Talia turned to glare at him but nodded. 'Somewhere glamorous, but not in the middle of a battle or anything?' she asked.

'I'll see what I can do,' Vic told her.

They were standing in a spacious, tastefully decorated apartment with a balcony. The door to the balcony was open, diaphanous curtains blowing in the gentle wind. They were staring out over a cityscape. It looked very small to Vic.

'I'm not sure where this is,' Vic said.

'It's New York,' Talia said. She was dressed elegantly in a tight, calf-length skirt, a striped blouse, stockings and heels, her black hair arranged into a bouffant style. One hand rested on her hip; the other held a cigarette holder with a lit cigarette in it. 'Before the war, I think.'

'*The* war?' Vic asked. 'You only had the one? What changed?'

'I'm not sure about the giant floating, glowing jellyfish, though.'

'I can get rid of them if you want.'

Talia turned and looked up at Vic. There was something different in her expression – something calculated that was starting to make Vic feel funny.

'No, it's okay,' she said. 'They're kind of pretty, assuming they're not going to attack us.'

'I don't think so.'

Talia moved closer and looked up at him with an expression Vic's neunonics told him was best described as 'coquettish'. She touched his armoured thorax with one perfectly manicured burgundy nail and ran it down to his abdomen.

'Can you look more human?' she asked, tilting her head.

This was a matter of pride for Vic. Humanophile or not, he was secure-ish in his identity as an insect. He always swore that he would never pretend to be anything he wasn't. He would stand firm.

He turned into a muscular human male with four arms and multifaceted crystalline eyes. He glanced at his reflection in the huge mirror over the fireplace.

'Shit,' he muttered. 'Scab's oversight. He probably thinks he's being funny.'

Talia reached up and traced around his eyes with the tips of her fingers. 'I think they're pretty,' she told him. 'And four arms gives us some options.'

She moved her hand down, placing it flat against his chest, and started pushing him backwards across the apartment until he stumbled against a chair and sat down hard. Then she climbed into his lap.

'Why?' he asked, though he found his human form was strangely breathless.

She hesitated for a moment. 'Because this isn't real,' she told him. 'It doesn't matter.' She kissed him. Being accustomed to mandibles, Vic wasn't quite sure what to do with lips. 'Relax,' she told him. 'I'm really good at this.'

33

Ancient Britain

The figure with the antlers turned and left the mound, disappearing into the mist and sunlight.

They had been blindfolded, which neither of them had been happy about, but both had agreed to. They stumbled through the woods for what seemed like a very long time, then were loaded into what felt like dugout log boats and taken upriver.

Finally their blindfolds were removed. They were standing on a little outcrop on the side of the narrow, fast-moving river, a shelter made of branches and ferns on the riverbank in front of them. Steam was leaking through the ferns.

'Strip,' one of their guards ordered.

Tangwen looked at the shelter, then at her captors, and started to undress. Kush didn't move. 'I don't think they're going to rape us,' Tangwen said. 'Not yet, anyway.'

Kush was looking at the steam coming from the shelter. 'I am more worried about being eaten,' he muttered. Tangwen laughed. Reluctantly, Kush started to undress. Tangwen found herself staring at his penis. Kush became aware of it and looked back at her. She didn't notice. He cleared his throat and she looked up at him, utterly unembarrassed.

'When we return to camp, you and I should—' Tangwen stopped, and her hand came up of its own accord to cover her acid-burned face. She turned away. Kush watched her, concerned. One of the warriors pointed into the shelter.

Inside the shelter, hot rocks bubbled away in a large, shallow stone bowl, filling the structure with steam. Something mixed with the water gave the steam an aromatic quality. Tangwen started to feel drowsy as sweat beaded the skin of her wiry body.

The steam was so thick and heady that it took them a minute to realise there was someone else in the shelter with them: an old man, twig-thin, long, wavy grey hair draped over his face, concealing his features. His thin, straggly beard was shaped into a point. He looked up at them through his hair. His narrow face was heavily lined, but his eyes were very much alive.

'I'm more impressive when I'm wearing a robe and antlers, I think,' he said. His accent was odd – Tangwen had never heard one quite like it, but she had no problem understanding his words. 'It's more difficult to lie when we're not hiding ourselves.'

'And there is magic in the steam that compels the truth,' Kush rumbled.

'I breathe the same steam that you do, Kush-who-is-not-a-demon.'

'I am Tangwen, hunter of the—'

The old man held up a hand. 'We are being cleansed. We are to be unborn. The steam will send away all the other spirits that surround you. The serpent.' He looked at Tangwen. 'And those of metal.' He looked at Kush.

Kush looked to Tangwen. 'I mislike this,' the Numibian said. Tangwen was not altogether happy herself.

'Is there a spirit bound to the skull you have brought with you?' the old man asked.

'The skull was taken fairly in battle,' Tangwen told the man. 'Its owner died well and should have returned to his god, his head held high.'

'If the spirit has not moved on to his god, then it has something to be ashamed of. It will be a weak and frightened thing and no threat to us.'

Kush gave a slight shake of his head.

'Are we not *civilised* enough for you, Kush-who-is-not-a-demon?' the old man asked.

We? Tangwen wondered.

'I meant no offence,' Kush told the man.

'I did not ask if you meant offence,' the old man told the Numibian, though there was no reproach in his voice.

'Your ways are not mine,' Kush muttered.

'And I am not a stupid man. One look at you could have told me that.'

Kush looked up and straight into the old man's eyes. 'No,' Kush told him evenly. 'You are not.'

'And see – already we are chasing falsehood away. Soon we will be able to talk as real people, and not the deceitful people we all must be outside this place.'

'This may not be the correct time to introduce ourselves in your rites, but I was told by a Persian Magi that names have power. You know ours, and I would know yours – unless you have something to hide,' Kush said, somewhat irritably.

The old man regarded him for a moment or two. 'Are you sure you're not a demon, Kush-who-is-not-a-demon?' he asked. Kush opened his mouth to retort. 'My name is Guidgen.'

Tangwen recognised the name. It was an old one. It meant Born of Trees.

After Tangwen had sweated most of the mud off – and the berry dye she had smeared on herself to call the serpent – they left the steam-filled shelter. Next they followed the old man's example by plunging into a deep pool in the fast-moving and very cold, river. They dried themselves with ferns, and the old man led them into the trees.

'Shouldn't we go clothed?' Kush asked.

'Were you born clothed?' Guidgen asked. Kush shook his head.

Guidgen was clearly another of the mad men this island appeared to breed so easily, Tangwen thought. She hesitated when they came to the gnarled, ancient, stooped oak. There was a hole in the earth beneath it and the oak's roots acted as a doorway to a cave. Tangwen had always liked her father's cave, but for the most part caves were to be feared. Wolves, bears, monsters and madmen all lived in caves. They were said to be the gateway to the Otherworld, and she knew from her own experience that sometimes gods made caves their home.

'It's not what you think. You're safe with me,' Guidgen said, not unkindly. Tangwen looked around but could see no more of the ash-covered warriors. She steeled herself and crawled into the cave entrance. Guidgen went to follow her but Kush stopped him. The old man looked at him questioningly.

'I'd rather you have to look at my arse than I at yours,' Kush told him, and then followed Tangwen into the cave.

At first it was pitch dark and cold, the smell of earth very strong. Gradually, Tangwen started to feel warm air against her skin. She could smell woodsmoke, and finally she made out a faint red glow.

She crawled out of the tunnel into a low earthen cave supported by a network of roots. A fire burned low and red in the centre of the cave. Tangwen thought it a little odd that the cave wasn't filled with smoke. It didn't feel like a place that she should fear. Rather it felt warm, oddly comfortable and strangely familiar.

Kush crawled into the cave, followed moments later by Guidgen. In the dim red glow they were little more than indistinct shadows. The ceiling was low enough that Kush was unable to stand up straight.

'This place is sacred to Cuda?' Tangwen asked. Guidgen nodded. 'But you clothed yourself as the Horned God.'

'We were under the trees,' Guidgen said, then sat down on the strangely warm earth, 'and he is Cuda's favoured son. I ask only that you respect this place. You are, however, not under hospitality. We do not know if you are friends or enemies yet, and it is difficult to trust someone who feels the need to assure people that he is not a demon,' the old man said, smiling.

'It's only because everyone on this island—' Kush started, but found both the Pretani were grinning at him.

'I am Tangwen, a hunter and a warrior of the Pobl Neidr. This is Kush the Numibian, a warrior from lands across the seas and far to the south. We come with a message from Bladud, whom some call the Witch King, of the Brigantes. It was he who made you the gift of the skull, which, by his word, took some effort in the taking,' Tangwen said formally.

'And you are a man just like us?' Guidgen asked Kush.

'Yes,' Kush told the old man.

'Only more civilised?' Guidgen asked.

'Are you mocking me?' Kush demanded.

'Yes,' Guidgen said simply. 'But I mean no ill. You may not be a demon, Kush-who-is-not-a-demon, but neither of you is normal. The blood of the gods, however weak, runs in your veins.'

Kush and Tangwen stared at him.

'I have not heard the name of your people,' the Numibian finally said.

'We are the *Tyleth Am Sgrech Cysgod*,' Guidgen said. Tangwen started at the name. The Tribe of the Screaming Shadows.

'That is an ill name,' Kush said.

'We are cursed people.'

'Are you their king?' Tangwen asked when she finally felt she could speak again.

'No,' Guidgen said, shaking his head. 'We have no king. I am a *dryw*, an advisor. Since there was some suspicion that you were consorting with creatures from Cythrawl, I was asked to deal with you.'

'Why are you cursed?' Kush asked.

'A bold question from those invading Ardu,' Guidgen said, though there was no reproach in his tone.

'Is truth only for us to give, then?' Kush demanded. 'You speak of it, but there are shadows here, shadows there. You name yourselves shadows and then make war on the sleeping.'

'We did not make war on them,' Guidgen said simply. 'We just

398

killed them. They were fruit hanging from the trees for the Horned God. We live in Ardu to be free of the tyranny of kings. And to answer your question, we were cursed because we were too *civilised*. Our king sought to build a city. He did not care that it was on land sacred to Cuda. He did not care that another tribe had better claim to the land.'

'We simply seek to pass through your land,' Tangwen said.

'I believe you,' Guidgen said.

'Then why make war on the landsfolk we protect?' Kush was becoming angry.

'Many of them are spear-carriers, and we killed warriors, too—'

'Nobody is questioning your courage—' Tangwen started.

'That is a lie,' Guidgen said.

Tangwen went cold and her hand reached for a dagger that was not there. Kush tensed, not sure what do.

'Think on what you said,' Guidgen warned. 'Think, before the anger takes you.'

Tangwen took several deep breaths as she tried to calm herself. 'I do not question your courage.'

'Because you know what it is to hunt. We give you the same chance we give a bear,' Guidgen told her.

'I question your courage,' Kush said. Guidgen smiled.

'But why attack us when all we would do is pass through your land?' Tangwen asked.

'Two reasons,' Guidgen told them. 'First, it is a lesson. It must be too costly to cross our land or others will try. I would see all of you destroyed to keep my people safe, to see this land unspoiled.'

Kush laughed bitterly, but Tangwen held up a hand to quiet him.

'And the other?' she asked.

'This Bladud, he wears the black robe of a false *dryw*?' Guidgen asked. Tangwen nodded. 'He is moonstruck with the sickness of greed. I could smell it on him. He would have more than he could see from the highest point in his land. He would make slaves of his fellows. He would pass through today, but tomorrow he would conquer us.'

Kush and Tangwen were quiet.

'I think he is right,' Kush said. Tangwen nodded. 'Why tell us this?'

'What I tell you will not make any difference.'

'Because you will kill us,' Tangwen said.

'That is a poor way to treat a guest,' Kush said.

'It would be,' Guidgen agreed.

'But we are not guests,' Tangwen said quietly. 'We have been offered neither food nor drink.'

'Your people are invaders. You are prisoners, and we do not keep slaves. All go to our gods.'

'I could snap your neck with my bare hands,' Kush growled.

Guidgen laughed. 'Now *that* is the truth,' the old man said.

'Kush,' Tangwen said.

'What?' the Numibian demanded.

'He is being courteous.'

Kush stared at the young Pretani woman.

'You are people of many different tribes,' Guidgen said as he poked at the fire, sending sparks into the air. Tangwen nodded. Kush just glared at the strange *dryw*. 'What is chasing you?'

Tangwen told him. Guidgen was quiet for a long time after she finished her story. He stared into the fire.

'That cannot be believed,' he said eventually.

Tangwen gritted her teeth, choking back an angry challenge. You did not threaten or harm a *dryw*, not even if they would be the one to peel the skin from your flesh.

Finally Guidgen looked up, his eyes catching the red glow of the flames: 'So it must be true.'

Bress rode his horse slowly into the valley along the muddy track beside the river. Britha rode next to him. The Lochlannach, silent and impassive, rode behind. It was raining hard.

It looked like all had come to see them. Row after row of dismounted warriors stood on the track and in the trees. Those on the opposite side of the river held slings, bows and casting spears. She was aware of people keeping pace with them in the trees. Behind the warriors came the lines of landsfolk. Almost all of them were armed, even if it was just a stick with a fire-hardened point. They stared at Bress and the Lochlannach with undisguised hatred. They stared at Britha the same way. She glanced over at Bress. She could not read the expression on his pale, beautiful face.

Bladud stood at the head of the army, his hood up against the rain. Nerthach was at his side. Behind him were more black-clad warriors in bearskin cloaks. She saw the emaciated but still regal Anharad of the Trinovantes, though there was no sign of Mabon. Borth the Tall and Eithne of the Iceni both stood on Bladud's left side. She looked for and found Germelqart. The Carthaginian navigator was watching her, studying her as if he was looking for something. There was no hatred there, but maybe a little fear.

Then she saw the girl and felt her heart do something strange. She could have been no more than eight years old, dirty, bedraggled, thin, ragged, hungry and very, very frightened. She was perched in a tree, watching the Lochlannach ride through the mud. Once she would have been too far away for Britha to notice, but not now. And Britha knew her.

She was the daughter of a family of landsfolk who had lived and worked in one of Ardestie's outlying farms. Britha had delivered her. The birth was something of a fight. She had been a sickly baby, and winter-born. Britha didn't expect her to last the white season, but she lived until spring and then grew up strong enough. She blinked back tears as she realised she could no longer remember the girl's name.

Bress glanced over at her as they brought their horses to a halt a little way in front of Bladud and his assembled warriors. Bladud put his hood down.

'I am Bladud of the Brigantes. I would say well met, but ...'

Bress just looked bored. Nerthach's face started to turn red, furious at the rudeness. The big warrior's hand went to the hilt of his sheathed longsword.

'Are you afraid to say your name?' Bladud asked. If the Witch King was angry, he was masking it well.

Bress turned to look at the black-robed man. 'I am here because Britha would see you spared, nothing more. Let's get on with this, or I will ride your people down right now.'

Nerthach's sword was half out of its sheath.

'Enough!' Britha shouted in the voice that brooked no argument. She might have been with the enemy, but Nerthach and the other Brigante warriors at least had enough respect for the *dryw* to hesitate. Britha glared at Bress. 'There may well be bloodshed this day, but you will treat these people with respect. Some of them did, after all, defeat your forces on the Isle of Madness and escape from the wicker man!' Her anger was not entirely for show.

Bress watched her for what felt like a long time. Finally he appeared to come to a decision and turned his attention to Bladud once more.

'I had heard of power. So far all I have seen is arrogance and rudeness,' Bladud said mildly.

'I am Bress of the Lochlannach,' he told Bladud, 'and whatever you feel is due to you, remember that you are not my equal. Will you let us pass?'

'I mislike looking up at a man,' Bladud said. 'It hurts my neck.'

Bress glanced over at Britha. She could tell he was irritated. He climbed off the back of his white horse and strode through the mud to stand in front of Bladud. The Witch King was not a small man, but Bress towered over him. He was of a height with Borth the Tall, though much thinner.

'You still find yourself looking up at me,' Bress said quietly.

'Aye, but you look like you'll snap in the first strong wind,' Nerthach said. There was laughter from the other Brigante warriors. Bress glared at the one-eyed warrior. Nerthach held his stare.

'Where are his scars?' Eithne asked. 'His smooth skin makes him look sword-shy.'

Britha shook her head. Eithne stared at the other woman and spat.

'I am no warrior because I prefer to give scars, rather than receive them?' Bress asked, glancing at Eithne's disfigured face. He looked up at Britha. 'How long would you have me tolerate this? These people are no match for us. They know that and would fight with words before they will draw iron.'

Britha caught Nerthach looking at Bladud, but the Witch King shook his head.

'Will you let us p—' Britha began.

The small figure darted out of the woods and leaped at Bress. Britha was already sliding off the back of her horse but none of the Lochlannach moved. Bress merely reached out his hand and caught Mabon in mid-air, by the throat. Mabon's eyes bulged out of their sockets, but the boy still tried to stab down with his dagger.

'No!' It was the Trinovantes woman, Anharad, who cried out.

Bress slapped the dagger out of the boy's hand. His long fingers were wrapped all the way around the boy's neck as he squeezed the life out of him.

Anharad ran to Bress. 'When the black *curraghs* came, his mother, father and two older brothers died fighting you. His sister wasn't strong enough. She died in our arms in the wicker man ...' Tears covered her face. It was obvious to Britha that this was a woman unaccustomed to begging.

'Do you believe he will be with them soon?' Bress asked.

The warriors surrounding Bladud were surging forward. Britha moved between Bress and the warriors, mostly to keep them alive. The Lochlannach still had not moved. They sat on their steeds, impassive.

'What treachery is this?' Britha shouted at them. The warriors stopped moving forwards. They were not quite ready to defy a *dryw*, not even a hated one.

'Enough!' Bladud shouted at the warriors before turning to Britha. 'He is but a child!'

'He is but a child wielding iron!' Britha shouted back, glancing

had killed all those they had not taken. He had to see for himself. He had to gauge the Lochlannach's strength, but he wasn't going to kill his 'strong right arm'. Bladud had just saved Nerthach's life and killed Borth, and the Witch King knew it.

Borth put on his helmet, transferred his longspear to the hand that already held his shield and picked up one of his casting spears. He pointed the spear at Bress as he walked forwards.

'I am Borth of a Hundred Battles, Borth the Head Harvester, the Child of the Red Man, and I will drink my beer from your skull.'

Bress started walking towards Borth, looking irritated. 'Is this the man I must kill to pass?' Bress asked Britha.

'You may fetch your helm, shield and spear,' Borth told Bress. The pale warrior didn't answer, just continued walking towards the huge Iceni. Borth looked confused for a moment. Then he threw his casting spear. Bress ducked. It narrowly missed Britha's horse and one of the Lochlannach had to deflect it with their shield. Borth transferred his longspear into his free hand and stepped forwards, thrusting the weapon at Bress. Bress quickened his pace, darting to one side, getting inside the spear's reach. He still did not have a weapon in his hand. Borth dropped his spear and reached for his sword. In one movement, Bress drew his sword and sliced up through Borth's shield, the iron blade of his almost-drawn sword and the tall man's cuir bouilli armour, opening the warrior's body from hip to shoulder. Bress sheathed his blade as he walked past Borth and came to stand in front of Bladud.

'Have you learned enough?' he asked, leaning down to whisper into the other man's ear. Borth's corpse toppled to the ground.

'Let them by,' Bladud said. People started shuffling towards the trees, making way for the Lochlannach. Bress turned away from Bladud and walked back towards the horses.

Britha was watching Bladud, but she could not quite make out the expression on his face as he observed Bress mount his horse. There was more than fear in his eyes, she knew. She climbed up onto her own horse.

They rode through the warriors and the landsfolk, who parted for them. The silence was broken only by the occasional sob. The little Cirig girl from Ardestie was still sitting in the tree. She watched Britha ride by. Britha saw that the girl recognised her.

34
Birmingham, 3 Weeks Ago

They were finding more of them. Or rather, Grace was finding more of them. She had used the Circle's resources to do an invasive city-wide Internet history check, looking at the most unpleasant content on the net, who was writing horrible things, who was creating horrible artwork – in short, anyone who was showing signs of a significantly deviant imagination. In a number of cases they found the brass scorpions, the Alpha- and Theta-wave recorders and transmitters. Silas appeared to have learned from Letchford, though, as none of them remembered seeing him. They also had no memory of the brain surgery they'd undergone to remove the brass scorpions, though they would perhaps have dreams of abduction experiences.

Control had sought ways to trace the Alpha- and Theta-wave transmissions, but as yet had found nothing. It looked as if the carrier wave for the transmissions was too ubiquitous to spot and blended into the background electromagnetic radiation of modern-day life.

Nanette Hollis's brain had been removed, but they found no traces of Silas in or around the Moseley Road Swimming Baths. He had not revealed his presence this time. Du Bois checked. It was less than a mile from the closest waterway to the baths, but then most of the city was just as close, or closer.

They were both in du Bois' room at the Malmaison Hotel. Du Bois was seated at the desk. Grace was lying on his bed with her boots on, much to du Bois' annoyance. They were transferring files back and forth between their heads, or rather between Grace's head and du Bois' phone, much to Grace's annoyance.

'He doesn't have enough time – he's working towards something and it's about to come to fruition—' Grace started.

Du Bois sighed. It was just more speculation. The case was all she thought about now, all she talked about. Going over the same things again and again.

'So we're agreed that Galforg was a misstep,' she went on. 'He killed the wrong person, he pretty much said so. Then Songhurst, Jaggard and Hollis. He thinks they're the real deal, psychic or something. So he takes their brains because he wants something from them, presumably their "power", because it feeds some element of his fantasy life. Then he puts transmitters in the brains of sick individuals. Why?' Grace was talking to herself. Du Bois had heard variations of this a dozen times since they'd dealt with Letchford and found Hollis. 'Does he think he's transmitting to the brains? Torturing them in some way?' She looked over at du Bois. 'You said he always goes for the pain.' Du Bois nodded. 'But why just torture brain matter? That doesn't make sense.' Grace went quiet for a few moments. 'Unless he doesn't think he's transmitting it to them. He thinks their brains are transmitting to someone or something else.' She looked over at du Bois triumphantly.

'Which doesn't make sense,' du Bois said. 'It's not possible.'

'Christ, Malcolm, if this job's taught us nothing more, it's that given enough technology, pretty much anything's possible. Besides, it doesn't have to work, he just has to *think* it does.' Then it was as if a light went on behind her eyes. 'He's building a beacon, like—'

'Hawksmoor,' du Bois finished for her.

Grace looked over at him. 'I'm not—' she started.

'Transferring?'

Grace was off the bed in a flash and marching across the room towards him. 'Fuck you, Dad! What have you brought to this? He might be swimming in the canals? Great, we'll look for bridges with billy goats clip-clopping across them, but that's not been much use so far, has it? At least I'm trying to think it through!'

'No,' Malcolm said calmly. 'You're not. You're wildly speculating in a bid to make the facts fit because you want revenge on someone who terrorised you, murdered your friends and family, and made you feel helpless. Except it doesn't fit. Hawksmoor's delusion was different. He was a driven man. A fanatic. He really believed in what he was doing. Silas is a sensualist and an egotist. He gets off on other people's suffering, power and, frankly, attention. While you were speculating, did you actually read the profile put together by several very powerful AIs using programs specifically written to profile Silas? Hawksmoor thought of himself as performing a grand experiment, a ritual, even. Silas is interested in spectacle, grand gestures, like what he did at the Manufactory. He does these things for gratification, nothing more.'

Grace opened her mouth to retort, then closed it again. She looked furious. Du Bois was pretty sure it was because she knew he was right. As she stormed out of the room, du Bois' phone vibrated on the desk. Grace stopped and concentrated for a moment. She glanced over at him, then grabbed her bike jacket and helmet from the bed.

'Why don't you come in the Range Rover with me?' du Bois managed to get out just as the door slammed behind her.

Du Bois was already receiving information from Grace as he drove – as quickly as the narrow, busy road would allow – towards the Druids Heath Estate. A number of missing-person reports had been called in to the West Midlands police. All the disappearances centred on Demesne House, a name that didn't really make sense to du Bois. Demesne House was one of the tower blocks on the estate. Two police officers had been sent to investigate. Only one of them had made it out. Beyond that, information was a little hazy as the police hadn't really wanted to speak to Grace.

He was driving through a basin on the Alcester Road lined with grass-covered verges, beyond which lay bland suburban housing. He could see the tower blocks of Druids Heath on a hill to the south. Through the haze of the cold but sunny spring morning, the tower blocks reminded him of megaliths. The haze was pierced here and there by blue flashing lights.

Minutes later he was being flagged down by an armed police officer as he pulled up next to the cordon of emergency vehicles surrounding Demesne House. The tower block was a nearly featureless grey concrete high-rise. There were a number of identical tower blocks in close proximity. Like the other towers, a car park and large grassy expanse surrounded Demesne House.

Druids Heath was obviously a run-down area. Many of the businesses, shops and what had once been quite a large pub had been boarded up and then vandalised. In addition to the tower blocks, the estate also contained rows of dilapidated terraced houses.

The police were dealing with a number of locals who were visibly upset. Presumably they knew people in the tower block. Du Bois could feel a palpable anger in the crowd, but he wasn't sure who it was aimed at yet. He suspected some of the local residents weren't great fans of the authorities.

He showed a Special Forces warrant card to the armed police officer who had flagged him down. He suspected it would be the quickest way to get what he wanted. He glanced over and saw a police armed-response team gathered near the tower block.

'Are they getting ready to go in?' du Bois asked. The officer he was dealing with didn't reply, though his expression told du Bois everything he needed to know. Looking around for Grace, he saw her talking to the chief superintendent. He could see by her gestures that she was less than pleased. Du Bois started walking towards them.

'... told you I'm an undercover operative, you've checked my credentials ...' Grace was saying to the chief superintendent as du Bois came into earshot. He noticed a white Mercedes Sprinter van parked close to Demesne House. It piqued his curiosity because of the heavy-duty winch mount on the front of it, which was far from standard on such a vehicle.

'How old are you, anyway – eighteen? If that?' the chief superintendent demanded. Grace just glared at the man. Du Bois quickened his pace. 'Look, little girl, we've got over a hundred missing persons – and rising – and an estate on the edge of a riot. More than enough to handle, without whatever your undercover freak show is about.'

Du Bois ran the last few steps and grabbed Grace's arm just as she was about to hit the chief superintendent in the throat, very hard. Grace spun around to glare at him, but calmed down enough not to cripple or kill the high-ranking police officer.

'Is the commissioner here yet?' Du Bois asked the red-faced chief superintendent.

'He's running this from HQ. I'm in command on the ground,' the chief superintendent told him.

Brilliant, du Bois thought. A pompous fool in command with a boss who liked to lead from the rear.

'Okay, you need to get the commissioner on the phone for me—' du Bois started.

'I need to do no such thing,' the chief superintendent retorted. The armed-response team was now running across the grass towards Demesne House. Grace pointed at them, a worried expression on her face.

'Look, I'm sorry we've pissed all over your jurisdiction,' said du Bois, 'but you need to let us handle this.'

'How? By doing nothing? Or by mutilating corpses?' the chief superintendent demanded.

The armed-response team had reached the main door of Demesne House.

There's a blood-screen surrounding the tower block. Du Bois received Grace's message direct to his mind.

'Okay, you need to pull your men back right now,' du Bois said, a trace of desperation in his voice. A shout of surprise from a member of the armed-response team drew his attention back to the building. They'd got the door open and a stream of blood was flowing out through the doorway. It looked as if the building was bleeding. The chief superintendent was staring at the blood, appalled.

'Over a hundred tenants, nine pints each,' Grace said.

'Pull your men back, now!' du Bois told the police officer. The armed-response team waded through the blood as they entered the tower block, weapons at the ready. The chief superintendent was still staring. He clearly had no idea what to do.

Then the screaming started. The crowd, almost as one, ducked when they heard gunfire. Du Bois watched the inside of Demesne House light up with multiple muzzle flashes, then grabbed the chief superintendent by the face.

'Listen to me – if any of your men fire on us, we'll fire back, and then I'm going to kill you. Do you understand me?' he demanded. The chief superintendent managed to nod despite the grip. Du Bois leaned closer. 'Do you believe me?' The chief superintendent didn't say anything, but du Bois saw the answer he needed in his eyes. He let go of the man. The gunfire had stopped.

Du Bois drew his Accursed .45 and checked the chamber for a round. There was still screaming coming from Demesne House. The sound echoed among the tower blocks. Grace drew one of her Beretta 92 FS Inox pistols, removed the fifteen-round 9mm magazine and replaced it with an extended twenty-round magazine from the ammo pouch on her belt. The screaming was cut off suddenly. Both of them knew that the armed-response team were all dead. Grace replaced the magazine on her other pistol as well.

'There's media here,' she noted.

Du Bois nodded. With a thought, he texted Control. They would have to D-notice the media, and probably hack or edit any footage that was shot as well. Control would not be happy with the public nature of what they were about to do. Grace checked that she had a round chambered in each pistol and that the safeties were off.

'Plan?' she asked.

Maybe if we'd had any prep time, du Bois thought. 'Can you think of anything more sophisticated than go in there, find Silas and shoot him a lot?'

'Try not to get our brains eaten?' Grace suggested. The chief superintendent was still staring at them, utterly lost for words.

'I like it,' du Bois said. Her earlier anger with him was forgotten. They had something to do now. Du Bois started running across the grass towards Demesne House, half-expecting to get shot as he ran. He wasn't sure if it would be by Silas or the police at his back, but as he ran, he heard the chief superintendent speaking to his men over the radio.

It wasn't quiet or subtle. Du Bois hit the door with his shoulder at a run. Safety glass cracked and metal bent enough to knock the door out of its frame. Du Bois went flying through into a small foyer and slipped over on the blood covering the floor.

Grace hurdled him and charged through the foyer into the base of the stairwell, where it was raining blood. She had both her pistols pointing upwards as the gore covered her.

Du Bois pushed himself to his feet, blood dripping off him. He moved quickly to the stairwell, his .45 at the ready, checking along the other corridors on the ground floor. He saw the bodies of a number of the armed-response team on the stairs. A quick glance told him they'd all been killed with a single well-aimed knife slash, and then their arteries had been cut. There were shell casings lying in the blood. The butcher-shop smell was overwhelming, a metallic tang of blood mixed with the stench of evacuated bowels. It could have been his first battlefield all over again. Looking up at the constant deluge of blood still pouring down, he saw bodies cable-tied to the railings all the way up the stairwell. Their arteries had all been opened, too. Silas had painted the interior of the building red.

Du Bois could feel the mass murderer's blood-screen interacting with his own like an itch, a cold war being fought at a molecular level as du Bois attempted to find Silas, and Silas sought to hide.

Where do we start? Grace asked in his mind.

'Malcolm, is that you?' The voice came from above, echoing down the blood-soaked stairwell. The accent was still there, but Silas's voice was deeper now. It had a rasp to it, as though he'd damaged it somehow in the last two hundred years or so.

Grace glanced over at du Bois and then looked straight back up the stairwell, trying to catch a glimpse of the speaker. Du Bois indicated that she should start moving up the stairs. She nodded and began climbing, both weapons at the ready. Du Bois followed.

'I was so pleased when I saw you outside. Tell me, who's the girl? When I consume her, will I find that she hates you as much as the archer did?'

Du Bois didn't answer. He just continued moving up the stairs, weapon at the ready, trying to use all his augmented capabilities to pinpoint where the sound of the voice was coming from.

'I don't really understand why you're here. Nobody cared about these people before I started killing them.'

They reached the second floor, and suddenly something was falling down the stairwell towards them. Both of them tensed, but neither fired. The armed-response-officer's corpse plummeted past them, bouncing off the guard rails and the bodies strapped to them. It hit the concrete at the base of the stairs with a wet thump and a splash of blood. Du Bois glanced down. Grace continued looking up the stairwell, watching for movement. Du Bois noticed that the pins and spoons were missing from several of the stun grenades on the police officer's body.

'Grenade!'

Both du Bois and Grace moved to the wall, crouched down and turned away from the stairwell. Du Bois closed his eyes, but even then the bright phosphorescent light still leaked through his lids. The noise was deafening, like thunder running up and down the stairwell, rattling doors and shaking the bodies tied to the railings. Augmented eyes and ears compensated for the light and the deafening noise almost immediately. Du Bois couldn't quite understand the play. He ran the last few moments back in his head. Then he realised the filtering effect on his hearing had allowed him to pick up something interesting, even under all that noise: glass breaking somewhere above him.

He ran past a startled Grace and pushed his way through one of the doors into a corridor with flats on either side. He heard the throaty roar of a powerful engine starting up. The Mercedes Sprinter. He reached the window at the end of the corridor, which looked out over the same side of the building where the unusual van had been. Grace was right behind him. He smashed the window and leaned out – the van was moving beneath him now. He aimed the .45 and started firing it rapidly, expecting to be taken out by an overzealous police marksman at any moment. The bullets sparked off the top of the van as it sped across the grass. The van was armoured. The slide flew back on the .45, its magazine empty.

'Coming through!'

Du Bois stepped back and away from the window as Grace hurtled past him and smashed through the remaining glass, dropping forty feet to the ground below. He heard her cry out in pain as she landed on the grass, but she rolled and came up firing short bursts from each of the converted, fully automatic Berettas. She was limping after the van as she fired, but the bullets were sparking off the speeding vehicle's armour.

Du Bois steeled himself and then leaped out of the window. While he was in mid-air the police woke up and started firing at the van as well. They were pouring bullets onto the vehicle, but none of the rounds penetrated the armoured body.

Du Bois hit the ground hard, a jarring impact that rattled his teeth and momentarily knocked the air out of him. He tried to roll but felt something give in his leg. Pain shot up the right side of his body. Grace dived and rolled back to her feet, moving close to the wall as rounds fired by the police chewed up the ground where she'd been standing a moment before. Du Bois was trying to get to his feet as his systems attempted to heal whatever the fall had done to his leg. A solid impact to his right side spun him around even as his clothes hardened sufficiently to stop the bullet penetrating.

He managed to stagger over to the wall next to Grace, who was busy reloading both of her pistols. Du Bois ejected the magazine on his .45, pocketed it and replaced it with a new one, working the slide to chamber the first round.

'I'm ready to start shooting police officers now,' Grace muttered through gritted teeth.

'Maybe not with so many cameras here,' du Bois suggested, though he agreed with the sentiment. There was shouting from the police lines, more gunfire, screams from the crowd, then a crashing noise and the unmistakable sound of panic, followed by the cries of the injured.

Du Bois' leg had repaired itself by now, and he risked running across the grass towards the Range Rover. Grace followed. She wasn't limping anymore either. The police didn't fire on them. They had other things to worry about – the Sprinter van had just crashed into the police cordon. The power of its obviously modified engine and the weight of the vehicle had sent a police van and a police car hurtling backwards into the assembled crowd.

Du Bois watched the Sprinter heading east along Druids Lane towards Alcester Road South.

'Security services. Don't fire!' du Bois shouted as he and Grace sprinted for their respective vehicles. At the same time he was requesting a direct satellite feed to be downloaded straight to his head from Control.

By the time du Bois reached the Range Rover, hauled the door open and scrambled in, the van was already out of sight. Grace sped by him on her Triumph Speed Triple, accelerating so hard that the front wheel had come off the ground. She was pushing her weight forwards, wrestling the bike back down.

Grace was also receiving the satellite feed direct from Control, which amounted to grainy footage of the Sprinter as it cut across the roundabout at the junction with Alcester Road South. It looked like the van had collided with a number of vehicles and just kept going.

Grace rode at speed through a tangled warren of streets, trying to cut ahead of the Sprinter, leaning low into the corners.

The Mercedes van drove through the rest of the traffic on the road as if it wasn't there, the vehicle's weight and power easily shunting the other vehicles out of the way as it used the heavy-duty winch mounted on the front like a battering ram.

Grace wove in and out of the carnage the van was leaving in its wake as it headed north, back towards the city centre. She slewed the bike onto one of the streets that ran alongside Alcester Road South, pulled parallel with the van and glanced over the grassy bank towards it. The cab's windscreen and windows were tinted.

Grace didn't notice the hatch in the van's side window drop open until she saw the muzzle flash from the three-round burst and felt the impact on her helmet, shoulder and side. Her clothes and helmet hardened, but she wobbled. Realising she was losing it, she tried to steer the bike towards the grass verge. Grace and the bike parted company. The bike slid across the grass. Grace did a half-tumble and landed high on her back, then followed her bike across the wet grass.

Du Bois mounted the pavement as he cut the wrong way across the roundabout. Both sides of the road were lined with dented or wrecked cars. He realised that unless he took a similarly blasé approach to human life, there was no way he was going to catch up with the van.

He saw Grace go down on the satellite feed. She would be fine unless the bullets being fired at her had a nanite payload.

'Do you need picking up?' he asked as the first flashing blue lights appeared behind him and he heard sirens.

'Ow, and no,' Grace finally answered. 'The bike's still running.'

On the satellite feed he watched her climb back on the Speed Triple, take off across the grass and drop back down onto Alcester Road South.

Du Bois' route analysis finished. He slewed the Range Rover hard right, off Alcester Road South, and accelerated. Moments later, he turned hard right onto a residential road that ran parallel with the Alcester Road. He continued accelerating, overtaking cars and forcing oncoming vehicles to brake hard.

The bike had lost one of its mirrors, the paintwork was messed up and, most worrying, one of the handlebars was a little bent, but it was still running. Grace wove in and out of busy traffic and the multiple car accidents the Sprinter was leaving behind it. She watched it hit an oncoming car head-on not far in front of her. The car's momentum was halted, then reversed, and it flew backwards into a shopfront. The van sideswiped a double-decker bus and made it wobble. It was still wobbling as Grace rode by. She knew the van's body was armoured. She was wondering about the tyres.

Grace pulled the bike out into the oncoming traffic to peer around the van, looking for an opening. The van moved to block her. Grace dropped a gear and then leaned in low, slewing the bike hard left, coming around on the inside of the van and then accelerating hard. The van veered hard left and tried to force her off the road. The side of the van touched Grace's elbow and she took the bike onto the pavement. Startled pedestrians flashed by.

Grace reached inside her jacket with her left hand and drew one of her Berettas. The van half-mounted the pavement as it tried to crush her into the shopfronts rushing by. Pedestrians were diving into the shops to get out of the way. Grace accelerated as she fired a long burst at the van's rear wheel, and then another at the front wheel as she overtook the Sprinter. The van closed the gap. Sparks flew and glass smashed as it scraped against the shopfronts, but Grace was already past. She leaned to the right, coming off the pavement and back onto the road. Grace aimed the gun behind her and fired off the rest of the magazine, mostly in frustration, at the van's windscreen. Sparks flew from it, but nothing much else happened. If her shots into the wheels had any effect, she couldn't see it.

In her remaining mirror, Grace saw a hatch in the front of the windscreen pop open and a gun barrel appear through it. She slewed the bike into oncoming traffic, weaving in and out as the driver started firing, the bullets ripping indiscriminately into the vehicles on the road.

Du Bois was driving the Range Rover at ridiculous speeds through narrow roads with cars parked on both sides, trying to catch up with the van.

'I need more gun,' Grace told him over their link. On the satellite and CCTV feeds, he watched her weaving in and out of traffic, taking fire from the van.

'Seven-six-two and a grenade launcher,' du Bois said.

'We'll need the weight of the jeep to force him off the road,' Grace told him.

It's not a jeep, du Bois thought automatically. 'Okay, I'm going to—' Du Bois slammed on the brakes. There was a car in the middle of the road. Du Bois left black marks on the Tarmac but managed to bring the Range Rover to a halt just in time to avoid a collision.

Grace sped up, trying to put enough distance between her and the Sprinter that he would stop firing at her. There was too much collateral damage in the way.

The road was mostly clear ahead as she roared through a junction with a pub on the corner. More shops and pubs lined the road, but they began to look nicer, more upmarket, the closer they got to the town centre. She glanced behind her and was appalled to see the Sprinter catching up. She twisted the throttle, coaxing more speed out of the bike as she wove between the few other vehicles on the road. Grace knew she was the one being chased now.

Du Bois stared. He couldn't quite believe what he was seeing. The driver of the car had stopped to have a chat with a pedestrian. He leaned on the horn. The man in the car gave him the finger and the pedestrian laughed. Du Bois thought about showing them the gun. Actually, he thought about shooting one – if not both – of them, but he managed to control his anger. He moved the Range Rover forwards until it touched the rear bumper of the car and then accelerated. The Range Rover pushed the car forwards, building speed, until du Bois saw a convenient space among the parked cars on one side of the road. He turned the wheel and put the car through the gap and into a wall. He stopped, backed the Range Rover out and resumed his course.

There was a park on his right. He braked mounted the pavement and drove up a tree-lined, steep grass bank. He picked up speed, heading for the path, scattering joggers and dog walkers as he roared through the park. The armoured Range Rover hit the locked gates at the end of the path at speed and crashed through them.

Grace leaned down so low that her shoulder nearly touched the Tarmac as she turned onto the Belgrave Middleway, part of the ring road surrounding the city centre. She knew the Sprinter wasn't far behind her.

It had gone wrong somehow. They were supposed to be chasing the van.

Ahead of her she saw a police car parked on one of the bridges that crossed over the road. She leaned low and swerved off the Middleway, heading up the ramp towards the bridge. There were two policemen, both armed – probably the only two armed-response officers in Birmingham who hadn't been at Druids Heath. She assumed they were waiting for the Sprinter. Grace mounted the pavement and brought the bike to a stop right next to the railing. She climbed off and left it idling, then pushed up the visor of her crash helmet.

'Gentlemen, I need one of your carbines and I'm afraid I don't have time to argue with you.'

'Miss, I need you to clear this area immediately!' one of the officers said, walking towards her, hand held up. Grace closed with him quickly. She kicked up at his Heckler & Koch G36 carbine with sufficient force to break it in half, catching him in the chin, powdering bone and causing him to spit blood and teeth. Then she brought her foot down on top of his head in an axe-kick, fracturing his skull and driving him into the ground. His partner was already turning towards her, raising his G36. Grace closed with him and grabbed the weapon before he could bring it to bear. She yanked it hard, dragging him towards her by its strap. Still wearing her crash helmet, she head-butted him, breaking his nose, then pulled the carbine's sling over his head. Grace was aware of the Sprinter getting closer. The police officer was staggering, pawing at her. Grace glanced at him irritably. She grabbed his Taser from its pouch on his webbing, pushed him back and Tasered him in the face until he hit the floor, twitching and drooling.

Grace brought the carbine up to her shoulder, which was a little awkward as she was still wearing her crash helmet. She aimed the reticle of the holographic sight at the Sprinter's armoured windscreen, directly over the driver's position. She fired short burst after short burst, but again the bullets just sparked off the glass. She continued firing as the van left the Middleway, heading up the ramp towards her. The magazine on the G36 ran dry, so she tossed the weapon. The van slewed around the corner and onto the bridge. Grace leaped on the bike as the van bore down on her. She put her right foot on the bridge's railing, screaming as she pushed with augmented leg muscles. She managed to lift the bike up and over the railings and jumped moments before the Sprinter ploughed through the spot where she'd just been standing. The vehicle ran over the two prone police officers and smashed into their car. Grace and the bike fell twenty feet to the road and hit it hard. The suspension cushioned the fall but the impact still drove the bike up into Grace. Her teeth clattered together and a few of them broke. Blood filled her mouth, which she spat out as the impact forced the wind out of her. She knew she'd torn something in her leg manoeuvring the bike over the railing. She'd also heard something crack on the bike as it hit the road, but the engine was still running as it bounced back up on its suspension. She heard the screech of tortured metal above her as the police car was rammed through the railings of the bridge and plummeted to the road.

Grace twisted the bike's throttle. As the bike lurched forward, she cried out as pain lanced through her leg. With a thought she released chemicals to deaden it. Her internal systems were already repairing the damage she had received.

The bike was handling sluggishly. It was picking up speed, but not quickly enough. On the other side of the road, she saw the Sprinter driving the wrong way down the bridge's on-ramp, cutting into the oncoming traffic and causing havoc. Grace twisted the Speed Triple's throttle, willing more speed out of it, but the van was gaining on her. It hit the central partition and lurched across it, bearing down on her. Glancing behind, the van filled her vision.

The Range Rover hit the Sprinter doing ninety miles an hour and pushed the van across the road. For a moment it looked like the Sprinter was going to turn over, but the driver managed to regain control.

Du Bois put the four-wheel drive between the Sprinter and Grace and matched speed with her bike. She reached over and grabbed hold of the railing above the driver's door. The Sprinter sideswiped the Range Rover, forcing it into the bike, and Grace pulled herself from the Speed Triple as it flew into the concrete wall at the side of the road. Somehow her feet found the Range Rover's running boards.

Then the Sprinter was gone. It had turned sharply right towards the city centre. Du Bois braked hard and slewed the Range Rover right. Grace held on for dear life.

She reached back and opened the driver's side rear passenger door. She put one hand on the top of the open door and the other on the roof of the speeding Range Rover, then pushed herself over the door and slid into the leather upholstery of the back seat. The door slammed shut behind her as it hit the wreck of a car left in the Sprinter's wake.

'Give me something to shoot this fucker with!' Grace screamed. Du Bois unlocked the concealed gun compartment in the back of the Range Rover with a thought. Grace leaned over the back seat, opened the hatch, grabbed the M320 grenade-launcher and pushed it open. She loaded a forty-millimetre high-explosive armour-piercing grenade, then pushed open the thick armoured glass of the sunroof and stood up on the back seat.

'Wait until you've got a clear shot, and watch for collateral damage,' du Bois shouted.

The Range Rover was weaving left and right as du Bois raced after the Sprinter, gaining on it now as it ploughed through traffic.

The Sprinter turned right on the Paradise Circus Queensway, driving into oncoming traffic. More cars swerved out of the van's way. One of the oncoming vehicles clipped the van and was launched into the air. Grace dropped back into the vehicle as the airborne car clipped the roof of the pursuing Range Rover, slamming the sunroof shut. Du Bois almost lost control of the vehicle, but managed to wrestle it back. Grace stared at the sunroof for a moment, then pushed it open and stood up again.

Brakes squealed and tyres smoked as the Sprinter slowed and turned left alongside the neoclassical town hall. The street was empty of people and traffic. Grace fired the grenade-launcher just as the van reached the end of the side street. The grenade hit the van in the rear right-hand corner. The explosion lifted the back of the other vehicle off the ground and swung it around. The van came to a halt in an open pedestrian area containing a shallow, stepped amphitheatre. Du Bois pushed the accelerator to the floor, intent on ramming the Sprinter, but astonishingly the van was still running. It shot forwards, and du Bois had to brake hard and slew the Range Rover around the corner. Pedestrians scattered.

'He's heading for New Street,' Grace said as she reloaded the grenade-launcher with a flechette round. Silas was going to drive the armoured van right down a busy pedestrian street. The van sped through the gap between Council House and the town hall.

'Down! Belt!' Du Bois downshifted and floored the accelerator again. Grace slid into the rear seat and tried to pull one of the seat belts on.

The Sprinter sped into Victoria Square, heading for the steps that led down to New Street. More pedestrians scattered. Du Bois hit the back of the van at the top of the steps, forcing it into a stepped fountain in an explosion of water and the grinding of tortured metal.

Grace hadn't managed to get the seat belt on properly. She was flung forwards and battered her face against the front seat. Her arm was caught in the seat belt, which stopped her momentum, but she cried out as it was wrenched out of its socket.

The Range Rover was grounded, see-sawing on the fountain's stone lip. The Sprinter tottered at the highest point of the fountain, and then toppled over, sliding down the fountain's water-covered steps.

Du Bois, furious now, was out of the Range Rover and running after the van. As he ran, he switched out the magazine in his .45 for the magazine of nanite-tipped bullets. He swarmed up onto the Sprinter, which was now lying on its side.

Grace managed to stagger out of the Range Rover, gripping her arm. She saw du Bois kneeling on the upturned van. He reached for the door to open it.

'No!' Grace screamed.

Du Bois was surprised to find the door unlocked. He pulled it open as he heard Grace. He was more surprised when he saw something that looked like a clockwork mannequin sitting in the driver's seat, and then the claymore mine went off.

Du Bois was blown high into the air as ball bearings tore through his flesh. Blackened meat landed, wetly, on the ground close to one of the Sphinx statues that watched over the square.

Silas crawled out of the canal, his clothes shedding water as he did so.

'Excuse me?'

Silas froze. The voice had a very soft Middle Eastern accent that Silas couldn't quite place. He turned slowly to see a nondescript-looking man, clearly of Middle Eastern descent, wearing a well-tailored but tastefully subdued suit and a keffiyeh headscarf. At first Silas wondered if this was just a passer-by, but then he realised his wards had been tricked. The demons that surrounded him, released from his blood, hadn't detected the man. Silas was immediately on his guard.

'This may sound like a strange question, but have you ever eaten the brains of an archer?'

'Who are you?' Silas demanded.

The man stepped forwards. Silas had a moment to see some kind of wriggling, metallic tendrils extend from the man's fingers before they rammed into his head. Silas sank to his knees, drooling.

Hamad looked down at the peace of filth whose secrets he was stealing. It was another weak link in the Circle's chain, another bit of information, no matter how old. He knew what the man had done and sought permission to kill him, but the Brass City refused. Silas was too valuable to them. He was keeping two of the Circle's operatives very busy.

He had not been easy to track, but the electronic realm all but belonged to the Brass City. They eventually separated the carrier signal for his strange Alpha- and Theta-wave transmissions from the background noise and triangulated his position.

Hamad took what he wanted from the sick man's mind, and a little more. Then he retracted the tendrils and let Silas fall to the ground. He might not have been allowed to kill him, but he had not been explicitly ordered against helping others do just that. He sent out a heavily occulted email to an old enemy.

35

A Long Time After the Loss

Cascade was a third-string Consortium world very much in the later stages of its industrial exploitation. Maybe a few hundred years away from becoming a gutted, skeletal planet like New Coventry, with an excess biomass too poor to get off the planet. The Consortium might then designate it a conflict resolution world if they needed a war, or if they just wanted to burn off some of the biomass.

It was nominally a shallow-water world, but the planet's vast hydrosystem had been so utterly polluted by run-off from numerous mining ventures and the inevitable subsurface conflicts over the mines that chemically it was problematic to describe the filthy, mostly-black, turgid liquid which covered the surface of the planet as water.

Cascade still had enough value left that the corporate authorities didn't want heavily armed ships breaching their atmosphere or, more to the point, their orbital-defence cordon. Scab could have bridged in from planetary Red Space, but the *Basilisk II* had been badly damaged doing that on Lotus Eater. Instead they docked at one of the *entrepôt* orbital stations, a slum of a habitat called the Tricorn.

After they found another asteroid to harvest, they used the *Basilisk II*'s smart-matter hull to extensively reconfigure the yacht's appearance. The only thing they couldn't do was change the signature of the drive that had originally come from the Church frigate, the *St. Brendan's Fire*. That was why they had chosen the Tricorn as their entry point: the Church was the only organisation capable of recognising individual bridge drive signatures. The Tricorn was the *entrepôt* with the least Church presence.

Like the ship, Vic, Scab and Steve the Alchemist were also disguised. Though there was only so much that could be done with a seven-foot-tall hard-tech-augmented insect. On the other hand, most insects looked the same to the other uplifted races.

They were restricted on what weaponry, armour, virals and

aggressive and defensive software they could take to the planet, and all weaponised nano-swarms were illegal. They carried the legal stuff openly, mostly sidearms and other hand weapons, and armoured clothing, plus two portable assemblers programmed with specific template builds. As for the other things they'd need, they smuggled in what they thought they could get away with and left the rest.

They became anonymous travellers, shuffling through the Tricorn's vast, grimy departure halls towards waiting drop-shuttles. As they were jostled and bumped, Vic glanced down at his human partner/captor and wondered how close Scab was to killing someone in this crowd. It didn't help that the walls were showing footage of the latest of the clone Scab's pirate atrocities. These were interspersed with stories about the Consortium blockade of and ongoing sanctions against Pythia for breaking its planetary quarantine. Scab was pointedly looking down, his eyes closed, chain-smoking and listening to something via a pair of ancient audio crystals. Vic was amazed at the restraint Scab was showing. He guessed his partner had finally found something important enough to encourage a modicum of impulse control.

The drop-shuttle was an ancient piece of shit with heat shielding so thin that Scab actually started sweating. His sweat, less toxic after the internal purge, still made smoking rivulets through his make-up.

The sun looked pale, distant and weak through the haze of pollution. Planetfall found them on one of Cascade's surface stations close to the Great Rift. The surface station's landing areas were above the foul-smelling, turgid gunk of the planet's all-encompassing ocean, so they took elevators down below the water, their internal systems compensating for pressure changes.

They actually had to walk to the carbon reservoirs in the laser-cut caves below the ocean. They transferred debt relief with their fake ID signatures to the AI system running the reservoirs and plugged in the portable assemblers. The custom templates began growing the bikes.

With the planet's resources dwindling, much of its population was itinerant and followed the mining work. They were cheaper to employ than automatons. With air travel restricted, mostly by wealth, and the oceans so polluted as to make water-travel difficult, the vast road network beneath the ocean was the quickest, cheapest and – more importantly to Vic, Scab and the Alchemist – the most anonymous way to travel.

The bodyglove bikes were long, low motorcycles with powerful internal gyroscopes, powered by miniature fusion reactors. Moulded to the rider or riders' shape, the armoured body slid over to completely enclose the rider.

'Ground transport is so primitive,' Steve muttered. Vic and Scab nodded.

Scab climbed into his bike, lying face down as the padding encased him. He wrapped his fingers around the backup manual control bars even as his neunonics established connection with the vehicle. The armour slid over him and locked into place. Scab's omnipresent P-sat, configured to look like a black sphere at the moment, sank into a port on top of the bike. Its AG motor could help with certain manoeuvres, and the P-sat's lasers would be the bike's only legal offensive weaponry.

Vic's bike was obviously larger. It had three in-line wheels, two at the back, one at the front. Vic lay face down, information from the bike's systems appearing in his vision as he established a neunonic connection. Steve stood over the bike, staring at it.

'I'm pretty much going to have to lie on you,' Steve complained. 'Also, I think this stupid body gets motion sickness.'

'We're here because of you,' Vic told the dolphin irritably. There were easier ways to do what they were trying to do, but as ever, Scab had a plan. 'Climb on, don't throw up on me and absolutely don't soil yourself, do you understand?' Vic told him. Steve nodded and climbed on top of the 'sect. The padding configured itself around them and the armour slid shut. They sent their information to Cascade traffic control, reversed out of the carbon reservoir cave and headed for the on-ramp.

They were doing two hundred miles an hour by the time they hit the road. To Vic it looked less like a road and more like a vast plain. Formerly seabed, it had been flattened and then covered with a molecularly bonded hardened concrete analogue. As far as the bike's three-hundred-and-sixty-degree sensor feed could see, lanes of traffic stretched out in all directions. The vast plain was interspersed with huge pillars with tunnels running through them to allow the passage of traffic. The pillars held up the ceiling covering the road system. The ceiling looked black but was actually transparent – the blackness was the sea above the road. Built during the joyous optimism of the mid-Colonial era, the grand engineering project designed to encourage tourism was now little more than a white elephant – and an accident waiting to happen. Vic decided to release a gentle relaxant. The road system was managing to make him feel both agoraphobic – he grew up in the confines of hive habitats – and claustrophobic at the same time.

They filtered through the busy traffic at speed, weaving between the other vehicles. For the bigger bulk-haulers or moving dormitory blocks, they simply joined the traffic speeding under them. Traffic authority and police contractors patrolled the gap between the road and the ceiling in G-carriers and hoppers.

'I still don't get the plan,' Vic said over an occulted 'face link as they wove in and out of the wheels of a huge mobile leisure complex. He could see smaller shuttle vehicles driving up the large vehicle's ramps into its parking bays. The shuttle vehicles would probably have come from larger domicile vehicles slaved to follow the mobile leisure complex.

'Please slow down,' Steve said. He did not sound happy. 'And can't you just drive in a straight line?'

'We're going to find Steve a new body,' Scab's reply came back.

'I get that. I even get why we're doing it this way,' though it feels like a long shot to me, Vic decided to not add. 'I mean overall. All right, we've got the most valuable commodity in Known Space, and yes, we're actually in credit as a result of this, but how is any of that helping? Rich as we are, we can't settle down anywhere, and we're still no closer to cashing in on Talia.' Not that Vic wanted to cash in on her. 'All we're doing is collecting strange people and strange things for no good reason that I can see. Have we got an exit plan?'

There was no answer for a long time and Vic gradually came to the conclusion that Scab wasn't going to reply. He was wondering if the business with Scab's clone was stopping his human partner/captor from thinking clearly. Or what passed for thinking clearly in Scab's world, anyway.

'The plan hasn't changed. We're auctioning Talia,' Scab eventually said across the occulted 'face link.

'Then why are we pandering to a chemist who's going to make us potent hallucinogens?' Vic asked as he swerved the bike around a cradled limousine with eight bubble wheels. The limo's cab was tinted and his scans detected an active privacy field.

'Key isn't a hallucinogen,' Scab said.

Vic tried to shake his head, aping a human gesture he'd observed, but the contours of the bodyglove's internal padding held him still. Well, that explains everything, then, the insect thought. The bike's three wheels inflated, becoming ball wheels, as they approached the Great Rift and they began receiving advisements on their speed from the Cascade Traffic Authority. Vic engaged the bike's magnetic locks, adhering the bike to the road, which looked as if it came to an end right in front of them. Vehicles disappeared over the edge, cabs and cargo bays swinging in their cradles to remain level, accompanied by a thundering noise that not even the filters on their augmented hearing could completely dampen.

They went over the edge into a canyon more than five miles deep. Multiple lanes ran up and down the Great Rift Road, and they saw more than a few vehicles come unstuck when their magnetic locks failed, some bouncing off other vehicles as they fell. Subjectively above the vertically travelling bikes, the ocean had become a vast, black, horribly polluted waterfall.

There was a jarring crash as a sliding vehicle, its magnetic locks having only partially failed, slid into the rear of Vic's bodyglove. As the bike slewed around, the ball wheels compensated by changing direction through the skid. Then they were travelling horizontally down the rift wall. The cradle on the small cargo vehicle that hit them hadn't moved when it went over the edge and its cargo tumbled down into the rift. The vehicle itself was hanging on by one wheel now. Through the bodyglove's sensor feed, Vic could see the lizard driver's terrified expression. Vic 'faced the vehicle and, finding its electronic defences to be rudimentary, he sent an override signal to the remaining working magnetic lock. The cargo vehicle fell off the road, to be pushed away by a safety feature that used the road's magnetic field to repulse debris. It would cause less chaos in the long run, Vic decided. Then Steve vomited on his back.

They took an off-ramp that led them behind the transparent, vertical road where a series of terraces containing towns and buildings had been cut out of the solid rock. Here the roadways were either horizontal on the terraces or diagonal ramps connecting level to level.

They found the place Scab was looking for about four miles down, a seedy apartment warren cut out of the rift wall. They parked the bikes as close to their destination as they could get, leaving their P-sats to guard the vehicles after initiating all the legal defensive systems they'd been allowed to equip the bikes with.

The shop was on one of the balconies facing the underside of the road. The continental-plate-sized waterfall looked like a solid wall of black, and only the noise told them it was moving. Even with audio dampeners they had to shout to be heard. 'Facing was an easier way of communicating, except that Steve, along with his hygiene strike, had refused to accept neunonics until he'd been given a dolphin body. The stench from the waterfall was also appalling to the point of dangerous, and their nano-screens had sent a number of toxic warnings to their neunonics. They had to force an upgraded portable nano-screen on Steve. Even so, the chemist looked decidedly ill.

Vic was still trying to wipe the vomit off as they approached the shop. The shopfront was a mixture of solid rock and armoured shutters covered in graffiti. Some of the graffiti was holographic, some cut into the stone with lasers. The blinking holographic sign was actually written in script, rather than showing an animation of the services the business proffered.

A strobe gun mounted on a mechanical arm appeared out of the wall to cover them when they 'faced to gain entrance. Scab kept 'facing debt relief until the heavily armoured door popped inwards and then slid open. They found themselves in an airlock covered by another strobe gun. They were extensively scanned. When the security systems attempted to take blood and DNA samples, Scab just 'faced more debt relief until they were allowed in. He paid enough that they didn't have to relinquish any weapons, either.

The inner airlock door popped inwards and slid open.

'There are much cheaper ways to get to see me,' a heavily accented voice said.

Scab stepped out of the airlock, followed by Vic and Steve. Inside, it was very humid. They were standing on a catwalk connected to a series of walkways over a number of protein vats that Vic assumed would be used for growing various soft-tech augments and replacements. Embedded in the wall were a number of clone tanks filled with a murky green and yellow fluid. Just over three-quarters of them contained shapes consistent with variants of the four uplifted races.

'No, no, no, I don't think so,' the Alchemist said, looking around.

'Shut up,' Scab told him.

Vic glanced up. The ceiling was a distant shadow, and the premises had obviously been expanded to subsume other apartments and commercial premises within the warren complex. The skeletal remnants of other rooms were still visible. More clone tanks had been embedded into the walls high above them, and strung between old supports, spars of rock, the walls and the actual ceiling was a network of heavy-gauge, weblike cables.

The cables moved as something slowly but agilely made its way towards them. Vic suppressed an instinctive feeling of revulsion. At first the shape made him think it was a distasteful hard-tech arachnid augment for a 'sect. But as it came closer, he saw that the eight-legged form was a mostly soft-tech augment coupled with a base human. The human arachnid was wearing some sort of smock and a hat. His eyes were the compound eyes of a spider but the lids had epicanthic folds. He had a tiny pointed goatee and a long wispy moustache. Each of his multi-jointed limbs ended in a further eight digits that could manipulate as fingers or thumbs, and each digit ended in some sort of tool or surgical device.

'I don't like going anywhere unarmed, and I don't like explaining myself,' Scab said.

'Careful,' Vic 'faced Scab. 'He doesn't know who you are, doesn't know your rep, so to him you're just another dick.' Vic was conscious of the stealthed arachnid automaton hiding high up in the net. More conspicuous were the three strobe guns on spipods moving around in the web. Vic liked the approach. One spipod for each customer and a stealthed surprise that probably would have fooled his sensors before they had become rich enough to significantly upgrade them.

Scab looked up at Vic. Scab was still wearing a suit, hat and rain-coat, but the ensemble was less unpleasantly garish than his usual efforts and much more like the suits 'normal' people would wear.

'You're Jonas,' Scab said, turning back to the cloner and soft-tech purveyor. The human arachnid nodded. 'We have a job for you. We need a dolphin with very specific specs and soft-tech augments. We'll also need neunonics, again to the spec we designate, a P-sat equipped with manipulators and one or two other things. We know your ability and your stock, and everything we're asking for is well within your capabilities. We will pay you well for your services. We also need it done very quickly and very discreetly, for which we will also pay handsomely.'

Scab 'faced over the instructions, and then both he and Vic con-centrated for a moment as they received feed from the bikes. The bodygloves' countermeasures and their P-sats were dealing with people trying to tamper with them.

'Hmm,' Jonas said in a manner that Vic felt was supposed to be inscrutable. He suspected the clone-technician was running some kind of personality created from a pre-Loss human racial stereotype. 'A dolphin? They are restricted. Mainly for Church use—'

'I've told you, we know what you can do, and what you've done before, and we'll pay you more than enough for your services to avoid the inevitable negotiations, because, frankly, they annoy me.'

'They're not for "Church use",' Steve said in exasperation. 'They work with the Church.'

'This is our friend Steve,' Vic said cheerfully. Steve glared at Vic but didn't correct the 'sect.

Jonas was looking at Steve with interest. Vic was pretty sure the cloner had worked out that the apparent human was actually a dolphin. This meant a Church connection, and nobody liked deal-ing with the Church, particularly as nearly all dolphins worked with bridge drives.

'This will be very expensive,' Jonas mused.

'Here's half the debt relief now,' Scab said.

So much for inscrutable, Vic thought when Jonas rocked back in his web after checking the sum he'd just received.

'I will have to source the P-sat and the hard-tech augments elsewhere. I will use discreet people I trust, pay them a lot of your money and order everything as separate components and templates to assemble here, if that is all right with you?' Scab nodded. 'And is there anything else I can get you, Mr ...'

Scab just shook his head, then reached into the breast pocket of his suit and drew out his cigarette case.

'Look, Scab—' Steve started. Too late he realised his mistake. Vic and Scab both turned to stare at him. Jonas froze on his web. Scab put a cigarette into his mouth and lit the inhalable poison as Jonas scuttled around in his web to face Scab. The human killer put the case back into his breast pocket, and suddenly his tumbler pistol was in his hand. The spipod-mounted strobe guns moved to cover Scab but stopped abruptly, presumably the result of an order from Jonas who would not be eager to antagonise someone with Woodbine Scab's reputation. The stealthed arachnid automaton high above remained still.

'I don't care,' Jonas said. 'I'm very greedy, and you're paying me enough not to care.'

Scab just nodded.

They became so tired of Steve's whining and trying to tell Jonas how to do his job that they sedated him. His new body was being speed-grown in one of the vats, the augments had already been spliced into it and his neunonics had crawled into the meat of the dolphin body's brain to better adapt to it as it grew.

They had no interest in preserving the human body, so Jonas had used an invasive nanite procedure to download and then imprint Steve's mind into the new body. All of which had taken the better part of a human-standard twenty-six-hour day.

Scab had spent most of that time almost completely still, crouched on the side of a catwalk near the edge of one of the vats. He had been chain smoking, and hadn't reholstered his tumbler pistol.

Vic had also crouched down, but only because it was a comfortable resting pose for his hard-tech-augmented body. Jonas scuttled backwards and forwards, checking on things. There was no doubt in Vic's mind that the arachnid human – or spider monkey, as Vic had started thinking of him – was more than a little nervous of Scab's presence. Scab had been allowed limited neunonic access to the cloner's systems so he could monitor what was happening. A number of items, including the components of the customised P-sat, had been delivered, but they'd all been left in the airlock.

Finally Steve's new P-sat rose into the air.

'Get me out of this filth,' Steve said. 'I need to be hosed down and put in the pool.'

Scab didn't acknowledge the P-sat communication. Vic assumed his partner/captor was starting to think their plan hadn't worked.

'Now you pay me and leave?' Jonas said. Scab turned to look at him. 'Please?' Jonas's voice sounded calm, but the calmness had a narcotic quality to it.

Scab stood up. 'What did you do?' Scab asked.

'Nothing,' Jonas said, but fear was starting to break through the cloner's drug-induced calm. The spider monkey swallowed hard and added some more drugs to his very nervous system, Vic suspected.

'Guys?' Steve asked. 'Seriously, how are you going to get me back to the ship on a motorbike?'

It was a good question, Vic conceded.

Scab pointed the tumbler pistol at Jonas. Jonas shrank away. The spipod-mounted strobe guns swivelled to aim at Scab, and the arachnid automaton practically plummeted through the web to crouch just above the human killer.

'Don't make things harder on yourself,' Scab told Jonas.

'You need to listen to him, spider monkey,' Vic added. He had straightened up as well. The big 'sect was a little insulted when only one of the strobe guns swivelled to cover him as he drew his triple-barrelled shotgun pistol with his lower-right hand, and both his double-barrelled laser pistols with his upper pair.

'I didn't do anything,' Jonas said, absurdly raising four of his hands.

Scab manually cocked the hammer on the tumbler pistol. It was an affectation, nothing more. The arachnid automaton tensed in its web and the strobe guns' six barrels started spinning up to speed.

'Oh, wait,' Scab said. Then he 'faced the virus to Jonas's systems. It was an expensive Pythian-made sequestration virus that had been extensively modified by Elodie. Jonas's systems were excellent. He was an illegal cloner and soft-tech augmenter at the top of his game. He could afford excellent defences, both physical – like the airlock, the automaton, the strobe guns – and viral, nanite and electronic. The expense of the modified Pythian software virus effectively outbid Jonas's electronic defences. In less than a heartbeat, Scab was in control of everything in the cloning facility. Vic still thought his partner/captor was being melodramatic when Scab had the strobe guns swivel to point at Jonas.

'You can't lie to me,' Scab told the spider monkey. 'There are only degrees of suffering now. You decide.'

Scab 'faced access to the external feed from the clone facility to Vic. The 'sect saw featureless automatons in anachronistic pre-Loss dress walking along the *terrace towards the shop, coming from both directions.*

'I'm sorry!' Jonas said.

'No. You got caught,' Scab said and pulled the trigger. The recoil jerked his arm up as the spinning bullet drilled into Jonas's head. The spider monkey fell, getting caught up in his own net. Scab 'faced a virus to scramble Jonas's neunonics, so the spider monkey would have to be cloned from a backup. He sent orders to the systems that would poison the soft-tech vats, kill the cloned bodies – except Steve's – and destroy any stored minds that were about to be downloaded into the bodies. He then modified the sequestration virus to utterly junk the facility's systems. There had to be consequences for messing with Scab. Consequences and collateral damage.

Steve, now in his new dolphin body, was thrashing around in his tank.

'Guys! Guys! Why does it always come down to violence with you people?'

Vic holstered both laser pistols as Scab made one of the strobe guns scamper over to the insect and leap up at him. Vic caught the heavy weapon. It would be a bit more unwieldy than his own as it didn't have the miniaturised AG motors to offset its weight. Then Vic 'faced a courier service with the best reputation for speed, security and discretion on the planet. Finally he left instructions with the arachnid automaton to protect Steve and overrode the airlock, popping both doors.

Even over the sound of the waterfall they could make out the sound of superheated air molecules exploding so rapidly that the noise of one detonation ran into the next. There was a near-constant red glow coming from outside where the exterior strobe gun was firing constantly. The one in the airlock was firing more intermittently as Scab and Vic marched through.

Outside, the narrow terrace was filled with the burned body parts of the featureless automatons, many of them still glowing neon from their overloaded energy-dissipation grids. Scab sent one of the spipod-mounted strobe guns ahead of him. Almost immediately it was tracking targets and firing rapid bursts of thin red light. Energy-dissipation grids lit up on the remaining automatons, dressing them in neon. One overheated and exploded. Scab kicked another over the stone lip of the terrace and fired into a third, point-blank, with his tumbler pistol.

Vic walked out behind Scab. His thorax and upper limbs rotated one way, his abdomen and lower limbs another. He started firing the strobe gun, concentrating the beams between two or three of the automatons at a time, overheating their energy-dissipation grids until they blew. A split-screen view from his neunonic targeting systems told him exactly where to place the shots, and he fired all three barrels of the shotgun he was still holding in his lower hands. All three tungsten solid shots hit one of the automatons and pierced its downgraded armour before the explosive charges blew. The automaton's torso went spinning away from its legs.

The other spipod-mounted strobe came scuttling out after Vic, spinning on its pintle, firing, covering Vic's back as more automatons scrambled up the rock face and onto the terrace.

Scab and Vic had done their homework. Any decent automaton would give even the most augmented bounty killer a run for their money unless they were in full military-spec combat gear. Mr Hat owned a small army of them, but other than his automaton deification fetish, Mr Hat prided himself on doing things by the book. Scab and Vic had been forced to downgrade their capabilities when they came planetside, and similar laws existed for automatons. Even so, Vic hadn't expected Mr Hat to risk so many of them as, expense aside, the automatons apparently worshipped the diminutive lizard.

Vic reloaded the shotgun pistol and flicked it closed. He spun his thorax around and fired the shotgun at the chest and head that was chasing after him using its arms as legs.

An automaton leaped over the lip of the terrace and landed on Scab, ramming him into the rock wall. Scab spat his cigarette into its eyeless face. The automaton grabbed the wrist of the hand holding the tumbler pistol and forced it down. Scab's metalforma knife appeared in his left hand and he rammed it up through the automaton's chin. Strands of the smart-metal blade, fed by the small assembler in the hilt, grew through the automaton's head as it staggered back. His wrist now free, Scab shot his attacker twice in the chest and kicked it away from him. He fired the last two rounds in the tumbler pistol's cylindrical magazine, then raised his left hand and fired the mini-disc launcher strapped to his forearm. The electromagnetically guided monomolecular discs flew out, cutting into the heads of the automatons and spinning around inside them. It wasn't enough to stop them, but it would give them pause. He flicked open the tumbler pistol's cylindrical magazine, slid in new rounds from a speed loader and snapped it shut with a flick of his wrist. He tore his metalforma knife from the head of the automaton as it fell to the ground and kept walking. The strobe guns were firing nearly constantly now. The automatons charging them looked like bright neon ghosts.

The bikes were surrounded by a number of people, some of them dead from laser fire, others just stunned, concussed or diseased. One of them, a male feline, his fur shaved and dyed in what Vic assumed were gang colours, was moaning and trying to stand. Scab shot him as he walked by, then ordered one of the slaved strobe guns to deliver the coup de grâce to the other still-living would-be bike thieves. They were likely too poor to have clone insurance, Vic thought.

All the strobe guns were running low on juice now. The automatons had ceased their attack. Vic wasn't sure if they had destroyed them all, or if Mr Hat had pulled them back because too many of his worshippers were dying. One of the strobe guns stood guard and Vic dropped the one he'd been using. It extended its spipod and scampered across the ground, then leaped up onto the bike. The remaining strobe gun attached itself to Scab's bike. With a 'faced instruction, the bikes allowed the strobe guns to connect to the universal hardpoint on their roofs, next to the P-sats. The bikes' miniature fusion reactors started recharging the rotary laser weapons.

The armour slid back. Vic and Scab lay face down inside the bikes, manoeuvred them around and made for the Great Rift Road's on-ramp. There were other ways they could have chosen – tunnels that would have taken them to other shuttle stations – but that wasn't the point of the exercise.

They hit the road doing speeds in excess of two hundred and fifty miles an hour, weaving in and out of the cradled traffic. Travelling vertically up the road, Vic felt like he was in a rocket.

The Amuser was on them the moment they left the on-ramp. Accurate fire from the oddly shaped ship's short-range anti-personnel weaponry lit them up. Vic was impressed at Mr Hat's pull, or perhaps his employer's influence. Probably the latter. The authorities had allowed the bounty killer to bring his ship not only into the atmosphere, but into the road system. Vic was just pleased that it looked as if the lizard wasn't permitted to use any of his heavy ordnance. Either that or he wanted them alive. That also made sense. They were the only link to Talia, after all, and it would explain why the automatons had appeared to go easy on them.

Assault-cannon fire chipped away at the bike. New armour was being regrown, but the carbon reservoirs were quite limited on a vehicle this size. The cannon fire sounded like someone beating on the bodyglove with jackhammers, every impact shaking the bike, the effects worsened because they were moving so quickly.

Strobe fire lit up the bike's energy grid, making it glow brightly, the speed of its movement leaving fractal lines of light behind it as it wove in and out of the vertical traffic. The Amuser's odd, flattened-octopus shape kept pace with them, pouring down constant fire. At the same time, the bike's electronic defences were fighting off hacks from Mr Hat as he tried to control their systems.

The strobe guns and the P-sats' lasers were firing constantly. There was no point firing at the Amuser; the strobe guns wouldn't even score it – ships were just too heavily armoured. Instead they were using the lasers as point-defence weapons against the assault-cannon fire. The lasers drew red lines to the incoming rounds, trying to take the pressure off the bikes' armour. They were, however, trying to intercept electromagnetically driven hypersonic rounds over short range, with mixed results.

Vic rode under an ore carrier and braked hard to match its speed. Scab joined him moments later. The Amuser moved up and over, then down and under the ore carrier, trying to get an angle of fire, but couldn't.

'So we just stay here, right?' Vic asked over the 'face link, hopefully.

'Sure,' Scab said. It was one of the most reasonable things Vic could ever remember his partner saying. They cruised along vertically at a hundred miles an hour, the bikes' armour re-growing from the badly depleted carbon reservoirs, the strobe guns and energy-dissipation grids cooling.

Then Vic saw them: the eyeless automatons crawling hand-over-hand on the ore hauler like insects, from above and below. Vic gunned the bike, feeding targeting solutions from his neunonics to the strobe gun as both he and Scab accelerated. The strobe guns spun in their mounts, firing rapid burst after rapid burst as the automatons leaped for them. They targeted the automatons closest to the bikes first, pouring fire into them at close range. The automatons turned neon, leaving fractal patterns of light in the air as they leaped and fell towards the bikes. Their energy-dissipation grids overheated and they exploded in mid-air. The explosions buffeted the bikes, and gyroscopes fought to keep them upright as they wobbled in the blast.

One of the automatons hit Vic's bike before exploding and the bike skidded. Suddenly it was on its side, spinning. Vic was losing momentum and starting to fall away from the road as the three bubble wheels spun, trying to get traction with the vertical roadway.

Scab slewed his bike left and right as the automatons leaped for him. Those that didn't explode in the sustained fire from the rotary strobe gun went tumbling into the rift below. He cut the bike hard to the right, causing other drivers to brake and swerve.

The wheels caught and Vic was upright again. He accelerated hard. The strobe gun was still firing, hitting automatons and other traffic alike. As he shot out from under the ore crawler, the automatons leaped for him, some missing, some hitting the road to be run over, others falling, bouncing off other traffic on the way down. They tried chasing both bikes, leaping from vehicle to vehicle, and they were fast, but not nearly fast enough to keep up. Vic was vaguely aware of the fight having caused a crash below him. Multiple vehicles smashed into each other, some of them spinning out into the air before gravity pulled them back down into the rift. One or two of the lighter, faster vehicles flew as far as the waterfall, only to be yanked downwards by billions of tonnes of water. Whomever Hat's employer was, he must have a lot of influence to keep the traffic authorities out of this mess.

As soon as they emerged from under the ore hauler, the Amuser resumed its attack. Vic tasked the strobe gun and the P-sat's laser to intercept the incoming assault-cannon fire, again with varying degrees of success. The cannon hits battered the bike around on the road, making it difficult to control. He could feel the heat from the overloading energy-dissipation grid even through the armour and insulating padding. He looked for another large vehicle to take cover under. Then he saw more of the automatons coming from above, leaping from vehicle to vehicle.

'Give me a break,' Vic muttered.

Mr Hat was receiving sensor feed from the Amuser as well as all the ship's active weapons systems and all his automatons. He could also see the ensuing chaos on the vertical Great Rift Road through the circular webbed window in the smart matter of the ship's gothic Command and Control centre. He was on his throne-like seat atop the extruded column that dominated the chamber. Mr Hat did not like the way things were going. He was losing far too many of his automatons. This was a wasteful way to treat them – ridiculous expense account aside, he was invested in them. He watched as they leaped from vehicle to vehicle, always heading downwards as the traffic was coming up. They landed on the vehicles with sufficient force to significantly dent bodywork.

Then he felt something press against the side of his face.

'The load in this needler is designed specifically to pull its way through your armoured skin. The neurotoxin will overcome your internal defences and you will die painfully.' As the female spoke, Mr Hat received warning messages that his neunonics were being hacked, successfully. 'You'll see the virus we uploaded into you. It will hide in your personality upload and aggressively pursue your backups. Maybe your insurance company will catch it, but me hacking your neunonics should be proof enough that it's a serious bit of code. I'm telling you this to try and stop you from doing something really stupid in response to my presence. I'm assuming your automatons are programmed for martyrdom if anything happens to you, but bear in mind that I just want to talk.'

'You have my attention, Miss Negrinotti,' Mr Hat told the feline. He was less than happy, and more than a little surprised, that both his and the Amuser's defences had been circumvented. He was, however, also intrigued to hear what she had to say. She looked a mess – what little was left of her fur was falling out in charred clumps. Whatever she'd been wearing – it looked like a lightweight spacesuit – had fused with her burned skin. She was obviously in agony and only being kept upright by her internal medical systems and an awful lot of drugs.

The automaton hit the road just in front of Vic. He braked hard, sliding under a heavy-cargo vehicle. The automaton bounced off the cargo vehicle and tumbled down into the rift. Vic braked and let the cargo vehicle pass over him before accelerating and steering around it. There were seven more automatons above, all making towards him. The strobe started firing again, trying to engage them all. Three of them leaped for him. Vic disengaged the electromagnetic locks on the bike's bubble wheels and the road pushed the bike away from it. The bike started plummeting down into the rift, wheels spinning. Two of the automatons fell past. Something heavy hit the bike in mid-air and Vic tasked the P-sat to fire at whatever was on the bike. Then he used the AG motor on the P-sat to try and guide the free-fall. The AG motor pushed the bike back towards the road and Vic reengaged the electromagnetic locks on the wheels. Vehicles seeing the bike falling towards them tried desperately to get out of its way, causing more collisions. More vehicles tumbled off the vertical road.

There was a shrieking noise as the automaton riding the falling bike tore the armour open. Vic hacked the bike's padding so he could move as the automaton reached for him. He spun his head around a hundred and eighty degrees to face the featureless automaton and reached under his thorax. He managed to draw his triple-barrelled shotgun pistol and push it between his body and the automaton's. The automaton grabbed Vic's head and started to squeeze. Vic fired all three barrels. The solid rounds penetrated the automaton's body and exploded, and it went spinning into the Great Rift. The AG motor managed to guide the bike back onto the road and the wheels hit the surface hard. Without the padding, all Vic's weight came down on his arm, which broke despite the armour and the reinforcement from his hard-tech augments. The bike spun downwards and across the road on its side. It bounced off a personal shuttle vehicle. Then a cargo vehicle ran over it. The bike's armour buckled but held up, crushing the body of the vehicle around Vic. Finally the bubble wheels got purchase and the bike righted itself, but it continued skidding as the wheels tried to get traction. He was heading towards another ore hauler. Finally the wheels caught, and a panicked, partially crushed Vic accelerated away from the oncoming traffic.

It was over now, Vic realised. With the bike's armour torn open, all Mr Hat had to do was fire on him. Above him he could see more of the automatons leaping towards him.

'I suspect the first thing we should do is call off the attack. I think the boys have had enough,' Elodie said.

'Agreed,' Mr Hat said, and with a thought he had the automatons cease what they were doing and stay where they were. He was aware of Scab having reached the lip of the Great Rift Road. 'However, you must tell me how you gained entry to the Amuser. You really shouldn't have been able to do that. I'm assuming EVA? Whilst I was docked at the Tricorn?'

Elodie nodded. 'A short EVA from the habitat. I spoofed your sensors and the suit was set up for stealth,' the feline intrusion-specialist told him.

'By the look of you, you rode the ship down during entry into the atmosphere. Some kind of insulating foam?' Elodie nodded again. 'So all you had to do then was override my airlock, spoof it so I didn't know about it, sneak past all my sensors, spoof a nano-screen and hide from my automatons – none of which you should have been able to do. You really are very good, aren't you?' Mr Hat said. Elodie's smile was more of a grimace. 'And you have a ridiculous amount of resources behind you.' At the base of the column, more of Mr Hat's automatons were slowly moving towards them.

'I'd advise against it -- your psych profile says you don't like taking unnecessary risks.'

'Does it say that I also don't like losing? Or being made a fool of?'

'Yes, it does. There's no shame in this. Your army aside, there's one of you and three of us, and whatever lies we may like to tell ourselves, we're all of a comparative skill level.'

'Did you trick me here?' the diminutive lizard asked.

'We knew the information broker Jonas used – an AI affiliated with Pythia. We bribed him so he'd only accept your bid.'

'I'd hope it was the highest,' Mr Hat said.

'With our contribution, it was.'

The automatons had stopped. Vic rode past them as they perched on vehicles, watching him with their eyeless faces. The Amuser had stopped firing as well. He rode over the lip. The bubble wheels deflated to a normal configuration as he made his way towards the shuttle station.

'So I suppose the question remains: why?' Mr Hat asked.

'We want the blank,' Elodie told him.

The lizard's snout wrinkled in confusion. 'Without his entangled twin, he only offers one-way communication with my employer, whom Scab can contact through other channels if he wishes. So why does he want the blank?'

'I don't know,' Elodie said. The lizard's voice-analysis software suggested she was probably telling the truth, and that there was an undercurrent of confusion and irritation connected to her lack of knowledge.

With a thought, Mr Hat brought the Amuser up over the lip of the rift and ordered his automatons to make for the closest shuttle station. He gazed out over the vast plain-like road. The vehicles on it looked like fast moving insects. He had the ship hover just beneath the transparent roof holding up the ocean.

'You must realise that my employer's a very powerful individual, yes?' Mr Hat asked. 'And he will be displeased about this, to say the least. Your threat is inconsequential compared to what he could do to me.'

'You'll weigh up the risks; we're a more immediate threat.'

Mr Hat considered this. 'My pride is wounded, Miss Negrinotti, but this really is a most interesting job.'

'I'd give it up. Woodbine Scab destroys everything he touches.'

The diminutive lizard looked up at her. 'Very well, I'll give you the blank.'

*

Scab, a partially mangled Vic – who had to be cut out of his body-glove bike – and a still-healing Elodie, escorting the blank – an eyeless human, idiot clone, biologically entangled to a twin somewhere – walked into the *Basilisk II*'s pool room. Steve, now in his dolphin body, was swimming in agitated circles.

'A courier!' his limbed P-sat shouted at them. 'You had me delivered! You had me fucking delivered!'

'You're welcome,' Vic groused.

36

Ancient Britain

When they left Cuda's bower they were blindfolded again until they were close enough to easily find the tracks left by the column. The survivors had travelled deeper into woods, into the land that Guidgen and his people called Ardu.

Guidgen had spoken with the *gwyllion,* and they had agreed to cease the attacks until the *dryw* spoke with Bladud and his people. As they made their way past the outlying guards, a number of them nodded at Tangwen and Kush as they walked by. The guards glared at Guidgen with suspicion and no little dislike. It was obvious that he represented the tribe who had been murdering their people as they slept.

As they walked into the camp, Tangwen saw four riders enter as well. They wore the garb, bore the weapons and carried themselves as warriors, but their armour looked ill-fitting, as if it had belonged to someone else originally. They dismounted as Bladud and Nerthach, accompanied by Anharad and her silent grandson Mabon, approached the riders. If they were warriors, as they appeared to be, then it was fitting that Bladud greet them. Even from a distance, Tangwen could see that the newcomers had experienced hard times in the recent past.

'That is Bladud,' Tangwen told Guidgen. He nodded, smiling as if he knew that already. As they walked towards the Witch King, they started to hear the conversation with the newly arrived warriors.

'I am Ysgawyn. These are my men – Brys, Gwynn and Madawg,' the apparent leader of the warriors said.

'That is all?' Nerthach asked, sounding a little confused. 'No deeds to your name, nor your father's name, or your tribe?'

'We are Durotriges from the south and the west,' Ysgawyn told Nerthach. 'We do not feel like great warriors. Our lands have been overrun by the spawn of Andraste and our people are dead, or worse.'

Bladud was studying the man, a look of concentration on his face. 'There is some truth to your story, but that is not all of it, I think,' he said.

Tangwen increased her pace, stooping to pick up a rock without breaking stride.

'Tangwen?' Kush said.

Tangwen pushed past a surprised Bladud and Nerthach. Ysgawyn turned. There was a moment of confusion but he realised her intent too late. As he started reaching for his sword, Tangwen hit him in the face with the rock again and again, riding him down to the ground, bloodying his mouth, breaking his nose and teeth. His three men reached for their weapons. Nerthach stepped forwards, pushing the youngest one, Gwynn, to the ground with his bulk as he drew his own blade. Bladud stepped back, watching impassively. Warriors were running towards the fight. Kush arrived first, axe at the ready. Ysgawyn's men were quickly surrounded. Tangwen was crouched over Ysgawyn. She spat in his face and drew her iron-bladed dagger.

'Tangwen!' Bladud's voice cut through the raised voices. Tangwen hesitated. Ysgawyn was staring up at her through the blood, furious. 'This is ill done.'

'These are the Corpse People. They make war on children and defenceless landsfolk. They kill for the sake of it and think they are dead. I am merely helping them with their belief.'

'Then let us face each other like warriors, when I have a sword in my hand, or is that too much of challenge for you?' Ysgawyn demanded. There were nods from among the warriors present. Tangwen spat in his face again.

'I'll give you the same chance you gave all the peaceful villages you sacked – not that you would have had the courage to do it if you hadn't been allies of the Lochlannach!' Tangwen hissed. There was more muttering from the surrounding warriors at the mention of the Lochlannach.

'I have heard of the Corpse People,' Nerthach mused. 'It is an ill name.'

'If Tangwen wishes to take this man's life, then any who object may do so to me,' Kush said. His voice was a low, menacing rumble. Guidgen had come to stand next to him. There was still a slight smile on the strange *dryw*'s face.

'Are you spying for them? For Bress?' Tangwen demanded.

'No,' Ysgawyn told her.

'This is ill done,' said Brys, the oldest of the Corpse People, a heavily built, grizzled man with long grey hair tied back into a ponytail. 'We have waged war and raided just like the rest of you, only we are better at it. If Ysgawyn, or any of us, have broken your laws, then we have the right to challenge.'

'Why aren't you with Bress and his master, the Dark Man in the flames?' Tangwen demanded.

'They betrayed us!' Ysgawyn shouted at her. 'Are you happy?'

Tangwen stared down at him with utter contempt. She raised the stone again and he brought up his hands to shield his face. Tangwen dropped the stone, then straightened and faced Bladud.

'If he gets in my way, or even irritates me, I'll kill him,' Tangwen told the Witch King.

'Tangwen, it is not for you to speak to Bladud—' Nerthach began. Kush opened his mouth to object.

'Let her speak freely,' Bladud said.

'As far as I am concerned,' Tangwen said, raising her voice so all could hear it, 'this man is beneath respect. He may be treated as people see fit. If he offends you, or breaks any laws, he should be killed out of hand, for he does not deserve anything more.'

'How convenient.' It was said in a low, rasping voice, little more than a whisper, but it still carried. Tangwen turned around to see the sallow, narrow-faced, oddly frail-looking warrior with a receding hairline who had ridden in with Ysgawyn. He had been introduced as Madawg. He was staring at Tangwen in a way that made her feel uncomfortable.

'Do you have something to say?' Tangwen asked, her hand dropping to the haft of the hatchet pushed through her belt. Madawg said nothing. He just kept watching her.

Nerthach offered his hand to Ysgawyn and pulled him to his feet.

'You help around here and you do as you're told,' Nerthach told the *rhi* of the Corpse People. 'Any trouble and I'll kill you myself – fair fight or not, it makes no difference to me, understand?'

Ysgawyn glared at the big warrior in his bear-fur cloak, but he nodded.

Tangwen turned to Bladud. 'This is Guidgen, a *dryw* of the *gwyllion*,' Tangwen told the Witch King.

Bladud offered his arm. Guidgen looked down at the hand. His smile grew a little wider but he did not take the proffered arm.

A short time later they were standing on a small earthen bank next to the mud track, some distance away from the main camp. Around them the leaves were just starting to yellow and the woods were soaked still from the overnight rain.

Bladud was opposite the wizened, still-smiling Guidgen, Anharad and Tangwen nearby. Nerthach was keeping watch, and Kush was also close by. Even Germelqart had come to sit quietly at the treeline after exchanging a few words with Kush in their own tongue.

'Thank you for coming to speak with me,' Bladud said. Guidgen nodded.

'I do not thank you,' Anharad said. 'You have acted in a cowardly manner. You have waged war on the sleeping and the helpless, killed children, and all this on people who have suffered enough. I think you are no better than these Corpse People.'

'Given the choice between doing the right thing and the survival of your people, what would you do?' Guidgen asked.

Anharad opened her mouth to answer but then closed it again.

'The Corpse People raided, the *gwyllion* are just protecting their land,' Tangwen said. 'I am not sure we would have done things very differently. When a stronger tribe comes to your land, you're left with cunning and fear to best them. We used to lead raiders astray in the marshes and pick them off one by one.'

'I am sure that Tangwen explained the situation?' Bladud said. Guidgen nodded. 'And you will join us?'

'We have not even decided if we will let you pass,' Guidgen said. 'We will certainly not be serving you.'

Bladud held his composure well. Tangwen couldn't help but smile. Anharad made a choking noise.

'Do you understand what is happening?' the Trinovantes woman demanded.

'Indeed,' Guidgen said.

'And you believe it?' Bladud asked. 'It can sound difficult—'

'The spawn of Andraste are less than two days behind you, and they kill or change everything in their path. Our scouts have seen them, and there is no way we can fight them.'

'Yet,' Bladud said.

'Then your people will flee?' Anharad asked.

'Perhaps,' said Guidgen.

'Are you trying to be irritating?' Anharad demanded.

'No, it is incidental.'

Tangwen laughed and Anharad glared at her.

'We are stronger together,' Bladud pointed out.

Guidgen shook his head. 'You, personally, are stronger, because you have power over these people. We would obviously be better off on our own. That is assuming the coming of Andraste's brood is not a good thing.'

Bladud didn't quite manage to keep a grasp on his composure this time. Even Tangwen was staring at Guidgen in shock.

'Guidgen, you are right to question, but we have seen these things,' Bladud said when he finally recovered the ability to speak. 'There is no reasoning with them – what they do not kill, they change and then enslave.'

'I would agree with all of that – with the exception of slavery,' said Guidgen. 'We think they are as much slaves as are the wolves in a pack.'

'Wolf packs have leaders,' Nerthach growled from where he was keeping watch.

Guidgen nodded towards him in agreement. 'We made the mistake once of gathering power, of living behind walls, of trying to be civilised.' Guidgen looked at Kush, who smiled and bowed towards him. 'It was a mistake. Now the trees walk and we can hear the Horned God's laughter echoing through their branches. We would be changed. What we are now would be no more, but we could better serve the Horned God, and through him Cuda.'

Bladud was already shaking his head. 'This is not of Cuda. This is a blight – it sickens her.'

'So you would have it, because your life is coming to an end and now a different life will be dominant. Tell me, do you think these things are evil?'

'No,' Bladud finally admitted. 'They are ... something else.'

'Fine,' Tangwen said. 'But you can't blame the old life for fighting back.'

Guidgen nodded towards her.

'It sounds like an excuse to *not* fight, an excuse for cowardice,' Anharad said, unimpressed.

'To do something of which we are very afraid?' Guidgen asked.

'Is that what you have chosen?' Bladud asked.

'It is one of our choices. We could also flee on our own, so we would not be laden down with the others you have gathered around you. We could join you and help with the burden of your responsibility. Or—'

'Fight us every step of the way so that you could sacrifice us to Andraste's children,' Bladud said. Guidgen nodded.

'Is he under hospitality?' Anharad demanded. Mabon was on his feet, hand on his knife, responding to his grandmother's obvious anger.

'Yes,' Tangwen, Kush and Bladud said as one.

'You fear a change,' Guidgen said. 'That is understandable, but it is not so clear a path for us as it is for you. Constant fleeing would appear to offer no hope.'

Bladud was smiling. 'I like you, Guidgen,' he said.

'I'm afraid I cannot say the same thing, for I know what you are,' Guidgen said.

Nerthach turned to stare at Guidgen, furious. '*Dryw* or no, it does not befit you to insult Bladud!' the big warrior told Guidgen. It was the first time the smile on the *dryw*'s face faltered.

'He did not insult me,' Bladud said thoughtfully.

'Is there hope for you as a people?' Guidgen asked.

'Yes,' Bladud told him. 'But it is slim. It will be hard, and dangerous, and we will not discuss it with you unless we are sure you are with us.'

Guidgen nodded. It was his turn to look thoughtful. 'And there are others here who know of this hope?' Guidgen asked. Tangwen frowned. It sounded like an odd question.

'Yes,' Bladud said.

'Very well. We will join you, we will help – on one condition,' Guidgen said.

'That I give myself to the land,' Bladud said.

'Enough of this,' Nerthach spat and started drawing his sword. Tangwen's hands went to her hatchet and her dagger. Bladud stepped between Nerthach and Guidgen.

'It is better that you cut me down than strike a *dryw* in my presence, do you understand?' the Witch King demanded. Nerthach froze. The big warrior was shaking with anger. Guidgen appeared to be perfectly calm and unafraid. The smile was back on the wizened *dryw*'s face as he looked around at the wet woods. Bladud turned back to Guidgen. 'Do I know you?'

'We have never met,' Guidgen told him.

'Why would you see my blood on the earth?'

'Because the oaks speak of you, and the words they whisper through their creaking branches are *bannog rhi*.'

'I have made no secret of this,' Bladud said. 'We are stronger together, particularly now, and if there is a stronger leader, they will take my place whether I want it or not. But these are things to discuss once we have found a way to deal with the spawn of Andraste.'

Guidgen's smile had gone now. 'That is a lie,' he said. Tangwen's breath caught in her throat.

'I'm warning you—' Nerthach began.

'Nerthach, enough!' Bladud said. He was angry now. 'Is this your idea of serving your people? Hide behind your status as a *dryw* to insult warriors?' he demanded of Guidgen.

'You do not wear a warrior's robe,' Guidgen said. 'And it is no insult to say what is, is. The actions you take now will help your claim as *bannog rhi*.'

'Fine, that is true, but I also think you underestimate how much I want my people and myself to live,' Bladud said after some thought.

'You would rule us?' Guidgen asked.

'I would have you join us.'

'Under your rule.'

'If you like.'

'It does not befit a *rhi* to obscure his words so.'

'Yes, then.'

'Would you conquer us if we will not be ruled by you?'

Bladud paused to think about the question.

'There is nothing wrong with a strong tribe conquering a weak one,' Nerthach said. 'That is the way of things. In the long run, the weak one will benefit from the strength of their conquerors. There is no shame in power and skill at arms.'

Guidgen was already nodding in agreement. 'Indeed, but then you can't blame the weak tribe for fighting back,' Guidgen told the large warrior. Tangwen smiled, hearing her words echo back to her.

'And if I made an agreement with you now?' Bladud asked.

'Would you? If we join with you, would you swear an oath never to return to Ardu, and to leave the *gwyllion* in peace?'

'Yes.'

'Which leaves us with two problems. You are an oathbreaker.'

'Enough of this!' Nerthach shouted. 'Get back to the woods and we will hunt your people like the animals they are, and when we find your homes, we will burn them. The only blood that will water the earth will be your own!' Spittle flecked the big warrior's beard. He was furious. It was only with supreme effort that he had not drawn his sword.

Guidgen's expression turned serious. He turned on Nerthach, pointing at Bladud. 'You see the robe he wears? Is he a *dryw* now? Does he serve his people as a *dryw*? Or does he wear armour and carry a sword? He stands between two worlds, lusting for power. And if you ever threaten me again I will use the blood of everyone you care about to paint the trees! Do you understand me, warrior who I will name brown-nose if he does not start thinking for himself?'

Nerthach stared at Guidgen, appalled. A satire and a curse from a *dryw* were no small thing.

'He speaks the truth,' Bladud said quietly. Nerthach turned to stare at his friend and *rhi*. 'I broke my oaths.'

'Out of necessity,' Nerthach said.

'They were still oaths,' Guidgen said mercilessly.

'The council are sitting in judgement on this very matter,' Nerthach said.

'You know the punishment,' Guidgen said.

'And now *you* lie,' Germelqart said quietly.

Everyone turned to stare at the quiet Carthaginian. It was Guidgen's turn to look angry.

'Watch your tongue, foreigner!' Guidgen spat.

'Your threats mean nothing to me,' Germelqart said. 'I am in no less danger now than I was yesterday, or the day before.'

'And I am not frightened of striking a priest,' Kush growled. 'Very hard, with an axe.

'You do not care about this oathbreaking,' Germelqart said.

The anger left Guidgen's face immediately, to be replaced once more by his wry smile. 'That's not entirely true.' The wizened *dryw* turned back to Bladud. 'You would make an oath with me today, but there will come a time when you will find a reason, a good reason to your mind, for why you had to come to Ardu and why you had to conquer us.'

Nerthach bristled but Bladud held his hand up to quiet the warrior. 'I never learned to foretell the future so I do not know what it holds, but you are right – that sounds like me,' Bladud said. Guidgen was nodding. 'Is that why you would see me given to the land?'

'That – and a king, even a false king, is a powerful sacrifice.'

'Surely being an oathbreaker would lessen the power of that sacrifice?'

'But increase its necessity.'

Tangwen couldn't shake the feeling that she had utterly wasted her time going to see the *gwyllion*.

'We will be enemies one day,' Guidgen said. 'But you have told the truth this day.' Guidgen opened his mouth as if to scream, and instead uttered a sound like a raven's call. The *gwyllion* walked out of the trees. Tangwen stared at them, appalled. She'd had no idea they were there. The others were also staring at them in shock. Even Germelqart and Kush. 'We are with you.'

Britha ducked under something that was half-tentacle and half-tree branch. Everything appeared to be moving so slowly. It gave her lots of time to react. She stabbed out with her spear, the red metal spearhead piercing the monstrous tree and releasing its own demonic venom into the idiot creature.

They charged into the living woods and into a mass of monstrosity. She could actually feel the magic of the Muileartach in the air, attacking the magic in her own blood, trying to change her. Her Otherworldly steed carried her at full gallop as she stabbed down to the left, to the right, and even over the horse's head. The horse snapped at anything that got too close.

Ahead of her, one of the Lochlannach had been torn off his horse and lifted into the air. He was pulled apart. Tendrils of red filigree from inside the body reached for its constituent parts, but the damage was too great. He hadn't even cried out. Britha rode through the shower of blood and viscera, laughing.

They charged the unstoppable advance of the Muileartach's spawn in a line and had been fighting ever since. She was aware of Bress hewing left and right with his long-bladed sword from the saddle of his own horse, surrounded by a near-constant arc of blood and ichor, moving with incredible speed to cut through the spawn even as they tried to mass against him.

Another of the Lochlannach was overwhelmed by the creatures. His horse toppled and he disappeared under a surge of crawling, slithering strangeness. It was like watching maggots eat a carcass.

Bress slewed his horse in front of her, hacking down with his sword quickly but methodically. Something like a fish or a slug with moss-covered, rock-like skin and tendrils around a mouth filled with rows of needle-teeth flopped across the changing ground on a bed of excreted slime. Bress's horse leaped over the creature. His cloak billowed out behind him and Britha caught a glimpse of the circular leather case slung across his back. She had seen it before. It had belonged to Fachtna, and he kept a spear in it. A very powerful weapon that he had used to kill a dragon.

Britha's horse leaped over fish/slug thing. In mid-air, Britha stabbed down with her spear, felt it hit and penetrate the creature's rock-like skin. Inside its flesh, the venom infused in her spear by the Red Chalice would war with the Muileartach's healing magic.

And then they were on the other side of the spawn's advance.

She looked around. Of the twelve riders who had accompanied them only five were left. They were all injured but healing quickly, though they would need to eat soon. One part of her was terrified, appalled at what had become of the natural order of things. The other side of her had never felt so alive as she had in that fight – and, if she was honest, she had felt a strange kinship with the creatures.

If only she could remember the name of the little girl from Ardestie she had seen back in Bladud's camp. She shook her head. That thought had come unbidden to her mind.

They were on what looked like a very strange plain. Perhaps it had once been farmland, or even forest – until the trees grew teeth, or beaks, and started walking. The Otherworld had appeared more natural, though the sky had been the ground and the other way around. This ground had a skin like a fungus and much of it was covered in a kind of grey mulch. Pustule-like growths pierced the fungal skin, many of them moving. Some had tendrils sprouting from them, or long tongues wriggling in the air. Here and there odd, misshapen creatures wandered around the strange plain. Britha was overwhelmed by disgust.

Bress wheeled his horse around and trotted towards her. He was looking past her, and she turned in the saddle to see the monstrous line moving away from them.

'I don't think they have a mind or even know they are attacking anything,' Bress said. 'I think they just attack whatever is in front of them. Maybe all they want to do is turn the things they meet into whatever they are.'

Britha suppressed a shudder. 'You're carrying Fachtna's spear?'

Bress nodded. 'He killed one of my giants. I will not underestimate him.'

'You beat him once without it. It is a powerful weapon.'

'He was not taken by the *riasterthae* when I fought him last,' Bress said, referring to the berserker rage that had transformed Fachtna when he fought one of the giants on the beach.

Britha looked less than happy at his answer. Bress kicked at his horse's flanks and it moved closer to Britha's steed. Bress leaned towards her.

'Assuming you didn't kill him, and it doesn't sound like you did, then I'm going to. If you're worried about how fair it will be then remember that you should only have to kill people once.'

Britha nodded, though it felt as if something had caught in her throat.

Bress stared at her expectantly. She looked around the strange landscape. Something like a large butterfly with fingers and an oddly human face landed on the head of her horse.

'It was this way, I think.'

Fachtna had been singing. He was no bard, but his voice was good enough and he could play a few instruments. He enjoyed sitting around the fire with his people, singing with them. Life had felt very simple back then. He didn't like the sound his voice made now. It was raspy, unpleasant, as if he had spit forever trapped in the back of his throat. His inability to sing saddened him momentarily.

He was on a ridgeline looking out over this strange, transformed land. Plants had become diseased pustules, animals had become plants and rocks walked. He felt movement and life under his skin and inside his body. His armour, which had fused to his skin, had eyes now, too.

The dead who had returned to life still walked with him. They had more earthy flesh now and looked more alive, though no more human up close.

He had been watching the riders approach along the ridgeline for a while now. There was something about them, something familiar. He recognised Britha first. Then Bress. He remembered that he hated Bress. No, that had been another Fachtna. Bress had killed him. He stopped and decided to wait for the horsemen. The dead stopped as well, swaying gently in the wind.

With difficulty, he pulled his sword free of its scabbard and his flesh. The sword that Britha ran him through with. Fortunately she had not triggered its power when she had done so, or he would probably be dead. He vaguely wondered if the sword still worked. It looked different now, warped somehow.

Britha and Bress reigned up in front of him. The five Lochlannach surrounded him and Fachtna's dead turned to face them. He wasn't sure if he'd made them do that or if they had done it of their own accord. The dead outnumbered the Lochlannach four-to-one but they were no match for the slave warriors, particularly as the Lochlannach were mounted.

Britha was staring at him in horror. Bress slid off the back of his horse, drew his long-bladed sword and strode towards Fachtna. Fachtna could not keep his eyes off Britha. Bress raised his sword to strike.

'Wait!' Britha called out. Bress hesitated for a moment, but his sword remained raised. He looked at her. 'Please,' she said to him. 'Let us talk first.'

'What have you done to yourself?' Fachtna asked, appalled. Her hair had gone from brown to red, she'd shaved half of it off, and he could see red, metallic sigils somehow tattooed on her flesh.

'What have *I* done to myself?' Britha asked in horror.

Fachtna started laughing and his other mouths joined in. It was a horrible wet, rasping noise. He touched the place where his face had flowed and melded with his neck, shoulders and armour, forming into bony ridges.

'You've fallen,' he said quietly. He turned to Bress. 'Do you control her now? Like the others?'

Bress stepped away from Fachtna, lowering his sword, and looked up at Britha. 'We should do this quickly,' Bress told her.

Fachtna could see the indecision written all over her face. Even with the small amount of time he had spent with her, it looked alien. Then it hardened.

'You helped them take my child,' she said.

'*Our* child, and I came for you. And we can—' Fachtna started. Some of his other mouths began to laugh.

'You killed a *dryw*,' Britha said, 'and they will execute you the moment you return.'

'Look at him,' Bress said. 'He is sick. They will burn him.'

'We can—' Fachtna started.

'We can what?' Britha demanded.

'Why are you with this filth?' Fachtna shouted, pointing at Bress. Britha actually flinched. 'He enslaved and then murdered your tribe, and now you ride at his side! Why?'

'Haven't you worked it out yet, boy?' Bress asked, and glanced back at Britha. 'She likes power. She would see us fight.'

Fachtna looked to Bress, his flesh literally crawling across his face.

'You will not touch my child!' multiple mouths screamed. He glanced up at Britha. 'Would you let him do to my home what he did to yours? Would you see many thousands more dead or enslaved?'

Britha leaned forwards in the saddle. 'They took my child,' she said, carefully enunciating each world. 'I would destroy your world if it meant getting her back.'

'The *drui* took your child. You would condemn others for that?'

'I will do what is necessary,' Britha said coldly.

'Help me. We can kill him, end this!' Fachtna was begging now. There were tears coming from the eyes on his face, and from the eyes on his armour. He pointed at Bress. 'He could heal me, make me whole again! We could go back. I could disguise myself and we could find our daughter!'

'So you can get back, then?' Bress asked quietly.

Fachtna stared at him, but his words were for Britha. 'You know he has the power to stop this, to stop the Muileartach's brood? To change the land?' Fachtna asked her. He flexed his toes, felt the changed earth beneath them. He started to draw it into himself.

'But I choose not to,' Bress said.

'I don't think you can remember the last time you made a choice,' Fachtna said quietly.

Bress opened his mouth to reply but instead just stared at Fachtna. The Goidel was growing in front of his eyes. His flesh was bulging and flowing like water, his features distorting, the eyes in his face and armour popping, mouths growing, whipping tongues sticking out of them, teeth becoming longer and sharper. Heat was pouring off him in waves. The normally fearless horses became nervous, pawing at the ground.

Britha remembered the *riasterthae* taking Fachtna on the beach, close to the wicker man, where he had slain one of the Lochlannach's giants. It had not looked like this twisted monstrosity, this abomination. Fachtna's sword started to sing, flickering, almost ethereal, but the singing was wrong somehow.

Fachtna's roar deafened Britha for a moment. Her horse reared, primal fear overwhelming the magics that had changed and controlled the creature. Britha struggled to regain control.

Fachtna charged Bress, who threw himself out of the path of the charge and rolled back up onto his feet. He spun around and ducked a blow that would have taken his head off. He parried another that nearly dashed his sword out of his hand. He ran backwards trying to avoid Fachtna's furious, frenzied attacks.

Bress tried to put distance between himself and Fachtna, but the berserker warrior charged him. Bress leaped up, bringing his legs into the splits position as Fachtna ran underneath him. Bress slashed the blade of his sword down the berserker's back, opening skin and revealing churning flesh and organs beneath. Fachtna continued running as Bress landed in a crouch behind him. Fachtna charged one of mounted Lochlannach and swung his sword. The shimmering blade clove through rider and horse. With a thought, Bress ordered the other Lochlannach to attack. They kicked their mounts forward.

'No!' Britha cried out.

Fachtna stopped and cocked his head, like a confused animal.

'Does this feel fair to you?' Bress demanded.

'This is single combat!' Britha shouted.

'Who do you want to win this battle?' Bress demanded, but the Lochlannach stopped moving towards the warrior caught in the *riasterthae* frenzy. Fachtna struck out again and again. Bress moved, dodging the blade when he could, parrying blows that sent him staggering and numbed his hands when he couldn't. Fachtna was faster and stronger, but not as coordinated. Despite the berserker's crazed attacks, Bress was just about able to anticipate them. His blade flicked out again and again, but he was too much on the defensive to land any powerful or killing blows. His sword opened horrible wounds in

Fachtna's flesh, but the flesh seethed and boiled beneath the wounds and then started to close. Bress was aware of Fachtna's legs bulging as he sucked up more of the earth from beneath his feet to replace the damaged flesh.

Bress leaped over one of Fachtna's sword-swings. The Goidel's ghost blade sang its discordant song through the air beneath him. Then Bress felt Fachtna's free hand close around his ankle and he knew it was over.

Fachtna yanked Bress out of the air and slammed him into the ground in an explosion of fungal-like earth. He stamped on Bress, the cracking of his bones echoing across the landscape. He battered Bress with his free hand before starting to slash at him with his shimmering ghost blade. The tendrils of red gold tried to close Bress's wounds, knit the flesh together, but Fachtna was doing too much damage too quickly. Bress howled. He sounded less like a man and more like a wounded animal.

'No!' It was a cry of anguish. Fachtna stopped. He shook once and then the spearhead exploded out of his chest. He looked down at the living metal trying to tear apart his flesh from within. Then he turned around with some difficulty. He saw Britha standing there as if her hands still held the haft of the spear that had just been torn from her grip. There was fear in her eyes. Tears running down her face. Fachtna stared at her, his own tears running from a bulging eye in his deformed head. The heat pouring off him was blistering Britha's skin. Bress was still screaming like a wounded animal. She staggered back away from Fachtna, and Fachtna merely watched her go. There was sadness in his many eyes. Then the dead flew at Britha.

Bress's body was working enough to move again. He reached for the case, opened it. He used the magics Crom had given him to try and soothe the ancient and irrevocably insane demon in the spear. Even then it almost overwhelmed him, controlled him. There were moments when he wasn't himself, when something old and malevolent possessed him, but that was all right, if he wanted to live. Then the spearhead grew, extending a long, thick haft which Bress grasped with all his strength.

'Britha!' Bress cried in a moment of control and threw her his sword. She caught it and started cutting down the earthen dead even as they charged her. Fachtna started to turn. Bress stood and rammed the sunspear into Fachtna's body. The flesh burned, melted, flowed, hissed and boiled. Fachtna's head split in two in a shower of dirty steam and bubbling flesh. His two separate halves fell to the fungal ground. Then Bress let go of the spear.

The Lochlannach had moved to engage the earthen dead, though Britha was hacking her way through them without too much trouble. The spear flew through the dead, the Lochlannach and their horses almost too quickly to see. Bress was no longer possessed. He was in control again. Britha screamed. With a thought, Bress cast the final part of the magics Crom had taught him regarding the spear. The spear stopped just as it was about to pass through Britha's head. It fell to the ground, and the ground caught fire. Bress redoubled the wards that protected him and ran to the spear. The spear fought him, the strange metal flexing, the heat blistering his skin. Its demonic mind tried to push its way into Bress's head, but he fought it back into its case, where it became still.

Bress managed to stumble to his feet and walk over to Fachtna's bubbling corpse. Deformed insect-like creatures were growing from the warped flesh and crawling away. He stared at the two halves of Fachtna until he saw what he was looking for – metal glinting within the flesh. He reached down and grabbed the two halves of the brass six-pointed cross which had wrapped itself around Fachtna's ribs. Bress concentrated and the metal unwrapped itself. He held the two uneven parts together and they fused seamlessly.

'That's it, isn't it?' Britha asked. The six arms sank into the body of the cross and it became a rod. Bress nodded. 'We could take it, go now,' Britha said, eagerness in her voice. 'Get my child.'

Bress turned to look at her. 'You know it has to go back to him, don't you?'

'No,' Britha said, shaking her head. 'I don't know that. I don't know why you have to serve that dark spirit.'

'He made me the way I am.'

'He' – she nodded towards Fachtna's bisected body, though she tried not to look at it – 'defied his *dryw* for our child.'

Bress swallowed hard. 'For your child, Britha, yours and his.'

'And if it was ours?' Britha demanded.

Bress looked up at her. He crossed the distance to her quickly and grabbed her arm. 'That can never be – do you understand me?' It was the angriest she had ever seen him. Then she realised it was fear disguised as anger. 'It would be the greatest crime. You must promise – if there is ever any child, you'll kill it!' Britha shook off his arm and backed away from him, appalled. 'There shouldn't be, it shouldn't be possible, but he plays his games.' There was a manic quality to Bress's voice. Britha wasn't sure if he was talking to her or himself.

'Give it to me,' she said evenly.

Bress fell silent and looked up, his eyes wide now. 'Tell me, did you come to me because you wanted me, or because you wanted power – and this?' he asked, holding up the control rod.

Britha forced herself to look at Fachtna's body. She was shaking with anger. 'I did this for you,' she said.

'*I* did this!' Bress roared at her. His voice carried across the poisoned, fungal land, causing strange misshapen creatures to take flight from living trees made of stone and insects.

'You would be dead if I hadn't ... if I hadn't ...' Britha's face crumpled. 'I killed Fachtna!' She sank to her knees, sobbing.

'Would you rather he had killed me?' Bress asked quietly.

Britha looked up at him. 'Of course I would! He was a friend, a lover, the father of my child. You are a monster, you murdered my people, but I—' She stopped and looked down again. 'Give me the rod, please.'

Bress turned and walked away from her.

37

Close to the Oceanic Pole of Inaccessibility, 2 Weeks Ago

More dreams. He used drugs to numb himself. He was becoming more like the clones, a zombie trudging through his day. Kneeling in the silt, every movement sending up little clouds of particulate matter, he was backlit by the lamps of an ADS as he used a handheld fusion torch to cut into the organic-looking basalt-like stone.

Lodup wasn't sure what made him look around. The light fixed to his mask caught the shape of the figure standing less than six feet from him, a human shape. Lodup jumped and scrambled back, ungainly in the mud. He dropped the fusion torch. It went out the moment it left his grip.

It emerged from the silt and was all over Lodup. It had dark, rubbery skin, eyespots and two comb-like cartilaginous protuberances protruding from its gaping mouth. Eight small, tendril-like barbels surrounded the mouth. The thing had only one nostril and its skull was misshapen, but as it grabbed for Lodup, its mouth open in what looked like a silent scream, Lodup realised it was Hideo.

The Hideo-thing held Lodup's face next to his, its proto-mouth opening and closing as if it was trying to say something. Its hands were all over Lodup. He realised that the hands had mouths on them that looked more human than the one in its face. They were opening and closing as well. Lodup grabbed for his dive knife, wrestling it out of its sheath. Then he realised the thing wasn't attacking him, and suddenly it was yanked off him. He started to subvocalize, to warn the ADS pilot not to hurt it.

It had touched their minds through the human-shaped hole in the world.

Overwhelming pain. She was looking down on the city, lashing out despite herself, destroying, killing with every movement, every spasm, as consciousness was replaced by the searing cold, the indescribable agony, the fury and the unthinking hate. She could hear her sisters screaming, too. Across the blue world, those who heard their cries either dropped dead or were driven irrevocably mad.

In the streets the weak minds simply died, blood shooting from their ears and eyes. The guardians killed in a frenzy. Even the oldest, the serpents, were succumbing to the madness, though not all of them.

Her sisters were sporing uncontrollably, and every spore carried the physical corruption born of their pain-induced madness. Diseased, nightmare forms grew from the fruiting bodies of the dead and the insane living alike.

One of her eggs flew into the air. Thunder echoed across the clear blue sky as it shot straight upwards.

One of her last conscious thoughts was recognition that her form had been diseased. A servitor, one of the serpents, had done this as it tried to cling to rational thought against the agony of its link with his mothers. She crushed its mind. Punished its betrayal. The disease coursed through the living city and all connected to it. Destroying their ability to enter the other place. The red place.

Then thought was gone. Instinctively she was aware that she was hardening, her skin, her flesh transforming. The cold, blue ocean washed over her. Even as she petrified, she knew she would not die. Instead she would be locked in the living stone.

Lodup was lying in the silt. The ADS stood over him. Bits of the Hideo-thing, which the ADS had just crushed, were raining down on him. Indescribable pain lanced through his skull and blood filled his vision. He opened his mouth and tried to scream into the sub-freezing water.

'To all intents and purposes, it is – was – a hagfish,' Siraja said.

Lodup was looking through the window into a sealed operating theatre where the bits and pieces of the Hideo-thing were being examined. Sprinklers kept the room wet, and it looked pretty miserable for the doctor and the two nurses into whose neural systems the skills of a medical examiner and marine biologist had just been downloaded.

Lodup had the mother of all migraines despite the vast quantities of painkillers they had pumped into him. His throat was raw and red – he'd only stopped screaming half an hour ago. The pain he had felt during his blackout was indescribable. Most of the blood vessels in his eyes had burst, making his eyes nearly all red, and scabs blocked his tear ducts.

Even though Lodup knew Siraja wasn't actually there, the

Mwoakilloan still turned to look at the dragon-headed representation of the habitat's AI.

'No shit?'

'It just happens to look like Hideo.'

'Oh, well, that's a *lot* more reasonable,' Lodup said. 'What the fuck is going on?'

'You had another blackout. What did you see?' Siraja asked.

'Can't you monitor my dreams?' Lodup asked. Siraja shook his reptilian head. 'The city. I think I saw its fall.'

It was difficult to gauge the expression of something with the head of a dragon, but Lodup thought he saw an eagerness there.

'How did it fall? Was it attacked?'

'Yes ... no ... I don't know. There was something there, something from ... somewhere else. No, it wasn't a *thing*. It was just coldness and pain ... I think their children, the things it made, the snakes ... They did something. Some kind of viral self-destruct.' Lodup felt as if his skull was about to burst. The pain was making him feel dizzy and sick. He staggered.

'Perhaps you should sit down, drink some more water, and then we can go through your dream in detail,' the draconic AI suggested.

'Why?' Lodup finally managed, meaning the Hideo/hagfish thing.

Siraja looked up and concentrated for a moment. 'I could make an educated guess, but I dislike guessing.'

'Do it anyway.'

'I think something – or someone – in the city was trying to contact you. Perhaps this Lidakika entity.'

'But it's already contacting me,' he said, tapping the side of his head and then wishing he hadn't.

'But are you listening, Mr Satakano, are you understanding? We found rudimentary larynxes in the creature's throat, wrists and ankles. I think something was trying to communicate with you in a more direct fashion. It used the material it had to hand and formed it into the shape of Hideo to make it more familiar to you.'

'There have to be easier ways.'

'Indeed,' Siraja said. 'And that is what worries us. We have had contact before. In fact, we believe that when people go "thatch" down here, it is in part due to contact of some kind with entities in the city. It is almost as if there is an attempt at subterfuge here, but who is fooling whom, we have no idea. That is why we have to fully debrief you now. If necessary, we might have to—'

'Who's in charge, Siraja?' Lodup asked.

Siraja regarded Lodup with his oddly expressive reptilian eyes. 'Mr Satakano—'

'Someone gave the order to call that thing from the black lake. There's someone above Siska. Who?' Lodup demanded.

'We have been very indulgent with you, Mr Satakano. Yes, we have done things that perhaps we shouldn't. We have taken liberties with your physical form, and with your mind, but you have been – and will be – generously rewarded for your services—'

'What happens if they wake up?' Lodup asked. He was looking down at the grass-like carpet being stirred by the warm, humid wind that blew through the habitat when it breathed.

'Do you feel that's likely?' Siraja asked.

Lodup looked up at the AI. *You're frightened,* Lodup realised. Aloud, he asked, 'You want to debrief me?' Siraja nodded. 'I'll only speak to the person who's in charge.' He wasn't sure but it looked as if Siraja was trying to master irritation.

'We have a great deal going on today—' Siraja started.

'Like what?' Lodup asked.

'A delivery of supplies,' Siraja said.

Lodup's eyes narrowed. 'I thought you were self-sufficient down here. If you can manipulate matter at a molecular level, then what do you need delivered?'

Siraja's sigh had a definite hissing quality to it. 'Curiosity is an admirable human quality, but you know that we cannot, and will not, tell you everything.'

'It's to do with the increasing number of suicides and people going thatch, isn't it? Something's about to happen.'

'Mr Satakano, that is enough,' Siraja said quietly.

'Are you going to threaten me now?'

Siraja glanced away from Lodup and rubbed the bridge of his snout with clawed fingers. It was a peculiarly human gesture that looked out of place.

'No, Mr Satakano. We would like to think that our relationship remains one of employer and employee.'

'Fire me, then,' Lodup said, looking straight at the dragon-headed AI's image. They stared at each other for a few moments longer.

'Go to the northernmost wet dock.'

'The floating-shed things?'

Siraja nodded. 'He will meet you there,' the AI told him.

Lodup still felt woozy and sick. Under normal circumstances he would never have considered diving in a state like this, but now it appeared that he was just as adapted, technologically, to life at this depth as he was physically adapted to live on the surface.

He left the biomed area and made his way through the carpeted corridors towards the moon pool. He saw Yaroslav heading towards him. With him were two other men, both solidly built and heavily armed. Like Yaroslav, they reminded Lodup of the Special Forces operators he had met.

The smaller, more wiry of the two had several days' worth of stubble, chiselled features and long brown, greying hair tied into a ponytail. His eyes were blue and his weathered skin suggested an outdoor life. The other had much blunter features and was more heavily built. His head was shaved, his eyes were cold and grey, and a patchwork of scars covered his face and head.

A number of Yaroslav's security detail followed the three men. They were escorting three carts with rubber caterpillar tracks, all of them loaded with glass-fronted medical freezers. Lodup couldn't make out what was inside the freezers through the swirling gases.

Lodup stepped to the side of the corridor to let them pass. He nodded at Yaroslav as he walked by, but the Russian ignored him.

Further on, Lodup found a similar scene. This time the caterpillar-tracked carts were moving things that looked like a weird cross between a standing stone and a server. Lodup glanced up the corridor along which the strange, guarded convoy was moving. He could see Siska talking to another woman. Like the other two newcomers he'd just seen with Yaroslav, the woman was armed. She was wearing combat trousers, combat boots and a sleeveless black T-shirt. Her long black hair had been braided into a ponytail, which had then been arranged into a noose, as he had seen Siska wear her hair sometimes. By far the strangest thing about the woman was the beaten-silver facemask she wore.

It felt obvious to Lodup that the woman was somehow related to Siska. As he watched them, Siska looked down the corridor towards Lodup. He couldn't quite make out the expression on her face.

Lodup walked into the moon pool chamber. The habitat had repaired itself since the granite construct's attack and showed little sign of ever having been damaged.

Lodup sealed his thermal sheath and pulled the hood over his head. Ignoring the hive of activity around him, he dived into the water. He experienced the now-familiar rushing sensation of water coursing through his chest as his internal cavities were flushed with liquid.

He brought his feet together. The individual fins melded and grew to form a rippling monofin.

He dived down and out of the moon pool, then headed north. Out in open water, he glanced behind him. He hadn't seen any new submersibles in the moon pool, certainly nothing big enough to carry the cargo he'd seen trundling through the habitat's corridors. The submarine docked to the side of the habitat was a surprise, however, particularly as it was docked at an airlock not present in the habitat several hours earlier.

The sub looked like a Virginia-Class nuclear-powered fast-attack boat. Except airlocks didn't come standard on them, either, and this one would be more than three thousand metres deeper than its maximum depth capability. Yet another question for the habitat's mysterious boss.

From the outside, the wet dock looked like a rectangular open shed made of thick, black metal. The odd angles suggested that the wet docks had some kind of stealth characteristics designed to shield them from surface detection. They were buoyant, and tethered to the sea-bed twenty five metres below by thick chains.

Inside the wet dock he saw one of piscean-shaped seed-pods. He remembered that the agonised thing he'd been when he blacked out had thought of it as an egg. It was, or had been, some kind of dormant offspring.

Its petrified skin was smooth to the touch with a number of ridged indents. Something about them made Lodup think they were sensory organs. The seed-pod was elegant and somehow beautiful, but also disturbing.

The wet dock was empty, though Lodup had noticed the dark form of one of the orcas – Marvin, he suspected – swimming lazily some distance from the tethered structure. A number of AUVs were patrolling nearby, but most of the security appeared to be concentrated around the habitat and the newly arrived sub.

There was a jarring piece of technology sticking out of the seed-pod's flesh which did not look like it belonged there. It appeared to have grown through the petrified seed-pod's flesh like a cybernetic cyst. As he watched, the airlock portal opened like an iris, the lock itself already filled with water. Lodup regarded it for a moment, uncertainty and a degree of fear creeping into him. But he had come this far, he decided. He finned into the airlock and arranged himself in an upright position as the water started cycling out. The thermal sheath shed excess moisture as the water level dropped until he was standing in a dry airlock. He pulled the hood off his head as the inner iris opened.

The space within was cavernous. In scale it reminded him of the cargo bay of an amphibious assault dock. The interior walls were coated with what looked like stainless steel. The ceiling was a curving dome that matched the exterior shape of the seed-pod and steel-covered ribs ran across it. All that seamless plating made him think of surgical instruments, but it couldn't disguise the organic feel of the huge chamber. Lodup was starting to feel like Jonah.

One end of the cavern tapered off where the ceiling curved down to meet the floor. The other end was a steel-covered wall studded with various bumps and protuberances. Lodup guessed that the steel covering the oddities was supposed to make them look like machinery, but once again their organic nature was apparent. Another iris door in the wall opened like an eye blinking and Lodup started walking towards it. His footfalls barely made a noise due to some odd sound-dampening quality of the chamber.

He walked through narrow corridors that half-reminded him of being in a submarine, and which also resembled some kind of steel-covered gullet. He found the man sitting on a work surface in a small cubby-hole. Inside the cubbyhole the metal had a definite biological look to it. It was moving, as if it was covering some kind of pulsing organ.

The man wasn't quite what Lodup had expected. He was wearing a thermal dive sheath, but it was split open to the waist, revealing a hairy chest and paunchy stomach. The paunch alone made him un-like anyone else working in Kanamwayso. He was a small man with dark, weather-beaten skin which made Lodup think he came from the Mediterranean region. He had shoulder-length straight black hair, streaked through with white, and a neatly trimmed goatee. He looked up as Lodup filled the doorway.

What surprised Lodup the most was that he recognised the man. He was the priest who laid the tall, beautiful boy down in the pool of green water, the pool that had contained some kind of snake-like creatures.

'I've seen you before,' Lodup said.

'That is not possible,' the man replied.

Lodup decided not to argue just yet. After all, in the normal surface world, telling people you recognized them from your dreams tended to sound strange.

'It's a spaceship,' Lodup said.

The man nodded. 'Very good,' he said.

Lodup couldn't quite place the accent but again, it struck him as Mediterranean. He stepped aside as the man walked past and headed further forward in the seed-pod.

'It's actually a biotechnological, extremophile, panspermic seed-pod that we've spent centuries reverse engineering to allow humans to at least steer it, if not pilot,' the man told him.

'You ... what? Cut them free, inject them full of nanites which hollow them out and then build the required interface technology?' Lodup asked.

The man glanced behind him. 'There's a bit more to it than that, but essentially yes. We have to convert extensively so the human mind can deal with living inside another organism like a tapeworm.'

'And if they wake up?' Lodup asked. 'I don't think they're sane.'

The man led him into another steel-covered room. At first Lodup thought it looked like a cockpit with windscreens, but he realised they were in fact monitor screens. There were also controls and rudimentary joysticks like those found in modern aircraft. The two seats looked like a cross between the bucket seats you would find in military aircraft, and the couches in the Command-and-Control centre back in the habitat.

'It would be piloted by direct neural link with the pilots we have been breeding. The manual controls are mostly in case something goes wrong, but I suspect they would only help psychologically in that eventuality. And to answer your question, we virally lobotomise them first. We effectively kill their minds. We murder the city's children, but I wonder if that is our greatest crime.'

'I saw you in my dream. When I blacked out,' Lodup said.

The man turned to stare at him. Lodup wasn't sure what he saw there – hope, fear, desperation?

'Where?' the man demanded. 'Here?' Lodup nodded. There were tears in the man's eyes. 'What was I ... I can't remember ... he took it from me—'

'I think you were some kind of priest. You were ... I don't know ... baptising a boy in a pool with snakes in it.'

The man staggered back until he bumped into one of the couches and leaned heavily on it.

'You can't remember any of it?' Lodup asked.

The man shook his head as tears rolled down his cheeks. 'What else?' he asked, in a voice choked with emotion.

Lodup was shaking his head as well. 'That's all I saw. What do you want from me?'

'He's always watching. I couldn't play my hand. I had to wait until the end.'

Lodup moved back and leaned against the organic steel. It felt warm. Wrong, somehow. 'Who are you?' he asked.

'My name is Germelqart,' the man told him, 'and I was born a very long time ago.'

'I got that,' Lodup said, gently. 'Who's always watching?'

Germelqart tried to answer, his mouth opening and closing, but it was as if something was preventing him from talking. More tears filled his eyes. Lodup pushed himself off the wall and moved towards the man, putting a hand on his shoulder.

'Are you all right?' he asked.

Germelqart looked up at the taller man. 'No. I was a spy, and now I am a traitor. I have lived among these people for millennia, just waiting to betray them. What kind of man does that, Lodup? Tell me that.'

Lodup stared at Germelqart. 'What have you done? What is this thing for? Exploration?' At the back of his mind, Lodup had convinced himself that he was involved in humanity's next big adventure.

'These are for an evacuation.'

'For whom?' Lodup asked.

'Humanity, or those lucky – or unlucky – enough to be going.'

Lodup went cold. 'Why would they need to evacuate?'

'Because this city is waking up. The suicides, the people going insane – those are the defensive spasms of waking minds. All are signs.'

Lodup stared at the other man. 'And you've betrayed this plan?' Lodup asked carefully. Germelqart swallowed hard. Lodup wasn't sure what he'd have expected of a man millennia old, but he still looked very human. Guilt was written all over his face.

'You have to understand something—' Germelqart started.

'Do I?' Lodup asked. 'Siska, this is Lodup, do you read me, over?' he said, sending the words as a packet transmission in a burst of low-frequency infrasound. There was no reply. He turned and headed towards the cockpit's doorway.

'Do you think I would be speaking to you now if there was the slightest chance that you could affect what I've done?' Germelqart asked. Lodup turned back. 'I can give you answers, if that is what you want.'

'And if I leave?'

Germelqart shrugged. 'I don't know,' he said.

'What do I have to understand?'

Germelqart turned one of the chairs around and sat in it. The chair configured itself until he was comfortable. He gestured towards the other. Lodup walked over and sat. The way it moved underneath him was disconcerting.

'The Circle was formed more than two thousand years ago to fight those who abused the alien technology. As you can imagine, at that time we thought it was magic. Gifts from the gods. We thought those who had been augmented by the technology were the children of gods – demigods, if you will,' Germelqart said. Lodup nodded, wondering at how much his world had changed in just a few short weeks, that he could accept such things so easily. 'As far as we can tell, when the disaster befell the city, some sort of self-destruct command was given.'

'Which petrified them,' Lodup said.

Germelqart nodded. 'Yes, but it also did something else. Each of these seeds has an organ capable of harvesting a great deal of energy. You understand that any space travel is limited by the speed of light?'

'So I've heard.'

'Well, this organ allows them entry into what is effectively another universe, a coterminous universe with different physical properties. Hyperspace. The self-destruct mechanism wiped out the Seeders' ability to use that organ, but not the organ's capabilities.'

'So they couldn't spread whatever drove them mad?' Lodup asked.

'Precisely. But one of them escaped before it could be affected by either the self-destruct mechanism or the corruption itself. We found it ... It was threatened ...' Germelqart's face was screwed up in concentration, as if he was desperately trying to remember something, 'By ... something. It hid the secret of how to access this other place inside a human. Very quickly the Circle's priority became protecting the bloodline that stemmed from that person.'

'As well as controlling the technology?' Lodup asked, trying not to make it sound like an accusation.

'Once, there were worse things than the Circle.'

'Once?'

'Well, such things probably still exist, but the Circle has changed. We are the most powerful organisation in the world. We have existed for over two millennia. Corruption was all but inevitable. We were the real science. Human efforts, whilst impressive, were ultimately irrelevant, so we recruited as many of the great minds as we could. But others always stumbled across the tech, and they needed to be prevented from causing great harm. That meant recruiting powerful people, and we had always relied on violence when we needed to. We were born in a violent time.'

'What happened?' Lodup asked, leaning towards Germelqart despite himself.

'The powerful took over. Don't get me wrong, I have nothing against the wealthy, particularly those who have worked for their money, but to get into our club these days, you have to be the worst, most ruthless kind of powerbroker. Instead of the greatest of Earth's minds going forth into the universe, it will be greedy rats leaving a sinking ship.'

Lodup leaned back again and took a deep breath. 'Okay, so it may not be exactly what you wanted, but it pretty much sounds like business as usual for humanity, and assuming the city waking up will be as bad as you think it's going to be, then at least humanity will survive.'

'It will be as bad as I think it is going to be—' Germelqart started.

'Things aren't the same as they were in prehistoric times. I accept that this city is full of all kinds of technology, but there's only so much good that will do you when a dozen or so nuclear-tipped torpedoes hit it.'

'You saw the thing in the black lake?' Germelqart asked. Lodup went cold. He nodded. 'We are not talking about unpleasant politicians or tyrants fleeing the planet. They are taking every lesson they have ever learned in social engineering about making people not care, about breaking up community and societal bonds, about control through greed, fear and envy, and they are going to spread it like a disease through the stars.'

'That sounds a little paranoid,' Lodup said.

Germelqart laughed bitterly. 'Does it? That's what I thought, until they wiped the minds of some of the greatest scientists, thinkers and artists in human history for storage space. You saw the servers?'

'The stone things that came on the sub?'

Germelqart nodded. 'They contain souls. The minds of those they are going to take with them. All of them conditioned. Did you see the freezers?' Germelqart asked. Lodup nodded. 'Clone embryos for the minds to be downloaded into when they're rapidly brought to maturation. A slave race for some of the biggest bastards in recent history.'

'Okay,' Lodup said, still not sure if he believed any of this. He was sure he didn't *want* to believe it. 'So what did you do?'

'Do you know what an *ifrit* is?' Germelqart asked. The word sounded familiar to Lodup but he shook his head. 'It's a type of *jinn*, a fire spirit. I've released invisible electronic *ifrit* into their storage systems to burn out their minds. I've introduced viruses carried by intelligent nano-swarms to infect all their slave foetuses. I've given the security details and locations of every Circle facility – in the world and in orbit – to the Brass City, and I've poisoned the well.'

Lodup was staring at Germelqart. He wasn't sure he understood everything the man had just said, but it hadn't sounded good.

'The well?' Lodup managed, his mouth and throat suddenly very dry.

'Every bloodline crèche has been hit with targeted virals. The Circle no longer has the ability to meld with the ships, to have them enter the hyperspace.'

Lodup swallowed hard. There were tears in his eyes now. 'It sounds ... it sounds like you've damned us.'

Germelqart leaned forwards. Strong fingers gripped Lodup's arm and Lodup looked down. Germelqart had rough hands, the hands of a sailor. He looked back up.

'Humanity would not have survived, not on those terms. We would not have been human any more.'

Lodup opened his mouth to answer. There was a sound like rapid coughing, and the keys of an old-fashioned typewriter being hit. Germelqart's face crumpled in on itself, suddenly becoming a red and unrecognisable mess. Something hot and wet spattered Lodup. Despite the large-calibre entrance wounds that had replaced Germelqart's face, the small man was still sitting upright, his entire form shaking. Lodup stared, horrified, as the man's internal nanites tried to rebuild his face, but just as quickly as the flesh healed, whatever was in the bullets' payloads ate it away again. Germelqart's ancient, augmented body lost the fight. He slumped back in the chair, then slid onto the organic-looking steel floor.

Yaroslav advanced into the cockpit, still wearing his thermal sheath – though his looked armoured – the smoking, suppressed Vector SMG still aimed at Germelqart. He stood over the small man. Put another two rounds into his chest and one more into his head.

'We can interrogate the corpse,' Yaroslav muttered.

'You're right,' Siska said from the doorway. Lodup looked up at her. 'He has damned us.'

38

A Long Time After the Loss

'No,' Benedict/Scab said quietly. 'I don't remember you.'

He was standing in the *Templar*'s Command and Control centre. He had changed little in C&C. He knew some of the crew had taken to decorating their cabins with grisly trophies, but that had never been his style. If anything, he had made C&C more anonymous, although the pools for the enslaved dolphins were starting to look rather polluted. He had to stop the crew from urinating and defecating in them. The nano-screens were having problems filtering out the smell.

'Myself and my two brothers were running a black cloning facility in the Sea of Ghosts—'

'I don't care, I really don't care. The only reason you're not being eaten by a nano-phage swarm is because there's still some ridiculous throwback ideal that I have to handle this one-on-one.'

The other man was in the body of a human Church militiaman. He was big, augmented, stripped to the waist. The sport fans among the crew had worked out the rules. No firearms or ranged weapons of any sort; no virals, swarms or toxins; no smart-matter blades or P-sats. Just dumb-blades and kinetic energy. The lizard with the home-assembled berserker augment had given him the most trouble.

'See, the thing is,' his challenger said, raising his voice, playing to the audience, 'you're not him. You're not the Scab that took down and killed my brothers—'

'And you, obviously,' Benedict/Scab pointed out.

'You're just a cheap copy wearing Church meat!'

'So are you,' Benedict/Scab said. 'But you're right – I'm not him, not any more, if I ever was. I'm something new.' He had found Mish Tullar's shrine to Woodbine Scab. He wondered absently if his acolyte would approve of what he had become. He suspected not. Mish had struck him as a purist. On the other hand, he was also pretty sure he got a lot more pleasure from life than Woodbine did. 'Wait a minute,' he said. 'You don't go to a Psycho Bank for running a black clone op. What else did you do?'

'We made copies of the uploads—' his challenger started.

'And dropped them into snuff immersions?' Benedict/Scab said, incredulous. 'You're a fantasist? That's basically a victimless crime. How do you expect to run this crew, let alone deal with me, if you've never actually killed anyone?'

'No – wait,' the man said, rattled. 'I have ... the things we did to—'

'All very masturbatory, I'm sure. I'm guessing your brothers did the heavy lifting, intellectually speaking?'

The challenger looked confused. 'What?' he asked.

Benedict/Scab decided that he needed to get this over and done with quickly.

There was a gunshot. The man's eyes went large. Then came the sound of drilling. He started to scream as smoke rose from the back of his skull. There was a cracking noise. The slow bullet penetrated the skull and exploded, splattering the man's surprised face all over Benedict/Scab. He turned to his first mate, St. John, a prolific conceptual spree killer who had been taken down by Crabber's bounty crew, so had no axe to grind with Benedict/Scab.

'Really?' Benedict/Scab enquired. St. John was in the body of one of the *Templar*'s C&C crew, which had received significant soft-tech and combat augments since he'd taken it over. A number of the possessing personalities from the Psycho Banks had been med- or biotechs. The *Templar* was also big enough to have assemblers with military and other restricted technology. They had been able to manufacture virals and nano-swarms to use on their raids, as well as personal hard- and soft-tech augments.

'He was wasting everyone's time.' St. John's human body looked very nondescript – average build, average features, average haircut.

'But now there's not a lot of his brain left, and we don't have the facilities to regrow it. We've wasted a body someone else could have inhabited.'

St. John's leadership challenge had been subtle. Benedict/Scab could tell by his first mate's body language that he knew he'd been discovered.

'I was going to kill him with a fork,' Benedict/Scab said, holding one up. 'Nobody gets killed by a fork these days.'

When St. John started to raise the tumbler pistol, Benedict/Scab was already moving. He grabbed the wrist of the hand holding the gun, then neunonically hacked the slow bullets. He rammed the fork into St. John's eye. His first mate screamed as vitreous humour and blood squirted out of the socket. Benedict/Scab locked up the hand with the pistol in it and then jerked it hard. The compound fracture of the radius and the ulna was violent enough to break through the hardening skin. Benedict/Scab took the tumbler pistol out of St. John's limp hand, then reached between the first mate's legs and shot him in the anus. Benedict/Scab stepped back. The reprogrammed slow bullet drilled up into St. John's stomach cavity and then exploded. The force of the explosion severed the spine and sent legs and torso flying in different directions. The legs slipped off the catwalk and into the filthy dolphin tanks. The torso landed, wetly, on the catwalk. St. John was still alive, blood bubbling out of his mouth.

'You can't fix that, either,' Benedict told the torso before he turned to his Lizard second mate. He could never pronounce the lizard's tribal name, so he just called him Harold. Originally downloaded into a human, Harold had found one of the few Church militia lizards aboard, exorcised the original possessing personality and then re-downloaded himself. Benedict/Scab was so impressed he'd promoted him. The lizard was formerly a tribal warrior who had never quite understood that you weren't supposed to hunt the talking sentient mammals nowadays. His clothes were made out of dyed human skin and tribal scarring covered his visible scales. 'You're first mate now,' Benedict/Scab told Harold. The lizard just nodded. 'Get rid of that.' He kicked at St. John's still living torso. 'The next job, we take the security detail alive for possession, and I want some quality control on the souls we're downloading. No more fantasists.'

Benedict/Scab returned to his chair. The padding moulded around him and the chair's AG motor lifted him up into the air. He was looking for the next target. Too many of them were paying ridiculous bribes to the *Templar* rather than fighting. He had to make an example of the next job. He opened the feed from the external sensors with a thought, then turned the smart-matter walls of C&C into screens and played the view from outside. They were bathed in red light.

The *Templar* came out of the red wound into Real Space and the tear closed behind them. The light cruiser was a long, heavily armoured behemoth of a ship. The external Seeder Church religious iconography on the ship's partially smart-matter hull had been reconfigured by the diseased minds of Scab's crew. The ship was now truly disturbing to behold. A demon ship.

The *Templar* emerged into light, close to a galactic core where space was filled with tightly packed stars clustered around a vast circle of blackness.

They had timed it perfectly. The luxurious cruise ship, run for high-echelon execs and visiting aristocracy, was approaching the bridge point. The cruise ship's smart-matter hull was already turning opaque as its carbon reservoirs pumped matter to the ship's hull, adding a layer of thick armour. Weapon batteries were growing through the hull – cruise ship or not, its passengers demanded a degree of security, which the cruise line had the resources to provide. That was fine. After all, Benedict/Scab wanted to make an example.

'Destroy their weapons, engines and the drive, then close with them and prepare to board,' Benedict/Scab said as he stood up. Part of the tediousness of commanding such a group of people was that he was expected to lead from the front. 'Remember what I said – I want combat-augmented flesh for possession, so take down the ship's private security details with as little mess as possible.' He was going to try and control the crew a little. Letting them indulge their own appetites was a thing to behold, but this time he wanted to send a message, he wanted an aesthetic for this job. He wondered how much of the cruise ship he could wallpaper with skin.

Steve the Alchemist had partitioned the pool. About a quarter of it was a plant-choked environment for the serpentine dream dragons. They spent most of their time submerged, coming up only occasionally for air, making ripples, their electrical display sparking across the surface of the water.

The Alchemist had been hard at work extracting and refining their gland secretions with the help of his custom P-sat, which was equipped with waldos ending in very delicate manipulators. At the moment, however, the dolphin had his head out of the water and was watching various media streams on the pool room's smart matter walls.

Vic and Elodie were both sitting on sunloungers on the edge of the pool watching the footage of the attack on the *Boredom*, a cruise ship operating out of one of the Consortium core worlds.

'He's hit too close to home,' Vic muttered. 'They've got to do something now.'

Because Scab had dropped out of view on the bounty killing scene and his recent exploits weren't common knowledge, there was speculation that Benedict and Scab were one and the same person. Vic knew that under normal circumstances Scab would track down some of the people doing the speculating and make examples of them.

'It's just one desperate bid for attention after another,' Elodie said.

'Daddy issues, anyone?' Vic said, his mandibles clattering together in his approximation of laughter.

'Oh, hi, Scab,' Steve said through his P-sat.

Vic looked around, assuming it was the dolphin's idea of a joke as he'd picked up nothing from his antennae, but Scab was standing in the entrance to the pool room in his shirtsleeves, suit jacket folded over his arms, staring at the smart-matter screens, shaking.

Vic released a cloud of pheromones so strongly redolent of the terror he felt at seeing Scab this angry that Elodie glanced over at him, eyebrows raised. Steve sank into his pool. The P-sat sank into the water with him.

'Why?' Scab managed. Vic didn't have the courage to speak at the moment. 'Elite ... ? Fleet? The Church?'

It was a good question. Benedict/Scab had access to an excellent warship and a crew of killers, but his hit-and-run tactics aside, the *Templar* was no match for a concerted effort from a Consortium, Monarchist or Church naval squadron, and one Elite could have dealt with the problem some time ago. Instead, the *Templar* mainly had to handle second-rate naval contractors or competent ships of roughly the same size and class. There had been talk of a group of bounty killers going after the *Templar*, but Vic couldn't see them getting that many different hunters to work together well enough to take it down.

'They're trying to draw you out,' Elodie said.

Vic was pretty sure Scab was eventually going to lose it and wondered if that would provide him with release. He concentrated and 'faced himself into Talia's immersion. He figured if he was going to die, he might as well do it there.

'We're going back to the monastery,' Scab said through gritted teeth.

'Why?' Elodie asked. There was no answer. When she turned back he had gone.

It was a strange place, too small for him even in his six-limbed, compound-eyed human form. It was filled with one-function devices that had to be operated manually. Everything looked either brown or grey, the colour washed out. It was covered with a patina of ash and it smelled worse than Scab after he'd been chain-smoking.

Vic had given Talia control of an immersion environment, but without neunonics she had to program it the hard way via the voice interface.

She was sobbing again, curled up in the hallway of the strange little domicile. In the lounge, a badly rendered facsimile of a human male was sitting in a seat, smoking a cigarette.

Vic stared down at Talia with concern. She looked up at him through her tear-stained eyes.

'I can't get the smell of stale cigarettes right,' she told him.

'Please let me take you somewhere nice?' Vic begged.

That just made her sob twice as hard. 'I ... I ... I ... can't remember what my mum's face looks like,' she finally managed to say.

Vic knelt down next to her. 'Let me show you some immersions of nice places, please. This just upsets you.'

'Ask Scab if I can come out. I'll be good. I promise I won't hurt myself. I'll do whatever he wants,' she begged.

'This really isn't a good time to be around Scab,' Vic told her. 'Even less so than normal.'

Talia stood and ran up the stairs into a room, slamming the door behind her.

It was the third time that some incarnation of Scab had killed her. She had awoken in one of the Cathedral's clone vats, and it had taken Churchman some time to calm her down. She wanted to deal with Benedict/Scab and then go straight back to hunting his father. She was furious. Churchman had talked her into doing something else.

This is better, she thought.

She was desperate to know how Church security, particularly electronic security, had been so thoroughly breached. She wondered initially if it had been a beyond-black op run by the Church itself to draw Scab out. If that was the case then she was unaware of it, which was unlikely, unless Churchman was somehow unaware of it as well.

Without any current insight and the trail going dead after Cascade, the Monk had instead turned to chasing down the heretical sect lead, though she knew it could be a red herring.

The cults tended to revolve around the use of S-tech and breaking the monopoly on bridge technology. Frequently they involved slavish devotion to the Seeders or other entities. Most of the time it was a load of rubbish, but some cults got disturbingly close to the truth.

The Church militant, aided by a substantial mercenary army, had wiped the majority of the serious and sizeable heretical cults out over a thousand years ago. Those that still existed tended to be small street sects or lone insane individuals. The Church had interviewed a number of the fringe lunatics in the past, seeking insight, and their ramblings were usually a mix of nonsense and, sometimes, surprising accuracy.

Woodbine Scab had run a street sect on Cyst. The cult had become large enough that the Consortium, with Church support, had put Legion troops down on the ground to suppress it.

What worried the Monk most about Scab's connection to a heretical cult was that they'd successfully transplanted a bridge drive, which meant the cult must have been Church once themselves. Ex-Church members always made the most dangerous heretics because their heresy was often the result of contact with S- or L-tech, or remnants of their servitors. Truth and knowledge had driven them insane.

One of their assets in the Monarchist systems had implied that Scab had somehow managed to break into the Monarchist Citadel. This would have required S- or L-tech, and even then she was quite surprised he was still alive. It happened shortly after the first time she and Benedict tried to contact Scab on Arclight.

She had managed to find a tiny bit of AV footage from a sensor outside the Polyhedron Club on Arclight, where she and Benedict had met Scab. The footage was grainy, indistinct, as if suffering from interference. It showed an old-looking baseline human male, waiting. The Monk zoomed in on the man's face and cleaned up the image. There was something wrong with the wrinkles on his head. She ran the image through several intelligent filters and was surprised by what she saw. She'd seen this sort of thing before, but not for a long time. Like everything in Known Space, S- and L-tech had become devalued. This, however, was godsware, a Marduk implant.

The man looked shipless and homeless – what the Consortium considered 'excess biomass'. She ran a search for him and came up with nothing. This was unusual in itself – there was something on everyone if you knew where to look or had debt relief to spend. She used an AI program to set up a false persona as a mid-level bounty killer and had that persona spread debt relief around Arclight.

She finally found a couple of ships' crewmembers who had been approached by the same man. From different ships, both provided AV data to prove it was the man she was looking for. He'd been looking to work passage to the New Coventry system. Both had refused him. Which meant that unless someone else had let him work passage and refused her fake bounty killer's debt relief – and she couldn't think of a reason why anyone would do that – then the man was still on Arclight. The Marduk implant, however, was not.

The later AV footage showed him with bloodied bandages around his head. He also looked more ill than he had in the original footage, as if he'd been ravaged by a virus and not completely healed yet. The Monk knew Scab had virus-bombed the habitat just after he'd killed the blank, but the virus he used was quite potent. If the man's surgical scars hadn't healed, it was unlikely that his nano-screen and internal systems could have fought off a virus as potent as the one Scab had used. Looking diseased was one of the reasons why he'd been refused a berth. She was also surprised that Scab hadn't killed him, mainly because he killed everyone else.

She checked on the New Coventry system. During its industrial heyday, the system had been the home of one of the three heretical cults capable of modifying, though not creating, bridge technology, until that cult had supposedly been destroyed by the Church militant.

The Monk piloted the modified bridge-capable long-range Trident fighter through the sprawling superstructure of the unregulated habitat. She wove in and out of the various tethered domiciles and docked ships, making for the centre of the habitat – a hollowed-out asteroid 'sect Hive run by the Queen's Cartel. The last time she'd been there, Scab had made his escape by hacking the habitat's defences, and those of the surrounding ships, to fire on the Church frigate she'd been aboard. It had not endeared the Church to the criminal syndicate that ran Arclight and the matter-mining refinery and S-tech prospecting operations in the system. That said, it didn't pay to ignore a polite request from the Church if you enjoyed the benefits of bridge technology.

She'd run facial-recognition searches through all the available sensor feeds on Arclight that she could buy access to but had found nothing. That was okay – it simply meant she would have to do it the old-fashioned way, by looking. She was used to that.

The Monk paid for a secure berth for the fighter and was met by a representative of the Queen's Cartel. She wasn't sure that the word *dapper* should apply to a worker 'sect, but it was apropos for this one. He was courteous but cold. Whether this was just his nature, or the result of the Cartel's displeasure at the Church's last visit, she wasn't terribly sure. She was provided with a guide: a spindly – the result of living in a zero-G environment – lizard hatchling of indeterminate gender with soft-tech compound insect eye implants. Her guide was called Fruitfly. She asked him/her where the shipless could be found in a place like Arclight, somewhere beyond the view of the sensors.

They located him in the third place they looked, in the cargo bay of a gutted old bulk hauler. Left to rot decades, if not centuries, before the tethered detritus of the habitat stretching out from its asteroid core had effectively grown over it. Someone had hooked up rudimentary life support, and a worn concertina umbilical that was not for the fainthearted connected it to the rest of the habitat. It was cold, the atmosphere thin and not properly scrubbed, and nothing could remove the stench of the unwashed, supposedly excess uplifts who called the place home. The zero-G environment allowed them to adhere shelters and ragged sleeping cocoons to all four of the cargo bay's walls. They'd also added a mezzanine cube structure, constructed from salvaged material, to create more living space. It never ceased to amaze the Monk that even though the uplifted races could create habitats like Arclight and giant spaceships, people were forced to live this way.

The man still looked diseased, partially consumed, his flesh mottled and necrotised. His neighbours gave him a wide berth, and those closest to him were the most wretched of the unfortunate living down there. He was wearing layers of filthy clothing and an old coat. The ragged wounds on his head, which to the Monk looked self-inflicted, still hadn't healed and were badly infected. She took one look at him and told Fruitfly that he – or she – could go. The strange spindly lizard child cocked his/her head at the Monk quizzically, then threw himself/herself towards the umbilical.

The molecular hooks on the Monk's tabi adhered her to the surface of the cargo bay wall and she knelt down next to the man.

'You don't look well,' she said. A number of advertising slogans were growing on his flesh, one of them weakly animated.

'I don't understand why,' the man said weakly.

'Why you're unwell?' the Monk asked.

'Why I *am*. I should not exist. I was a vessel. I saw such things, such wonders. Now I am nothing.'

'Who did you give the godsware to?' she asked. He stared at her blindly. His eyes were filled with cataracts. 'The eyes – who did you give the eyes to?'

'I have no eyes.'

'But you did. You would have been able to see fields, understand them.'

'I gave them to the harbinger.'

The Monk stared at the sickly man. *Does he mean Scab?* she asked herself. Everything they had on Scab suggested that being a street sect leader on Cyst was just a phase he went through. He had shown no interest in religion when he served in the Legions. There was little information regarding his time in the Elite, but certainly since becoming a bounty killer he had, if anything, demonstrated contempt for religion.

'Do you have a name?' the Monk asked.

The man gave this some thought, his facial muscles twitching. 'Why would I have a name?' he asked.

'This is really important. Where did you get the eyes from?'

The man considered the question. 'God.'

The Monk leaned away from him. Retrieving the information she wanted would require interrogation by people and systems much more adept at that sort of thing than she was. She didn't think he was being purposefully obtuse, and she was pretty sure he knew something, but his mind was fractured. She would take him back to the Cathedral. They could do something for him physically, as well.

Then she realised what was wrong with the picture. The wounds, the viral ravages, the frigid, shitty atmosphere: he should be dead. And he had no nano-screen. She went cold.

'There's no way you can still be alive,' she said.

A tear trickled out of the corner of one of the man's cloudy eyes. 'I am a vessel,' he told her simply.

She drew one of her blades – black hilt, long silver blade, like an old pre-Loss bayonet. She grabbed a handful of his stinking clothes and slit them open with the blade. Then she cut into his pallid, diseased flesh. The 'man' gave no indication that he felt it. There was no blood. Instead, she saw something move underneath his flesh.

'Everybody out now!' she shouted, but she knew they wouldn't listen. She made a decision. It was a risk, but they had to get something from this or it was just another lead going nowhere.

'Sorry,' she told the man. She tried to grab him by the hair but it came away in clumps. Instead she pushed his head down against the cargo bay bulkhead and put the blade against his neck. The knife cut through brittle, dry flesh and bone with an unpleasant crunching noise. She pulled the head off the neck stump and looked into the skull. Nothing. She hoped he had at least rudimentary neunonics or this was all for nothing. Then something black and viscous surged up out of the dry neck wound. She snatched a thermal grenade from her belt and dropped it, then kicked off from the bulkhead.

'Grenade!' she shouted. Then people started to move. The thing inside the man's body writhed, its amorphous, changing form breaking the flesh apart. The grenade went off and the thing was cleansed by fire.

The bath chair rolled across the obsidian floor in silhouette. Bright-light pollution flooded in through the window that looked out over the core planet's low orbit. His employer was sitting behind the bare marble table.

'There was really no need for you to come personally,' the tall man said.

'I felt an explanation was in order,' Mr Hat replied. 'I was outbid.'

'You were outsmarted,' his employer said.

Mr Hat shifted uncomfortably in his seat. 'Perhaps—' he began.

'There is no perhaps about it. You were too eager. I have reviewed the information you sent ahead. Scab would not make a mistake like that. It was bait.'

'These things are easy to sit in judgement on in retrospect—'

His employer held up a hand. Mr Hat went quiet, almost despite himself.

'Being outsmarted by Mr Scab and his cohorts does not concern me as much as your apparent unwillingness to learn from your mistakes.'

'Learn from my mistakes? Then you're not going to ...?'

There was a dry chuckle from the other side of the desk. 'Why would I? You are a valuable asset in which I have invested a great deal. You are already in place. Anyone new I would have to bring up to speed. The loss of the blank is regrettable, but it may open a channel of communication I had hitherto thought lost. I am a businessman. I cannot afford too many more failures like this, but the consequences are only the loss of my patronage, and the loss of payment. Now, I understand you suffered your own losses. Do you wish to continue in my employ in this matter?'

'Unequivocally,' Mr Hat said.

His employer nodded. 'Excellent. Now, I have a confession. I, too, have made a mistake. I underestimated the good uses to which Scab would put the resources they gained during that farce of an auction on Pythia. I must see that you have access to similar resources.'

'Thank you,' Mr Hat said. Clearly surprised.

'Now, I'm sorry, but you must excuse me.'

'Of course.' Mr Hat turned his bath chair around with a thought and headed for the two huge marble slabs that acted as a door to the office.

When the bounty killer had gone, his employer darkened the smart-matter window, dimming considerably the incoming light. He stood up and walked down a small passageway to an antechamber. It was bare except for a chair. On the chair sat a twitching, eyeless blank.

'So. What it is you want to tell me?' the tall man asked.

The blank opened his mouth to speak.

39

Ancient Britain

Britha stood on the fungal plain, leaning on her spear. She had been running for the better part of three days and nights, but she wasn't out of breath. She was, however, hungry enough to start scooping up gobbets of earth and stuffing them into her mouth. She had become visibly thinner and frailer. The running, the simple act of putting one foot in front of another had managed to keep her thoughts at bay: the warped father of her daughter, dead at her lover's hand. Bress walking away from her with the only hope she had of ever seeing her child again. Sitting on the floor by Fachtna's steaming, still-mutating corpse, she had almost given in to despair. It was anger at herself, at her weakness, and thoughts of her child which forced her back onto her feet and started her moving.

In the distance she could see the shaking treeline. The Muileartach's spawn looked like a swarm of devouring insects. She had passed numerous strange creatures as she ran, insects with human faces, winged stag-like creatures with cloven hooves, screaming trees, but they had mostly left her alone. She did not think that would be the case when she tried to make her way through the front ranks.

She saw a rider galloping towards her, clouds of fungal matter billowing out from under its hooves. The closer it came, the more deformed it looked. For a moment, Britha wondered what her life had come to that the flayed fusion of horse and rider, its sword and shield now protrusions of bone, had become so commonplace it neither appalled nor frightened her.

The creature slowed, coming to a halt a short distance from her.

The *gwyllion* had taken them off the main track and through the forested land of Ardu. Guidgen told them that the track wound through the forest, whereas they could show them a more direct route.

After Bladud, Anharad and the others had met with Guidgen, Nerthach and Anharad told Tangwen about the meeting with Britha and Bress. Her heart sank when she heard that Britha had joined with Bress. The strange northern *dryw* had been their strongest ally against the Lochlannach. Tangwen was convinced they had enslaved her with their magic, but Germelqart very quietly told her that he did not think this was the case. The Carthaginian was of the opinion that Britha had made the decision voluntarily. This had left Tangwen feeling more than a little angry with the other woman.

They had been walking through the woods for three days now and their supplies were close to running out. As night fell, they set up camp among the trees, and the warriors took turns standing guard through the night. The *gwyllion* were doing their best to help forage for more food, but as the survivors became weaker they also became slower. The sense of despair in the camp was greater than ever, a feeling that they were only forestalling the inevitable.

Tangwen heard angry shouts from the southern part of the camp, followed by iron sliding from leather. She grabbed her bow and sprinted through the woods. She saw others running towards the shouting and sounds of violence.

They found the monstrosity rearing in a small clearing. Warriors jabbed at it with longspears, but the wounds they made closed almost immediately. It was similar to the deformed thing they had fought in the mud between the Isle of Madness and the mainland. Tangwen didn't realise she was touching the acid burn on her face. Then she noticed the rider on its back, behind the thing's human torso. Britha. Her finger appeared to be embedded in the back of the creature's head. The *dryw* looked frail and emaciated. Tangwen shuddered. She had seen Britha look like that before – it was her hag-like aspect – though she had not seen the woman with half her head shaved, and the red metallic sigils in her flesh were also new.

When Britha tore her finger out of the creature's head, Tangwen caught movement at the end of the finger as tendrils of metallic red filigree were sucked back into the stump of her middle finger. Britha slid from the creature's back, ducking under a wild swing from the creature's bone shield. As Britha straightened up she rammed her spear into the thing's body, just below the horse head. Britha continued pushing upwards. The creature reared on its hind legs and toppled over.

Warriors and landsfolk alike stared at the black-robed woman. Britha put one foot on the creature's corpse and wrenched her spear out. There was a collective gasp and even warriors backed away from her as the spearhead's metal tendrils re-formed into a more conventional shape.

Tangwen held her ground but stared warily at the spearhead for a moment. Then she marched forward. Britha, sensing movement, turned as Tangwen slapped the other woman, hard, and the sound of flesh hitting flesh resounded through the trees. Another collective gasp rose from the growing crowd. Whatever else Britha was, she was clearly a *dryw*. You weren't supposed to strike a *dryw*. Britha's head whipped back, an expression of fury on her face. Then Tangwen punched the other woman as hard as she could. It felt like hitting wood, not flesh. Britha hit the ground. She was back on her feet a moment later, furious.

'I am a *dryw*!' she shouted at Tangwen. The skin around her mouth darkened for a moment before it healed and the blood on her lips was sucked through her skin. Her knuckles were white around her spear. Tangwen dropped her bow and drew her hatchet and dagger. Suddenly Kush was at her side, his axe in hand.

'Prove it!' Tangwen spat. 'Help your people. Help the land.' Even in the darkness, Tangwen thought she saw a look of shame on the other woman's face.

'What is this?' Bladud's voice was quiet but somehow still carried. Tangwen continued to glare at Britha as the Witch King walked forward, Nerthach, as ever, at his side.

Britha stared at him, trying to control her anger. 'You would have people bear arms against a *dryw*?' she demanded.

Bladud glanced down at the dead creature. 'A *dryw* who rides demons into our camp. A *dryw* who, while she may not be our enemy, is certainly on his side. But you are right – I would not have my people bear arms against a *dryw*.' He glanced at Tangwen, who showed no sign of putting up her weapons. Bladud took a step towards Britha. 'I, on the other hand, will gladly kill a *dryw* and pay the price in this world and the next if it means protecting my people.'

There was another collective gasp. Britha was staring at intently at Bladud. Tangwen couldn't quite read her expression.

'I am no longer in your enemy's council,' Britha said.

'And how can we trust someone who changes sides as often as you do?' Bladud asked.

Britha's face hardened. 'I have not acted against you or yours, and I have dealt fairly with you. I made no oaths to you, or to Bress.'

'But you made oaths to your people,' Tangwen snapped.

Britha turned on the younger woman. 'Who are all *dead*!'

Kush looked at the warriors and the survivors. 'I see them all around you, and this isn't even my land,' the Numibian said.

Britha turned to Bladud. 'What would you have of me?' she asked.

'Your oath,' Bladud told her. There were mutterings from the assembled crowd.

'The *dryw* do not swear to kings!' Britha said angrily.

'Take her head,' Anharad said as she emerged from the trees, one hand gripping Mabon tightly to try and prevent him from doing anything rash. She glanced down at the corpse of the twisted creature and shuddered before spitting and making the sign to avert evil.

'All are welcome to try,' Britha said.

A quiet voice said something, but it was lost among the arguments, threats and counter-threats from Britha, the assembled warriors and the landsfolk.

'Quiet!' An authoritative voice cut through the furore. Tangwen looked around and eventually saw Guidgen standing in the trees. He was wearing his antler headdress and holding his staff. It was difficult to tell because he was standing in the moon shadow of a tree, but Tangwen didn't think the *dryw* was smiling right now. *Gwyllion* warriors flanked him on either side. Tangwen caught a glimpse of Bladud's face and he did not look happy. As the noise died down, Guidgen turned to Germelqart.

'Carthaginian?' the old *dryw* asked.

'Do you have a way to fight your goddess's spawn?' the navigator asked.

'But we cannot trust her!' Anharad shouted. Bladud held up his hand for quiet, watching Britha.

'You may take my blood—' she began.

'As we did on the Crown of Andraste?' Tangwen asked. Britha nodded. 'It was barely enough then, and there were two of you. It will not be enough now.'

'What is the enemy's greatest weapon?' Germelqart asked.

She was tempted to say Bress himself.

'It is not a weapon,' Britha said, 'but it is the source of their power. They have a chalice.'

Germelqart nodded as if this did not surprise him.

Bladud addressed the crowd: 'Please return to your responsibilities, or rest. We will gather the people we require.'

People turned and started to shuffle back towards the camp.

'Why should they leave?' Guidgen asked. 'This affects all here, them as much as you.' The survivors and the warriors turned back to look at Bladud. The Witch King couldn't prevent an expression of irritation from creeping onto his face.

'Some things require secrecy,' Nerthach said.

'Why?' This time it was Germelqart asking the question.

'Because if we decide to do something, it would do us ill if the enemy discovered it,' Nerthach said patiently and slowly.

Germelqart smiled at the warrior's good-natured if patronising attitude. 'I understand that, but who here would betray us other than the one we are going to talk to anyway?' The navigator pointed at Britha. She remained impassive. 'And if I die by betrayal, then so be it. I would prefer that to being transformed.' Germelqart pointed at the corpse of the creature Britha had killed. 'We're in no more danger than we were this morning. The only difference is that now there is hope.'

There was muttered agreement from the assembled crowd.

'Our hope will diminish if we are betrayed,' Bladud pointed out.

'And there are Corpse People among us,' Tangwen said, though she couldn't see Ysgawyn in the trees. Then she heard a dry chuckle.

'Bress would not look to see me again. Nor I him, except perhaps on the edge of my sword, but that does not matter. He does not care what you talk of, or what you do, nor would he listen for the telling. You're no threat to him.'

Tangwen finally located Ysgawyn. He was standing with his remaining three warriors, unarmoured, on a small rise just under the trees. All four Corpse People were in shadow.

'I will aid in this,' Ysgawyn told them. His three warriors nodded their agreement.

'For a chance to gain the power for yourself,' Tangwen spat.

Ysgawyn shrugged. 'And how does that make me any different from this one?' He nodded towards Bladud. 'With his show of false threats against a *dryw* whilst he has the crowd's ear?'

'Bitter tongue! Deceiver! Spreader of strife!' Nerthach spat. He drew his sword and made his way towards Ysgawyn. The *rhi* of the Corpse People did nothing. Tangwen noticed Madawg shift slightly, his hand touching the hilt of his sword. She also noticed that Britha had a smile on her face.

'Enough of this,' Bladud said. Nerthach kept moving. 'Nerthach!'

The big warrior stopped then and turned to Bladud. 'No, enough is enough! Strength and power are nothing to be ashamed of – the Brigante know this! I am sick of these dogs nipping at you. You have led these people, kept them safe, and when they insult you, they insult all of us. This fool dies!'

'Are you still my oath-sworn man?' Bladud roared.

'Let him kill the worm,' Tangwen said.

'Enough!' Bladud roared again. Now all eyes were on him. 'If you believe you are stronger than me – and I include you in this,

her arms and face. She was sure the symbol of a Z-shaped broken spear entwined with a serpent that covered much of her upper back had once been blue. Now it had the same look as the rest of the sigils: a smooth, red, almost flesh-like metal.

They constructed a frame from branches gathered by the *gwyllion*. Guidgen first offered a sacrifice of his own blood to the earth, to appease the Horned God for calling on other magics in his woodland realm. Then they hung Britha from the frame by her feet and cut her at the ankles, the wrists and the neck, to bleed her like a sacrificed calf. Bowls made of ash, willow, beach and oak were arranged to collect the blood from the ankle and wrist wounds. A bowl of bronze collected the blood from the neck. All the while Guidgen kept watch, burning various herbs and mumbling the words of protective magics to himself.

Tangwen remembered the first time she saw something like this, when she found Britha and Fachtna hanging by their feet. She had been appalled at their apparent sacrifice. That was not even one moon ago, but she was a different person now.

Bladud came to watch the proceedings when he wasn't attending to other duties. Tangwen had noticed him deep in conversation with Nerthach more than once.

When the blood stopped flowing, they cut Britha down and wrapped her black robe around her. The other eight who were to accompany her to Annwn joined Tangwen. They dipped sword and dagger blades, spearheads, arrow tips, her own hatchet blade, Guidgen's sickle and Germelqart's skull-topped mace in the blood-filled wooden bowls.

Finally they were presented with the bronze bowl of Britha's neck blood. Though Tangwen had drunk of her serpent-father's blood, somehow this still felt wrong, like dark magic. She saw Sadhbh and Nerthach looking at the bowl with disgust on their faces. Kush and Germelqart appeared less than happy at the prospect of drinking from it. Even Guidgen seemed unsure. Only the two Corpse People appeared to relish the chance to drink the powerful *dryw*'s blood – Brys, the powerfully built, scarred, grey-bearded and grey-haired veteran, and Madawg, the balding, sickly-looking warrior.

'Where is your king?' Tangwen asked as she watched Madawg drink from the copper bowl.

'My understanding is that the amount you drink makes no difference to the power you receive,' Guidgen told the frail-looking Corpse People warrior. Madawg stopped drinking from the bowl, his mouth stained with Britha's neck-blood.

'Perhaps I like the taste,' Madawg said, grinning, and passed the bowl to Brys, who drank and passed it to Nerthach, who just stared at it.

'He has sent his two best remaining warriors,' Brys said.

'This one does not look much like a warrior,' Nerthach said, glancing down at Madawg.

'And yet I have the courage to drink of the *dryw*'s blood, and you do not,' Madawg said.

'Are you not a follower of Cocidius, the Red Man?' Guidgen asked Nerthach. 'He is red because he is covered in blood.'

'Aye, covered in it, not drinking it,' Nerthach muttered, but he glanced at Madawg, who was smirking. The Brigante steeled himself and drank from the bronze bowl. He wiped his mouth with the back of his hand and passed the bowl to Sadhbh.

Finally all the others had drunk and the bowl was passed to Tangwen. She stared at it. She knew this was the blood magic of the Lochlannach. The ritual might have changed it, controlled it, but it was still the magic of demons from the ice in the far north. The magics she had fought against, the magics that were used to enslave. She feared enslavement more than she feared death, perhaps even more than she feared transformation by Andraste's spawn.

'It is not a good thing that we do, but this will not make us what we fear and hate,' Germelqart said softly, as if he had read her mind, but it was more likely Sadhbh's contemptuous sneer that made her drink from the bowl. The blood was still hot and tasted of metal, and seemed almost eager to be drunk – it practically surged down her throat. Then fear gripped her as she felt something move inside her. She could see the dots of fire moving through the blood of her companions.

Tangwen felt good, she had to admit, strong, fast. The night felt somehow alive, vibrant. She could see clearly in the dark, hear insects on the wing and distant hunting owls in flight. She could smell the food from the feast, the fire, sweat, leather, metal, the sap of the trees and the scent of the flowers. She felt very different, but for some reason the change did not worry her.

Bladud had arranged the feast. Tangwen knew she should feel guilty for the food that she and the other eight gorged themselves on, but she did not. That said, the amount Britha ate was appalling. In front of their eyes, she devoured the survivors' meagre supplies and what the *gwyllion* had been able to hunt, and her frame filled out as they watched. She had been carried to the food in a weakened stupor, barely able to grab at it and stuff it into her mouth. Now she looked strong and healthy, though there was still little colour in her pale skin.

They were seated around a fire pit over which the remains of a deer was cooking. A cauldron bubbled over another nearby fire. Nerthach was next to Bladud, who ate little. Tangwen sat next to Guidgen, Kush next to her. Germelqart was on the other side of Kush.

'Where is your friend?' Guidgen asked, and then belched loudly. Tangwen bit off another chunk of meat from the haunch of venison she was eating. She didn't think she'd ever eaten so much in her life before, but still she wanted more. Tangwen looked around the fire pit. Britha was no longer there.

'She's not my friend,' Tangwen muttered, and then took a mouthful from a horn of ale.

'I think that, whatever else she has said and done, once you have shared certain ... troubles, there is a bond,' the elderly *dryw* said.

'She betrayed us,' Tangwen said stubbornly.

'She also saved us,' Kush pointed out. Germelqart had stopped eating and was looking at Tangwen. She could not read the Carthaginian's expression.

'Would you do me a service, Tangwen serpent-child?' Guidgen asked. Tangwen nodded. There was little choice in the matter when a *dryw* asked something of you. 'It worries me that she is not here. Would you go and see if you can find her?'

Tangwen wanted to say no. Instead she reluctantly got to her feet and went to do as Guidgen bid her.

'It is true. I have been to the Otherworld, but I am no child-thief.'

Tangwen could hear the exasperation in Britha's voice. The northern woman was talking to Anharad among the wet trees. There was a small girl with the older woman, one of the few survivors from the wicker man who had made it this far. The child had never uttered a word that Tangwen had heard. She and Anharad had taken it in turns looking after the girl before they met up with Bladud's forces.

Mabon was nearby, perched on a rock. His knife was in his hand and the boy looked like he was ready to pounce.

'I could not care less if you were the bride of the sun and the moon himself – leave this girl in peace, or Bladud will know why,' Anharad spat. Tangwen could tell that the older woman was frightened. The little girl was, too – she was shaking like a leaf and staring at Britha wide-eyed, but to her credit she did not cry.

'Do you think your Witch King frightens me, woman?' Britha demanded.

'What do you want of the child?' Tangwen said, stepping forwards. Both Anharad and Mabon jumped. Britha did not. Instead she turned to Tangwen. She opened her mouth to say something, then appeared to think better of it, and her expression softened.

'She is of the Cirig,' Britha told her.

'Your people?' Tangwen asked.

'She may be the last one,' Britha said.

'So she says,' Anharad spat.

'I will cut out your tongue if you name me a liar once more,' Britha declared.

'I'll call you—'

'Anharad!' Tangwen said, desperate to get the other woman's attention before she said something Britha would have to act on. 'Please, peace. We are about to walk into the Underworld and all is shouting.' Anharad subsided into an angry silence. Tangwen looked at the child. 'She is strong, she does not cry and she lives, despite all. Isn't that right?' The girl still clung to Anharad's leg, but she was staring at Tangwen now. 'Do you remember me?' Tangwen asked. Slowly the girl nodded.

Tangwen pointed to Britha. 'Do you remember this woman?' she asked. 'You do not have to be afraid of her. She cannot hurt you here.' The girl looked up at Britha, her eyes wide. Tangwen saw the look of recognition in her eyes before she nodded. 'Do you remember her from your own lands, before you were taken?' Tangwen asked.

'Tangwen!' Anharad hissed, but the little girl nodded.

'What is her name?' Tangwen asked Britha.

'I ...' Britha started and then made choking noises. Tangwen was surprised to see tears rolling down the northern woman's face. 'I can't remember.'

Anharad was staring at Britha with an expression of surprise on her face. Tangwen got her attention and nodded. Anharad scooped the child up and headed back to camp. Mabon leaped off his rock and followed.

Tangwen stopped Anharad as she passed. 'Would you speak with this woman again?' Tangwen asked the child. The little girl nodded.

When Anharad, Mabon and the child had gone, Britha broke down sobbing and sat hard on the wet earth. Tangwen stared. She could see Britha following a path to power, even betraying them for that, but she did not know this sobbing woman.

Tangwen knelt down next to her and put her hand on Britha's shoulder. The other woman looked up at the hunter.

'What?' Tangwen asked.

'I've failed that girl so much ...' The sobbing intensified, wracking her body. It looked like something she had been holding in for a while 'There was a child ...' Britha managed. Tangwen held her tightly.

Birmingham, 2 Weeks Ago

40

Birmingham, 2 Weeks Ago

Silas awoke face down in the mud, frightened. He had no idea what had happened. He had no idea why he was lying on the path next to the canal. The last thing he could remember was climbing out of the water.

This wasn't supposed to happen to him. He was as a god among these people. Nothing should be able to hurt or even inconvenience him. Nothing should be able to toy with him like this. Make him feel how he made others feel.

Had he been compromised? It didn't make sense. If he had, why hadn't he been killed and captured, why had he just been left there? He should move, flee, go somewhere else, even another city, but he was so close. There was too much to lose if he stopped now.

Grace was crouching down, hugging her knees, in the corner of the derelict warehouse. She wiped away tears and snot with the back of her hand as she watched the blackened piece of meat that was du Bois try to regenerate in the back of the Range Rover.

Grace had managed to free the Range Rover and load du Bois into the back of it. She hooked him up to emergency matter/energy packs, which looked like IVs but contained matter that could be converted to regenerate damaged flesh, and concentrated calories to help power the conversion. They were the last hope for Circle operatives if they were very badly damaged. Taking a point-blank blast from a claymore might have been too much, however.

Grace flinched as du Bois started to cry out in agony. Then a grin split her face. She stood up and walked towards him, pulling the cap off a syringe with enough morphine in it to stun an elephant.

'You were right about the grand gestures,' Grace said. She sounded subdued. Du Bois had put on replacement clothes that he kept in an overnight case in the back of the Range Rover. He had been badly hurt before, close to death, but he was very surprised to have survived this time. The technology in his body was suppressing biochemistry and psychology, which, quite reasonably, wanted him to go into shock. He was still shaking. He was sitting on the open tailgate of the Range Rover with a tartan car blanket wrapped around him, as if that would make everything okay. He was clutching a mug of strong, sweet tea.

'I couldn't quite work out why he did what he did in Demesne House,' du Bois said. 'I think you're right. He is like a rudimentary Hawksmoor. He was trying to brutalise the city, he wants it afraid so he can harvest that fear somehow.'

'Or he thinks he can,' Grace said. Du Bois nodded and took another sip of his tea. With shaking hands he put a cigarette into his mouth. Grace had to light it for him.

'He might be able to move around the city unseen, but a van can't materialise out of thin air.'

With a thought, Grace sent the information she had gathered to du Bois. He accepted it without using the phone as a buffer this time.

Grace had sifted through all the CCTV camera footage she could gain access to. The white Mercedes Sprinter van's first appearance was in Heath Mill Lane, in Digbeth, just south-east of the city centre. When du Bois stopped shaking, they took the slightly battered Range Rover there.

Heath Mill Lane was the location of Robert Jaggard's exhibition. Du Bois found himself standing on the road bridge over the Grand Union Canal again. It was a grey day, overcast sky but no rain, and neither particularly warm nor cold. It was a nondescript day. He still couldn't shake the feeling that the canals were involved somehow. He wasn't sure why. Perhaps it was Silas's age, the era he was born into. Du Bois remembered the changes, technological and social, and how uncomfortable he had been with them. The canals were such a part of that time, feeding the industry that had transformed this and other cities. Du Bois glanced up at the much higher red-brick bridge next to the road bridge. A train thundered by overhead, heading into New Street Station. The canals had been so quickly superseded by the railways. Grace's era.

Du Bois also knew that this area was close to where Silas was caught on CCTV leaping from the train after he'd killed Jaggard. As far as du Bois could tell, that was one of the few mistakes Silas had made.

He felt his phone vibrate in the pocket of his leather coat. He closed his eyes, an unnecessary affectation, and accessed the text. It was an address on Heath Mill Lane sent by Grace. Du Bois turned to look towards the Digbeth Road.

The garage did maintenance on the city's black cabs.

There was an empty space in the cramped environs of the garage big enough for a van. The mechanics were all underneath the platform lifts. The lifts had been lowered onto them, crushing them. Du Bois looked down at the mechanics. In many ways they were little people to him, unimportant, but all they'd been doing was trying to make a living, to look after themselves and their families. He found that he didn't feel angry, just very sad.

His blood-screen finished analysing a residue of something remaining in the garage. He turned slowly to look at Grace, who did look angry.

'How can they not know where it is?' Grace demanded. 'Even if they've lost it, they should be able to pick up its energy signature from orbit.'

They had found trace nanites that could only have come from the Red Chalice.

'He's here,' du Bois said. They'd called the murders in to the police and were standing in a nearby alleyway close to where the Range Rover was parked. Both of them were leaning against the wall, smoking.

Grace nodded. 'I know,' she said quietly. Around the corner they could see the glow of the flashing blue lights, hear the occasional siren and the raised voices of the police.

Du Bois was mentally checking the various dead letter email accounts that he used around the world. It was for something to do more than anything else. He knew they were close, but he couldn't see how to make the leap to actually finding Silas.

'What are we going to do?' Grace asked.

'We're going to find this bastard and kill him,' du Bois said.

'And if he has the Red Chalice ... ?'

Then du Bois found the anonymous email. He assimilated its contents, double- and triple-checked the information. He tried tracing it, but it had been occulted so effectively that it might as well have just blinked into existence in his protected account. He checked it for subtle viruses and found nothing. He shared its contents with Grace. Grace looked over at him.

'Do we tell Control?' she asked.

'They either know already or don't care,' du Bois said. He walked to the Range Rover, unlocking it with a thought. He opened the tail-gate and unlocked the concealed weapons locker.

'What do you want?' du Bois asked Grace.

The Fazeley Street Gasworks had been touched by the gentrification of the Digbeth area. The huge red-brick Georgian edifice on the banks of the Grand Union Canal had been renovated and turned into a conference centre, complete with an upmarket café. The two brick outbuildings attached to the gasworks had been left to rot, however. Their walls were crumbling, and the wrought-iron arches which held up what was left of the roof looked extensively rusted. Du Bois and Grace entered stealthily through holes in the wall.

Du Bois had the folding stock of his .45 calibre Heckler & Koch UMP against his shoulder as he checked his surroundings. He had attached the M320 grenade-launcher to the mounting rail beneath the SMG's barrel and loaded his Accurised .45 pistol with his only magazine of nanite-tipped bullets. He knew that Grace had done the same with one of her Berettas. She had du Bois' M1014 semi-automatic Benelli shotgun at the ready.

The outbuilding was an old retort house where coal had once been heated to produce gas. They skirted piles of rubble, their weapons twitching up and down, left and right, barrels following their line of sight. The retort house felt empty and looked undisturbed. They could hear the sound of cars on Fazeley Street, which ran parallel with the canal on the other side of the gas works, and there were smokers chatting outside the conference facilities. It looked like a very normal day, in a very normal world. Even if all the overheard conversation was about the massacre at Druids Heath, the chase and the subsequent explosion in Victoria Square.

Du Bois signalled a stop. He was beginning to wonder if he'd been set up as he glanced around the rubble-filled building. Then his blood-screen snagged something.

Silas launched himself off a rusted iron arch, falling silently through the air and the nanites of du Bois' and Grace's blood-screens, his coat-tails flapping out behind him. He clutched a large, stylised, silver-bladed knife in each hand. Du Bois turned, bringing his SMG to bear smoothly, his right hand moving forwards. A hard kick into his shoulder. The popping noise of the underslung grenade-launcher firing. The flechettes from the forty-millimetre grenade barely had time to spread out as they tore through Silas's flesh, shredding it, creating a cloud of blood behind the killer. Screaming and red, Silas landed on du Bois, knocking him to the ground, slashing wildly with both knives.

Grace swung around and started firing the Benelli rapidly as she moved towards Silas and du Bois. Silas jerked as the first cloud of buckshot hit him, then the second round knocked him off du Bois. Grace was shocked when Silas stood up. She continued firing. Liquid red metal was pouring out of his exposed flesh, knitting it together and sealing it. He was glowing with an inner red light. She had fired all eight rounds from the shotgun before the first ejected cartridge hit the ground. Silas turned and ran. In one smooth motion, Grace let the shotgun drop on its sling and drew the Berretta with the nanite-tipped bullets from her left-shoulder holster. She held the weapon two-handed, for accuracy, and fired. Silas dived into a pile of rubble. The shot missed. She holstered the pistol and drew the other Beretta, which contained conventional rounds in its magazine, with her left hand. She backed towards du Bois, looking all around for Silas while reloading the shotgun's tubular magazine with her right hand.

'Malcolm?'

'Christ!' Du Bois' flesh looked in flux. As soon as his wounds healed they reopened as the nanites Silas had coated his blades with warred with du Bois' own defences.

Grace opened her mouth to say something, but instead spat blood all over du Bois. The tip of the blade pierced her chest as Silas grew out of the earth behind her. She dropped the shotgun cartridge she'd been trying to load into the Benelli. Silas opened his mouth to say something and Grace elbowed him in the face. Silas staggered back, more from surprise than anything else, and Grace back-kicked him with enough force to send him flying through the air. She continued turning, firing the Berretta with the conventional rounds at Silas. There was a little glint of red metal after each round hit. Du Bois managed to roll to his knees and bring up the UMP, firing rapid, short bursts at Silas. Grace drew the other Berretta and fired it once, but Silas was sucked into the earth again and her second nanite-tipped round missed. She collapsed into the dirt, dropping the conventionally loaded Beretta. She managed to reach behind and awkwardly pull the knife out of her back, crying out in pain, blood spraying from the wound. She felt the nanites from Silas's blades attacking her defences, trying to consume her own nanites and kill her. Sweat beaded her skin, a sensation she hadn't felt in years, as her body became a battlefield. Grace dropped Silas's knife. She didn't see the fingers that wrapped themselves around its hilt and pulled the weapon into the earth. Du Bois staggered to his feet, changed magazines on his UMP while standing over her.

Then the screaming started. It wasn't audible. Instead it tore through their heads. Blood filled their eyes and ran from their ears and noses. Du Bois staggered but managed to remain on his feet. Grace's hands went to her ears, though she was still holding one of her pistols in her right hand. It felt as if something was tearing them apart at some fundamental level. Nausea threatened to overwhelm them. Insects made from shards of razor-sharp glass were eating their way out of their guts. Amongst the screaming they could hear horrific, discordant music, and the air in front of them was squirming as if it was alive. They felt more than heard the howls of agony coming from people outside the retort house.

Silas grew out of earth next to them, holding his knives crossed over his chest. He was weeping tears of blood. More blood ran from his nose and ears.

Du Bois staggered away from Silas, firing short burst after short burst from his SMG into the murderer.

'Isn't it beautiful?' Silas said, barely staggering as round after round hit him.

'You have to keep him occupied,' Grace heard du Bois say in her mind. Her defences had just about won the battle against Silas's blade-delivered nanites and she could almost move through the pain and nausea. She raised her Beretta and fired twice. One of the nanite-tipped rounds caught Silas in the leg, the other in the hip. He barely registered them, but then nanites in the hollow points immediately started to attack his systems. Silas kicked the Beretta out of Grace's hand, shattering the weapon and every bone in her hand. She managed to grab the shotgun's pistol grip somewhat awkwardly with her left hand. She jammed the shotgun barrel up into Silas's stomach as he reached for her and fired again, and again. The nearly .70 calibre solid shot blew chunks of his flesh out through his back, but he reached through the muzzle flashes and grabbed the barrel of the weapon. Grace let go of the shotgun, drew the knuckleduster-hilted fighting knife from under her right shoulder and cut the sling that connected her to the shotgun as Silas yanked it towards himself. Grace kicked off backwards in a one-handed flip. She barely felt the pain of putting all her weight, for a moment, on her still rapidly healing right hand. As she flipped she grabbed the conventionally loaded Beretta and came to her feet with the gun in her right hand and the fighting knife in her left. Even through the pain and nausea she was wondering what the fuck du Bois was doing.

Du Bois sank to his knees, praying to a god he knew didn't exist. He grabbed the tanto from its sheath and cut down the artery on his wrist. He was finding it difficult to concentrate through the screaming in his head and the pain, which he heard and felt at some level more fundamental than the physical. He managed to force his body to increase the flow to the artery, the pace of his heartbeat picking up as he started to spray blood in pulses onto the dirt. It was a quick, dirty, nasty matter-hack. He told the nanites coursing through his blood to do one simple thing. He told them to do it over and over again. It became part of his prayer. An invocation.

Grace backed away rapidly from Silas, firing burst after burst from the fully automatic Beretta. Silas stalked after her, the wounds healing almost as quickly as the bullets hit him. His flesh looked like a cascade of molten metal, a bizarre, living, internal lava flow. The slide locked back on the Beretta – the extended magazine was empty. Silas swung the Benelli shotgun that he was still holding by the barrel. The weapon's pistol grip caught Grace in the side of her head with enough force to knock her off her feet. She hit the ground, hard. Silas dropped the shotgun. Grace's vision was blurred – there was more than one Silas reaching for her, and it hurt too much to focus. Despite the screaming that tore through her mind she was aware of the earth moving. The piles of rubble became landslides.

Du Bois was wasting away. So much of his vitality, so much of his constituent matter, was spurting in weakening crimson arcs onto the dirt in the retort house. It was working, though. He could feel it moving in the dirt beneath him, the dirt that had been its womb. It had worked because du Bois' blood incantation had been an order, a summoning, rather than an attack. It was growing through the dirt. It was made of brass, wood and glass bell-jar-like protrusions, displaying a design ethos from an earlier time, showing the insane but skilled craftsmanship of its creator. The bell jars contained slide-mounted slices of brain, an unintentional mockery of circuit boards, stemming from Silas's failure to understand the world into which he had been freed. The transmitters looked like Tesla coils. The body was that of a mechanical, armoured brass scorpion, presumably to protect the transmitter. Silas's signature design.

Du Bois stopped bleeding into the earth with a thought. The brass scorpion took a step towards him. It was easily the size of the Range Rover. Brass pincers snapped together as a sting-tipped tail curved over its back. Weakly Du Bois reached for his UMP. He pushed open the grenade-launcher, ejecting the spent flechette grenade as the scorpion's sting arced down towards him.

Grace was aware that something had risen from the earth behind her. She kicked up from the ground. Her motorcycle boot caught Silas in the face as he reached for her. The blow, with augmented leg muscles behind it, was strong enough to powder even reinforced bone. Silas staggered back as his 'demons' raced to rebuild the front of his skull. Grace kicked out at Silas's knee and broke it. He staggered again but somehow didn't go down, balancing on one leg. Grace slashed at his face with her fighting knife, opening the flesh down to the still re-forming bone. She slashed again and again. Each time the wound closed as quickly as she made it. Her own systems appeared to have just about beaten the invading nanites. The knife wound in her chest had closed, but she was still weak.

The sting caught du Bois in the upper chest and drove straight through and out at the small of his back, destroying his right lung, stomach and one kidney, but missing his spine. The sting injected its nanite venom into him on its way through. Du Bois' head shot back and he vomited what little blood he had left as he cried out. The scorpion lifted him up off the ground with its tail, du Bois still howling in pain, impaled on its sting. The tail moved him towards one of the pincers, which reached for his head. It started to get dark. Behind the scorpion, du Bois could see the air blackening and squirming like multiplying bacteria. Cracks appeared in the bricks, stress fractures expanding along the wall, the result of the matter of parts of the wall simply ceasing to exist. Through the pain du Bois still, somehow, had the presence of mind to be afraid. He managed to drop the forty-millimetre high-explosive armour-piercing grenade into the open breech of the underslung grenade-launcher and shut the weapon.

Grace skipped up onto her feet. She threw the empty Beretta towards the wreckage of her other pistol and drew the other fighting knife. Silas staggered towards her, slashing at her face. She parried with the knife in her left hand, punched Silas in the face with the knuckledusters on the hilt of the right-hand knife, and slashed him with the blade of the same weapon. She kicked him in the knee again, hearing something crack. Brought her leg up and side-kicked him. Grace cut at his face, he parried, she slashed repeatedly at the arm wielding the parrying knife before going after his face with both blades, cutting it again and again, keeping blood pouring into his eyes regardless of how quickly he healed. She felt herself getting weaker. She saw her skin necrotising. It started to flake away, to be sucked into something horrible behind her. Silas was laughing.

Du Bois was watching himself rot, his desiccated flesh being sucked towards the squirming black space behind the scorpion. It had been called by the slices of the minds in the bell jars, which were transmitting the worst images imagined by the city's sickest minds. Du Bois managed to weakly aim the grenade-launcher at the bell jars on the scorpion's back. He squeezed the trigger. The scorpion bucked under the impact of the grenade as it pierced its armour. Then the grenade exploded inside the scorpion, damaging the jars with their slices of brain and the tesla coils. The scorpion flicked its tail instinctively and du Bois flew through the air.

The concussion wave from the explosion knocked Grace forward into Silas. She head-butted his nose, slashed at his face with both blades and plunged them into his chest. Then she let go and ran.

Du Bois hit the wall and slid down it. He was surprised that he was still, somehow, able to function. His own nanites were just about holding their own against the scorpion's nanite venom, though his flesh was bubbling and writhing. He managed to draw his Accursed .45 and aim it at the scorpion as it turned towards him. The writhing blackness consumed the wall and everything beyond it like rapidly replicating hungry maggots.

Grace threw herself to the ground and grabbed at the remains of the Beretta Silas had shattered. She yanked the magazine from what was left of the pistol's grip, grabbed the other Beretta she'd thrown down earlier, ejected the empty magazine and slid in the magazine filled with the nanite-tipped bullets. She spun around. Silas was almost upon her.

'Put all the nanite rounds into the Scorpion,' she heard du Bois' weak voice beg her in her head. She had a moment to take in the scene – the brass scorpion, the squirming, consuming absence of light behind it, du Bois weakly trying to lift his arm.

He managed to raise his .45 and squeeze the trigger. He fired again, and again, until the slide came back empty and the pistol was just making clicking noises. The nanite-filled hollow points exploded against the scorpion's armour and began eating.

Grace put two rounds into Silas, then shifted aim and put the remaining nine rounds into the scorpion.

'No!' Silas reached down for Grace. Long fingers wrapped around her neck and yanked her up into the air.

Du Bois tried to stand but collapsed to the ground.

Silas rammed his remaining knife into Grace's guts, trying to push the blade up into her chest cavity.

Du Bois pawed weakly at his UMP, which was still hanging off its sling.

Grace cried out in agony. It was a barely conscious action: she grabbed at the two knives she'd left sticking in Silas and wrenched them out. She rammed the right-hand blade into his mouth, breaking teeth, the point of the nine-inch blade exploding out through the back of his skull. The left-hand blade she stabbed into the arm holding her. Silas staggered back, dropping Grace into a pool of her own viscera. He tried to howl out of a mouth filled with tempered steel, clawing at the hilt.

The black squirming thing was gone. Some of the wall adjoining the conference centre next door collapsed but there was little rubble – parts of the two buildings had simply been consumed. The scorpion collapsed to the ground. It looked as if it was melting as the nanites ate at it, converting its matter at a molecular level into more nanites, which further consumed it.

Silas, still staggering backwards, wrenched the knife out of his bloody mouth, then howled again as he yanked the knife out of his arm.

'I'm going to fuck you to death with your own knives!' Silas managed through a mouth gummed up with red liquid metal as it tried to repair the damage she'd done.

'Go and f—' Grace started, holding in her guts. Her own nanites were trying to heal her and fight off the ones attacking her. 'Sick ... fuck.'

The 40mm HEAP grenade caught Silas in the side and sent him spinning through the air. The grenade exploded, almost tearing him in two. It left a hole in his midriff, exposing his spine. Red filigree tendrils shot out from his stomach cavity and wrapped themselves around his vertebrae.

The recoil from firing the grenade had knocked the weakened du Bois off his feet. Grace looked over to where he lay. Blood bubbled around her partner's mouth as he struggled to breathe. She managed to turn her head and look at Silas. He was still moving weakly. Silas opened his mouth and emitted an inhuman-sounding howl. She watched the filigree lashing out into the earth to use its matter to rebuild his body. Grace looked down at herself. The wound in her stomach had almost closed, although she was still a mess internally. Nanites were fighting a number of wars in her feverish flesh, but her innards probably weren't going to fall out if she stood up.

Grace staggered over to du Bois. He looked up at her, his blue eyes full of pain but still alert. He was a mess. Multiple wounds, including a large one in his upper-right chest, weren't closing. The wounds also looked dry. She reached down and grabbed his belt buckle, removing the concealed punch blade. The blade was designed to disintegrate into nanites on command after it was stabbed into flesh. Du Bois looked up at her and nodded. Grace staggered away from him.

Silas was clawing at the ground as Grace tottered towards him. A disturbing amount of his body had been regrown but he wasn't able to move yet. He was still making noises like a wounded animal. Grace cut the palm of her right hand open with the punch dagger and then collapsed onto her knees next to Silas. Silas moved his head to look at her with pure hate.

'It was nearly over ...' Silas managed. 'I'm going to—'

Grace spat in his face. Then she rammed her hand into Silas's rapidly healing wound. She felt the tendrils of living red filament wrap around her hand and wrist, piercing her flesh. She tried to ignore the pain as best she could. Silas was howling and writhing at the violation. Her fingers wrapped around its stem. She used the blood on her hand to hack his flesh. Then Grace tore the Red Chalice out of his stomach cavity, where Silas had crudely implanted it, along with the red, living filaments, which retracted into the chalice. Silas howled in agony again. Grace raised the punch knife, preparing to plunge it through his skull. The bullet blew her hand off. Crying out, she collapsed onto Silas.

The wiry man with weather-beaten skin advanced rapidly, keeping Grace covered with the suppressed M14 rifle. There was still smoke rising from the weapon's barrel. The newcomer had a stubbly beard, and greying hair tied back in a ponytail.

'Sorry, Grace,' he said. He had an American accent, New England. 'I had to stop you stabbing him.' Holding the rifle at port with one hand, he reached down and dragged Grace off and away from Silas as gently as he could. She was still conscious, sobbing. The American then moved back to Silas. The serial killer was trying to push himself up on his arms. The American put a booted foot against his chest and forced him back to the ground. 'You just stay put, you piece of shit,' the American told Silas. He was standing where he could keep an eye on Grace and du Bois.

'Josh, what the fuck?' Grace spat through the pain. She was losing flesh as her systems fed on her matter to heal the extensive wounds she'd received. She was hungry. She saw du Bois trying to push himself into a sitting position with some difficulty.

'Orders, Grace, you know that. I'm really sorry, but your blood was up. If I thought you'd have listened to me I'd have asked.'

Du Bois' laughter was devoid of humour but had a horrible bubbly quality to it as he spat blood down his chest. 'You shooting your own side is getting to be something of a habit, isn't it, Josh?' he asked weakly.

'Once every two hundred or so years doesn't sound like much of a habit to me,' Josh said. 'How are you doing, Malcolm? You don't look good.'

'Fuck this,' Grace said, her voice still full of pain. She used her left hand to push herself to her feet, then cradled the stump of her right hand in her left. The Red Chalice was lying in the dirt at her feet, forgotten. She started walking towards Silas. Josh brought the M14 to his shoulder and levelled it at her.

'Are you out of your fucking mind?' Grace demanded.

'Please, Grace, be reasonable.'

'I *am* being fucking reasonable!' Grace shouted at the American. 'Have you any idea what that evil fucker's done?'

'Let us kill him,' Malcolm managed.

'I'm afraid not, Malcolm, and I'm sorry we keep having this conversation.' The voice was incredibly deep. Mr Brown walked into the retort building. He glanced at the hole in the wall, looking through into the next building. He was wearing a finely tailored dark-coloured business suit and leaning on a thick stainless steel staff. Four IV-style bags hung from the top of the staff; tubes connected each bag to a main tube, which ran into the left arm of Mr Brown's business suit. As they watched, one of the bags was deflating in front of them, its contents – a clear liquid – running down the tube and, presumably, into Mr Brown's arm.

The Pennangalan was at Mr Brown's side in her beaten-silver facemask, carrying a Sig Sauer 716 Patrol Rifle with an underslung grenade-launcher.

'Why?' du Bois asked, desperation and pain mingling in his voice. 'The Circle has enough pet killers. Enough grotesques.'

'Like Grace and yourself?' Mr Brown asked.

Du Bois managed to glance over at Grace. She was still cradling the stump of her hand, but had started looking around for a weapon.

'He will escape, do this again, you know that,' du Bois said.

'Malcolm, do you really think we have that much time?' Mr Brown asked.

'Then why's he so important?' du Bois asked. The first IV was empty and the second was starting to deflate. 'We deserve an answer.'

'You probably do,' Mr Brown conceded. 'But you must have realised that I am going to erase the memory of my explanation from your mind.'

'Fuck you!' Grace spat.

Mr Brown grimaced, as if the profanity bothered him.

Silas was making keening noises, trying to stand again. Josh slammed him down into the dirt with his boot and told him to shut up. There was obvious disgust in the American's voice.

'He is a Bad Seed. A member of an S-tech-infused bloodline. One that we, or rather I, have driven insane,' Mr Brown told him.

'Why?' du Bois asked.

'He is a harbinger.'

'Of what?'

'Pain, all of it,' Mr Brown said sadly.

'You're as mad as he is,' du Bois said.

'Do you know how we drive them mad?' Mr Brown asked, ignoring du Bois' remark. 'We make them just sensitive enough to really feel what's going on around them. What do you think that says about humanity?'

Du Bois looked down. He started to laugh but ended up coughing instead. When the spasm subsided, he asked, 'Do you know the one trait in people that I have constantly underestimated?' Mr Brown raised an eyebrow quizzically. 'Kindness.'

This time it was Mr Brown who laughed. The second IV bag was empty and the third started to deflate.

'When it comes, nobody will see me any more,' Silas said.

The American slammed him down into the dirt again. 'I thought I told you to shut up,' Josh said.

'We're on the wrong side, aren't we?' du Bois said.

Grace was looking between him and Mr Brown.

'No, but every time I've explained it to you in the past, you haven't seen it that way. Your race will cease to be soon.'

'The evacuation ... ?' Grace said, her voice sounding small.

'Oh, the people we take with us will look and sound human, but we've learned the control lessons taught by the parasites that humans think of as their leaders in this grand era. They will wear silk collars, but they will be no less a slave race for it.'

Du Bois and Grace stared at him.

'Malcolm's wrong,' Grace said. 'You're madder than him.' She nodded towards Silas.

'Why do this?' du Bois asked, trying to keep a pleading tone out of his voice. 'We had the thinkers, the scientists, the artists, philosophers—'

'And bastards like you to keep everyone in line,' Mr Brown said. 'Because humans, though they may have forgotten it in this era, are extremely capable of resisting when they put their minds to it.'

Du Bois looked between Josh and the Pennangalan. 'And you're both all right with this?' du Bois asked. Then he noticed that Josh was looking at him with an expression of disgust on his face. Du Bois had never quite forgiven the American for shooting him at the

Manufactory, but there had always been a degree of respect for each other.

'The Pennangalan is more Naga-tech than person, and Mr Ezard' – he nodded at Josh – 'has just heard an entirely different conversation.'

'I am going to kill you,' Grace told Mr Brown evenly.

Mr Brown sighed. 'And I think your partnership has reached its logical conclusion. You've both questioned orders, broken doctrine and acted of your own accord too often. I think you bring out the worst in each other.'

'I don't agree,' Grace said.

'You do understand that I can reprogram people, don't you?' Mr Brown asked. Grace clutched her head. Du Bois looked on, horrified, as blood seeped out of her ears. Then the expression on Grace's face changed and she turned on du Bois with an expression of total hatred.

'You bastard!' she screamed at him, tears pouring down her face as she stormed towards him. The Pennangalan interposed herself between Grace and du Bois. Josh was running towards her. 'I'll fucking kill you!' Grace was shouting at him. 'How could you? How could you!'

Josh grabbed her by the shoulder before she could push past the Pennangalan.

'I'm so sorry, Grace,' Mr Brown said. 'I would see him punished as well, but I need him alive, just a little longer. I wouldn't make you suffer so if it wasn't important.'

Grace turned and gave Mr Brown a look of utter contempt. Then Mr Brown stopped and concentrated for a moment, his face filling with concern.

'We're being attacked,' Mr Brown said. 'We need to go, now.'

'C'mon, Grace,' Josh told her. 'He'll get his, I promise.'

Du Bois was staring at them, appalled. 'Grace, look, they've done this to you—' he started

'They!' Grace screamed and tried to break free. The Pennangalan slung her rifle over her shoulder and grabbed Grace with both hands. She started pulling Grace bodily out of the retort building. Josh let them go, then went and retrieved the Red Chalice from where it was lying on the ground. Then he walked over to du Bois.

'Josh—' du Bois began.

'You want to regenerate? Then I think you'll need to eat some dirt.' Josh kicked du Bois in the head as hard as he could. Du Bois slumped to the ground, barely conscious. Josh turned and walked back to Silas, stuffing the Red Chalice into his jacket as he did so. The killer was mostly healed now. Josh yanked him to his feet and marched him out of the retort house.

Some time later, du Bois started shovelling dirt into his destroyed mouth.

Du Bois parked close to the lifts in the hotel garage. Only a few people saw him staggering from the Range Rover, but they stared at his filthy, blood-covered clothes and his emaciated appearance. If people had subsequently called the police, none had come to speak to him.

Du Bois managed to shower. Then he called room service and ordered a great deal of food. He spent several hours gorging himself until finally he started to feel better and his body began to bulk out again. All the while he was trying to think where he was most likely to find Mr Brown.

He would need nanite-tipped bullets if he was going after Mr Brown, but that was okay, he knew a way to make them. He slid a magazine into the .45, chambered a round and holstered the pistol. He picked up his bag and headed for the garage and the Range Rover.

As du Bois climbed into the Range Rover, the pain felt as if his head was being split in two. His vision filled with white light.

Du Bois sat in his Range Rover, looking around. He was in Birmingham, he knew that, but he couldn't remember how he had got there. He quickly audited himself. He was missing about four weeks of memory. The last thing he remembered was being in Pohnpei, and recruiting Lodup Satakano for the Kanamwayso operation. He had worked that job alone, just like he always did. He started beating on the steering wheel, the roof, the armoured window, the dashboard, flailing wildly and violently.

'Again!' he shouted. 'A-fucking-gain!' He repeatedly hammered the horn. The few people in the underground garage were staring at the Range Rover.

Eventually he managed to calm down. He understood that some missions were so sensitive they were classified even from the operatives who worked them. It still didn't stop him from feeling utterly violated when it happened.

Malcolm's phone rang. He answered it.

'We need you in London,' Control told him.

41
A Long Time After the Loss

Vic escorted Talia into the stone chamber in the monastery. He was pretty sure it was the place where his clone tank had been but there was no sign of it now. Instead there were three uncomfortable-looking stone benches. Two of the red-robed monks stood against the wall, cowls hiding their features. There was no sign of the black, viscous liquid in the transparent, floating container. Vic was thankful for that. Something about the liquid disquieted him.

Scab was leaning against the wall. Talia looked at him. Vic wasn't sure if she was hurt, frightened or angry. Probably a combination of all three.

'I won't try and hurt myself,' she told Scab.

'Didn't you enjoy the immersion?' Elodie asked. Vic couldn't shake the feeling that there was a degree of cruelty in the feline's question.

'It didn't work,' Talia said simply.

'You'll like this, there's drugs,' Vic told the human nat, hoping to cheer her up.

'And you'll be sold soon,' Elodie added. Vic half-expected Talia to burst into tears. Instead she just turned and looked up at Vic. The 'sect knew she was asking him to kill her. It wasn't self-pity, she just didn't want things to get any worse. Talia hadn't even asked about the eyeless blank in the white linen suit and Panama hat sitting on one of the benches. Or the scorpion made of living brass nestled into the flesh of Scab's right arm.

'Will that thing be any use where we're going?' Vic asked Scab. He'd always hated the Scorpion, partly because it was an arachnid and partly because it hated him – and everything else.

Scab ignored Vic. He turned to Elodie and nodded. The feline smiled. Her prehensile braid darted out.

'Ow!' Talia cried. The stinger on the end of Elodie's braid had embedded itself in Talia's arm. Talia tried to slap the feline but Elodie caught the human girl's hand easily. Vic was already moving towards the two women to separate them.

'Relax, Vic,' Elodie said. 'I was just taking some blood.'

Vic stopped. Talia glared at the feline. The tension was broken by the arrival of Steve's P-sat carrying a tray with its manipulators. On the tray were three vials containing a brackish-looking liquid.

'Can I come with you, please?' Steve whined. 'After all, I made it.'

'The dream dragons made it, you refined it,' Scab said. 'I've programmed the ship. If you want to use your P-sat, it needs to return to the *Basilisk* now.'

'He can go instead of me,' Vic offered. Scab handed Vic one of the vials and gave another to Talia. He watched them both expectantly. The vial's smart matter unsealed the top and Talia knocked back the contents.

Scab turned to Vic. 'Now.'

Vic shook his head, opened his mandibles and drank the liquid in the vial.

There was a brief falling sensation, and it occurred to Vic that he should have sat down before drinking the vial of Key. Talia got there first. They were in a bar or café. Floors of bare wooden boards. Small tables with low stools around them. Several tables held complicated-looking devices filled with water, with tubes running from them that emitted smoke. The bar was polished dark wood, and behind it were racks of dirty bottles. The air was hot and dusty. An open door led to a balcony that looked out over a *souq*. Beyond the *souq* was a complicated city made up of a jumble of architectural styles, everything from adobe and handsomely carved wood to red brick, glass and steel. There were bamboo houses, tree houses and houseboats, and rising above them were domes and minarets. Jungle grew up, around and through the city like a fungal infection.

All sorts of strangeness inhabited the *souq*. Humans with insect heads; centipedes with human faces; oiled, heavily armed gladiators with stylised facemasks and impractical weapons. Green mists floated though the marketplace, mingling with the clouds of smoke rising from it. And everywhere were beautiful young men of every conceivable shade, colour and size that humanity had to offer. The place appeared to be a combination of drug hallucination and monosexualist fantasy.

Talia was looking around. 'Are we in North Africa?' she asked, confused. She was wearing a long, simple, elegant dress with a blue and gold diamond pattern on it. She had no make-up on and her hair was a dark brown colour, long and straight.

'Where?' Vic asked. He was bereft of augmentations, a natural 'sect, yet he was somehow still able to stand up and function in the apparent 1G. He wore a light summer suit, a short-sleeved shirt and had a trilby on his head. He was carrying a Browning Automatic Rifle and had a number of other weapons in various holsters. He moved to the door and glanced out over the *souq*. He could see steps leading down to the marketplace.

Scab walked into the café through a curtain from the back room. He looked much as he had back in the stone chamber, but here his look fitted in better. He laid a Thompson sub-machine gun down on the bar. Vic glimpsed movement under the arm of Scab's suit jacket, the flash of a brass leg burying into flesh.

'Are we all in the same hallucination?' Talia asked, her voice touched with awe.

'Yes,' Vic said.

'No,' Scab said.

'Now this,' said an impossibly deep voice from a table in a window bay, 'this is very civilised.' The table held one of the water pipes and the man was sucking on one of its tubes. A bubbling sound came from the device and then he exhaled smoke. The man was nearly as tall as Vic but managed not to look too uncomfortable on the tiny stool he was sitting on. He was also quite thin. His skin was so black that it appeared to absorb light. Vic assumed it was a cosmetic augment. He wore a light linen suit, an open shirt with no tie and a Panama hat. 'This I thank you for.' He took another hit on the water pipe.

Seated at the table across from him was a human boy who looked to be in his mid-teens, wearing loose-fitting white cotton trousers, his chest bare, head shaved. He was sound asleep. The restful expression on his face and his porcelain skin made him appear somehow beatific.

'I know you,' Vic said to the obsidian-skinned man, desperately trying to remember the man's name. They had worked for him before, but there was something about him he could never quite remember. Vic wasn't sure how that was possible with his neunonics. He should have perfect recall of everything he'd witnessed, but he couldn't even remember this man's name. He noticed that the man was toying with a ring. A speck of material floated over a tiny and complex array set in the ring.

'Is that antimatter?' Vic asked in awe. Talia was looking back and forth between them.

'In a Penning trap setting, yes,' the man said. His voice was so deep, it felt like it was causing pleasant vibrations in the surrounding atmosphere. 'And you may call me Patron.'

Vic nodded as if all it made sense now. Patron took another hit of the bubbling water pipe.

'Are you here to buy me?' Talia asked in a small voice.

'Yes, but I assure you that it's not as bad as it sounds,' Patron said, a pained expression on his face. 'We need access to certain genetic data. You will be exceptionally well treated, and protected.'

'Free?' she asked.

'We will attempt to furnish you with as much freedom as possible, but part of your protection will mean—' he said apologetically.

'A gilded cage,' Talia said.

'I find that very few people use their freedom for anything worthwhile, and would you be free in this age?'

Talia's mouth turned upwards in a small smile. She gestured over her shoulder at Scab with her thumb. 'At least you're nicer than this prick and his bitch girlfriend.'

Vic followed her gesture, and then went cold when he saw Scab shaking with rage.

Scab raised his arm and pointed at the boy. 'What is that?' he managed to ask. Vic had assumed it was Patron's sex toy. He noticed that Talia was looking between the sleeping boy and Scab now, a smile spreading across her face.

'This, Mr Scab, is merely the fulfilment of a promise. You were paid handsomely and you betrayed me. I had an agent of mine warn you in the Living Cities. Proliferation is to be your punishment.' Patron gestured at the sleeping boy. 'Hence the Innocent.'

'Ohmigod!' Talia squealed. 'He's like you, only nice.' Vic was already moving. She looked at Scab. 'You're so cute!'

Vic managed to interpose himself between Scab and Talia before Scab could get to her. He didn't know what violence in the hallucination would mean in the real world but he didn't want to find out. Talia, realising she'd gone too far, was backing away from Scab. Even Patron had his hand up, a worried expression on his obsidian features.

'We are so close,' Vic told his partner/captor. Scab was still staring at the terrified Talia, but he backed off and lit a cigarette.

'He is a social experiment,' Patron said. 'I wanted to know what you would have been like if you had grown up happy and well adjusted, cared for, instead of running feral on Cyst. Would you still have become a monster?'

'I want it dead, before we even start,' Scab said, still shaking.

'Obviously not,' Patron said. It was very clear that he wasn't the slightest bit frightened of Scab.

'How can it remain pure and fight?' Scab asked.

Vic was confused. 'That guy?' Vic said, gesturing at the human boy. 'He couldn't fight his way out of a wet fart.'

'Tailored nightmares. He lives through them,' Patron told the human killer. Scab shook his head and lowered his eyes. Vic wasn't sure, but he thought Scab looked sad. He had no idea what was going on, and then it hit him. He turned and looked at the sleeping human, appalled.

'He's Elite?' Vic asked. Patron nodded.

'He has to die,' Scab spat.

'Perhaps,' Patron said.

'What's wrong with you?' Talia demanded angrily.

Scab turned on her. 'You don't know what I dream of.' He pointed at the Innocent. 'That is wrong. It's an abomination.'

'Who are you?' Vic asked Patron. He was more than a little confused and frightened by Scab's outburst.

'To all intents and purposes, he's the chairman of the board,' a voice said from the balcony.

They looked around. Vic cursed himself. In all the excitement he had forgotten to keep an eye on the steps leading up from the *souq*. Surveillance was a lot easier when he had access to all the sensors in his antennae and a P-sat to help him. The figure standing in the doorway wore a light summer suit, the jacket folded over his arms. His skin was transparent and his flesh had a violet bioluminescent quality to it. Vic wasn't sure if it was the same spokesperson Scab and he had met when they visited the Living Cities on Pangea, but perhaps that wasn't important. The hive mind in the Living Cities shared everything and knew everything the others did. Since the attack on Game, the Living Cities were the dominant power in the Monarchist systems, and it was believed that they controlled the remaining Monarchist Elite.

Patron gave the newcomer a look of naked contempt that bordered on disgust. Vic felt that was unfair. If this was the Elder, the representative Lord of Pangea for the hive mind, then Vic had liked him/them when he'd met him/them. In fact, he/they had been one of the few reasonable people he'd met recently.

'This is clever,' the Elder said to Scab. 'I'm assuming this is the real auction, yes?'

Scab nodded.

'Should there even be an auction?' Patron asked. 'I hired Scab to deliver something to me.' He pointed at Talia. 'And there she is.'

'Do you guys even get that I'm a person?' Talia asked.

Scab was shaking his head absent-mindedly.

'I am afraid you are also a commodity,' the Elder said, not unkindly. 'All I can do is apologise, but I assure you that you will be well looked after.' Then he turned to Scab. 'May I sit down?' Scab ignored him.

Vic gestured to a table. 'Please,' the 'sect said. The Elder sat down. Turning to Patron, Vic said, 'Can I ask you something?'

'Why Scab and you?' Patron asked.

Vic nodded, then pointed at the Innocent. 'You have access to Elite. Why not send them?'

'I wanted it done a little less overtly than that.'

'Oh, yes,' Vic said, practising sarcasm. 'Scab is the soul of discretion.'

'And yet nobody has known of my involvement until now,' Patron pointed out. Vic had to admit that was true, though he had been sure there was board-level involvement somewhere along the line. Patron glanced over at the Elder. 'I underestimated the childishness of the Absolute—'

'You can glare at me all you want, but we are not the same person,' the Elder said. He sounded a little peeved.

'I didn't think the aristos would use their Elite so quickly,' Patron told Vic.

'You know my price,' Scab said. 'And you have to kill that,' he said to Patron, pointing at the Innocent. 'In fact, that would be a good way for you to start the negotiations.'

'We might be able to come to some arrangement regarding the Innocent, though I am rather fond of him. He is a prodigious killer whilst he sleeps. I will not, however, be making you an Elite and turning you loose. In fact, I am disappointed that you want something as paltry and tawdry as mere physical power. Power is there for the taking. If you want to be an Elite so badly and you want the Innocent gone, then come and work for us. You can replace him. I will not be paying you anything more because we already have a deal,' Patron said. 'I'm hoping to avoid bandying around undignified threats but proliferation is still a possibility. In fact, you already have a cult following as a bounty killer and an ex-Elite. We could probably make it quite lucrative. Collectible designer Woodbine Scabs. The market research has come back quite favourably.'

Vic shuddered at the thought. Scab looked over at the Elder.

'We will make you into an Elite,' the Elder said.

'Are you insane?' Vic shouted despite himself. Scab turned slowly to look up at his big 'sect captive/partner. Vic hung his head and fingered his BAR. 'Sorry, Scab.'

Scab looked back to the Elder. 'A free Elite?' Scab asked.

The Elder looked a little uncomfortable. 'It's not that simple—' the Elder started.

'In terms of resources both the Monarchists and ourselves can only sustain three Elite each. If he makes you one, and you go your own way, then I will destroy him,' Patron said.

'We would need you to fight for us,' the Elder said, 'though of your own free will, of course,' he added hurriedly.

'That's exactly the same offer I made,' Patron pointed out. 'And frankly, you working for the Monarchists is just one spoiled child doing the bidding of another.'

'I don't care if they destroy you,' Scab told the Elder.

'You don't think we'd go after their Citadel?' Patron asked. 'Which you'd need to sustain you.'

'You know, I'm starting to think that you're just not very bright,' Talia said. Vic was making gestures for her to be quiet with all four of his limbs, behind Scab's back. 'Oh, what?' she demanded. 'He's either going to kill me or sell me. What difference does it make what I say?'

He can still hurt you, Vic thought.

'Has it occurred to you that he just likes watching both of you fight?' Talia demanded. Vic thought that was as good a motivation as any for Scab.

A human walked in. He was wearing a black suit and shirt with an odd white collar, and had short blond hair and bright blue eyes. Vic raised the BAR to his shoulder.

'A bit melodramatic, isn't it, Mr Matto?' the man asked as he moved around the bar and started pouring himself a drink.

'I brought you here for security,' Scab snapped at Vic. He drew his Webley .455 revolver with one hand and his Broomhandle Mauser with the other.

'I've always wondered if those really work here,' the man said.

'They work,' Vic and Scab said together.

The man glanced down at the Thompson sub-machine gun on the bar. 'Probably shouldn't have left that lying around, then, should you?' the man asked.

'Do I know you?' Talia asked. Her face was scrunched up in confused concentration.

'I don't think we've ever been formally introduced,' the blond man said. Then he looked around at the café. 'Do you know, I think my sister knew Burroughs? In the 50s, though I believe he was frightened of women.'

Vic, Scab and Talia stared at the man.

'Are you a priest?' Talia asked.

'He's *the* priest,' Patron said. He didn't look at all pleased to see the priest, though he showed the man none of the contempt he had for the Elder.

'Mr Chairman, always a pleasure.' The blond priest raised his glass. He glanced over at the Elder, a look of distaste on his face.

'You're Churchman,' Scab said.

'A pleasure to meet you, Mr Scab. In fact, I've been trying to meet you for some time now. I believe you killed a friend of mine.'

'Not so much that she couldn't be cloned,' Scab said. 'The *Templar*?'

'We'll deal with the *Templar* the moment we have Miss Luckwicke,' Churchman said and bowed towards her.

'It's been a while since I was this popular,' Talia muttered.

'What are you doing here?' Scab demanded. Vic was sure it was the first time he'd ever heard Scab sound unsure of himself. There were a lot of firsts involved in this. Scab was well outside his comfort zone, and Vic could only imagine that this would end in a severe psychotic episode.

There was a dry chuckle from Patron. 'Do you not think that we've been doing this for a while?' the tall obsidian-skinned man asked.

'After all, where did you get the know-how from? One of my ex-employees, perhaps?' Churchman asked. 'I'm intrigued – how did you work it out?'

'St ... the Alchemist, he was a bridge tech, not a chemist,' Scab said. 'Key is either involved in bridge technology, or more likely a by-product, because the Alchemist retained some residual knowledge of it after he escaped you, even after the Church conditioning had kicked in.'

'Unlike Miss Luckwicke, I don't think you are stupid, Mr Scab,' Churchman said. 'You may be a screaming red psychotic, but you have an enquiring mind. Have you any idea how rare that is these days?' Churchman glanced at Patron as he asked this last.

Vic had been puzzling through something. The thought was just out of reach. 'Are we in Red Space?' Vic asked.

'Not quite, Mr Matto,' Churchman said.

'We're not hallucinating?' Talia asked. Then frowned. 'It feels a little specific for a hallucination.'

'What's going on, then?' Vic asked. 'Where are we?'

'Unknown Kadath, Interzone, arguably Wonderland,' Churchman told them after a moment's thought. Vic and Scab looked confused. Talia, on the other hand, was pleased that she actually knew what someone was talking about for once. 'It's what we see in the corner of a dream or glimpse on potent drugs. It is the designer-mutated space-time fabric of an engineered universe, or rather the minds that engineered that universe, and it has been explored by creative minds and the ferociously hallucinating a long time before crude metal ships found it. Key, the secretion from the dream dragons' glands, augments and guides a naturally occurring chemical in the brain called dimethyltryptamine.'

'DMT?' Talia asked. Churchman nodded. 'Hmm, I think I've taken that.'

'I find myself unsurprised,' Churchman said.

'It was intense.'

Patron was shaking his head. 'When did you become such a romantic?' he asked.

'I'm starting to appreciate things,' Churchman said. Vic was surprised to hear sympathy in his tone. 'I wish you could, too.'

Patron looked out of the window, over the *souq* and the confused-looking city, but Vic had seen the expression of anger on the obsidian-skinned man's face.

'And are you here to offer a bid?' the Elder enquired.

Churchman shrugged. 'Actually, I was wondering if I could nick a fag,' he said to Scab. Scab looked at him blankly. 'A cigarette.' Scab reached into his suit jacket pocket and removed his cigarette case. He offered one to Churchman, who took it. Scab lit it for him. Churchman inhaled deeply and then exhaled the smoke. 'So good,' he said. Vic shook his head.

'Enough of this,' Patron said, standing up and walking over to Scab. 'Listen to me. I can make your dream a reality with such totality – your *true* dream, not this foolish power fantasy that you know can never be realised. That is just an excuse to fail again, to self-destruct.' Patron paused before speaking again, carefully enunciating each word: 'I can take your pain away.'

Scab swallowed hard, and again Vic saw something new in Scab's facial expression, something he'd never thought to see on Scab's face. Vulnerability. Vic had spent most of his recent existence living in fear – of Scab, the Church, the Consortium, the Monarchists – but somehow what he had just seen scared him the most. Churchman was watching the exchange carefully as he smoked his cigarette.

'Whereas we have offered something tangible,' the Elder said in exasperation, 'rather than vague promises' – he nodded towards Patron – 'and spiritual well-being' – he nodded towards Churchman.

'I have offered nothing,' Churchman pointed out.

'If you want succour, then join with the collective in the Living Cities,' the Elder said irritably.

'I am a disease,' Scab told the Elder. 'Do you have anything to offer?' he asked Churchman.

'I don't think there's anything we have that you want,' Churchman said, 'and I can't see an appeal to your benevolent nature being a great deal of use.' Scab turned away from him. 'Unless you want answers.' Scab turned back to face Churchman.

'Answers to what?' Vic asked.

'You're not seriously considering his offer, are you?' Patron demanded. Scab didn't reply. He was studying Churchman. Churchman's face was impassive.

'I think we should go with him,' Talia said, meaning Churchman.

Patron sighed. 'Being reasonable just doesn't work, does it? You have no idea how much you owe me,' the obsidian-skinned man told Scab.

'What does that mean?' Scab demanded. Vic noticed his partner/captor's fists were clenched, knuckles whitening.

'Do you accept my bid?' Patron demanded.

Scab glanced between Churchman and Patron. Again Vic saw the indecision on the human killer's face. Vic suddenly started to feel mounting terror about Scab accepting Patron's bid.

'There is a time limit on this,' Patron said. Vic cringed. He saw his partner's face harden. Too late, Patron realised his mistake. Patron straightened up and took a step back. 'Very well. Did it not occur to you that we knew of this place? I mean, if he could find you ...' Patron nodded towards Churchman.

Vic watched in horror as smoke billowed out of two corners in the café. The Innocent opened his eyes and sat up.

'Father, I had a dream,' he told Patron.

They leaped out of the corners. They were indeterminate, quadrupedal, crystalline, not fully present and painful to look at. It was as if they were warping local space. Vic brought the BAR to his shoulder and started firing. The bullets elicited little puffs of strangely crystalline smoke that dissipated into hard-to-see places. Patron reached out and took the Innocent's hand, and they disappeared. One of the crystalline entities leaped. The Elder stood up. The entity leaped through him and the Elder collapsed, his cleanly severed head falling from his shoulders. An acrid, chemical smell filled the air.

Churchman turned and walked into the back room. The other thing leaped at Scab. Scab swung his right arm at it. The Scorpion's sting tore out of the sleeve of his suit jacket and violated the space where the thing was leaping. There was a strange, discordant, unnatural-sounding howling.

'Dancing with tears in my eyes,' Scab said.

They were back in the stone chamber in the monastery. Patron was standing over them. Some very competent-looking people in light-combat exoskeletons had the two monks and Elodie down on their knees and were covering them with assault cannons. The Innocent was standing next to Patron, clothed in the black, liquid glass of Elite armour. He held his weapon, now in a rifle configuration, loosely in his left hand. Something about his body language suggested to Vic that he was asleep. He was twitching as if he wasn't enjoying the experience.

'You were like a beacon,' Patron told them.

Vic glanced over at Talia. She looked terrified. He would try and kill her, but with an Elite present he didn't fancy his chances.

'We have a sizeable fleet outside. You need to know this is over, and I want you to remember that you could have been reasonable.'

Scab narrowed his eyes.

The cave smelled of meat and the copper tang of blood. The Lochlannach lay dead or dying. Guidgen walked among the injured, harvesting their throats with his sickle, muttering prayers and invocations to the Horned God.

Nerthach looked around at the dead Lochlannach, grinning, spattered with blood. 'This is a good day's work,' the big Brigante warrior said.

They killed two horses riding hard to the cave entrance that led to Annwn, in the shadow of the Mother Hill, but they had brought spare mounts. They came in as stealthily as they could, boiled leather armour and scabbards oiled against creaking. All of the warriors had eschewed metal armour, and even Nerthach, the largest of them, had made little noise. It didn't matter. There was some kind of ghost fence. Tangwen felt it, and she knew the others had as well. It was like walking through cobwebs. Crom Dhubh knew they were there.

They killed the two sentries quietly at the entrance and rushed into the cave mouth, but the Lochlannach were waiting for them. The nine of them fought like children of the gods of war, and the slave warriors in the service of Crom Dhubh fell to the power in their weapons.

Tangwen watched, crouched over a corpse, as Britha walked deeper into the cave. She was surprised by how far she could see into the darkness, though the colours had become strange. She took a step back when Britha turned to look at her and the *dryw*'s eyes glowed. It was only then that she really understood that the other woman was a demon, what she herself and the others had become. She stood up and followed the *dryw*. Slowly, one by one, the others did the same.

Tangwen wasn't sure when they crossed over into Annwn but she was certainly there now. Once she would have been afraid clinging to a rock wall in a chasm above nothing but darkness. But now her eyes saw in a ghost light, and her companions had become spirits of white and green. She wondered if Brys and Madawg were happy now they were in Annwn.

Where once she would have moved cautiously, feeling for hand- and footholds, she followed Britha's movements with confidence. She even leaned away from the rock face to look up at the others. Only Britha had kept her spear; the other spears and staffs had been left up at the top of the chasm. Nerthach and Brys had their large shields and Madawg his smaller, lighter shield, slung or strapped to their backs. Likewise, Kush's axe was strapped across his back.

Tangwen kept climbing down. She could see the black water below her now.

They put their weapons into the two large, upturned shields and pushed out into the black waters of the lake, following Britha, who appeared to know exactly where she was going.

Tangwen was cold to her very bones, but although she did not really feel it, this did not stop her shivering. She felt like they had been swimming for a very long time. Gradually she was able to make out the island ahead of her. With each stroke she saw a little more of it. With every stroke the charnel smell was a bit stronger. She heard muttered curses and the sound of people trying to spit as they swam. Guidgen was praying. She could not imagine anywhere further from the reach of the Horned God. She was disgusted when she noticed that Madawg was smiling. She could not read Britha's expression, and this worried her.

She glimpsed small, misshapen, bent-over figures moving around in the shadow of the horrible tower of bone. Strangely regular-looking rootlike structures ran from its base and into the water. Behind the island, there was a faint, pale glow coming from the water. Then they started swimming through the boneless corpses, pushing them aside as they bumped against them. She watched the small twisted figures leaping from body to body, feeding on them. They looked like deformed children, but Tangwen assumed they were *dorch*, evil, diminutive spirits that consumed the flesh of the living and the dead alike. Tangwen tasted bile in the back of her throat. Both Nerthach and Germelqart vomited into the water, but managed, somehow, to keep swimming.

Then they were at the island, crawling up onto muddy stones. The tower of bones looked as if it had grown from the rock. There was something both fragile and actually quite beautiful about it. The *dorch* kept their distance, swaying, watching them with eyes like black pools. If they moved towards the *dorch*, the small creatures backed away. Tangwen walked around the tower. On the opposite side of the island she was surprised to discover that the light was coming from under the water. The water looked clear, and she could see the rock bottom of the lake. There was a circle of stones, and beyond that some other structure that she couldn't quite make out.

'Where is this chalice?' Nerthach asked. His voice sounded obscenely loud in this still, dead realm. 'I like this place not.'

'It was at the summit of the tower the last time,' Britha said.

'It is not there now.' The voice was like a sickness in the back of their minds, but at the same time was soft and deep, somehow seductive. Tangwen saw him walk out of the water. He was tall, taller even than Kush, and his skin was the colour of pitch. It hurt her head to look at him. She backed towards the others, and they advanced slowly towards her. In one hand Crom Dhubh clutched the chalice of red gold. Tangwen could just about make out its contents, bubbling away inside. None of the red, liquid metal seeped out, regardless of how he tipped the chalice. In the other hand he held a black-bladed sword with a strangely complicated-looking hilt that projected light down the black blade. It made a slight humming noise.

Crom Dhubh held the chalice up. 'Is this what you have come here for?' he asked.

'That can help us heal the land,' Guidgen said. '*You* could heal the land.' The *gwyllion dryw* took a step back when Crom Dhubh looked at him.

'It is not my nature,' the Dark Man told him. Nerthach spat and made the sign against evil. Crom Dhubh looked at him for a moment.

'What is your nature, then?' Guidgen asked.

'I am pain,' Crom Dhubh said.

Sadhbh laughed. Tangwen cringed.

'A hollow warrior's boast, nothing more,' the Iceni warrior said. Tangwen had to give the Iceni woman her due, she was doing better at hiding her fear than she was.

'I don't think you understand,' Crom Dhubh said.

'Are you anything more than a whispering, mocking spirit?' Britha demanded. Crom Dhubh's head wrenched around to look at her.

'I thought you had made your deal with my slave?' he asked. Britha did not answer, and Tangwen could see pain etched on her face. 'Tell me, how will you now oppose me without a fifth-dimensional parasite consuming your mind?'

Britha looked confused.

'I am not sure what you hope to gain here,' Crom Dhubh said. 'Go or stay, you are merely postponing the inevitable. The only worthwhile thing you can do is take your own lives.' He turned and walked back towards the water.

'You're not going to try and kill us?' Britha asked, surprised.

Crom Dhubh stopped but he did not turn around. 'Why would I offer you the release that my ... that I cannot achieve myself?'

'It is nothing to you to save our land, is it?' Guidgen asked.

'No,' Crom Dhubh admitted. 'It makes no difference to me at all. I have what I need.'

'You're going to the *Ubh Blaosc*?' Britha asked. Germelqart looked over at her from where he stood behind Kush. Crom Dhubh did not answer.

'And what is it you have come for?' There were shouts of surprise and shuffling as people changed position. Bress, wearing only shirt, trews and boots, was standing by the edge of the water, one hand on the hilt of his sword. He held a bronze rod in the other hand.

'Take me with you,' Britha said. The others muttered.

'Traitor!' Nerthach shouted at her. He started towards her but Bress moved to intercept.

'It will be the last thing you ever do,' he told the Brigante warrior. Tangwen squeezed her eyes shut. Britha had told her of the child, and his father, and how the *dryw* had taken her. Though she had no children of her own, she could understand why Britha wanted to cut a deal with Bress, and with his master.

'If I have walked you into a trap, tell me the purpose of it!' Britha said to Nerthach. She sounded tired.

'You would trade us for what you want!' Sadhbh spat.

Crom Dhubh laughed. Deep and sonorous, the noise was devoid of humour. 'What makes you think you are so important?' the Dark Man asked.

'We have defeated you once,' Kush said.

'You changed things. If you could see from my perspective you would understand inevitability, and how utterly inconsequential we all are. You more than me.'

'I tire of this,' Nerthach said. 'We have killed their men.' He pointed at Crom Dhubh. 'This one is a coward.' Then he pointed at Bress. 'And this one is no more of a warrior than any of us.'

'You fool, that one is as a god!' Brys hissed at the Brigante warrior, meaning Crom Dhubh. Nerthach spared the grey-bearded warrior a look of contempt.

Bress wasn't listening to Nerthach's words, however. He was staring at Britha.

'Please,' she whispered.

'Your friends are about to kill themselves,' Bress said quietly, his face an impassive mask.

'I hate you,' Britha told him.

He nodded. 'It is for the best.'

The Dark Man was watching Britha and Bress closely. There was more humourless laughter. Tangwen couldn't understand why Crom Dhubh was laughing but she saw the look of horror on Bress's face.

Nerthach strode across the island toward Crom Dhubh. The Dark Man watched him approach.

'This is the single greatest thing you will ever do in your life,' Crom Dhubh told the big Brigante.

'I will not even think of you as I drink from your skull,' Nerthach told him. He raised his sword to strike. Crom Dhubh stabbed forward with his sword. It touched Nerthach's shield. A painfully bright white light flared and Nerthach came apart as a silhouette.

Tangwen found herself lying in the water, staring up at the tooth-like protrusions of rock on the cavern ceiling, screaming. It felt like the acid burn she had received from fighting Andraste's spawn, only much, much worse. The entire front of her body had been charred. Slowly she started to feel better. The blackened dead skin flaked off into the water, and her armour, which had fused with her scorched flesh, was being pushed out of her by pink new meat. Now more than ever, her power, the capabilities of the demons in her flesh imbibed from Britha's blood, frightened her. This was not natural. She should be dead.

She could see the others now. She had been the closest, but all of them, even Bress, had been knocked down. Kush and Germelqart had also been blown back into the water and were crawling up onto the island. Somehow the tower was still standing.

There was no sign of Nerthach. Crom Dhubh was still standing where he had been, the sword down by his side.

The pain gone, her flesh healed, Tangwen started swimming back towards the land.

'We have no choice now,' Guidgen was saying. The old *dryw* sounded frightened, really frightened, as if he was only just holding it together. 'We must have it.' As Tangwen reached the island, the others were shuffling around, half-heartedly preparing to attack Crom Dhubh. No one wanted to be the first to strike. Tangwen crouched low. All she had to do was deliver a killing blow without the sword touching her, but like the others she could not quite make herself attack the Dark Man.

Bress moved away from Britha to stand between Crom Dhubh and the others. He still held the rod in his left hand.

'This bores me,' the Dark Man said and turned towards the water. Sadhbh threw a dagger at his back. Bress stepped into its path, grunting in pain as the blade embedded itself just below his shoulder. Sadhbh was already moving, drawing another dagger, her short sword in her right hand. The others surged forwards. Bress drew his long-bladed sword one-handed. He stepped to the side and continued swinging the blade up as it cleared the scabbard. Sadhbh didn't even notice that she no longer had forearms before Bress reversed the blade and cut off the back of her skull. Madawg was close behind Sadhbh. The frail-looking warrior was surprisingly fast. Bress thrust his sword at him, but Madawg reversed direction, grabbed Brys and pulled him in front as a human shield. Brys all but ran onto Bress's blade, a look of surprise on the old warrior's face. As Bress wrenched his blade free, Madawg put his hand on Brys's shoulder and jumped into the air over his dead comrade's head to stab at Bress's face. Bress jerked his head back, but Madawg opened a line of red on his porcelain skin. Madawg rapidly backed away. Brys's body slid off Bress's blade and fell to the ground. Tangwen was almost on him, but she was brought up short by Bress's sword. She backed away. The others were doing likewise. Tangwen had never seen a swordsman like Bress. Madawg had been lucky to cut him, even if he had to sacrifice his fellow tribesman to do it.

Crom Dhubh had continued walking towards the water. He stepped forwards, his toe touching the pool, making it ripple.

'Hello, Sotik,' Germelqart said. Crom Dhubh stopped moving. 'I can't believe you didn't realise I was here.'

Crom Dhubh stopped and turned around. 'I was wondering if you'd have the courage to speak. I never knew your name.'

'Germelqart will suffice.'

'I do not think that was the name you went by then.'

'It is who I am, who I have been for so long now.'

All the others were staring at the Carthaginian.

'Tell me, were you in my wicker man?' Crom Dhubh asked. Germelqart nodded. Crom Dhubh glanced over at Bress.

'He had no way of knowing,' the Carthaginian said.

Crom Dhubh stalked towards the small navigator. The others made way for him despite themselves and Germelqart took an involuntary step back.

'And if I asked you why?' the Dark Man asked.

'We had no idea. You were so full of promise. We sought to communicate—'

Crom Dhubh stared at Germelqart. Tangwen could see so much pain on the Dark Man's face that just for a moment she felt sorry for him. Crom Dhubh squeezed his eyes shut, holding the chalice in a tightly clenched fist in front of Germelqart's face. When he opened his eyes, Tangwen was amazed to see tears rolling down his cheeks.

'It would be easiest for me to kill you, all of you. None can know,' he said. Now Tangwen could hear it in his voice. It sounded as if the Dark Man was in considerable physical pain.

'Know what?' Tangwen asked. Crom Dhubh's head spun around, and he gave her a look so filled with malice that she actually took a step back.

'Give them the chalice, kill me.' Germelqart said.

Crom Dhubh laughed.

'No,' Kush said and made to move to Germelqart's side. Bress walked across to stand by Crom Dhubh, facing the Numibian. Kush readied his axe.

'You are my sacrifice, are you?' Crom Dhubh asked. 'I could kill you and keep the chalice, you realise?'

Germelqart swallowed and looked around. 'I do not think you are the creature of spite you pretend to be.'

Crom Dhubh stared down at the smaller man. 'There is nothing left of who I was, and you never knew me. I've had a thousand names and been a thousand people since then, and I will be a thousand more before I am done. You may not have the chalice. You can live with your guilt a little longer, but you may not speak of me.'

To Tangwen's ears, he almost sounded like a *dryw* pronouncing a curse. Crom Dhubh dropped the sword and then moved like a striking snake. Wriggling black tendrils extended from his fingers and he rammed them into Germelqart's head. She could see them moving under the navigator's skin.

Kush was moving. He swung his axe at Bress, who was in his way. Bress parried the blow. Tangwen was running. Madawg was looking for an opening. Kush caught the blade of Bress's sword on one of the blades of his axe and yanked hard, pulling the sword out of Bress's hand. Bress continued moving forwards, ramming his long-fingered hand with its long, pointed nails into Kush's chest cavity. Through armour, through hardening skin and bone, his fingers closed around Kush's beating heart and he tore it out.

'No!' Tangwen cried and flew at Bress. He backhanded her,

powdering the bone in her jaw, sending her spinning through the air. Kush toppled to the muddy rock.

Madawg reached for the Dark Man's fallen sword. Crom Dhubh tore the metallic tendrils out of Germelqart's head and kicked Madawg. The sound of the frail-looking warrior's ribs breaking echoed through the cavern. Madawg arced up high into the air from the force of the blow, landing in the cold water.

Germelqart sank to his knees, staring at Kush's body. The damage was too much for even the newly imbibed magics to overcome.

Tangwen threw her hatchet from her crouched position. Bress batted it out of the air. When he turned to check on Crom Dhubh, Britha ran him through with her spear. Then she spat in his face.

'At least I looked in your eyes!' she told him.

Bress spat blood down his chest as he looked at the haft of the spear sticking out of his body. 'You have to promise me you'll kill it,' he said. It sounded like begging. He sank to his knees. Britha stared at him. She looked down at his left hand, but the bronze rod was gone.

Tangwen ran past them, leaning down as she ran to grab Bress's sword from the ground. She swung the sword two-handed at Crom Dhubh's left arm as the Dark Man was turning to face her. The sword severed his arm. Crom Dhubh stared at her impassively. Tangwen had to resist the overwhelming urge to apologise.

Guidgen stood on the arm and grabbed the Red Chalice. With some difficulty, he managed to wrench it free of the severed arm's fingers. Crom Dhubh was still staring at Tangwen. She backed away, colliding with Germelqart.

'We have to go,' the hunter whispered to him. She was terrified. She had angered a god. Terrible things happened to mortals who dared to anger the gods. She dropped Bress's sword.

Guidgen dived into the cold lake with the Red Chalice. Crom Dhubh reached down and picked up his severed arm. Britha was staring at Kush's body.

'Germelqart! Britha! Please!' Tangwen pleaded.

Crom Dhubh held his severed arm to its stump and the black flesh started to knit together. Tangwen glanced around and saw Germelqart. Britha cast one last look at Bress, still coughing blood before turning and diving into the lake. Tangwen ran to the Carthaginian and dragged the navigator into the cold, black waters.

Crom Dhubh reached down and grabbed the haft of the spear protruding from Bress's chest. His will crushed the will of the demon in the spear. The head of the weapon re-formed and he slid it out of Bress's chest without causing much more damage.

Bress fell forwards onto all fours, spitting blood. Crom Dhubh went to stand on the island's rocky shore and watched them swim away from him. Eventually Bress managed to stand up and stagger over to join the dark man.

'Where is it?' Crom Dhubh asked. Bress held up his left arm. The flesh distended and the control rod grew through Bress's skin. 'Send the hounds,' he said, meaning the transformed children, 'or the giants. Bring back the chalice. Leave the ones they call Germelqart and Britha alive.'

Bress spat out more blood. 'You need to decide which one of your machinations you care about most,' Bress said. 'Without the chalice, Britha will be consumed by the Muileartach's spawn. That particular plan of yours will not come to fruition.'

Crom Dhubh turned to look at Bress. Bress would not meet his eyes.

'If only you knew what a mockery you truly are,' Crom Dhubh told him. 'Very well, let them go. It makes no difference to me.'

Crom Dhubh turned and walked away, leaving Bress standing alone by the edge of the dark waters.

43

Close to the Oceanic Pole
of Inaccessibility, Now

The images were coming faster now. Cold, murky, dark water. A modern coastal city viewed through the mud. He suspected it was in the UK somewhere. It looked familiar. Something was alive in the mud. Something ancient and—

He was stalking back and forth in his room. Features contorted, the ends of his fingers covered in blood, turning to look at the wall, except he was the reflection watching himself scream, his throat moving unnaturally as if the cries had a physical presence and was trying to get out. Then he turned away from the wall and picked up the diamond-bladed dive knife from the bed. He sank to his knees. His eyes rolled up into his head. He looked as if he was praying, or speaking in tongues. He brought the knife up to his temple.

He was standing on a blackened plain. The sky was red.

Everything was light, and agony.

Coldness, and nothing.

Lodup opened his eyes. He was breathing fast and hard, gulping down air. He was on the bed in his room. The lights were flickering, sometimes leaving him in total darkness. His eyes were trying to compensate. Geothermal power and backup fusion reactors meant that this was not supposed to happen.

The room smelled funky. He had been confined there for two weeks, ever since Germelqart was shot, and had left the room only to be interrogated. Not verbally. He was sedated and given what they called a neural audit. Other than the nurses and a doctor in the medical centre, the only people he'd seen were Yaroslav and Siska. Siska was distant, Yaroslav angry. There was a sense of despair about them that neither had been able to hide, however. It was as if they were just going through the motions. Even Siraja had been strange with him.

It had been a frightening two weeks. He heard shouting, screams and gunfire more than once. Nobody told him anything, but listening at the door he guessed that the suicides and the number of people going thatch were increasing. He spent most of the time watching junk media on his wall screen and doing what exercise he could, though his body didn't really appear to need it these days. He had been trying to deaden the fear by numbing his mind. It hadn't worked.

There was dried blood on his pillow. He touched it, and then touched his head and his ears. He found more on his temples and in both ears, and on his T-shirt, but no sign of a wound. He assumed that the nano-technology running through his body had repaired any wounds. He half-remembered the sickening crack of a skull being pierced.

His dive knife was lying on the floor. There was dried blood on the blade and still-wet blood in a pool on the floor around it. He climbed off his bed and got down on all fours to inspect the knife and the blood, his vision still trying to compensate for the flickering light. There was something else there – a clear, viscous liquid. Just a tiny drop of it among the blood, but not mixing with it in any way. Lodup gingerly picked up his dive knife and poked the clear liquid with the diamond tip of the blade. It moved like mercury.

'Siraja?' Lodup said out loud. There was no answer. Then he realised he was receiving no information at all from the habitat. He tried turning on the media library. Nothing. He appeared to be completely cut off.

Then he noticed the door. There were bloody fingermarks all over it. It looked as if he'd been clawing at it. He checked his fingers – more dried blood but no wounds. He realised he felt hungry. Then he remembered what happened yesterday when he ordered food. It had appeared crawling with maggots, something that categorically shouldn't happen when your food was entirely synthetic and assembled at a molecular level.

Lodup realised he wasn't alone. He turned and threw himself at the bed in shock, but the figure was there behind him as well. Siraja, pointing at him in the flickering light, his draconic maw wide open. Suddenly the noise was deafening. It sounded like a million agonised voices but there was a strange electronic quality to the sound. Lodup saw faces growing through the AI's skin, all of them talking in a language Lodup had never heard which hurt his head to hear. It was formed of sounds he didn't think he could make. Then he realised that Siraja wasn't subjectively in the room with him. He was on the screens, an image of him on each wall as if he was trapped in there. Then the image was gone. He felt as if he could still hear the voices, and the obscene language.

He actually flinched at the sound of a crack appearing and running all the way around the four walls of his room and his door. The door juddered open a little. Lodup knew that the synthetic diamond-analogue from which the habitat had been grown shouldn't crack like that. He stood up and moved over to the door and peeked through the small gap. The lights were flickering, a few of them hanging down from the ceiling. Outside, the dormitory plaza looked as if it had been extensively trashed and he saw smears of blood, a lot of it, on the walls and the floor. He couldn't get much of an angle to see properly, but he was sure there was a body lying on the ground just out of sight.

He backed away from the door and sat down on his bed. He could feel a strange kind of pressure building in his head and the flickering light was starting to get to him. Judging by what he had seen outside, calling for help wasn't a good idea. He might be safest in his room, but with no food he wouldn't last long. He stood up and walked into the shower cubicle/wet room and tried the tap. What came out of it was thick, and black, and viscous, and there was no way he was drinking it. He returned to the bed. He reached for the dive knife.

He used the knife to jemmy the door open far enough to squeeze through it.

Outside on the balcony overlooking the plaza, he saw that the damage was extensive. Apparently he'd slept through a very violent riot. A number of the light strips weren't working, and in the flickering gloom he could see four bodies, three clustered around a fourth – one of Yaroslav's security detail.

Lodup listened hard but heard nothing except a steady dripping noise, which he hoped wasn't blood. The crack in the wall worried him. If the structural integrity of the habitat was failing, there was only so much time left before it was crushed. He didn't want to be inside if that happened. Then he realised he no longer felt the strong compulsion to stay that he'd experienced before. He'd always known it was some kind of conditioning, and now it was gone. Now he desperately wanted to get out.

He moved over as quietly as he could to the four bodies. Three were worker clones – he recognised one of them as the clone of someone he'd worked with in the Kwajalein Atoll. It looked like they'd charged the security guard and he'd shot them, then shot himself.

Lodup pushed the clones aside and, with some difficulty, took the security guard's integrated webbing and body armour off and put it on. The webbing/body armour held a sidearm, ammunition and non-lethal weapons in various pouches and holsters. Lodup then picked up the suppressed .45 calibre Vector SMG and checked the magazine. Some of the rounds had obviously been fired, so he pocketed the magazine and loaded a fresh one. He checked the underslung M26 Modular Accessory Shotgun System. There was one cartridge missing from the five-round box magazine. He decided he could live with that. It looked like the shotgun was loaded with solid shot. He'd had basic weapons training when he'd joined the Navy, but his knowledge of the sub-machine gun was something that had been programmed into him.

Lodup moved forwards, SMG at the ready, checking all around him as he went. He would make for the moon pool, and then make his decision.

They were just standing there, about two hundred of the clones, their backs to him, staring straight ahead. They were in the destroyed plaza of the dormitory block next to Lodup's. He had to go through the block to get to the moon pool.

They hadn't given any indication they knew he was there. He was crouched behind an overturned genetically modified palm tree, staring at their backs, trying to remember to check around him as well. His heart felt like it was trying to beat its way out of his chest. This was the same plaza where he'd seen a number of them congregated around a stone effigy taken from the Kanamwayso. The effigy was still there, but they didn't appear to be praying to it any more.

He knew there were other ways to get to the moon pool aside from through this dormitory block, but he wasn't sure of them. He realised he had become too reliant on Siraja doing things for him.

He knew that if they turned on him, despite the fact they appeared to be unarmed, he wouldn't stand a chance. Also, he didn't relish the idea of shooting a lot of people, whether they were clones or not. He'd noticed a number of bodies scattered around the upper levels of the balcony. More than a few of them were security guards, and they showed the signs of having been subjected to significant violence.

Lodup swallowed hard and glanced behind him. The way back through to his own dormitory block was still open. He couldn't sneak past them without being noticed.

Gun levelled at the clones, he moved back through the jammed-open doors into his dormitory block, then used one of the doors for partial cover. He swallowed hard. He knew he should be sweating, but the modifications had made his body a lot more efficient.

'Hey!' he hissed. There was no response. He knew he'd been too quiet. 'Hey!' he said a bit louder, his heart hammering as he did so.

He knew this was a profoundly stupid thing to do. 'Hey!' he shouted. His human voice sounded out of place here, a violation, somehow. There was no way they couldn't have heard him. He had the strong urge to look behind him. He spun round, Vector at the ready, but there was nothing to see. He turned back to the plaza full of drones. They hadn't moved.

'Shit, shit, shit, shit,' he muttered quietly to himself. He didn't feel as if he could move. He had to force himself to take a step over the lip of the hatch back into the plaza. He moved forward as quietly as he could, hating every tiny jingle or rattle his gear made. As quietly as he could, he made his way towards the closest stairway that led up to the balcony levels. He had to pass quite close to one of the clones. On the one hand, he wanted to look away. On the other, he knew he had to cover them. He did it quickly. He felt close to panic. He was breathing hard again, but not from the exertion.

He went up the stairs quickly and moved along the first balcony. The balconies felt like the safest option – he didn't want to walk through the clones. He couldn't bring himself to look down at them, but he could still see them in his peripheral vision, standing stock still, and their presence was a palpable pressure.

Something about the image wasn't right. He found his head slowly turning to look at them. Their eyes. They were black. No pupil, iris or sclera. They looked like black pools. Something about the eyes reminded him of the thing that had come from the black brine sump.

He returned his attention to the balcony. Sal was standing in front of him. She hadn't been there the moment before, and he hadn't registered any movement. Her eyes were the same as all the others'. Despite her eyes, it was still quite difficult for him to point the gun at her.

'Sal?'

She did not reply but she was definitely looking at him. He glanced down into the plaza. Now all the other black-eyed clones were facing the balcony, staring up at him. He swallowed again, tried to control his breathing. He felt rooted to the spot.

'Sal ...' His voice was cracking. 'Please, I don't want to hurt you.'

He forced himself to take a step forward. She did nothing. Then another, and another, until he was standing right in front of her. She still hadn't done or said anything, but she was watching him intently.

'You're not Sal.' Because Sal was dead. *Hideo told you she was dead*, he thought, and he hadn't seen her since he was presented with her scalp.

There was no response. He stepped to one side and moved past her. Nothing happened. He tried to resist the urge to flee. He failed.

He finally managed to gather the courage to stop running in the corridor that led to the moon pool. He checked behind him, and then remembered to bring the Vector up as he did so. He had felt their eyes on him as he ran along the balcony, down the stairs and out of that dorm block. The other dorm blocks were empty. Although he'd found more dead bodies, more blood and signs of violence, a lot of the clone workforce was still unaccounted for.

A number of bodies lay on the grass-like carpet of the corridor. He had come out with nothing on his feet. It was foolish, he realised, but force of habit. He rarely wore shoes, or boots unless he knew he needed them. There was, in theory, no glass in the habitat for him to stand on. He noticed that the warm, grass-like material of the carpet was longer. If he stood in one place for more than a couple of seconds, he felt the grass adhering to the soles of his feet, and there was a sucking sensation as he moved away.

He heard whale song. Just for a moment. It sounded wrong, warped somehow, twisted.

The bodies in the corridor were mainly members of the security contingent. They all appeared to have been the victims of violence, but it was difficult to tell for sure because they looked partially melted, or eaten, and there was a white, weblike growth over them. In horror, Lodup realised that that the weblike growth was coming from the carpet. It was consuming the bodies, recycling them.

The habitat shifted under him and then lurched violently.

He looked up and saw a wave of water rolling down the corridor towards him. He fought the urge to panic, again. If this was the habitat depressurising due to loss of structural integrity, for whatever reason, it would collapse in on itself like an aluminium can run over by a truck. If it was just the habitat shifting position, he might still be in with a chance. The freezing-cold, clear water rolled over his feet, came up to his ankles and then started to recede. Lodup breathed a sigh of relief and pulled his feet free of the disconcerting carpet. He brought the SMG up and continued to move cautiously towards the moon pool.

Lodup stared. The ADSs and submersibles looked like they had partially rotted away. They were missing huge chunks of their superstructure, as if something had taken bites out of them. The gun towers were also decaying – Lodup could see inside them. Something appeared to be growing through one of the larger submersibles, creating bizarre shapes, stillborn monsters caught in the distended bodywork of the machine.

He found Deane on the bulkhead opposite the door to the moon pool. The dive supervisor had been crucified. It looked like spikes had grown from the bulkhead through his wrists, his ankles and his side. He was missing his left hand. On the bulkhead above him, the words *I died for your fucking sins* had been written in a thick smear of blood. *Your fucking sins* had been crossed out and replaced with the words *nothing at all.*

He would not be using one of the submersibles to get out of here. That left free-swimming. He knew his modified body could adapt and survive the ascent, but that would leave him more than sixteen hundred miles from the nearest island. Without food and water, not even his augmented body would survive. He was wishing they'd just cloned him.

He noticed his skin was itching.

Movement caught his attention in his peripheral vision. There was something in the water. He was too frightened to move. He managed to turn his head. Something swam out of sight under the habitat. Something with a wedge-shaped head. Something at home in the water. Something armoured, spurred and clawed. Lodup started backing away from the moon pool.

It exploded out of the water. Lodup caught a glimpse of a huge maw filled with titanium teeth, camera-lens-like eyes, a face covered in white scar tissue and armour. He threw himself back, triggering the SMG in a long, wild, one-handed burst. The killer whale's maw snapped shut where he'd been the moment before. It didn't stop moving towards him, breaching itself, opening its huge maw again. Lodup scrabbled backwards through the shallow water that had swamped the deck. There were things growing out of the orca's flesh and armour, moving shapes trying to break free. Give birth to themselves. Some rational part of his mind was aware that this was Big Henry, leader of the tribal pod that was supposed to provide security for Kanamwayso and the habitat.

There was a crashing sound as another armoured orca buckled a metal pontoon jetty as it swam through it. It surged out of the water and Big Henry was yanked back, the other orca's maw sunk into the pod leader's flanks. Power-assisted titanium bit through mutated battleship armour and Big Henry was dragged under the water. Lodup scrabbled backwards some more, then managed to stand up and aim his weapon into the surging moon pool. There was blood in the water but no sign of either of the whales, or anything else. The other whale had been Marvin. His sub-killing orca stalker had saved him.

Something made him turn to look up at the Command and Control centre's window. It wasn't shuttered. Siska was standing there looking at him as if he was an idiot. She beckoned him. Her eyes were normal.

Lodup stepped over another body. The weblike growth from the carpet had entwined itself around the metal stairs, then grown up as far as the dead security guard and started to consume her and her gear.

Lodup moved the rest of the way up the stairs, his weapon at the ready. He looked along the corridor to C&C – the door was open just enough for someone to squeeze through. He glimpsed movement on the other side of the door. He glanced the other way along the corridor but saw nothing. He knew if he stepped off the stairs, he would be in the line of fire of anyone in C&C.

'Hey!' he hissed. 'Who's there?'

'Keep your voice down and come to us.' The voice was unmistakably Yaroslav's.

'How do I know you won't shoot me?' Lodup asked.

'If there is anything wrong with you then I will kill you, but I will check first. You need to approach with your weapon down – do you understand me?'

Lodup glanced back at the stairs. He was having problems stepping out into the corridor. He knew Yaroslav wouldn't have the slightest compunction about killing him if he felt it necessary. Assuming that Yaroslav was even himself. On the other hand, he knew something of what was waiting for him in the rest of the habitat.

He stepped around the corner and didn't die. He was still holding the Vector but pointing it towards the floor, as instructed. He advanced slowly, and as he got closer to the door he could see the Russian security chief on the other side of it, covering him with his own SMG.

'Pass the weapons through to Siska,' Yaroslav said.

'I'm not comfortable—' Lodup said.

'If you do not, I will kill you,' Yaroslav told him. Lodup believed him.

In the light coming through the crack in the door from C&C, it was difficult to tell if there was anything visibly wrong with Yaroslav. His eyes looked normal, as far as Lodup could tell. Lodup pulled the sling for the SMG over his head and passed the weapon through the gap. Siska's hand appeared to take it.

'Now keep your hands high, where I can see them, and step through,' Yaroslav told him.

Lodup did as he was bid. Yaroslav moved back as he entered C&C, making sure that Lodup was never close enough to grab for his weapon. Siska was standing to his right, slinging the Vector over her back. Lodup counted a number of bodies in here, most of them C&C crew who had been killed in their couches. One or two had made it off their seats before dying and were lying on the floor. All of them had been shot. All of them looked deformed. Their flesh had been growing into grotesque new shapes.

Against one of the walls was a stack of weapons and ammunition. Against another was a large quantity of survival packs, which presumably contained emergency rations. He also noticed a pair of collapsible cots, sleeping bags, torches and a number of plastic jerrycan-style containers filled with water.

'What happened to them?' Lodup asked, nodding towards the C&C crew.

'Lace your fingers behind your head and get down on your knees,' Yaroslav told him. Again Lodup didn't immediately comply. He was sure he was dead when Siska drew one of the curved daggers from the sheath on her belt and approached him.

They're just as crazy as the rest, Lodup thought in a panic. He started to move.

'I will shoot you in the face!' Yaroslav snapped.

'It's all right,' Siska told him. Somehow it wasn't very reassuring. She ran the razor-sharp blade across his face. His skin hardened protectively in response, but she pushed the blade through. Lodup cried out in pain and jerked back. Siska brought the blade to her mouth and licked it, tasting the blood. She concentrated for a moment. 'He's fine,' Siska told Yaroslav, who didn't look convinced. Siska handed Lodup his Vector back. 'You can get up now.'

Yaroslav lowered his SMG. Then Lodup noticed the head on a stick. He backed away from it, bringing the SMG up. Yaroslav shouldered his own Vector.

'Wait!' Siska cried.

'What the fuck is that?' Lodup demanded.

Siska's hands were up, making calming motions. 'I know you're frightened, but I need you to calm down, okay?'

Lodup's eyes compensated for the low and flickering light coming from the moon pool. Germelqart's head was impaled on the end of a wooden staff. His face had been reconstructed. The wood looked very out of place down here. Parts of the staff were moving, pulsing, as if they were alive, as if they were organs of some kind.

'What the *fuck* are you doing?' Lodup demanded.

'We can tell you everything, but you need to calm down or Yaroslav is going to kill you,' Siska told him. Germelqart's mouth was moving. He was speaking nonsense syllables over and over again, talking in tongues. Lodup lowered the SMG. Yaroslav followed suit.

'Maybe you should give me that?' Yaroslav suggested. Lodup shook his head. 'I think you will eventually force me to shoot you if you keep hold of it.'

Lodup ignored him and focused Siska. 'We took his head, barbarous as that may seem in this age. He had nanite neural systems, ancient ones. We were going to interrogate him.'

'So you put his head on a stick?' Lodup said, incredulously.

'It wasn't supposed to be a stick,' Yaroslav muttered. 'Towards the end ... Siraja ...'

'I saw him,' Lodup said. Yaroslav and Siska exchanged a look. 'What? What's going on?'

'What do you think?' Yaroslav said. Lodup glanced out of the window. He was standing directly across from Deane's crucified body.

'Those things, in the city – they woke up?' Lodup asked. Siska nodded. 'How b—'

'How bad is it?' Yaroslav asked, then he started to laugh, a full belly laugh. He walked away from Lodup to look down into the moon pool.

'We have the most sophisticated biological, electronic and physical defences on the planet,' Siska told him. 'When whatever happened, happened – and I'm not even sure they're entirely awake – they went through our defences as if they didn't exist. Hacked Siraja, matter-hacked the vehicles and the weaker parts of the habitat, meat-hacked the clones and the orcas. We closed down as much of the system as we dared—'

'But a corrupt and insane Siraja now controls our life support,' Yaroslav added. 'At any point he may lower the ambient pressure, and we will find out what it's like to be in a car compressor. Assuming he doesn't just turn off our air.'

'Is there some kind of rescue protocol?' Lodup asked. 'Like the Virginia-Class sub I saw?'

'The Circle is in complete disarray,' Siska told him. 'We're still reeling from the attack on our facilities.' Lodup looked over at Germelqart's head. 'He was a deep-cover agent for a group who call themselves the Brass City. He spent more than two thousand years establishing that cover, all to destroy our last hope of survival as a species.' Yaroslav was glaring at Siska. 'It doesn't matter now!' she snapped at the head of security. 'In the highly unlikely event that Lodup gets out of here, he can run naked yelling our secrets through the streets of San Francisco for all I care.'

'Why did you bring him here?' Lodup asked.

'We hoped he might have something useful to say,' Yaroslav replied. 'He hasn't so far, and he is starting to get on my nerves.'

'Well, okay, never mind the Circle – does the US government know? The Navy?'

Yaroslav started laughing again. 'Oh, they know, they know all right,' the Russian said.

Siska glared at him. Lodup looked at her askance. She sighed.

'One of the first things it did was splice itself into the TPE,' Siska told him. Lodup stared at her in horror. The TPE – or Trans-Pacific Express – was the submarine telecommunications cable that connected Asia to the US.

'You mean it just hacked everything connected to the TPE?'

'That *is* everything,' the Russian growled. 'No military communications; every ship and plane system useless junk at best. The global economy is gone. Any form of electronic communication is gone, and frankly that is the best-case scenario.'

Lodup was staring at the Russian in horror as Siska cradled her head in one of her hands.

'What could be worse?' Lodup managed. The habitat shifted again and he glanced down into the moon pool. Water was surging out of it in waves and washing into the rest of the habitat, but it appeared to be the result of movement rather than imminent depressurisation.

'Imagine your phone rings and something impossibly ancient, and alien, screams its madness at you.' Yaroslav moved closer to Lodup until they were nose-to-nose. 'Tell me, Lodup, do you know anyone with a phone?'

'That's enough,' Siska snapped.

'Anything we do is just delaying the inevitable now,' Yaroslav said as Lodup stepped back from him.

'Then put a gun in your mouth, you miserable Russian bastard,' Siska snapped.

'I think I'd like to resign now,' Lodup said. Yaroslav gave a snorting laugh and went to check the door. Siska smiled for a moment, but it was quickly gone.

'Why now?' Lodup asked Siska. 'I thought you had more time.'

'So did we, though we knew it was close. Something happened in Portsmouth.'

'Virginia?'

'In the UK.' Siska glanced over at Deane. 'We think another mind, a Seeder, woke up. The others in the city sensed it and it roused them.'

Lodup thought back to the seed-pod he had seen in his dream, the one that had escaped when the city had been petrified.

'Why are we unaffected?'

Yaroslav was laughing again, but there was no humour in the sound. 'We are not unaffected,' he said.

'Myself and Yaroslav, we're different from the clones.'

'How?' Lodup asked.

Siska opened her mouth but hesitated.

'Go ahead,' Yaroslav said. 'You're telling him everything else, and he's dead anyway.'

'We have drunk from ... we were augmented by an ancient and very powerful device called the Red Chalice. We are different, more powerful than the clones.'

'Who were mass-produced to do a job,' Lodup said.

Siska nodded.

'It was still all a bit too much for Charles, though, wasn't it?' Yaroslav said. Lodup glanced over at the Russian, and then at Deane's crucified body.

'What about me?' he asked. He felt rather than saw Yaroslav and Siska exchange a look. He was still staring at Deane's body. He had never decided if he liked Deane or not. He could never quite get a grip on what the dive supervisor was actually like. He did not deserve his fate, however. None of them had, clones or not.

'We don't know,' Siska finally said. 'You're the original you, but your augments are much more like the clones' than ours.'

'I found something, a clear liquid. It was strange. I think I dreamed I did some kind of rudimentary surgery on myself. When I woke up all my comms connections were gone.' He turned back just as Yaroslav and Siska were exchanging another worried look.

'It sounds like the carrier solution that neural nanites are suspended in. But to utilise this you'd have to know to isolate them, and then order the other nanites to reject them—'

'And then cut through my own skull?' Lodup asked.

'Or blow your nose, or have it seep out of your ear, or in a tear, whichever you're most comfortable with,' Yaroslav said.

Lodup closed his eyes. 'Is that why I'm okay? Because I've cut myself off from the comms?'

'You think home trepanning is okay?' Yaroslav asked.

'Perhaps,' Siska said, sounding unconvinced. Lodup opened his eyes and looked at her expectantly. 'Or it was something to do with your dreams, your communication with Lidakika. Something out there is trying to protect you.'

'You mean there's a sane one?' Lodup asked. Yaroslav laughed again. He was starting to irritate Lodup now.

Siska shook her head. 'I think there may be a tiny facet of sanity among all that intelligence out there,' she said.

'All that insane, *alien* intelligence,' Yaroslav corrected.

'Is there any chance, anything at all?' Lodup asked. Yaroslav snorted with laughter.

'If there's any chance, any hope to be had, it lies with the converted seed-pods. We destroyed their infant minds. They might not be affected by the madness,' Siska said.

'But without the navigators, without the bloodline—' Yaroslav started.

'You mean to go out there?' Lodup said, incredulously pointing down into the moon pool.

'We wouldn't survive for a moment,' Yaroslav said. Better to put a—'

Siska turned on him. 'Then do it! Take a nanite-tipped bullet, put the barrel of your gun in your mouth and pull the trigger! Forty-seven years! Forty-seven years I've known you, Piotr, and I have never realised until now what a fucking coward you are!' The Russian bristled but said nothing. 'What possible difference does it make if we hide in here, eking out the last of our supplies, either waiting for those things to come in here and get us, or wasting away, or getting meat-hacked and our forms rewritten, or killing ourselves, or going outside and getting killed by what's out there? Are you that afraid of the unknown?'

'Yes,' Yaroslav said simply. 'Everyone is.'

'He's right,' Lodup said. 'And we still need to go outside.'

The clone workers were neutrally buoyant dots arranged in the water all around the city. Among them were the AUVs and the ROVs, their shapes changed, warped, and among *them* the wedge-shaped armoured servitors. Massive rootlike structures grew from the city and ran deep into the seabed, deep into the Earth's crust. The roots pulsed as they fed.

The water was full of what looked like particulate matter, marine snow. Lodup realised they were actually spores.

The city was moving. Huge basalt tentacles with screaming faces growing out of them reached up from the depths towards the light far above. They swayed gracefully, like seaweed.

The black thing had grown out of the sump. It looked like a bare winter tree made of liquid. It was moving, as if in a gentle breeze.

Hanging in the water, Lodup, Siska and even Yaroslav just stared.

Portsmouth, UK

Her body was bumping up against a partially submerged car parked next to where the beach used to be. He waded through the water and grabbed her sodden leather jacket. Even this far away from any houses he could still hear all the phones in Portsmouth ringing.

Nearby he heard screaming. He looked up and saw something living growing from the body of a woman it was simultaneously consuming. He raised the SA58 FAL carbine to his shoulder and felt the gun kick against him as he fired. He put a three-round burst into the woman, then another into the thing growing from her before the body could fall into the water.

Beth awoke to the sound of gunfire. Du Bois looked down at her. 'We need to go,' he told her.

44
A Long Time After the Loss

It happened quickly. The cylinder fabricated to look like brass, wood and glass which contained the black, viscous fluid floated into the chamber. Patron looked up, frowning. Elodie started to move. The cylinder exploded and semi-liquid, oil-like pseudopodia shot out from it. At the same time, the two monks exploded, oily pseudopodia shooting out from the black, semi-solid masses of their protean bodies, their voluminous red robes disintegrating around them. Whatever the pseudopodia touched dissolved rapidly.

Elodie rolled forward, one hand coming up to sweep away the assault cannon trained on her by the military contractor. The sting in her prehensile braid darted out and stabbed the blank.

For a moment the Elite stood there, swaying, as the black, oily mass surged around him. Any pseudopodia that touched his glass-like armour flinched away from it, smoking. The Innocent analysed the contacts, released virals, nano-swarms, even electronic warfare, cycling through all his options, searching for a way to harm it. Then he raised his rifle-configured weapon and started firing. Bullets with exotic payloads, charged particles, decoherence matter-hacks, DNA-scrambling meat-hacks, even exotic bandwidth lasers tore into the pseudopodia.

The military contractors were dissolving, being consumed by something utterly inimical to life.

Patron's suit dissolved. His face was a mask of fury as he reached for Scab to utterly end him. Scab swiped at him. The Scorpion's sting tore through the sleeve of Scab's jacket and slashed open a rent in Patron's flesh. Beneath the skin was dead flesh and void. Patron took a step back. Surprised. Scab's other arm began to glow from within. The energy javelin shot out of the hard-tech housing in his arm and Scab rammed it into Patron's stomach. Patron now began to glow from within. He looked down at Scab and started to laugh. Then the blank began to scream.

Talia's blood had been carried around the blank's body by nanites so aggressive that most of his veins were haemorrhaging. Under his nearly translucent porcelain skin, blood was spreading like a dye. The blank's S-tech-augmented mind shone like a beacon. Patron joined in the screaming. He sounded like he was in agony.

Vic drew his triple-barrelled shotgun pistol and levelled it at Talia. Elodie saw what was happening, but she was already throwing a syringe. It hit Talia in the neck.

The Innocent had turned his rifle into a two-handed sword and was hacking at the pseudopodia as they shrank away from contact with the weapon. Vic found his targeting solution. Scab blew the wall of the chamber and Vic, Talia and Elodie were sucked out into space. Some of the contractors' remains were sucked out with them, but the pseudopodia snagged them, dragging them back in to continue consuming them.

The emergency-vacuum-survival nanites Elodie had injected coursed through Talia's otherwise natural human body. The others' augmented bodies would keep them alive for a short period of time.

Tumbling through space, they had a moment to take in the massive size of the englobaling Consortium fleet. Fighters, corsairs and intership shuttles were tiny dots of light between the frigates, cruisers, carriers and the city-sized behemoth that was a capital ship. Manoeuvring engines glowed as they moved in a slow, graceful ballet around the monastic habitat.

Holes appeared in and around the monastery habitat. Space looked like a rotting, honeycomb void. Wriggling, maggot-like absences of colour came through the holes, consuming everything, reaching for the fleet. The fleet, in return, made space a storm of light and force, and sent more matter to be consumed.

A red rip bordered with a pulsing blue light opened in space. Elodie reached for and grabbed Talia, hugging the convulsing, haemorrhaging human to her. Behind them all the spectrums of destructive energy were being explored as distended, maggoty voids touched the first of the fleet and started to consume it. Manoeuvring engines burned brightly as the fleet, in disarray, tried to escape the void-things.

Vic had no idea why he wasn't dead. The three P-sats sped through the wound in space. Vic, Elodie and Scab reached for them, grabbed extruded handholds and were pulled through the rip into Red Space.

Patron stood in the vacuum among the hungry living voids, screaming silently, in agony.

*

The *Basilisk II* was waiting for them, its mouth-like airlock open. Vic was angry and scared. Scab had managed to call the things they'd first seen when they destroyed the Seeder ship that Talia had been linked to in Red Space. They appeared to have more destructive power than an Elite, and somehow Scab could influence it. Things just kept getting worse and worse. This wasn't even considering the fact that the man who had hired Scab initially – Vic couldn't remember his name – had taken an energy javelin in the stomach and not died. It didn't matter how augmented you were, you died when someone cut you open with a coherent-energy weapon.

The P-sats took them into the airlock which closed behind them, and air cycled in as the smart-matter chamber sank into the floor of the cargo bay. Vic glanced down at Talia. Burst blood vessels covered her visible skin but she was gasping down air, kept alive by the nanites Elodie had injected her with. Elodie was standing over the human with an expression of contempt on her feline features. Scab was looking deeper into the ship. Vic decided to fulfil his promise just as he started receiving warnings from the motion detectors on his antennae and his P-sat.

'Something's wrong,' Scab said, drawing his tumbler pistol and spit gun. Vic rotated his thorax and pointed his triple-barrelled shotgun pistol at Talia. Something fell from the roof, kicking Elodie and Scab hard enough to send them sprawling to the ground as she fell past them. Vic fired the weapon with a thought. The gun went off on the floor, where it was lying, still held in the hand on the end of his newly severed arm. The barrels weren't pointing anywhere near Talia when the weapon went off. The recoil shot the limb backwards across the airlock's deck.

Scab had flipped back onto his feet. The flechette penetrators fired by the shotgun pistol hit him in the leg. Some of them beat the hardening armour of his suit trousers, embedded themselves in his hardening skin and then exploded. Scab's leg was blown out from underneath him.

Surprised, Vic had a moment to take in the white-hot glowing end of his new stump, and then he was drawing both of his double-barrelled laser pistols with his upper limbs. Combat-exoskeleton-clad figures were appearing in the cargo bay now, levelling assault cannons, double-barrelled, flechette-loaded automatic EM-shotguns and strobe guns at them as they decloaked.

The Monk was crouched over Talia protectively, a thermal blade designed to look like a bayonet in each hand. Vic wasn't sure why he hesitated.

'I want to live!' Talia cried. Vic froze.

Scab had the tumbler pistol pointed at the Monk and the spit gun pointed at Talia.

'For someone with a death wish, Woodbine, you work very hard to stay alive,' the Monk said.

'I like doing things on my own terms,' Scab replied.

'Unfortunately, you're getting predictable. How many times have you pulled this trick? You need to remember that we were the ones who taught it to you in the first place.'

'That's fair,' Scab said, nodding. 'How'd you find us?'

'We didn't find you, we found the monastery in the severely corrupted neunonics of one of the heretics. The one who delivered the Marduk implant to you on Arclight,' she told him. Scab was nodding. 'The *Basilisk* is being surrounded by our ships as we speak.'

'I know,' Scab said. Vic was surprised that the Church was still letting him speak to the ship. 'And St ... the Alchemist is dead.'

Vic found that he was utterly ambivalent about this bit of news.

'He committed suicide when we came aboard,' the Monk said.

'Fair enough. Get your people off my ship, back your ships away, you and her stay as hostages until we're clear. I'll kill you, but I won't mess up your cloning,' Scab told the Monk.

'This is stupid,' Elodie said. She put her hands up. 'Don't shoot, I'm out of this.' She pointed at a far corner of the cargo hold. 'Cover me if you want but I'm going to stand over there, okay?' She walked across the hold under the guns of the Church militia.

The Monk was shaking her head in exasperation. 'All we want to do is talk,' she said, the frustration telling in her voice.

Vic levelled both his laser pistols at Scab.

'You sure?' Scab asked. Vic just nodded. Scab lowered his pistols and gave a Vic a look of utter hatred. Once it would have terrified Vic beyond the capacity for thought or action, regardless of the drugs he took to try and cope. Now it was just another day with Scab.

'Look, you've got control of your ship. Keep your weapons. Just try not to be a tedious wanker until we get to the Cathedral, okay?' the Monk asked. Scab was holstering his weapons. He nodded, once, then with some difficulty he stood up and hopped from the cargo hold. Vic lowered his lasers.

The Monk relaxed and looked down at Talia, sympathy and concern on her face. She ran her hand over Talia's face.

'Beth?' Talia asked. The Monk nodded. There were tears in both their eyes. 'What have you done to your hair?' Talia asked. Beth pulled Talia to her, hugging her tightly. 'I'm so sorry.' Talia sobbed into her sister's shoulder.

The Monk had shared something with the *Basilisk II*'s personality-spayed AI, and the ship piloted itself through Red Space using occulted beacons for guidance. A carrier, two heavy cruisers and an assortment of smaller ships escorted them on their journey. All the ships shared a similar baroque design and had religious reliefs and statuary on their hulls. They were still warships.

They congregated in the pool room. Scab had turned as much of the smart-matter hull as was possible transparent. Though, curiously, he'd kept the window as well, and they were all bathed in the red glow. He had stripped down to his boxers but kept his hat and weapons on. He was also wearing a pair of sunglasses. He was lying on one of the poolside loungers on a heroin nod, only just about able to smoke a cigarette. A medical fabricator was regrowing the missing parts of his leg.

Elodie fixed herself a drink, and then another. Vic assumed that, like him, she had also picked a relaxing narcotic from her internal supplies to help unwind and cope with the situation.

Vic was also lying on a lounger, his remaining arms crossed. The fear of what Scab was going to do as a result of his betrayal hadn't kicked in yet.

Talia was crying a lot. Mostly from relief. The Monk – Beth was her name, apparently – was holding her, comforting her now that an amount of first aid had been administered.

The Church militia were still aboard but keeping a discreet distance. Vic wondered if this was so they wouldn't damage Scab's pride any further.

The dead dolphin floating on top of the pool was a bit depressing.

'You'll want to see this,' Beth told her sister. She took Talia's hand and led her around the pool to stand by the transparent hull.

It loomed out of the red gas, a huge edifice carved from a massive asteroid. It was one single building more than a hundred miles long in the shape of a cross. The main body of the cross was about twenty miles wide, the crossbar fifty miles wide, and it stood about fifteen miles high. One end of the cross was semicircular in shape.

Massive windows ran down the length of the huge building decorated with static, highly stylised images. Flying buttresses grew out of the walls, their bases carved from smaller satellite asteroids. Each buttress was topped with a tower containing sensor arrays and comms gear. The towers also had various weapon emplacements and landing pads big enough to take the largest drop shuttle or intership transport. The entire building was covered with religious statuary. It was a vast, technological, Gothic, pre-Loss cathedral writ large.

'How did you call those maggot-things?' Beth asked as the *Basilisk II* flew them down the length of the Cathedral. Many ships of all shapes and sizes were docked with the massive habitat, two of them capital ships. A third capital ship was ponderously making its way towards the Cathedral through the clouds of Red Space.

'Are you expecting trouble?' Elodie asked.

'She told Vic about something that happened to her,' Scab said, nodding towards Talia, his voice slurring slightly. 'Someone, possibly some kind of sensitive, drank her blood and destruction ensued. I wanted to see what would happen if her blood was given to a blank.'

The *Basilisk II* banked around the front of the Cathedral, various weapon batteries tracking them. Their carrier escort peeled away but the two cruisers stayed with them. Part of the huge circular window at the front of the Cathedral opened and the ships flew in.

They were bathed in a warm orange light. The interior of the Cathedral was a vast open space. They flew over a statue the size of skyscraper carved to depict what everyone thought of as a devolved Seeder: a six-armed, armoured, spurred, wedge-headed creature, crucified on a six-armed cross. Beth asked the *Basilisk II* to magnify part of the smart hull. Through the clouds in the far distance they could see another similarly sized statue, this one a bearded human male, obviously in pain, wearing a crown of thorns. The figure had been crucified on a tesseract.

There were a number of Church ships in the Cathedral, which obviously had an atmosphere. Many of them were surrounded by platforms with vehicles, automatons and uplift crews working on them.

Much of the apparent floor of the Cathedral was taken up with vast pools. P-sats zipped over the surface of the waters, doing the bidding of the dolphins that swam in them. There were also thousands of flying vehicles moving between huge, open-plan platforms teeming with activity. Connecting the various platforms were a network of walkways and tracks for some kind of mass-transit system.

Beth asked the *Basilisk II* to relay the sound from outside, and they heard tranquil organ music echoing through the vast building/habitat. Even Scab looked up at this.

When the *Basilisk II* reached the junction where the crossbar cut across the vast building, the yacht started circling down towards a plinth-like landing pad. Close to the landing pad were vast pipes the size of skyscrapers, which appeared to have been grown out of the stone. At the base of the pipes was a huge keyboard. A gleaming figure was playing the organ. The *Basilisk II* landed as the music finished, the last notes echoing throughout the huge building.

Beth took her sister by the hand. Vic got up and followed. Elodie shrugged and decided to do the same. They walked through the ship and down the ramp at the front of the yacht. Moments later, Scab joined them, buttoning up his shirt.

The organ was some distance from the landing platform. They watched as a mechanical arm unfolded, picked up the figure that had been playing the organ and carried him across the several-miles-deep drop to the platform, then deposited him right in front of them.

At first they thought it was an automaton. It was a bulky, squat, ten-foot-tall, roughly humanoid-shaped armoured body. It looked to have been made of gold, inlaid with other precious metals to form beautiful but abstract patterns. There was a bulbous glass-like bubble where a head or at least a neck should have been, but it was tinted and they couldn't see into it. It was clearly some kind of protective exoskeleton.

'Miss Negrinotti, Mr Matto and Mr Scab, you are most welcome,' a jovial, booming male voice said. Then he turned to Talia, who looked terrified. He reached for her with a huge mechanical gauntlet, but she shrank away. He apparently thought better of it and pulled his arm back. 'And Miss Luckwicke, you have led us a merry chase,' he said, more thoughtfully. 'You are most welcome as well. I am Churchman.'

Patron tumbled though dead space, frozen tears on his face. A hand wrapped in black liquid glass closed around his wrist. He opened his eyes.

45
Ancient Britain

In the end, Madawg lived. His ribs were healing even as he landed in the water. They swam away from the island spending every moment assuming they were about to be attacked from behind, or below.

They might have been powerful and imbued with Otherworldly magics, but they still knew fear as they climbed out of the chasm and left the Underworld.

'All will know of your actions,' Guidgen told Madawg as they climbed out of the valley. 'Including your king.'

'And yet I live,' Madawg said, a sly smile on his face.

Some of their horses had broken free, but they did not take the time to track down the valuable horseflesh. Instead they rode south, hard, making for the northern part of the Ardu.

Britha felt numb. For most of the frantic ride she had been thinking of nothing. Her body ignored the cold, the pouring rain, the discomfort of the galloping horses, one of which died underneath her, pitching her into the mud.

Numbness was better than the confused feelings she had for Bress. He had a sword in one hand and the key to seeing her daughter again in the other. His cruelty in denying her the key was born of his slavery, his cowardice. She hated him the most for that. She knew he felt for her, as she did for him, but it was not enough to make him stand against the mockery that was Crom Dhubh.

She had been cold before, calculating. A practical woman, she knew that the chance of her ever seeing her daughter again was almost non-existent. They lived in a harsh land. Landsfolk and warriors alike lost children all the time. Once, she believed they were taken by the cruel gods that the Pecht had eschewed, as punishment for their lack of sacrifice. Now she was sure it was just the rigours of life that stole the young and innocent. She should put her child aside. She should return to her responsibilities. She shouldn't just wear the mask. She should live it, try to redeem herself – in her own eyes, if nobody else's. But she knew she would always be wearing the mask. She would play her part, but she would never give up on her child.

Her hand dropped to her stomach. What had Bress meant when he told her to kill it? She glanced up as they rode. It took her a moment to find the moon hidden behind dark clouds. It was little more than a sliver. Britha cursed.

The last part of the journey was so thickly wooded that they had to lead the horses through on foot. Following Guidgen's directions, Tangwen led the column down a steep slope into a narrow valley choked with undergrowth packed between the trees. It was pouring down with rain, but the ground underfoot hadn't become boggy yet.

As they made their way along the concealed muddy track, Britha felt as if she was in a different land. Suddenly there was a break in the greenery. They came to a deep, muddy ditch with sluggish water running through it, and beyond that, on a large mound of earth, was a hill fort.

'I had not thought to see this here,' Britha admitted quietly to herself.

Madawg was looking all around him. 'This is foolish – the trees are too close to the fort,' he said. The others had mostly been ignoring him because of his conduct in Oeth, the Place of Bones.

'Assuming you can ever find it,' Guidgen said.

'And after you had been harried all the way through the woods by people who know the land,' Tangwen added.

'Not even those we have brought here will be sure of the way,' Guidgen said, nodding towards the open gates of the fortress. The survivors of the wicker man and those who had joined them fleeing the Muileartach's spawn had set up camp within the wooden walls of the fort. 'Though doubtless Bladud will have tried to memorise it.'

'It is still folly,' Britha said irritably. 'These people can't stay here.'

Guidgen looked over at the other *dryw*. 'How much further do you think they can go, and to where?' he asked.

Britha was becoming more and more frustrated. Guidgen had placed the Red Chalice in the centre of the *gwyllions'* fort, drawn a circle around it in the dirt and then poured salt around the circle. Finally he placed the skulls of some of the *gwyllions'* strongest fallen warriors and greatest enemies at regular intervals around the circle. A ghost fence. Bladud was furious when he saw what the elderly *dryw* had done.

All were summoned – warriors, landsfolk, the survivors and the *gwyllion*. When Britha looked around, most of the *gwyllion* were standing on the palisades, looking into the hill fort which was now teeming with people. Most of them carried casting spears, bows and slings.

'Aren't we under hospitality?' Britha asked.

Guidgen looked over at her. 'I hope you're not questioning our hospitality,' he asked softly. 'It may have been a while since we allowed strangers into our home, but I think we still remember the laws.'

Britha assumed he deliberately left unsaid the obvious consequences of anyone else breaking their hospitality.

Bladud was on the other side of the circle from where Britha was standing by Guidgen. He was wearing his robe, hood up, surrounded by the bearskin-cloaked warriors of the Brigante. She looked around and found Ysgawyn sitting on the steps leading up to the palisades. Madawg and Gwyn were standing above and below him, respectively, still armed. Ysgawyn had been told of Madawg's actions in Oeth. If Ysgawyn reacted to the news, it had not been publicly. Like the Brigante, the Corpse People were in full armour and carrying weaponry. The Muileartach's spawn were less than half a day away. As the survivors became increasingly exhausted, they had slowly been losing ground. That was why Bladud had agreed to bring them to the *gwyllions'* fort.

Bladud was beside himself with grief when he heard about Nerthach.

Tangwen had been nearly silent on the way back. The young hunter and warrior had changed a lot in the moon since Britha first met her, but she supposed she had as well. Britha could read the grief over Kush's death in Tangwen. She had also liked the dark-skinned foreigner. He had helped save her life in the wicker man. She wondered how close Tangwen and Kush had become.

Britha had also seen Germelqart weep for his fallen friend when he thought no one was looking. With both Hanno and Kush gone, the Carthaginian was on his own in an unfamiliar land.

'It is obvious to me that the Red Chalice should belong to the Brigante,' Bladud said. The muttering in the crowd started straight away.

'Quiet!' one of the Brigante warriors shouted, playing the role of Nerthach for Bladud.

'We are the strongest of the tribes,' Bladud continued when the crowd settled a little. 'We have protected you, and we have paid the greatest price for the Red Chalice.'

There was more angry muttering from the crowd.

'Greatest price?' Guidgen asked. Britha rolled her eyes. It was a question that would only bring strife, one designed to manipulate people against Bladud.

'Nerthach fell,' Bladud said simply.

'So did Kush the Numibian,' Tangwen snapped irritably. 'And Sadhbh of the Iceni.' Shouts of agreement came from the Iceni warriors in their lynx headdresses. 'And Brys of the Corpse People.' Britha glanced at the three remaining Corpse People, but Ysgawyn and the others remained silent.

'None was so great as Nerthach' Bladud said. 'None had fought so many battles, won so many victories, harvested so many heads or had so many stories told of him. To him will go the hero's portion in Annwn.'

Tangwen bristled. 'And Kush was his match,' she said, her voice brimming with emotion. 'I forget, Witch King – are you *dryw* or *rhi*? You appear to be one or other as its suits you.' She ignored the threats from the Brigante warriors.

'I am a *rhi*,' Bladud told her, anger in his voice.

'Then one more insult about Kush and I will take your head. Do you understand me?'

'Brave words from one who has drunk of this one's blood,' Ysgawyn said, gesturing at Britha. Using neither her name nor title was a slight, but she let it pass. There would be strife enough for all in this gathering. She only hoped it would be over before the Muileartach's spawn were upon them.

Britha saw exactly what had happened here. Ysgawyn sent Brys and Madawg rather than go himself so he could court favour with Bladud. He had sought power and given the Witch King his support.

'I meant no insult,' Bladud said evenly. 'Kush was a staunch warrior, for a foreigner, but I will drink from the chalice and then kill you, if you still wish it so.' Tangwen opened her mouth to say something but Germelqart's hand was on her shoulder, and he was whispering in her ear.

'Carthaginian, in our lands it is not courteous to whisper when all have gathered to speak openly,' Guidgen called, not unkindly.

Germelqart bowed towards the old *dryw*. 'My apologies. I merely said that Kush would not have wished for this. He had no interest in boasting beyond what was necessary to be taken seriously.'

Britha sighed. She understood how difficult it was to get disparate tribes to cooperate, but had these people been hers and prepared to listen to her, she would be having stern words with them right now.

This was not the time for warrior boasts and manouvering for power. *Shouldn't have betrayed their trust, then,* she admonished herself.

'We would not see the Brigante with the Red Chalice,' Guidgen was saying as Britha started paying attention again. 'It is tantamount to saying that the Brigante will rule us now and for ever.' There was muttering among the crowd, and more than a few nodding heads, warriors and landsfolk alike.

'We are merely showing courtesy here,' Bladud pointed out. 'I still remember how to break a ghost fence, and whilst I have tried to reason with you, we can take the Red Chalice whenever we choose. The songs of our fallen notwithstanding, we deserve it because we can take it, and hold it.'

'You will be resisted,' Guidgen said, sadly.

'If we are to fall upon each other with sword and spear, it would be quicker for us to cut our own throats,' Britha said.

'Then stop being foolish,' Bladud said.

'It is not foolish,' Guidgen said. 'I think you would be a gentler Lochlannach.'

There were sharp intakes of breath and Brigante warriors tensed. The *gwyllion* warriors on the palisade walls shifted, readying themselves.

'This is poor hospitality,' Bladud spat. 'No more, I say. A *dryw*'s position is to advise, not to insult. Any more of this and I will strike you down and pay the consequences, and this is no hollow threat for the ears of the crowd. A man can only tolerate so much.'

Guidgen walked towards Bladud. He dropped his staff, unhooked his sickle from his belt and dropped that as well.

'I renounce the right of vengeance. There are to be no consequences to Bladud's actions in this matter,' the old *dryw* called as he approached the Witch King. 'I thought only to speak what I believe to be true. If you believe you have been wronged under our hospitality, then strike me down.'

Britha couldn't help but smile and shake her head. 'Now who is speaking for the crowd?' she muttered to herself. She glanced over at Tangwen. The younger woman looked irritated.

There were more gasps when Bladud punched Guidgen as hard as he could. The blow knocked the old *dryw* off his feet and he hit the ground, the wind knocked from him and his jaw was hanging askew. Almost immediately there was a clicking noise as Guidgen's jaw reset itself. Bladud stepped forward and offered the *dryw* his hand. Guidgen accepted it, and the Witch King pulled the much smaller man to his feet.

'I was a poor student among the groves,' Bladud said. 'Go and pick up your staff and your sickle, you old fool. There is nothing between us.' Guidgen smiled and retrieved his staff and sickle.

'If not Bladud, then who?' Anharad asked. Mabon was crouched close to his grandmother, silent, watching. The girl from Ardestie was also with the Trinovantes woman. Britha still felt an ache in her chest every time she saw the girl. Britha wondered who Anharad was backing in this. She was not aware enough of the politics of the southern tribes to know if the Trinovantes and the Brigante were allies or enemies.

'It is clearly a relic of the Otherworld,' Britha said. 'We stole it from Oeth, in Annwn, from Crom Dhubh himself.' Many spat and made the sign against evil. She did not because she didn't think the gesture made any difference. 'This chalice is clearly the responsibility of the *dryw*.'

'Who? You?' Anharad demanded. 'You cannot be trusted!'

'I will not warn you again,' Britha told the older woman. 'I will tear your tongue from your head if you speak to me this way once more. I do not care what you think of me, but you will respect my position.'

Anharad opened her mouth to retort angrily but Ysgawyn spoke first.

'You would be as well to say that we, as the children of Arawn, should look after it,' Ysgawyn said from the steps.

'Britha is actually a *dryw*,' Tangwen pointed out. 'You are just fools who believe your own lies regardless of the evidence of your senses. But try and take the chalice, and you will find that your skulls will not even be worthy of joining the ghost fence.'

It was as direct a challenge to Ysgawyn as any had ever heard, but the *rhi* of the Corpse People just smiled. 'All will be settled,' he said. Then he pointed at Britha. 'But this one served her own purpose in the Place of Bones, so I'm told.'

'I did not say I should have the chalice,' Britha said. 'I have drunk from it already. I say only that its responsibility should fall to the *dryw*, who serve all, and not just one tribe.'

'It would do little good on the Isle of Shadows,' Bladud said. 'And we would not see it in your hands, or Guidgen's. I, on the other hand, was trained as a *dryw*.'

'One thing or another, Witch King, or you'll confuse us,' Guidgen said. There was a little laughter. Bladud bristled but said nothing. 'I am a good choice. We have no designs on power. We keep ourselves to ourselves, and we are well hidden.'

'No,' Bladud said.

'I thought not,' Guidgen said.

'There will be no tomorrow for you all to fight over if we do not decide soon,' Tangwen said.

'And who gets to drink from it?' Britha asked. All eyes turned to her. 'They will be powerful, no matter who holds the chalice.'

Immediately more arguments broke out. Britha cursed herself, but it was something they had to bear in mind. Bladud had a point, but so did Guidgen. The only way she could see it working was for the *dryw* to decide how and when the chalice should be used. The problem was that Bladud didn't trust Guidgen, and nobody trusted her.

'You would be slaves,' Germelqart said quietly. Britha only heard him because her hearing was so much better since she had drunk from the chalice.

'Quiet!' Britha used the voice that cannot be argued with. It brought silence. She looked expectantly at the small Carthaginian, who in turn looked uncomfortable.

'Do any of you know how to use it?' the navigator asked.

'Do you?' Bladud demanded. Germelqart nodded. 'How?'

'Will you tell me the secrets of the *dryw*?' Germelqart asked.

'He might, if he thought it would earn him power,' Guidgen said. Bladud turned on the elderly *dryw*. 'I am sorry. You did not deserve that – ask of me what you will in compensation.'

'It's a foreign trick,' Ysgawyn said nodding towards Germelqart. 'Nothing more.' He made it sound as if this was something that should be obvious to all.

'The ... magics in the chalice are still ... attuned to the Dark Man,' Germelqart said. 'You must change this.'

'Then we may drink from it?' Bladud asked.

'If you wish,' Germelqart replied.

'Or make stronger weapons? Weapons that could harm the spawn of Andraste?' Guidgen asked.

'You could do that now, though there would be a risk,' Germelqart said. 'The weapons would be ... possessed by devils. They would speak to you, trick you, try to make you do their bidding. You see only the power, but there is a cost. The chalice could just as easily be the ruin of you.'

'But you could save us from that? How kind of you,' Ysgawyn said, his voice dripping with sarcasm.

'I think that if we can attune it, then we can heal your land,' Germelqart said. All eyes were on him.

'At what price?' Ysgawyn asked.

'If you mean who should have responsibility for it, then I would give it to the one who's showed the least interest in both the chalice and power in general. The one who has time and time again acted in the best interests of your people, no matter the cost,' the Carthaginian told them.

Britha found herself nodding along with Germelqart.

'And who is this paragon?' Ysgawyn demanded.

'Tangwen,' Germelqart said. All eyes turned to the young warrior. Tangwen looked astonished. At all the attention, her hand came up to cover her face, but Britha's blood had healed the scar. Both Bladud and Guidgen were looking at the young woman thoughtfully.

'Tangwen the young, Tangwen serpent-child. Tangwen serpent-tongue, more like. What foolishness is this?' Ysgawyn spat. 'I think not.'

'Then isn't it the way of your people to challenge her?' Germelqart said. Britha was starting to think that not only was the Carthaginian very cunning, he had a seam of iron running through his backbone as well.

Ysgawyn snorted with derision. 'Aye, let me drink of her blood first' – he nodded to Britha – 'and we'll see how much of a warrior she is when she faces someone on equal terms.'

'Gladly,' Britha said. This appeared to take Ysgawyn by surprise.

Tangwen opened her mouth to say something.

'Tangwen!' a voice shouted from the crowd. It was Twrch, the timid but powerfully built Parisi metalworker.

'Tangwen!' another voice cried. It was Duach. His friend Sel was nodding in agreement. Both of them had borne Essyllt's litter. As Brigante landsfolk, both were defying their king. More among the landsfolk and the survivors were taking up the call and shouting her name. Britha found herself smiling. It made sense. She glanced over at Guidgen. He was looked happy with the idea as well.

Bladud raised his staff and motioned for quiet. Eventually the chanting died down.

'I cannot say this pleases me,' Bladud said, 'but I believe it is the best compromise we can come to on this day, in the time we have.'

All eyes turned to Tangwen. Tangwen shook her head, looking less than pleased. Britha could see the fatigue in the younger woman.

There were shouts from the sentries, warnings being relayed from scouts in the woods. Guidgen listened and then turned to the others.

'They are not far now,' he told them. The rain had stopped and the sun was trying to break through the clouds. A ray of light appeared in the sky. 'I think Nodens blesses us,' Guidgen said.

'I think Nodens offers us hope, nothing more,' Bladud said.

A figure ran into the fort and collapsed in front of Guidgen, one of the *gwyllion* scouts. His mouth had distended and run around the side of his face to join with a hump. As they watched, the hump opened its multiple eyes. Guidgen looked appalled. He stepped forwards and brought the point of his sickle down on top of the man's head. There was a crack and the curve of the blade pushed the point through the scout's head and out of his mouth in a spray of red. Guidgen rested a foot on the scout's shoulder and jerked the sickle free. The weapon had been washed in Britha's blood. The iron was absorbing the blood, bone and grey matter on the blade.

'Burn the body?' Bladud asked. Guidgen nodded. Both of them turned to look at Tangwen.

'That was one of our scouts. We are out of time,' Guidgen told her.

'Remove the ghost fence,' Tangwen told Guidgen. 'Give the Red Chalice to Germelqart.' Muttering started up among the crowd. 'We have no more time! Challenge now or keep your tongue still behind your teeth!' Everyone went quiet. Britha noticed a lot of the older warriors nodding. 'What do you need of us?' she asked Germelqart.

'Protection,' Germelqart said. 'And someone to go with me.'

'Go! Go where?' Ysgawyn snapped. 'We give this foreigner the chalice and it will be—'

Tangwen said nothing. Instead she drew her hatchet and her dirk and faced Ysgawyn. The *rhi* of the Corpse People fell silent. Madawg took a step forwards but Ysgawyn put a hand on his shoulder. Tangwen turned back to Germelqart.

'In truth, I don't like the idea of you going anywhere with the chalice, either,' she told the Carthaginian.

'My body will be right here with you,' Germelqart said. 'It is only my spirit that will travel.'

Tangwen nodded as if she understood. Britha suspected it was more to ease the minds of those who watched than out of genuine understanding.

'Before you leave, the chalice must change the weapons that we have so they can harm the spawn of Andraste,' Tangwen told him. Britha was sure the other woman was making it up as she went along, but it made sense. 'Who will you take with you?'

Germelqart turned and looked at Britha. Britha nodded. It was right. Whatever her losses, however selfishly she had behaved, she had to begin to serve again. There was some muttering, but it was silenced by Tangwen's angry stares.

'Then I will stand over you,' Tangwen said.

'Should we drink of the cup?' Bladud asked. Britha was impressed that as a king he had the sense to listen to those who knew more than he did. 'I ask only because this will be a fierce fight.'

'I think that will make you a slave of Crom Dhubh,' Germelqart said, 'though I cannot be sure of this. The same is to be said of the weapons, but there is less risk when the devils are in wood and metal than when they are in the flesh ... I think.'

Bladud nodded, as though satisfied with the answer.

The fort was chaos as they prepared for the fight. The youngest of the children and the oldest of the elderly were against the wall of the fort furthest from where the spawn would attack. They were to be defended by the eldest of the children and the more capable of the elderly. Everyone carried spears.

Germelqart had cut himself and bled into the chalice, then placed it on the ground, its red liquid contents churning. The Carthaginian told them to dip their weapons into the chalice. A long line had formed. Some of the warriors had insisted on precedence. Tangwen spat in the face of the most vocal one. It was a quick fight. Tangwen was still carrying around his dripping severed head. Britha had not approved of the death. The warrior, one of the Iceni and a friend to the huge warrior Bress had killed, would be missed. She did, however, understand the necessity of it. Bladud and Guidgen had then gone to stand at the end of the line.

They had, however, given precedence to spears and arrows. The more distance there was between them and the spawn, the more chance they had. As soon as swords, spears and arrows were placed in the chalice, the red-gold filigree shot out of the vessel and started wrapping itself around the weapons. The arrow tips, the spearheads, the blades – all came away with a red sheen to them.

Then the weapons began to speak to them. They thirsted for blood. They wished to feel flesh around them. The first killings came as the weak-minded, to Britha's thinking, succumbed to the whispers. They attacked other defenders and had to be put down themselves. Again Tangwen had been there to take heads and display them as warning to others. Most kept their weapons to hand but would not touch them until they needed to. Britha noticed that some of the warriors had looks on their faces that suggested they relished what they were hearing.

Britha had too much time to think. Short of a few harsh words to those who were proving difficult, there was little she could do to help until the weapons had been prepared.

Since she saw the moon, she had begun to feel the change within herself. She knew it was true. She understood what Bress had meant, the great crime against the future of which he had spoken.

'Britha?'

She looked up to see Tangwen standing in front of her. She was covered in mud and blood and now carried three severed heads in her left hand. Her right held her dripping hatchet. She wore woad on her face, like the majority of the warriors present. The Corpse People had limed themselves and painted their eyes black, but Britha struggled to take them seriously now. She herself wore the reds and darker dyes on her face, ritual rather than war-markings for her skin. Though she did not think it mattered now, perhaps it gave comfort to those who watched, made them think she knew what she was doing.

'I'm sorry—' Britha started, but Tangwen was shaking her head.

'We do not need a weak Britha now,' the younger woman told her. Britha had been standing under one of the palisades, sheltering from the rain that had started again and turned all to mud. The rain was dripping down Tangwen's face, making her woad run. 'We need the daughter of Andraste, we need the cannibal hag, the throat-cutter, the bear-slayer.'

Britha closed her eyes. Tears trickled out unbidden, only to be sucked back in through her skin. She opened her wet eyes and nodded.

'You used to frighten me. Do so again.' Tangwen moved to leave.

'Wait,' Britha said. Tangwen hesitated. 'You are going to stand over us?'

They could both hear shouts from the wall. The woods beyond had started to move. Tangwen turned back to the other woman. Britha handed Tangwen her spear. It wasn't the one she carried to Oeth. That weapon she had left in her lover's chest. This had belonged to Brys. The grey-bearded warrior had dipped it in her blood but left it at the top of the chasm before they climbed down. Britha had taken it to defend herself when they fled Annwn.

The hunter looked to the spear, and then to Britha. 'When this is done I will come with you,' Tangwen told the other woman.

Britha almost burst into tears. Instead she made a hiccoughing sound and immediately admonished herself.

'My blood has not come,' Britha blurted out. She was not sure why she told Tangwen, particularly now.

Tangwen looked taken aback. 'Whose?' Tangwen asked.

'Bress's.' Britha resisted the urge to look away from the other woman as she said his name.

Tangwen considered what she'd been told. 'Better decide if you want this one to live,' Tangwen said. Then she turned and walked towards Germelqart. Britha walked with her.

Germelqart was sitting cross-legged in the centre of the fort. They wanted to be far from the wall, but not too close to the children and elderly. He was soaked through and covered in mud, the Red Chalice on the ground in front of him. Britha sat down opposite him. Tangwen drove three casting spears into the mud in a triangle around the pair of them and the chalice. Then the young warrior impaled the severed heads she had been carrying on the points of the casting spears. Next she drove the spear Britha had given her into the ground so she could grab it easily. She would have done the same with her arrows but rain was not good for flights or bowstrings. The arrows stayed in their quiver, covered, though this would only protect them from the damp to a certain degree. Her bow remained unstrung for the time being.

'I have given this a lot of thought,' Germelqart said, looking up, rain dripping down his face. There were more shouts from the palisades. Britha heard the sound of bows being loosed. 'I really hate your land.'

Britha smiled. 'What do we do?' she asked. She realised she was afraid, though she knew she must not show it. None of her dealings with the Otherworld had ever gone particularly well.

'Blood,' Germelqart said.

'It always is.'

There was more shouting. Those with bows loosed again and again. There was a horrible screeching noise, and then a shadow fell across them. Britha glanced up to see something deformed in the sky above them.

'Britha!' Germelqart said. Britha glanced back down. Tangwen was staring up, stringing her bow. 'The blood will form a ... connection between us and the ... spirit of the chalice.' He drew a copper blade across his palm. The blood welled up and he made a fist over the chalice. The blood began to drip into the vessel.

Quickly Britha drew her iron-bladed dirk and did the same. The sharp blade cut through her skin as if it wasn't there. She clenched her fist over the chalice, dripping blood.

'How do you know these things?' Britha asked.

'I have drunk of the Milk of Inanna.'

Britha heard the demons in her blood, their cries in her head and her vision was suddenly divided into tiny squares. She saw Tangwen, an arrow nocked on her bowstring, raise the weapon, aim up and then loose. Everything stopped. There was the sensation of falling backwards. Then darkness.

For a moment, Britha thought she was still in Oeth. She was standing in a tower of bone, except these bones were red and made of metal. She could see through the bones but outside there was only darkness. There were metal stairs within the tower of red, but they stopped and started randomly and didn't connect. Britha was standing on such a set of stairs. She peered over the edge. The tower went down as far as she could see. Looking up, it was just the same. Germelqart was not with her.

Tangwen loosed the arrow into the strange thing in the sky. It looked to be a hawk with the legs and head of a stag. She shot it with two of her arrows. The thing tried to continue flying, but instead plummeted to the earth, impacting in an explosion of mud. It was still flapping around pathetically. Tangwen walked over to it and put her bare foot on one of its antlers to hold it still. Like many of the warriors, she had gone barefoot because of the wet conditions. This way her toes could grip the mud and wet ground. She brought her hatchet down on the thing's head, again, and again, until it stopped moving.

She put her bloodied hatchet through her belt, then stood on the thing's deformed carcass and tried to pull one of her arrows out. The other had broken in the fall. She managed to yank it free and looked at the head. It was a mass of still-writhing little metal tendrils, which receded and re-formed into a red iron arrowhead.

She glanced up at the palisade as she returned to where Germelqart and Britha lay in the mud. Beyond the walls the woods were moving more violently now. She could hear the bellows, roars, howls and other strange sounds from the spawn. She could see more shapes in the skies, and shadows of the largest of the monstrosities beyond the wall. The archers were firing constantly now. The air beyond the walls was black with arrows.

She could see Germelqart now. He was far above her on one of the steps, but he was upside down from her perspective. He looked strange. A trail of images of his form followed behind him on the stairs, as if his every movement had left an echo in the air. As Germelqart gesticulated, his movements left after-images. Britha glanced behind her and realised the same thing was happening to her.

He appeared to be deep in conversation with something she

couldn't quite make out, a thing of shadow. There was the suggestion of a twisted, stooped, dwarf figure, with eyes and a mane of red metal.

'Germelqart!' Britha shouted. She expected her voice to echo among the metal. Instead it was as if the sound had been swallowed.

Then Bress walked over the platform at the top of the stairs she was on. He seemed to have come from underneath the platform.

One of the landsfolk defenders on the palisade succumbed to the spear she was wielding. She turned on the archer next to her, putting distance between them so she could run him through. Tangwen shot an arrow through the back of her head. The writhing arrowhead burst out of her face.

Another staggered away from the wall with something trying to grow its way out of his spine. Tangwen put an arrow through the growth and into the man's chest. He collapsed to the ground, his dead flesh still moving. The arrows were too far away to retrieve.

Beyond the wall she could see more distinct shapes, monstrous heads, flailing tentacles, huge deformed limbs. The archers had almost run out of arrows. She wondered how many of the spawn lay dead on the other side of the wall. The warriors were throwing their casting spears now, but they were running short, too. Tangwen could not see many faces but she knew she was looking at the backs of people in terror. Most were shaking, even the warriors. For many this was the first time they had been confronted with the true insanity of Andraste's spawn.

'You're not Bress,' Britha said. Bress did not have eyes that were pools of liquid red metal, and his hair was not made of strands of living, moving red filigree.

'Is Bress your god?' the figure asked. He sounded like Bress, except there was an odd metallic quality to his voice.

'No,' Britha said sharply.

The figure looked at her quizzically. 'Usually people see their gods,' the figure told her.

'My people do not have gods,' Britha said. 'Are you the spirit of this place?'

The figure considered the question. 'I will say yes.'

Britha looked at him suspiciously. 'Is it the truth, though?' she demanded.

'Is it your way to come to someone's home and call them a liar?' the figure asked.

'No,' Britha said. 'I apologise. My name is Britha, I am a *dryw* of the

Cirig, of the Pecht. We come from the North.' *Though we are no more,* she thought.

The figure narrowed his eyes, concentrating. 'I have heard these names before. They are soft, warm things inside which hard metal can live,' the one that looked like Bress said.

Britha flinched at his words. 'What would you have me call you?' she managed.

'Goibniu.'

Tangwen actually ducked when she heard the tearing, crashing noise as something leaped onto the wall. A sound that was half-squawking and half-human cry rent the air as the thing was done great violence by the defenders.

Some kind of liquid splashed against part of the wall, and there was more screaming as the defenders staggered back, falling off the palisade, flesh and armour smoking, skin bubbling as it slewed off them. There were things clambering over the wall, and larger creatures behind them, grabbing at the top of the spiked palisade with massive deformed limbs and pulling it down. Tangwen started loosing arrow after arrow. The demons in her flesh and the demons in her arrows whispered to her where to place each shot. It was difficult to miss despite the rain, wet flights and a wet bowstring.

On other parts of the wall people were staggering back, their flesh twisting, growths sprouting from their skin. The walls were beginning to warp. There was a whooshing noise and another part of the wall was engulfed in sickly green flame. Panicking, the defenders ran, falling from the palisade into the mud, their flesh transforming as they burned. Others untouched by the flames fled as well. Tangwen could understand that. She felt the need to run, felt her bladder turn to ice. But others stayed. They stabbed their longspears at the things on the other side of the timber wall. When the heads of their spears pierced the spawn they grew into the wounds, tearing up the spawn from inside. They slashed at the things reaching for the wall with swords that bit deep. Tangwen helped where she could, loosing arrows into creatures that were about to take the defenders unaware.

'Why do you look like that?' Britha asked Goibniu.

'So you will understand,' the spirit wearing Bress said.

'Why do I look like this?' she asked, waving her arms, leaving echoes in the air.

'So I will understand.'

'What are you?' Britha asked, frustrated.

'Perhaps I am your god,' Goibniu said.

Britha glared at him. 'Why do you serve Crom Dhubh?' she demanded.

'Because he found us, and because he is strong.'

'We have taken the Red Chalice from him. That makes us stronger.'

Goibniu smiled. 'Or more cunning, or luckier, or he was merciful, or he played his own game. I am aware of things beyond this realm.'

'Is he a god?'

'He is a servant. Or a victim.'

'Of what?' Britha asked. Her curiosity was getting the better of her.

'Something born of the light.'

'I don't know what that means. Can you speak plainly, in true words?' she said forcefully.

Goibniu's face screwed up in either consternation or concentration. 'I am trying. We came from before. We have little in common, and I am but a remnant.'

'Of what?'

'Of our creators. Those who forged us. The Lloigor.'

And then he showed her. He unfolded in front of her. His form was both growing and collapsing into impossible places of lines and angles she couldn't quite see, which were painful to look at. Light poured from him. Pain lanced through her head. She started weeping blood, but she could not turn her eyes away. She was in awe. It was like the first time she saw Teardrop, his crystalline mask, only this was more than some hungry parasite. This was beautiful.

'And we are but a poor changeling to them.'

Tangwen fired her last arrow into a one-eyed, one-legged, one-armed creature that had hopped up onto the wall. It fell off, disappearing from view. She was vaguely aware of the terrified children crying behind her.

There was another whoosh and most of the front of the fort was engulfed in the sickly green fire. Behind the wall, Tangwen could make out the shadow of something with a head like a horse's skull and the neck of a serpent. It spread its crow-like wings, flapping them, emitted shrieking sounds that made her wish she had arrows left. She dropped her bow and pulled Britha's longspear from the mud. Immediately it started to whisper to her. Immediately Tangwen felt less frightened. The spear told her of its hunger.

As she watched, the Brigante turned as one and leaped from the palisade. Bladud wasn't wearing his robe now. He was wearing iron mail and a bearskin cloak like the rest of his warriors. The skull of a bear that he had killed himself was set onto his helmet. His cloak caught fire as he leaped. Bladud landed and tore it off, stabbing at the cloak as the green fire imbued it with deformed life.

'Hold here!' Bladud cried. The wall across the entire front of the fort was torn down. The monstrosities crawled, ran, slithered and flew into the fort. Behind her the children screamed. In front of her, some of the warriors and landsfolk screamed as well, fleeing the line.

Tangwen pushed her feet deeper into the mud. There was a smile on her face. She could feel the demons in her blood fighting against the magics of Andraste that filled the air. Ahead of her, in the line of warriors and landsfolk, she could see flesh and armour start to warp. There were things growing out of them, bursting through skin, changing them. Some lost control and started stabbing at new mouths, eyes, entire heads. Others stood and held even as they were being transformed.

Goibniu resembled Bress again, which made him easier to look at, in some ways. The blood was still drying on Britha's cheek. Her head still ached.

'Who is Germelqart speaking with?' Britha asked.

'Ninegal,' Goibniu told her.

'Who is Ninegal?'

'Me.'

Britha shook her head. None of this was making much sense. 'You are aware? You know what is happening outside?' she asked.

He nodded. 'It has driven its own children mad,' he said.

Britha stared at him for a moment but had no time to go into it. 'Will you help us?'

'What would you have of me?'

'Can you ...' Germelqart had spoken of this but she could not see how it might be done. The land would not fit in the Red Chalice. 'Can you return the land to what it was?'

'Yes,' Goibniu said simply.

Britha stared at him. 'That's it? No bargain? No price?' All dealings with the Otherworld had a price.

'I am a tool, nothing more.'

'Thank you,' she said, and cursed her weakness as the relief surged through her and tears sprang to her eyes again. 'Can you return me, and my friend?' she asked.

He nodded. Then: 'Britha?' he asked. She looked up at him. 'I am alone. All my people are gone.'

'Mine, too,' she told him, but then she remembered the little girl.

Tangwen rammed her knife into something's head and there was an audible crack as the point of the blade pierced the skull. The mouth growing from Tangwen's own neck and shoulder was cackling insanely. She put both hands on her spear and rammed it into one of the beaked walking-tree monstrosities, running at it, pushing the spear in as deep as she could. The spear howled through her blood, into her skull. The spearhead branched out through the tree-thing's body, hungry for the slaughter, searching for a way to kill it.

A one-legged monstrosity landed in front of her. It clawed at her with thick, ragged nails on its single hand, tearing deep rents in her face. Tangwen barely felt the pain. She spat her own flesh into its eye, yanked her hatchet from her belt and used it to open the thing's head, splashing herself with its gory contents. She grabbed her knife from the dead thing's head and jammed it into neck of another. Iron branches exploded through the bark-like skin of the tree-thing and it fell to the ground, crushing spawn and human alike. Tangwen bit the nose off whatever it was she had just stabbed in the neck and spat it away from her. She embedded her hatchet in the head of something slithering towards her with a thousand tiny legs and a human face. Then she grabbed for her spear, tearing it out of the tree-thing.

A flailing tendril hit her hard, sending her spinning through the air. She landed close to where Britha and Germelqart lay. She could see their flesh starting to transform now. Britha's arm was slowly turning into a tentacle. Feathers and eyes were growing from Germelqart's head.

The Brigante and the *gwyllion* were fighting next to her, trying to keep Britha and Germelqart safe for as long as they could. Many of them were just being stomped into the ground by things too large for them to fight. The rest of the warriors were in a ragged line across the fort, trying to keep the creatures away from the children, though many had run. Tangwen wondered if those who stayed had done so because they were damned or driven mad with battle lust by the cursed weapons they carried, or were just the bravest people she had ever met.

Bladud was fighting like a demon, moving with speed and ferocity, cutting down anything that got close to him. All the more impressive when Tangwen remembered he had not drunk of Britha's blood. His sword arm, his entire body, must ache, he must have been gasping for breath, soaked in sweat. He cut at something that looked like a twisted man with antlers, driving it into the ground and then striking down, again and again, with his red iron blade until the thing stopped moving and started to come apart. Bladud had another face growing out of the back of his bald head. He tore his shield off his arm as it grew teeth and bit at him.

She saw one of the lynx-headed Iceni land on the back of one of the man/horse things and stab at it in a frenzy, shrieking as she rode it to the mud. Then a tree-thing stomped on her.

Duach and Sel dragged a one-legged hopping creature to the ground. Twrch beat its head in with a hammer.

Guidgen was being cagey, waiting for his moment to dart out from among his naked warriors and strike with his scythe. He watched for those in trouble and stepped in to help whilst the rest of the *Gwyllion* fought around him in a frenzy.

Tangwen stood up. A hoof caught her in the head as another rearing man/horse thing came down on her. The force of the blow drove her into the ground and everything went dark for a moment. She heard screaming. The mouth in her neck was trying to eat the mud she was lying on. Her face didn't feel as if it was on straight. She was nauseous. She heard someone shouting her name.

She managed to look up. Mabon was hanging from the creature's neck, stabbing at it again and again. He must have leaped at it over the thing's weapons. He must have charged it from where he had been guarding the other children. Anharad was next to her. The terrified Trinovantes woman had Britha's spear in her hand. She pushed it into the monstrosity's flanks. The thing reared and then toppled sideways.

Tangwen searched around for a weapon. Any weapon. The dragon with a horse's skull and a crow's wings reared up over them. Tangwen saw a longspear with a red iron head lying in the mud. Warriors went flying as they were swept out of the way by the deformed walking trees. As the horse-skulled dragon opened its mouth, Tangwen pushed herself to her feet, grabbed the spear and ran. She used the corpse of the horse/man creature to launch herself high into the air, towards the dragon.

Germelqart and Britha opened their eyes. Germelqart looked down at the Red Chalice.

The alien artificial intelligence that lived in the immersion environment inside the L-tech device set the process in motion. It pulled matter through the bottom of the ancient but powerful assembler, converting the base carbon molecules into a functioning nano-swarm and spraying them into the air.

The L-tech nanites met the biological nanites, which were the product of the Seeders' malfunctioning and corrupted terraforming process. It began to reprogram the biological S-tech nanites, transforming them at a molecular level, returning them to their constituent parts where it could, or into base carbon where it couldn't. It spread quickly among the corrupted terraformed life. Part-spore, part-disease. Flesh, bark, blood, sap, plant fibre, wood, mineral and chitin began to separate, collapsing, slewing to the earth in clouds of ash-like carbon dust as the artificial intelligence took Britha at her word. All the while it fed on matter from the earth.

'Run!' Germelqart shouted as he got to his feet.

Britha tried to push herself up but found her arm had partially transformed into a tentacle. It was agony as the demons in her blood sought to reverse the transformation. Panic took her as she thought of the child in her stomach.

Tangwen, unarmed, covered in blood and ichor, deep wounds in her face, was suddenly standing over her. She leaned down and grabbed Britha, dragging her to her feet. Tangwen reached for the Red Chalice.

'No, leave it!' Britha cried, and then it was her dragging the reluctant Tangwen back. All around them the ground was collapsing, as if the earth beneath it had been sucked away. The Red Chalice was quickly sinking into an ever-expanding crater. The walls of the fort started to fall into the crater.

'Break!' Bladud shouted. The line of warriors turned and ran, heading for the back of the fort. A door had already been opened in the wall and the children were streaming out of it. The running warriors were struck down as they fled, often sent flying into or over the walls, their bodies broken as they bounced off trees. Beyond the walls, the line of spawn stretched as far as the eye could see in either direction. But they were slowing. Starting to rot, melt or simply fall apart. All the while the Red Chalice fed on the earth.

Britha saw the child from Ardestie standing by the rear wall, crying, hugging herself. Britha scooped the child up with her good arm and carried her from the *Gwyllion*'s fort, away from the monsters.

Epilogue
The Walker

Hand-over-hand, he pulled himself up over the rocks past towering, hollow iron fingers reaching for the red sky. On the other side of the vast ridge he could see the glow of the city's lights now, flickering and surging.

Stones rained down on him and he heard movement above. Hanging on with one hand, he reached behind him to take the hilt of his sword and loosen the blade in its scabbard.

A scrabbling noise, bone on scree. The dataghosts watched as the creatures launched themselves at him. Their flesh was sparse and they looked almost skeletal, a biological design for an environment with few resources. Their once-human skulls had grown into a protective shell that covered their backs and was connected to the rest of their bodies by a membrane of skin. They were pitch black in colour, to help absorb any heat.

They were parasites. Like everything else. He was a vibrant source of heat, energy from calories, raw materials, even devices. It was no surprise that they attacked him. Even though there was little chance of them hurting him. It was no surprise that they gathered so close to the city, either.

He pulled himself up, landing on a sloping ledge as he drew his sword. He caught the first of them in mid-air. It came apart as the sword flew through it. He kept moving forward, wielding the sword two-handed, their shells cracking, bones breaking. They were soft, brittle mockeries of what had once been but he never dropped his guard, never once took his victory for granted. The dataghosts stood in silent witness, recording everything.

When they were all dead, he looked through their broken bodies for the most intact of their skull shells. He found four that were good enough. He dribbled into them, exuding a copious amount of trans-lucent saliva. The saliva ate the remaining dry flesh and used the transformed matter to harden the soft, brittle material. Then he tied them together through their eye sockets and continued making his way up the rocky path. He was no less a parasite than anything else, and soon he could use the hardened skull-shells to bargain for the service of screaming demons.

Soon he would see the city.

Acknowledgements

A lot of people helped get this book into shape.

I would like to think Jamie and Patti Arthur and the rest of the Arthur family and staff at the now sadly closed Village Hotel on Pohnpei for their hospitality and for sending me research material on Nan Madol and the island itself.

Scottlan Fanning, Jennifer Dupuy, Jake Busby, Chuck Griffin, Candra Malta and Valerie Finney for adopting a wandering Brit in the South Pacific. I also want to thank Chuck for his insights into commercial diving (any ridiculous flights of fancy are my fault not his).

Thanks to Anthony Jones and Tanya Baldwin for hospitality and suggestions whilst researching Birmingham, and to Matthew Strange and James Adey in their capacity as native guides of the same city.

Thanks to the following writers for support, advice, in poor Stephen's case actual collaboration (nothing illegal) and sometimes just staying up late and drinking at conventions: M.D. Lachlan, Chris Wooding, Stephen Deas and particularly to Peter F. Hamilton and my arch-nemesis Hannu Rajaniemi for their comments on Age of Scorpio.

Thanks to my excellent agent Robert Dinsdale at A.M. Heath for his support.

Thanks to Simon Spanton, Charlie Panayiotou, Gillian Redfearn and Sophie Calder at Gollancz and to my editor Marcus Gipps for going above and beyond on this and other projects, it's much appreciated.

Thanks to Lisa Rogers for all her hard work on the copy edit.

Thank you for the support and sarcasm from my friends, family, and members of the gaming community, particularly to my mum and dad and to Yvonne for her continuing evil brand of patience.

Again, and I hope I never forget to say this, I am thankful to everyone who buys a copy (or gets one out of the rapidly shrinking number of libraries) of anything I write and particularly to those who comment or review, good or bad, online. Thank you.

Finally, during the course of writing this book Iain Banks passed away. I did not know Iain but I have been reading his books for many years and he has been a huge influence on me, and not just my writing. He was taken way too soon and is a huge loss to literature, SF and otherwise.

Turn the page for a preview
of the sequel to *A Quantum Mythology*:

The Beauty of Destruction

Prologue
The Walker

The twisting, multi-storey bridge had uselessly violated the rock of the ridgeline. The Walker was almost used to the nonsensical angles, the shadowy corners that stretched away from the eye, the optical illusions that weren't actually illusionary. He clambered through an irregular arch, only banging his head twice, and made his way across the bridge, high over terraced spore fields that weren't what they had once been.

The city was the last bastion of life. The remnants of humanity had flocked here when there had been nothing else left, though they were little more than animals now. They had separated into subspecies – herd, predator, parasite humanity – but they remained in the city. Urban living, it seemed, was part of some shared race memory; the fleeting pretence of something approaching civilisation.

The Empty Bridge was still one of the main thoroughfares into the city, though it saw little use these days. The Immortal Mr Jenkins was still there, however. He was something between a rat and a monkey, with a narrow, buck-toothed, but undeniably human face. Sometimes he claimed to be a witch's familiar, or a particularly wilful homunculus, and at other times he claimed to be the King of the Rats. Mr Jenkins was standing on the bench that ran down the deceptively crooked bridge in one of the more low-ceilinged areas. He was absently turning the bodies of a number of spitted, blackened, rat-like bodies over a small rubbish burner while looking towards the living tombs at the centre of the city.

'Mr Jenkins?' the Walker said cautiously. Mr Jenkins turned and ran an appraising eye over him before a smile appeared on his face.

'I'm pleased to see you. Such a day for visitors. I don't think the stones themselves can remember the last time that happened.' He was eyeing the skull shells that the Walker was carrying. 'Now, what can I do for you on such an auspicious day?'

'Food and screaming demons,' the Walker said.

Mr Jenkins narrowed his eyes. 'I see. The skulls bonded?' the grotesque little creature asked.

The Walker nodded.

'One will get you something to eat and two more will get you the bound service of a demon.'

'I need more than one,' the Walker said irritably.

'I don't doubt it, I don't doubt it at all. Well yes, I 'spect we'd all like an army of screaming demons for a hardened skull-shell or two, but that's not the way economics works, is it? With the emphasis on economy, and don't you go thinking you can negotiate with a sword, you know there's more of me where I came from. Besides,' he waved at two of the cooking rat-like things, their faces deceptively human, 'these are fresh. Me wife, queen of my harem and my heart mind you, just popped them out last week.'

The Walker tried to remember a time when this would have disgusted him, but frankly he needed to eat.

The centre of the city was bathed in hard destructive light from the red heavens. Twisted spires, which had reached for the blood-coloured sky, started to fall. Mr Jenkins watched, appalled. The skull shells clattered onto the bench next to the creature.

'Now,' the Walker said.

'Right you are.' Mr Jenkins turned and ran into the inky blackness of one of the bridge's oddly angled corners. The Walker watched the spires fall as he chewed on one of the cooked creatures. Moments later Mr Jenkins reappeared from the darkness. The lines around his small grotesque eyes had deepened, there was more white in his fur.

'They don't like what's happening,' Mr Jenkins said, between grunts of exertion. He seemed to be tugging on the corner's inky darkness. 'They know the city's sleep has been disturbed.' Slowly the darkness started to coalesce into a form.

1
Ancient Britain

Tangwen stumbled through wasteland that had once been dense forest, before collapsing to her knees in a cloud of grey dust that defied the weather. Tears ran from her eyes as she vomited.

There was a dividing line. Just to the north of her the forest started. Everything south was a grey wasteland that the driving rain was turning to mud. All along the demarcation line were the crumbling remains of the creatures that Crom Dhubh, the Dark Man, had drawn from Andraste's poisoned womb. The warped forms created from the beasts, plants and even the rocks of Ynys Prydain, the Isle of the Mighty, were returning to their original state, robbed of the animated life the goddess's magics had provided.

She touched her neck. It itched painfully as the mouth that had grown there during the battle with Andraste's spawn started to heal over with new skin. When the goddess's magic, her seeds, had tried to transform Tangwen into one of her brood.

She drew a painful breath as sobs wracked her body. A shadow fell across her. She wiped the vomit from the corner of her mouth with the back of her hand and looked over her shoulder. Britha was standing there holding the little girl from her village. The one who had survived the wicker man, the march north, and Andraste's spawn. Neither the girl nor Britha looked like they were ever going to let go of each other. The girl was quiet. She had seen too much to cry. Britha grimaced in obvious pain; some of her flesh still had a life of its own.

'I remembered her name,' Britha said quietly. 'It's Caithna.'

Tangwen nodded. She tried to speak but could form no words.

'I've killed too much ...' Tangwen finally managed. Britha looked down at the younger woman and nodded. She gripped Tangwen's shoulder with her free hand. The skin looked pink and raw, new, almost as if it was still in flux. 'What now?'

'Now? Now we start to fight each other.'

Tangwen nodded again and looked down. A small flower had grown through the mud.

There was little of the *gwyll*'s fortress left. Whatever the Muileartach's spawn hadn't pulled down had collapsed into the crater created by the Red Chalice. All that was left was one of the watchtowers and part of the rear wall. Despite the rainwater trickling down the side of the crater the chalice was still where they had left it, in a growing pool at the bottom. Britha was sure she could make out the raindrops that hit the red metal turning to steam.

They had wasted no time. The warriors and the survivors were regrouping in the woods to the north of the ruined fortress. Those who wanted the chalice, who wanted the power it offered, were all here regardless of their fatigue.

Britha was disappointed to see that Ysgawyn, *rhi* of the Corpse People, was still alive. His warband had burned and murdered in Crom Dhubh's name, back when they had thought it meant power. They had changed sides when their master had abandoned them. Now that his retinue numbered only two warriors the *rhi* was looking for any opportunity to increase his fortunes. Of all of them Ysgawyn looked the least weary from his exertions in the recent battle.

Guidgen was the *dryw* and leader in all but name of the *gwyllion*, the forest tribe whose land they were on. He looked ready to collapse into the crater, despite being one of those who had drunk of Britha's blood to receive the gifts of the chalice's magic. The bearded, wizened old man may have been imbued with the powers of speed, strength, vitality and healing that the cup offered, but it was obvious the battle had taken its toll.

Germelqart, the short, once portly, Carthaginian trader was tugging at his beard, a worried expression on his face. He was looking anywhere but down into the crater at the chalice. It had been Germelqart and Britha who had spoken with Goibhniu, the god in the chalice who had claimed to be the servant of other greater gods long since gone.

Anharad, the highborn Trinovantes woman who was friend to

Tangwen and had helped lead the survivors to eventual safety, was trying not to glare at Britha. The Pecht *dryw* knew that the older women hated her for siding with the Lochlannach, the Otherworldly raiders. They had slain Anharad's family and imprisoned her in the wicker man as part of the sacrifice to the Llwglyd Diddymder, the Hungry Nothingness, the dark god that Crom had tried to summon to eat the sky.

Mabon, Anharad's grandson, the only surviving member of her family, remained close to his grandmother. Britha saw that he had a shortsword now and had clothed himself in a patchwork of boiled leather armour. Despite the raggedness of his attire he held himself as a warrior, though Britha knew he had not said a word since his parents had been killed and he had been taken as prisoner from the boys' camp.

Britha noticed that Anharad was standing quite close to Bladud, known as the Witch King. The heavy-set, bearded bald man wore the black robes of a *dryw* once more, despite having been cast out. Britha knew that Bladud, *rhi* of the Brigante, had ambitions to be the *bannog rhi*, the high king of the Pretani. He wanted the chalice for himself.

Finally there was Tangwen. The younger woman, a small, wiry warrior and hunter with spiked hair from the Pobl Neidr, the People of the Snake, swayed on her feet as if she was about to pitch forwards into the crater. This was despite the fact that she had drunk of her blood as well. Britha could see the ravages of the magic on Tangwen's wiry form. It had fed on her flesh – she looked emaciated and would have to eat soon. Warriors and landsfolk alike had decreed Tangwen should be guardian of the chalice.

Along with Britha, still holding onto Caithna, they formed a rough circle standing around the edge of the crater. Britha had no illusions about why Caithna would not be parted from her. The girl had been frightened of her but terrified of the spawn of the Muileartach. In such times it made sense to seek the protection of someone as frightening as the Pecht *dryw*.

There were so many of them missing. Kush, the Numidian warrior, had been killed by Crom Dhubh in Oeth, the Place of Bones. Sadhbh, the Iceni scout, and Nerthach, Bladud's right hand, had fallen in the same place. Teardrop had been killed by the Ettin in the wicker man. She herself had helped Bress kill Fachtna, her lover and the father of her daughter – now taken from her by the *dryw* of the Ubh Blaosc. She touched her stomach as she thought of her stolen daughter. She knew that Bress, Crom Dhubh's champion and warleader, held the control rod that would allow her to open a trod back to the Otherworld where the *dryw* of the Fair Folk kept her unborn child. She would take the rod from Bress if she could. From his corpse if need be, as they had both done with Fachtna. Old lore and newer magic, however, told her that she was once again with child. The dread she felt at this was because the father was Bress.

Her people were gone. Cruibne, her *mormaer*, Feroth, the war leader and all but a father to her, Talorcan, the quiet tracker. And Cliodna. So many in such a short period of time.

'The blood of our fallen hasn't yet cooled. This is unseemly,' Guidgen started. The *dryw* was right but Britha had respect for his cunning. Guidgen knew he was fatigued. He would want more time to recover so he could bring all his wits to bear on the coming argument. Bladud, however, was as much warrior as he was *dryw*. He thought to strike while his enemy was weakened.

'And yet you are here,' Ysgawyn pointed out in a tone less courteous than one would expect when speaking to a *dryw*, even for a *rhi*.

'If this isn't resolved quickly then it will cause trouble among us, and we still have a greater threat,' Bladud said. Britha could hear the fatigue in his voice as well, but something told her that he had planned this before the battle.

'It has already been resolved,' Guidgen said. 'Tangwen has guardianship of the chalice until the threat has passed.'

'Tangwen did an admirable job in safeguarding the chalice and protecting Germelqart and Britha while they worked their magics; we owe them much, but the agreement held until we had dealt with Andraste's Brood. This we have done. We need to decide what happens with the Red Chalice now,' Bladud told them.

'You said it yourself,' Guidgen muttered. 'Tangwen was a worthy guardian, let's leave her as such.'

Britha glanced at Tangwen's face. She did not think the younger woman was listening to them. Britha had seen the same look on warriors before. She was locked in a prison of fatigue and the memory of her experiences. This would have been the first time she would have had the luxury to reflect on everything that she had seen, everything she had done, since the wicker man, if not before.

'I notice this time we are not having this discussion in front of everyone,' Britha said.

Bladud looked over the crater at the black-robed *ban draoi*, meeting her gaze easily. 'Nor do I have my warriors at my back,' he pointed out.

Britha noticed Anharad and Ysgawyn nodding. *No, but you brought allies*, she thought.

'There is still the matter of the Lochlannach and Crom Dhubh. Let us leave things as they are until we have dealt with them and then we can fall on each other.' Guidgen's tiredness was telling in his lack of subtlety. There was no trace of his normal wry smile.

'Some of us are strong enough to keep going even after the exertions of battle,' Ysgawyn said.

Bladud glanced over at the *rhi* of the Corpse People. He did not look pleased. Guidgen closed his eyes. For the first time since Britha had met him he looked his age, his normal vitality gone.

'I did not see you in the battle, *rhi* of two,' Guidgen said, then he opened his eyes, bloodshot. He stared at the bristling Ysgawyn.

'Enough of this,' Bladud growled, raising his voice enough to be heard across the crater, over the rain. 'I am well aware of the threat that Bress, the Lochlannach and this Crom Dhubh pose ...'

'Are you?' Britha asked. Normally she would not interrupt a *rhi* in such a way. It wasn't that she lacked the authority to do so. It was just that it showed a lack of respect to their station. 'You have not fought them. They raided little of your land, as far as I can tell. You were not at the wicker man. I think you know little but what you've been told.' Caithna was growing restless in her arms. Presumably cold and hungry, but the young girl showed no sign of wanting to be put down yet.

'If we are to fight them then more of us will have to drink from the chalice,' Ysgawyn said, almost managing to keep the eagerness from his voice. Britha glanced at Tangwen. Normally the young hunter would counter anything said by Ysgawyn; she had borne witness to the depredations of the Corpse People, she hated them and their *rhi*. Instead she just swayed on the edge of the crater, looking up into the sky, the rain falling on her face.

'We will certainly need the magic of the chalice to fight the Dark Man,' Bladud said, and then spat to avert evil. 'Magic that must be shared.'

'And controlled,' Guidgen said. He pointed at the chalice. From their position on the lip of the crater they could see its bubbling, liquid, red metal contents. 'We have the means of our own destruction here if we are not careful.'

'Control requires strength,' Bladud said. 'We have proven time and time again that we are the strongest.'

'Bladud has our support,' Ysgawyn said. Again it was a sign of Guidgen's tiredness that he laughed in the so-called *rhi*'s face.

'All three of you? That's an impressive warband.' Britha could not hide the contempt in her voice.

'And where are the people you swore to serve?' Ysgawyn asked. 'Is that the only survivor there in your arms?'

Britha opened her mouth to retort, but no angry words came. He was right, after all.

'The Iceni are with me,' Bladud told them. This was significant. After the Brigante, the Iceni were the largest tribe that had answered Bladud's summons to fight the monsters. They were powerful and warlike.

'And the Trinovantes,' Anharad said. Mabon nodded at his grandmother's words.

'And you can speak for them?' Guidgen said.

'I have some influence,' Anharad said.

'We are to be wed,' Bladud told them, and suddenly he had the attention of all but Tangwen. Britha guessed that Anharad had underplayed just how important she was to her tribe.

'Congratulations,' Britha said.

Guidgen laughed bitterly. The old *dryw* turned and looked to the south at the plain of mud that used to be his people's wooded land.

'After we have dealt with the Lochlannach you will need strong allies,' Bladud told the old man. 'All the southern tribes will.'

'Allies yes, rulers no, tyrants certainly not,' Guidgen said. 'And we have already had this discussion. The chalice was given to Tangwen to safeguard because we would have fallen on each other with sword and spear if we did not. Nothing has changed. We still have a threat that we need to deal with.'

'So you see war between us when we have dealt with the Lochlannach?' Bladud asked. Britha sensed a trap in his words.

'There will be war if you insist on ruling all,' Guidgen said angrily. 'There is always war when a *rhi* wants to own more than they can see from the highest point of their land. We should use the chalice and then throw it into the deepest part of the sea.'

'Things like the chalice have a way of finding their way back into the hands of mortals,' Germelqart said quietly.

'We need its power to defeat the Lochlannach,' Bladud told them.

Britha laughed bitterly. 'You are assuming that you can defeat the Lochlannach,' she said.

'Andraste's spawn and the Lochlannach have proven that we need to be united ...' Bladud said as if Britha hadn't spoken.

'But not ruled—' Guidgen started.

'I understand the danger of the chalice's power,' the Witch King continued. Ysgawyn turned to look at Bladud, distrust written all over his face. Bladud ignored him. 'Can we come to an accord?'

Guidgen peered through the rain at the Witch King. 'An accord that will benefit you, no doubt,' he said.

'Of course.'

'I don't mind an agreement that benefits you and yours; I object when it is to the detriment of all else.'

'Bladud may have forgotten that your people crept into our camp as we slept, slit throats and stole the blood of many, including children,' Anharad started. Bladud was making calming motions with his hand. 'I have not. You need to remember that he can take the chalice whenever he wants.'

Britha saw Germelqart sigh. She understood how he felt.

'We would murder him and flee with the chalice.' Britha was surprised at just how strong Tangwen's voice sounded. She was staring straight at the Witch King. She was more surprised when she looked up and saw Bladud smiling.

'At best it would bring dissension in your forces before you face the Lochlannach,' Britha added.

'Indeed,' Bladud said. 'Before the battle we sent messengers out to all the tribes asking them to meet us in the valley of the Mother Hill where the entrance to Annwn and the Place of Bones is. We could also send a message to Ynys Dywyll. I am assuming that you will abide by the judgement of the council of *dryw*?' Bladud asked. Britha knew Ynys Dywyll, or the Island of Shadows, was a place far to the west where the southern *dryw* were trained. It was also home to their council and arch *dryw*.

Guidgen did not answer. Britha could tell by the firm expression on his wizened face that the old *dryw* was less than pleased. Britha wasn't sure what Bladud hoped to gain from this. He had betrayed the *dryw* when he had pursued power as a warrior, leader, and ultimately *rhi*. She had heard that he had been satirised, censured and then cast out, though he still wore the robes and used the influence. She could not see the council on Ynys Dywyll ruling in his favour if they were anything like the *dryw* in her homeland to the north.

'And you will accept the council's judgement in this matter?' Guidgen asked.

'Of course,' Bladud said. Britha knew that if Guidgen refused then Bladud would have reason to turn on him and the *gwyllion* for rebelling against the council. The Red Chalice was a thing of power; magic and the Otherworld should be their responsibility anyway.

'I'm surprised you would seek their guidance,' Guidgen said suspiciously.

'I do not have to,' Bladud said.

'We all had a part in retrieving it,' Britha pointed out.

'Aye, while you tried to betray us,' Ysgawyn spat.

Britha looked down to hide the look of shame on her face. She had tried to bargain for the rod she needed to return to the Ubh Blaosc and her stolen, unborn daughter.

'And you weren't there,' Tangwen said, staring at the *rhi* of the Corpse People.

'We could claim it as a spoil of war from you,' Bladud said evenly. Suddenly everyone went very still. The only sound was the rain in the trees just to the north of the ruined fort and the constant drip of water as Bladud's threat settled in. Britha noticed Tangwen's hand go to the hatchet pushed through her belt. She felt Caithna grip her more tightly.

'Or?' Guidgen managed between gritted teeth.

'Or we seek the guidance of the *dryw* and we leave the chalice in the hands of Tangwen and Germelqart until they send someone to make judgement.'

'Britha as well,' Tangwen said, slurring the words slightly in her tiredness.

'She cannot be trusted,' Bladud said. He sounded almost sad. Tangwen opened her mouth to protest.

'He's right,' Britha said. *I would give the chalice back to Bress if I thought it would mean I could see my daughter.*

'The Red Chalice is the responsibility of the *dryw*,' Bladud said, glancing over at Britha as he did so.

'I grow tired of this; speak plainly,' Guidgen told Bladud. 'What do you want?'

'Your support,' Bladud said.

'Against the Lochlannach? Gladly.'

'I mean your oath of loyalty.'

Guidgen stared at Bladud. Britha had never seen the old *dryw* so angry before. She suspected that he would have struck the Witch King, had it not been for the muddy crater in the way.

'False tongue! Deceiver! Liar!' the old *dryw* spat. Bladud narrowed his eyes but controlled himself with great restraint. They weren't words you called a warrior lightly. 'You swore—'

'That we would not conquer you. We are negotiating over the Red Chalice. Have the events of the last moon taught you nothing? Show me a stronger leader and I will step aside. Or he may challenge me and kill me in single combat.'

'We will aid and follow your leadership for—'

'No!' Now Bladud became angry. 'This does not work! You know this does not work! If everyone wants one rule for themselves we are divided.' He pointed at Guidgen. 'That is just you putting your arrogance and the arrogance of your people before the good of all!'

Guidgen stared at Bladud. The old man was shaking with rage. Britha had to give Bladud his credit. Guidgen was wily but Bladud had completely outmanoeuvred him.

'I will take this to my people,' Guidgen muttered with little grace before turning and stalking out of the ruins.

Bladud watched the old *dryw* walk away before turning and nodding to Britha and then starting to walk back to camp himself. Britha wondered how much it cost him to leave the chalice at the bottom of the muddy crater. That said, it would not be seemly for him to scrabble around in the mud. Ysgawyn smiled and then followed the Witch King.

'The child,' Anharad said, nodding towards Caithna.

'I will look to her,' Britha told the other woman. Anharad looked less than sure but started back towards the temporary camp. Mabon followed. 'Her name is Caithna!' Britha called. Anharad stopped. Something in the set of her shoulders told Britha that the other woman was feeling her age. The highborn Trinovantes woman did not turn around, and after a moment or two she continued on her way.

Britha sagged, overcome by a sudden wave of fatigue, and she realised just how hungry she was. She looked to Caithna. The girl had fallen asleep.

'I do not mislike Bladud ...' Germelqart started.

'But you would not trust him with the chalice,' Britha supplied.

The Carthaginian navigator nodded. 'I do not think I would trust anyone with it.'

'Except yourself?'

Germelqart looked up at her. 'I would not trust myself with such a thing.'

Britha noticed that Tangwen was staring down into the crater at the chalice with a look of loathing on her face.

'I had better go and get it then,' she muttered quietly to herself. She started to climb down into the crater and almost immediately slipped. By the time she had made her way through the mud to the chalice she was covered in filth from head to foot. Her fingers curled around the red metal and she lifted it out of the mud.

He felt heavier with each step up the bone spiral staircase. It had been several days since the Dark Man's last summons had crawled into the back of his head like a sickness. Bress hoped each time that it was the last. That his master would finally let him go, but he knew that it would not be the case this time – if indeed it ever would be.

Crom Dhubh was standing on the top of the tower looking out over the boneless, drifting bodies in the huge subterranean lake. There were no carrion eaters here, and little current to carry them away from the isle of rock that the skeletal tower grew from, deep in the huge cavern.

'They did it, didn't they?' said the pale warrior with the long silver hair. He held his master's gaze when the Dark Man turned back to look at him. 'They defeated the Muileartach's Brood?'

'I was as much their father as that slug was their mother,' Crom Dhubh said, his voice a silk corruption. 'Does my children's destruction please you?'

'They will come for you,' Bress said.

'It does not matter, they can do nothing to me. Your Lochlannach can distract them until I am ready. The war will not be fought here.'

'You will travel to the Ubh Blaosc?' Bress asked.

'Me? No, they could destroy me. You will travel there. You will die there, but you will make the Ubh Blaosc's location known to the Naga.'

'How?' Bress asked, showing no reaction to the news of his imminent death. If anything, he found himself struggling not to show excitement at the prospect.

Crom's expression of consternation looked alien on his face. 'That is the question.'

'You called them before.'

'Relics from this world. The Ubh Blaosc is too far.'

'What of the one in the cave, to the south and east?'

'A frightened old creature, if it still exists, if my children did not consume or transform him. I have not heard his mindsong again. No. I think the answer lies in the body of the dragon.'